D1627248

CONDENSED BOOKS

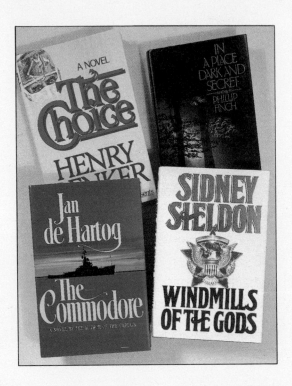

With the exception of actual personages identified
as such, the characters and incidents in the fictional
selections in this volume are entirely the product of
the authors' imaginations and have no relation
to any person or event in real life.

THE READER'S DIGEST ASSOCIATION LIMITED
25 Berkeley Square, London W1X 6AB
THE READER'S DIGEST ASSOCIATION
SOUTH AFRICA (PTY) LTD
Reader's Digest House, 130 Strand Street, Cape Town
Printed by Petty & Sons Ltd, Leeds
Bound by Hazell, Watson & Viney Ltd, Aylesbury
Original cover design by Jeffrey Matthews FSIAD
For information as to ownership
of copyright in the material in this book see last page

Reader's Digest
CONDENSED BOOKS

THE CHOICE
by Henry Denker

Dr. Walter Duncan is a brilliant and dedicated orthopaedic surgeon at University Medical Center. To patients like Amy Bedford, a pretty young tennis player forced to come to terms with bone cancer, he seems like a miracle worker.

But suddenly, Walt's private world crumbles around him when his eleven-year-old daughter, Simone, falls desperately ill. Professionally powerless, Walt is as terror-stricken and helpless as any parent. Even more so. For as a doctor, he knows only too well what can go wrong when agonising choices have to be made.

A moving story of inspiring courage, unbearable loss and the ultimate power of love.

THE COMMODORE
by Jan de Hartog

The seafaring novel at its best—a man against the elements, being tested to the limits of endurance. But there is an added poignancy—Commodore Martinus Harinxma is seventy years old, and suffering from hypertension. He is hauled out of retirement to act as adviser to an inexperienced Chinese crew on board the world's most powerful, technically sophisticated ocean-going tugboat—but a tugboat that has a fatal design flaw.

The voyage of the *Isabel Kwel* across the storm-tossed Atlantic is beset by problems and subterfuges. And Commodore Harinxma is forced to face new realities—the ruthless world of big business and his own ever-increasing years.

IN A PLACE DARK AND SECRET

by Phillip Finch

A teenage girl disappears. Is she a runaway, as the police suspect? Or has she been kidnapped—or worse? The answers are hidden from the outside world in a place where no one can find them—no one except the madman who has made the girl his prisoner. Even skilled police detective Howard Warner is stymied by the lack of evidence. Meanwhile, time is running out for both kidnapper and captive, and in the secret place where she is hidden away, one very frightened girl discovers that her survival may well depend on her own cunning.

A suspenseful new thriller that transforms today's "missing child" headlines into a gripping drama.

WINDMILLS OF THE GODS

by Sidney Sheldon

Here is the latest breathtaking bestseller from Sidney Sheldon, one of the world's most popular authors.

From the moment Mary Ashley, a Kansas college professor, is nominated as American ambassador to Romania, she and her family become pawns in a sinister game of international intrigue . . .

Who are the powerful but unseen masters of the game? And why are Mary and a handful of other innocent victims being stalked across the globe by Angel, the deadly assassin who never fails?

An electrifying story of intrigue and adventure that will keep the reader spellbound right up to its explosive conclusion.

the
CHOICE

A CONDENSATION OF THE BOOK BY
HENRY DENKER

ILLUSTRATED BY TED LEWIN

A tennis star at fifteen, Amy Bedford has dreams for the future that are sky-high. On the courts she has confronted many challengers and overcome them. But now she faces a terrifying new adversary—bone cancer—and she is forced to make the most important choice of her life.

Her sympathetic surgeon, Walter Duncan, guides Amy in her decision. A father himself, "Dr. Walt" has dreams for his own young daughter. But these may be shattered when he too must make a heartrending choice . . .

CHAPTER 1

In Surgery 3, on the fifth floor of University Medical Center, Dr. Walter Duncan was experiencing more difficulty than usual implanting the titanium prosthesis that had been designed for the sixty-eight-year-old patient. Restraining his frustration, working diligently and with great strength, Duncan finally succeeded. Once he had tested the appliance—a hip piece—and was assured it would respond easily, he began to close the incision.

He glanced up at the wall clock. Already past five. He knew now that the problem he had encountered with this patient had made it impossible for him to appear at Simone's school for her very first performance in her class play. Emily would be there, of course. But for Simone that was no special treat; her mother was always there. But Daddy . . .

Walt Duncan could already visualize the look on Simone's face when he came upstairs to kiss her goodnight. She would insist that she understood why Daddy couldn't be there. But the look in her moist eyes would belie her acceptance.

Having closed the incision and carefully packed and splinted the hip to immobilize it, Walter Duncan removed his mask, ripped off his thin surgical gloves and tossed them into the refuse can. He hurried out of surgery and heard himself being paged.

He picked up a wall phone, announcing briskly, "Duncan!"

"Walt?" A familiar voice greeted him softly. It was the voice of his scholarly mentor and longtime friend, Dr. Simon Rosen.

"Yes, Sy."

"Look, I know you're busy. So tell you what—I took a liberty. I hope you don't mind. When you get to your car in the parking lot, you will find a file. Take it home. We'll talk in the morning. OK?"

"Of course, Sy."

"Good. Now get going. Maybe you can make it before Simone's play is over. And give her a kiss for me."

"How did you know about—" Walt started to say.

"My godchild is in her first big role in a school play and I'm not supposed to know about it?" Sy Rosen demanded. Then he urged, "Now get over to that school, Walt!"

ON HIS WAY TO THE SCHOOL Walt realized that Emily must have called Sy, urging him to get her husband out early on this special afternoon. As he drove, Walt thought back to the day he had first met Sy Rosen. Having completed medical school and two years of internship, Walt had applied for a place as resident on the orthopaedic service at the hospital.

Ever since Walt was a boy, he knew that he was destined to study medicine. But his devotion to the speciality of orthopaedics was the result of his experiences in Vietnam, where as a lieutenant he had often stood alongside his wounded men when they were being treated at a forward medical unit. He had marvelled at military surgeons who possessed the skill to mend broken, torn and shattered limbs. To be able to make mangled young bodies whole again had become, to Walter Duncan, a doctor's finest work. On his return to civilian life he entered medical school and soon learned that if orthopaedics was to become his speciality, there was only one hospital and one man he could aspire to serve: University Medical Center and Dr. Simon Rosen.

During that first interview Walter Duncan was a very surprised young man. Most surgeons as famous as Rosen had a reputation for being busy and brusque. But Rosen was soft-spoken, taking the time to acquaint Walt with the rigorous life of a surgeon on his orthopaedic service. Clearly, he was not the kind to *demand* total dedication—he expected it without demanding.

Walter Duncan would discover later that Sy Rosen had no close family and had never married. Many times Walter thought that if Sy had had a wife and children, they would have felt grievously neglected.

Regardless of his own personal life, Rosen was always solicitous of Walt's obligations to his family. On the day Walt's daughter was born and became his namesake, Sy Rosen had sent gifts to her and to Emily. Nor had he ever failed to do so on Simone's eleven birthdays and Christmases since.

Sy Rosen was now past his own days of active practice and had been honoured with the title of professor emeritus. He was, in fact, considered

10

the prime consultant for all difficult orthopaedic cases in the entire Midwest. Many times his fingers itched to operate on patients he had to pass on to younger men. The toughest cases he referred to Walter Duncan. He looked upon Walt not only as a protégé and successor but as the son he'd never had.

WHEN WALT FINALLY ARRIVED at his daughter's school, the empty parking lot told him all he needed to know. He turned his car homeward. He debated stopping to pick up a gift for Simone. But he had become aware that such diverting little bribes were not nearly as effective as they had been when Simone was younger.

By the time he arrived home, Simone had already had an early dinner and gone up to bed. It would have done no good to explain to his wife why he was late. She'd heard the excuses before. Besides, her beautiful face, her pale blue eyes, her silence were a more telling rebuke than any words she might have said in return.

He asked only, "How was she?"

"Wonderful. She was so into her part that for the first few minutes I didn't even know it was her."

"Is she still awake?"

"Unless she fell asleep crying," Emily said softly.

That was all the spoken rebuke there was. He climbed the stairs, making himself all kinds of promises. A long vacation, the three of them together, when school was out for Easter. Summer at the latest. Scheduling his surgeries even earlier in the morning, so he could be home for dinner more often.

He was full of righteous resolutions of this kind by the time he arrived at Simone's door. When he knocked, there was no answer. He opened the door gently.

The room was dark except for the slant of light from the hallway that fell across her bed. Little Simone was lying on her side, her blanket drawn tight around her. He knew she was not asleep, not in so tense a posture. He approached her bed and knelt down beside it. He whispered, "Baby?"

She clenched her eyes tightly. He kissed her on the cheek. She opened her eyes. Emily was right. She had been crying.

"Baby, I'm sorry." She did not react. "Mom tells me you were terrific. I wish I'd been there to see. Tomorrow at breakfast you must act out your whole part for me. OK?"

She did not reply. He kissed her again, then buried his face in the soft, warm crook of her neck. Finally her hand stole out from under the blanket to embrace his hand.

"Next time?" she bargained. "Promise?"

11

"Next time, baby," he said.

She kissed him. "You need a shave, Daddy," she said. She turned on her other side and drifted off to sleep.

AFTER DINNER, IN THE DEN with Emily, Walt skimmed the case history Sy Rosen had given him. He held up the X-rays to his desk lamp. He studied the results of the scans. He was puzzled that Sy had asked him to get involved. It was not a case in which he would have recommended surgery. Yet the surgery had already been performed. And to judge from the file, it had not been performed well. It was too late to correct anything now.

Why, then, had Sy given him this file to review? And why had the names of both patient and surgeon been removed?

He would ask Sy in the morning. By the time he looked up to pay some attention to Emily, he discovered that she had gone to bed. If he neglected his daughter, he was even more neglectful of his wife. Always on the assumption that she understood the demands of his career.

WALTER DUNCAN HAD FIRST laid eyes on Emily Ingraham as she was entering the library at University Medical Center. It was just after he had begun to serve his residency. She was a petite, attractive young woman and seemed extremely serious. A nurse possibly, or a med student, he thought. She possessed a face of small but perfectly matched features. With her dark hair and her black-framed spectacles she appeared to be sober, dedicated, intent on a mission.

He stood alongside her at the librarian's desk and heard her ask for an outdated medical textbook. His curiosity stirred, he volunteered, "If you're looking for information on the proper treatment of tuberculosis, I can suggest a much better book: *Miller on Thoracic Disease.*"

She had turned to look up at him, a hulking six foot three inches tall, with shaggy hair. She noticed that he had a strong face and a jutting jaw, but his brown eyes softened the total impression. Her first glance reflected resentment at his intrusion. Then she smiled, her face turning from merely pretty to warm and inviting.

"If you want the latest and best," he added, "ask for Miller."

"Well, if I ever do want the latest and best, I will," she said, turning back to the librarian to renew her request.

Walt Duncan watched her start off towards the stacks to which the librarian had directed her. He could not resist. He followed and reached her just as she was straining to take down from a high shelf the book she wanted.

She succeeded, but as she turned away she collided with him. They both apologized. Then he proceeded to lecture her. "Young woman, if

12

you are interested in the treatment of tuberculosis, you will get nothing but a lot of misinformation out of that volume. The treatment of tuberculosis has changed radically since that time." He took the volume out of her hands.

"Now, just one minute—" she started to protest.

"Look, tell you what I'll do. I will personally introduce you to the chief of thoracic medicine here. He will tell you everything you want to know. But this book is a waste of time."

"I want that book," she insisted.

"I have noticed one thing about women, particularly young women. They are most stubborn when they are most wrong," he said, replacing the volume on the high shelf with ease.

"Is that your speciality, Doctor? Studying women?" She started to reach for the textbook again, standing on tiptoe.

"My speciality is going to be orthopaedics, and I can tell you now that straining to reach that way is not doing your lower back any good." He took down the volume but did not hand it to her.

"I have noticed one thing about doctors, particularly young doctors. They are most stubborn when they are most wrong," she mimicked.

"What does that mean, Miss . . ."

"Ingraham," she informed him. "Now, Doctor, if you were less intent on *telling* me and more on finding out what I want to discover, we might get on a good deal better!"

"You want to learn the best treatment for tuberculosis," he declared.

"In 1927," she added.

"In 1927? Why would anybody—"

"Because, my dear young doctor, I am in the process of editing a novel that takes place in the 1920s, and I want to check some of the author's facts."

"Is that what you do, edit novels?" he asked, intrigued.

"With a BA in English lit. what better could I do?" she asked, taking the book from him and starting towards a reading table.

He followed her. "Miss Ingraham, do you also happen to have a first name?"

"Most people do. Emily."

"Emily Ingraham. I like the sound of that. Tell me, do you ever edit novels about orthopaedic surgeons?"

"Not so far," she said.

"Too bad. I could be a great help there."

"Well, if I ever do, I'll call on you, Doctor . . ."

"Duncan."

"Ok, Dr. Duncan." She continued towards the table.

Disappointed, he called, "Don't you want to know my first name?"

She pretended to consider her reply, then said, "I suppose, whether I want to or not, I'm about to learn it."

"You sure are. Walter," he declared.

"Walter Duncan, orthopaedic surgeon. I like the sound of that," she said, smiling impishly.

A bit sheepishly he admitted, "I'm not really an orthopaedic surgeon yet. Not board certified, that is. I'm in training under Dr. Rosen. Simon Rosen."

"The way you say it, it seems I should be familiar with his name."

"Yes. Because he's the best there is. If you'd like to meet him, I can arrange it."

"Can you?" she asked, pretending to be interested.

"He runs a Wednesday-night seminar at his home. For a small group of selected residents. We talk about developments in orthopaedics. Then there's coffee and cake and usually some gossip about hospital politics."

"Does he permit outsiders?"

"Well, for someone as pretty as you, I'm sure Sy would make an exception. Are you free Wednesday evening?" he asked.

"If I can finish editing this novel, I will be."

"I'll pick you up. Say, around seven?"

"Seven," she agreed, and wrote out her address for him.

After that first Wednesday evening Emily Ingraham became a regular at Sy Rosen's seminars. By the time she and Walter married, Sy Rosen was close enough to both of them to serve as Walter's best man, since Walter's father was dead.

"I WENT OVER THAT FILE, Sy," Walt Duncan reported as he seated himself across the desk from the elderly consultant.

"And?" Sy asked, tugging gently on the narrow fringe of white beard that bordered his ruddy face. "Anything trouble you?"

"The dates."

"For instance?" Sy asked.

"The first examination of the boy, the initial X-rays and the EMG, all in the space of three days. Then four days later, surgery. Too fast. Much too fast."

"Yes, it seemed a little hasty to me too," Sy agreed.

"I should have thought the surgeon would have tried to avoid operating. At least until more conservative measures had failed to relieve the patient's pain. It seems to have been nothing more serious than sciatic pain down to the left foot, accompanied by some muscle weakness. Both of which might have responded to rest, medication and other noninvasive treatment. But surgery—" Walt shook his head. "Sy, I'd hate to tell you what I suspect."

14

"Me too. Smacks a little of greed, doesn't it, Walt?"

"Surgery performed for the doctor's benefit, not the patient's," Walt said. "And the surgery was botched. Unfortunately, it's beyond repair. I wouldn't know how to cure the dropped foot that has resulted."

"He'll never control that foot again," Sy agreed. "He's only eighteen, and he'll have to wear a brace the rest of his life."

"Sorry, Sy," Walt said, handing back the file.

Sy did not reach for it. "Keep it, Walt. Study it further. Because we have a decision to make."

"Decision? There's nothing we can do to repair the damage."

"This file was sent to me by the young man's attorney. There is a very large malpractice suit involved here."

"They want expert testimony; is that it?"

"That's why it was sent to me," Sy informed him. "But that old buzzard Worthington, in cardiology, tells me that my heart is no longer up to the strain of testifying."

Walt was aware of the purpose of Sy's statement. They both possessed the same righteous anger towards surgeons who practised their profession as if it were a trade. Walt knew he must volunteer to go to court.

"OK, Sy. So long as it doesn't cut too deeply into my time."

"Don't you want to know who the patient and the doctor are?"

"It doesn't really matter." Then, taking his cue from the grave look on Sy's face, he did ask. "Who was the surgeon?"

"Enright."

"Peter Enright?" Walt asked.

Sy nodded.

"I never did like his work when he was on staff here." Suddenly a thought occurred to Walt. "Say, this didn't happen at University Medical Center, did it?"

"No. At the hospital where he served just before he got here. Frankly, if I'd known about it, he'd never have been accepted. Thank heavens he's gone. Even so, it won't do the reputation of this hospital any good if they hang this on Enright."

"I know. For the rest of his career it will say on his record, 'Formerly of University Medical Center'. That can't be avoided. But there is the patient to consider, and the harm done."

Sy nodded once more.

"And we can't let this hospital's reputation become a shield for unnecessary and careless surgery, no matter who was at fault," Walt said. "OK, Sy, I'll definitely testify."

"Thanks, Walt. Believe me, if I could do it myself, I would. I'm old enough, prestigious enough to take the flak. But, unfortunately, too old for the job. Too old for so many things these days," he said sadly.

WALT DUNCAN WOKE, lay there a moment, then became aware that he was in bed alone. Where was Emily? Usually he left her half awake as he kissed her and went on his way to the hospital for early surgery. He turned on his side to look at the clock on the night table. Four minutes to eight. He started to move quickly, then realized, Today is Sunday.

He had promised Emily that this would be a special Sunday. A whole day devoted to Simone. For Emily had warned, "She's going to forget what you look like."

Walt came down to breakfast to find Simone fed and awaiting him. She was dressed for some form of active sport. Tennis, he hoped. He was fairly good at that. All through breakfast he listened to her relate the events of her week. School. The birthday of a friend. An exam on which she had received a B plus.

When he had finished eating, Simone went to the hall cupboard and brought out the equipment for their game. Two curved sticks. And a hard black rubber ball. So it was to be field hockey, he realized. He had never played the game.

Simone led the way outside. Fortunately, it was a fine, dry, springlike day. The grass made a soft, fragrant cushion on which to fall and roll whenever they made contact. When Simone instructed her father in the strategy of the game, he pretended to be a slow and uncoordinated pupil so that she could become impatient with him and display her superiority.

In one moment of physical contact Simone winced and seemed to catch her breath.

"Did I hurt you, sweetheart?" he asked.

"No, I'm fine, Daddy," the child protested.

"Let me see," he said.

She turned to him. He pulled her shirt out of her shorts and discovered a black-and-blue mark on her side.

"Well, how did you get this? Practising hockey at school?"

"I guess," she said.

"You'd better be more careful from now on," he said. "Now, shall we take Mommy out to lunch?"

Later, while Simone was changing clothes, Walt said to Emily, "Do you think hockey is too rough a game for girls?"

"I played it and grew up rather well," Emily said. "Why do you ask?"

"Simmie's got a bad bruise on her side. Like someone hit her with a hockey stick at school."

"Nobody hit her with a hockey stick," Emily said.

"How can you be sure?" he asked.

"Because official school practice only starts next week."

Before he could pursue the matter, Simone appeared in the doorway, wearing a pink dress that he favoured.

"Ready, Daddy?" she called to him, smiling.

"Ready!" he called back.

On the drive to the restaurant Simone kept up a frivolous chatter, asking him riddles and playing word games with him. But all the while Walt kept thinking, Watch that bruise on her side. For some undefinable reason it troubled him.

IT WAS FOUR O'CLOCK in the afternoon three days later. Since arriving at the hospital that morning, Walter Duncan had performed surgery on three patients, been called into consultation on four others and had had a chance to eat only half the sandwich Claudia, his secretary, had given him before he made his rounds. Clad in a white coat, he was leaving his office when Claudia intercepted him. He was wanted on the phone.

"Later, Claudia!"

"It's Dr. Rosen," she said.

Walter Duncan came back to his desk to take the call.

"Walt," the old man said. "In this modern age things happen faster than they used to. We've already got some flak."

"Flak?" Walt asked, puzzled.

"Russell," was all Sy said, and all he needed to say. James Rowe Russell was the only trustee who had inherited his place on the board of trustees. His father had been the prime mover in building University Medical Center, having been its most generous donor. Thus the current Russell looked upon the institution as virtually his own possession.

"What does Russell want this time?" Walt asked.

"He's heard about the case against Enright."

"How?"

"Enright's lawyer figured if he could involve Russell, he'd bring pressure on any doctor who was considering testifying."

"So?"

"Russell would like to talk to you," Sy warned.

"OK," Walt said. "I'll call him."

"Right away," Sy suggested. "Give him time to brood about it and he'll be five times as angry by morning."

AT THE SAME TIME that Walt Duncan had Claudia place his call to James Russell, tennis practice was under way at Midvale High School under the watchful eye of Lars Olafsen, whom everyone called Swede. Swede had been physical education instructor and tennis coach at Midvale High for more than a generation. His hair, which had been the colour of standing wheat when he started, was now white as snow. But his blue eyes were as sharp as ever when he paced behind the courts watching his pupils practise.

His boys' teams of the past had earned their share of citywide and statewide honours. This year his team again promised to go all the way to the state finals and was even a fair bet to win the championship. However, unlike previous years, this time his players had a shot at the girls' title too.

His ambitions for a double title rested mainly on the excellent strokes, good eye and graceful style of fifteen-year-old Amy Bedford. Deceptively slender for a girl who hit so powerfully, Amy reminded old Swede of some of the greats he had seen when he was young. She could not only win the state championship, he thought, but she might go on from there.

This afternoon Amy seemed to be having an off day. Swede noticed that when she came off her right foot after shifting her body weight, she betrayed a slight limp.

When she came to the side of the court to towel her wet and pretty face, Swede suggested, "Enough for today, Amy?"

"Why?" she asked, almost resentful.

"You're losing your smoothness, your ease of stroke."

"I'm trying to work it out," Amy said.

"Work what out?" Swede asked, taken by surprise.

"I've got a slight pain in my right leg," Amy admitted. "But I'll work it out before the tournament. So don't worry, Swede."

"OK, Slugger," Swede said, smiling and resorting to her pet name. "Just don't push it too hard."

Later that afternoon, after his charges had deserted the courts, showered, dressed and were leaving the school, Swede Olafsen watched as Amy Bedford strode down the corridor towards the open doors, her trim figure silhouetted against the afternoon sunshine. She walked with a slight limp too.

He must watch her closely for the next few days.

JAMES ROWE RUSSELL, a man in his late fifties, was generally described in the media as a wealthy philanthropist. But his main activity was running the medical center.

At this moment Walt Duncan was facing him, considering how to respond to Russell's question: "If you're so sure of your opinion about this lawsuit, wouldn't *most* surgeons feel the same way?"

"Most honest surgeons, yes," Walt granted.

"Then it shouldn't be hard to find other experts who would testify on behalf of this patient," Russell said. "Why must it be a doctor on the staff at our particular hospital?"

"The file was originally sent to Dr. Rosen. Why, is quite obvious. What orthopaedist in this part of the country has a better reputation? When, for reasons of health, Sy was advised not to appear, he turned the matter over to me."

"And, of course, you couldn't refuse. You never refuse him anything, do you?" Russell asked.

"We generally agree," was all that Walt replied.

Russell's face became ruddy as his anger simmered. "Let me put the matter directly, Duncan. It would do this institution great harm if you were to testify against a man who had once been on the staff here."

"It would do this institution even greater harm if it became known that we concealed the truth out of a mistaken sense of loyalty to a former staff member whose standards are less than professional."

"It is not this hospital's job to take part in lawsuits," Russell protested. "Particularly lawsuits in which we are not involved. This happened at another hospital and to a man who is no longer our responsibility."

"Mr. Russell, I believe that any time the practice of medicine is less than it should be, it becomes the responsibility of every physician to point that out!"

Walt rose from his chair to pace as he continued. "I know what you're thinking, Mr. Russell. And I don't blame you. A big verdict against any hospital raises the cost of insurance for all hospitals. And the malpractice insurance for this hospital already runs into hundreds of thousands."

"More than a million!" Russell corrected.

"Over a million, then," Walt conceded. "And why? Because for years the profession tried to sweep its failures under the rug by virtually blacklisting any doctor who dared testify on behalf of an unfortunate and damaged patient. And now, giving vent to their outrage, juries have been handing down large, multimillion-dollar verdicts. Well, the answer isn't to go back to the old ways, but to practise a standard of medicine higher than before."

Both men knew that the last word in this particular encounter had been spoken.

LATER THAT AFTERNOON, on his way home from the hospital, Walter Duncan stopped at the law office of Andrew Silverstein, to confer with him for the first time about his testimony in the case. A small, dapper man, Silverstein seemed well prepared for Walt's visit and displayed a level of expertise in the surgical problems involved that would have done credit to any physician.

Home again, late again, Walt reproached himself as he pulled his car into the driveway. No one answered his cheery call from the front door.

He went to the kitchen. Neither Simone nor Emily was there. He went to the foot of the stairs. "Hi! Anybody up there?"

"Daddy?" came Simone's voice. It seemed tense.

He bounced up the carpeted stairs, reached the door of her room and discovered Emily sitting on the bed, alongside Simone, who lay on her stomach. "What's wrong?" he demanded as he drew close to the bed.

"She has another black-and-blue bruise. On her arm this time," Emily said, pointing to an irregular blemish on the inner side of her daughter's left arm.

"How in the world could she get hit with a hockey stick there?" he asked, leaning over to examine the spot. He flexed Simone's arm, which moved easily, then pressed the bruise. He finally concluded, "Playing hockey with your friends again before school practice starts? Let's stop for a while."

"But, Dad—"

"There are other forms of exercise at least as good and not so dangerous." Before the child could continue the argument, he kissed her and said, "Your father was a tennis player in college, and it didn't do him any harm. Did it?"

He smiled and finally she smiled too. "No, Dad, it didn't."

"Tell you what. If you want to take tennis lessons, I'll ask Swede Olafsen at the school to make you his special pupil. Private lessons. With a new racket. OK?"

"OK," Simone finally conceded.

EMILY SAT OPPOSITE HIM as he ate his late dinner.

"How did it go today?" she asked.

"The usual," he said.

"I mean that session with the lawyer."

"Oh, that. Pretty well. Why?"

"I ran into Millie Enright today. She ignored me."

"Sorry," Walt said. "But it can't be helped."

"Walt, are you sure her husband handled the case that badly?"

"It's plain from the patient's history. There was no need for immediate surgery, if at all. And the condition the patient was left in proves the surgery was done badly."

"I don't understand. If Enright is so inept, how come he was accepted on the staff at the medical center?" Emily asked.

"And was asked to leave very soon thereafter, don't forget."

"Still, there must have been some reason for accepting him in the first place," Emily insisted.

"Frankly, that troubled me too. Before going to see Silverstein, I looked up Enright's file. With the recommendations he had, any hospital in the country would have grabbed him. So I called Dick Forester. Enright was on Dick's orthopaedic service before he came to us. And Dick didn't have much good to say about him."

20

"But you said they gave him such a great recommendation when he left," Emily argued.

"Of course. Dick admitted he had to do it. His trustees insisted, to avoid being sued by Enright if Dick wrote the letter of *condemnation* he was itching to write. That's what hospitals do in these litigious times. Send off their failures with praise and a sigh of relief, saying, 'Let him become some other hospital's problem.' "

His appetite gone, Walt pushed back his plate and stood up.

"I made some chocolate mousse," Emily said.

"No thanks, hon. I've got too much reading to do."

He kissed her, and before starting for the den, he said, "Keep an eye on Simone. I don't like those bruises."

CHAPTER 2

Swede Olafsen was watching his charges work out when he noticed that Amy Bedford, who had been about to serve, suddenly turned away from the baseline and hurried to the fence. Her young body seemed to convulse. Swede ran towards her and was still some paces away when he realized the girl was vomiting.

"Amy! What is it, Amy?" he called out.

She turned away, embarrassed, and began to weep.

"Easy now, Amy. Easy does it," he whispered when he reached her. "Come with me." He shepherded her towards the door to the gym.

She was seated in his office, looking guilty, when he asked, "What did you have for lunch?"

"I—I didn't have any," she said.

"What was it, then, nerves?" the coach asked. "You don't have any cause for nerves, Amy. I've never seen a girl better prepared for the state finals."

"I—I think it was the aspirin," Amy admitted.

"Aspirin. Why aspirin?" Swede asked.

"The pain in my leg. It wouldn't go away. So I started to take aspirin. I took six tablets this morning," she confessed.

"That would be it," Swede observed grimly. "Get up, Amy. Let me see you walk away from me."

The girl complied. He watched as she walked towards the door of his long office. There was no question. She still manifested that limp.

"Still hurts, doesn't it?" the coach asked.

"Uh-huh," she said, half looking back at him.

"Worse than before?"

"Yep."

21

"Come on back," he said. "Now, first thing, no more aspirin. There's no sense trying to hide pain."

"But I want to be ready to play," Amy protested. "I need that title to get into some of the more important tournaments."

"Amy, dear, your health is more important than any title. So let's try a few days of rest. Then we'll see."

After she departed, the coach sat there, staring in her direction. Then he turned to the phone, dialled a number long familiar to him, and asked for Sy Rosen.

In moments Rosen was on the phone. "Hi, Swede. What's up?"

"Sy, I've got a girl on my squad. Amy Bedford. She's having a little pain."

"Pain? Where?" Sy asked.

"Right leg. You see—"

"Where in her right leg?" Sy interrupted.

"Seems to be just below the knee. In the front. It must be bad, because she's been overdosing with aspirin."

"Swede, send her in. I'll have her X-rayed. Probably nothing. But let's make sure."

"Thanks, Sy. She's my best. With a good chance of going pro."

"X-RAY? WHY, DARLING?" Marion Bedford said when Amy told her. "For a slight pain in the leg? Let me see."

She knelt beside her daughter and ran her fingers up and down the area just below Amy's knee. "There's no swelling," Mrs. Bedford concluded. "I'd better call Dr. Corey before we do anything. What did you say that doctor's name was, the one Swede mentioned?"

"Dr. Rosen. Simon Rosen," Amy said.

Mrs. Bedford placed her call to Amy's pediatrician and had to hold on for some minutes. During that time she nervously brushed back the strands of her long, blonde hair. Though she had attempted to minimize the problem, instinctively she feared there was something terribly wrong. Her concern anticipated her husband's attitude, which he most often expressed with considerable impatience. "Darn it, Marion, I work all day and part of the night. It's your job to run the house and take care of our daughter. I hope that's not too much to expect."

Thus Ed Bedford rid himself of all responsibility for the care of his daughter, whom he loved but whom he felt unequipped to deal with. A workaholic, he was much more at ease at the large machine-tool business he owned.

When Charles Corey came on the line, Marion Bedford explained the situation. He asked only one question. "Whom did Swede recommend?"

"A doctor at University Medical Center named Rosen."

"Sy Rosen?" Corey asked.

"Yes, I think so."

"She couldn't be in better hands. Just tell Rosen to call me when he gets the results."

"RELAX, AMY," Rosen said. "It *is* Amy, isn't it?"

"Yes, sir," the girl said, playing nervously with her fingers, which rested in her lap.

To put the girl at ease, Rosen said, "It seems you and I have some things in common, Amy. We both have the same tennis coach. Or had. I don't play much any more. But when I did, Swede was my coach. Well, now, he tells me you are having a little pain in the leg."

"Yes, sir," Amy responded.

"Just where?" Rosen asked, leaning forward in his chair.

Amy drew a circular line below the knee of her right leg.

"Aha," Rosen said. "Get up, child. Walk to the door and back."

Amy followed his instructions. When she was seated again, the elderly surgeon knelt beside her and palpated the area of pain. There was no swelling, but his sensitive fingers detected a very slight difference in surface temperature between that area and the lower part of her leg.

"Well," he said, pretending to be casual, "let's have a go at that X-ray. Mrs. Kruzsik, my nurse, will take you down there. And afterwards I'll call Dr. Corey and tell him what I find."

Sy Rosen watched as the girl walked out of his office. Damn it! he thought. Why do I always have to look at the dark side? It could be nothing. Yet, years of instinctive hunches warned him otherwise.

WHEN WALTER DUNCAN opened the door, he found the consultation room dark. Sy sat in a corner. Even in the darkness Walt could tell the old man was grim and deeply concerned.

"Sy?" Walt asked. "You wanted me to look at a set of X-rays?"

"They're mounted on the viewing screen. Take a look."

Walt approached the wall of opaque glass, snapped on the back light and studied the two X-ray films of the long leg bones of a patient. It took no longer than a few moments. He turned to Sy.

"X-rays like this aren't definitive. Still . . ."

"Still *what*?" Sy asked.

"I can't fool you. Biopsy. That's the only way to be absolutely sure. Who's the patient?"

"A fifteen-year-old girl named Amy Bedford."

"Say, isn't she the young tennis player I've read about? One of Swede's protégées?"

"That's the girl."

"Good Lord!" was all Walt could say. Then he asked solemnly, "Whom do we talk to?"

"Chuck Corey's her pediatrician," Sy said. "I'll call him so he can inform the family. Will you take on the case?"

"Of course," Walt said, knowing that of all cases the ones involving young people were to him the most taxing emotionally. Especially since Simone had been born, each time he treated a child, it was as if he or she were his own.

IT WAS EARLY EVENING BEFORE Dr. Corey, a busy pediatrician, could return Sy's call. The conversation was brief.

"Chuck, Walt Duncan's going to take over Amy Bedford's case. Would you arrange for her to have another X-ray right away?"

"Another X-ray?" Corey asked, puzzled.

"Her chest this time."

At the word "chest", Corey's quick mind came directly to the point. "What do you suspect, Sy? Metastases to the lungs from osteogenic sarcoma?"

Sy could hear the grimness in Corey's voice. "We only suspect, Chuck. We don't know for sure."

"I'll get her in for chest X-rays first thing tomorrow," Corey said. "What next?"

"Biopsy. If it confirms what we suspect, then we'll do bone and CAT scans. If it is a sarcoma, it may not be primary. We have to make sure it isn't a metastasis from another part of her body. About her family: how do we handle that?"

"Her mother is a good, strong woman. Has to be. Because her father is a highly-strung workaholic who'd have you believe he's all business. But from my experience I think he does it to cover up. The man can't handle personal problems. So I won't guarantee how he'll react. When the time comes—" Corey corrected himself. "*If* the time comes, I suggest we hold a joint consultation. You and Walt to answer the technical questions, of which Bedford will have plenty. And me to reassure them. But first I'll get those chest X-rays and explain the need for the biopsy."

SY ROSEN AND WALT DUNCAN were in the darkened room staring at a wall-size viewing screen on which were displayed Amy Bedford's X-rays. As they moved from one film to another, the only encouraging aspect was that the chest films Corey had sent over showed that the girl's lungs were clear.

"Schedule that biopsy as soon as possible, Walt."

Walt studied the films as he observed, "Blind-needle biopsy won't do. Not in a case like this."

Sy agreed. "Open-incisional biopsy is the way. Especially in this case."

When Walt Duncan arrived home, Simone was upstairs, getting ready for bed. He went up quietly, hoping to catch her unawares and make a game of his late homecoming. He found her in her bathroom, standing before the full-length mirror in her nightgown, feeling another one of those contusions, this one on her shoulder. Damn, he thought, I said she was to give up hockey.

He surprised her when he said, "I hope you hit back this time."

Simone turned to her father. "I think I banged into the door of my locker," she said. "But I can't remember."

He held out his arms to her, and she came to him. He kissed her goodnight, at the same time examining that bluish spot on her shoulder. He pressed it. She did not react in pain. He looked into her face.

"Something wrong, Daddy?" she asked.

"No. Nothing. Just get into bed. It's late."

With no word of protest the child obediently went to her room and climbed into bed. He lingered only long enough to kiss her again. Then he went down to the den, where Emily had his predinner drink waiting.

"Did you know Simone had another one of those things, on her shoulder?" he asked.

"No," Emily said. "She gave up hockey, you know."

"Did she make much of a fuss about it?"

"No. Which surprised me," Emily admitted. "I thought she'd be her usual rebellious self. But maybe she's maturing faster than we think."

"Maybe," Walt said. "Does she look the same to you?"

"Of course," Emily said. "Why shouldn't she?"

"Isn't she pale?"

"Light-skinned brunettes always seem pale," Emily said. "They used to say that about me when I was a kid. Now, bring your drink to the table. Dinner's ready."

"OK," he said, preoccupied.

SY ROSEN DID NOT WISH to alarm the Bedfords unnecessarily before all the medical evidence was in. Especially since he had been warned of the volatile nature of Amy's father. So her biopsy the next week was treated as a routine bit of minor surgery. But five days later, when the pathology report reached Sy's desk, it confirmed that patient Amy Bedford, fifteen years old, was the victim of a full-blown case of aggressive osteogenic sarcoma.

When Walter Duncan read that report, he scheduled the bone scans and CAT scan without delay.

It took several phone calls and one meeting postponed at the last minute before Ed Bedford, his wife, Marion, and their daughter, Amy, could be assembled in Sy Rosen's consulting room along with Walter Duncan and Chuck Corey.

Warned of Bedford's proclivity for wanting technical answers, Sy relied on the X-rays and body scans to make the first explanation. "You see here, Mr. Bedford, on this X-ray, this dark shadow?"

"Yes," Bedford said impatiently. "What is it?"

"Evidence of a neoplasm. An unnatural growth."

"Unnatural," Bedford repeated. "Which means what?"

"A tumour," Sy explained. "A tumour of the bone. Now, on these bone scans you can see this hot spot—"

"Hot spot!" Suddenly Bedford stood up and interrupted. "Are you telling me that that thing in my daughter's leg is a cancer? Impossible! Fifteen-year-old kids do not get cancer!"

"Ed, please!" Marion Bedford said. Though she was on the verge of tears, she tried to comfort her daughter by reaching for her hand.

"Look," Bedford exploded, "I'm no dummy! Just tell me the facts." He turned on Corey. "How could such a thing be there? Lord knows Amy's in your office every year, like clockwork, for a complete physical! How could you miss such a serious thing?"

Walt Duncan rose to his full six foot three and seized Ed Bedford by the shoulders. "Hold on, Bedford!" Bedford glared up at him. He seemed poised to swing out at Walt. Instead, he merely continued to stare, appearing to shrink in size, and became far less belligerent.

In a calmer voice Walt continued. "Mr. Bedford, this is an insidious disease. No doctor can suspect it until there are symptoms. And cancer is not solely a disease of the ageing. Fifteen-year-olds do get cancer. So forget all your preconceived notions and listen. Very carefully. Because a choice has to be made here today. The most important choice in your daughter's life."

Chastened by those words, a pale, sweaty Ed Bedford sank back into his chair. Walt Duncan stayed on his feet, addressing himself to Amy. He could see how her father's uncontrolled reaction had shaken her.

"Amy, I won't minimize the seriousness of your disease. It is a nasty business. And I won't lie to you. *It can be fatal.* But it can also be treated. In several ways. That's where you and I have to make a choice."

Out of his despair Ed Bedford muttered, "The Kennedy boy . . . They took his leg, amputated it."

With a soft gasp Amy started to weep. Her mother put her arms round her. Walt Duncan quickly dropped to one knee beside the tearful girl. He took her hand.

"Amy, I didn't use that word. Nor did Dr. Rosen nor Dr. Corey. I said we have a *choice.* Yes, amputation is one alternative. Maybe the safest one. But there is another way."

As if she had not heard, the slim, fair-haired girl continued to weep.

"Now, listen to me very carefully, Amy. This is what the other way consists of: for the next six to eight weeks we will put you on a regimen of chemotherapy. If that succeeds and causes the tumour to shrink, I can then perform an operation. Dr. Rosen will be there. Dr. Corey will be there. We'll work as a team. During that operation I shall remove the part of your calf and thigh bones that is cancerous and in its place insert what we call a prosthesis—a long metal device made of strong, lightweight titanium. If we have to, we can even replace your knee."

"If it works, will I be able to walk?"

"If everything goes well."

"Will I be able to play tennis again?" she dared to ask.

"Not as well as before," Walt replied.

"Then that's my choice," Amy said at once.

"Not so fast, my dear," Walt said. "First, this won't be easy. Second, there are no guarantees. I must be completely honest with you. Those sarcoma cells may have already spread from your leg into your bloodstream. Fortunately, your lungs are clean. They are the area of the body most vulnerable to these cells. So we may have caught this in time. But I want you to know all the risks. We are going to be honest with you all the way, Amy."

Such complete disclosure gave the girl increased confidence in Walter Duncan.

"Now, Amy, if you choose this procedure, you must be willing to undergo a year of chemotherapy, surgery, physical therapy, and all the pain and suffering that goes with it. In a word, if you make this choice, you must be prepared to give us one year of your life. It's a gamble. But if you give us that year, we have a good chance of getting you well."

"A whole year?" she asked.

"A whole year. Forget tennis. Go to school only when you can. Your main job will be to help us get you well and healthy again. What do you say?"

Amy hesitated, then said, "All right. I'll do it."

As if he had gained confidence from his daughter, Ed Bedford nodded too. "Just help my little girl get well," he said.

"We'll do our best," Sy said. "First step, we want Amy to arrange a meeting with our oncologist, Dr. Rita Bristol. She'll explain all about the chemotherapy. I've already called her secretary. She's expecting you."

"Amy," Walt suggested, "why don't you and your mom go down the hall to Dr. Bristol's office?"

Ed Bedford realized it was a request that he remain. Once the door was closed, he reached into his inner coat pocket and took out his chequebook.

"All right, gentlemen. How much money to start with?"

"That's not the reason I wanted you to stay on, Mr. Bedford," Walt said. "Financial matters will be handled in due course. But we want to impress something on you. Your daughter is about to undergo an arduous process. Chemotherapy has some very distressing side effects. She's going to need all the courage she can muster to see it through.

"What she needs from you is not money, but guts. A show of strength, from which she can take strength. If you have to shout in anger or denial, go down to your office. If you have to cry, go into the bathroom and cry. If you have to curse fate because of what's happening to your daughter, do it out of her hearing. What we want from you is a smile. A genuine smile that says, Stick with it, Amy, and we'll all make it. Let her know how much you love her and that you have confidence that she'll beat this.

"Above all, don't ever give her the feeling that by getting sick she's let you down. You loved her before; love her more now. She needs it. And always remember, no one was to blame for this. No one could have prevented it. It just happened. That's all."

When Walt was finished, Ed Bedford nodded humbly. After some moments of silence he rose and started for the door. There he stopped and turned to face the three physicians.

"They didn't know. Not Amy. Not her mother. But I've been putting aside bonds for three years now. To finance her first year on the tennis tour. Twenty-five thousand dollars' worth. Now it's all yours, gentlemen."

Irked by the man's crass assumption, Walt Duncan asked, "What if we said it will take ten times that much?"

"It's there. You name it, you got it," Bedford said. "Only do something. Save her!"

THE EVENTS OF THE AFTERNOON had affected Walt Duncan even more than he realized. The face of Amy Bedford followed him as he went on his rounds and when he sat in consultations. It was with him so persistently that he finally asked his secretary to call off his last two appointments so he could get home in time to have dinner with Simone and Emily. For he had realized that, different as their vocations might be, Ed Bedford and Walt Duncan had something in common.

IT WAS AN ENJOYABLE DINNER for all three of them. Simone talked elatedly throughout the meal. More than once Walt had to urge, "Darling, your chicken is getting cold. We'll have plenty of time to talk later." But the child insisted, relating everything that had happened to her in school not only that day but the day before as well. To his dismay, Walter realized her excitement, the sparkle in her eyes, was really a rebuke. She was taking advantage of every moment with him because the opportunity to have him to herself was so rare.

When she left the table, she stopped in the archway. "Come up and kiss me goodnight later?"

"Of course, sweetheart," Walt said.

As soon as he had finished his coffee he started up the stairs. He found Simmie's door partly open. He peeked in, intending to make a game of it. But she did not respond. He came to her bedside. She was already asleep. She must have been very tired. He bent down to kiss her on the cheek.

When he came down to the den, Emily said, "You came home early tonight."

He smiled. "Come home late, it's taken for granted. Come home early, I have to explain."

"It's not just that. Something happened to you today."

"Yes," he admitted. He told her about Amy Bedford. "I may have overpromised her. But I felt I had to reassure her."

"What *are* her chances?"

"Good," he said, then moderated that to, "Well, not exactly good. There's already an eighty-three-per-cent chance that the cancer could have spread into her bloodstream. But there's a possibility the chemo will counteract that."

"If it doesn't?" she asked.

He hedged, saying, "We'll know soon. Six weeks, eight. The tumour will recede or it won't. That'll dictate what we do next."

"So that's what brought you home early?" Emily remarked. "Simone was beside herself with excitement. She surely made the most of it."

"Wore herself out, it seems," Walt said, smiling. "She been going to bed early recently?"

"Come to think of it, she no longer pouts when I tell her not to watch television. Just goes right up to bed."

Walt settled down to study some lab reports he had received that afternoon. In the morning he would have to get together with Rita Bristol, the oncologist, to establish a treatment plan for Amy Bedford's chemotherapy.

And, he remembered with annoyance, he would soon have to appear in court to testify in the malpractice suit against Peter Enright. He did not look forward to that chore at all.

EVERYONE AT UNIVERSITY MEDICAL CENTER considered Rita Bristol a very private person. Aside from her impressive curriculum vitae, which included a record of excellent service with two hospitals in the east, no one at the hospital knew a great deal about her. She was an attractive woman, tiny, dark-haired. She had a reputation for being quite unemotional as well as very open and direct about the course of treatment she prescribed for her patients.

Today, as she faced Amy Bedford and her mother, Dr. Bristol was her usual brisk, efficient self. She wore her black hair in a coronet, which served as an elegant frame for her precise features.

Amy sat as still as she could manage. Her mother sat beside her. Aware of their enormous tension and fear, Dr. Bristol did her best to start the meeting on an optimistic note.

"Amy, I suppose you've heard horror stories of what happens when a person gets chemotherapy. Mostly they tend to be exaggerated. That is not to say that it will be pleasant. Because there will be a war being fought in your body. The good guys are the chemical agents we give you. The bad guys are the cancer cells. And, as in all wars, the innocent sometimes get hurt. So, yes, there will be times of discomfort. Nausea. Vomiting, even, for a time. But none of it as bad as you've heard.

"The main purpose you and I have is to shrink that tumour in your leg. If we can do that, then Dr. Duncan can do his operation. So, every time you feel like quitting, remember our aim. OK?"

"OK," Amy murmured, barely audible. Then she asked, "What happens if it doesn't shrink?"

Dr. Bristol was taken by surprise. Unaware of what Walt Duncan might have said, she answered, "In that case there won't be any choice. Dr. Duncan would have to amputate."

A cold hand seemed to grip and twist Amy Bedford's stomach. She turned to her mother. But Dr. Bristol intervened.

"Amy! I didn't say that will happen. I only said if you and I failed, it would happen. So it is most important that we each do our part. Every time you feel like your insides are being torn apart by the chemo, know that you are suffering in a good cause. Discomfort now, stress now, can mean that operation in just weeks. And then a whole new life."

Amy faced Dr. Bristol and took comfort from the look of conviction in her deep, dark eyes.

"Now, Amy, this will be our routine for the next eight weeks. You will have to have nine doses of a chemical called methotrexate, administered intravenously."

"Will I have to be in the hospital?" Amy asked.

"Only three days at a time. One day to get the treatment. Two days so we can monitor the effects."

"Miss three days of school at a time," Amy said.

"We'll work out something with the school, Amy. Home lessons. A special curriculum. Now then, I've arranged a room for you in the Pediatric Pavilion."

30

"I'm fifteen!" Amy protested.

Dr. Bristol smiled. "I'm afraid in medical circles we still consider that a proper age for the pediatric service. So, Monday morning. Eight o'clock!"

CHAPTER 3

On Saturday Amy woke early out of a dream of which she could only remember protesting, "I'm too young, too young." She lay awake, exhausted, her bed damp with sweat.

Vestiges of her dream began to come back to her. She had been protesting to a tall, shadowy person who hovered over her. "I'm too young to have this, too young to be so sick."

She breathed deeply, wiping the sweat from her tense face with the palms of her hands. Monday, she suddenly thought, I will have to report for the first dose of that stuff that Dr. Bristol talked about. Metho something. Which does all kinds of hateful things. What if it's all a waste?

She turned on her side and became aware again of that slight but persistent pain in her leg. To her, the enemy was the pain, not the disease. She had no proof of the disease.

Besides, she told herself, a girl can't be training for the state finals one day and be threatened with death the next.

Before she would submit to the horrors of chemotherapy, she would do a little investigating of her own. She slipped out of bed and and went to her closet. She opened the door, which had a full-length mirror. She stood before the mirror and put her right leg forward, turning it first one way, then another. She noticed no swelling. No deformity. She pressed it and pinched it. She felt nothing except for that annoying pain that persisted day and night. But, she thought, after strenuous training for the tournament it was only natural that her leg might hurt.

She had played before, despite pain. There was no reason she could not do so again. She determined that she would.

She pondered whether it was too early to phone, then decided to risk it. She slipped down the stairs on bare feet. She noticed no light in the kitchen, which meant no one else was up yet. She went into the den, sat at her father's desk and used his phone.

She was prepared with exactly what she would say if Brent Martin's mother answered. Fortunately, it was Brent himself.

"Brent? Amy."

"Oh, hi. Where you been the last few days?"

"You know Swede. I had this pain in my leg, and he wouldn't let me work it out. I guess I'll have to do it on my own. So I wondered, this being Saturday, could you and I rally for an hour or two?"

"If Swede said—"

"Not on the school courts. The public courts. In the park," Amy said. "Please, Brent?"

"For you, Amy, OK. Want me to pick you up?"

Amy considered that for a moment before she said, "No. I'll—I'll meet you there. About nine."

WHEN AMY APPEARED at the public courts, she looked well dressed in her navy blue and red tracksuit. The colours contrasted with her blonde hair and her blue eyes. The trim cut hugged her adolescent body in a flattering way.

She waited apprehensively for Brent, afraid he might not show up. But at nine, as promised, he appeared, carrying his racket and a net bag bulging lumpily with used tennis balls. It was evident from the look in his eyes that he liked her.

"Are you sure it's all right?" he asked as they stripped down to their tennis shorts.

"Of course it's OK. I feel great," Amy assured him.

They started warming up from the baselines. He hit long, easy strokes, the sort that Amy liked to return with equal strength. Soon they widened the area of play, some of Brent's shots reaching the corners of the court. Amy scampered after the ball, mostly making it in time to strike a good return. Sometimes, though, she could barely get her racket on it. Brent came to the net, ostensibly to put the ball away on a volley. But once there, he tapped his racket on the tape and asked, "Amy?"

"Yeah?" she responded, breathless.

"You're not getting to the ball like you usually do."

"I'm just warming up," she replied tartly, walking towards him.

"You're already warmed up," the young man said. "Something's wrong."

"Nothing's wrong. Just get back there and play."

"Are you sure—" he started to say.

"Brent, you're worse than my mother when it comes to nagging! Now, get back there," Amy insisted.

She started back to the baseline. As she walked away from him Brent noticed the same limp that had disturbed Swede Olafsen. Brent felt he should make her quit. But he knew how headstrong Amy was. If he didn't practise with her, there wasn't another boy on the team who would refuse. He decided to continue.

"Let's play a few games," she called out.

"Sure," Brent responded. "Serve!"

32

They played for about twenty minutes, accelerating their pace, increasing their strokes, testing Amy to her limit. But she stayed in the set, determined to show him that she was as good as ever.

She was at her own baseline, waiting to receive Brent's serve. It was shorter and somewhat softer than she expected. She came in to meet it and sent it back deep to him. She then raced in to reach the net, but her right foot went down under her. She fell forwards, sprawling on the green concrete, scraping her knee. The pain was so sudden that despite herself she cried out. Brent raced to the net, vaulting it to reach her. He knelt beside her, saw the bad scrape and the blood seeping to the surface. Over her protests he lifted her in his arms and carried her to his car.

"Please don't drive me up to my door," she begged.

"I'm not going to let you walk," he said.

As Amy feared, when they pulled up at her house, her mother was waiting at the front door.

"Please, Brent," Amy whispered. "Don't make it any worse by trying to help me to the door."

"OK," he said. "But tell her the truth."

"We were practising. Why would I lie about that?"

"I don't know. But I have a feeling it was wrong."

She opened the car door and slipped out. By the time she reached the front door, her mother's face had changed from mere concern to great distress. She assisted Amy into the house and sat her down. She was appalled by the sight of torn skin and blood on the diseased leg. But without a word of recrimination she went to the phone and placed a call to Dr. Corey.

"Call Dr. Duncan" was the pediatrician's advice. "I want him to see Amy at once! Do you understand? At once!"

"WELL, WELL," WALTER DUNCAN said as lightly as he could manage while he stared at Amy Bedford's right leg.

She looked up at him from the examining table, trying to read his expression. He did not seem as alarmed as her mother had been, or Dr. Corey. In truth, he was more agitated than both of them.

"Just tell me how it happened," Walt said, tenderly palpating her leg.

She admitted practising, stressing how good it had felt. Yes, there was still a little pain, but it seemed to lessen as practice progressed. When she described her fall, she insisted it was just one of those accidents that will happen on a tennis court.

"So you see, Doctor, the pain had nothing to do with it."

"Amy, it really doesn't matter how it happened. Whether it was due to tripping on a step or getting out of a car is not important. The only thing that does matter is that you didn't break your leg. Because if you had

33

broken it, we would have had no choice. I would have had to amputate. Today."

She stopped breathing. She could feel her skin tighten. Then she thought, He's only saying that to scare me. But when she looked into his eyes, she knew he was telling her the truth.

"Amy, right now, from what we can determine, those cancer cells are all confined to one area. But should a fracture occur, they'll break out and start rampaging through your body. The only safe course then would be to remove the leg."

Amy began to tremble. Duncan placed his hand on her shoulder and continued. "I only said that would happen if there had been a fracture. So, while you're having chemo, I will have to insist that you wear a leg brace."

"A brace? Like a cripple?" Amy asked.

Walter Duncan corrected, "A brace, like a young woman with a dangerous condition that we want to cure."

"Would I have to wear it all the time?"

"Yes."

"You mean even those days when I can go to school?"

"Yes."

"Then I won't go! I don't want them to see me like that."

"Amy, I've already called Hans Metterling down in our surgical appliance department. He's there now, even though it's Saturday, and he's waiting to see you."

HANS METTERLING'S WORKPLACE in the basement of the hospital seemed to be a disorderly jumble of metal parts and pieces. There were vices and clamps in which some of those pieces were in various states of preparation. Sketches lined the walls. Metterling gestured Amy to be seated. He did not attend to her at once, but concentrated on filing down a metal part.

Finally he turned to her. "Ah," he said. "*Und* now. Dr. Duncan has told me about you." His accented words seemed a rebuke. "A young girl running around on a tennis court, trying to break her leg. Vell, ve are not going to let that happen."

He peered at her over the high-intensity lenses he wore when he worked. "Say, you really are beautiful, like Dr. Duncan said. Vell, for pretty girls old Hans makes a very pretty leg brace that vill be light as a feather. You like that, young lady?"

Amy tried to nod, but could not.

"I know, I know," he went on. "You are thinking, Vat will my friends say? A young girl like you, valking around with a leg brace. Vell, two things you can do. You can tell them you don't give a darn what they think. Or else you can wear jeans and they vill never know. Myself, I would wear the trousers. Now . . ."

He gently took her right foot, extended her leg and studied it. Then he began to mumble to himself, making what seemed to be hieroglyphic notes on an old pad on his worktable. Using a tape and callipers, he measured her leg at various points. It seemed to Amy that he jotted down hundreds of figures.

Finally the old man smiled and stared at her over his glasses, revealing a twinkle in his eyes.

"Ve come for a fitting in four days, no?"

"Yes, yes, Mr. Metterling."

"Hans," he corrected. "Hans."

AMY BEDFORD lay in her hospital bed. Her nervous fingers played with the hem of the sheet that covered her. She stared at her mother, who stood at the foot of the bed trying to smile encouragingly. Amy smiled back. For she felt that if she did not, her mother would soon begin to cry.

"You're going to be fine, fine," her mother kept repeating. "Before you know it, you'll be playing tennis again. Swede told me so."

Amy nodded, though she was thinking, Please, God, make her leave. She doesn't know what to say. She keeps making up things. Swede never said that.

To Amy's relief, Dr. Bristol entered, followed by a nurse who carried a tray of medications and hypodermics.

"Mrs. Bedford, please?" Dr. Bristol dismissed her.

Marion Bedford nodded, trying to smile. "I'll be waiting outside, Amy darling."

The oncologist filled a large hypodermic with a colourless fluid.

"Amy, this is methotrexate. Before we're through, you'll hate that word. But remember all the while, this is the stuff that's fighting those cancer cells."

She tightened a length of thin, tan rubber tubing round Amy's bicep until the vein on the inner side of her arm stood out. She washed the area with an alcohol swab to sterilize it. Then slowly she injected the powerful fluid into her.

"There we are. First treatment," Dr. Bristol said. "There'll be nurses available. Just press that buzzer. We know what you'll be going through. Meantime, you can read, listen to the radio, watch television. Now, anything I can do?"

Amy hesitated before saying, "Yes. Please send my mother home." The doctor's noticeable resistance made Amy explain, "I'd like to have her here. But it's too much for her. Too much."

"Amy, let her stay," Dr. Bristol suggested.

"She feels so helpless; she makes up things to say. Trying to give me courage. And it doesn't."

"I can only suggest she go. I can't force her," Dr. Bristol said.

"Then do that, please," Amy pleaded.

IN THE AFTERNOON, some hours after Amy had received a second injection of methotrexate, she began to feel the first waves of nausea. She reached for the buzzer. But as she pressed it the feeling overcame her. A nurse raced into the room.

"Nurse—nurse—" Amy began to say, but the words were drowned in another wave of sickness. The nurse held a stainless-steel basin to her lips, embracing the girl with her free arm. "It's all right, Amy," she murmured. "This is par for the course, so don't be afraid."

The first siege was over. Perspiring, Amy lay back in the bed.

"We'll get some clean things and you'll feel better," said the nurse, and she left quickly. Before she returned, Amy heard her door open quietly.

"Amy—" her mother ventured.

"Gee, Mom, not now. I'm a mess."

"I know. The nurse told me. Anything *I* can do?"

The nurse came back. "Out of bed, Amy," she said briskly. The woman quickly stripped the bed and remade it with fresh linen. She then shook out a clean gown. "Out of that one, Amy." She held out the gown, and Amy slipped into it. "Now back into bed."

The nurse placed another pillow behind her head and said, "There. Good as new, aren't we?"

"Until it happens again," Amy said.

"Don't feel embarrassed. You're doing just fine." She turned to Marion Bedford, inviting her to leave. "Mrs. Bedford—"

"No, please," Amy interjected. "I want her to stay now."

"Of course," the nurse said.

The door had closed again. Marion Bedford stood at the foot of Amy's bed. She strained to observe her daughter, to see if she could anticipate the next wave of nausea. In a while Amy began to feel that evil stirring in her stomach, the burning in her throat. "Mama!" she cried.

Marion Bedford lunged for the steel basin, held it to her daughter's mouth and embraced her quivering young body as the girl retched again.

The spasm gradually passed. She had sweated through her fresh gown. She was breathing hard. But for the present it was over. Her mother turned to set aside the basin.

"Mama?" the girl said softly.

"Yes, dear?"

"Hold me, Mama. Hold me for a little while."

"Of course, baby. Of course."

THERE HAD BEEN SEVERAL changes of gowns, but no need to change bed linen again. Between them Amy and her mother had mastered the problem until it became a routine. At times Amy was able to lapse into snatches of sleep.

When Amy woke the last time, it was dark outside.

"Is it night? What are you still doing here, Mom?"

"It's not late. And Dad's on his way. He's going to pick me up."

"Oh. Good!"

"You need to have your dinner. Dr. Bristol was here. She said you should eat."

"I don't feel like eating," Amy protested.

"She said try anyhow. I'll buzz for the nurse."

In a short while the nurse placed a tray on the bed-table and raised the bed so Amy was in position to eat.

The girl surveyed the bland food. "Yuck," she said.

The nurse smiled, then said as she left, "Give it a try, Amy. Please?"

Amy tried. The food was tasteless. But she realized why it was all so bland. Any spice at all would start the unhappy process all over again. She ate as much as she could and was still staring at the tray when the door eased open. Her father peeked in.

"Daddy," she said.

He embraced her with his right arm, for in his left arm he held a package. "I had my secretary scour the town for it, darling. Wait till you see." He unwrapped it and produced a small black object, somewhat bigger than a portable radio. "How's that?"

"What is it?" Amy asked.

"Your own private television set. See the size of that small screen? You can watch television from any position you're in. You don't have to lie on your back and stare up at that set on the wall. And it gets great reception. Here, let me show you!"

He plugged the cord into the wall socket, pressed the on button and waited for the screen to light up. Finally it did. He switched the channels. Unfortunately, not one channel produced an acceptable picture. He was enormously disappointed.

"I'll—I'll take it down to the office. Fritch is great with anything mechanical. He'll figure out what's wrong." Then he changed the subject. "Well, how did it go today, darling? Mom told me you had some rough moments. But you look fine . . . fine."

To ease his discomfort over the gift, Amy said, "It's not as bad as people said it would be. Is it, Mom?"

He noticed the tray. "You didn't eat very much, darling. Hospital food. No wonder. Listen, I'll order some decent food in for you. You name it, you got it."

The phrase was familiar to Amy. She had heard her father use it on the phone many times with customers. Poor Daddy, she thought. Doesn't he know any other way to deal with people?

To relieve him of his promise, Amy said, "It's really good food. Tastes better than it looks. I like it."

At the same time she prayed, Please make him go before I have another attack of nausea. I don't know if he could stand it.

Dr. Bristol came to her rescue as she entered briskly, dressed in street clothes, evidently on her way home.

"Ed, this is Dr. Bristol," Marion Bedford said.

"Howdy, Doctor," Bedford said. "How's our little girl?"

"Based on what I saw and heard today, I'd say she is doing very nicely. She gets her medication when she should. Reacts when she should. Now, if I can suggest, I think she might want to get prepared for a night's sleep. What do you think, Amy?"

"Yes, yes. I'd like that."

Ed Bedford kissed his daughter, gathered up his gift and started for the door. "I'll get this fixed for you, darling," he said.

Marion Bedford kissed her daughter and followed him.

Once they were gone, Dr. Bristol said, "What was that?"

"My own private, personal television set."

"Does it get channels the others don't?"

"No. My father's not good at picking out gifts for girls. His secretary usually does it for him. She must have run out of ideas."

"Well, he tried. That's the important thing," Dr. Bristol said consolingly as she pushed away the bed-table.

"You didn't eat much," she said. "It's natural not to want food now. But make an effort. Whatever nourishment you can gain is worth it. We need a strong girl for that operation."

She started for the door, but Amy called to her. "Doctor—"

Rita Bristol turned back. "Yes, dear?"

Amy hesitated before asking, "When will we know whether . . . well, whether all this was worth—" Before Dr. Bristol could answer, the door opened behind her and Walter Duncan entered the room.

"How's our patient doing, Rita?"

"She's on target," the oncologist assured him. "She was about to ask me something you are better qualified to answer. Amy?"

The girl hesitated again, then asked, "When will we know if all this— the chemo, the nausea—was worth it?"

"Six weeks, seven, eight at the most. But don't worry about that now. Just follow the routine Dr. Bristol's laid out—"

Before he could finish the girl burst out, "If it comes to a time when you have to—to take my leg, let me die!"

"Amy!" he rebuked strongly.

"No. I mean it!" the girl insisted. "I couldn't stand the look in his eyes."

"Whose eyes?" Walt asked.

"My—my father's."

Walt glanced at Rita Bristol, then moved closer to the bed.

"Amy, listen to me. I'm a father too. I have a little girl. Not as old as you. But I know how fathers feel. No matter what happens, he's always going to love you."

"You don't understand," the girl protested. "He has never got used to having a daughter. He wanted a son. He wanted someone to play football. And grow up to go to business school. And take over his business one day."

Walt laughed. "Amy, women do that now. Go to business school. Take over businesses."

"He wanted a son," she insisted. "That's why I took up tennis. To make him proud. It got his attention. Now, if something happens—and you know what that something is—he won't want a daughter, not a one-legged daughter."

"Amy, Amy, come now," Walter Duncan said.

But the girl turned away from him to hide her tears. Walt reached out to draw her to him. He embraced her, held her, and against his better judgment said, "Amy, I gave you my word. One year of your life and I'll cure you."

CHAPTER 4

Seven weeks had gone by. Amy Bedford had appeared at the hospital periodically for her infusions of chemotherapy. The treatment had advanced beyond methotrexate. Dr. Bristol had put her on vincristine, a more powerful drug. Amy had borne up well, enduring all the suffering inherent in the treatment. She attended school on those days she felt able, though both she and her teachers had resigned themselves to the fact that she could no longer keep up with her classmates.

Always, secretly, she counted the days. She marked them off on a calendar that she kept hidden in her desk drawer. In four more days the doctors would take those crucial bone scans and X-rays that would reveal whether or not the tumour had shrunk.

Every day she would pose before the mirror, turn her leg this way and that to see if she could determine some change. The most recent scan did not indicate that the tumour had shrunk, but to Amy the leg did look thinner. Perhaps that meant the thing was shrinking. But then, all of her was thinner.

She no longer weighed herself on her mother's bathroom scales. It frightened her. Antinausea drugs had no salutary effect, so she suffered days when she was sure that more came up than she had eaten. With all that, losing weight was inevitable. She had only one consolation: a few more days and she would know if it all had been worth it.

The night before she was to return to the hospital she stirred in her sleep and woke. After staring up at the ceiling of her room, still sleepy, yet sleepless, she turned on her side. As she turned, her right arm fell easily to the far side of her pillow. Her hand felt something that made her start. She reached across and turned on the light. She saw them—loose strands of her blonde hair across the pink pillow. What she had been warned might happen had begun. A gush of tears came to her blue eyes.

After some minutes of weeping she determined to face the worst of it. She threw back her blanket, rose and went to the mirror. It was not as bad as she had feared. Her hair seemed as thick as always. She felt relieved. She was tempted to tug at some of the strands to see if they would come loose in her hand. She decided not to risk it. Instead, she picked up her hairbrush and started to give herself a vigorous brushing.

She continued until the brush suddenly felt strange in her hand. She put it down to flex her fingers. They felt tingly, then numb. She picked up the brush once more, but she lost her grip. It dropped noisily to the dressing table.

Terrified, she ran from the room and burst into her parents' bedroom, crying, "Mom! Mom! I'm paralysed!"

Startled, Marion and Ed Bedford woke suddenly. Marion bolted from the bed, embraced her sobbing daughter. "Baby, darling, now calm down. And tell me."

"The brush, the hairbrush. I couldn't hold it; it just fell," Amy said, through her tears.

"Amy, let me see your hand," her mother said.

Amy held out her right hand.

"Move your fingers."

The girl opened and closed her hand.

"There. See! You are not paralysed."

"But it tingles, and I can't hold anything."

"I'll call Dr. Duncan!" her father said, jumping out of bed.

"Ed! Ed! Not at this time of night."

"If my daughter is in trouble, I don't care what time it is."

THE PHONE BESIDE the Duncans' bed broke the night silence. Walt instinctively turned in its direction and lifted the receiver. "Duncan," he announced.

"Dr. Duncan," Ed Bedford assailed him. "My daughter is in trouble."

"Who is this?"

"Bedford. Ed Bedford."

Walt sat up suddenly. "What kind of trouble is Amy in?"

"Her hands. She can't hold anything—"

"Put her on the phone!" Walt ordered. He waited until he heard Amy sobbing. "Amy, can you hear me?"

"Uh-huh," she managed to say through her tears.

"Just listen to me, dear, and answer yes or no. Do you have any feeling in your fingertips?"

"Uh-huh."

"Is there a tingling?"

"Some."

"Listen closely, Amy. You are having what we call neural toxicity. The drug vincristine that Dr. Bristol had to give you sometimes produces such aftereffects. But it's just a passing phase. Now, you go back to sleep. And don't worry. The numbness will pass. I promise you."

WALT SAT ON THE EDGE OF THE BED. He glanced at the digital clock: 5:16. Too early to get up, too late to go back to sleep. Besides, he had to leave even earlier than usual this morning. Starting at seven thirty, there were four patients to be operated on. Then a meeting of the Tumour Board to discuss the treatment of a number of cancer patients.

Complicating his life even further, that Enright trial was in progress, and the attorney Silverstein had notified him that he could be called to testify any time now. And finally, at the end of this day, would be Amy's scans and X-rays.

He showered and dressed as quietly as possible. It was still dark out when he stopped by Simone's bedroom to kiss her goodbye. As he bent close to her she opened her sleep-shrouded eyes, said, "Goodnight, Daddy," and slipped back into sleep.

He kissed her on the forehead and was about to rise when he realized that she was warm. He placed his hand lightly on her forehead. Low fever, he diagnosed. Not alarming in a child. Yet it disturbed him. He must leave a note for Emily.

DR. WALTER DUNCAN PREPARED to study the latest X-rays of Amy Bedford. The room was dark. He slipped three sets of matching X-rays into the wall-long viewing glass. He flipped on the light. First he studied the set of X-rays taken on Amy's initial examination. Then he examined the second set and finally the third set.

He had no need to spend much time on her lung X-rays. They were perfectly clear. Encouraging sign. He stared long and hard at the matching films of her leg. Unfortunately, they were too much alike.

42

After two arduous series of chemotherapy treatments there was no clear sign of tumour shrinkage.

His train of thought was interrupted when the door opened suddenly. Dr. Bristol came in, saying, "I heard Amy's new set of X-rays are ready."

"They are." Walt pointed to them with no enthusiasm.

The oncologist gave her eyes a moment to adjust to the darkness. Then she compared the films.

"What do you think, Rita? Another series of chemo?"

"It can't do any harm. We might be on the verge of shrinking the darn thing. Be a shame to quit now."

"Can she take it?" Walt asked.

"She's had a bad time with the stomach upsets, but I think she's still game. If you can delay the leg surgery for three more weeks without endangering her life, I'd say let's go for it."

"I'll talk to her," Walt Duncan said.

AMY BEDFORD AND HER MOTHER were waiting patiently in Amy's hospital room when Walt came in. The teenager sat up straight, trying to present an image of health.

He was well aware of her attempt to look good, even though she clearly was not the same patient he had first examined weeks ago. Her pretty face was thinner. Her blonde hair still hung freely, but it was much sparser than before; a few bald spots were evident on her pink scalp. Still, she stared up into his eyes, asking, begging for some good word.

"Hi, Amy," Walt said, trying to appear casual. "Dr. Bristol and I just had a go at your X-rays. We think we're on the verge . . ."

"Verge," was the only word Amy repeated, but it encompassed all her disappointment, all her shattered hopes.

"We haven't given up, Amy. We'd like to try another series of chemo. Add still another chemical."

"More chemo," Amy said, her eyes glistening with tears.

"Amy," Walt Duncan said, taking her hand, "I know what you've been through. I know—"

"You don't know anything!" the girl exploded in a mixture of anger and tears. "You don't know what it's like to look into the mirror and ask yourself, Is this really me? This isn't my face. I never looked like this before. I get up in the morning and find my hair on the pillow. Lots of it. I'll be bald soon!"

"Amy, please," her mother begged.

But Walt Duncan gestured her mother to silence.

Tears streaming down her face, the girl continued. "I won't go through any more. I can't. I can't face them."

"Can't face *who*, Amy?"

"The others. The guys and girls in school," she confessed. "I can't let them see me this way. I can't." She lost control completely and wept freely. "Just let me die."

"Amy!" her mother said in a hushed whisper.

But Walt's look said, Let her cry. Let her say anything she wants.

Soon the girl was sobbing less and wiping away her tears. Her first words were, "I bet I look even worse now. I'm a wreck."

"You are not a wreck," Walt corrected. "You are a young woman with red eyes, which will look perfectly natural as soon as you get over this crying jag. Now, are you telling me that you won't go back to school? I said you could go. And you *should* go."

"Not the way I look!" the girl said defiantly. She reached to her hair and came away with strands of it in her hand. "There! See!"

"So that's it," Walt said. "OK. Just wait here!"

When he came back, in his hand was a light green surgeon's cap. He slipped it over Amy's blonde hair at a rakish angle and invited her mother's opinion. "How's that?"

"It does have a certain flair," Mrs. Bedford said.

He went to the medicine chest in the bathroom and opened the mirrored door. "Go on, take a look, Amy."

The girl ventured towards the mirror, looked at herself and finally conceded, "It doesn't look too yucky."

"It looks darned good!" Walt Duncan said. While she was staring at herself in the mirror, he continued. "Amy, what do you say? Are you game for another series of chemo? I believe it could do the trick."

She did not reply at once. She was reliving those days and nights in the grip of medication, feeling her guts being torn out.

"Amy," Walt Duncan coaxed, "I believe we can still do it."

Finally she set her jaw and nodded.

"Good!" the surgeon said, then signalled Marion Bedford to join him in the hall outside.

"Mrs. Bedford, I don't want your daughter to become a recluse. I want her back in school. Does she have any special friends who might help?"

"There's one boy. Brent Martin."

"Isn't that the young man she was with when she took that bad fall?" Walt recalled.

"Yes, that's the one."

"Tell him to call me," Walt said.

A FEW DAYS LATER, near the end of the afternoon, Walt Duncan pushed open the door to his office to find a tall, blond young man in the waiting room. It was Brent Martin.

"Mrs. Bedford called me," he said. "If it's about that practice session, I

44

tried to discourage Amy from working out. But she was so determined. If you know her, you know she's determined."

"Determined?" Walt said. "Come into my office, Brent."

Once the young man was seated, Walt said, "Amy's overdetermined about some things. And not determined enough about others. She's refused to go back to school."

"Is she allowed to?"

"She's not only allowed to, I want her to. We've got to keep her spirits up. I think you could help."

"Anything you say, Doctor."

"Talk to her. Get her coming back to school. It won't be easy for her. She's very self-conscious about losing her hair and not looking as good as she did. It's your job to tell her that her hair and weight will come back, that she'll be a very pretty girl again. In a word, Brent, you have to be a cheerleader."

The young man nodded soberly. Then he asked, "But how can I even get to talk to her? Since all this started she's shut herself away from all her friends."

"Some people do," Walt conceded. "They feel cancer is something to be ashamed of. Do you know of any friend of hers who could change her mind?"

"Swede, I think. Swede could do it if anyone can."

"OK, Brent. Your first assignment, talk to Swede."

He was at the door when Walt suddenly said, "Brent!" The young man turned. Smiling, Walt tossed him a surgeon's cap.

"What do I do with this?"

"Convince Amy to come back to school, and I'll show you."

SWEDE OLAFSEN ARRIVED at the Bedford home in the early evening. Marion Bedford answered the door. As soon as she recognized Swede her eyes welled up. "She won't see you. She won't see anyone," she warned.

"Tell her that I need her help," Swede said.

Mrs. Bedford hesitated, then asked him in and started up the stairs. Swede waited. Finally Mrs. Bedford came down.

"It's OK. But please don't stare at her. She's losing her hair, and she's very sensitive."

"I've been dealing with youngsters for years, Mrs. Bedford. I know how sensitive teenagers can be."

She led Swede to Amy's bedroom door, and he knocked. After a moment came Amy's soft, hesitant voice. "Come in."

He pushed the door open. In the unlit room he made out her form. She was sitting huddled in a chair in a corner.

"Amy," he began, "I know you're not feeling well. And I wouldn't bother you, except I have a problem. With you out for this season I've got to rely on Carole Wallace."

"Yes," Amy said. "I thought so."

"Well, you can tell a girl she's number one, but that's a long way from making her feel like it."

"What can I do?" Amy asked.

"Carole admires you, always has. If you could tell her how good she is, it would help."

"I'll call her if you want." Amy offered.

"You can't tell her how she's doing unless you watch her."

"That would mean I . . ."

"That's right, Amy. You would have to come back to school."

"Back to school. I can't do that."

"Why not?"

"Because . . ." The girl seemed to draw back into the darkness even more.

"If I didn't need your help, I wouldn't ask," Swede said. "You know what a state title means to the school. And I've been thinking about retiring. I sure would like that trophy in the school gym before I leave."

"I'll think it over," was all she would say. Then, as the tall, white-haired coach turned to leave, Amy called to him. "Swede—"

"Yes, Amy?"

"I know what it means to you. So, OK, I'll do it."

BRENT MARTIN WAITED down the block from the Bedford house. He had been waiting since a quarter to seven in the morning. Finally he saw the front door open. Amy and her mother came out. For an uneasy moment it seemed that Amy might change her mind and go back in. But then she started down the path.

As he overtook her he slowed down, trying to make his discovery appear accidental. "Hi! Amy? That you?"

She half turned to face him. He was pleased with the way she looked, with the way she wore that surgeon's cap. It sat perched on her head at a jaunty angle, fixed in place with hairslides. She was thinner, but she was almost as pretty as ever.

"Hey, you look great, Amy!" Brent said enthusiastically.

"You think so?"

"I sure do. Love that hat," he said. "Carry your books?"

They were a block away from the school when a classmate, Pam Sanford, who had been appointed lookout, spied them. She raced to their first-period class and said, "OK, guys. They're on the way!" At once everyone dropped into a seat.

46

Amy and Brent entered the building and walked down the corridor. When they were at the door to their classroom, Brent could sense Amy withdrawing within herself. He gripped her arm, and they both started into the room.

The sight that greeted Amy made tears of relief come to her eyes. Every girl in the class was wearing a surgeon's cap, neatly held in place by slides or grips. And they were smiling. One girl cried out, "Amy!" and started towards her for an embrace. Soon all the girls crowded round her, welcoming her.

As arranged, their teacher, Mr. Hitchins, entered the room late. Pretending his usual pedagogic severity, he said, "Well, now, shall we risk learning something about American history today?" Then he smiled and said, "Welcome back, Amy Bedford."

CHAPTER 5

Two more weeks had gone by. It was another day, another early morning. Walter Duncan was standing at the kitchen table downing his coffee when Emily came in, drawing her robe round her.

"Hi, hon. Did I wake you?" he asked.

"No," Emily said. "I'd love to make you some breakfast."

"Thanks. But I've got to be in the operating room before seven. Then have to spend half my day in court. That Enright thing."

"I hope it doesn't get messy."

"Whenever a doctor botches a case, it gets messy," Walt said. "Anyhow, my part of it should be over today." He kissed her. "By the way, Simmie getting a cold?"

"Not getting, got," Emily corrected.

"Take her temp. If she's got any fever, keep her home."

HE WAS PULLING into the parking lot at the hospital when he suddenly braked. He sat there itemizing in his mind the isolated facts he had noticed about his daughter during recent months: slight fever, paleness, compliant attitude, those bruises. Could a doctor become so immersed in his own specialization that he forgot all those other symptoms he knew so well as a houseman?

No time for that now. He had to scrub for surgery.

After he had finished his three cases for the morning and changed from OR greens back into his own clothes, Walt went down to his office. As soon as he opened the door his secretary, Claudia, greeted him with a message.

"Mr. Silverstein called. He needs you in court after lunch."

"I'll be there," Walt replied. "How long will you be here?"

"Late as you want. Something up?" the young woman asked.

"Remind me."

"Of what?" she asked, puzzled.

"Just remind me. I'll know what," he said. "Oh, by the way, Amy Bedford. Her new X-rays?"

"I checked. She's in radiology right now."

"Good. I'll stop by and see them after court."

Once he had left, Claudia printed in large letters on a sheet of plain paper THIS IS TO REMIND YOU, then mounted the sign prominently on his desk.

AS WALTER DUNCAN entered the courtroom he saw at once that Dr. Peter Enright was seated at the counsel's table alongside his lawyer. Walt realized he would have to confront his hostile former colleague while giving testimony.

Walt was in the witness chair and had taken the oath when Andrew Silverstein, counsel for the eighteen-year-old plaintiff, came forward to ask, "Doctor, will you please tell the jury your background and credentials?"

Walt recited the details of his education and experience.

Silverstein then turned to the bench. "Your Honour, is there any objection to Dr. Duncan's qualifications for giving expert opinion in this case?"

The judge addressed the opposing lawyer. "Counsel?"

"No objection," the defence attorney replied as he seized his pencil and yellow pad, ready to frame the questions he would put to Walt on cross-examination.

"Doctor, have you made a study of the entire file in this case?" Silverstein asked.

"I have."

"And have you examined this young plaintiff seated here?"

"I have," Walter replied.

"Will you tell the jury the condition in which you found this young man?"

"The general state of his health was good. But he suffered a noticeably dropped left foot."

"Did you determine the cause of that condition?"

"I did. It is clear from the patient's file that the fifth lumbar spinal nerve root, what we call L-five, was severed in an attempt to remove a herniated disc—the result of an apparent football injury. When you sever the L-five, a dropped foot will result, and a patient loses the ability to control his step. A permanent brace may be necessary."

"In your opinion, Doctor, is the severing of such a nerve during this procedure the result of faulty medical and surgical practice?"

Walter Duncan looked at Peter Enright, who stared back at him, half defiant, half fearful. Walt replied firmly, "There is no doubt of it in my mind. The treatment performed here was not in keeping with the standards of medicine and surgery practised in this community."

"Now, Doctor, if a young man of sixteen and a half, who had been injured in a football game and suffered sciatic pain extending down to his foot, and showed signs of muscle weakness in that leg, came to you for treatment, what would you have done?"

"First a complete examination to determine the extent of the injury," Walt said.

"Dr. Enright did that, didn't he?" Silverstein said.

"Yes, he did," Walt conceded.

"And would you also have taken X-rays of the patient?"

"Of course."

"Well, didn't Dr. Enright do that?"

"Yes, he did," Walter said.

"Didn't he go even further and do an electromyogram to test nerve conductivity to the painful leg?"

"Yes, he did."

"And would you have done that?"

"Yes, I would," Walt replied, growing a little impatient.

"Then, Doctor, in your expert opinion, how was the treatment of this case faulty?"

Walt realized now that Silverstein had cleared the way for him to testify in detail. He launched into his explanation, speaking directly to the jury.

"The X-rays and the electromyogram could serve only one purpose: to reveal the source of the pain, the herniated disc. Now, faced with that finding, a careful doctor doesn't rush in and do surgery. You confine the patient to bed—to rest that area, reduce the inflammation of the nerve that is causing the pain. If that doesn't work, you put the patient into traction. Either at home or in a hospital. In other words, you give that young body a chance to heal itself. Four weeks, five, six, if need be. Only then, if bed rest and traction have failed, a good, careful surgeon would consider invading the patient's body. Surgery is the last thing you do, not the first."

Walter Duncan shifted in his chair to face the counsel's table at which Peter Enright and his lawyer sat.

"And if you do surgery, you do it carefully! You don't leave a young man with a dropped foot and a leg brace for life!"

Silverstein waited patiently until Walt Duncan had finished. "Would you say then, Doctor, that the defendant in this case was guilty of malpractice?"

Walter Duncan nodded, then said, "Yes. Yes, I think there was malpractice."

"Thank you, Dr. Duncan."

For another forty-five minutes Walter Duncan endured a gruelling cross-examination by Peter Enright's lawyer. But he didn't budge from his testimony.

On his way out of the courtroom he passed the counsel's table and Peter Enright. The surgeon glared at him. But Walt rushed by to get back to the hospital, where two new patients awaited him and there were his post-op rounds to make. He raced down the three flights of stairs to the street, where he slid into his car.

As he drove he felt himself in the grip of such an unusual compulsion that he had to force himself to slow down. At the traffic light he realized the source of his urgency. He must conclude his day as quickly as possible and get home. To Simone.

HE HAD PARKED HIS CAR and was starting for the side entrance to the hospital when Alan Bridges, a colleague on the orthopaedic staff, emerged.

"Hi, Alan," Walt greeted him.

"How did it go?" Bridges asked.

"Go? What?" Walt asked, confused for a moment.

"'What?'" Bridges repeated angrily. "Is that all it meant to you? Something to do and then forget?"

"What are you talking about, Alan?"

"I am talking about what you've just done to every doctor who does orthopaedic surgery!"

"Oh, you mean testifying," Walt said.

"Yes! That's what I mean. You and Sy may think it's a highly ethical thing you two conspired to do. But I would like to remind you what legal cases like this can mean to our malpractice insurance premiums, which are sky-high already. And who knows how much higher they will go!"

"Alan, before you go blowing off steam, did you examine the patient's file? Did you see the patient?"

"I didn't have to. I take it for granted that given a certain number of surgical procedures there is going to be an accident here and there, an unexpected outcome."

"This was no accident. It was lousy surgery!" Walt exploded.

"And if it was?" Bridges demanded. "To help one kid, you decided to penalize thousands of surgeons. You and Sy made a very foolish choice when you decided to step into that case!"

"Sorry you feel that way," Walt Duncan said, pushing his way through the door.

"I'm not the only one who does!" Bridges called after him.

It sounded like a threat. But Walt Duncan had no time to consider it. Rounds. New patients. Then home. Simone.

AT THE CLOSE of his end-of-day rounds the beeper in the breast pocket of Walt's white lab coat summoned him. He picked up the nearest telephone. "Duncan," he announced.

"Walt, this is Sy. Come to my consultation room at once!"

When he arrived, the room was dark except for the light from the viewing screen. That light was filtered through a number of X-rays and scans that hung in pairs. As soon as Walt saw the dates on the X-rays he knew who the patient was. March 14, 1986. May 25,1986. Amy Bedford's first X-rays and now her latest, taken early in the day.

"Take a look, Walt. Take a look!" Sy invited.

Walt stared at the films. Each set, before and after, proved one thing: Amy's invasive tumour had shrunk.

"That's all we have to know," Walt said.

"Schedule her. Right away," Sy said.

"Right!"

WALT RETURNED TO HIS OFFICE. Though it was past seven o'clock, he found his secretary still waiting.

"Claudia, what are you doing here at this hour?"

"The way you asked me to remind you this morning, I thought I'd stay on and remind you in person. What can I do for you?"

"Get Amy Bedford on the phone. If her mother is there, have her pick up the extension."

As he continued on into his office the intercom buzzed.

"Doctor, Amy and her mother are both on the phone."

"Thanks, Claudia. Now go home!" He pressed the lighted button to pick up the line to the Bedford home. "Amy?"

"Yes, Doctor." He could sense the expectation as well as the fear in her young voice.

"Amy Bedford, from now on I am going to hold you up as an example to all my patients who have to suffer the slings and arrows of outrageous chemotherapy."

"Doctor—" Amy started to ask, but dared go no further.

"Yes, Amy. You did it! Dr. Rosen and I just went over your X-rays and scans. The tumour has shrunk enough for us to agree that surgery is now indicated."

"Oh, Doctor—" The girl broke into tears.

"Doctor," Marion Bedford interjected, "when do you want her at the hospital?"

"I'll arrange OR time and a room in the morning. The operation will surely be within the week. Meantime, let's all feel that we've won the first battle in a long war. Sleep well tonight, Amy."

"Thank you, Doctor. Thanks so much," the girl said.

As Walt hung up the receiver he saw Claudia's reminder. He hesitated before he turned to the wall of medical textbooks behind his desk chair. He pulled down a large volume, searched through it and began to read:

> . . . frequently presents itself with an abrupt onset of fever. Patient may seem listless, compliant. Ecchymoses and other skin changes may appear. . . .

He allowed the volume to drop to his desk. For the signs and symptoms he had just read related to a disease that, like osteogenic sarcoma, attacked the young in far greater numbers than the old: acute leukemia.

Like all parents confronted by such a terrifying possibility, his first reaction was to deny it. There were differences between these signs and the ones Simone presented. The book also said, "Bleeding from the mouth and nose may be present." Simone had none of that. "Enlargement of the liver and the lymph nodes . . ." He must palpate her for that as soon as possible.

All the way home he considered ways in which to carry out his purpose without arousing concern in his wife.

He turned into the driveway, came in through the garage door and called, "Hi, hon! I'm home!" Emily called back to him from upstairs. She came down to greet him with a kiss.

"Simmie still awake?" he asked as casually as he could.

"We were just going over her book report for tomorrow. You know, she has a real talent for using words. I wouldn't be surprised if some day she turns out to be a writer."

"I'll go up and say goodnight to our budding genius," he joked.

As he reached the top of the stairs he saw the light at the base of her door go out. He had wanted to get to her before she settled down for the night. He knocked.

"Simmie, it's Dad. Can I come in?"

"Of course, Daddy."

She did not turn on the light, expecting, as on most late nights, he would kiss her and snuggle a bit before she went to sleep.

He approached her bed, sat down on the edge, leaned towards her and kissed her. "Baby," he said, "how are you feeling?"

"Fine!" she replied.

"Any more of those black-and-blue marks?" he asked.

"No."

"I don't believe it," he said, pretending to protest.

"I'll show you," she said. Eager to prove herself, she reached for the lamp on the night table and turned it on. She pulled up the top of her pyjamas, exposing her back to him.

"Go ahead, Daddy, look!"

He made a close examination and found no blemishes. He started to massage her back, asking, "There, how does that feel?"

"Great," she said.

As he massaged he turned her gradually until she was lying on her back. He continued rubbing, eventually concentrating on her stomach, especially the area just below her ribs. There he pressed firmly until she squirmed in slight discomfort.

"Sorry, baby," he said. But his sensitive fingers had detected a slight enlargement of her liver. He gently rubbed her neck so that he could palpate her lymph nodes, but he could detect nothing.

Further observation is demanded, he decided.

Emily came upstairs to call, "Walt? Dinner's ready." She entered the room, discovered them and asked, "Something wrong?"

"No," he said. "Just giving a little relaxing massage." He turned to Simone. "Now, baby, get to sleep."

THREE DAYS LATER, attired in his white lab coat, Walter Duncan strode down the hall of the hospital basement to the workshop of Hans Metterling. There he found the technician studying a titanium appliance he had crafted to fit specifications determined with the aid of a highly ingenious computer. Hans demonstrated the slender, shiny device that would replace Amy Bedford's diseased bones. It flexed easily at the knee joint, which was made of a strong, durable plastic that should last Amy for years, possibly for her lifetime.

Walt examined it carefully, then asked, "How much leeway?"

The old craftsman proceeded to demonstrate how expanding rings on the prosthesis could lengthen it. Amy Bedford's X-rays indicated that she had some growth left in her. When that occurred, Walt could perform fairly simple surgery and lengthen the prosthesis with a few turns so it could keep up with the natural growth of her other leg. If all went according to plan, she would never be forced to suffer awkward walking or running.

If all went according to plan.

That reservation overshadowed all of Walt's thoughts.

Hans wrapped the prosthesis tenderly in its plastic covering, presented it to the surgeon and said a soft, very sincere, "Good luck, Valter. She is a nice girl."

With the device in his possession Walt Duncan faced his last and usually most difficult presurgical obligation. He stopped by his office. Claudia had a long legal form waiting for him. He took it and started up to the second floor of the Pediatric Pavilion.

As he had requested, the Bedfords were waiting at their daughter's bedside. Walt could tell at a glance that Marion Bedford had not slept the whole night. Her eyes betrayed it. Ed Bedford was by his daughter's side, seated on the bed, holding her hand.

"Amy," Walt said, "I want you to meet something that is going to become a part of you. You might even want to give it a name. Like Hansi. Why not? The Academy Awards are called Oscars. The TV awards are called Emmys. Well, this is a Hansi."

He carefully removed the plastic wrapping and presented the silver-coloured device, holding it up, flexing the knee joint.

"See how it moves—easily, naturally, like your own knee joint. And it's yours, yours alone. It wouldn't fit anyone else in this world. And tomorrow it will become a part of you for the rest of your life."

Walt rewrapped the device as he spoke, to be free for his next step. He felt the upper left hand pocket of his lab coat to make sure the paper was there. "Hansi wasn't the only reason I asked for all of you to be here today. We have a formality to complete before surgery can be performed." He presented the single printed sheet.

"This spells out the procedure I am going to perform, and that you agreed to. Amy, since you're still a minor, legally it should be signed by your father or your mother. I want you to sign it too."

The girl glanced up at him. She then looked to her father, who seemed as puzzled as she, and as tense.

"Amy, despite all the advanced tests, in a case like yours, when we go in surgically, we can still be confronted with findings we did not expect."

"What kind of findings?" her mother demanded immediately.

Amy gripped her father's hand tighter.

"Amy, I want you to read this sentence," Walt said, running his finger along the form.

Her father intervened. "I'll see that first!"

Walt surrendered the form to him. Ed Bedford read the words. Slowly he lowered the page. He stared at Walt Duncan. In a strained voice he said, "I thought this was being done to avoid what's written here."

"It is," Walt said. "But as I said, we can't be sure until we get in there."

"I want to see it," Amy demanded.

Walt took the paper from her father and gave it to the girl. She stared at it. Walt's finger pointed to the words: "We understand and consent that if it is deemed medically indicated for the patient's health and survival, the surgeon is authorized to perform an amputation of the area involved."

"Amputation." Amy was barely able to utter the word. "But you said, Give me a year . . ."

Walt leaned close to the girl. "Amy, yes, I said, 'One year of your life and I'll cure you.' And I will do my darnedest to accomplish that. But I have seen what can happen in the operating room. A surgeon goes in armed with all the best data and knowledge, but he finds that nature has tricked him. What seemed like healthy bone or tissue turns out not to be. Then the surgeon has no choice. He must save the patient's life."

"If you take off my leg, I don't want to live!"

"Yes, Amy, you do want to live," Walt said. "You're too brave, too fine a person to want to give up your life now. Amy, sign this. Your signature may not have legal importance, but it's important to me. Because it is your expression of faith in your surgeon."

Amy stared at the document and shook her head. "I can't," she protested. She turned to bury her face in her father's shoulder. He patted her gently on the cheek, stared across her at Walt.

"Doctor, do you need this in order to proceed?"

"We can't do surgery without an informed consent."

"You'll do your best to save her leg?"

"You know I will."

"OK," Ed Bedford said more calmly than Walt had expected. "My daughter's life means everything to me." He took a pen out of his inner breast pocket, and holding the form against the wall, he wrote his name more shakily than he had ever done before.

Receiving the signed form, Walt asked softly, "Amy?"

"I can't. I can't," she repeated.

CHAPTER 6

It was late in the afternoon. Marion Bedford sat in the leather lounge chair in the corner of the hospital room, staring at her daughter, who lay on top of her bed. They had not spoken for more than an hour. They had not even tried to console one another. They did not know how. Eventually Marion Bedford became aware that Amy's breathing had settled down. She had dozed off. Thankfully, Mrs. Bedford slipped out of the room to make some inquiries at the nurses' station.

Amy was still dozing when her door eased open. She woke and turned towards the door, expecting the nurse, more medication, another test. She found a young man in his twenties, tall, quite good-looking.

"Amy Bedford?" he asked, pausing in the doorway. She nodded. "May I come in?"

"Yes."

He came to stand at the front of her bed. "My name is Josh Tedrow. Dr. Duncan asked me to stop by. Mind if I sit down?"

"No," Amy replied, puzzled.

He crossed the room to the lounge chair. "Walt said that with surgery approaching you might be feeling a little queasy."

"After all the chemo I've had, queasy is a very small word for what I feel," Amy said.

"Isn't it hell?" the young man remarked. He rose from the chair, approached Amy. He leaned against the foot of the bed. "I'll bet there were times when you said, 'If this is getting cured, I'd rather die.'"

"More than once."

"And times when you felt so lousy that you wanted to call Walt and curse him out?"

"More than twice," Amy said.

"Well, I actually did it," he said, moving to the chair by her bed. He sat down and crossed his legs. He leaned in her direction, as if to impart a secret. "I got him on the phone one night. I told him to hell with his chemo, with his surgery and with him."

"You, you had surgery?" Amy asked, surprised.

"Yes. Same as you're going to have," he said.

"But, you . . ." She did not say it.

She did not have to. He said it for her. "I look all right. I move well. And you never noticed." He patted his left leg. "This is the one. Now I do everything I want. Walk, run, swim, sail, golf."

"He asked you to tell me this, didn't he?"

"Part of my deal with him. If he cured me, I promised I would do this every time he asks." Tedrow smiled. "It's the best deal I ever made."

He uncrossed his legs, rose from the chair, took her hand. "Amy, I was just about your age. Just as scared. Just as debilitated from the chemo. Just as hopeless in some moments, wondering why God had picked me. But then Walt would come in, with his big smile, his confidence, and I'd say, I'm going with him all the way. I'm reaching for life, and he's going to help me get it!"

"You went through the same thing—all of it?" Amy asked.

"All of it. And here I am, six years later. You can do it, Amy. Just go into that operation tomorrow saying that, believing that."

Her mother came into the room. Tedrow winked at Amy. He turned and said, "Mrs. Bedford, she's going to be OK." He left.

Once the door closed, Marion Bedford asked, "Who is he?"

"Josh Tedrow."

"Isn't he a little old to be a friend of yours?"

"Maybe. But he is. He is."

There was a soft, almost apologetic knock at the door. Mother and daughter both turned. The door eased open silently. A ruddy-faced, white-haired man peered in, smiling.

"Swede!" Amy cried out, her first impulse one of joy to see her old coach. Then her blue eyes filled with tears.

"I came to wish you luck tomorrow," Swede said. He smiled. "Like before a big match. You know, those nervous minutes before you go out on the court. When everything feels tight, and your hands are cold. Let me have your hands."

She held out her hands to him. He took them in his, and they were indeed cold.

"Good," he said. "I like it when a player is nervous before a match. One should never be overconfident."

He was rubbing her cold hands as he talked.

"Tomorrow, that's going to be like a match. So you be up for it. Say to yourself, No matter what I find when I wake up, I will face it. I will overcome it. Remember the first time you went to the finals? I said to you, 'Play one point at a time. Don't look back at your errors. Don't look forward to the next game. Play this point.' You believed me. And you did win. You went all the way. Because you knew that to lose a point, or even a game, is not to lose the whole match. Every time you come up to that service line, it's a new point. Well, tomorrow is like that, Amy. If you lose a point or two, there's still the whole match left to play. Right?"

She stared into his delft-blue eyes. "Did Dr. Duncan ask you to come here?"

"No," he said quite simply and honestly.

"Someone did," she insisted.

"Yes. Your father," Swede admitted.

"My father?" She seemed surprised.

"He said he couldn't do it. He didn't know how. But he wanted someone to say to you, No matter what happens tomorrow, there's a whole life before you. He wants you to go into that operating room with the same eagerness, the same fight as when you go into a match. And come out the same way, no matter what happens."

"I may never be able to play again. Or run. Or even walk straight again."

"Amy, my dear, is that what you think life is? All those things you said, they disappear anyhow. Slowly perhaps. But the time comes when all of us can't play any more. But we live on. We find our place. We do the best we can with what we are. That's what life really is. Whether we are sixteen or sixty, we do the best we can. You've always done that. That's why you're a champion. Be my champion tomorrow, Amy. Promise?"

She began to weep but managed a smile and nodded.

"That's my girl," Swede said. He kissed her wet cheeks.

BEFORE WALTER DUNCAN LEFT the hospital for the evening, he dropped in to Amy's room to say goodnight. He found her alone.

"How do you feel, Amy? Ready?"

"Josh Tedrow was here today," she said.

"Nice young man, Josh."

"You cured him. He said he made a deal with you. To come speak to any patient you asked him to."

"He's never turned me down. Never too busy. He's lived up to his part of the bargain. And you will too."

"Me?"

"Yes. That's the only thing I am ever going to ask of you. That when you're cured, you'll do the same—give some other kid the courage it takes when he's coming up to the wire."

"I wouldn't know how to do that," Amy said.

"When the time comes, you'll know," Walt said confidently. He patted her hand. "Ready, Amy?"

"I'm ready," she said with conviction.

"Good," he said. "See you in the morning."

When he was at the door, she called out, "Doctor? That form you wanted me to sign. If you still want me to, I'll sign it now."

He stared at her. She stared back. Smiling. The look in her clear blue eyes was strong and determined.

On the way back to his office to check on late calls Walt realized that his momentary satisfaction with Amy's signature on the consent form had turned to a disturbing sense of guilt.

By the time he reached his office, he realized why. His emotional involvement in Amy's case had roots deeper than were first apparent. Amy had become like a second daughter to him. But he also had concerns about his own daughter.

He wondered, Am I being a parent instead of a physician? I should already have turned Simmie over to another doctor. Well, I will. But first one more test. Without alarming Simmie or Emily I will do it. Tonight.

"I'M GOING TO TAKE A BLOOD SAMPLE from Simmie," he said to Emily. When his wife reacted with surprise, he explained. "I think that cold may have left her with a low-grade infection. I'd like to track it down so we can treat it."

"Good idea," Emily agreed. "Want me to help?"

"Would you?"

While Walt Duncan prepared a hypodermic, Emily broached the subject to Simone.

"Darling, Daddy only wants to get the littlest bit of blood from you. So he can take it to the hospital and have it analysed. That way we can get rid of your cold."

Emily held Simmie on her lap while Walt deftly inserted the needle into a vein in her thin arm. He drew up the plunger slowly, filling the glass tube with bright red blood. He injected the blood into a small specimen phial and sealed it.

In the morning he would give it to Victor Ogura, the hematologist in the hospital for whom he had the highest regard.

VERY EARLY THE NEXT DAY Walter Duncan stopped at Ogura's office, where the Japanese hematologist was already at work.

"Hi, Vic."

"Walt," was all Ogura said as he turned from his microscope. "What's up?"

Walt handed him a phial with blood, which had been kept under refrigeration since the night before.

"Oh, OK," Ogura said as he took the phial.

"Vic, as soon as you know, call me."

"Of course. What are we looking for—sarcoma cells?"

"Just tell me what you find. OK?"

"OK." Something about Walt's evasiveness made Ogura ask, "Who is it, Walt? Special patient?"

"No. Routine. Just tell me."

"I'll run it through right away."

AT SEVEN AM AMY BEDFORD was wheeled through the doors of a large operating room into what seemed a maze of overhead lights and electronic instruments. She felt herself being lifted off the stretcher and onto the operating table. She stared up at the lights. They blinded her for a moment. She looked about and saw no faces, only eyes and masks. From behind one mask came a familiar voice. "Amy . . ."

It was her pediatrician, Dr. Corey. The man standing beside him had warm, compassionate eyes that she recognized.

"Dr. Rosen?"

"Yes, Amy." He then proceeded to introduce every member of the masked team and identify their functions during the surgery.

The anaesthetist was affixing monitoring sensors to Amy's body as Walter Duncan entered the OR from the adjacent scrub area. He held up his hands, and a nurse pulled thin surgical gloves down over his outstretched fingers.

"Ready, Amy?"

"Yes, Doctor," she said.

He gave the anaesthetist a head gesture. The man proceeded to feed barbiturates into an intravenous drip in her arm. While Walt waited for a signal from the anaesthetist, he glanced at the wall clock. He felt almost as if he had another pressing engagement. It was not his habit. Once he was in the OR, he had no time frame. Only the patient under his hands mattered. Suddenly Walt realized he was wondering not about the operation but about how far along Victor Ogura was with the specimen of Simone's blood.

The anaesthetist began signalling. The patient was under and ready. Walt did not respond by word or action.

"Walt," the anaesthetist prodded.

Even Sy Rosen noticed. He bent closer, to ask in a whisper, "Walt, you all right?"

"Of course I'm all right. Why?"

"Well, I've never seen you hesitate like this. If you're not feeling well, let's not begin."

"I'm feeling fine. Fine!" he protested, and held out his hand.

Scalpel in hand, Walt knew that from this moment on he must forget about everything except Amy Bedford, whose future would depend on what happened in the next three or four hours.

He would be battling nature, which could be tricky and cruel in such situations. No one could predict what he would find. Any of a dozen times during the procedure if he found tissue, arteries, veins, nerves or edges of bone to be cancerous, he would have no choice but to amputate.

With such concerns in mind Walt Duncan made the first long, frontal incision from Amy's midcalf to halfway up her thigh. Carefully he retracted the tissue to reach the femoral artery and then the vein. Walt teased them away from the area of bone, peering closely as he examined them. He could breathe a bit easier. There was no sign of tumour attached to either long vessel.

That hurdle passed, he then concentrated on the sciatic nerve. Again, clean. Now with the same exquisite care he examined the peroneal nerve. Luck was with him. Clean.

He was staring down now at the exposed bones, from mid-calf to mid-thigh, the patella, or kneecap, joining the two. Careful measurements had delineated the area of cancerous bone. He marked off the limits of diseased bone and a safe margin of healthy-appearing bone below the tibia and above on the femur. Now he had only one shot at it. If he cut through the bones and the seemingly safe margin turned out to be involved with cancer cells, again he would have no choice. Amputation. So this next move had to be perfect.

He stared at the markings he had made, Finally he held out his hand. The chief nurse passed a high-speed electric saw to him. At the designated places on the tibia and the femur he cut swiftly, cleanly. He removed the patella and passed it to the nurse to be saved for later in the procedure.

Now came the ultimate test, which would decide Amy's fate during the operation. Walt scooped out samples of bone above and below the excisions. He dispatched a nurse to the lab for an immediate frozen section to determine if the margins were healthy. It would take minutes, long minutes that would seem like hours, until the pathologist would phone back his report.

There was nothing to do but wait. Walt Duncan looked up at the wall clock. It had been more than an hour since the surgery had begun. During that time had Ogura examined Simmie's blood sample? Let it be benign, Walt prayed. Let all those signs and symptoms turn out to be just that, signs and symptoms that did not add up to any dread diagnosis.

Sy Rosen detected his uneasiness. Unaware of Simmie's condition, he said, "Don't worry, Walt. I think you got it all. You certainly left safe margins."

Walt did not appear to be encouraged, Sy noticed.

The phone rang. Every head in the operating room turned in its direction. A nurse answered it. She smiled, looked to Walt and nodded. He did not accept that as the final word. He approached the phone. The nurse held it to his ear.

"Peter. Walt. Let me have it."

"Clean," the voice came back. "All samples clean."

"No question?"

"Not in my mind. Of course we'll put it through the regular lab procedure. But I've never seen cleaner."

"Thanks, Peter."

Walt returned to the table. The chief nurse passed him the shiny titanium prosthesis. He flexed it at the knee to reassure himself that it would work easily, comfortably. That done, he drilled an indentation in the top of Amy's tibia and packed it with surgical cement. While the cement was still fresh and soft, he sank the pointed lower end of the prosthesis into it. Once he had safely anchored it there, he extended the upper end of the device and locked it onto the lower end of Amy's femur. The metal skeleton was now firmly entrenched.

He signalled the nurse for the patella that he had removed earlier. Using small, strong stainless-steel screws, he affixed it to the plastic knee joint of the prosthesis.

Next he worked slowly, gradually manipulating the muscles of Amy's calf over the prosthesis. He then proceeded to bring the skin over the muscle and close the incision. His final step was to encase Amy's entire leg in a Jordan splint—a cast with Velcro closures—so he could open it easily to observe how the wound was progressing.

Amy Bedford was now ready to be removed to the recovery room. As she was being wheeled out Walt Duncan ripped off his surgical gloves.

"Excellent, Walt. First-rate surgery," Sy said.

Dr. Corey, Amy's pediatrician, patted him on the shoulder. "I don't witness much surgery. But I know an artist at work when I see one. Shall we go up and see the Bedfords? They'll want to know. You know how parents are."

Walt wanted to reply, Yes, yes, I know very well how parents are. Today more than ever. Instead, he said, "Of course. They'll want to know right away."

CHAPTER 7

A dozen times Walter Duncan looked at the message he had found on his desk when he finally returned to his office. "Dr. Ogura called. Call him. Urgent." A dozen times Walt tried to interrupt the pressures of his own practice to make that call. Twice he did. Only to discover that Ogura was out.

It was just past six o'clock in the evening before the two doctors could make contact.

"Vic, what did you find?"

"Walt, can you come down to my lab for a minute?"

"Of course. Right away."

Walt raced down three flights of stairs. He was breathless when he burst into Ogura's lab.

"Vic, what is it?" he demanded.

"Walt, I don't know what this patient is seeing you for, but I would consider this the more serious problem. I suggest we take a bone-marrow sample, and—"

"Bone-marrow sample?" Walt interrupted.

"Yes. It's clearly indicated by the abnormal blasts in the blood smear. Walt, what's the matter with you?"

"It—she—" Walter tried to say.

Aware that his colleague's face had turned pale, Ogura said, "Walt, here. Sit down." Walt sank into the chair. His face was now not only pale but damp as well. "Are you all right?"

Walter Duncan nodded. He breathed slowly but shallowly, trying to regain control. Then he said in a soft, hoarse voice, "Vic, the patient—is not a patient."

Confused, Ogura asked, "Then, who?"

"Simone," Walt said in a whisper.

"Oh my God!" Ogura replied.

"Tell me everything," Walt insisted.

"Findings like these demand a bone-marrow sample so we can make a definitive diagnosis."

"What's your educated guess?"

"Leukemia," Victor Ogura said. "I'm so sorry, Walt."

Walter Duncan nodded and turned away.

"Have her in. Let's take that marrow sample. Then we'll know a good deal more," Ogura said. "Walt, these days the percentages are much better than they ever were. When I first started in—"

Walter Duncan interrupted, exploding. "Don't quote me percentages! I am only interested in . . ."

He said no more and fled the lab. Victor Ogura debated what he should do now. Finally he placed a phone call. When he received an answer, he said, "Sy, can I come right up and see you?"

Sy Rosen found Walter Duncan in his office, staring out of the window at the evening darkness. He had not responded to the sound of the door being opened.

"Walt, Victor just told me," Sy began.

No response.

"Walt, I know it's like a knife in the heart. And nothing I might say can change it."

Walt Duncan remained silent.

"Someone has to tell Emily."

Without turning to face him, Walt said, "I will tell her tonight."

"And Simone? What will you tell her when you have to bring her in for the bone-marrow biopsy?"

"As little as possible," Walt said. He turned to face Sy. "She won't know the truth until I can't keep it from her. And don't argue with me, Sy. She's my daughter! Can you understand that? No, I guess you can't understand that."

He was venting his frustration by attacking his friend and mentor, by pointing out Sy's life as an unmarried, childless man. He recanted at once. "I'm sorry, Sy. Forgive me?"

"I forgave you even before you asked," Sy said. "Nor do I blame you. There is no torment worse than seeing loved ones facing death and being unable to prevent it."

Something in Sy's voice forced Walt to look into his eyes.

"Yes, I know. I was already a young physician in Poland when we were taken away. My whole family. I had been expelled from the staff of the

64

hospital in Breslau. So I went home to get my mother and two sisters out of the little town in which my father had been the village doctor before he died. I had a plan to get them safely to Switzerland. I was too late.

"We were held two long days and nights in the synagogue, which had been turned into a prison. Afterwards they marched us to a railway siding. And up the ramp into the cattle cars. Another three days on the train. Cold. Without food. Without water.

"We ended up in two camps. One for women. One for men. Separated only by a high fence of barbed wire. We could almost touch each other. I watched them always. My mother, my two sisters. I could also watch the smoke rising from the row of chimneys. And I knew that door.

"They disappeared one by one. My mother first. Then Esther. And finally my little sister, Miriam. All I could do was watch. And you want to give me lessons in frustration, in hopelessness?"

"Sy, you never told me."

"I had no reason to tell you—until now," the elderly man said. "My boy, if I may suggest, do tell Emily. Tonight. Gently if you can. I will arrange for Simone to have that bone-marrow biopsy before the week is out. But first, Emily."

DINNER WAS INTERMINABLE. Walt tried to smile and laugh as Simone mimicked one of her teachers. He watched every mouthful of food she ate, as if nourishment could influence her condition.

He could barely wait until it was time for her to go up to bed. He went with her, watched her get ready, kissed her, tucked her in. At the door he turned for one last glimpse. She peeked from beneath her coverlet to smile at him. He blew her a kiss.

Surely Simone did not exhibit the signs tonight. Perhaps it would all turn out to be a laboratory mistake, he thought, then realized he was thinking like a parent again, not like a surgeon. Victor Ogura did not make such mistakes.

Walt waited until Emily joined him in the den. He had rehearsed several different ways he could introduce the subject. Emily circumvented all of them by asking, "All right, Walt, what is it?"

Taken by surprise, he merely glanced at her.

"Walt, I am not a fool. Yesterday you took a blood sample from our daughter. Tonight you act very strangely. All through dinner you laugh a little too often and too heartily. You can't take your eyes off Simone. Now, what is it?"

"Darling, sit down," he said simply.

She slid into a chair opposite him. "Tell me!"

"There is a possibility—no, I won't lie to you. There is preliminary proof that Simone has leukemia."

Tears welled up in Emily's eyes, but she did not cry. She was determined not to. "And?" was all she could say.

"I'll have to take her into hospital so we can do a bone-marrow biopsy on her."

"Will it hurt?" was the first question Emily asked.

"I'll make sure that it won't," he promised.

They were silent for some minutes before he said, "These days they do miraculous things with chemo in juvenile leukemia."

"Children still die, though," she said quietly.

"But the odds are in her favour. Seventy, eighty per cent, for certain types of leukemia," he said encouragingly.

"Which means that one out of every five dies," Emily said.

"We'll make sure she isn't one of them," Walt said as firmly as his surgeon's mind would permit.

He was relieved that she had not cried. For if she had, he knew he would have broken down too. Slowly, silently, they went to bed.

IT WAS STILL DARK when he woke. He felt the bed. He was alone. He rose, went down the stairs, whispering, "Emily?" There was no answer.

He went into the den. There he found Emily. She was in a chair, crouched into a ball, her nightgown pulled around her.

"Been up long?" he asked.

She shrugged.

"You mustn't make it seem worse than it is."

"Why did it happen to her?" Emily asked.

"Nobody knows."

"X-rays. I've read that X-rays can cause cancer. Especially leukemia. Didn't that happen in Hiroshima? All that radiation from the bomb, didn't the leukemia rate go way up?"

"Up," he admitted. "But not so much as people believe. And what's that got to do with Simmie?"

"Her braces," Emily said. "Orthodontics calls for frequent X-rays. To make sure how things are progressing."

"Emily, darling, a child does not get enough X-rays in the course of such treatment to affect anything," Walt said.

"If it wasn't X-rays, what was it?" she persisted.

"We don't know. We may never know. So there's no use pursuing that. We've got to look ahead. To the definitive diagnosis. To the treatment. To the results."

"But, if—" Emily started to say, then began to tremble and finally sob for the first time since he had told her.

Walt lifted her out of the chair to embrace her and warm her. As he held her he pressed his face against her head and spoke softly.

"Darling, Simmie most likely has leukemia. The question is, What do we do about it? We see her through the biopsy. If the results are bad, we put our heads together and arrive at the best treatment. And then we see her through that."

She nodded but continued to weep.

"Now come back to bed. You have to keep up your strength for her sake as well as your own. Simmie's going to need you a great deal in the months to come. The chemo. And whatever else they have to do."

He led her up the stairs and past Simone's room to their bedroom. He made her take a pill that would allow her to get some sleep. Once the pill had had its effect, he slipped into Simone's room. He sat in her too-small white rocking chair and stared at his daughter. She slept peacefully, unaware of her parents' fears, her innocent face lit only by the glow of the nightlight.

"YOU'LL BE EASY WITH HER," was Walter Duncan's instruction to his colleague, Herbert Coleman, who was scrubbing to go in and secure bone-marrow samples for Simone's biopsy.

"Walt," Sy Rosen intervened, "I'll be there. Emily will be there. We'll see that Simone feels secure and safe."

"I'd be there myself—" Walt started to say.

"Walt," Sy interrupted, "you have patients waiting."

Walt hesitated a moment, then realized that he had better leave. His presence might distract Coleman. Sy would see that his godchild was made as comfortable as possible.

A short time later Walt peeked into Amy Bedford's room to see if she was awake. She was. She lay on her back, staring up at the ceiling. Her cheeks were wet. Despite his own concerns, he could tell this child needed cheering up.

"Well, Amy, good news!" he announced as he entered.

She turned to him.

"We got the lab reports back," he said.

"I thought you got the lab reports during the operation."

"Those reports were OK. But we don't stop there. We take thirty samples along the bones we removed. And we submit each of them to examination to see if they're clean. And you passed! One-hundred-percent perfect. Now, let's look at that wound."

He opened the closures of the temporary cast that encased her leg. He studied the long, red scar, his keen eyes searching for any sign of improper healing. Her leg looked fine. As he closed the cast he said, "That wasn't so bad, was it, Amy?"

"Doctor, are you all right?" she asked.

"Of course I'm all right. Why do you ask?"

"I don't know. Today you seem different somehow."

"Me? Different? I'm fine," he insisted, forcing a smile.

"When you first came in, I thought something was wrong. I mean, it seemed that you were trying to sound optimistic because you didn't want to scare me."

"No such thing, Amy. Everything is fine. So far, you're having what we like to call an uneventful recovery. Boring, almost." He laughed, hoping to entice her to laugh. But she did not.

It shows, he thought as he left the room. My mind is not with my patients. It's up there with Simmie and Coleman and what he'll find.

EMILY DUNCAN HAD SURRENDERED her young daughter to Sy Rosen. He led the child into the treatment room and held her to reassure her while Dr. Coleman administered a local anaesthetic to her arm.

Once the anaesthetic took effect, Sy turned the child's face towards his own as Coleman picked up a long, sterile, stainless-steel needle. He inserted it into the skin of her arm, pressed the needle until he could feel it pierce the bone and sink into the soft area of her marrow. He extracted a few drops, placed some on a glass slide and deposited the rest in a test tube along with heparin to keep it from clotting. Coleman repeated the process four times in different parts of her body.

The procedure was carried out without pain to the patient and with a minimum of fear. Sy returned her to her mother.

"I'll take her home," Emily said. She grasped little Simone's hand and started out, but stopped to look back at Sy with a plea in her eyes: don't find anything.

By the time Sy returned to the treatment room, Coleman was viewing the samples on the slides under the microscope.

"Well?" Sy asked.

"Take a look," his colleague urged.

Sy studied the slides carefully, one after another. When he raised his head from the microscope, he stared at Coleman. It was obvious they had both reached the same discouraging diagnosis.

"We—we can't be too hasty about this. Let's submit the samples to electron microscopy," Sy said.

Coleman knew it would not reverse the diagnosis. But he agreed. "Sure, Sy. Right away. I'll call you with the results."

WALT TRIED TO CONTINUE with his rounds. But he could not. He was approaching a patient in room 517 when he suddenly turned to the elevator. He rode to the main floor, left the elevator and started down a long corridor of doctors' offices.

He entered the one with a bronze plaque reading DR. SIMON ROSEN.

68

"Is he free?" he asked Bridget, Sy's secretary.

She could tell by the look on his face that it would do no good to say that he wasn't. Walt continued on into Sy's private office, where he found him studying the file of his next patient.

"Sy?" Walt asked anxiously.

The elderly man looked up, dropped the file onto his desk and knew that the moment had come to speak some distressing truths to a man on whom he looked as a son. "Walt, sit down."

It was hardly necessary for Sy to say anything else. Walt knew that the diagnosis was among the worst and the prognosis could not be much better.

"Walter, we have to await confirmation from the path lab. But if I had to render an uninformed opinion, I would say acute myelocytic leukemia."

Walt was aware of the sweat forming on his brow, his cheeks and his neck. His hands went cold.

"It's not the end of the world, Walt. Leukemias are amenable to treatment. Vincristine, asparaginase, prednisone in heavy doses. We can have that thing on the run in weeks."

Walter Duncan nodded in a vague manner that was meant to end the discussion. He rose. "I've got a patient waiting," was all he said, and he left.

THE NEXT MORNING, while Sy Rosen was studying a set of X-rays in his darkened consultation room, his phone rang. He was annoyed at the interruption and hoped it was not James Rowe Russell, calling to discuss the verdict that the jury had rendered in the Enright malpractice case. Sy answered with impatient gruffness. "Yes?"

"Sy?" the tentative voice of Emily Duncan asked. "I have to talk . . ." She could not finish and began to weep.

The elderly man waited until she had recovered. "Emily, my dear, what can I do?"

"I have to see you. Alone. Away from the hospital."

"Of course. Let me take a look at my diary." His finger raced down the entries. "This afternoon at two?" he suggested.

"At two . . ." Emily considered. "Yes, Simmie will still be in school then. Do you know the tearoom just outside the shopping precinct?"

"I know the place. I'll be there," he promised.

THEY FOUND A TABLE in a corner and ordered quickly, to be rid of the waitress. Emily kept herself under restraint until they were served and alone again. But Sy could detect her deep nervousness.

"Emily, dear, exactly what do you want to know?"

69

She appeared relieved not to have to initiate the conversation.

"I—I went to the library yesterday," she began.

"And what did you discover there?" Sy asked.

"First of all, there are two kinds of acute leukemia."

"True."

"And one is much worse than the other. The worse of the two is called acute myelocytic leukemia. AML the books kept referring to," Emily said.

"Right," Sy agreed, awaiting the next question with considerable trepidation.

"The kind that Simmie has—is it AML?"

Sy paused before answering. For if Emily was asking, there was every indication that to spare her the worst news at once, Walt had hedged on the specific diagnosis. But if she was asking so direct a question, Sy was compelled to give her a direct answer.

"Yes, my dear. Simmie's *is* a case of AML," the old man said, "I hope you can understand Walt for being considerate of your feelings, for giving you time to adjust."

She nodded. Tears began to seep from her eyes. She wept silently. Embarrassed, she used her napkin to dry her cheeks.

"Tell me," she finally said. "Tell me everything. Because I have to know how to behave towards my child. I'll promise her anything. I'll lie if I have to. But I myself have to know the truth."

"Emily," the old doctor said, reaching across the table for her hand, "lying might not be the way."

"I don't want her to suffer emotionally as well. I have to be able to tell her that treatment can help."

"You can tell her that without lying. We can't be sure, but the treatment may help. So until it appears to fail, you can truthfully say it can help. As for the discomfort of the treatment, there is no purpose to lying. It's much better if you tell Simmie about all the difficulties she will face and then say, 'But Mommy will be with you all the time. We'll see it through together.'"

She nodded slightly, accepting the doctor's counsel, then said, "I want to know what it will be like. I have to prepare myself as well as my child."

"As you wish," Sy Rosen said. "Years ago—twenty-five, thirty—a child like Simmie with AML would last, at best, three months. But in the years since then, we have made great strides. We can induce remission in about seventy per cent of AML cases, wipe out leukemia cells, restore normal bone-marrow functions. Unfortunately, the difficulty in AML cases is that most patients with that form of the disease, after remission, eventually relapse."

"Most patients," she repeated breathlessly.

70

"We're trying new forms of chemotherapy. And there is always the possibility of bone-marrow transplants."

"If that's what it takes, I can give her some of my bone marrow."

"We're getting ahead of ourselves," Sy said. "Let's see how things develop."

"Is there anything else I should know?" she asked.

"Yes. Percentages, remission rates, cure rates mean nothing. What happens to your daughter is the only thing that counts. And that we have to discover day by day."

She nodded thoughtfully and wiped her eyes again.

"More important, remember to show her smiles, courage, love and, above all, hope. I have seen cases where doctors have given up but the patient has not, and the patient has outlived some of the doctors. Medicine is still an inexact science."

Emily looked at her watch. "I have to pick Simmie up at school."

They rose from the table. He kissed her on the cheek. He watched her leave. And prayed for a miracle.

CHAPTER 8

The weekly meeting of the Tumour Board convened at ten o'clock, five days after Amy Bedford's surgery, two days after Simone Duncan's diagnosis.

This evaluation of Amy Bedford's condition and the planning of her future treatment depended on the final pathological evaluation of the bones excised by Walt Duncan during surgery. The board, consisting of a hematologist, an oncologist, a radiologist and a surgeon, in addition to Sy Rosen and Walt Duncan, read the pathologist's report.

It confirmed the original diagnosis. "On microscopic analysis," the report stated, "it was found that ninety per cent of the tumour cells had been killed by the chemotherapy and that the tumour itself was not close enough to the edge of the excised portion to constitute a danger."

Walter Duncan looked in Rita Bristol's direction. She nodded, saying, "We'll continue with the same regimen of chemo."

The next case to be put before the board was that of the patient Simone Duncan. The results of Victor Ogura's early observations and the bone-marrow biopsies led the board to agree that the conventional approach to AML was indicated.

Dr. Bristol suggested heavy dosages of vincristine, asparaginase and prednisone for a period of four weeks. This regimen should induce remission in most leukemia cases. To avoid a swift recurrence of the disease, Simone would later have to receive consolidation therapy, involving a different mix of chemicals, to destroy those cancer cells that had survived the first phase.

After the case of Simone Duncan was discussed, Walter Duncan excused himself suddenly from the meeting. He fled down the corridor. Moments later he heard his name being called.

"Walter, Walt . . ." It was Sy.

The old man caught up with him. "Walt, you can't let it get to you now. We have to give the treatment a chance. It's the least you can do. Don't start acting like a typical parent."

"Sy, I've discovered that I *am* a typical parent. Except for one difference. I know all the things that can go wrong. So forgive me if I act like what I am. A worried father, a terrified father."

TO ESTABLISH A WARM RELATIONSHIP between doctor and young patient, Walt Duncan brought Rita Bristol to Simmie's room in the Pediatric Pavilion of the hospital. While Emily stood at the foot of Simmie's bed, Walt made the introductions.

"Simmie, darling, this is Dr. Bristol. She is a very nice woman. And a friend of mine. So you can consider her a friend of yours too. You do what she tells you, and you're going to be fine."

He tried to avoid Emily's eyes as he forced a smile. "We'll leave you two to get acquainted."

Throughout the morning Walt adhered to his rigorous schedule of examinations, consultations, studying X-rays and arranging for surgery. All the time he felt as if he were dragging with him an extra burden. It was a shadow, a presence that followed him, clouding his thoughts. When he thought about it, he knew it was his daughter, in room 209 in pediatric. With an intravenous drip in her young, slender arm, infusing what he hoped would prove life-saving chemicals into her body.

Twice he found a reason to go to the Pediatric Pavilion, to drop in and see how Simmie was bearing up. Each time he found her in bed, holding her favourite dolls, the inverted IV bottle feeding the chemo into her drop by drop. She seemed in excellent spirits.

Aware of his concern, Simmie tried to reassure him. "It doesn't hurt, Daddy. I hardly know it's there."

"Terrific. That's my girl," he said, kissing her and tousling her dark hair. At the same time he was keeping track of the time. Two more hours, three, and the aftereffects would commence.

Early that afternoon, after his first surgical case and with half an hour before his next scheduled operation, he stripped off his OR greens and hurried back to his daughter's room. He found her in the arms of her mother, retching into a stainless-steel basin. He slipped into Emily's place, took his daughter's frail young body in his arms and held her close, as if to impart his strength to her. Her body seemed to relax, but only a little. She breathed more deeply.

"Better, baby? Better?" he asked softly.

She tried to nod, but suddenly another wave of nausea welled up in her. The phone rang. Angrily he said to his wife, "Don't answer the damned thing!"

It continued to ring. Emily lifted the receiver.

"Yes. Yes, he's here . . . I'll tell him." She hung up. "That was surgery. Your next patient is ready. You have to scrub."

Reluctantly he surrendered his child to her mother. He kissed Simmie on the cheek. "Mommy will be with you, so don't worry, baby. Don't worry."

TWO HOURS LATER Walt Duncan stood at his daughter's bedside, staring down at the sleeping child. Emily stood beside him.

"Will it happen again?" she asked in a whisper.

"Not till they give her another dose of vincristine," he whispered back. "Poor kid. Exhausted. But at least she can sleep now. You ought to go home and get some rest yourself, hon."

"I'd feel better staying here, in case she wakes."

"All right," he said, understanding. Then he left the room and exhaled wearily, exhausted from the strain of keeping his fears from his wife.

He started on his rounds. This was a big day for one of his patients. Amy Bedford would be getting out of bed this afternoon. On her feet. Both of them.

He entered Amy's room, calling as cheerfully as he could, "OK, lazybones! Today's the day you have to get out of bed."

"Can I?" Amy asked, starting to move.

"Not so fast, my dear. First a little lecture. I wouldn't be Dr. Walt if I didn't precede everything with a lecture, would I?"

He tried to laugh, but Amy noticed that he could not.

Walt presented her with crutches. "These are the old-fashioned kind that fit under your armpits. The reason for that is, you are to walk without putting any weight at all on your right leg. So let's get these adjusted. Sit up, Amy."

She moved slowly, carefully, to a sitting position. Then, bringing her legs to the side of the bed, she sat up.

"Easy now, my dear," he coached.

She started to rise as he slipped one crutch under her left arm, then under the right. The crutches were a bit too high. He knelt beside her, loosened the screws of the adjustable slides and set them at the proper height. Then he observed her carefully as she let her body rest on the rubber tops of the crutches.

"Good, very good. Now let's review your new regimen. What we did with the surgery was to remove the origin of your cancer. But cancer is a treacherous disease. We can cut it out and there can still be cancer cells floating through your bloodstream. So we have to track them, hunt them down, wipe them out."

"How do we do that?" Amy asked.

"Chemotherapy."

"More chemo?" she asked.

"Yes, more chemo. Not for at least three weeks. Because chemo right now would interfere with your leg healing. But after that, every two or three weeks."

"Every two or three weeks!" she echoed.

"Yes, Amy. For at least eight months," he said. "Remember, I said this would take a year. The next eight months are part of it."

"I was planning on going back to school full-time."

"Not now, Amy. Go when you can. But don't even try to take your exams. You're not ready yet."

She nodded, but her eyes became moist.

"And I'll want your lungs X-rayed every month."

"Why?"

"If those darned cells are at work in your body, that's the most likely place for them to show up."

"And if they do?" She hesitated to ask.

"If they do, we cut them out. And continue with the chemo."

"If I'm still alive, that is." She stared at him directly, asking to be contradicted.

"Amy, you've come this far in good style. Don't start feeling sorry for yourself. Not now. Believe me, compared to some cases I know, you're doing extremely well."

"Doctor," she replied, then hesitated, wondering if it would be impertinent to ask. She decided to risk it. "Doctor, are you all right today?"

"Of course I am. Why do you ask?"

"When you just said, 'compared to some cases I know', somehow it seemed strange, the way you said it."

He realized that this teenager was a great deal more perceptive than he had thought. Or else he was more transparent.

"Yes, Amy. You're right. That case I know, she's my daughter."

"Oh?" Then Amy dared to ask, "Is she very bad off?"

"She could be," he admitted.

"Is she here in the hospital?"

"On this floor."

"Would you mind— I mean, is she allowed to have visitors?"

"I think she might welcome that, Amy."

"If it's not too far, that'll be my first walk."

"That would be very nice. But don't overtax yourself. Your muscles aren't as strong as you think. It'll take time. So don't overdo it."

"I won't, Doctor. I won't."

ONCE LEFT ALONE, Amy Bedford reached for the crutches that leaned against the side of her bed. She slipped them in place, thinking, I'll have my walk before Mom and Dad arrive. Then when I do it for them, they'll be surprised. It's time they had a happy surprise.

She rose to her one good foot, rested her full weight on it, made sure her right foot did not touch the ground. She hobbled towards the door and realized it was an awkward process and she had better be very careful.

After just enough steps to take her to the door, she decided not to venture down the hall to visit Dr. Walt's little girl. She was relieved to return to her bed, far more tired than she had expected.

Where, she thought, where is all the energy, all the strength I used to have? Chastened, a bit frightened, she lay back in bed.

In keeping with hospital regimen she was given an early dinner. Afterwards she tried to interest herself in a magazine, but her ability to concentrate seemed to have failed her too. It was almost dark outside, one of those late spring evenings when dusk seems soft and benign. The traffic sounded far away. The human traffic in the hall was at a lull, just before the invasion of nighttime visitors.

In all her days here in the hospital Amy had become skilled at reading the sound of footsteps. Now she could hear her parents' footsteps approaching—her father's sharp, staccato steps and her mother's, hurrying alongside. Amy raised herself, edged to the side of the bed, sat up, reached for her crutches, fixed them firmly in place under her arms, and rose. She was determined that when they came in, she would be facing them.

As usual, her father preceded her mother into the room. His prepared smile gave way to a look of surprise and delight. "Amy! You're standing. Marion, look, she's on her feet! Isn't that terrific?"

Unreservedly he crossed the room to his daughter, carefully embraced her and kissed her on the cheek.

"OK, AMY, LET'S SEE YOU walk today," Walt Duncan said.

Amy started towards him on her crutches. He watched, trying to detect if inadvertently she was putting any weight on her right leg.

"Perfect, Amy. Now we are going to put on a walking leg brace Hans has designed for you. You'll wear that until I evaluate you again five weeks from now."

"Are you telling me I can go home?" Amy asked.

"Yes!" Walt said. "But you have to remember two things we're going to be watching: healing and, even more important, any sign of infection."

"Why are you so worried about infection?" Amy asked. "I won't do anything dangerous."

"Amy, you'll be getting chemo every few weeks. While the chemo is chasing those cancer cells, it is also weakening your immune system. That's why I keep harping on infection," he explained. "Now, I've called your mother. She'll be coming for you this afternoon."

"Then I'd better see Simmie before Mom gets here."

"Simmie told me you were in to see her. Several times. She likes you."

"I like her too," Amy said. "She's very pretty and bright. What's actually wrong with her? No one would say. Except I can tell by their attitude it's serious."

"It is," he admitted, "but we're doing all we can."

"That means it's very serious. Doesn't it?"

"I'm afraid so," said Walt.

AMY BEDFORD MADE HER WAY down the corridor on her crutches, which she now handled with confidence. As she reached the open door of Simone Duncan's room she heard, "Mommy, why don't you go down and get some lunch? I'm feeling great."

"I won't leave you alone," her mother was saying as Amy entered.

"You won't have to, Mrs. Duncan. I'll stay with Simmie while you're gone."

"See, Mommy, you can go now," the child said encouragingly.

"Well, OK," Emily Duncan said as she bent to kiss Simmie. "I'll be back as soon as I can, darling."

The two young people waited until Emily Duncan was gone.

"I'm glad you're here," Simmie whispered. "I need someone to talk to. Do you mind?"

"No. Go ahead. Talk!"

"I don't think they're telling me the truth."

"Of course they are. Your daddy has told me the truth all along. He's very up-front about everything. Good and bad."

"Then maybe your bad isn't as bad as my bad."

"What do you mean?"

"They tell me things. Like what kind of chemo I'm getting. And what to expect it's going to do to me. And for me. But there's one thing they don't tell me."

"What's that?" Amy asked.

"Am I going to die?" Simmie said. "They don't say anything about that. So I keep wondering. Did you wonder about that too?"

76

"That. And worse. Like losing my leg," Amy confided.

"Is that worse than dying?"

"I used to think so," Amy said. "But I do know how you feel. I went through all that. Worrying. At night. When you're alone. No matter how much they visit, and talk, come nighttime you're alone. And you think of all those things they try so hard not to let you think about."

"I know," Simmie said. "I never tell my mom how I feel about dying. She's cried enough as it is. If I told her, she'd come apart."

There was a knock on the door. Both girls turned.

It was the nurse with the IV that would begin the next phase of Simmie's chemotherapy. Amy leaned close to Simmie.

"Don't worry. I know it's awful when all this is going on. Just remember it's always over. Always." On impulse she embraced the younger child. "Your dad's a wonderful man. He wouldn't let anything bad happen to you." She hobbled out of the room on her crutches.

WHILE MARION BEDFORD gathered up her daughter's belongings and packed them neatly in the small suitcase, Walt Duncan was issuing instructions. "And after she returns for her fourth course of chemo, we will do a complete bone scan." He turned to Amy. "We take no chances, do we?"

"No, Dr. Walt."

"Now, Amy, remember. Don't push things. Healing is a slow process. Keep that brace on. Walk carefully."

Mrs. Bedford had closed the suitcase. It was time to go.

"I'll remember, Doctor," said Amy. "And thanks, thanks a million." Impulsively she kissed him on the cheek, but in so doing, lost control of one crutch and fell against him. He caught her. "Amy, that's what I mean. Don't make any sudden moves. Slow. And sure. That's your prescription for now."

"I know. I'm sorry. I just had to thank you."

There was a knock on the open door. They turned. Brent Martin was standing in the doorway. "Can't I help in some way?" he asked. "Carry your bag or your flowers?"

"Brent, how nice of you to come," Mrs. Bedford said.

"I just thought you might need a hand."

Walt watched with considerable satisfaction as Amy moved out under her own power. Brent and her mother followed. None of them were as aware as Walt how great a part luck had played in bringing Amy Bedford this far. Only he knew how many times along the way her treatment, his surgery, could have been frustrated by an unwelcome, even fatal development. And such devastating possibilities must still be reckoned with, he knew.

MARION BEDFORD turned her silver Mercedes into their driveway and stopped near the front door. Brent was close behind on his motorbike, so when Amy opened the car door, he was there to help her with her crutches and assist her along the brick walk to the house.

When they got to the front door, Amy was breathless from exertion. Brent reached for the shiny brass door handle. He pressed down; the latch gave easily. He pushed the door open for her and stepped back. Amy hobbled in.

She had managed only four laboured steps into the hall when she was surrounded by the excited voices of her classmates. "Welcome home, Amy!" From the living room on her right and from the dining room on her left they rushed out to greet her.

Not only Amy but her mother was taken aback. After the first moment of surprise they looked at each other and both of them began to laugh and cry. "This is just wonderful," Marion Bedford called out. "But shouldn't you be in school at this hour?"

"We are," one of the girls said. "It's all been arranged. This is a class in social studies. On how to be a good neighbour and friend."

"Well, in that case, I'd better order in some food, lots of food, to judge from the size of this group."

"Too late," another girl called out.

"It's already been done," Brent explained. "We had to get your husband's permission to get in. When he found out why, he just took care of everything."

CHAPTER 9

Simmie had had her fourth series of chemo and had been back in hospital for what had become routine tests. The test results were not encouraging. Oncologist Bristol decided that strong chemicals must be administered while the patient was still able to tolerate the effects. As soon as possible, she would put little Simmie Duncan on adriamycin.

When she announced her decision, Walt detected that she was being slightly less than totally frank about her fears. It was his job now to play the same sad game with Emily.

SIMMIE HAD BEEN PUT TO BED. They were in the den when Walt said, "I had another talk with Bristol today."

"What did the Iceberg have to say?" Emily asked.

Walt tried to laugh. "I thought only patients called her that."

"She's a machine. A computer. Such and such results from the lab, and she grinds out those chemicals like a slot machine."

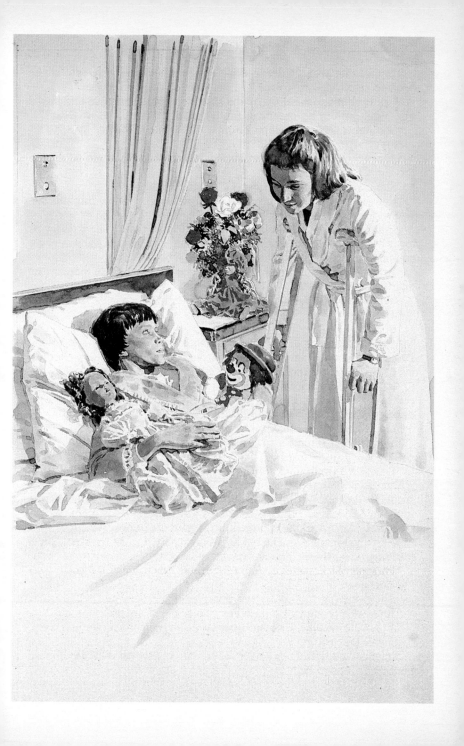

"Emily, that woman deals with the worst illnesses there are. If she became emotionally involved in each case, she'd go to pieces."

Walt took his wife gently by the shoulders, held her close and kissed her. While still in his embrace, Emily asked, "What did Bristol say?"

"She wants Simmie back in hospital. This time to stay."

"Stay?" Emily asked. "What for?"

"A new kind of chemo. Very strong. Bristol thinks it might do the job this time."

"She used those words, 'to stay'?" Emily asked.

"For the course of the chemo. It's a protective measure. Em, darling, you're trembling. What's got into you?"

"I don't know," she admitted, breaking free of him so she could wipe away her tears. "Those words, 'to stay', made it seem as if she was never coming home again."

"Bristol's doing all she can. We're all doing all we can. But there are no guarantees," he said.

She nodded. "When does she want her there?"

"Tomorrow."

THE NEXT MORNING Emily Duncan took her daughter back to the Pediatric Pavilion. She carried a suitcase with Simmie's nightclothes, robe and slippers. And Matilda, her favourite doll.

As they stepped into the elevator they met Mrs. Amiel, a young, rather pretty blonde. Her son had occupied a room adjacent to Simmie's during her previous hospitalization.

"Good morning," Emily said. "How's David doing?"

Inhibited by Simmie's presence, Mrs. Amiel said, "Oh, fine. He's getting along just—just fine."

"I'm glad," Emily said.

But over Simmie's head the two mothers exchanged glances. Mrs. Amiel's eyes betrayed her hopelessness. Still, she tried to smile. Emily thought, She was so pretty two months ago; now she's aged not months but years. Am I looking at myself a few months from now?

The elevator door opened. The women parted quickly, Mrs. Amiel hurrying down the corridor to see her young son.

"He's very sick, isn't he, Mom?" Simmie asked.

"Yes, dear."

"Then why did she say he was doing fine?"

"Just—just trying to keep up her own hopes, I guess."

They were passing an open door when they heard a familiar voice. "Simmie, that you?"

Simmie went to the open door, peered in to discover Amy Bedford in bed, an IV in her arm.

80

"Amy!" Simmie was delighted to see her.

"Yes. I'm back for mine. You too?"

"I guess so," Simmie said.

"Well, I've got only four months to go," Amy said. "Look, when they get this IV out of me, I'll come visit. OK?"

"Oh, sure!" Simmie said. "Please!"

THE NEXT DAY AMY BEDFORD was given a complete bone scan. After it was over, she was free to go to the solarium, catch up on school assignments, or visit. She chose to visit.

The little Amiel boy was still here. She always looked in on him when she came back for chemo. But when she reached his door, it was closed and there was a sign, NO VISITORS. She hesitated, then turned and started down the hall, leaning on her stick. Her progress in that regard had pleased Dr. Duncan. She was now permitted to rest twenty-five per cent of her weight on her right leg while wearing a brace and using the stick for support.

She made her way down the corridor with great care to Simmie's room. The door was open. Amy looked in. Simmie was in bed, her doll clutched in her arms. Amy watched for a moment and realized that the child was asleep. She decided to go in.

She stood at the foot of the bed, leaning forward to get a closer look at Simmie. She was pretty, Amy thought. Dark-haired and with small, exact features, like her mother's. When she grew up, she would look like her mother. Yes, if she grew up. If?

Amy wondered, Why am I thinking something like that suddenly? Is it because of the way she looks? So thin, so pale, and her cheeks so sunk in. She wasn't like that the first time I saw her. But then neither was I before they started me on the chemo. She'll get over it. As I did. And maybe they'll get her a wig, like I have now. Do they have wigs for kids?

The nurse wheeled an electrocardiograph machine into the room. She smiled at Amy and was about to speak, but the older girl signalled that Simmie was still asleep.

Amy turned on her stick and started out of the room, glancing at the medical equipment and thinking, I never need anything like that when I'm getting chemo. I wonder what's wrong.

EMILY DUNCAN HAD DRESSED hurriedly and was on her way to the garage when the phone rang. For an instant she considered refusing to answer. But it might be the hospital. "Hello."

"Emily, dear." She recognized her mother's voice. "Emmie, Dad and I have been talking it over, and we feel we should be there—"

"Mother, please. I don't think it's wise. Walt doesn't think so either.

Not with Dad's heart condition. So you just stay out there in Arizona until we send for you."

"And when will that be?" her mother asked. "When it's too late?"

"Don't say that!" Emily rebuked her mother.

"Well, what are we to think? The only reports you give us are so vague. And there's no real sign she's getting better. We think we should come," her mother insisted.

"No!" Emily said bluntly. "I have to spend all my time with Simmie. So, much as I love you, I cannot run a household for you and Dad. I have time for only one thing now, my daughter!"

"Are you *forbidding* us to come?" her mother asked, her hurt obvious in her strained voice.

"If you want to put it that way, Mother, yes, I am forbidding you. Now I have to go to the hospital. I'll call you later."

The conversation with her mother had unnerved her. On her way to hospital Emily had to make an effort to drive carefully. By the time she arrived, she felt under control. Sufficiently so to acknowledge that her mother's love for Simmie, her dad's love for his granddaughter, were no less than her own. She must try to be more pleasant and understanding.

Her sense of control was severely shaken by what confronted her as she entered Simmie's room. The child lay on her back, an IV in her arm. Fixed to her chest were the familiar sensors that Emily identified immediately as necessary for an ongoing electrocardiogram. Sy Rosen was leaning over her bed.

Oh no, Emily trembled, has her heart given out?

Whatever self-control she had been able to muster deserted her now. "Sy?" she asked through her tears.

He gestured her to go out into the corridor. Once the door was closed, she asked, "What happened?"

"Nothing. That equipment is to prevent anything *from* happening," he explained.

"They're doing an electrocardiogram. That means a heart attack."

"Emily, please, before you start imagining the worst, let me explain. Dr. Bristol is now using a more powerful drug on Simmie. Adriamycin. It sometimes produces side effects. Tachycardia. Very rapid pulse. Skipped beats. So while they administer the drug, they also monitor her heart to make sure none of those things occurs."

"And if they do occur?" Emily demanded.

"She stops the treatment at once," the surgeon said. When Emily did not respond, he said, "You believe me, don't you?"

She finally nodded. "I'm sorry, Sy. But I just had a run-in with my mother on the phone, and I guess it undid me."

"She wants to come, eh?"

"Yes. What do you think?"

"I'm the wrong one to ask. Frankly, if you and Walt had moved out to California when he had that offer from UCLA, and Simmie was this sick, I'd come. Whether you said to or not. So I know how grandparents feel." He smiled. "Not much help, am I?"

She kissed him on his wrinkled cheek. "I'll call Mother back."

"Good. After all, your daughter needs you now. But you are also a daughter. So there's no shame in needing your mother."

TWO MONTHS LATER Amy Bedford returned to the hospital for another series of chemo. Another X-ray. She knew the routine well by now and figured there were only three X-rays to go, two more scans, possibly three, and eight more series of chemo.

A year ago she was a healthy, strong young woman whose sole aim in life was winning the state tennis championship. Now she was an emaciated, almost bald young woman who was lucky just to be alive.

But she *was* alive. And determined to stay that way. Not only for herself, but for her mother, who was so devoted, and especially for her father. Lately, he had revealed depths of feeling that she had not suspected, finding time to call and visit her every day she was in hospital.

Amy made her way down the corridor to the room assigned to her. She still depended on her stick. But only until she had progressed sufficiently in her physiotherapy programme to build up her hip and leg muscles.

It was early. The trolleys were still in the corridor, ready to receive empty breakfast trays. Amy looked for her room and noticed that she had just passed a door with a name card reading SIMONE DUNCAN. So Simmie was still here. Strange. The last time she had asked Dr. Walt about his daughter he had said, "Oh, she's coming along. Coming along."

BEHIND HER CLOSED DOOR Simmie Duncan lay in bed, clutching her doll Matilda, waiting for her mother to arrive. The nurse had been in to take her breakfast tray and remind her cheerfully, "No chemo today, sweetheart. Isn't that good news?" Simmie had tried to laugh, but the muscles of her stomach ached too much from three days of vomiting.

Some day soon, she thought, I'll be going home, and then all this will stop. The needles. And the doctors. So many doctors. The way they smile at me, they must think I'm a dummy. And Uncle Sy. Even when he smiles, his eyes tell me how serious it is.

Outside the door she could now hear the usual morning noises: the trolley that rolled softly from door to door collecting the empty breakfast trays, the scurrying rubber-soled footsteps of the nurses.

Suddenly she heard the sounds change. Footsteps seemed to stop; then they all moved rapidly in the same direction. There was tense whispering, which made Simmie sit up and lean in the direction of the door, straining to listen. There were other sounds now. She recognized the voice of the floor supervisor as she said, "We'll get the certificate filled out later. Meantime, move him off this floor."

Curious, and free of the confining IV and the electronic sensors, Simmie Duncan slipped out of bed. She went to the door to peer out into the corridor. She heard sounds once more. Voices. Footsteps. Then she saw a rubber-wheeled stretcher pushed by a young student nurse. On the stretcher, completely covered by a white sheet, was the form of a child.

Through wide, frightened eyes Simmie watched until the small procession passed out of sight. She felt cold suddenly. She began to tremble. She turned back to her bed, crept in between the warm sheets and reached for Matilda. She held the doll close again and lay still until she pulled the covers up over her head.

When Emily Duncan came in for her usual morning visit, she found her daughter still covered that way.

"Honey, what are you doing?"

"Just playing games with Matilda."

"Come out. Let me see how you look this morning." Simmie wriggled up out of her hiding place and smiled.

"That's my baby," Emily said, but she could read fear in the child's eyes. "Honey, what is it? Something wrong?"

"No, I'm fine, Mommy. Honest. Just . . ."

"Just what, darling?"

"Can I go home?" Simmie burst out.

"Home?" Emily repeated. The question caught her by surprise. "That depends on what Dr. Bristol says."

"What if she says I can *never* go home?" Simmie asked.

"Why would she say that?"

"Because maybe they'll always find new things to do to me."

Emily sat on the side of the bed, took her child in her arms and brushed back her thinning dark hair. "Simmie, darling, the doctors are trying new things because that's the way they'll discover the right thing that will cure you."

"They don't cure everybody," Simmie said.

Emily felt her own body stiffen. "No, darling, the doctors can't cure everybody. But when they find the right thing, they will cure you."

Just after lunch, once Simmie had fallen asleep, Emily went to the nurses' station. There she discovered that early that morning young David Amiel had died of his lung disease. That sweet, gentle little boy, not yet nine years old. Of one thing she was sure. When Simmie woke, she would have to talk to her about it. She would not allow her to go on concealing her fears.

SIMMIE MOVED IN HER SLEEP, then opened her eyes. "Mommy?" she asked, to make sure.

"Yes, baby, I'm here. Would you like a drink?"

"No, thank you," Simmie replied.

The child lay still, then started humming to her doll.

"Simmie, did something unusual happen early this morning?"

"Early this morning, something . . . oh, yes. Someone, some child must have died."

"How do you know?"

"I heard sounds. So I got out of bed. I went to the door. I peeked out, and I saw this stretcher. There was a . . . there was someone small, covered by a sheet."

"You know Mrs. Amiel?"

"Oh, yes. She's a very nice woman. Was it . . ."

"Yes. Simmie. It was her son, David."

A look of fear slowly darkened Simmie's pale, thin face. But she said nothing.

"Simmie, when you saw that, did it frighten you?"

"Uh-huh," she said very softly.

"Is that why you were hiding under the covers?" Emily asked.

"I wasn't hiding," Simmie said. "I was—I was trying to see how it felt."

"How what felt, darling?"

"How it felt to be lying on that stretcher all covered up. Dead."

Emily fought hard to control her impulse to embrace the child. She knew that any overemotional reaction from her would only serve to frighten Simmie even more.

"Mommy, how *does* it feel?"

"I don't know how it feels. But I know one thing. There is no pain."

The child thought a moment, then nodded and seemed reassured.

"It's nothing to be afraid of, Simmie. Because it is something that is going to happen to all of us one day. It's as much a part of living as being born. You know, soon after you were born, Uncle Sy held you when you were christened. And he gave you that gold bracelet that we're keeping for when you grow up. When he brought it to the house, he said to me, 'Em, I won't be there by the time Simmie gets married. But I would like for her to wear this on her wedding day.' What he meant was that everyone dies at some time. He thought his time would come before you were old enough to get married. And he wanted to be remembered."

"When he said that, was he afraid?"

"No. He wasn't afraid. He seemed like a man who had completed his life's work and was content to die," Emily explained.

"Was David tired, and did he want to rest?"

"Yes, that's one way of saying it, darling."

CHAPTER 10

Rita Bristol laid out the data on Sy Rosen's desk.

The old man tugged at his small goatee, reluctant to examine the material. Finally he picked up the pages and studied the data. The results were even worse than he had feared.

Poor Simmie, he thought. That innocent, bright child, to be faced with a white count so low. And her platelet count even lower. Both counts severely diminished by the chemo, inviting the possibilities not only of infection but of hemorrhage. That's the trouble with chemo. It attacks healthy cells as well as the cancer. The very white cells and platelets relied on to fight disease became victims of the chemo. Yet the diseased cells had not been wiped out.

Sy tossed the pages back onto the desk. "All right, Rita, what are you suggesting?"

Dr. Bristol looked down at the old man, at his watery eyes, which made no secret of his torment.

"Extreme cases demand extreme measures. Superlethal doses of radiation and chemo to wipe out all of the malignant cells, and also her own bone marrow. Then infuse healthy donor marrow to reconstitute her body's immunologic systems."

"Total body irradiation," Sy said, indicating his reluctance.

"I'll prescribe prednisone, of course, to counteract any swelling of her brain," Dr. Bristol said.

"You realize, Rita, that Simmie has no siblings."

She nodded.

"Then you also realize the risks," Sy said.

"I never said she was an ideal candidate for a bone-marrow transplant. But I know what her chances are now. None. I would like to do histocompatibility tests on Walt and his wife. And use the marrow from whichever one is the closer match to Simmie. Of course, I'll take this to the Tumour Board. But first someone should discuss it with Walt Duncan."

"I will talk to Walt at once," Sy said.

Dr. Bristol started to gather up her lab reports, but the old man laid his hand on hers. He said, "You know how bad the odds are?"

"In this case there is no option."

He nodded. Rita Bristol took her reports and started out of the room. At the door she stopped to remind him, "Of course, once the superlethal doses of radiation and chemo start, I'll have to confine Simmie to reverse isolation."

"Of course."

WALTER DUNCAN TOOK THE NEWS with no show of emotion. Sy almost wished his protégé would break down, cry, curse, or explode in fury at the Fates. But Walt listened as if receiving reports concerning a stranger.

"I'll speak to Emily," was all he said as he started for the door. Then he turned slowly to face his mentor, and Sy could see the gleam of tears on the younger man's cheeks.

"Emily is no fool. She will know how desperate we are. Only one step away from giving up altogether."

"Walt, would it help if I told her?" Sy asked.

"No. This is something she deserves to hear from me."

THAT EVENING, AFTER HE HAD SEEN all his patients and left instructions for his morning surgery, Walt found two messages in his office from James Rowe Russell, the hospital's powerful board chairman. Obviously Russell assumed that Walt was avoiding him, for his second message read, "I will wait in my office until I hear from you." That made it an obligatory call. Walt telephoned Russell's office.

"Oh, Duncan," Russell began, barely able to conceal his hostility.

"You called me, sir. What can I do for you?"

"You can listen to a letter I just received from the hospital's attorneys. 'We have been informed that the verdict of two million dollars against Dr. Enright has been upheld on appeal. Less than an hour ago we were notified by the insurance company that for the forthcoming year malpractice premiums for all hospitals in this district will be increased one hundred and fifty per cent.'

"Duncan," Russell went on, "next time you feel the urge to place your ethical duty above common sense, think about this experience. Think twice."

"Sir, are you threatening me?" Walt asked.

"*Advising*, Duncan, *advising*," the man said coldly.

Before Walt could react, Russell hung up on him. There was nothing to do now but pick up Emily and take her home. And tell her about Simmie. And bone-marrow transplants.

THEY WERE HALFWAY HOME. Nothing had been said. When they stopped for a traffic light at the edge of a shopping centre, Walt asked, "Do we need to pick up anything?"

Emily did not answer.

"Em? Darling?" He turned to her, to find her weeping silently. "Em, please . . ." She shook her head, continued to weep, powerless to hold back the tears. He wanted to embrace her, but the light changed to green. He drove on slowly.

"Em, you mustn't give up. There are still things we can do," he said reassuringly. He glanced at her. She was staring straight ahead, her eyes still moist. "In fact, I was going to tell you. We both have to be tested. Tomorrow, if possible. They have to find out which one of us is most histocompatible with Simmie."

He expected her to ask why, but she remained silent.

"You see, there's a procedure called a bone-marrow transplant. It's really miraculous the way it works. In leukemia the body's own immune system doesn't produce the proper number of healthy, disease-fighting white cells. The fault is in the bone marrow. So what we can do now is eliminate completely Simmie's faulty bone marrow, using heavy concentrations of chemo and radiation. Then we take bone marrow from a compatible healthy donor, like you or me, and inject it into her, intravenously. Eventually the transplant stimulates the growth of new, healthy bone marrow in the patient."

He awaited Emily's reaction. There was none.

"Of course, during the treatment there are some difficulties. When they wipe out Simmie's bone marrow, they also wipe out her body's resistance to disease. So, during that time she has to be in what we call reverse isolation. She will be moved to a small suite with a little anteroom separating her from the outside. There will be facilities for visitors to wash. And sterile gowns to wear. But you can spend just as much time with her as you do now."

They had arrived at the house. Walt went into the den to mix himself a drink. Soon he heard Emily's steps behind him.

"Drink?" he asked.

"Walter," she said, "what does GVHD mean?"

He had to grip the whisky bottle firmly so as not to drop it. Where had she come upon that term? And if she knew enough to ask what it meant, she must know a good deal more about bone-marrow transplants than he had suspected.

"GVHD," he began. "That's graft-versus-host disease."

"What does it *mean?*" she insisted.

"Well, there are transplant cases where instead of achieving the desired result, the graft starts to attack the host—the patient, that is."

"So a transplant could do more harm than good," she said.

"Now, honey, you know that any treatment, even the surgery I do, can sometimes backfire. We do the best we can."

"And when the best is no better than the worst?" she demanded. "What about those times?"

He knew now that he had to address her fears directly. "Em, how did you run across GVHD?"

She stared at him, angrily at first; then gradually her anger gave way to tears. "I'll have that drink now." She went to the nearest chair and sank into it. He mixed her drink and brought it to her.

"This afternoon," she said, "I went down to Sy's office. I heard him talking to Dr. Bristol. He said, 'Rita, about Simmie. Do you think a bone-marrow transplant will do any good?' She said, 'Sy, you know the odds. Even in cases where the match is from an identical sibling, forty to fifty per cent develop GVHD.' And Sy said, 'Yes, I know. And once established, GVHD is virtually resistant to treatment.'

"After that I went down to the hospital library. And I asked for the latest information on bone-marrow transplants. There are all kinds, I discovered. Transplants from the patient's own marrow when he or she is in remission. Then marrow from an identical twin, or from a partially matched donor. Is that right?"

"Yes, yes, that's right."

"The worst odds, the lowest cure rate, is when they transplant marrow from a partially matched donor."

"It's true that the ideal match would be from an identical twin. But there's only the two of us who have a chance of being histocompatible with Simmie. We're doing the best we can."

"Not exactly, Walter," Emily said.

"There isn't anything else left to try!" he protested.

"That's precisely what I mean. We're at a time when little lies won't do any longer. When being considerate of my feelings won't wash. From now until the end of this I want to know how bad it is. I want to be able to be honest with my daughter. She is very intelligent, very sensitive. Only the other day—" The glass dropped from her hand and fell to the carpet.

"Em—"

"Only the other day she asked me, 'How does it feel to die?' "

"Em!" He went to her, pulled her up from the chair and held her as her body shook from sobbing. "Darling, please."

Through her tears she was able to say, "From now on I've got to know the truth, the whole truth."

"Of course, darling. Everything. But just hold fast to the thought that it isn't hopeless yet. Difficult. Against the odds. But not hopeless."

"Will you tell me when it is?" she challenged.

He hesitated only briefly. "Yes, yes, I'll tell you."

ONCE EMILY AND WALTER DUNCAN had both given samples of their blood and bone marrow, it became clear that Emily's genetic characteristics matched Simmie's more closely than Walter's. Unfortunately, even Emily's were not perfect.

"I've seen closer matches," Victor Ogura said to Sy Rosen and Rita Bristol. "If only there were a sibling."

Simmie Duncan now had to be prepared for the transplant process. It was a debilitating procedure, commencing with intravenous doses of the chemical cyclophosphamide for two consecutive days. Being a very powerful drug, it had the unfortunate and more taxing aftereffects of such drugs. For two days Simmie was racked with even more sickness.

After those days of agony were over, there remained six days of superlethal radiation. For the transplanted marrow to have an opportunity to succeed, the patient's body must be almost completely clean of all cancer cells. Since there are areas of the body where the most powerful chemotherapy cannot penetrate, radiation was relied on to accomplish that end. Total body irradiation, TBI, one thousand rads a day of it.

FRAIL LITTLE SIMONE DUNCAN completed her six days of radiation. On the following day Emily Duncan was subjected to being a bone-marrow donor. She lay on her back in a small operating room, a surgical drape covering her body. The anaesthetist had decided to put her under completely, as much to combat her emotional state as to render her impervious to pain.

Once the patient was anaesthetized, Dr. Bristol reached for the sharp-pointed stainless-steel instrument that resembled a long hypodermic needle with a flat cap at the top.

The nurse turned Emily on her side, giving Rita Bristol access to her exposed lower back. The doctor then started to push the sharp, hollow instrument into the bone of Emily's pelvic girdle, the area most productive of bone marrow. She pressed with considerable force until she felt the bone give way and knew that she was now into the softer marrow-rich area of the bone.

Having achieved that, Dr. Bristol removed the flat cap from the needle and signalled the nurse for a glass syringe. The doctor screwed it into the top of the inserted needle. Slowly she pulled up the plunger. Soon she had accumulated a hypodermic full of a mix of bloody, serumlike marrow. She emptied it into a sterile test tube and sealed it. Then she repeated the procedure three times.

Several hours later Dr. Bristol infused the marrow intravenously into the arm of Simone Duncan. If nature and luck were with them, Emily's marrow cells would circulate through Simone's bloodstream, eventually to find a home in the marrow cavities of the sick child's bones.

After that it remained to be seen whether her immune system would begin to produce healthy marrow on its own.

EMILY'S PARENTS, Charles and Madeline Ingraham, arrived on the Monday afternoon following the infusion of healthy bone marrow into Simone Duncan. Since Emily insisted on remaining at her child's bedside, the Ingrahams took a taxi directly from the airport to the hospital. Without warning, Emily found herself confronted by her mother and father, who stared at her through the glass window of the small anteroom. It was obvious that they were startled to find their granddaughter in isolation. Emily came out to greet them.

As always, her father moved to embrace her. She moved back.

"Be careful, Dad. This gown has to remain sterile."

"Yes, sure," he said, but it was clear he felt rejected.

"Em, why sterile gowns?" her mother asked. "What's going on here? And why weren't we told?"

"Mother, please! I can't take time to explain now. But if you want to see Simmie, you'll have to wash your hands thoroughly and put on one of these gowns."

They washed with care, then slipped into green sterile gowns. They waited in the doorway until Emily said, "Simmie, darling, guess who came all the way from Arizona to see you?"

"Grandma, Grandpa," the child said weakly.

"Right, Simmie," her grandmother said, drawing close to the bed. She half turned to Emily, asking permission to embrace her grandchild. Emily nodded. Madeline Ingraham gathered the child up in her arms. "Oh, Simmie, how good it is to see you again. Oh, child—" Her reserve deserted her. Shocked by the sight of her granddaughter, the poor woman broke into tears. Emily was sympathetic, but to protect the child, she ordered, "Dad, take her out of here!"

"Maddy, come." He put his arm round his wife and guided her out of the room.

Emily knelt at the bedside. "Grandmother's so glad to see you, Simmie, that she broke down and cried. But just think, they came a thousand miles to see you."

The child stared at her through eyes sunk deep into her painfully thin face. "Do I really look so bad?"

"Of course not, baby," Emily said, quick to reassure her. "It's just that the last treatment hasn't had time to take effect. You have to understand how Grandma feels. Being so far away and worrying about you, it was such a relief to see you that she broke down."

"She'll come back, won't she?"

"Of course. Just give her time to gather herself together."

"And Grandpa too," the child said.

"Both of them," Emily promised.

SHE FOUND THEM in the visitors' waiting room. In one corner Charles Ingraham hovered over his wife, who sat facing away from the other visitors, hiding her tears in her handkerchief.

"Maddy, Maddy," he pleaded.

"I can't help it." She went on shaking her head and crying.

Emily drew close to them. Her father looked at her. He moved aside. Emily placed her hands on her mother's shoulders and turned her about.

"Mother, listen to me." Her mother stared up into her eyes. "You are going back in there. You will smile. And you will talk to Simone of pleasant things. I don't want her to see how startled and frightened you are. Walt and I don't do that. And we won't let you do it."

"But the way she looks. It's plain to see—"

"Plain to see *what?*" Emily demanded angrily.

Madeline Ingraham glanced at her husband, then turned back to her daughter. "She's going to die."

"This last treatment hasn't had time to work yet," Emily insisted. "It'll take weeks, several more weeks, before we know."

"Maddy," her husband said, "do as she says. Wash all signs of crying from your face and go back into that room. Visit with Simmie like you used to when she was little. But do not let her see your fear. I'll be along in a minute."

The woman appeared to resist, but then, as she usually did, she yielded to her husband's judgment. Once she had left the room, he took his daughter by the hand and looked into her eyes.

"Now you tell me, Em. Is it as bad as it looks?"

She tried to nod.

"Is it true that this last treatment hasn't started to work yet?"

"It'll take a few more weeks before we know."

"Then I'll tell you what I'm going to do. I'm going to take your mother home. Back to Arizona. You've got a tough enough job as it is. You don't need to keep pretending for our sakes as well."

"Thanks, Dad. For understanding," she said.

"Look, darlin', your ma's worried—desperate, in fact. We both are. She'd do anything to save that child. Don't forget, Simmie's as much part of us as you are. Now, I'll do my best to keep your mother in hand. But don't think I feel any different than she does."

Emily reached up, drew his face down to hers and kissed him.

"I know, Dad. I know. We each have to see this through in our own way. But stay a day or two longer."

"OK, baby. You can depend on me."

"Thanks, Dad."

THREE WEEKS HAD PASSED since the injection of Emily's transplanted bone marrow into Simmie. Early each morning Emily appeared at the hospital and spent the day with her ailing daughter. Each day she watched, expecting some miraculous change. She found none.

Most days she held her retching child while Simone suffered reactions to the methotrexate that she had to endure to help her body deal with the foreign bone marrow. At the same time, Emily, along with Walter and Sy, kept searching for warnings of the GHVD they all dreaded.

Despite the discouraging statistics, which Walter no longer attempted to keep from her, Emily kept hoping, seeking signs of improvement. Even during the first two weeks, when she had been told there could be no visible change, she had insisted she detected signs of recovery.

Several times each day Walt hurried in, scrubbed, gowned himself and visited with his daughter. He embraced her, talked to her, told her funny stories about his own childhood and made her laugh. But all the while he held her he felt her body growing lighter, her skin barely covering her fragile skeletal structure.

Sy Rosen came by often to smile at his namesake and encourage her, to nod reassuringly to Emily. And he saved all his suggestions for Dr. Bristol. Each day he cornered her in her office.

"Well, Rita, what?" he asked simply.

"We don't know yet," she would say.

"Don't know or don't want to say?" Sy retorted. "Is her system beginning to respond, to produce healthy cells?"

"The signs are not encouraging, Sy."

"And GVHD? Any indication?" Sy asked.

"Not yet."

"If you think it will occur, why not switch from methotrexate to cyclosporine? Or prednisone?" he urged. "They're both effective in preventing GVHD."

"*Sometimes* effective," she corrected.

Sy nodded, accepting her modest rebuke. "Rita, please let me know. If there's anything I can do . . ." The old man had run out of words. Nothing he could say would influence the outcome.

ON THE TWENTY-SIXTH DAY after Simone Duncan had received Emily's transplanted bone marrow, nurse Corinne Scammon took Simmie's temperature as part of the usual morning routine. Scammon glanced at the reading and stopped suddenly.

She held the thermometer up to the light: 101.2. Since Emily stood at the foot of her daughter's bed, Scammon said nothing, shook down the instrument and placed it back in the alcohol.

She went directly to the floor phone and paged Dr. Bristol. The doctor did not answer at once. But within the hour she came up to the pediatric floor to search out the nurse, who was now engaged in inserting an IV into the arm of Amy Bedford. Amy was back for her routine chemo treatment and her monthly lung X-ray.

Dr. Bristol came into the room. "You called me, Scammon?"

"The patient in two twelve."

"Yes?" Dr. Bristol asked urgently.

"One o one, point two," Scammon said.

"Thanks. I'll have a look." Rita Bristol hurried away.

"Nurse," Amy said, "the patient in two twelve, isn't that Dr. Duncan's little girl?"

"Yes."

"Maybe I'll drop in later if I'm able."

"I wouldn't drop in. Not today," the nurse said.

"Oh, I know all about scrubbing and wearing a gown—"

Scammon interrupted. "I wouldn't. Not today."

A SHORT TIME LATER Sy Rosen sat back in his old creaky desk chair. He tugged at his white goatee as he stared across the desk, hesitant to ask. "OK, Rita. What?"

"She has a fever of one o one, point two."

"Any other signs?"

"Indications of exfoliative dermatitis on her back, slight abdominal distension with sensitivity."

"Any signs of hepatitis?" Sy asked.

"Not yet," she said. "But there is a detectable weight loss."

Sy Rosen nodded sadly. "The classic signs. GVHD. Shall we increase the methotrexate?"

"I'm giving her all she can tolerate now."

He nodded, accepting her appraisal of the situation. "Rita, if you had to say, what would you estimate are the chances of reversing GVHD in Simmie's case?"

"Based on my experience, between very bad and none at all."

"Then you consider her terminal?" Sy asked.

"The slightest infection, a hemorrhage—anything could do it."

After Rita Bristol left, Sy Rosen put in a call to Walter Duncan. He was told that Dr. Duncan was in consultation and had left orders not to be interrupted. Later, Sy thought. With what I have to say, later will be good enough. Soon enough.

WALTER DUNCAN HAD BEEN SUMMONED down to radiology by Dr. Wiswell, who was in charge of Amy Bedford's X-rays and scans. For comparative purposes Wiswell had mounted on the wall of glass all the sets of Amy's X-rays.

"Walt, take a look," was all Wiswell said when Walt arrived.

The radiologist turned off the overhead lights, flipped on the back lights. Both doctors moved slowly down the line of films.

Clean, clean, clean, Walter noted silently. Until he came to Amy's most recent set of X-rays. There Wiswell had circled a shadow that did not appear on any previous films.

"Damn it!" Walt said. "She was doing so well."

"Fortunately, it's encapsulated."

"Fortunately?" Walter Duncan shot back angrily. "What's so fortunate about having a metastasis? I thought we had this thing beaten! But it never ends."

Walt realized that Wiswell was staring at him. He became self-conscious. "Sorry. I just wasn't expecting this. I'll talk to Levin in thoracic surgery. And, of course, to Amy and her folks."

ED AND MARION BEDFORD had both arrived at the hospital within half an hour of Duncan's call. They waited anxiously for Walt's arrival.

"Has Duncan said anything to you?" Ed asked his daughter.

"Only that he wants to speak to us all together."

"Probably some new kind of treatment," her father said. "Maybe to help you with your physiotherapy."

He smiled confidently. Nevertheless, he kept mopping his face with a handkerchief that was already limp. The air in the room grew dense with unspoken fears.

Finally Walt Duncan entered. "Sorry to keep you waiting. But I had things to do down the corridor. Mr. Bedford, Mrs. Bedford, Amy, what I have to say will sound discouraging at first—"

"Doctor, what is it?" Amy asked anxiously.

"Amy, we have discovered something in your last X-rays. A spot. Metastasis."

"You're saying she still has the cancer?" Ed Bedford looked as if he had been betrayed.

"Mr. Bedford, I am saying that, as in many similar cases, the cancer has spread to her lungs. That is not so serious as it sounds. Because this particular kind of cancer when it hits the lungs is encapsulated, and we can just cut it out, leaving the lung intact."

"What if the disease is still there—" Ed Bedford started to say.

"That's why we do chemo for a whole year," Walt explained. "To chase down those cells and wipe them out."

"But you didn't wipe them out!" Bedford said accusingly. He started to mop his face again. "You don't know how it feels to be the father of a sick child. Helpless, that's what it feels like."

"I think I know the feeling, Mr. Bedford." Walt turned to Amy. "Now, Amy, we are going to have to operate again. This time I'm asking Dr. Alvin Levin to do it. He's an excellent thoracic surgeon. He's done many cases like this. I will scrub with him and I will be there all the time. The main thing is, Amy, don't think that this is an unusual development. We hope against it. But we do anticipate it. And the odds are in your favour." Walt took her hand. "Amy, you've been a real trouper through all of this. So I want you to know the truth. Patients with one metastasis in the lung, and no other involvement, have a seventy-per-cent chance of surviving. Living five years and beyond for a totally normal life. Seventy per cent. Those are darn good odds."

Amy nodded soberly.

"So you have to go with us the rest of the way. Surgery. Chemo—a new one we call cis-platinum. With your courage and determination you can make it."

Amy stared into his eyes and nodded. "OK, Dr. Walt."

"Good. Because Dr. Levin has an opening in his schedule tomorrow morning. We should do this at once."

He patted her on the cheek and had started for the door when Bedford called to him, "This Levin, he's the best?"

Walt turned. "If my child could be helped by lung surgery, I'd pick Levin. Does that answer your question, Mr. Bedford?"

Within two hours of Walt Duncan's visit the preparations for Amy Bedford's second operation were under way. In midafternoon Dr. Alvin Levin came in.

When Levin introduced himself, Ed Bedford, who had remained with Amy, stared at him before shaking his hand. "You're pretty young."

"Beats being just pretty," Levin said, smiling. "Don't worry, Mr. Bedford. I've been briefed on Amy's case. I know what to do. And I do it very well. By this time tomorrow it will be over. Amy will be in intensive care, and we can all breathe easier."

He approached the bed. "Amy, I've had a chance to study your X-rays. Based on those, we go in, retract your ribs, reach that sucker and remove it easier than coring an apple. Of course, your parents will have to sign the usual informed consent."

"Will it say anything about—about amputation?" she asked.

"No. This time there's absolutely no possibility of that," Levin promised. "See you in the morning, Amy."

CHAPTER 11

Sy knew the Duncan family routine these days, knew it only too well. At the end of a long day Walter went straight to Simmie's room, exhausted but determined to greet his young daughter with an optimistic look on his lean, lined face.

By that time Emily had fed Simmie what little she could eat, had tucked her in, sung to her, kissed her and waited until the child drifted off to sleep. She then sat by the bed, holding her cold, wasting hand, observing her shallow breathing. Walter would arrive, wash carefully, slip into a sterile gown and enter the room silently. Most times his wife would signal him not to talk. He would watch Simmie sleeping, as if he could determine her condition by mere observation.

As the dread illness was sucking the life out of his daughter, so were the demands on his wife draining her. He knew that fatigue, loss of sleep and loss of weight were factors that in combination could bring on nervous exhaustion, even a total breakdown. Emily ate nothing by day. At night, whether they ate at home or went out, every meal ended with the tears she had held back all day.

That evening, knowing the Duncans could be found in Simmie's room, Sy called the nurses' station on the second floor. The nurse came in to say softly, "Dr. Rosen asked if you would both stop by before you left."

When they arrived at Sy's office, the old man had spread out before him the reports from Dr. Bristol and the lab. He motioned them to take seats. Emily sank into a chair. Walter remained standing.

"Em, Walt, I have conferred with Dr. Bristol. There is no doubt that Simmie is experiencing a GVHD reaction. Bristol has already put her on cyclosporine. But—" He paused, sighed, then said simply, "She has virtually no chance at all. No chance."

"I failed her," Emily said softly, as if to herself.

"Em, no!" Sy refuted.

"I failed her. Whatever it was she needed from my bone marrow, I didn't have it to give."

Walter looked at Sy Rosen, whose face reflected his shock at Emily's reaction. Walter put his arms round her and held her in a tight embrace.

"Em," he said softly. "Em, you didn't fail. Medicine failed. We don't yet know enough to defeat this terrible disease. If anyone's to blame, we doctors are." He shepherded her out of the office. Sy watched them leave, shaking his head with grim concern.

THEY WERE IN THE HOSPITAL parking lot. Walt was unlocking the car door when Emily suddenly said, "I'm not leaving."

"Em, you've got to get some sleep," he insisted.

"I'll sleep in a chair in her room," she said, starting swiftly back towards the Pediatric Pavilion.

He raced after her, caught up, seized her. "Em, you can't. You'll disturb her. She needs her sleep too."

"She needs her mother. When doctors fail, when medications fail, a child needs her mother more than ever."

Violently she broke free and ran towards the entrance. He caught up with her at the door. She struggled with him, summoning strength he did not know she possessed. If she was that determined, he knew he had better acquiesce.

"I'll get a camp bed set up for you," he finally said.

A NIGHT MAINTENANCE MAN found a camp bed. As quietly as possible Walter set it up alongside the child's bed. Simmie stirred, opening her eyes just long enough to ask, "Daddy? That you?"

"Yes, baby. Now go back to sleep."

Once Emily was bedded down, Walt started for home. He got as far as the front door of the hospital but decided to remain. He found one of the small rooms where residents on night duty usually slept. He lay down. After all these years, he thought, here I am again, sleeping in the residents' quarters. I remember those days when I used to think ahead, to the future. We'd get married, Em and I. Have children. Have a house. I had it made.

Had it made. That terribly misleading phrase.

Simmie, oh Simmie, what a life I had planned for you. Did you know that I have a fund set up for your college education? Before that, we'd take trips to the most beautiful parts of this country. Then to Europe. I'd take time off. We'd go together. All the things I never had, you were going to have, Simmie. Everything.

Yet, here I am, afraid to go home to an empty house. Afraid that when I get home, I'll race up the stairs to your room to kiss you goodnight. But you won't be there. I'll go into the den to be with your mother. And she won't be there.

So I am here in this little room. Half my life gone, and I'm back where I was so many years ago. Walter Duncan, who had it made.

THE NEXT MORNING IT TOOK a moment for him to realize where he was. An instant later he recalled he was due in the OR to assist at Amy Bedford's lung surgery. He must shower, have coffee and get to surgery. But first he would call in at Simmie's room.

He entered the anteroom of the isolation suite, prepared to scrub and slip into a sterile gown, but what he heard from inside the room made him pause. "Simmie, darling, if you could have anything in the world, what would you want?" Emily was asking.

"Home, Mommy. I want to go home."

"Home?" Emily equivocated.

"I want my own room again. My own things again. My toys, my books." As if confiding a secret, she added, "I don't like this place, Mommy. I'd rather be home."

"All right, baby. If that's what you want, Mommy will take you home."

Walter's impulse was to blurt out, "No, Emily! You can't do that!" Instead, he remained silent. No purpose in upsetting the child. He would discuss this with Emily later. He slipped into a gown, forced a hearty smile and entered the room.

"Good morning, sweetheart," he greeted his daughter.

"Daddy, guess what? Mommy's taking me home. Won't that be terrific!" She smiled, a bare flicker of a smile, actually.

"Yes, yes, that's fine," he agreed. "Of course we have to talk to Uncle Sy about it first, though."

"Do we?" Emily challenged.

"Yes, Em," he said. "We have to."

"Oh, he'll say yes," Simmie interjected confidently. "He never says no to me about anything."

"We'll see, baby. We'll see," Walter said.

The nurse came in with Simmie's breakfast. It gave Walter a chance to gesture Emily outside the room, where he asked, "Em, how could you promise that? We can't take her home."

"Why not?" she asked sharply.

"Now more than ever she needs medical care."

"Why?" Emily demanded. "What can they do for her now? Nothing. Sy as much as said that last night. Well, she is going home. Where she wants to be. With the things she loves. Where she has lived all her life. Home, Walter, home!"

"Em—" he started to plead.

"She is going home. Today!" Emily declared with finality.

He could not stop to argue, for he was overdue in surgery. He said only, "Don't do anything until I get back."

"I'll wait that long," Emily said. But she was more determined than he had ever seen her before.

AMY BEDFORD WAS SEDATED but still conscious when Walt entered the operating room in gown, cap and mask.

"Amy," he said, leaning over her.

She looked up into his eyes. "Hi, Dr. Walt. Last night, before I fell asleep, I was thinking—"

"Yes, Amy?"

"Simmie. How is she?"

"She's getting along, Amy, getting along."

The anaesthetist spared Walt the obligation of enlarging on the lie when she said, "Doctor, I need access to the patient now."

Walt patted Amy on the cheek. "You'll be OK. When you wake up, that thing will be gone and you'll be good as new."

During the surgery Walt admired Levin's skill. The young chest surgeon handled tissue carefully, yet worked with great efficiency and speed. He removed the cancerous lesion from the lung, dropped it into a stainless-steel basin and had it rushed to the lab for a preliminary biopsy to make sure it was not a fresh carcinoma but a metastasis from the original sarcoma.

Ten minutes later the word came over the OR phone. Yes, metastatic osteogenic sarcoma. That meant there was no need for further surgery, and it was safe for Levin to close.

"SY, IT'S UP TO YOU to talk Emily out of it," Walt insisted. "Talk to her, Sy. She'll listen to you."

"What should I tell her?"

"Tell her she absolutely cannot take Simmie home! We have no facilities at home. Even with twenty-four-hour nursing we can't do anything for her there."

"Walt," the old man said, "we can't do anything for her here."

SIMONE DUNCAN WAS HOME once more, in her own bed, under a bright coverlet of red and white floral design. She looked about her and inhaled. "It smells so sweet here, Mommy," she said.

Her mother nodded, smiling, holding back tears.

"It's good to be home." Then Simmie added, "They won't be doing anything to me here, will they?"

"No, darling. Now, would you like something to eat? Some cereal, perhaps?"

"No. Some—some pancakes? With lots of syrup."

"Of course, darling. I'll go down and make them right away," Emily promised. She started for the door.

"Mommy?"

"Yes, dear?"

"Cindy . . ." She pointed to the doll on the top shelf of the bookcase opposite her bed. "You remember, Daddy brought her home for me that time he went to California."

"Of course," Emily said. She reached for the brightly dressed doll with flaxen nylon pigtails.

Simmie cradled the doll in her arms, straightening its plaits. "Hi, Cindy. Did you miss me?" she asked. "Well, I'll be here from now on."

Emily turned once more to start downstairs to prepare the pancakes. She had not taken two steps out of the room when what she heard arrested her sharply. "Cindy, would you like to belong to Kimmie, or maybe Lynne? You can choose." Emily drew against the wall, out of sight.

"Or should I let Kimmie choose? She's my best friend. We went to day

100

camp together. You'll like her. Maybe what I'll do is give you to Kimmie. And give Oscar the Clown to Lynne. Then there's my ice skates. Who'll I give those to?"

Emily was tempted to rush into the room and protest, No, no, you mustn't! Instead, she leaned against the wall and wept silently as she heard her daughter softly dispose of what she considered her most precious worldly goods.

SIMMIE WAS DOZING when Emily entered her room carrying a tray with hot pancakes.

"Simmie?" Emily said gently to wake her. "Pancakes! The way I make them on Sunday mornings. Don't they smell great?"

The child ignored her invitation and said, "Mommy, tell me again, how does it feel when you die?"

"Who said anything about dying?"

"Does it hurt?" the child persisted.

Emily realized that for her child's peace of mind the time for pretence was over. She set the tray aside on Simmie's desk and took the child in her arms. "No, darling, it doesn't hurt. In fact, when it happens, there's no pain at all. All the pain is over."

"Before—is there pain before?"

"If there is, we'll get Dr. Bristol or Uncle Sy to give you something and you won't hurt any more."

"Or feel sick in my stomach?"

"No. There'll be no more of that either, sweetheart."

The child lay still, absorbing what her mother had said.

"How does it happen, Mommy?"

Emily found herself unable to answer.

"Is there anybody here?" the child asked, explaining her question, to Emily's relief.

"Of course, darling. I'll be here. Daddy. Maybe Uncle Sy. One thing is sure, you won't be alone."

"And after? What happens after?"

Emily could not control her tears. She let them roll slowly down her cheeks as she talked.

"After—we'll still be here. You won't be alone."

"Will I ever see you again, Mommy?"

"Sometime, somewhere we will be together again."

"It feels so sad to be away from you for a long time," the child said.

She became aware of Emily's tears on her own cheek. "You crying, Mommy?"

"Uh-huh," Emily admitted.

"Is it all right? To cry, I mean?"

"If you feel like it, darling, it's all right to cry."

The child turned to her mother, buried her face between Emily's breasts. Soon Emily felt the warm, moist tears of her young child seep through her dress.

After a time Simmie asked, "Mommy, can Kimmie come to visit? And Lynne? I'd like to give them some things."

"I think it'll be all right. I'll check with Dr. Bristol."

The child seemed reassured. Suddenly she asked, "You're sure I won't be alone, will I, Mommy?"

"No, darling. When it happens, you won't be alone."

FROM THAT NIGHT ON, Emily slept alongside her daughter. By the fourth day, once Simmie had been stabilized in her new environment and had her intravenous drip connected to feed a drug to ease any pain, she was allowed to have visitors.

For a brief time, encouraged by the presence of her two friends, Simmie became animated. She told them of her adventures in the hospital. The treatments. The nurses. Some of the funny things that had happened. And that nice girl, real grown-up, who had become her friend—Amy Bedford.

"Did you know she was the tennis champion of the high school? She could even beat some of the guys in the team. She came to see me lots of times."

Emily listened, encouraged by her daughter's sudden spurt of energy. Perhaps in her own environment, surrounded by her friends, she would thrive. To prevent Simmie's exhausting herself, Emily announced, "Girls, time for cookies and ice cream!"

Neither of them appeared to have the usual eagerness for sweets. Somehow they sensed that this might be the last time they would see their friend. Before they departed, Simone disposed of her possessions as she had planned. Then, gifts in hand, they started to leave.

"Don't go," Simmie pleaded. "What I have isn't catching, is it, Mommy?"

"Of course it isn't catching. But you need to rest now. It's been quite an afternoon, and you need your nap."

After they were gone, Simmie talked on while Emily straightened the covers about her.

"They liked their gifts, didn't they, Mommy?"

"Yes, darling. They loved them. It was very sweet and thoughtful of you to do that."

"After I'm gone, will they remember? I mean every time they look at their presents, will they remember me?"

"With the gifts or without, they'll remember you. We'll all remember you. You will never be forgotten, or alone. You'll be with us always. In our minds. In our hearts."

Reassured, the child closed her eyes and drifted off to sleep.

As SIMMIE'S CONDITION continued to deteriorate, Walter Duncan came home from the hospital earlier each day. Sy covered for him in consultations and in Tumour Board meetings. On many cases Sy did Walt's post-op rounds.

Every moment when he was home and Simmie was awake, Walt spent in her room. He regaled her with stories of his youth, his schooldays, and of his own parents, who had died years ago.

One night Emily listened to her husband trying to keep up a running commentary on his childhood, which Simmie always called the olden days. I almost wish he would stop, Emily thought. It's painful to see him try so hard to pretend. Some moments he seems to believe he can reverse the inevitable. Under the pretext that Simmie needed her rest Emily was able to shoo Walter from the room and to bed for the sleep he too so desperately needed.

On THE SIXTH DAY of the third week after Simmie's return home, early in the morning while it was still dark, Emily was wakened by her daughter's voice.

"Mommy . . ."

Emily responded sleepily. "Yes, darling? What would you like? Some water? Fruit juice?"

"Mommy, I'm so warm, so wet"—Simmie's voice seemed suddenly muffled—"and I'm so tired."

Emily became alert. With a startled move she reached behind her, found the bedside lamp, flicked it on. Then she saw it.

Blood was seeping from her daughter's mouth, tracing down her chin and onto her nightgown.

"Simmie!" Emily cried out taking the child in her arms and rocking her. "Walter! Walt!" she called desperately. For she knew. She had read enough to know this was one way it could end. A massive hemorrhage. She began to weep.

"Don't worry, Mommy. I'm all right. It doesn't hurt. It's like you said, it doesn't hurt."

Walt came rushing into Simmie's bedroom. He saw what was happening. He raced to her bedside, tried to take the child from her mother's arms, to examine her. But Emily resisted.

"No, no. I promised her. I promised. . . ." She kept protesting and weeping.

Firmly yet gently Walt separated the two. With the child in his arms he realized it had happened. What had threatened for so long had finally happened. He held her, rubbed his large, strong hand across her soft, thin cheek. The struggle was over. The pain. The agony of the treatments. The battle within her wasted body. It was all over. His child was finally at peace.

CHAPTER 12

The funeral of Simone Duncan, aged eleven, was held on Saturday morning. Several of Simmie's friends attended, in the company of their parents. Kimmie brought the flaxen-haired doll Simmie had given her. Emily's mother and father were there, having flown in from Tucson.

The ceremony in the church was brief. The choral group of her class in school sang two songs. The minister recounted the high points of Simmie's too-short life.

Afterwards Emily and Walt followed the coffin up the aisle of the church towards the bright, sunny day outside. Behind them were Sy and other colleagues from the hospital. As they reached the last row of pews Walter noticed Amy Bedford, leaning on her stick. Next to her was Brent Martin.

At the cemetery there was only Walt, Emily, her parents and Sy. The minister spoke a simple prayer. He turned to Walt, signalled an attendant to hand him the first, symbolic spade of earth. Walt could not bring himself to take it. Again the minister urged it on him. Walt stared down into the grave but did not move.

Sy stepped forward, took the shovel into his own hands and sprayed the fresh brown earth over the coffin. Emily's father took the shovel and did the same. Still, Walter Duncan did not move.

On the ride back from the cemetery Emily and the Ingrahams sat in the back seat of the limousine. Walt and Sy sat on the folding seats. No one spoke. What was there left to say? Several neighbours were waiting for them when they arrived home. Despite Walt's orders, they had prepared a meal for the mourners, few as they were.

Lunch too was eaten in silence. Walt ate little, excused himself early and drove off.

"Probably gone to the hospital," Sy said. "Maybe it's the best thing for him at a time like this."

Later, in Emily's garden, her father conversed with Sy. "Dr. Rosen, was there anything that could have been—"

Sy interrupted. "We did everything. Everything."

After some minutes of silence Ingraham said, "I—I'll have to change my will now."

104

"Me too," Sy said. Then he asked, "What college did you pick out for her?"

"I was thinking maybe she would have liked Arizona State. Some place where we could have seen her often. Or even UCLA. That's only an hour's flight from Tucson." They were silent for a long moment before Ingraham asked, "You?"

"I picked out the University of Chicago. For the same reason. It's only an hour's flight from here." Then he added, "I hope you don't mind my thinking I was her grandfather."

"From what Emily's told me, you deserve the privilege. 'Sides, every child is entitled to two grandfathers."

"I'd better go," Sy said. "To do what I can to relieve Walt of his obligations, today of all days."

Sy was on his way to his car when Walt pulled into the driveway. Sy approached him to say one last word of sympathy and noticed that Walt was taking files, books and several framed diplomas out of his car.

"Walter, what's the meaning of this?"

"I don't think I'll be going back there. Emily needs me now. She's been through hell. I've got to make up for it."

"Walter, listen to me—" Sy started to say.

"Sorry, Sy. I've made up my mind. I left instructions about my cases that are still due for surgery. Pendleton will take care of those. If his schedule is overloaded, find someone else."

"Walt, I know how you feel," Sy said. "But—"

Sharply Walt interrupted. "You can do one thing for me. Amy Bedford. I would like you to take on her case yourself."

"Of course. But Walt, that does not address the real issue. You. You have to come back!"

"Why?"

"You owe it to the profession. To your patients. And, in the end, to yourself."

"I owe? I owe no one anything!" Walt exploded. "Simmie! Yes. I owed her. I owed her a lot more than coming home late, when she was already asleep. I owed her a lot more than kisses she never knew I gave her. Well, I have nothing left now except Emily. I owe her all my time, all my love. She needs it. You can see that for yourself."

The ready answer was on Sy's tongue, but he knew it would make no impression on a grieving man as guilt-laden and tormented as Walt Duncan was at the moment.

So Sy limited himself to a hand on Walt's shoulder and a soft, "Well, we Jews have a mourning ritual called *shivah*. For a week a man does not leave his home. Does not wear shoes, but slippers. Does not sit on his usual chair, but on a low stool. In the biblical tradition he makes a symbolic cut in his coat, as in the ancient rending of one's garments. But after seven days a man puts aside his mourning and returns to life. He does not forget the dead, whom he prays for. But he resumes his life. I will not mention this again for seven days. But after that I must."

"It won't change my mind," Walt insisted.

"I will be back in a week, Walter," Sy said.

IN A FEW DAYS Sy called Emily to ask, "Is there anything I can do for you? Is there something you need?"

"Nothing. The neighbours have all been very kind."

"And Walt?" Sy asked.

He heard Emily pause. Then she confessed, "The first two days he greeted visitors. But since then he's been spending his time in Simmie's room. When I ask him to come down, he refuses, saying, 'I'm making up for the time I should have spent here.' Sy, I don't know what to do."

He could hear her gasp and begin to cry.

"Emily, I'll come by and talk to him."

Later Sy Rosen knocked gently on the closed door to Simmie Duncan's room. There was no response. He turned the knob and pushed the door open. The room was in darkness. The blinds were down and shut against the daylight. Sy discovered Walt in a chair beside Simmie's small bed.

"Walt?" Sy challenged.

"Your week isn't over yet," was Walt's response.

"I can't wait," Sy said. "We are having problems at the hospital."

"I'm sorry. Dr. Walter Duncan is no longer available. His time is now his own."

"You have to go back to your work sometime. Why not now?" Sy demanded.

"If I go back—and I say *if*—I will not go back to that hospital. I will never set foot in that place again. I'll take Emily away, somewhere where she can forget all this. It's the least I owe her!"

"Walt—"

His protégé shut him off. "No, Sy. No more do I put aside my needs, my wife's needs, for the sake of others. No more!"

IT WAS NIGHT. Walt had not turned on any lights. He had not answered the telephone. He sat in the den, feeling neither hunger nor thirst. Feeling only the stillness in the house. He rose from the chair, went upstairs to look for Emily.

He found her in their bedroom, holding a hanger of clothes. On the luggage rack was an open suitcase.

"Em?"

"I think maybe I want to go away from this place."

"Where?"

"I don't know. My mother's maybe. Somewhere. Every time I pass Simmie's room I think, Part of me, the marrow from my bones, attacked her, killed her."

He took the hanger out of her hands, tossed it aside, enfolded her in his arms.

"No, Em, no. That transplant was her only chance, a desperate chance. We all knew that. You did everything you could. Em, we've got only each other now. And I need you very much. Because I too am going to start a new life. If there's going to be any going away, let's go together. There's nothing to keep us here any more. I'm not going back to the hospital. I told Sy. I may not ever practise surgery again. Or medicine. I owe them nothing!"

He raised her face and kissed her on the lips. He pressed his face against hers. "Did you mean what you said about not going back to the hospital?" she asked.

"I meant it."

DR. SIMON ROSEN had just completed his checkup of Amy Bedford. Her X-rays were clean once more. The surgery on her lung had accomplished its purpose, and healing was excellent. "All right now, Amy," he said. "Let's see you walk the length of this room, back and forth, without your stick."

Amy looked at Sy, then at her mother. She rested her stick on the examining table. One foot before another, she started away from them towards the far wall of the narrow room. The prosthesis within her leg supported her full weight. She was not as smooth as she would be one day. But she was on her own.

"Amy, you're on the last lap. A little more chemo and physiotherapy, and your year will be up."

"My year?" she said. "It seemed like a hundred years!"

"I know, child, I know," Sy said.

"Dr. Rosen, can I play tennis again?"

Sy smiled. "Amy, my dear, can you? Yes, in time, I suppose so. Should you risk it? Not if I were you. Sure, we have replaced a prosthesis before. Do we like to do it? We always like to avoid unnecessary surgery. So I would pass up tennis."

Amy nodded solemnly as she considered Sy's advice. Then she brightened. "Doctor, I'd like to show Dr. Walt that I can walk on my own. If I went by his house, would he see me?"

Sy paused a moment, then nodded. "Yes, I think that would be a very good idea. But call him first."

While Amy was in the dressing room slipping out of her patient's gown and into her own clothes, Sy said softly, "Mrs. Bedford, does your husband play golf?"

"When he finds the time. Why?"

"A girl like Amy, so athletic, needs something to take the place of tennis, which can conceivably be a dangerous sport. The sudden starts and stops. The possibility of falling. Golf could serve a double purpose. It would channel her talent into a safer sport. And it would bring father and daughter closer together."

Mrs. Bedford nodded, smiling. "Dr. Rosen, golf together could be a *very* good idea."

"WALT, THERE'S A CALL FOR YOU," Emily said, leaning into Simmie's room, where he still spent most of his time.

"I don't want to talk to anyone," he said.

"It's Amy Bedford. She wants to talk to you."

"Amy. OK. But she's the only patient I'll talk to."

He went down to the den to take the call. He listened to Amy, but refused to see her. Only when she pleaded, did he finally acquiesce, with great reluctance.

Emily said, "You ought to put on some respectable clothes."

He nodded grimly but went back to Simmie's room.

"BRENT, YOU HAVE TO DRIVE ME, you just have to," Amy Bedford said over the phone.

"I'd love to, Amy, but I don't have wheels. My car's in dock. And my mom is at the same lunch as your mom. So there's no car here."

"I could take a cab," Amy said, "but I wanted you to be there when I show Dr. Walt. After all, you're part of this, you know."

"Hey, I got an idea. Why don't we go on my motorbike?"

"Motorbike? I haven't been on that since before all this started. It'll be like old times."

"Oh, one thing. You have to wear a helmet."

"Of course," Amy said.

BRENT MARTIN WAS EXTREMELY CAREFUL, making sure Amy was properly in place on the rear seat of his motorbike. He waited until she had strapped her helmet in place, then took off for the suburb where the Duncans lived.

The trip was uneventful until they were within a few blocks of the Duncan house. A large transcontinental moving van came up on their left side. Brent slowed down to allow it to pass. Once it went by, he resumed his former speed.

Then, without any signal, the van turned right into Brent's path. Brent jammed on his brakes, but the momentum was too powerful for him to stop in time. His motorbike crashed into the turning van.

WITH SIRENS BLARING, three squad cars converged on the scene of the accident. Moments later an ambulance pulled up. The technician in charge leaped out of the back while the driver hauled out a stretcher.

"What have we got here?" the technician asked a policeman.

"Two kids," the officer replied. "Lucky they had helmets on. But the boy seems hurt real bad."

The technician knelt over Brent Martin and made a swift appraisal of the boy's condition. He called out to the driver, "Bring the spine board!" Very carefully, with the technician supporting Brent's head, they lifted the boy onto the rigid spine board and carried him to the ambulance.

The technician now had time to examine Amy. He concluded that apart from shock she had come through the experience with no discernible physical injury. But he insisted that she come to the hospital, where there would be a follow-up diagnosis.

As soon as Brent Martin was carried into the emergency room at University Medical Center, the resident called for a single lateral cervical X-ray. While the X-ray was being processed, the resident asked Brent, "Feel any pain, son?"

"Yes," Brent whispered.

"Let me see you move your legs. The right one first."

Brent's response was barely discernible.

"The left one now," the resident ordered.

Brent tried but could not move it.

"Now your arms. Right one first."

Brent responded with great effort.

"Now the left," the resident said, though he had already formed his diagnosis. He called to the nurse, "Get me someone in orthopaedics!"

From the examining table on which she lay, Amy Bedford called, "Get Dr. Rosen! Please!"

"Simon Rosen?" the young physician asked. "You know him?"

"I'm under his care now."

"Why didn't you say so? Nurse, find Dr. Rosen!"

Minutes later Sy Rosen came racing into emergency, asking breathlessly, "A patient of mine? Where?" Before they could tell him, he spied Amy Bedford.

The young doctor tried to get his attention. "Dr. Rosen, this other patient . . ."

But Sy brushed by him to reach Amy. He performed a careful examination of her right leg, which seemed intact and uninjured.

"Amy! Stand up!" he ordered. "Let me see you walk."

In ripped and slightly bloody jeans, Amy Bedford proceeded to walk up and back. Relieved, Sy Rosen said, "Good, Amy! We'll X-ray you. But that leg seems OK."

He turned to the younger physician. "Now, Doctor, what's on your mind?"

"This patient over here," the man said.

"Let's have a look."

Very carefully Sy Rosen examined Brent Martin.

"He needs surgery," Sy said. "And right away. Get me Pendleton, or if he's busy, Harvey or Bridges. Meantime, get hold of Clemmons in neurology. We'll need a neurosurgeon to assist."

CHAPTER 13

Minutes later Dr. Alan Bridges hurried into the emergency room.

"You sent for me, Sy?"

"Alan, have a look at this young man."

Sy and Amy stood aside while Bridges made his assessment of Brent Martin's condition. Amy was in tears. Sy tried to comfort her, putting his arm round her. She kept crying and saying, "It's all my fault. I asked him to take me to see Dr. Walt. Will he die?"

"Amy, we don't know yet. But there are other things to worry about. Like what happens if he lives."

"What do you mean?"

Before Sy could answer, Bridges turned from the table. His glance to Sy indicated he would rather not discuss the patient's condition in the presence of the young woman. Sy led him to a corner of the room.

"We've got to do a total spine X-ray—" Bridges began.

"Of course!" Sy interrupted impatiently. "What else? Dislocation of the spine. Possible spinal-cord injury. Loss of movement in the legs."

"Partial, but clearly discernible. But you know that. Why did you send for me?" Bridges asked.

"We have to do surgery on him at once!" Sy said.

"Surgery? In a case like this? Not me!"

"What do you mean, not—Bridges, are you telling me that you *refuse? I'm ordering you to!"

"Dr. Rosen," Bridges replied formally, "need I remind you that you are no longer chief of orthopaedic surgery?"

Furious, Sy Rosen seized Bridges by the lapels of his lab coat. "Bridges, as one doctor to another, I am asking you to do surgery to reduce the injury to that boy's spinal cord."

Carefully choosing his words, Bridges said, "Dr. Rosen, in my professional opinion the chances of the patient's recovering from the surgery indicated in this case are so slight that I do not think the risk to the patient is justified."

"You don't think the risk to the patient is justified? Or you don't think the *doctor* wishes to risk it?" Sy asked angrily.

Without another word Sy went to the wall phone. He barked an order at the operator. "Get me Walt Duncan. At home!"

He held on, glaring at Dr. Bridges. Amy stood at the examining table, holding Brent's hand. He had lapsed into unconsciousness.

Sy spoke into the phone. "Hello, Walter . . . Oh, Emily . . . Won't come to the phone? Damn it, there's no time now for even a week of mourning. You tell him I must talk to him!"

No one in emergency dared to move.

Finally Sy Rosen said, "Walt, I want you down here at once. An emergency. The kind in which minutes can count. We've got a trauma case that demands decompression of the spinal cord by open reduction. And from what I can see, there is constrictive bony tissue that could leave this young man a quadriplegic."

"Sy, I told you—" Walter started to say.

"Walt, it's a young man you know. The young man who helped you with Amy Bedford. Now he needs your help!"

"That young man? Brent something?"

"That's him. Walt, you know what can happen to nerves under pressure for any length of time. Come down here! Fast!"

Walt had never been able to refuse Sy Rosen. Finally, this time proved no exception. "All right, Sy. I'll be there."

"Good. And Walt . . . ."

"Yes?"

"Let Emily drive you down. Just to make sure."

Walt Duncan hesitated. "OK, Sy, OK."

IIN TWELVE MINUTES Emily Duncan's car pulled alongside the ambulance dock. Walt Duncan, with a four-day growth of beard, dressed in old corduroys and a crumpled shirt, stepped out and started up the concrete steps to the emergency room.

With Emily trailing behind him he entered and nodded to Sy. While he was washing he became aware of Amy's presence. "Sy, was Amy involved? Was she hurt? What about that leg?"

"The leg seems fine. It's the young man I'm worried about."

Walt turned to the examining table. Applying only the most delicate touch, he proceeded to evaluate Brent Martin.

He turned to Sy and to Alan Bridges, who stood just behind the elderly doctor. "You've got to go in and decompress him. There's no other chance."

"Then do it," Bridges said.

"Not me, Alan. After what I've been through these last days, I wouldn't trust my own hands. You have to do it."

"Do I? Would you like me to cite the statistics in cases like this when surgery is done perfectly? The mortality rate? The patients who survive but lose motor ability in all four limbs?"

"Alan, look," Walt pleaded, holding out his large, trembling hands. "I can hardly keep them steady. Alan?"

Sy Rosen intervened. Grimly he said, "No, Walt. It's no use. You are looking at a new breed of doctor. Who, between taking a risk to give his patient a chance at a full life and choosing to save his own hide, chooses the coward's way out."

"Don't you call me a coward," Bridges shot back. "I didn't create this system. You know that if I operate and this boy dies or is left paralysed, there could be a multimillion-dollar malpractice suit against me. Everything I worked for, security for my wife, education for my kids, would go down the drain."

Walt Duncan turned on Bridges. "What are you, Bridges? A businessman or a doctor?"

Bridges answered in carefully selected words. "I do not think this patient presents a justifiable risk for decompression surgery. Especially when some self-righteous saint like you might go into court and testify against me. As you did against Enright."

"Some of you will never forgive me for telling the truth, will you?" Walt demanded.

"Gentlemen, I have given you my professional opinion," Bridges said. He left the room.

"Walt?" Sy asked.

He had no need to ask anything more. Walt knew what that meant. If surgery was to be done, it had to be done at once. He felt his hands at his side, still trembling. Whether in anger or nervous exhaustion, he did not know. But he could not move to accept Sy's challenge.

Sy looked at Emily and hoped she would intervene. Slowly she came towards her husband. She put her hands on his shoulders.

"Walt, he's a young man, a kid, really. He's got years ahead of him. You have to do it."

"I—I no longer *have* to do anything," he said. "Besides, I don't think I can. Not any more."

"All the skill you had, did that disappear in just a few days?" she said. "Walter, what if surgery could have saved Simmie and a doctor had refused to do it?"

112

His eyes welled up with tears. He asked softly, "Did anyone get in touch with Brent's folks?"

"I did," Amy said.

"Then they should be here any moment," Walt said, as he turned to Sy. "I'll start scrubbing. You get the informed consent. Meet me in OR."

He started out of the door. Sy went to Emily. "Thanks, my dear. You said all that he needed to hear."

OPEN REDUCTION. THE PHRASE went through Walt's mind as he scrubbed. It meant the delicate procedure of removing pressure on the nervous system of a trauma victim. Bits of sharp, jagged bone must be carefully separated from the spinal cord, while trying at all times not to damage the nerves themselves.

All through surgery Walt would be aware that in a case like this Bridges was right. The odds were always against the surgeon.

Sy came alongside him to scrub. "Clemmons in neurology has agreed to assist. He'll be right up."

"Good man, Clemmons, good man," Walt said.

Once Walt had thrust his hands into the rubber gloves, he began to feel more at ease. This was what he was used to. Despite the surprises that might confront him when he got inside the patient, he felt equipped to deal with them. Far better equipped than he was to deal with the sorrows of his personal life.

With Clemmons at his side and Sy across the table from him, he proceeded with considerable delicacy to lay back flap after flap of skin, tissue, and the dura mater, which protected the spinal cord.

He had reached the area of the damage. It was patent to the naked eye that bone splinters from crushed vertebrae were pressing on the spinal cord. Allowed to remain even for a few hours, they would result in irreversible paralysis.

He consulted Clemmons with a look. Clemmons nodded. Walt began the intricate task of extracting the tiny splinters from Brent Martin's spinal cord. That done, he proceeded to perform the fusion that would prevent any future damage. The nerve had been decompressed. What happened hereafter was in nature's hands. If all went well, the boy could have a promising future.

They wheeled the patient out to the recovery room. Walt Duncan tore off his rubber gloves and tossed them into the waste container. As he untied his surgical mask he became aware that Sy was staring at him, his face still masked, only his blue eyes exposed.

"Good work, Walt," Sy said.

"Beautiful work," Clemmons said. "That's a very lucky boy. I hope he appreciates it."

Sy was stripping off his gloves and mask. "Walt," he said, "as long as you're here, I wonder if you would do me a favour. I've got a little boy in pediatric. Take a look at him?"

Walt pondered the request. "OK. Just this once."

"That's all I ask," Sy said. "But please shave first. And comb your hair. You look like a rock star, not a surgeon."

AFTER WALTER DUNCAN carefully examined the slight ten-year-old patient, he glanced at the boy's case history, then gestured Sy to join him outside the room. "Sy, you didn't need my opinion. His X-rays and scans tell the whole story. Osteogenic sarcoma."

"What do you suggest?"

"Chemo, of course. Right away."

"I've had him on chemo. Eight weeks now."

Walt asked the crucial question. "Did the tumour shrink?"

"Noticeably," Sy said.

"Then it's obvious; go in and do a resection."

"Of course, Walt, that's what we ought to do, but there's a problem," Sy said. "When you looked at the boy's file, did you catch his address? St. Mary's Foundling Home."

"An orphan?"

"Not that lucky," Sy said. "An abused kid. His name is Thomas Mangan. The court took him away from his parents. That's also why the doctors were late in detecting his sarcoma. They assumed his pain was a residual of the abuse."

"Natural mistake. But it's not too late."

"Fortunately. However, this is a charity case. Who can I ask to operate without a fee? One of our eminent surgeons who drive sixty-thousand-dollar Mercedes? You know the excuses I'll get. Walt, just this one last case is all I ask. He's a nice kid."

"He's a nice kid all right," Walt said. "But we're determined, Em and I, to go away. Somewhere. To forget."

"Are you going to leave all your memories behind? Going to forget Simmie too? What happened to my family was over forty years ago. Do you think I ever forget?"

Walt evaded replying by saying, "I'll do the little boy's case for you. After that, I want to be free. Free!"

TWO DAYS LATER Walter Duncan and Simon Rosen stood alongside each other at stainless-steel sinks, scrubbing with antiseptic green soap.

"Quite a kid, isn't he?" Sy said.

Walt seemed taken by surprise, lost for the moment in the details of the surgery he was about to perform.

Sy explained, "The boy you're going to operate on. Considering what he's been through, he has terrific spirit."

"Makes you wonder," said Walt. "Don't his parents realize what a precious gift they've been given? What's going to happen to him?"

"I'm depending on you to determine that, Walt."

"I mean after we do the surgery. Let's assume that he makes a good recovery; what happens to him?"

"I don't know. I guess the courts decide."

"I hope they don't give him back to those parents," Walt said. "Those healed fractures on his X-rays show he must have been abused since infancy." He paused. "I'll never forget the look on his face, the eagerness in his eyes, first time I examined him. They were pleading, Like me, love me, accept me. How could anyone raise a hand against a kid like that?"

The two doctors proceeded into the operating room. The resection on the boy was long and intense, but it went well. The titanium implant that Hans had designed fitted perfectly.

As Walt was stripping off his surgical gloves Sy said, "Long as you're here, take a look at Brent Martin."

"You said he was recovering nicely," Walt countered.

"He wants to see you. He asks for you."

BRENT MARTIN WAS LYING IN BED, his neck fixed into a rigid position to avoid risk to his spinal cord. When he heard his door swing open, his eyes strained to see who it might be. He was delighted to see that it was Walter Duncan.

"What's up, Doc?" Brent tried to joke.

"That's what I came to find out," Walt said. "How do you feel?"

"Considering I am in this torture chamber, not bad."

Walt drew back the covers. "Let's see you move your toes." Brent complied. Walt then palpated his legs, pinching gently to induce automatic responses. "Good." He grasped Brent's right hand. "Press. . . . Good. Harder. . . . Very good." He repeated the same procedure with Brent's left hand. "You're doing great, son."

"Doctor, I've been hearing things. I mean, from what I heard, if you hadn't volunteered to operate on me, I might be completely paralysed by now. Is that true?"

"Any halfway good surgeon could have done it, Brent."

"I understand at least one good surgeon refused."

"There was some disagreement on what should be done," Walt admitted, continuing his examination.

"When I think I might have had to spend my life in a wheelchair, I—I get cold sweats."

"Well, it's not going to happen. You'll be OK," Walt said.

The door opened suddenly. Walt could hear a familiar voice calling out, "Brent . . . Oh, Dr. Walt, sorry."

"Amy! You're not using your stick," Walt said, smiling.

"No. And look." She proudly walked the length of the room. "How's that?"

"Wonderful! Just great, Amy."

"Remember, you said, Give me a year of your life? Well, we did it in only eleven months!" she boasted.

"We sure did. From now on, nothing to do but build up that leg with exercise, get a checkup every three months and a bone scan every six months."

"And no more chemo!" Amy exulted.

"You're a free woman, Amy. You can take up your life again. Even tennis, if you're very careful."

"I've been thinking about that. I've decided in favour of golf."

"Good idea."

"Dad thinks so too. He says it'll give us a chance to spend time together."

"There is one other thing, Amy," Walt said. "One obligation you have. Remember, I said you'd have to talk to other patients?"

"Yes."

"Well, come with me. You'll excuse us, Brent, if I borrow Amy for a little while?"

"Just make sure to send her back."

As they walked down the corridor Walt said, "Amy, there is a boy in two twenty-nine. He's just had your kind of surgery. He's only ten. And very scared. So he needs all the courage you can give him. OK?"

"Depend on me, Dr. Walt."

He pushed open the door to discover a nurse feeding the boy cold fruit juice through a straw. She left the room, and Walt said, "Thomas Mangan, I want you to meet another patient of mine, Amy Bedford."

"Hi, Tommy."

"Amy, walk up and down for Tommy. Let him see what he's going to be like very soon."

Amy walked the length of the boy's room, holding herself as erect as a fashion model and moving almost flawlessly.

The boy raised his head off his pillow to watch, his blue eyes wide with wonder. "You had the same thing—" he started to ask.

"Even worse, Tommy," Walt said. "And look at her now. Well, I'll leave the two of you to get acquainted. Amy, drop by my office after you've talked to Tommy."

As he closed the door behind him he heard her saying, "You are the luckiest kid in the world to have Dr. Walt as your doctor."

WALT HAD RETURNED TO HIS OFFICE. There was an urgent message from Sy Rosen. "Call at once!"

So that's his game, Walt thought. To snow me under with so many new cases that I'll abandon my plan.

He lifted the phone and dialled. When Sy answered, Walt said, "Listen, you old faker. I know exactly what you're up to. And it won't work. Emily and I are going away. And we are not coming back! Got it?"

"Not even for the ceremony?" Sy asked.

"Ceremony? What ceremony?"

"Well, I hold here in my hand an announcement from James Rowe Russell himself."

"Sy, I am no longer interested in anything James Rowe Russell has to say. He can run this hospital any way he pleases!"

"You could at least pay me the courtesy of listening to his announcement. I quote: 'On Friday afternoon next we will hold a special ceremony in the main auditorium of this hospital to celebrate receiving a gift of two hundred and fifty thousand dollars for the Walter Duncan Research Fund. This grant is to be devoted to such orthopaedic research as the honoree deems beneficial.' . . . Walt?" Sy asked. "Are you still there?"

"Still here. And speechless. Who in the world would do something like that?"

"More quote: 'The moneys come to us through the kindness of Bedford Industries and Mr. and Mrs. Edward Bedford.' Unquote. Walt, how would it look if you weren't there?"

"Well, I guess you're right, Sy. OK. I'll be there. But I'm not making promises beyond that."

"I didn't ask you to, did I?" Sy replied. He hung up, smiling.

Walter Duncan hung up his phone too. He hesitated only a moment before dialling. "Em? Darling, I hate to ask this of you. But we're going to have to put off our trip for a little while."

"Walt, I know. Sy called me first. I said it was all right."

"Em, you know what I thought? If it's all right with you, I thought I would ask them to change it to the Simone Duncan Research Fund."

"I think that would be wonderful. I want people to know that there was such a person as Simone. And to remember her always." He could detect a hint of tears in her voice.

"Em, why don't you drive down here and we'll go out to dinner together? You haven't been out in so long."

"I'd love to, darling."

"And while you're here, there's someone I want you to meet. He's ten years old. And he's got big problems. Medical problems. But other problems too. He's practically alone. They had to take him away from his parents."

"Take him away?" Emily questioned.

"The court has forbidden his parents to have any contact with him. He was abused. Badly abused."

"Oh, no!"

"What he needs now, as much as medical care, perhaps more, is to know he's not alone. He needs someone to visit him. Spend time with him. To let him know that there are kind and loving people in this world. Mostly, that he is worthy of being loved. I've never seen a kid who needed it more. Em?"

"Of course, darling. I'll be there as soon as I can."

THE SECOND FLOOR of the Pediatric Pavilion had settled down for the night. All visitors had departed. Walt and Emily arrived at room 229. Walt knocked softly. He eased the door open.

"Tommy? Still awake?"

"Yes, Dr. Duncan."

The boy edged up in bed despite the confining burden of the Jordan splint on his left leg.

"Tommy, I want you to meet my wife, Emily."

The boy stared at her through his blue eyes. He smiled shyly.

"I hope the two of you will get to be good friends in the next few weeks. And will stay good friends for a long time. A very long time," Walter Duncan said.

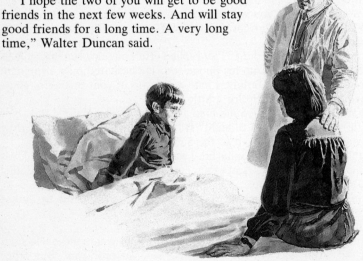

HENRY DENKER

"She was a beautiful young woman of twenty-three who stepped off the elevator and walked toward me as normally as anybody would," recalls Henry Denker. "It was remarkable."

"She" was Pegeen Mularchuk— the real-life model for the character of Amy Bedford in *The Choice*. A research technician at The Hospital for Special Surgery, in New York City, Pegeen was introduced to Denker while he was doing medical research for his book. As an author who specializes in medical and legal fiction, Denker has spent many hours over the years reading technical journals, visiting hospitals and interviewing doctors. But this was the first time he had done his research with someone who had actually experienced the trials of a character he was creating.

Like Amy Bedford, Pegeen was a bright, active girl in her teens when she was told she had osteogenic sarcoma in one leg. Like Amy, she endured months of chemotherapy. And even with the love and support of family and close friends, Pegeen felt the same emotional trauma that most patients undergo throughout their treatment. Pegeen too had successful surgery on the affected leg, and soon after followed an arduous regimen of physical therapy and exercise to restore her natural walk. Recently married, she is now completing her studies in biochemistry at New York University.

As for his own future, Henry Denker plans, simply, to write more books. That should come as good news to readers, for *The Choice* marks this popular author's seventh appearance in British Condensed Books. A native New Yorker, Denker lives in Manhattan with his wife, Edith.

THE COMMODORE

A CONDENSATION OF THE BOOK BY

Jan de Hartog

ILLUSTRATED BY JOHN BESWICK

Martinus Harinxma has the sea in his blood and a lifetime of maritime service in the tugboat profession behind him. Now living in retirement in the south of France, this Dutch master mariner and ex-naval commodore is given the chance to return to the sea, for one last epic voyage on the very latest ocean-going tugboat, the *Isabel Kwel*. The daunting task before him is to tow a giant dry dock through the Atlantic stormbelt to Rio de Janeiro—but this is not all. Under certain conditions the tugboat rolls precariously and is in grave danger of capsizing. What's more, her officers and motley Chinese crew seem an untrustworthy bunch—almost as untrustworthy as her owners. Nevertheless, befriended by a mischievous rat and a canary called Pete, the Commodore accepts the challenge . . .

Chapter One

The call came a few days before Christmas, while my wife, Sylvia, and I were having one of our Darby-and-Joan tiffs. I was decorating the kitchen of our bungalow in the south of France with holly and tinsel, the radio was bellowing carols; she had sausage rolls and mince pies in the oven and looked apple-cheeked, like a Russian doll. We were expecting two sons, one divorced daughter, one daughter-in-law and six grandchildren for the holiday; the tiny house was going to burst at the seams. I was not looking forward to it.

I stood teetering on a wobbly chair, putting up a paper garland; the radio, turned up to enough decibels to fill a stadium, blasted "Halleluja!" from Handel's *Messiah*. "If I hear one more 'Halleluja'," I said, "I'm going to kick the set."

She said, "Don't talk nonsense," and opened the oven door, and the smell of Christmas hit me like a blast. "You're turning into a cantankerous old cuss in your old age, Martinus. Why don't you go for a walk with the dog? Go on." She dumped a load of mince pies onto the counter. "Take Héloise. It'll do you both good."

"The last thing I want right now is to go for a walk with that hysterical mongrel. She'll hang herself in the junipers with that ridiculous Christmas ribbon."

"See what I mean?" She turned back to the oven. "Ever since you left the sea, you have become very irritable."

"Rubbish!" I said. "I left the sea nine years ago. I'm only ever irritable at Christmas."

The phone rang. Sylvia gave hard starboard rudder and headed for it. That would be one of her women friends; maybe it was not a bad idea to take off for a while.

As I put on my overcoat, I heard Sylvia say behind me, "It's for you. KITCO." With a steely look in her eye, she added, "Mr. Kwel."

He had called me only once since I retired, and that was to invite me to an old captains' reunion, eight years ago. I took the phone.

"Commodore Harinxma?" a girl's voice asked. "One moment, please. Mr. Arnold Kwel for you."

"Harinxma?" I recognized the imperious voice at the first word. "How would you like to take one of our ships to Rio de Janeiro as an adviser to the new captain?"

"Excuse me?"

"It's the *Isabel Kwel*. She has been sold to Taiwan and is about to leave, with a crew of Chinese. We've been contracted by the new owners to provide a skeleton staff as far as Rio de Janeiro, to show the captain and the other officers the ropes. What do you say?"

"But, sir, I've been out of the service for nine years!"

"Come, Harinxma," the imperious voice said with a hint of impatience, "don't question my competence. If I say you are the right man, that means you *are* the right man. Can you be in my office tomorrow, ten am, to talk it over? It's for six weeks. You'll be well paid." He mentioned a figure; it was generous indeed.

"I'm flattered, sir, but it's Christmas, we're expecting the family from Holland, it's the only time of year when we're all together—"

"If you're a normal human male, Harinxma, you'll welcome an escape hatch. Get yourself to the airport; your plane leaves at five thirty. You'll have a room on arrival at the Schiphol Hilton. Tomorrow morning at nine hundred hours you'll be picked up by limousine; we meet at ten in my office. Don't bring any gear, we'll provide that."

"Don't let him seduce you, the wily bastard!" my wife whispered hotly, as if she had heard every word; she sounded ready to explode.

"Well? What do you say?"

"I'd like to talk it over with my wife, sir."

"Never mind your wife, man! Make up your own mind for once!" No one had spoken to me like that for a long time. Come to think of it, no one ever had except this old man.

"I'll call you back within the hour, sir."

"Harinxma, you're a fool. You always were, even though it's been a well-kept secret between us. If you'd rather rot in the hills in your bungalow for two, I'll look elsewhere. Good day." He hung up.

"Well, let's have it," Sylvia said.

I told her what old Kwel had told me, or most of it.

"All right, let's talk about it."

"No, Syl. I have to think this over first, alone." I opened the door. "Come on, creep."

"The animal's name is Héloise!" she cried after me.

Once out in the open, the dog sprinted off into the heather and I ploughed my way to the top of the first hill, where I always sat down to catch my breath. I gazed at the haze on the distant hills, the blue brushstroke of the Mediterranean on the horizon. Despite the season, it was hot out here; the hills quivered with heat. The air was perfumed with the scent of lavender.

Kwel's offer came as a total surprise. I had put the sea behind me nine years before, and never looked back. I had moved from Holland and bought a charming little house in the south of France, in a new development especially geared to the needs of retired executives and their wives. I had created an entirely new life for myself, and my wife was happy. Now, here was that old man again, whom I had thought I'd shaken off after almost half a century in his employ.

My old life suddenly faced me once more: the telephone calls, the hasty packing, the rushing off to some port on the other side of the globe to tow some incongruous floating structure across the ocean. An exciting life; but enough was enough. The hell with old Kwel and his imperial stance, his devious ways; the man was a maniac, all shipowners in the towage business were maniacs. I was astounded he was still alive; he must be in his eighties.

I turned back to the bungalow, where Sylvia sat sipping a glass of sherry at the dining table. She was smoking a cigarette, something she had not done for some time. "Martinus," she said, "I have thought it over. I think you should go and find out what all this is about."

I couldn't believe my ears. "Why? You don't think I *want* to, do you? I've been gone nine years! Time hasn't stood still, the new tugboats are very different from the ones I was used to. I don't feel competent to act as an adviser on a type of ship I have no experience of."

She gave me an absent-minded look and puffed at her cigarette with touching unfamiliarity. "How long did he say it would be?"

"Six weeks."

"And what is he paying you?"

I told her.

"Then I want you to do it," she said firmly, stubbing out her cigarette. "Six weeks, on a modern ship, to Rio! You'd be silly not to take it."

"But what would *you* do all that time? I can't leave you now, at Christmas, with all the children coming..."

She waved it away. "Don't worry. I've done it all my life. Once Christmas is over, I'll go and stay with Ella and Tim, and wait for the new baby. It's perfect timing. Also, the money is very good. Maybe now we can build that new guestroom; the grandchildren are growing. Call Kwel and tell him you'll go and look it over."

I gave in and called the head office in The Hague. I would come but I would reserve the right to turn it down if I found I couldn't hack it.

OUTWARDLY, THE HEAD OFFICE of the Kwel International Towing Company in The Hague had not changed: a patrician building in the heart of the city that looked like a government office. It seemed incongruous that this should be the nerve centre of the largest tugboat company in the world. Only the faint glitter of antennas and electronic receiving equipment against the stormy sky indicated that it was the communication centre for a fleet of two hundred ships, ninety of which were oceangoing tugboats dispersed all over the globe: some on salvage stations in places like the Firth of Forth, the Gulf of Oman, Trinidad; others towing, alone or in convoy, colossal floating objects for thousands of miles. Once upon a time I had been part of that fleet, crawling at a snail's pace across the oceans on voyages of up to six months, all the while telling myself it was the only life for me.

I stepped from the windy, rainswept street into the marble hall with the old-fashioned porter's booth and the ancient lift that I remembered so well. The porter, twenty if he was a day, gave me the kind of look immortals under thirty reserve for the elderly, pressed a button on a communication board and muttered, "Someone to see the old man, a commodore somebody. OK." He turned to me and said, "Someone will meet you here in a few minutes. Please wait over there—Commodore." He said it as if it were a joke.

The title of commodore had been discontinued after I left the service. I had been boosted to the lofty rank during World War II, when Arnold Kwel had sent me, looking ludicrously young, to take on the old *Isabel Kwel*. The only way he could give me some weight to throw around in my dealings with the British navy, which had chartered the ship, had been by giving me the nonsensical title and advising me to grow a moustache. I had lost the *Isabel*, but the title had stuck.

"Commodore Harinxma?" A strikingly elegant woman in her early forties was standing before me. I rose.

"I've come to take you to Mr. Arnold. The lift is this way."

I had expected a sumptuous office, as in the past; my reaction was one of shocked surprise. The room was dingy and dark, with a window opening onto an airshaft. Old Kwel was sitting behind a desk topped with cracked plate glass. I barely recognized him, he seemed to have aged twenty years. But his eyes were unchanged: bright blue, unflinching, sizing me up. "So there you are. Sit down," he said. "Cigar?"

126

The ritual had not changed. "Thank you," I said, although the only cigars I had ever smoked were the ones he had forced on me during the rare audiences he had granted me over a lifetime.

He opened a box and I selected one. Now he would ask me to hand it to him so he could snip the tip off with the little surgical instrument dangling from his watch chain, before lighting it for me with his gold lighter. But a woman's hand entered my field of vision and broke the spell of the past "Excuse me, Commodore." She took the cigar from me and carried out the surgical procedure, and it was she who proffered the flame.

"Let's get down to brass tacks, Harinxma," he said with a hint of impatience. "I told you the gist of it on the phone. The *Isabel* is a new ship, built especially for work in the North Sea oilfields. As you may have noticed even in your golden ghetto on the Riviera, the bottom has dropped out of the oil market, so we decided to take an offer we received from a shipbreaking company in Taiwan, who want to use her in their line of work. Miss Bastiaans has prepared a folder which will give you all the pertinent information on the *Isabel*. Captain Fransen, our head of operations, will furnish more details if you need them. The ship is now in Flushing, and I have arranged for you to make a test run with Captain Bron, one of her previous masters, tomorrow morning. I suggest you go to your hotel now and study the material Miss Bastiaans will give you. After lunch Captain Fransen will visit you at your hotel to answer any questions you may have; after that you go for your medical, get your injections, and sign the Articles."

"I'd prefer to postpone that until after we've made the test run, if you don't mind."

His blue eyes snapped at me. "Harinxma, it's time you recognized your own idiosyncrasies. When I first promoted you to captain, you spent half an hour protesting you were unsuitable. When I promoted you to commodore, you reacted as if I had made an indecent proposal. Don't start the old routine. You wouldn't be here if you didn't want the job. All we need now is my grandson's blessing. He's officially in the driver's seat these days. All right, Harinxma. Let's go."

He walked with a quick, shuffling gait to the door; Miss Bastiaans opened it for him. She accompanied us to the lift and helped him step inside, which he did like an old heron. We went down one floor, out again, and headed for a door in a hallway much more impressive than the one upstairs. In the past his own office had been here somewhere.

It was the same one; I recognized it the moment we entered. It was a strange experience. This was where the old man had ruled the largest tugboat fleet in the world for over forty years, undisputed master of the international trade. Now, a nondescript young man was sitting behind the ornate desk. He did not bother to rise, but gestured at a couple of chairs in front of the desk. "Good morning. I gather you're the one who's taking our *Isabel* to Talcahuano."

"Rio," the old man snapped. "And mind your manners." Miss Bastiaans helped him sit down, gently, and left the room.

The young man rose and held out his hand. "I'm Jim Kwel. You are Captain . . . ?"

"This is Commodore Martinus Harinxma," the old man said. "He has been with the company for fifty years. I thought you'd done your homework."

The young man smiled at me. "Commodore, how do you do?" His hand was firm and cold; he sat down again. "I presume you've been advised of the delicate nature of the assignment?"

"I'll thank you to leave the handling of this matter to me," the old man said, with such authority that I felt it in the nape of my neck. "Commodore Harinxma and I have worked together for a long time, we're used to each other. This is just a formal introduction."

The young man responded to the rebuke with a thin smile. "I appreciate your help, Commodore. I gather you'll be arranging the details with my grandfather, so all that's left for me to do is wish you Godspeed and happy sailing."

The old man rose. As if she were a cat who could locate a mouse through a brick wall, Miss Bastiaans came in before he was able to move. He did so more nimbly than before; it was obvious that he had had a basinful of his grandson. He shuffled to the lift. As we stood waiting he said, out of the blue, "Well, see you at dinner."

"Excuse me, sir?"

"Dinner! I expect you for dinner! To meet the Chinese owner! The car will be at your hotel at six thirty. Don't keep it waiting." The lift arrived. "We're going up," he said. "Are you coming or going?"

"I think Miss Bastiaans has something for me, sir."

"Ah, yes."

The gate slammed shut. As the shaking old cage slowly made its way back to the top floor, I wondered what the delicate nature of the assignment was that young Kwel had mentioned, causing his grandfather to slap him down.

MISS BASTIAANS HAD THE FOLDER on the *Isabel Kwel* ready for me in a briefcase, and had booked me into a hotel in the port of Rotterdam, where I would find the water bailiff, the doctor and the outfitters, and from where the *Isabel* would leave three days from now. She supposed I would want a quiet hour at the hotel to study the contents of the folder, then a light lunch for which she had booked a table in the restaurant of the hotel; Captain Fransen, KITCO's head of operations, would be at the hotel at fourteen hundred hours. He would arrange transportation for the test run with the *Isabel* tomorrow morning and give me the programme for the rest of that day—supposing I were to accept the assignment. She gave me a ravishing smile; I was quite smitten with her.

She took me downstairs to the waiting limousine and made sure I was safely seated before handing me the briefcase. Then she said, again with that ravishing smile, "There you are, Commodore. See you this evening." She shut the door, gave the driver a curt signal, and we drove off.

In the hotel everyone seemed to have been advised of my arrival. KITCO must have some clout here; I was treated like a VIP. I decided to follow Miss Bastiaans's advice and have a quiet hour in my room before going down to the restaurant. I looked at the material on the *Isabel* from Miss Bastiaans's folder.

There were a lot of press clippings; the ship must have made quite a splash when she was launched. *Vessel from the Space Age ... the mightiest tugboat in the world ... marvel of modern technology ...* But judging from her specifications, I thought she was less a marvel than a monster. Her dimensions were massive: length 270 feet, width 62, and a draught of 30. Her bridge, in a break with tradition, was midships rather than on the forward quarter. Instead of a mainmast, she carried what the brochure referred to as *the paradise tree*. It looked indeed like a tree full of electronic whiskers, globes, reflectors and dish antennae. It was placed on a walkway between her two squat stacks. One thing was obvious: if any ship in distress were to give as much as a rabbit squeak within a thousand-mile radius of this monster, she would be able to go pounding towards it at the speed of an express train within minutes.

But the *Isabel Kwel* was not designed for work with oilrigs in the North Sea, as the old man had led me to believe. She was a fully-fledged ocean-going vessel, designed for long-distance towing and salvage work. Why had he presented her to me as something she patently was not? His grandson's casual remark about "the delicate nature of the assignment" came back to me. Something did not smell right.

AFTER LUNCH I RETURNED to my room to study the material on the *Isabel Kwel* again, in preparation for some judicious grilling of Captain Fransen, head of operations.

In my time I had known a number of his predecessors, usually ex-captains who stayed on after their retirement and, instead of slowing down, found themselves caught in a man-killing job which not only made them the target of everybody's gripes, but sent them all over the world on a succession of emergency missions which, in my experience, turned even the most laid-back character into a nervous wreck. However, they knew everything that went on on board each of the ninety-odd ships under their management; Fransen was likely to know more about the *Isabel Kwel* and her crew than the owners did.

I must have dropped off, for it seemed only minutes later that the telephone rang. A smoke-hoarsened voice asked, "Harinxma? This is Fransen. Shall I come up to your room, or are you coming down?"

"Oh, hello," I said, gathering my wits. "If it's all the same to you, I'd rather you came up, it's more private."

"Okeydoke." He put the phone down.

At first sight Captain Fransen ran close to type, only he seemed younger than the ones I had known; a tall man in his fifties, as thin as a rake, with a sallow face and bags under his eyes. He wore an old-fashioned fedora on the back of his head; a cigarette drooped from a corner of his mouth; his wet raincoat had tar and grease marks on it.

"Hello there," he said, coughing.

We shook hands. He sized me up with tired blue eyes and said, "You don't remember me, but we've met before. Do you mind if I take this rag off and order something to chase the chill? I've just been to Flushing to put the pig back in operation for the test run you asked for." He threw his raincoat onto the bed, tossed his hat after it, slumped in the only armchair in the room, stretched and yawned. "Sorry," he said. "I missed out on a night's sleep. Came in from Hong Kong this morning at four o'clock."

I ordered a bottle of whisky and two glasses, then asked, "Where was it we met before?"

"Oh, I was Number One on board the *Clara* when you took those two lock doors to Valparaiso in sixty-six. We were tailholder of the second tow."

"Ah, yes, I remember. You've come a long way since then."

"Don't let's talk about *that*." He coughed, and lit another cigarette with the butt of the old one. His hand shook. "It's high time I got out of this rat race," he said, grinding out the stub in the ashtray. "One day Hong Kong, the next Newfoundland, then you sweat your guts out in New Guinea, and when you come home your wife says in a strangled voice, 'While you were gallivanting with the boys, Liza died and I cried my eyes out.' Liza, for your information, was the cat. Well, another two years and it's retirement for me. What's it like?"

"It's OK, as long as you make sure you turn your back on anything to do with the sea or ships. I said to my wife the other day: a retired tug driver is like an alcoholic on the wagon. One glass and you're hooked again."

He gave me a tired look. "What made you fall off the wagon, friend?"

I shrugged. "I haven't really. I'm just sniffing the wind."

There was a knock on the door and a waiter came in with a bottle and two glasses. Fransen poured himself half a tumbler, which he downed in one. Then he pulled a dog-eared notebook from his inside pocket and

130

flicked the pages. "Tonight, I gather, you're living it up with the old man and the Chink. Early tomorrow morning you'll be picked up by taxi and taken to Flushing, where the pig will be waiting to carry you off into the great blue yonder, oinking away."

"I gather you don't care for the ship?"

I must have touched a sore spot, for suddenly he lost his cool. "Hell! Who does? For nine months we've all been yodelling about her being a marvel of technology, but the trouble is she rolls like a barrel, vibrates something terrible—a mechanical pig, that's what she is, dreamed up by a student fraternity of architects. She was meant to tow drilling platforms in the North Sea, but before she was even finished the oil market went kaput, they stopped drilling, and there she was: redundant before she was launched. '*Super tugboat of the 21st century*', the PR brochure says."

"Well, that's what she is, isn't she?" I asked innocently. "According to the description I read, she could do a lot more than push and pull oilrigs about. If ever a ship was designed for salvage work on the high seas, it would be this one, I'd say."

He shot me a blue glance like the dart of a kingfisher. "Don't ask *me*. I've had it, and the business is dying anyhow. No objects left to tow, too much competition."

"Why was she sold?" I asked. But he wasn't listening, or chose not to. "How many captains has she had so far?"

He gave me another of those looks. "Three in all. First Bartels, an egghead with tinted glasses who resigned after her maiden voyage and became a teacher at Amsterdam Naval College. Then mad Bron, otherwise known as 'Beast Rufus', who could handle the pig all right, but who's used to treating tugs like stockcars. They put him on station in Durban, where he started to abuse her on salvage operations—at least, that's what young Jim Kwel and the architects called it. So they slapped on restrictions, Beast Rufus got mad and walked out. They flew Haversma down to take over—you may have known him: sixtyish, short, bald, little melon belly; he had the *Cornelia* for fifteen years."

"I know of him, but we never met."

"Well, he brought the ship home and was given a string of barges for the Gulf, but he died in Aden—shot by a mugger in the streets. By that time the Kwels had already decided to sell her to Taiwan. At a loss, of course. The worst of it is that they have a second one exactly like her under contract, almost on the stocks."

He took another slug, lit himself another cigarette, glanced at his wristwatch and said, "Oh-oh! I've got to go. Let me give you the rest of the programme for tomorrow. I'll pick you up here at the hotel around four hundred, four thirty, so take it easy tonight. I've had meals with the old man myself; make sure you have a seeing-eye dog to take you home, like the Bastiaans woman. I must say, with a shapely all-rounder like her, I wouldn't mind being blind myself."

"What do you mean?" I asked, startled. "Are you telling me the old man is *blind?*"

"Didn't you know?" He looked amazed. "Blind as a bat, man! Well, see you tomorrow, bright and early." He slammed the door on his way out.

Old Kwel blind? I couldn't believe it. Those blue eyes had stared at me exactly as I remembered from way back when we were both young. But then, there was the way Miss Bastiaans had guided him, and the cigar-snipping and lighting ritual which she had taken over. I felt so affected by old Kwel's blindness that I had to force my attention away from him to run through the things Fransen had told me. It was obvious that something was being kept from me, something about the ship.

There was one way of finding out. I called the hotel switchboard and asked for the Naval College in Amsterdam. A surly male voice informed me that the school was closed for the Christmas vacation. I asked for the private number of Captain Bartels, one of their teachers, and was given a number in Leiden. I dialled it myself. A man's voice came on the phone: reticent, cagey. "Yes? Who is this?"

"I'm Commodore Martinus Harinxma, retired. I wonder if I could come and have a word with you about an assignment that I've been offered."

"What assignment?"

"I've been asked to act as an adviser to the new captain of one of KITCO's ships that's been sold to Taiwan. I gather you commanded her once."

"What ship?"

"The *Isabel Kwel.*"

He hung up on me. I sat staring at the phone for a few moments; then I called the hall porter to inquire about trains to Leiden.

THE WEATHER SEEMED WILDER in Leiden, a mere twenty miles north of Rotterdam. When I came out of the station the wind pushed me off the kerb. I took a taxi to the address I had found in the telephone directory. The house turned out to be a suburban semidetached villa with a small front garden. I rang the bell and the door opened a crack. A man's voice asked, "What do you want?"

"I'm Commodore Harinxma. Sorry to disturb you, Bartels, but I thought you might be willing to give me some information, to help me decide whether to accept that assignment or not."

There was a silence, during which I was observed through the crack. The whole thing was ludicrous. I'd had enough. "Look, friend," I said, "the way you carry on tells me enough. I'm sorry I bothered you."

I was halfway down the garden path when the voice called after me. "Harinxma!" I turned round. In the doorway stood a bald, stoop-shouldered man in a business suit, with tinted glasses. "Come on in! When I tell you the story, you'll understand why I have to be cautious."

I stepped into a little hall which smelled of cats.

"Good to meet you at last," the bald man said, holding out his hand. "I know of you, of course, but somehow we never met while you were still with the company." We shook hands; his was soft and clammy.

In the living room he contemplated me for a moment through his tinted glasses, then he said, "If you'd been ten years younger, I would have told you to go fly a kite."

"Would a younger man have had less of a problem with this assignment?" I asked.

"I would have left a younger man to face the consequences of his own choice. Now, what is it you want? Information, or my advice?"

"Information first, I suppose."

"Well, I'll give you my advice unsolicited. Don't touch it."

His bluntness began to lack charm. "All right," I said, "let's have it. What's wrong with the ship?"

"Ah—that's a good question! That's what everybody's been trying to find out, from the architects down to yours truly. If we knew that, it would be a different ball game. As it stands now, your guess is as good as mine. All I know is that whoever sails her as master had better be on the ball twenty-four hours a day, for if he turns his back on her, chances are she'll kill him." He paused. "You do realize that what I'm going to tell you has to remain between ourselves?"

"Depends what it is. Let's start with the facts," I suggested. His dramatics turned me off. Off the top of my head I would have said that one of the problems of the *Isabel Kwel* had been her first master.

"Well," he began, "let me tell you my own story. When I was given command of the new ship, of course I was pleased. I'd visited the ship in the yard, I'd taken a special course in computerized navigation. I was sure that this was the future, that I was going to open up the twenty-first century for the ocean-towing business. Her maiden voyage was from the Clyde to Central West Africa, towing a hotel structure, four hundred and fifty thousand tons. It was to be a landmark trip: for the first time in history, Lloyd's of London allowed a single tug to tow a structure of that size by herself. Our first oiling station was La Coruña. Up to then, everything had gone beautifully, the ship handled like a dream. Pretty impressive ... We bunkered in the bay, picked up the tow again and headed out. I don't know if you're familiar with La Coruña?"

"I've been there a few times."

"Well then, you'll remember that the channel runs virtually true north, and that at a given moment you have to make a ninety-degree turn heading for Point Herminio or you pile up on the shoals."

"I remember."

"Well—I completed the manoeuvre. Everything was hunky-dory. I was right on course, slightly northwest. When I came out of the shelter of the shoals, a moderate northwest swell caught me on the starboard bow. And then it happened."

He gave me an expectant stare, so I asked, "What did?"

"She went crazy. Suddenly she started to roll. She had rolled quite a bit before; I mean, she's definitely a tender ship; but all of a sudden, out of the blue, she started to roll out of control. Everybody on the bridge had to cling to the nearest handhold merely to remain upright. Downstairs was chaos. And all in a matter of minutes, seconds. I had no time to reflect. My gut reaction was to take the ship off automatic and kick her off course. That took care of it, but I had no idea what had happened, nobody had. It was stunning, totally unexpected: a three-thousand-ton vessel suddenly rolling like a barrel. I knew that if I'd waited a minute longer, she would have turned turtle." He paused. "Well?" he asked, as if I had missed a cue. "What do you say about *that?*"

"Incredible."

"I'll sum it up for you in one word: unseaworthy. I realized at that moment, unbelievable as it seemed, that the newest, most expensive, most powerful tugboat in the world was unseaworthy."

"My God," I said, picking up my cue.

"I wouldn't believe it at first. I told myself that every ship has an angle of incoming seas at which it may start to over-roll. I didn't even mention it in the log, for I didn't know how to put it without making myself look like a fool. Well. To cut a long story short, it happened again. Off the coast of Africa, in one of those sandstorms that are worse than fog. That's why I was on the bridge, although it wasn't my watch. It blew! From zero to force nine in ten minutes, and the sea picked up just like *that*." He snapped his fingers. "So I said, 'Let's take her up a couple of points. Three points. Four.' We must have been about four points up from our course when, *whammo!* She started to cycle again with a vengeance, much faster and more—more malevolent than the first time. She just did it again: rolling out of control up to capsizing point in two or three minutes flat, perhaps less. I don't know. But this time, at least, I knew what to do: I kicked her off course with the bow thruster. That brought her back under control. I don't think I'd have made it on the wheel alone, she was that fast.

"Well, I stayed on the bridge during my off watches from then on. I had a deckchair rigged up and slept there. The weather was good, she behaved beautifully again, but I couldn't trust her any more, so I started to write a report in which I summed up the whole thing. But then I realized: damn it, if this report gets into the wrong hands, what'll the result be? She'll lose her certificate of seaworthiness, and then she'll be worthless, the company will never be able to sell her except for scrap. So I tore up the report, and wrote another one in which I said how satisfactory the ship was, blah, blah, blah, but that there were some morale problems among the crew which could best be discussed in a private meeting with the directors. Now, wouldn't you think that was a normal, rational request?"

"I would."

"Believe it or not, they never picked up on it. More than that: nobody from head office would speak to me. I was relieved of my command, and I was so insulted that I resigned."

He certainly had my attention now.

"After Beast Rufus, who had her only for a few months, Haversma took over the *Isabel*. I liked him, so I thought I owed it to him to tell him the whole story. He listened, but I simply couldn't get through to him that this incredible vessel, this tug driver's heaven, was a killer. And the oddest part of it was this: the men who had been on board when it happened had all been scared out of their wits by the rolling, but the moment I hinted that the ship might be a killer, Bingo! I was stonewalled, as if I had committed treason by mentioning it. I've never been able to understand the psychology of that. Can you?"

I could, but I wanted to keep him going. "No."

"Well, there I was: the only man in the entire world who had this bee in his bonnet about the *Isabel Kwel*. She left for the Gulf with a string of barges, and for a couple of weeks there was no news; then I heard that Haversma had been shot by a mugger in Aden. His mate took over and continued to the Gulf. Shortly after she came home, she was sold."

"What was the mate's name?"

"Slobkous. Maybe now you understand why I said to you, 'Don't touch it.' Someone your age has no business on board a ship that has to be watched twenty-four hours a day or she'll sneak up on you and turn turtle. You're married, are you?"

"Yes."

"Be wise, go home and enjoy your life, the way I'm doing. It's like being in heaven, after all those years of banging around the globe—"

As if she had waited for the cue, a smiling Mrs. Bartels came in and beamed at her husband.

"What do you think—should we tell him about the visit from the Chinese?" he asked.

She gave me a look, a swift, expert appraisal. "Why not?" She rummaged in a sewing table and handed me a visiting card. It was a discreetly expensive business card with black and gold embossed letters: *Kao Hsiung Steel and Shipping Co, Charlie S. Chung, President.*

"This man turned up a week ago in a chauffeured limousine—he was charming, a perfect gentleman. He asked me if I'd be interested in the job they've now offered you: to sail on the *Isabel* as an adviser to the Taiwanese captain and his staff, as far as Rio."

"And what did you say?"

"Well, you'll understand now that the last thing I wanted was to get back on board that pig, but I had to watch my step. I didn't want to mess up whatever deal KITCO was arranging with him. So I said I'd have loved to do it, but that I was a teacher now. Then I began to realize that he didn't want me for that job at all—"

"He just wanted to find out about the ship," his wife concluded.

"I don't quite get it," I confessed.

"It's elementary, Harinxma: all the time, he was watching my reactions—he tossed that bait at me to see if I'd spit it out. He waited for me to say: 'On *that* ship?' and then he'd have pressed for details."

"So you think, Bartels, that the new owner of the ship knows he has a problem?" I said.

"Of course he does. He must have a spy at head office, they all have. But my guess is he doesn't know exactly what the problem is, and, frankly, neither do I. She's either top-heavy, or she has a fault in her underwater design that results in her going into that cycle under certain circumstances. And that not once every fifty years, but at least once every trip." Bartels slapped his thigh to indicate I had used up my welcome. "Mind what I said, Harinxma! All this was strictly confidential!"

I moved to the door. He opened it with ill-disguised alacrity and bade me farewell.

ONCE I WAS SITTING ON THE TRAIN back to Rotterdam, I thought about Bartels's story. Was it possible that a modern vessel, certified seaworthy by Lloyd's of London, could be a time bomb in the way Bartels had described? Could the *Isabel Kwel* be suffering from a, so far, undiscovered lethal fault?

Only one element in Bartels's story made me believe she might be: the reaction of the members of his crew to his suggestion that the ship was "a killer". Their reluctance to admit it had mystified him; with me it rang a bell. That was exactly how we had behaved on the Murmansk run during World War II. All convoys to Russia were decimated by the German navy and the *Luftwaffe*; of one convoy of forty-nine ships only two had arrived in Murmansk. Yet, to hear us talk in the pubs in Iceland and the Orkneys, it was all a huge lark. Never, ever, would any of us admit that he was scared witless. For what could you do about it? Get off and walk? The crew of the *Isabel* had responded in the same way. After all, jobs were not that easy to find. And anyway, the captain, whoever he was, always found a way of dealing with the *Isabel*'s fault. What had really spooked them was his admission that he hadn't.

As I was staring at the bleak landscape, the assignment's problems unravelled in my mind. Whatever was the matter with the *Isabel Kwel*, she would need a top-notch tugmaster of considerable cool and stamina, not a seventy-year-old with hypertension. And why should I mess with her? I had a loving wife, a happy home life among congenial people, hobbies

The train braked for the central station in Rotterdam. I took a taxi to the hotel. When I went down to the lobby two hours later, on my way to old Kwel's dinner party, I was determined to get out of the assignment. My age was a good excuse; I didn't expect any problem.

The limousine was waiting to take me to Mr. Kwel's home in Wassenaar, about twenty minutes away. It was a large, dark house surrounded by tall pines that were waving in the strong wind. A butler opened the front door for me.

"Good evening, Commodore. This way, please." He moved across half an acre of Persian carpet towards a pair of heavy oak doors.

In a panelled, high-ceilinged room ablaze with chandeliers, three people were huddled in front of a fireplace. At my arrival, a woman in an evening gown crossed the room to greet me; she looked regally elegant, diamonds and all. "Hello, Miss Bastiaans. Nice to see you here."

"Let me introduce you to our guest. This is Mr. Chung, owner and president of the Kao Hsiung Steel and Shipping Company, Taiwan."

"Nationalist China, Miss Bastiaans," old Kwel snapped petulantly. A small, rotund Chinaman rose, wreathed in smiles, with the twinkling black eyes that make women want to adopt Chinese babies. "So happy to meet you, Commodore Harinxma!"

The butler advanced on me with a tinkling glass of something on the rocks, on a silver salver. "Well, Harinxma," Kwel said, raising a glass of orange juice, "here's to our future cooperation."

Was this the moment to tell him? I decided not. "Cheers, sir—Mr. Chung."

Miss Bastiaans disappeared; old Kwel, the Chinese and I were alone under the chandeliers.

"Harinxma, I told my friend Mr. Chung all about you, and he is pleased that you are the one to take the *Isabel* to Rio for him. He's left all the arrangements to us, but if you have any questions for Mr. Chung personally, this would be the time to ask them."

Well, here it came. "I'm sorry, sir—Mr. Chung—but after studying the material on the ship and thinking over various aspects of the assignment, I have decided that it's not for me."

The old man shot me a furious glance. If I hadn't known he was blind, I would have been intimidated, as in the past.

"What nonsense is this? What are you saying?"

"Mr. Kwel, I am seventy years old. I left the sea nine years ago. In those nine years, tugboats have changed beyond—"

Suddenly he let me have it, and despite his age he still packed a wallop. "Harinxma, I'm sick and tired of you posturing as an old man! God damn it, I'm twenty years older than you are, and look at me: I'm ninety, and I'm still in control of a company that employs over twelve thousand people! A ship is a ship, period. I don't give a damn what high-tech gadgets they load her bridge with, a ship needs a captain, and when it comes to that vessel you're the best captain I have. That's how I sold you to Mr. Chung. So, stop talking drivel, have another glass and start making sense. Mr. Chung, what do *you* say?"

Mr. Chung purred, "Commodore, you'll be sailing under the flag of Nationalist China. In our culture, people your age are revered for their wisdom and their experience."

"And you won't be in actual command of the ship anyhow," the old man added. "The whole operation is meant as a training exercise for the Chinese captain and his staff. And you'll have plenty of assistance from four other advisers provided by us, all volunteers: first mate, chief engineer, radio officer and bosun. Your trainees will be experienced Chinese officers and sailors provided by Mr. Chung."

"A captain, two deck officers," Mr. Chung enumerated, "two radio officers, three engineers. The crew is made up of fishermen from a small island off the Chinese coast, their ancestors have been sailors for three thousand years. The supplementary crew is from a neighbouring island and equally experienced."

"Supplementary crew?"

"The ship will be towing something minor. We need a supplementary crew to man the towed object."

Something minor that needed a supplementary crew. Like a battleship?

Mr. Chung cried, "Come, Commodore! Six weeks, purely in an advisory position! First-class flight home! And if your wife would enjoy it, a South American vacation. We'll be happy to fly her to Rio."

"In any case," the old man concluded, "you have a trial run tomorrow. Take the ship out for a spin, find out how she handles. Then, if you still think she's too much for you, we'll talk again. Now, let's relax and enjoy each other's company."

"Commodore?" It was Miss Bastiaans, smiling down on me; she had floated back in, unnoticed. "How about another whisky?"

Well, I might as well; my getting a little high wouldn't make any difference. "Very kind of you. Thank you."

After dinner in a candlelit room, and coffee and liqueurs in the library, Miss Bastiaans rose, a picture of svelte elegance, floated towards a grand piano, sat down, and started playing one of Chopin's nocturnes.

You should always mistrust your reaction to performers when you have been drinking: even the most hackneyed piano player in a bar will sound like Vladimir Horowitz after three Scotches, a bottle of wine and a Napoleon brandy. But there could be no doubt that she played very well.

I sat gazing at the old man in his corner, straight as a ramrod, head back, his imperious profile back-lit by the flames of the log fire. To my surprise, I discovered that I was fond of him, despite the fact that he was an unmitigated rogue. Now, mellowed and maudlin with booze, I was suddenly overcome by a sense of loss, of farewell, and the strange feeling that I was looking at this old man who had dominated my life for over forty years for the last time.

When the last notes had faded into silence, the two men applauded politely and I joined in rather passionately.

"Harinxma," the old man said suddenly, "whatever you do, don't allow them to play music for you on your deathbed. It'll drive you crazy."

Miss Bastiaans's voice asked charmingly, "Another brandy, Commodore?"

I looked up at her. I should have had the sense to refuse, but I was so smitten by her that I said, "Thank you. Thank you very much," and handed her my glass in defeat.

Chapter Two

The telephone roused me from a deep sleep. It was still dark and I had a splitting headache. I croaked, "Hello?"

A voice asked, "Harinxma? Are you ready?"

"Who's this?"

"Fransen. We're having a test run this morning, remember? I've got a taxi waiting outside with one of the architects. Come on, get dressed and come down."

I hoisted myself upright, had a quick shower, staggered round the hotel room pulling on my clothes, took my blood-pressure pills; when I bent over to put on my socks and my shoes, I was hit by an attack of hiccups. I must have really hit the bottle last night.

In the lobby a scarecrow rose from one of the chairs in the murk and loped towards me. "Well, there you are! Ready for a bit of fun?"

All I could do was look at him with bloodshot, baggy eyes. He took me by the arm and asked, "Are you OK?"

"Of course. Why shouldn't I—hic—be?" It sounded convincing but for the hiccup.

"I see," he said. "Dinner with the old man. Before he went blind, he must have got a kick out of seeing his guests swim out through the door under water, singing."

The moment I stepped outside, the gale grabbed me; it had picked up considerably overnight and must be force ten by now. "Hang on, Harınxma," Fransen shouted against the wind. "In you go!"

He opened the door of the taxi, which was nearly ripped out of his hand by a gust, and shoved me inside. I landed sprawling on the lap of a shadowy passenger in the opposite corner. "Did you hurt yourself?" a small voice asked.

"No-o," I said with a hiccup. "I'm fine. How do you do? My name's— hic—Harinxma."

"This is Baron Balthasa van Beusekom and Beverdingen," Fransen said from the front seat.

"Most people call me BB," the voice said apologetically.

"I see. Well, how do you do?"

The taxi took off. I sank into the corner of the back seat and closed my eyes. My head throbbed, I was still plagued with hiccups and I cursed myself for the crazy notion that I might have taken on this assignment even under the best of conditions. I belonged at home now.

"You don't know Beast Rufus, do you?" Fransen bellowed, calling me back from a daydream of walking Héloise in the perfumed hills of home. "You're in for a treat, Harinxma! He's a character, all right! He's probably the best salvage captain around, but we're having a hell of a time trying to keep him operating within the law! He's a card!"

About the last person I fancied meeting on this bleak, unspeakable morning was "a card".

After an hour's drive we arrived in the harbour town of Flushing, and drew up on the deserted quayside. I saw the silhouette of a tugboat outlined against a wild sky full of racing clouds turning blue in the dawn. Fransen had been right: at first sight she did indeed look like a pig. Her two stacks, side by side and close together, crowded the bridge and looked as if they were leaning outwards, like ears. The squat snout, the ungainly body, the absence of the long, low sweep of an aft deck which to me had always been associated with tugboats, confirmed my overwhelming first impression: ugly. Her "paradise tree" with its dish antennae, radar reflectors, globes, coils and whiskers, a mysterious complex of electronic eyes and ears, glinted faintly in the dawn.

Fransen helped me out of the taxi and I started towards the *Isabel Kwel*, my hair whipping in the wind. She was colossal, towering above us like a pier with a lighthouse. When we arrived on deck, we found it empty. For a tugboat about to leave, this was unusual. Fransen stepped across a high threshold into a dimly lit corridor. I followed him and caught a first whiff of the smell of diesel fuel.

There was more: the faint stench of overflowing toilets, the odour of breakfast being slung together by a disgruntled cook somewhere below decks, smells that would have filled me with nostalgia if they hadn't confirmed my conviction that I was going to be seasick the moment the ship nosed out of port.

Fransen opened a door and said, "Well, here it is: the bridal suite."

I stepped into a cabin the size of a living room, with a wide view of the wild morning outside. A leather settee, leather club chairs, a coffee table and a room divider on which stood potted palms and a glass statue of a winged nude about to take off with a tugboat under her arm.

"I'll see if he's awake," Fransen said, and disappeared behind the palms.

I looked round the captain's dayroom. The walls were adorned with prints of previous *Isabels*. I found my own 1940 one among them: an ungainly bull of a ship with everywhere livable bunched up forward. It seemed incredible now that as a young man I had been in love with that ship. It was suddenly a moment full of meaning: an old man, holding his breath to suppress the hiccups of geriatric inebriation, face to face with the ship he had loved, the young man he had been.

"Good morning."

I turned round and found behind me a huge, red-bearded man with mean little eyes who sized me up with all the sunny charm of a rampaging gorilla. "I'm Rufus Bron," he said, holding out a hand. "You want to take the old girl out for a spin?"

"That's the idea. How do you do, Bron?"

His extraordinarily discomfiting little eyes drank in the spectacle of the old wino before him, then he said, "What you need, Harinxma, is a hair of the dog."

"No, no! Thanks, but for God's sake, no!"

My cry must have lacked conviction, for he went to a fridge, grabbed a crock of Dutch gin and a couple of glasses, filled them with surprising dexterity considering he was holding two in one hand, held out his fist to me and said, "There you go; never again." He plucked one of the little glasses from his fist and tossed it back. I had no choice but to do the same.

The neat gin hit my stomach lining like liquid fire; I needed all my control not to howl like a dog.

"Here," he said, proffering the crock. "Have another one."

"No, for God's sake ...!"

"Believe me," he said with authority, "it takes two."

I knuckled under and committed suicide right in front of his eyes by knocking back another dose of the national beverage which Sylvia, even after forty years, refused to ingest.

"Well, let's get going," my host said sunnily. "The weather's just right, nice swell rolling out there. I'd better tell you, she separates the men from the boys. What this ship needs is a horse trainer, not some egghead clutching a computer manual." I gathered this was a delicate dig at his predecessor, Bartels. He turned to Fransen. "I hope the skeleton crew you dug up for me is up to this," he said as if he hoped they weren't. "Has any of them been on board her before?"

"Oh, yes," Fransen said with ready assurance. "The chief has, and the mate has."

"What about the ABs?"

"They'll be OK. All they have to do is cast off, isn't it?"

"Come and see," Beast Rufus said, putting an arm round his shoulders and taking him outside for what seemed like an execution. Startled by a chirrup behind my back, I looked round and saw, for the first time, a canary in a cage suspended from the ceiling. I had missed that one. I followed the others to a companionway, which led to a lower bridge looking like the promenade deck for first-class passengers on an ocean liner. Then up another companionway, which emerged into the wheelhouse.

I recognized it from the photographs in the brochure, but they hadn't done it justice. The space was much larger than I had expected, glassed in on all sides and filled with an esoteric assortment of computerized equipment and five television screens. I was welcomed by the architect called BB and by two middle-aged characters, one of them in white coveralls, who were introduced as Mate Valk and Chief van der Molen.

Bron turned to the mate. "You Number One? OK, let's get out of here. Somewhere quiet first, so Harinxma can find out what she's made of. You take her first. I want Harinxma to see how she handles."

He and I stood in a corner while the *Isabel* headed out into the inner harbour, which was ruffled by the wind. Now, shredded clouds raced overhead; the wind-frisked water was restless, with small angry waves glinting like fish scales in the early light.

The moment the ship, buffeted by gusts, entered the outer harbour, Bron said, "OK, let's do some baton-twirling," and took the wheel from Mate Valk. "Chief? Grab hold of those thrusters. Number One, give me half speed on both engines." The ship gathered speed.

"OK, give me a starboard bow thrust, full speed."

"Aren't you going too fast for that?" the young architect, BB, asked.

"Shut up," Bron said. "OK, Chief, do as I say."

The chief pulled the handle of one of the thrusters. The ship veered sharply to port, heeling slightly as she did.

"OK, that's enough. Give me full speed on both mains."

"In harbour?" Fransen asked incredulously.

"Who's sailing this ship, you or me?"

The ship shivered and gathered speed, heading straight for the quay-side. Bron allowed her to virtually climb the basalt; then he ordered, "Stop engines," strolled over to the thrusters and did something that made her veer away at what seemed to be the last moment.

"OK, Harinxma," he said. "You take the wheel and feel what she's like. I'll handle the thrusters. You do what I did and you'll be in for a surprise."

Well, I thought, what the hell, I might as well put this monster through its paces and see what twenty-first-century tugboats are like. I got hold of the wheel, startled by its tiny size and its total lack of resistance. It spun easily, yet the three-thousand-ton colossus responded instantly.

"What speed do you want, Harinxma?" Bron asked, at the controls.

"Let's start with half ahead." The monster moved massively ahead. I worked the wheel and felt the huge body swing to starboard instantly. "All right," I said, "full ahead on both engines."

"Coming up," Bron replied.

With a surge that took my breath away, the giant ship blasted off for the opposite quay. I headed her away towards the open with my heart in my mouth. She responded with such abandon that she heeled in the bend and stuff on the chart desk started to slide. I straightened her out and said, "Starboard half ahead, half astern port."

"Too brutal!" the architect's voice shrilled from his corner.

"Shut up, boy," Bron said as if he were silencing a pet. "Try the thrusters, Harinxma, stern to starboard, bow to port."

"OK, give me that."

Bron worked the handles of the thrusters, and the result was almost magical: the giant ship spun around like a London taxi. I was so taken aback by it that I let her make a full turn before I took her back in hand. "God!" I said. "How about that?"

"I told you." Bron grinned with satisfaction. "And this is only the beginning. Sweat her some more, then we'll take her out for a spin."

So, with mounting exhilaration and a feeling of awakening that I cannot describe, I proceeded to put the *Isabel* through her paces. I felt her respond to a touch, a word, a daring command, as if she had been waiting for just this: to turn on a sixpence, whip round, charge, double back, trot, gallop, skitter and stop dead within a ship's length—and that over and over again.

The gale swept the outer harbour. The spray of the fury outside streaked through her rigging, bursts of silver in the steel-blue morning light. Rain lashed the windows of the wheelhouse, but through her clearview disc I had an unobstructed view of the world outside. There was not a moment in which I did not feel totally in control.

"Well?" I heard Bron ask by my side. "What do you say?"

"I've never known a ship like her. She's incredible."

"Welcome to the club," he said, "of two." He slapped my shoulder.

144

"Now let's take her out into the real world. Chief, you'd better go down to your shop, we're about to start riding her in earnest. As for you two," he said, addressing Fransen and BB, "find a corner to jam yourselves into." Fransen obeyed; the baron shook his head. "All right, take her out, Harinxma."

I headed her towards the pierheads, where white horses came storming towards us, manes flying.

"Hang on," Bron said, clutching the handles of the thrusters. The ship nosed out. After a few rearings, her bow reaching for the clouds, she suddenly started a stomach-sinking lunge over to starboard. It was totally unexpected. BB came hurtling by and ended in Bron's arms. I wanted to head her into the seas, but Bron shouted, "Let her do her worst, Harinxma! You'd better find out now!"

The ship, of her own accord, swung slowly to port and took the incoming swell on the starboard bow. She heeled over deeply, making everyone on the bridge reach for a handhold. But instead of swinging back, she went on heeling to an alarming degree. Things started to crash to the deck. Finally, at what felt like the last moment, she hovered on one ear, seemed to hesitate, then swept back with sickening speed, like a swing returning. She remained on an even keel for only a second or two, then began to heel over to starboard. I clung to the wheel as she lurched deeper. Incredulous, I felt my grip slipping. I admit I was scared.

Then Bron stopped the engines. That really made her do her worst; she wallowed in the troughs of the wild swell like a sick cow, making us all hang on to our handholds for dear life. Fransen cried, "Bron!"

"Shut up!" Bron bellowed. "Harinxma! Let her shake her guts out!" There was little else I could do. Down below, I could hear cries of anguish. Everything loose in the interior of the ship must have started a life of its own. When the next row of white horses came storming towards us, everybody on the bridge braced himself for another sickening roll but suddenly, magically, she righted herself and rode the waves like a gull.

It seemed a fluke. A second row came storming at us; again, instead of making a sickening lunge to starboard, the *Isabel* straightened up and rode the rolling hill of water beautifully. Then I realized how Bron was doing it: with the thrusters. He was compensating the ship's wild gyrations with their tremendous counterthrust. "Take the thrusters, Harinxma!" he shouted over the roar outside. "Wait for me to call 'yes', then give full power on both thrusters, countering her swing!"

We changed places, and Bron started to dare the sea. Full speed, half speed, full speed astern, swerving, sweeping, playing a brontosauran game of bumps-a-daisy with those killer waves. Each time she started her suicidal rolling cycle, he yelled, "Yes!" and I gave counterthrust from bow and stern, full power. The ship shuddered and shook; each time one of those waves slammed into her, I expected the paradise tree above us to come crashing down, but she obeyed him like a broken-in horse. It was one of the most ingenious feats of seamanship I had ever witnessed. And so simple! Why hadn't Bartels thought of this?

"All right," Bron shouted, "your turn!"

I waited for the ship to hover on even keel before I made a dash for the wheel; Bron skidded to the thrusters.

Now I started to dare the sea. The feel of the ship was different: there was a controlled frenzy to her power; she felt like a racehorse straining to start down the track. I searched for the critical angle of attack of the incoming seas; when she started her stomach-sinking cycle, I shouted, "Yes!" and she instantly obeyed, without hesitancy or disorientation. After about an hour of this, she had leaped through all the hoops I could devise for her. I headed back to port with Bron for a pilot. She moored like a dream; thrusters, I decided, were man's greatest invention since the wheel.

When the lines were ashore and snugged down, I felt forty years old, and I realized I was hooked.

The alcoholic had fallen off the wagon.

AFTER I HAD RUNG DOWN "Finished with Engines", Bron took me along to his dayroom. He groped among the palms, turned on the hi-fi, and poured two shots from the frozen crock. He raised his glass at me and said, "Well, here's looking at her next skipper. Godspeed and happy sailing." He tossed back his drink. I tossed back mine; it nearly tossed me against the wall.

"Well, I don't know about that," I said, feeling as if I were speaking in tongues of flame. "She's supposed to have a Chinese captain."

He waved that notion aside. "You'll be the captain, Harinxma, don't kid yourself. No amateur can handle this bitch. It needs a man like yourself, with guts. To you, she'll be a breeze, but that took—how many years?"

"As a captain? Thirty-five."

"Well, there you go. I'll have this cabin straightened up for you. There's a dandy bedroom, a bathroom, television, the works. When are you coming on board?"

"I suppose tomorrow or the day after. But I'm not going to live here. It's the captain's."

"You're the commodore, aren't you? Let him take the first officer's cabin, it's better than anything he's likely to have lived in up to now."

I felt it was time for me to leave. "I'd better get on my way. Thank you for this morning, it was very instructive. Where are you going now?"

"First I'll take this bucket to Rotterdam. Later today I ship out on

146

the *Fiona* for Cherbourg . . . I'll do some pushing and pulling in Indonesia while I wait for a hotel structure that has to go to the Marquesas out of Singapore. So I'll be busy."

"Well, if I don't see you before you leave, Godspeed and happy sailing. And thanks again." We shook hands.

In the corridor I ran into Fransen. "Are you ready?" he asked. "I won't be going with you, I need another couple of hours here. You can call for a taxi from the harbourmaster's office at the end of the dock. Lunch at your hotel; at fourteen hundred you're expected at the outfitters', half an hour later at the doctor's for your medical, then at the water bailiff's for the signing of the Articles. At eighteen hundred you interview your chief engineer, mate, bosun and radio officer at your hotel. I'll be there to tell you about them. See you then."

I set out in a taxi for the station. On the empty platform, I found the baron waiting for the next train. I joined him on his bench and asked, "Well, how do you feel?"

I expected him to be pleased, relieved that his ship's flaw had turned out to be manageable. "You've designed a beautiful ship. She's without doubt the most responsive and nimble tugboat I've ever handled."

He shook his head. "Martinus, I'm not in the business of designing toys for megalomaniacs to show off with. She was designed to be a ship, not a death-defying contraption that can only be handled by a stunt man. Those thrusters were never intended to act as stabilizers. There's a fault in her hull design, and we must find out what it is before we start building her sister ship."

"How far are you on with that one?"

"She's in blueprints, ready to go on the stocks." He lit a cigarette. "The *Isabel* is a prototype, her hull embodies an entirely new concept. The problem is that under specific circumstances her stability suddenly diminishes, for no apparent reason."

"What are those circumstances?"

"That's the problem! We could find that out only by field tests, but old Kwel is worried about her losing her certificate of seaworthiness. So he sold her. And here we are, my colleagues and I, suspended in mid-leap, so to speak. We begged him to give us the ship for just a month, a week, two days. But he wouldn't hear of it."

"What could you have done in two days?"

"Test her, test her, the way you did. Get you or Bron or somebody in your class to put her through her paces in weather like this, and we would be there with our instruments making observations. Actually, of course, we should test her not in one but in a whole series of gales, gradually increasing her stability by taking down first the paradise tree, in sections, and if that doesn't solve it, working our way down."

"Let me get this straight," I said, not quite believing my ears. "Are you suggesting that you should crash-test the ship by demolishing her—a twenty-million-dollar ship—from the top down?"

He dropped his cigarette and ground it out with his foot. "Never mind," he said. "Sorry I drew you into this. Forget it. By the way, all this was strictly confidential. If any of this ever got to the wrong ears. . ." He lapsed into a gloomy silence.

The train arrived. We found window seats opposite one another and sat gazing at the bleak, flat landscape swept by squalls. I mulled over the whole business. The euphoria of the trial run gradually ebbed away. Yet as far as I was concerned, there was now no reason for me to turn down the assignment. With luck, we would have reasonable weather through the Bay of Biscay at this time of year; after the Cape Verdes it would be plain sailing. And I was confident now that I could handle the ship. Then another thought struck me. Somebody should warn the Chinese captain of the *Isabel*'s suicidal quirk, demonstrate to him how to cope with it once she started her dangerous cycle. The one to do it would be me.

As the train entered Rotterdam's central station, I decided not to tell Sylvia the whole truth. She would react very differently indeed to this pleasant little assignment if she knew that the *Isabel Kwel* was a killer.

THE UNIFORMS THEY GAVE ME to try on at the outfitters' later that day were embarrassingly gaudy. The blue one had gold rings up to the elbows and the white one solid gold shoulder tabs; the cap was the size of a helipad, its visor encrusted with scrambled egg. As I stood gazing in the mirror, the attendant came with a double bank of battle ribbons; after he had pinned them on, I knew what I looked like: a Soviet admiral about to review the May Day parade from the top of Lenin's tomb. But this was what Mr. Kwel had ordered. He wanted me to make an impression on the Chinese.

I signed and acquiesced to the admiral's uniforms, but ordered a blue jacket without distinctives on my own account.

The medical examination was conducted by a young doctor who called me "Pop", gave me the fastest checkup known to medical science, said, "You're OK, but too fat," listed my hypertension medication on the form and commented, "Keep up these pills or you'll be in trouble."

While I was there, I thought I might as well ask about my overnight tremors. "I wake up in the middle of the night sometimes with a sort of trembling inside my muscles, mainly my arms."

"Oh?" he said. "Hold out your hands." I did. "Are you a heavy coffee drinker? A teetotaller?" I said I was neither. "Well, it would need a full neurological checkup but I'm pretty sure I know what your problem is. It's called booze."

I protested that I hardly drank at all, at home. He shrugged his shoulders. "I'm not going to argue with you, all I'm saying is: lay off the booze and you'll stop trembling. And while you're at it, lay off all coffee, sugar, fats, cholesterol and salt—I mean all. Exercise daily, and the chances are you'll be able to cut down on your medication after a month and toss the lot overboard after three. But you'd rather take the pills, no?" When I didn't protest, he signed the form, slammed a stamp on it and bellowed, "Next!"

By the time I got back to my hotel, I was ready to collapse for an hour, but there was a message at the desk that a Captain Fransen was waiting for me at the bar. I found him installed in a booth with a bottle of whisky and two glasses.

"Well," he said, "the pig's in the harbour; she's all yours." He poured himself a Scotch. "If I were you, I'd move on board tonight. Bron had the bridal suite readied for you. Why don't you nip over there after the interviews and establish squatter's rights?"

"Interviews?"

"The skeleton staff, remember? In about ten minutes you get your first mate, here in the bar, man by the name of Slobkous. Then Bosun Schoonmaker, Radio Officer Harlingen and Chief Alberts, twenty minutes apart. If you don't like any of them, let me know and I'll see if I can come up with an alternative." He lit another cigarette, pulled out his dog-eared notebook and flicked the pages. "Now, tomorrow. Caterers at six hundred hours, then linen, bedding, fuel, water, health inspector—the whole shebang. And to make your bliss complete: at fifteen forty-two— some hope!—your crew arrives from Taipei by KLM. Thirty-five bodies, all Chinks. There'll be a bus to bring them to the ship, so be prepared."

"I'd like to meet them at the airport. I always made it a practice to welcome relief crews at the airport when they were flown in."

"But these are Chinese!" He shook his head. "OK. I'll send the bus to pick you up. Fourteen hundred all right?"

"Fine with me."

"Now, day of departure. One hour before cast-off: pilot on board, and the captains of the two harbour tugs who are going to help you leave town. Out with the tide and off to Antwerp, where you pick up your tow: one thirty-thousand-ton dry dock for Talcahuano, Chile. Don't worry," he added, seeing my face, "the *Isabel* could pull three of them and never know the difference. Anyhow, you're getting off in Rio; up to there it's going to be a breeze."

"And thereafter?"

He shrugged his shoulders. "That's not your concern." He polished off his drink. "Well," he said, rising, "I'm off to Bahrain. If I get back in time, I'll fly out with the Belgian pilot to meet you in Rio. Here—the list of names of the characters you're about to interview. Have fun." I watched him disappear into the lobby.

A thirty-thousand-ton dry dock through the Roaring Forties? Those Chinese had better be good.

Ten minutes later a thickset, middle-aged man with a bulbous nose, clearly a sailor, entered the bar.

"Mate Slobkous?" We shook hands. The barman came for the order; when offered a drink, Slobkous shook his head and said, "No, thank you. I'll have a tomato juice."

He gave me a run-down of his past few years. He sounded all right, the list was respectable, I liked his manner, yet there was something that worried me about him. His lack of ambition struck me; but it might have been sheer laziness. Well, with two Chinese mates at his beck and call, he could spend his watches on the bridge in a hammock, as far as I was concerned, so I hired him.

The moment he left, a huge hulk loomed over me; I looked up and saw a Nordic face, with high cheekbones. He must be the bosun. He held out a hand the size of a frying pan and said, in a voice loud enough to stampede cattle, "Hi there, Ome! How are ya?" He pumped mine; when he put his other one on top of it, I winced.

"Sit down, Bosun Schoonmaker, sit down!"

He sat down and the barman turned up to take his order.

"Beer?" I asked. "Gin?"

"What are you having, Ome?"

"What's this 'Ome' business? Is it my nickname now?"

He suddenly became self-conscious. "Hasn't it always been?" he asked. "I thought you were always called 'Ome Tinus'. You don't mind, do you?"

"Hell, no. I just thought—well, never mind." Without my knowing it, I had acquired the name "Ome Tinus" in the fleet. *Ome* was the colloquial Dutch word for uncle, suggesting an avuncular presence bringing candy for the baby. Well, maybe that was what I had become.

"Well, tell the man what you want to drink," I said.

"What are you having, Ome?"

"Tea."

"I'll have tea, too," he said loyally.

I discovered that he had sailed with me years ago on the *Henrietta*; then we got down to the technicalities that were his province: hawsers, mooring lines, grease, paint, wire brushes, all part of the tender loving care of a ship. Suddenly he asked if I had a personal steward; when I replied that only the captain had, he said, "Let me take that on, Ome. I'll go on board now and see that you're comfortable."

"That's very kind of you, Bosun. You might start by cleaning out the canary's cage. We'll talk about the rest tomorrow."

150

A tall, blond young man appeared at our table. "Excuse me—are you Commodore Harinxma?"

"I am. Who are you?"

"My name is Joop Harlingen, sir. I'll be your radio officer. That's to say..."

The bosun rose, and after pumping the young man's hand, left for the *Isabel*.

"Do you want to see my dope sheet?" The young man pulled a sheet of paper from his pocket and handed it to me.

I was interested to see one trip with Captain Bron on the *Fiona* on his list. "Well," I said, handing the sheet back to him, "you know it's not going to be a normal run?" I explained the setup, including the Chinese crew and the Taiwanese flag; he listened intently. The barman came; this time I ordered sherry and Harlingen followed my example. When it came, he raised his glass. "Well, Commodore, here's looking at you."

He was an amiable chap and I saw no reason to be pernickety about him, but there was something: nervousness, an uncertainty. It might be the ship. I asked casually, "You know about the *Isabel*?"

He gave me a sliding look. "Oh, yes," he said. "Everybody does. I mean—about her problem and so on. Doesn't take long for that kind of thing to get around in the fleet."

"Then why did you volunteer?"

He looked surprised. "I'm sorry, Commodore, but I didn't volunteer. I was told to make this trip or else."

"Or else what?"

"Well—I might as well tell you. I had a problem in the past. A sort of a black mark. Nothing serious, but—well, you know the way it is."

"Would you mind telling me?"

"Not at all. I was serving under Beast—er—Captain Bron on board the *Fiona* in the Med. Another company ship, the *Hester*, was within range and while I was chatting to her radio officer I said something out of line about the company. Well, it seems a lot of people were listening in, and there were, well, problems. Captain Bron threw me off the bridge. So if you feel that you'd rather not have me..."

"I don't give a damn," I said. "As far as I'm concerned, I'll be happy to have you on board."

"Thank you, sir." He rose. "Thanks a lot," he repeated, as if I had done him a big favour.

I wandered over to the bar. I needed a bit of exercise after all these disclosures. The bosun seemed straightforward enough, but I was pretty certain that something about Mate Slobkous was not quite kosher. I wondered what the chief engineer's criminal record would be, or, God knew, his trail of broken engines.

"Commodore?"

I caught sight of a face grinning at me in the mirror behind the bottles, and it gave me a shock—it was like seeing a ghost. But when I turned round to face him, the spell was broken; the man simply looked like someone I had once known. "Hello there," I said. "You must be the chief engineer?"

"Yessir!" He grabbed my hand and shook it warmly. He was a keen, brown-haired, blue-eyed boy in his late twenties.

"Sit down, have a drink."

The bartender put a glass in front of the young man, who raised it and said, "Well, here's looking at you, sir."

"Cheers. By the way, what's your name?"

"Pieter Alberts, but my shipmates call me Porks."

I stared at him, thunderstruck; I *had* seen a ghost.

He added, "It was my dad's nickname too, as you know. Nobody knows how he got it, but—well, everybody just picked it up. You do remember him, don't you?"

I had had time to recover. "Of course I do. Good engineer. Where is he now?"

"I'm afraid he passed away a year ago."

"Sorry to hear that. What of?"

"Just old age, I guess. He was over seventy. You were together on the Murmansk run, weren't you?"

"Yes."

"I know all about that. My dad never stopped talking about how you tried to tow the last remaining freighter while all hell was breaking loose, and how the old *Isabel* went down."

"I see." I wondered if Porks had ever owned up to his son that he himself had been the cause of the old *Isabel*'s sinking, by getting his engine signals mixed up while under stress.

"That torpedo must just have been an unlucky hit," the boy continued, looking in the mirror behind the bottles as if his father was gazing back at him.

I decided not to mess up old Porks's reputation. What he had told his son was his own business, and the whole thing was more than forty years ago anyhow.

"What made you join this ship, Porks?"

He gave me a boyish grin. "You did, sir. When I heard that you were going to be in on it, I decided I wanted to find out who my dad had been talking about all these years."

It was a touching remark, and I would have been sincerely moved if I myself hadn't undertaken the job only two days ago. Despite the speed of the grapevine, there was no way he could have heard about my involvement, volunteered to join the ship and come down from the Firth of Forth, where he'd been on standby, in forty-eight hours.

I began to wonder what the charming boy had done, for KITCO to send him to the penal colony called *Isabel Kwel*.

AFTER YOUNG PORKS HAD LEFT, I should have gone to the restaurant and had dinner; but I decided to ring Sylvia first, from my room. By now I had been on my feet since four in the morning, and after a brief, loving chat with Sylvia while lying on my bed, I barely managed to reach up to put the phone back before I dozed off. When I woke after what I thought had been a few minutes, it was ten o'clock. I packed in a hurry, went down to sign the bill, and asked the porter to call for a taxi.

I was off-loaded at the *Isabel*'s gangway. The ship looked wide awake under her floodlights but I saw nobody on deck. I lugged my bags on board and headed for the captain's quarters.

It took me a while to find them; I finally opened the right door and stepped across the high threshold into the dayroom with the palms and the glass winged nude with the tugboat under her arm. I carried my bags round the room divider into what seemed to be an office, with a desk and a swivel chair, a computer on a stand and a couple of filing cabinets. From there a door led into the bedroom suite, which was spacious, with a wardrobe, a chest of drawers and a low bunk, wider than the ones I had been used to. There was a connecting bathroom with toilet, washbasin and shower.

After my meeting with the ship's officers, the thought of calling the whole thing off recurred to me. Rationally speaking, I was out of my mind to undertake this assignment. The ship had a serious problem, to put it mildly; the staff seemed to have been put on board as punishment for past transgressions; old Kwel and his grandson were involved in some underhand business in connection with the deal; and a thirty-thousand-ton dry dock was one hell of a mass to haul across the Atlantic with a bunch of inexperienced Chinese—they must be inexperienced or they wouldn't have needed me.

Yet here I was, Adam under the paradise tree, seduced by a big, shiny apple—the ship. Anyone who wanted to stop me taking this ship to Rio would have to shoot me.

I asked myself why. The main attraction was the ship, not despite her fatal flaw but because of it. I wanted to pit my wits, my experience and my tenacity against her deadly secret; I wanted to be the one ultimately to tame her.

I set out on a tour to familiarize myself with the ship's layout. I had to do it now, for tomorrow she would be swarming with people and I would be up to my eyes in other business. Deciding to start from the top and work my way down, I took a series of companionways until I emerged in the windy, wide-open space of the flying bridge.

On the inboard side of each stack was a set of rungs that led to the walkway on which was rooted the paradise tree, with its multiple radar scanners, dish antennae and other esoteric equipment, as well as four searchlights and the air horn. The paradise tree was very much larger and higher than it had seemed from the quayside.

The navigation bridge deck, one flight below, was in effect the wheelhouse I had seen earlier. But I used the opportunity to go round it once more at my ease, taking in all the equipment, the chart desk, the bank of dials and instruments almost as wide as the wheelhouse itself, the nerve centre of the ship. Then, one flight below, the bridge deck proper: the covered part a storeroom containing the steering engine and other machinery, the open part a wide deck with the tanks of compressed air, the cradle of the foremast boom and the navigation lights. One floor below that, the forecastle deck with my quarters and those of the first officer and the chief engineer, as well as the hospital.

As I explored the rest of the accommodation, opening doors and turning on lights, I came upon the radio room and spotted the first sign of life since I had come aboard: a smoking cigarette on an ashtray beside a telex keyboard. "Sparks?" I called.

"Looking for me?"

Joop Harlingen peered round the edge of the door behind me, a look of bewilderment on his face, and I remembered that radio officers were no longer called "Sparks" in the fleet, but "Marco".

"How are you making out?" I asked.

"Oh, OK—only I don't have a mattress in my bunk. I suppose my predecessor had some orthopaedic deal that he took with him when he left. OK if I use the hospital for tonight? I suppose they'll give me a mattress tomorrow."

"Help yourself. I'm just getting my bearings. That your cabin?"

"Yes, want to see it?"

I followed him inside. It was a pleasant little bed-sitter with a double bunk, a couch, a desk and an armchair. As he was the only one who had owned up to having had a "minor problem", I felt I could broach the intriguing subject of the penal colony with him. "Just a matter of interest: I gathered you wouldn't have accepted the job on this ship if you'd been free to choose?"

"God, no," he said with feeling. "Seems the union prohibits placing its members on foreign-flag vessels unless they volunteer. There weren't any volunteers, so they shanghaied those with black marks."

"Is her reputation that poor in the fleet?"

"Poor? Everybody knows she's a killer bitch. I was planning to resign

154

until I was told they'd hauled a real old expert out of mothballs—out of retirement—to take her in hand, and I thought, Well, let's give it a whirl. I love this radio room, lots of new stuff."

"Expert in what, exactly?"

"Ships like her. The handling of killer bitches. Are you? Sir?"

"I have survived to be seventy, that may be indicative of something."

"Seventy?" His face was a study.

"Don't worry, Marco, you're going to be all right. Goodnight. See you in the morning."

"Goodnight, Skipper."

It was a long time since anyone had called me that.

As I continued my tour of the ship I came upon a second sign of human life in this vast rabbit warren: the smell of coffee. It guided me to a galley like the well-equipped kitchen of a modern hotel; the homely bulk of the bosun loomed among the gleaming array of pots and pans, ranges and microwave ovens.

He was pouring coffee into three ship's mugs. "Hi, Ome!" he cried when he saw me. "Just making some Java for the two officers. I didn't know you were on board yet. Would you like some?"

"Don't think so, Bosun; I'm turning in soon. Thanks all the same."

"Pleasure, Ome. You go to bed and I'll bring you up a nightcap."

"Very kind of you. Happy to have you aboard, Bosun. See you later."

I came across the young engineer on the next deck down, the main one, after having worked my way through crew's quarters, laundry, shower room and "recreation area", a state-of-the-art gymnasium with rowing machine and exercise bicycle. I found Porks brandishing an oilcan in a vast space dominated by three sets of winches with flanges higher than a man.

"Evening, Porks. Just nosing around. This is the towing-winch room, I gather?"

"Yup. Those two babies hold about a mile of nine-inch hawser each, and that one a hundred and eighty feet of double nylon stretcher with a forty-two-inch waist. They're worked from the control room upstairs and observed by television cameras with screens on the bridge."

"Quite a plant." In fact, I had never seen anything like it; it was like the engine room of a space rocket. Suddenly I found myself in the role of adviser to Captain Kirk of the starship *Enterprise*.

"Come and have a look at the generator room," he said. "You haven't seen anything like that either, I bet."

He opened a door on the other side of the monster winches and took me down a passage to the engine room, or rather its control centre, which was an observatory separated from the engines by a double glass wall. It was lined with banks of dials and switches.

"When we're running full power," Porks said beside me, "we'll need earmuffs to go in there, for it's a screaming hellhole."

"What exactly was the trouble you had, Porks?" I asked casually, as if we had been discussing it.

He became quite still, then turned to look at me; his face was his father's. At first it looked as if he wasn't going to answer, then he said, "I threw a wrench at him. It just grazed his scalp. But he yelled as if I'd knocked his teeth out."

"Who was this?"

"My chief. On the *Antonia*. He was a bully. He'd been bugging me ever since I came on board. I happened to have that wrench in my hand and— well, you wouldn't believe the song and dance. Captain Fransen flew in and I was put on standby. And now this. It just isn't fair."

"What's wrong with this?"

"Wrong? To be shipped out on her is like being sent to Alcatraz! She's been a killer from the moment she was launched." He looked up at me the way his father used to. "Think we're going to make it, Skipper?"

"Don't worry, Porks," I said. "Everything's going to be all right."

I left him motionless, staring after me, and made my way back to the bridal suite. I had barely had a chance to undress when the bosun turned up with a mug.

"Chocolate and rum. It'll make you sleep," he said. "You need it, you're an old man; if you won't look after yourself, someone has to do it for you. Now, you settle down, go to sleep. And don't worry, the others won't disturb you."

"But—"

I should have voiced a moral protest, but exhaustion got to me. I was vaguely aware of the mug being taken from my hands, then the soft click of the door.

I was about to go under when I became aware of the vibration of an engine deep down in the ship: the giant generator. I lay there, my mind a blank, feeling that faint vibration, the living body of the ship. I tried to catch an elusive memory, in vain, before drifting off into sleep.

Chapter Three

When I woke next morning, I found the bosun standing beside my bunk, proffering my breakfast. In all my forty years as a tug driver I had never had breakfast in bed.

He put the tray on my lap and poured a generous helping of cereal into the bowl. After the cereal there were rolls, jam, cheese, two boiled eggs and three slices of gingerbread. Enough to incapacitate a horse.

156

"Coffee coming up."

By the time he came back, I was picking at the eggs. "This is splendid," I said, "but too much."

"Aw, come on, Ome! You've got a busy day ahead, you need your strength. Well, I'll leave you to it." He went.

I wondered, while dressing, where Mate Slobkous was. He obviously hadn't arrived yet.

I barely had my jacket on when they arrived all at once: the fuel barge, the water boat, the safety inspector, a man with a clipboard from the health department, a truck full of mattresses, pillows, blankets, sheets and messroom linen. Everyone had chits and forms for me to check and sign in triplicate.

Despite the bedlam, the bosun managed to set up a sandwich lunch for everybody in the messroom. Porks, Harlingen, the bosun and I were there, but not Mate Slobkous. I was due to be picked up by the airport bus in less than an hour and couldn't leave the ship with this circus in full swing; I would simply have to call the office and find out where the hell the man was. I was halfway down the gangway, heading for the telephone kiosk, when a taxi drew up and Mate Slobkous climbed out, as relaxed as a slow-motion movie. I was furious, but decided to play it cool.

"Slobkous," I said, "you'll have to look after things here. I have to leave for the airport, to meet the crew."

He said calmly, "No problem," and paid the driver.

I went to dress up in my new uniform with the gold-leafed cap, then I boarded the bus.

At the airport I found only the Taiwanese consul, a pompous little man, and his Girl Friday waiting to welcome the travellers. She had a crew list with her, full of Chinese characters.

The plane landed on time. The crew came through customs lugging cardboard boxes tied with rope and string bags full of clothing. All of them had new bright yellow oilskins over their arms and were, despite the winter cold, wearing T-shirts with the names of American universities. There seemed to be an awful lot of them; they lined up in a double file in the arrival hall, blocking the traffic. As I was looking for their captain I noticed a woman, a grinning old crone with stringy white hair and tiny eyes in a wrinkled face. I turned to the consul. "Are these all crew members?"

"Yes, yes," he replied, preoccupied with his list.

"Would you kindly introduce me to the captain?"

"Ah, yes, of course." He whispered to the girl, who pointed to a name on the list. The consul called, "Captain Cho, please!"

A very young man in a new-looking business suit came towards us. "Captain Cho, this is Commodore Harinxma, your adviser."

The young man gazed at my white hair, the massive gold rings on my sleeves, the fruit salad of battle ribbons on my chest, the cap with the scrambled eggs, and muttered something that sounded like "Good God!"

I held out my hand. "Captain, it's a pleasure to be of service to you."

He took my hand gingerly and said, "Honoured Commodore, it—it is an honour." He bowed.

I thought it might help if I chatted him up a bit. "Tell me, Captain, who is the lady?" I nodded at the old woman surrounded by solicitous Chinese.

"Ah, the cook, Honoured Commodore, Ma Chang, relative of all lower ranks, except those gentlemen over there." He indicated a group of ten men standing noticeably apart from the rest. Instead of university T-shirts they wore black jumpsuits and they looked menacing.

"They are from a different island," the captain said in a whisper. "The others do not like them. They are hop-hops."

"Excuse me?"

"They go on towed object. Hop-hops."

"Ah, runners. How—"

The consul cut me short by shouting something in Taiwanese. He must have ordered everyone into the bus, for they all picked up their belongings and followed the airline stewardess, like a herd of clockwork gnomes.

I followed them into the bus and sat down on the front seat. There were indeed an awful lot of them, for some had to stand. Then I saw the ten grim men in black seated at the back of the bus in splendid isolation, surrounded by empty seats.

The ride back to the harbour seemed long. The Chinese captain, sitting beside me, did not appear to be interested in conversation. Halfway through the town, I asked him, "Tell me, have you sailed with these people before?"

He looked up and gave me a toothy smile. "No, Honoured Commodore. They are fishermen. Mr. Chung got them from the government. They have no work, all the fish are dead. Mercury."

"They have never sailed on board a tugboat?"

"No, Honoured Commodore."

I wondered what had possessed Mr. Chung to select this inexperienced crew for a difficult tow of many months, part of it through the worst storm zone on the globe. By the time we arrived on the quayside I had decided to telephone the office at the first opportunity, for to start towing a thirty-thousand-ton dry dock with this crew seemed foolhardy. But first I had to get them installed on board.

They all formed a line again the moment their feet touched the ground; in the centre stood the old woman. The ten black jumpsuits lined up a short distance away, scowling. Captain Cho gathered round him a group of other young men in new business suits; together they advanced on me.

158

"Honoured Commodore, these are the officers," the captain said with obvious pride. "Number One!"

One of the young men stepped forward and bowed. "Greetings, Honoured Commodore." So it went: Number Two, Chief Engineer Liu, Chief Two, Chief Three, Radio Officer One, Radio Officer Two, and the bosun, one of the T-shirt brigade, a huge brute with BRYN MAWR stretched across his chest. After this I went to welcome the jumpsuits, who glared at me with varying degrees of detestation. I went back to the crowd of happy fishermen, and shook hands with them all: Amherst, Vanderbilt, Cornell, Yale, Harvard—the T-shirts would make it easy for me to keep track of them, as long as they didn't get mixed up in the laundry. When I reached the lady cook, I saluted and said, "My name is Harinxma, I am the senior adviser."

She looked up at me with an odd, unfocused gaze and lifted both hands as if she were about to touch my face. Then she smiled, showing that she lacked four front teeth, and bowed.

"You speak to me, Captain, I speak the English," a cheerful voice said. "She no speak English, I speak the English very good."

It was a grinning little man in jeans, with a nameless T-shirt. "I your butler. Speak and I will tell her what you say. Speak. Now."

Captain Cho joined us. "He is number-one steward, Commodore."

"Steward," I said, "welcome. Glad to have you on board. Please tell the lady likewise."

The steward quacked and lisped at her. While he did so, I called to the ship, "Slobkous! Porks! Harlingen! Bosun! Join me, please!"

They were all watching from the bridge deck, fascinated. When they joined us, I made the introductions then, turning to my men, I said, "You sort out who belongs in your department, then show them their quarters."

I headed back to the hate-filled leader of the runners. "Would you and your men please follow me on board? We'll show you your quarters. Tomorrow you'll move onto the dry dock."

He stared at my jugular, then aimed the guns of his black eyes at the crowd of happy fishermen. It was as if he hit them physically; they all fell silent and stared at him, their faces blank. It was a look of such contempt that I could not mistake its meaning.

One thing seemed obvious: I could not put the two groups together in the confined space of the crew's quarters or there would be problems. Head office would have to find lodgings for this lot for the night. In the meantime I had better put them back on the bus until I had sorted things out with The Hague. I headed for a telephone box. The tension on the quayside was tangible: all the officials and workmen on board the tugboat were lined up at the rail, watching the spectacle, spellbound. I walked past the now motionless rows of fishermen and entered the phone box.

159

When I was put through to Miss Bastiaans I said, "I think you'd better trace Mr. Kwel for me. I have over thirty-five Chinese here, which means they're spilling out of the portholes, and ten furious runners spoiling for a fight. I'm willing to improvise, but this one has me stymied. Besides, I have other things to do. Find Mr. Kwel and tell him it's urgent."

She said she would see what she could do.

I crossed the now empty quayside to the gangway and glanced at the bus. The runners were sitting inside in taut repose, staring ahead. At the top of the gangway I was welcomed by Slobkous. "Everything is under control," he said. "They're down in the cabins, nesting two to a bunk. Everybody's taken care of except the captain and the steward, they're waiting for you in the dayroom."

"Good work, Slobkous. Happy Hour at six for the staff, Chinese included. Spread the word."

"Will do."

I went to my cabin. In the dayroom I found Captain Cho and the steward waiting for me. I said to the steward, "Go and find the bosun, he'll instruct you how to serve drinks and so on."

"I know how to serve drinks. I was barman in Mah-Iot Hotel, Kao Hsiung! Very fine, big tips!"

"Well, splendid. Now get out."

He stared at me as if he couldn't believe his ears, but he left.

"Captain," I said, "tell me about yourself. What's your background?"

"I was captain of one of Mr. Chung's tugboats. Number One was my mate. The engineers are off other tugboat. Big tugboat."

"Harbour tug, I take it?"

"No, we sail out to sea to pick up big ships. But not big as this. This is beautiful ship, Commodore. Very honoured." He bowed sitting down.

"Thank you. I suggest you and I go up to the bridge in a moment to look at the layout. But, first, this suite is yours by rights. You are the captain, these are the captain's quarters."

He appeared horrified at the suggestion. "No, no, Commodore! This is *your* cabin! I wish not to be here! I am not real captain, only tit-you-lar. You are captain until I have learned."

That was not what had been arranged, but I didn't want to enter into an argument with him. I'd take it up with old Kwel later. I rose. "Very well, then, let's go upstairs."

He followed me to the bridge, where there was a lot of activity. Captain Cho stared at the display of controls, dials, scanners, viewers, television screens and flashing electronic figures in awe. And no wonder. The first time I had set eyes on this wheelhouse, it had looked to me like the control room of a nuclear plant, but I was not prepared for the intensity of his reaction. He looked at me, aghast, and cried, "No! I cannot! I cannot command this ship! I am not qualified! I have licence up to one thousand tons. Mr. Chung mislaid me! He said, 'Tugboat is tugboat, Dutch one is like the one you now command, only bigger.' He not said—*this!*" He made another sweeping gesture.

"But I assure you—"

"No! I will not!" He walked to the companionway; there he turned to face me. "You are a commodore. You sail this. I cannot. I am not qualified. All these buttons, switches, clocks, I not understand. I refuse. Point. Blank." He started on his way down.

I could not let this farce continue. "Captain," I said, "if you do indeed have a tonnage restriction on your licence, then we have a problem. You will have to call Mr. Chung on the telephone and settle the matter."

"No," he said tonelessly. "I have dispensation."

"You mean you're licensed up to one thousand tons, but received dispensation from that restriction?"

"No matter, I *feel* not qualified. I come here, I look and see, and I say: not qualified."

"OK," I said, tired of him, "when my director calls, I'll report all this to him. You do as you see fit."

Back in my dayroom, I took a deep breath and crossed to the window to have a look at the quayside. The bus was still there with its hostile runners. The whole thing was ludicrous. Two crises already before we were even under way! There was a knock on the door and Miss Bastiaans entered.

"Commodore? Mr. Arnold is here."

"Where?"

"In the limousine on the quayside. He is not good at climbing gangways."

"I'll come."

We went down the corridor together. I was struck by the silence on board; a few minutes earlier the ship had sounded like a bazaar, now you could hear a pin drop. The old man must have decked out the limousine with flags of the royal house.

When we came out into the open and started down the gangway, I saw the limousine. It was without flags, but the way it was parked did seem regal: it was smack in the middle of the railway tracks, so that any train clanging down the quay would have to stop and ask for permission to proceed.

The old man was sitting in the back seat, a rug over his knees.

"Commodore Harinxma is here, sir," Miss Bastiaans said.

"What is all this?" the old man asked testily, gazing at me with his oddly youthful eyes which saw nothing at all. "Why have I been called here? In the past you were always able to solve problems on your own, Harinxma. It's no longer my ship, we're just providing services."

"It's a case of an unqualified captain, sir. I don't think I can sail, under the circumstances."

"Don't talk rubbish," he said. "Get in. Close the door."

I obeyed. I said, "The Chinese captain insists he is only the titular master and will not assume command, so instead of serving as adviser, as agreed, I would in effect be acting as master. It means that I would have all the responsibilities of a master and none of the rights."

"No, Harinxma. You'd be given all the rights and none of the responsibilities. The Taiwanese captain is responsible by law, as he is listed on the manifest as the master. You have been assigned to assist and advise him. What you do is this: you take command until further notice, but before each decision or order you ask him if he wishes you to demonstrate the procedure. It will cover you, and you can go on acting as master for as long as necessary. Just make sure the man is physically there, and defer to him whenever feasible."

It sounded reasonable, but I didn't want to end up in an ambiguous situation. "I'm afraid I can't go in for that, sir."

He gazed at me. Even though I knew he was blind, I couldn't help feeling the weight of his regard. Then he said, "Harinxma, what I am about to say is to go no further. You *must* sail this ship for me, as far as Rio de Janeiro. The deal has not yet been finalized. Mr. Chung will pay in full only after the arrival of the tow in Rio de Janeiro."

"But—"

"Stop butting in! Your task is to see that the ship gets to Rio without any complications. It's not going to be difficult. You may have a little rough weather at this time of year as far as St. Vincent; there you enter the trades. With a minimum of vigilance on your part, her flaw is not likely to show up. The Chinese captain should be ready to take over in Rio. It sounds like a mere case of stage fright."

My first reaction was anger. "Sorry, sir, I cannot be a party to that. I'll have to warn the Chinese captain about her flaw."

He took a long time before answering. "Right," he said finally. "What exactly were you planning to tell the Chinese captain?"

"That, for reasons unknown, the ship has a tendency to roll out of control under a certain combination of circumstances. There is a way of counteracting this, but it needs practice and constant vigilance. I'll put the man through the drill as often as is feasible, until he has mastered it. Always supposing he pulls himself together and starts to function as a master within a reasonable period of time—say, before the Cape Verdes. If, in St. Vincent, he still refuses to accept responsibility, that's where I get off."

He thought it over. "That sounds reasonable. Just don't dramatize. Stay with the facts. Show him how simple it is to correct the rolling. Cast

off the tow somewhere between here and St. Vincent and demonstrate it to
him. Now, what else did you want to see me about?"

"The runners, sir. There is so much tension between them and the crew
that, even if I could find room for them, I can't have both groups on the
ship without danger of trouble. What do I do with them? They're waiting
in a bus, over there."

"Send them ahead to Antwerp and detail your first officer to accompany them. Miss Bastiaans will take care of lodging and transportation.
Talk to her. Anything else?"

"No, sir."

"All right." He sank back into the cushions. "Call Miss Bastiaans."

She was standing within earshot; she came at once. I explained the
problem with the runners.

"I'll arrange with the consul to send them ahead to Antwerp. If you
could delegate someone to accompany them—"

"I'll send Mate Slobkous."

"Ah, good. Godspeed, Commodore, happy sailing."

She slipped inside the limousine and closed the door. The car moved
away, leaving me standing centre stage, master of the *Isabel Kwel*.

I went back on board, yearning for a few moments of peace and solitude
in which to reflect, undisturbed. But when I closed the door of my
dayroom behind me, the canary trilled and warbled in its cage. I filled its
little tray with seed from a bag which the bosun had bought. While doing
so, I began to realize that thanks to the old man's manipulation, I was now
virtually in collusion with KITCO, and whoever else in this murky business
had an interest in getting the ship out of their hair with no questions asked.

What bothered me was Mr. Chung's role in all this. During the evening
at Kwel's house he had struck me as a tough and astute operator; now it
began to look as if he had had a flawed ship foisted on him—deadly
flawed. Or perhaps he had outsmarted old Kwel, having his dry dock
towed to Rio by a boat on which he had only an option; at which point he
would cancel the deal on the basis of the ship being unseaworthy, with his
tow halfway to Talcahuano for free.

When darkness fell, we all gathered in my dayroom for Happy Hour.
Porks turned up with Harlingen and the radio officers, two smiling
Chinese youths. The bosun trained the Chinese steward as to how to serve
drinks. "Not so much gin. They've got a ship to sail!" The steward
dropped two glasses, then a bowl of peanuts; each time he said, "Hopla!"

The Chinese mates and engineers did not show up, but they joined us for
dinner in the officers' lounge. After the first awkward minutes a conversation started among the engineers, leading to the drawing of engine parts
on paper napkins.

After the meal we dispersed for the night. I undressed, took a sleeping pill and climbed into bed. The harbour tugs were due at four in the morning. I could do with a good night's sleep.

But my mind was churning, it was hard to settle down. Also, there was an unholy racket on board. Porks and his colleagues were trying the engines again, jerking the ship back and forth, setting the mooring lines screaming. There were Chinese noises everywhere: laughter, giggles, tuneless music. All the floodlights were on, turning night into day beyond my window. I went to see what the devil they were up to and saw Asian figures scurrying in and out of shadows at a crouching run. Then some joker set the foghorn blaring. I rang the bridge.

Somebody picked up the phone and said, "Meow? Sing kwan, meow."

"Whoever you are, stop that noise! And cut those damn floods! Go to sleep, man, we sail before sunrise!"

"Meow, kwang."

It became quiet.

Then dark.

The engines stopped.

It was a miraculous transformation. I had said "Quiet" and it became quiet, "Dark" and it became dark.

I was, once again, Master after God.

Chapter Four

Early the next morning, before daybreak, two harbour-tug captains turned up in my cabin to take us out onto the river.

The Chinese steward served coffee with gingerbread under the eagle eye of the bosun. The pilot arrived, a hearty fellow smoking a cigar smelling like a smouldering haystack. I sent the steward to find Captain Cho and ask if he would please join us in the dayroom. When, after ten minutes, there still was no sign of the young man, I went to the first officer's cabin, where Captain Cho had taken up residence, and knocked on the door.

After the third knock I heard a sound I interpreted as an invitation to come in. When I opened the door, the first thing to hit me was the sickly-sweet smell of alien tobacco smoke. Captain Cho, in striped pyjamas, was sitting upright in his bunk, reading a little red book. When he saw me, he scowled and sucked his pipe.

"Captain, your presence is needed on the bridge," I said.

Smoking, he stared at me before he spoke. Then he said, "No."

There comes a moment in this type of situation when something has got to give, so I said, "Captain, this will get us nowhere. If you refuse to sail this ship, even with my guidance, I'll have to send the harbour tugs home and call Mr. Chung in Brussels. Make up your mind."

The mention of Mr. Chung seemed to make a difference. "Oh," he said.

"Get some clothes on and come to the bridge. I'll sail the ship, but you must be there, and I must ask your permission before I can give any commands or make decisions. That is the law." He went on staring at me.

On the bridge, in the dim light of the chart lamp, I found the pilot and the Chinese first officer. The bosun was at the wheel. A bevy of Chinese sailors, in T-shirts despite the bitter cold, were standing by at the bollards.

"Number One," I said to the first officer, a slight young Chinese with intelligent eyes, "Captain Cho is due any minute. Your place during this manoeuvre is on the fo'c'sle, to keep an eye on the mooring lines. Number Two should be on the aft deck."

He said, "Yes, Commodore," and was about to sprint off. I had to stop him if I wanted to play this by the book. "Hold it!" I called. "Wait until Captain Cho is here; he'll give you the order."

Captain Cho appeared, his face turned to stone.

"Captain," I asked, "do you wish to take over, or would you prefer me to go through a demonstration of this vessel leaving port?" It was a ridiculous question; in no way could I make it sound realistic.

"Proceed," he said stonily.

"Thank you, Captain." Well, from now on I could forget about him. "Number One, to the fo'c'sle," I said; the young man darted off. I went to the aft window and saw Number Two there in the white cone of the floods. "She's all yours, Pilot."

"Thank you." He pulled the mike down from the ceiling and said, "Let go fore and aft."

From the loudspeaker overhead came a variety of noises: quackings, chortlings, giggles. It was as if by some turbulence in the ether he had tuned in to the dormitory of a girls' school. Number One was not on the fo'c'sle yet.

Captain Cho had come up behind the pilot. "I will tell them."

"Don't they know what 'let go' means?" the pilot asked, amazed.

"They speak no English at all."

Captain Cho took up position underneath the mike and gave the mike a blast of highpitched chatter; the Chinese on both fore and aft decks sprang to life. The moorings were whisked on board and coiled on deck with the speed of an Indian rope trick. One harbour tug swung ahead of us, churning; the other dropped astern, and the ship nosed out into the river. A liner was passing as we came out, a gigantic cluster of stars. There was a lot of small traffic: lighters, motor launches and barges, pushing bow waves almost as big as themselves, on their way to the yards and wharves downriver.

The tugs cast off and the pilot rang for half speed as we headed towards the open sea with our backs to the dawn. The steward served coffee and sandwiches, half of which he dropped on the floor, saying, "Hopla!" He then wiped them on his trousers and put them back on the plate. Captain Cho pouted in his corner.

It was daylight when we passed the outer buoy. The swell hit us and the *Isabel* came to life.

A black launch slung with tyres came pitching and wallowing towards us, dipping the white letter "P" on its bow into the water. "Well, Commodore," the pilot said, "I think this wraps it up. It was a pleasure taking you out. Now, if you'll sign this chit for me, I'll mosey off." I rang down the speed to Dead Slow for him and said, "That should be signed by the master."

"Oh, I see." He took his book of chits to Captain Cho, who frowned at it. "Sign here, Captain," he said, indicating the spot. "If you can't sign your name, make a cross. The commodore will certify it's yours."

"What is this for, please?"

"Now, don't make any problems, Captain. My launch is waiting."

When Cho had signed, the pilot said, "Captain, Commodore, Godspeed and happy sailing. And *lots* of luck," he added morosely.

"Thank you, Pilot."

I went onto the port wing to watch his launch depart. I gave them a thankyou wail on the horn, went back into the wheelhouse and rang up the speed to Full Ahead, with demonstrative self-confidence. No point in advertising the fact that I had had no more than a two-hour crash course on this spaceship's bridge and knew, in fact, as much about her gadgetry as did Captain Cho by now—if he had been watching the pilot, which I doubted.

"All right, Bosun. Another mile or so and I'll give you the course. For the moment, steady as you go."

"Aye."

"Captain Cho, let's have a look at the chart."

I went to the desk and plotted the course for the Scheldt River entrance, en route for Antwerp. Cho watched me without a word, then retired to his corner again. I gave the bosun the new course and strolled out onto the port wing. In the distance I heard the ship's bell strike four twins. A voice beside me said, "All right, Commodore, I'll take over the watch, if you're ready."

It was Mate Number One. Captain Cho had disappeared.

This was a surprise. Young Number One looked completely at ease, as if for him to take over the watch was the most normal thing in the world. Well, I couldn't sail the ship all by myself, so I said, "Very well, thank you. The course is two ten. We're running at full speed. Call when you sight the Scheldt pilot."

"Yes, Commodore." He went back into the wheelhouse.

The bosun came out, furious. "Ome! There's a slit-eye who wants to take my place at the wheel!"

"Bosun," I said, "that's the idea. And stop calling these people slit-eyes, dammit!" I went into the wheelhouse and saw Number One arguing with a tiny Chinese sailor labelled Whittier.

"He's too short, Commodore," Number One said.

"Bosun, get a crate or something."

Mumbling, he lumbered off and came back with an empty orange box. "Try that, boy-o," he said.

The little helmsman climbed onto the crate and clapped his hands in childish delight. It infuriated the bosun, who came towards me with a face of thunder. "All we need now on this bridge is a skipping rope!"

"They have to work it out among themselves, Bosun. Don't try to run their lives for them. We have troubles of our own."

"Ain't that the truth!"

When Mate Slobkous was back on board and had arrived on the bridge with the pilot who was to guide us up the western Scheldt, the ship got under way again. Shortly after this Slobkous took me quietly aside. "I have news for you. The dry dock we're taking on is pregnant."

"I beg your pardon?"

"A thirty-thousand-ton derelict, and a yacht welded inside, derelict too. That tow is going to fall apart at the first blow."

"But that's ridiculous!"

"You're telling *me!* The yacht goes to Punta Arenas, the dry dock to Talcahuano."

If I hadn't had the option of leaving the ship in Antwerp, I would have reacted with shocked indignation.

At that point the western Scheldt pilot joined us and asked how things were in Rotterdam. I told him, and we chatted until the Antwerp harbour pilot came on board. He was accompanied by Fransen, who entered the wheelhouse in a chain-smoking frenzy, shook me by the hand, waved at the Chinese mates and said hello to Slobkous. Captain Cho was not on the bridge.

"Sorry, Harinxma," Fransen said, "I intended to come on board earlier, but I just flew in from the Gulf. I'll set you on your way, then I'm off to Glasgow."

"I gather from Slobkous that the dry dock has a yacht inside."

He lit a new cigarette with the stub of the previous one and muttered, between puffs, "Don't worry about that. We'll go and have a look at the dock together. It won't take us a minute. By the way, for a runner captain you have a man called Harry Keerie, known as Harakiri. He's good, but as ornery as a mule."

"How big is the dock?"

"Big."

"Slobkous says thirty thousand."

"Bigger than that. Thirty-five."

"And what about the yacht it has inside?"

"Come and see for yourself."

The pilot had moored the ship at the quay in the heart of town. We walked down the alley between the sheds to the main basin of the yard, where a huge dry dock was moored. Lit up by the yard's floodlights, it looked to be in a terrible state of neglect. Its ribs showed, its plates were buckled and streaked with rust. High up on its flank I spotted the remnants of what must have been a company name: A.G, the rest obliterated by rust, and, a yard or so lower, NES. This brute was at least forty thousand tons.

"Don't break your neck," Fransen said, as he led me across an acre of scrap iron to a gangplank slanting upwards to the floor of the dry dock. The interior was lit up jerkily by the blue sheet lightning of welding. I caught my first glimpse of the yacht: a beached whale trapped inside a steel canyon. It was a substantial vessel with a clipper bow, a bowsprit complete with figurehead, and a name: *Queen of Persia*. I estimated it at a thousand tons, yet it looked small in the canyon between the dock's walls.

The dock floor was crowded with welders and longshoremen, dragging chains. A figure detached itself from a group round a welder and advanced on us. "Hi there, Slobbo!" the creature cried. "How are you?"

Someone behind me said, "I'm OK. How are *you?*"

I turned round and saw Slobkous standing behind me. "Harakiri, meet the commodore," he said.

"Glad to meet you, Keerie," I said. "I gather you're the runner captain for this trip." We shook hands. He was a wiry, straw-blond character, in his forties; in the welding light he looked like a demon with a blue face and green hair.

"You know we're due to leave at three hundred hours?" Fransen asked.

"If the Belgians are through welding on my extra eyes by then," said the blue demon.

"How are they doing?"

"Slow. Tell me, Commodore, Captain—what do you want me to call you?"

I had dealt with runner captains all my life; they were a proud and independent lot. "Harinxma to you."

"OK. Want to check the struts, Harinxma?"

"I'd like to." Despite my tiredness, I had to establish a relationship with the runner captain before we sailed, as I wouldn't meet him face to face again before Cape Verdes. Until then our only contact would be by walkie-talkie.

"Harinxma," he said as we walked down the length of the ship, "have a good look at these struts. The structure seems solid enough, but the struts themselves are on the light side, if you see what I mean."

The distance between the flanks of the yacht and the walls of the canyon was about sixty feet. Horizontal struts, supported by vertical stanchions every twenty feet, had been welded on at the height of the yacht's deckline.

"Leaves a lot of play, if you see what I mean, Harinxma. Where's this box going anyway?"

"Punta Arenas is the destination of the yacht, the dock continues to Talcahuano," Fransen said.

"Good God! So I'll be hitting the Forties twice with this coffin?"

"The second time there'll be no yacht inside."

"Well, what do you think, Harinxma? Is this structure secure? If we get one of those gales, there's going to be blue water in here."

"Not enough to give flotation."

"I suppose not. Now, would you like to have a look at the yacht? I've bedded the Chinks down in the staterooms."

"All right, Keerie, lead the way." Leaving Fransen with the welders, I followed the runner captain up a narrow articulated gangway that led from the dock floor to the deck of the yacht.

"How are you getting on with the Chinese?" I asked.

"OK. They know their job."

He took me down a dim, evil-smelling corridor lit only by an oil lamp at the far end. "There you go," he said, pointing at closed doors. "Private staterooms, one for each Chink." There was an imposing door at the end of the corridor, which he opened with a flourish. "Welcome to my cabin!"

It was a large stateroom. Its ceiling, covered with ornate gold scrolls, reflected the light of two oil lamps. One wall showed a mural of nude female figures, some of them disfigured by moustaches and beards. The centrepiece of the room was an oval bed with a narrow, unmade mattress like a dog's mat; this must be where Keerie slept. There was a built-in dressing table and mirrored wardrobes; the floor was covered with a carpet pockmarked with burn holes and dark spots of dampness. The place smelled like Roquefort cheese. "What this needs is a couple of women," Keerie said. "Mind if I import some talent?"

If he'd really been planning to bring women on board, he would have kept it to himself, so I replied, "Do whatever you like, Keerie, as long as you have a second-in-command to take up the slack."

"As a matter of fact, I think I may have. Their *mandur*, or whatever you call him, looks a mean devil but he knows his way around. He had the lamps lit, his people housed, watches organized, before I could say a word. He may slit my throat while we're under way, but apart from that, I think I drew lucky."

170

"Thanks for the tour," I said. "How do I get back to the gangway?"

"Glad you could manage a visit." He slapped my shoulder. "This way."

He took me back into the corridor with its closed doors. One of the doors opened and I found myself face to face with the steel-eyed Chinese who had confronted me on the quayside. He had not gained in charm in the meantime. "Good evening," I said. "Good to have you aboard."

He gave me one of those looks that are supposed to kill.

"I hope you found everything all right for you and your crew?"

He didn't reply, just stared at me.

Keerie helped out. "If he didn't, he'd be the first to tell us, by the look of him. Wouldn't you?"

He did not react, other than by shifting his killing gaze to the man with whom he would have to spend two months on board this hulk. When I wished Harakiri "Godspeed and happy sailing" before going down the companionway, it was more than an empty phrase.

Downstairs, I found Fransen waiting for me. "Better get to bed, Harinxma," he said, rubbing out a cigarette with his foot. "I suggest you let the harbour tugs winkle this thing out of here and you take over in the channel."

"All right. Let them prepare the bridle with throw-line attached, and I'll take over as soon as I have room."

"You'll have plenty of room," Fransen said, as we walked to the edge of the dock. "They're holding up traffic in the narrows for an hour tomorrow morning."

We edged down the gangplank and walked back to the *Isabel.* As we approached, I saw a white delivery van parked at the foot of the gangway. Two little girls looking like twins peered at us from the window of the driver's seat, one sucking a lollipop.

A man came down the gangway. "You Commodore Harinxma? I put the basket in your salon."

When we entered my dayroom, I found on the coffee table a handsome basket of fruit with a card attached to its handle: *Happy Christmas and bon voyage, Charlie Chung.*

"Well," Fransen said, "you have to hand it to him. The Kwels wouldn't do this in a thousand years."

"That reminds me, I must call my family tomorrow, to wish them a Happy Christmas."

I ushered him out and undressed. A few minutes later I was bedded down, and went out like a light.

I WAS WOKEN BY BANGING on the door. It was Slobkous with the tugboat captains. They turned out to be thirsty; I put the Chinese steward to work fuelling them while I paid a visit to Captain Cho.

I found him sitting up in bed in his striped pyjamas, smoking his pipe, reading his little red book. He welcomed me with his stonewall look. I wondered what the little red book was. *Quotations from Chairman Mao*? It would fit the picture of adolescent rebellion.

"Well, Captain, how about coming with me to inspect the bridle before we sail?"

He puffed at his pipe.

"Look, Cho," I said flatly, "if you don't want to accept command, that's your problem. I'll sail the damn thing. But, God damn it, I need you on the bridge to satisfy the law. So make sure you're there. We sail in twenty minutes."

I had made more diplomatic speeches than that in my time, but it would have to do. After paying a hurried visit to the dock to inspect the bridle I went back on board and found my staff gathered in the dayroom for a pre-departure Happy Hour.

Slobkous was having an apple, Porks and Harlingen were into gin. The Chinese steward dropped two bowls of peanuts and one gin and tonic, yodelling "Hopla!" each time; Porks started to call him Hopla. It was not exactly an atmosphere of international brotherhood, but I did not feel like preaching at them.

The Flemish tugboat captains finally left with so much gin in them that it seemed impossible they could navigate the high threshold, let alone their vessels. I sent Slobkous to present my compliments to Captain Cho and request his presence on the bridge. When I reached it, he was standing in his corner like a statue. The pilot was there; I introduced them to each other. Then I spoke the magic formula: "Captain Cho, do you wish to take charge of this operation, or do you wish me to demonstrate the departure procedure for you?"

He made a gesture which I interpreted as acceptance. I said to the pilot, "Well, let's get this show on the road."

"Let go fore and aft," the pilot said into the mike. This time Bryn Mawr, Brandeis, Whittier and Loyola knew what the command meant; all Number One had to do was watch.

I revised my opinion of the Stone Age fishermen; they were very good. Out in midstream, we made fast to the dry dock, an angular mass ten times the size of the ship, blacking out the glitter of the waterfront. The Chinese worked the lines deftly while the four Belgian tugs churned away to keep the dock in the centre of the channel. Once again I was startled by the *Isabel*'s tremendous power. To tow a dry dock this size with just one tug was in itself an innovation to me; in my time it would have taken at least three. But I couldn't remember having come up to speed this fast, even with three ships. When I put on Full Speed Ahead to get the massive load behind me moving, the *Isabel* seemed to growl and hunch her shoulders, then proceeded to whisk the dock and the four tugboats along with a forward surge that took my breath away. When there was sufficient forward momentum I rang the speed down to half. Then I went to the aft window of the wheelhouse and looked at the black citadel behind us, with its red and green lights winking among the stars.

"Captain, tea." It was the Chinese steward.

"Thank you." Nice feeling, to hold a heavy ship's mug again.

I stayed on the bridge well past the end of my watch. The stars were paling in the blue of the dawn and the River Scheldt had widened into the vast pewter plain of the estuary when the tugs cast off. I gave them the farewell-and-thank-you blasts of our horn; when they responded, their braying sounded puny in the immensity of water and sky. I put the engine on Full Ahead; the short hawser was whisked out of the water. By then Slobkous, who had turned in for a shut-eye an hour earlier, was back on the bridge.

"If anything comes up, don't hesitate to call me. I'll just be having a nap on the couch in my dayroom," I said.

"Will do."

"Good watch, gentlemen."

Captain Cho had disappeared. The bosun reluctantly handed the wheel to little Whittier on his orange box and accompanied me down the companionway. "I'll bring you a nice mug of hot cocoa, Ome."

"Good idea, Bosun. But no rum this time."

As I entered, the canary was tweet-tweeting at the dawn. I filled the feeding cup and said, "Well, here we go, another trip. How about some breakfast?" The bird came fluttering down and started to peck furiously, throwing most of the seed on the floor.

I suddenly remembered it was Christmas Day. I should call my family. I picked up the phone and punched the number of the radio room.

"Harlingen, Harinxma here. Could you get a number in the south of France for me, or are we still under shore restrictions?"

"No, that's OK. One second . . . OK, let me have the number. It'll take just a couple of minutes." As I gave it to him the bosun came in with a mug. "Here you go, Ome. Nice and hot. Have you taken your pills?"

"Who told you about my pills?"

"Well, I watched that slit-eye unpacking— "

"For God's sake, Bosun! Stop calling these people slit-eyes! Call them what it says on their T-shirts. Thank you, by the way. This is delicious."

"Pills," he said, like a wife.

"They're in two boxes on the top shelf of my wardrobe. Bring me a white envelope from one box and put the other in the fridge."

As I shook the pills into my hand, he asked, "What's in the brown envelopes?"

173

"They're for suppertime. The white are breakfast."

"Do you have enough for the trip?"

"Each of the boxes holds four weeks."

He frowned thoughtfully. "H'm. That should take us as far as Rio." He turned at the door. "Happy dreams, Ome. I'll cover the bird. By the way, I'm calling him Pete."

The telephone rang. "I've got France for you, Skipper."

"Dad?" It was my daughter Helen's voice.

"Hello, honey! Nice to hear you. Happy Christmas!"

"Happy Christmas, Dad! We miss you! Are you all right?"

"Sure. This ship is a lazy captain's dream. I'm lolling on a couch in a bridal suite right now."

"You're *what?*"

"Never mind. Are you OK? How are the kids?"

"They're fine. They all want to talk to you. . . ."

So it went on, one instalment of grandparental bliss after another, including the dog, which they somehow got to bark.

I took my pills, then went to look at the fruit basket. I picked up an apple; it had a piece nibbled out of it. I checked the others. All had been chewed by mice and displayed with the good side up. I turned the basket over on the couch. Half the space inside was taken up by a false bottom with a hole in it. On closer scrutiny, it looked as if that too had been gnawed out by little teeth. I pulled the cardboard out and—"*Good God!*"

There, leering at me, sat a small rat.

The door opened, the bosun came in. "Ome! What the hell—"

"Look!"

We both stared at the rat incredulously. As it sat among the chewed-up remains of the fruit basket, it yawned, scratched itself, stretched, totally unfazed by our proximity.

"Hold it!" The bosun ran into my bedroom, came back with a boot and raised it to clobber the beast. The rat looked up at him, unimpressed, then it looked at me, yawned and hopped onto the back of the couch.

"You filthy—"

"No! Don't!" I stopped the bosun, not out of tender feelings but because of the mess it would make. The rat strolled along the back of the couch, laying a row of little mines.

A voice said behind me, "Him house rat." It was the Chinese steward. "Stroke him," he said to me. "Him know people."

When I hesitated, he fetched one of my pencils from the desk and scratched the rat's back with the rubber on the end. The rat seemed to like that; it rolled onto its back.

"I'll get a bucket," the bosun said. "Then I'll whack it one and toss it over the edge." He made for the door.

"No, Bosun! It's obviously tame. It must have belonged to the fruit merchant's little girls."

The creature jumped onto the bookshelf and perched on top of Bowditch's *American Practical Navigator*.

"Well?" the bosun asked. "What shall I do with the filthy varmint?"

I looked at the rat on the Bowditch. It looked back at me. "Let's leave it there, for the time being."

He snorted, and left. I lay down to sleep. The rat observed me like a contented little sphinx while Pete the canary squeaked and rattled his beak along the bars of its cage in what seemed to be a frenzy of jealousy. I heaved myself back to my feet, went to fetch a towel from the bathroom and covered the cage with it. Sleep came the moment I lay down, as if someone had covered my cage with a towel as well.

THE TELEPHONE RANG; it took a few moments of orientation before I answered it. "Harinxma."

"Skipper, sorry to wake you." It was Slobkous. "We're entering the Channel and there's a lot of traffic. I thought you might like to be around. I'm turning in."

"I'll be right up." I looked at the clock: I had slept three hours. The rat was asleep on Bowditch.

In the wheelhouse the Chinese mate number one welcomed me, smiling and bowing. "Good morning, Commodore." No sign of Captain Cho.

It was cold on the outer bridge, a chilly day. Massive cumuli, pregnant with rain, came sailing across the slate-coloured sea from the cliffs of North Foreland on the horizon. I looked at the dry dock. We were still on the short hawser; the citadel, tigered with rust, loomed just behind us, with the ancient yacht inside its ramparts. She looked like a dragonfly caught in a web, with all those struts and stanchions welded onto her from the walls of the dock and, higher up, the trelliswork of the dock gates. Through the binoculars I saw runners at work on the starboard wall, at the foot of a flagpole with two black balls and a black diamond between them, the international sign for a tow. I decided to try to raise Harakiri, and switched on the walkie-talkie.

"Dry dock, this is *Isabel*. Do you read?"

I had to try three times before his voice replied, "*Isabel*, this is *Agnes*. I read you loud and clear, over."

"Who is *Agnes*?"

"This box, Harinxma. That's what it says on her flank, isn't it?"

I remembered the odd letters on its flank, partially obliterated by rust: A.G . . . NES. Tugboat crews usually attribute a personality to the object they are dragging along and the ritual process was again taking place. "Righto, *Agnes*. All well on board?"

175

"Affirmative, *Isabel*. Godspeed and happy sailing, over."

"Godspeed and happy sailing, *Agnes*. Over and out." I turned to Number One. "From now on, write '*Agnes*' in the ship's log when referring to the dock. Tell the next watch."

He looked nonplussed, then he said, "Very well, Commodore."

To him, it was all part of the Mysterious West.

Chapter Five

During the days that followed, I discovered that to sail with a Chinese crew was a novel experience indeed.

They filled the corridors with the smells of their cooking and played strange music on the intercom, interminably. The Chinese officers were courteous and correct, but declined to take part in Happy Hour and announced, the second day out, that they preferred to take their meals with the crew in the messroom, so we decided to have our meals, cooked by the bosun, in the officers' lounge.

Captain Cho regained self-confidence to the point where he took a regular watch in rotation with his two mates, but each time he turned up on the bridge there was a notable change in the atmosphere. From the moment he appeared, he strutted and snarled and made what were obviously snide remarks to crew members, who reacted with good-natured bewilderment and proceeded to ignore him.

I shared my watch with Number One, the keen young Chinese first mate. He never lost sight of me, followed me wherever I went, but we rarely exchanged more than a casual word. The only Chinese member of the crew with whom I had any personal contact was Hopla, the steward. He was much in evidence, eager to serve sandwiches, polish shoes and gossip.

Inevitably, the Dutch staff closed ranks and became a tightly knit group more quickly than would normally have been the case. All crews new to a ship develop a private language; in our case, "pencil" soon became "rat-scratcher" and the dayroom—where the rat, now called Louis, ruled the roost—became "Louisville". Louis turned out to be an amazing creature. He was friendly and well-mannered. When drinks were served, he would hop onto the coffee table and eye the snacks, but he always waited to be offered one. His daytime roost was on top of Bowditch, where he lay in wait for me from the moment I left. On my return he would make a flying leap and land on my shoulder—a startling experience the first few times, but I soon got used to it. Thenceforth, while in my quarters I walked around with a rat on my shoulder.

Considering the time of year, we were lucky with the weather. After

Gris-Nez the convoy proceeded slowly southward through lovely frosty days of silver light and sky-blue sea. The dry dock was far behind us now, on a long hawser. I didn't see much of Harakiri or his crew through my binoculars, but every day during Happy Hour I would make contact with him via the walkie-talkie.

Throughout those dreamy days and star-haunted nights the *Isabel Kwel* behaved impeccably, but I knew that the day of reckoning must come sooner or later.

I telephoned Sylvia every few days. Thanks to the wizardry of the paradise tree, she and I spent more time chatting, during that first week, than if I had been at home. The rest of my free time I spent watching TV from the comfort of the couch.

We arrived off St. Vincent Island in the Cape Verdes just before nightfall. Early next morning, the pilot came on board with Fransen. *Agnes* was moored to the buoys in the Porto Grande and we went to the fuel dock behind the breakwater for oiling. When we had passed through customs, Fransen took me to a quaint little restaurant in the small town of Mindelo.

After we had ordered drinks, I said, "Well, the Chinese captain is a dud. He stays in his cabin most of the time. When he does take a watch, he carries on like Lord Nelson at Trafalgar. But his actual value as a master is zero. You can't let that bungler sail into the Forties with this ship, this dock!"

He shrugged his shoulders. "Who can't? It's got nothing to do with us, he's Mr. Chung's baby. The ship is registered in Taiwan, the crew is Taiwanese. *Your* job is to see to it that that ship and tow get to Rio. Is the man stopping you from doing that?"

"No, but—"

"Are the other deck officers OK?"

"Yes, but, like the crew—"

"Now listen, old buddy!" Suddenly he was laid-back no longer. "Your instructions are to advise the captain. It's nothing to do with you if the man can't take advice, or won't, or is incompetent. You advise, and report to me; I report to KITCO, they report to Chung. If Chung wants to know more, he'll ask. Until he asks, you shut up. You're messing in a very delicate situation." He raised his glass. "Cheers."

I was getting mad. "You ought to be ashamed of yourself! Delicate situation? It's like sending a carful of kids out into a rainstorm with a drunken driver."

"How's the pig been behaving?" he asked, taking off nimbly at a tangent.

After three weeks in a lazy captain's dream I no longer looked upon the *Isabel* as a pig. "She's behaved well, but the weather has been good."

"Well, good. Now let's talk business. I've arranged for the caterers to deliver tomorrow at six hundred hours; by then you should be back with the dock and ready to sail ..."

We talked shop during the rest of the meal. Captain Cho was not mentioned again.

AFTER THE CAPE VERDES we hit the trades. Wind and sea didn't amount to much as both were moderate; but to do what I had to do, this was the best I could offer between here and Rio de Janeiro.

I began by calling Captain Cho to my dayroom for a preparatory talk. I explained the problem of her suicidal rolling and the thruster operation in detail, with drawings. His attention was almost caught despite himself, but Louis chose that moment for a flying leap onto his shoulder from the Bowditch. That tore it; Captain Cho jumped to his feet with a shriek and shook the rat off as if it had been a boa constrictor. After that my efforts were ineffectual. The only hope of getting through to him was by showing him in practice, with his hands on the thruster handles, the kind of mischief the ship could get up to. I invited him to accompany me to the bridge for a demonstration. He accepted with ill grace.

The demonstration went smoothly, but not dramatically enough to bring home to Cho how dangerous the self-feeding cycle of the *Isabel's* rolling could be, under more severe conditions. After my portentous preparations the actual exercise took no more than half an hour and was a distinct anticlimax, from which Captain Cho walked away as if he had resisted the overtures of a soothsayer. He really was a pompous little ass.

I decided to stop pussyfooting around and simply write to Mr. Chung telling him, as diplomatically as possible, that his pet captain was a public danger. The decision gave me a measure of inner peace, and I set about writing the letter. But I had barely started when, nine days out of St. Vincent, something happened that blew me right out of the water.

Breakfast in bed had been served as usual by the bosun. Louis was ogling the tray, ready to jump onto it for his morning treat as soon as the coast was clear. The bosun, who had gone to get my pills, came back and said, "Sorry, Ome. No more pills in the box, only empty envelopes."

"OK, get the next one from the fridge."

He went to the dayroom and came back with another box.

"Look at this," he said. "Nothing but empties in this one either."

"That can't be! I packed two, we finished one! It must be full!"

"It is, but all these envelopes are empty."

My heart skipped a beat. I stared at the two boxes of empty envelopes. There had been a four-week supply in each. Like every elderly man who has to take two lots of pills each day, I had worked out a system, but an excess of zeal for economy had made me put the envelopes back into the box after swallowing their contents, so I could use them over again until they were worn out, instead of throwing them away and getting a new lot each time. In the hurry of packing, Sylvia or I must have picked up a box of empties, thinking it was full.

"What now?" I remembered the young doctor in the water bailiff's office: "Keep up these pills or you'll be in serious trouble." What kind of trouble? I had never gone without pills since a specialist had diagnosed mild hypertension, fifteen years ago. It had not remained mild: new pills had been added and their dosage gradually increased over the years. All I could do was wait and see; maybe nothing would happen. Just to put my mind at ease, why not take my blood pressure now, since I always travelled with a kit? I was only ten minutes late with my breakfast pills. So I took it, as a baseline to measure from, in case it went up.

To my surprise, my blood pressure was high. Why should it be? I had just been lazing around. Nerves obviously. I should take my mind off it, go to the bridge as I would normally do at this time.

I went to the bridge, busied myself with the chart, checked the compass, then hurried back to my dayroom and took my blood pressure again. But it was higher than it had been half an hour earlier. I took two tranquillizers and lay down on my bunk. The tranquillizers began to take effect: I was beginning to feel drowsy. Sleep. Sleep...

I awoke feeling that I had slept for hours, looked at my alarm clock and saw it had been seven minutes. I took my blood pressure again. It had risen another point. My God! I must *do* something.

I got up, dressed and went back to the bridge. Nothing had changed, only the sun had risen a little higher above the horizon. In its low light *Agnes* threw a long shadow on the glassy sea. We had passed through the trades; there was not a ruffle, no flying fish; in waves this low they could not take off.

Back in my dayroom, I took my blood pressure again. Higher still! God, how high could it go without popping a vein in my brain? I could think of nothing else. Every ten minutes or so I took my blood pressure. And it got worse. How I lived through Happy Hour I had no idea; I carried it off somehow.

After supper, when my watch came up, I had a headache. I didn't feel like going to the bridge. I went to my dayroom instead.

My bosun was there, observing me unobtrusively. He was like an elephant trying to hide behind a palm tree. I said, "For God's sake, Bosun, what do you want?"

He looked hurt. "Nothing, Ome. You don't look well to me, that's all. I just want to help."

"All right, get Mate Slobkous. And Mate Number One. Tell them to come and see me."

He left. I was standing in my bedroom in my dressing gown and pyjamas when Slobkous and Number One came in. I told them I wasn't feeling well. That I wouldn't be coming to the bridge for a while. I asked Number One if he could handle things: the Chinese took it in his stride, but Slobkous looked worried. There wasn't much else he could do.

I climbed into bed, lay staring at the ceiling for a while.

"Co'dore, sir ...?" I opened my eyes. Hopla was standing beside my bunk, a small, wizened man of an alien race. "Co'dore sick?"

"Not sick," I said. "I'm going to sleep. Goodnight." I turned my back on him. I was going to die. No man could have blood pressure that high and live. I would be buried at sea by Slobkous. I felt tears welling up, a flood of tears over everything. I took three sleeping pills, gulped them down and zonked out, falling like a stone into oblivion.

In the middle of the night, groggy with pills, I had a vision. A horrible old crone with a toothless grin was bending over me, touching me. I cried out and tried to struggle free of the hallucination, but it persisted. Then I heard a voice. "Co'dore! Let her look at you! She doctor! She help you!"

I stared at the vision in disbelief. It was the old Chinese cook, saying, "Wang kwai. Wang kwai." Beside her stood Hopla, who said, "She doctor. You tell her where pain is."

The old woman held up a small white carving of a male figure and pointed at its stomach. "Kwai?"

"She want to know: pain there?"

I found myself shaking my head. "Hypertension," I said.

They frowned in puzzlement.

Wearily, I pointed to my heart, made a gesture of squeezing an artery with my fist. "Woosh, woosh!"

Both of them looked baffled. They conferred in earnest whispers. I closed my eyes and said, "Go away."

There was more whispering. She moved towards the foot of my bunk.

"She want to see feet, Co'dore."

Hopla lifted the bedcover and bared my feet.

"Please, Co'dore. She read feet to find why you ill."

The old woman took hold of my left foot and started to press the sole. "Kwai?" She pressed another spot. "Kwai?"

"Ouch!" A fierce pain shot up my leg.

She grinned and babbled Chinese.

"What does she say now?" I asked Hopla.

"She says she find trouble. Now ask permission to do one more thing."

I gazed at the old woman with the gap in her teeth. She seemed to go into a sort of trance; then she produced a wooden bead dangling from a string, put her left hand on my abdomen and, eyes closed, let the bead swing back and forth. She slowly moved her hand up my abdomen; suddenly the bead swung clockwise. She opened her eyes, then moved her hand higher up my body, the bead swinging. When her hand was over my heart, she closed her eyes once more.

She stood like that for a while, eyes closed, bead swinging, then she opened her eyes, gave me a toothless smile and babbled something.

"She say· she know trouble now. She say: can cure."

Babble-babble.

"Food. Special food she will cook for you."

More babble.

"You not eat, not drink anything else."

She went on babbling in short bursts, and he translated. "She say: you cured in two moons. . . . She say: you better tomorrow. . . . She say: you eat wrong food. Wrong drink. . . . Smoke too, very bad. . . . She say: bad food, bad drink, bad smoke insult spirit of heart . . ."

"But tell her it's incurable! It can only be controlled by pills, and I've run out of them! I'm dying!" I cried in anguish.

She looked at me with kindness while he tried to translate my cry of despair by rolling his eyes and letting his head drop in a gross pantomime of death.

She nodded and smiled at me. Hopla said, "She say: Co'dore no die."

"But she nodded!"

"She nod; mean no. Co'dore no die. No. No." He nodded vigorously, then shook his head. "This mean: yes."

Suddenly the whole thing had turned into a farce. What could an ignorant old woman from a remote Chinese island who nodded "yes" for "no" possibly know about modern medicine, or about hypertension?

"She say: you must make peace with spirit of heart. . . . She say: think of it as healthy, young, strong, beautiful. . . . She say: you must tell heart, 'Sorry I offended you, heart. Forgive me, heart.' "

"Thank you," I said to her, feeling sick. "You're very kind."

She gave me a toothless smile, packed up her paraphernalia and turned to leave. Hopla respectfully opened the door for her, bowing, and followed her out.

I gazed at the ceiling. My head throbbed. My ears whistled. I could feel my faltering heart labour in my chest. I grabbed my blood-pressure gauge and put on the cuff. Higher still! It was as if death was standing in the doorway, like a man. I dozed off.

I had no idea what time it was when the first of the witch's meals was brought in by Hopla: three small bowls, each filled with a different-coloured sludge. There was a strong smell of cats. Hopla looked triumphant. I tasted a spoonful of the concoction; it tasted of nothing. "Get the salt, Hopla. It's with the glasses in the dayroom."

"No! Ma Chang say no salt! No sugar! Only what she put on tray."

"A dash of salt is not going to make any difference. Get it."

But he stood his ground. "No! If you eat salt, spirit of heart will be offended."

Weakly, I ate it, saltless, in his presence. Each of the three dishes contained a revolting sludge that slithered slimily down my gullet.

When I had finished, he said, "Good. Ma Chang happy. Lie down, Co'dore. Back in two hours with next meal."

When he'd gone I lay listening to the throbbing of the engines, the creaking of the wardrobe as the ship heeled in a slow roll, the footsteps overhead on the bridge. I dozed off.

After a while I woke up and took my blood pressure. It had certainly gone down a little.

I STAYED IN BED for what seemed like days, nights, eating cat-smelling sludge with a sense of devotion, dozing off at intervals. No one came to see me. Someone must be keeping them away.

I woke up at dawn. Next day? Two days? I didn't know. Louis woke up too, stretched, rolled onto his back, waiting to have his stomach scratched. As I obliged, I became conscious of piercing squeals in my dayroom. Pete the canary had probably not been fed. I stood up cautiously, expecting to keel over. But there was no sense of giddiness. I walked slowly into the dayroom. There was Pete, screeching, hopping around in his cage, throwing out sawdust. As I stood filling his cup, I suddenly realized it was the morning watch; it should have been myself and Number One. Maybe I should put in an appearance, it would reassure him to see me on my feet again.

On my way back to the bedroom I passed the desk with the computer. I switched it on. The small black screen came to life. I stared at it, transfixed. It couldn't be . . . But there it was: the day, the date, the hour. I had been sick for no more than eight hours.

When I opened the door, I found Hopla squatting in front of it, asleep. He leaped to his feet. "Co'dore feel good now? Feel good?"

"Where is everybody? I haven't seen anyone for hours!"

He pointed proudly at his chest. "Me! Me say: No! Stop! Otherwise everyone go in: chief, Mr. Mate, Fat Bullock—"

"Fat who?"

"What you call? Bosun. Very angry, want to feed you hot chocolate. What do I do? Say not allowed, Ma Chang feeding him. . . ."

I went up the companionway to the bridge. It was a glorious early morning, a young blue dawn with a new moon just above the horizon. The still-hidden sun lit up feathery ridges of cloud, red and gold. It was like returning from a year in a dungeon.

The wheelhouse was still dark. I said, "Good morning, gentlemen."

182

Two singsong voices replied, "Good morning, Commodore," from the shadows. They were Number One and Number Two, at the chart desk.

"How are we doing?"

The light over the desk was switched on; its greenish glow lit up their faces. A delicate hand pointed at a cross on the pencil line of our course. "Our position ten minutes ago, Commodore. Course two eighteen."

"Good progress since the Cape Verdes, Number One."

"Yes, Commodore."

"Isn't this your watch off, Number Two?"

"Yes, Commodore...." He gave me a sliding look, then glanced towards the back of the wheelhouse.

Captain Cho was standing where he always stood when I was on the bridge, in the starboard aft corner by the radar console. The green light thrown up by the screen was faint, yet there was no mistaking the expression on his face. It was a look of triumph and contempt.

"Good morning, Captain," I said.

"You better have look at your Mr. Slobkous."

"Why?"

He didn't reply, just gazed at me with that look of contempt.

"He's in his cabin, Ome," a voice said from the shadows. I hadn't realized the bosun was there.

Something in his voice made me say, "OK, let's go."

I accompanied him down the companionway, into the corridor that led to the mate's cabin. When we were out of earshot of the bridge, I asked, "What's going on?"

"He's—he's sick, Ome. He's lying on his bunk, unconscious."

It was dark when I opened the door. It took me a moment to adjust my eyes, then I saw Slobkous lying on his back on his unmade bed. He indeed looked unconscious. I hurried to his side; his eyes were half open. Heart attack? Stroke? The ship heeled slowly; I heard a rolling sound behind me. I looked and saw an empty bottle rolling on the deck. The bosun picked it up and handed it to me without a word. *Odschi Dschornia Imported Russian Vodka, 100% proof.*

"And have a look at this," the bosun said. He pulled out a drawer under the bunk. It was stuffed with empty bottles. He must have been an alcoholic of long standing. As the Russians know from generations of experience, vodka is the one booze you can't smell on a drunk's breath.

"Did you know about this, Bosun?"

"Well ..." He looked unhappy.

"He's a notorious drunk, isn't he? That's why he never made it to captain?"

"Well—I guess so, Ome ... Frankly, Ome, however you look at it, after

183

this he'll be no good to you. He'll either be out for the count, or a roaring lunatic throwing things at anyone who comes into his cabin."

In the past I could have coped with that, but not now. I was too old. The only way I could help him was by not reporting it to Fransen. We would have to make a concerted effort to get him sober and spruce him up before we arrived. Until then I would sail the ship alone.

I returned to my dayroom; when I entered, it felt as if I had been away for days. Louis jumped onto my shoulder from Bowditch; Pete hopped and warbled, ruffled his feathers and dragged his beak across the bars of his cage. When I reached inside, he hopped onto my finger, sounded a tiny discordant trumpet, and strutted up and down.

I wondered what my blood pressure was. I went to fetch the gauge and was about to put the cuff on my arm when the thought struck me, What's the use? High or low, I can't deliver this ship and all who sail on her into the hands of Captain Cho. So, better not to know.

I went out on deck and threw the gauge overboard.

I didn't stay around for the splash.

Chapter Six

I hadn't been down to the main deck since Rotterdam. As I made my way through the maze of corridors the next morning, I discovered that the *Isabel* had been transformed into a Chinese ship.

The galley had changed beyond recognition. Instead of the kitchen of a modern hotel where order and efficiency reigned, it now was a steamy Oriental mess. Ma Chang stood at the range, her hair tied in a knot, dressed in a shapeless smock and perspiring heavily. A dozen pots and pans stood bubbling on the stove; on washing lines strung from wall to wall, bundles of dried herbs were swinging. On the table there were Chinese bowls with chopsticks, a basket of what looked like severed ears, a teapot and a vase of flowers. The moment she saw me she stopped stirring, bared the gap in her teeth and dried her hands on her smock. I took off my cap.

"I've come to thank you, ma'am. You probably saved my life." To express my gratitude I took her hand and kissed it. It smelled of the sludge I was still ingesting six times a day. She stared at me with an expression I couldn't interpret. Then she reached up and touched my cheek. "Woo poos," she said, as to a favourite cat. At least, that's what it sounded like.

She guided me to a stool, poured a bowl of tea for me, patted me on the shoulder, pointed at the bowl, then returned to the stove and gave a startlingly raucous shout. One by one pyjamaed sailors appeared in the doorway. Each received one of the pots from the stove and took it away.

184

After the last one had left, she went to a corner shelf, brought a second bowl to the table, pulled up a stool and sat down facing me. She poured herself a bowl of tea and raised it for a toast. "Woo poos," she said, grinning.

On an impulse, I said, "Meow."

That broke her up. "Hoo hoo! Hoo hoo!" she hooted, pointed at me and said, "Meow!" She seemed to consider it the joke of the century. Tears rolled down her lined face, which she dried with the back of her hand. Then she looked at me with her bright eyes and her face took on an expression that in my part of the world would have been interpreted as fondness. She reached across the table and once more touched my cheek.

Even though she could not understand the words, I tried to get across to her some idea of my appreciation. "You worked a miracle. For fifteen years I've been stuffing myself with pills, but you just gave me a series of mysterious dishes, and now look at me; better than I've felt in years." I raised my tea bowl. "Madam, thank you. Godspeed and happy sailing."

She stared at me as if she had understood every word, raised her bowl and made a little speech of her own. I had no idea what the words meant, but the faces in the doorway chorused what I took to be the equivalent of "Hear, hear!" So I raised my bowl in their direction. "Godspeed and happy sailing to you too, gentlemen."

I was getting carried away; it was time to get out of there. I put my cup down, and was about to take my leave when someone appeared at my side. It was Bryn Mawr, the Chinese bosun. "Wa djin joh," he said, and pointed at the door. He must want to show me something. I followed him into the corridor, where the others joined us. We proceeded down to the far end, to the messroom.

A crowd of them were seated at the long tables, having their meal. There was a hubbub of laughter and conversation, but they fell silent when they saw me in the doorway. Bryn Mawr took me to the nearest man, whose T-shirt said Swarthmore, told him something, pointed at me, then pointed towards the galley. I understood he was reporting what he had seen. The man rose, bowed and said, "Won Chang."

I shook him by the hand and, trusting my luck, said, "Glad to know you, Won Chang."

He smiled. "Han chi, Omi."

"H'm. Yes," I said, taken unawares. Heaven knew when they had picked that up.

I went down the line, each man rising, bowing and introducing himself, and saying, "Han chi, Omi."

Suddenly I came upon Mate Number One. He rose, smiled and said, "Happy to see you here, Commodore. This is a surprise."

"Why should it be? These men are all my nephews now. Or so it would seem. *Ome* means uncle."

"Ah ..." He turned and obviously relayed the information, as I heard the word "Omi" several times. They all laughed and applauded.

"Woo!" I cried, in an excess of zeal.

For a second they looked at one another, stunned, then they shrieked, raised their bowls once more and shouted in unison.

"Woo! Woo, Omi!"

After the applause had died down, I asked Number One under my breath, "What does 'woo' mean?"

He hesitated, then replied. "In their language it means 'to perform the act of procreation', Commodore."

"Fancy that," I said.

MY VISIT TO THE GALLEY and the messroom signalled a change in my relationship with the Chinese crew. When I appeared on the bridge, Captain Cho scurried, but Whittier, the little helmsman, in answer to my "Good morning, gentlemen," climbed off his crate, bowed and said, "Omi." The "woo" joke was flogged to death by one of the crew, a low-

186

browed AB called Wellesley, who could not meet me without bellowing, "Woo, Omi!" and killing himself with laughter.

Apart from the odd transgression, I stuck religiously to Ma Chang's diet. To the utter astonishment of the Chinese crew, I sometimes even wandered into the lower regions of the ship in search of the exercise bicycle in the gymnasium. I later recalled the young doctor's advice: "Lay off all booze, coffee, sugar, fats, salt, cholesterol, and I mean all, and you'll be able to cut down on your medication after a month, and toss the lot overboard in three."

That was, in effect, a pretty good description of Ma Chang's diet.

After twenty-two days at sea, we arrived off Rio de Janeiro.

It was early in the morning. The white high-rises of Copacabana and Ipanema were emerging from the morning mist; above them towered the mountains. I recognized the Sugar Loaf, the Pico do Coronado, vaguely discernible in the young light, with its statue of Christ. Standing at the rail outside the wheelhouse, I gazed nostalgically at the most beautiful city in the world.

The pilot launch, a black dot in the golden haze, came foaming towards us and swung alongside with Fransen and the pilot.

"Good morning! You're headed for the general anchorage north of Enxadas Island," Fransen said, as he appeared on the bridge.

"Ah, good morning. Good morning, Pilot. Enxadas Island? In the old days we used to anchor off Viana, where the docks are."

"Can't be done any more, not for a tow of this size," Fransen said. "You'll see a lot of changes."

We became involved in the intricacies of the docking operation while Captain Cho stood frozen and forgotten in his corner. We shortened the hawser and entered the bay, surrounded by busy police launches that treated us as if we were towing a floating atom bomb. The day became hotter as we moved slowly up the channel. Four harbour tugs came barrelling at us, the pilot's walkie-talkie began to speak and snarl in Portuguese.

Once *Agnes* was put to bed by the tugs, the *Isabel* cast off and headed for the fuel docks. When the hoses were in and fuel oil was gurgling down the pipes, Fransen said, "Well, I have some business to attend to, but how about lunch at my hotel? Noon, in the bar at the Lancaster, in Copa?"

"OK, see you." I watched him hurrying down the dockside in his scruffy raincoat, the fedora on the back of his head.

I FOUND FRANSEN at a window table in a bar overlooking the beach and the ocean. After drinks had been served, I said, "Fransen, as I told you before, Mr. Chung cannot send that flawed ship through the Forties with her present captain. If he does, I'm going to raise bloody hell."

He lit a cigarette, inhaled deeply and said finally, with puffs of smoke, "I have to tell you something, Harinxma, which has to stay between ourselves. Mr. Chung, we've found out, has insured the ship for her full replacement value."

"So?"

He frowned. "Come now! A man buys a ship with a serious problem, at a bargain-basement price. He puts on her an untested crew from some remote Chinese island, which means no union and no next of kin who might raise a stink, a staff that still have to learn the ropes and a captain who's a dud. Then he insures her at full replacement value, strings a tow with maximum windage behind her and sends her to the Forties. Now, how does that smell to you?"

"Don't be ridiculous, Fransen. If that ship turns over in the Forties, nobody will come off alive. You're talking about forty-five people!"

"I'm talking about twenty million dollars. That's an awfully big jackpot."

As the idea sank in, I rejected it out of hand.

"No, I won't buy it. The way I see it, the whole history of the ship is one of bungling and last-minute improvisations. It's obvious that young Kwel rammed her through before her concept was tested, and when she turned out to be a lemon, his grandfather sold her to the Third World. No, I'm going to tell Chung that the insufferable, incompetent Cho has to be replaced by an experienced, functioning captain. Even if Chung is the megalomaniac amateur I think he is, he'll realize the danger. I'm phoning him this afternoon."

Fransen took an envelope out of his pocket and handed it to me. "You'd better read this first." I tore open the envelope.

Commodore M. Harinxma, by hand, private and confidential

The letter was written by hand and signed "Arnold Kwel". It was obvious that Miss Bastiaans had taken his dictation in longhand. Why? To make it look personal? Because he wanted to make sure there were no copies?

Dear Harinxma,

During the past half century our relationship has grown into one different from that between owner and master; together, we have seen so much and lived through so many ups and downs in our profession that I think by now we have become friends as well as fellow workers in the same vineyard.

I liked that: it was like Baron de Rothschild telling one of the peasants pressing his grapes with their feet that they were united by a common purpose and in the process of becoming friends.

It is on this basis that I want you to continue in your present position on board the *Isabel* as far as Talcahuano. My reason for this request is as follows.

After the war, Holland never recovered her monopoly in the deep-sea towing business. We are still among the first, but we have to fight to defend that position. The only way we can remain competitive is by being at the head of the pack when it comes to modern tugboats, which means building bigger, more powerful and more sophisticated ships. We have managed to do just that for the better part of a decade; now, with the *Isabel Kwel*, we have run into what is potentially a deadly snag. The ship, despite or possibly because of her mould-breaking originality, has a design fault which renders her unsuitable for the kind of work in which we specialize, therefore we have been forced to sell her. However, we must find out exactly what that fault is and correct it in the design of the sister ship which is now on the drawing board. Already the new ship is far behind schedule; unless we locate and identify the fault within the next few months, we'll fall behind in the race. It would mean the end of Holland's glory as we know it, to which you and I, each after our own fashion, have devoted our lives.

Given the fact that you are now virtually in command of the *Isabel Kwel*, I am asking you to continue as her acting master through both the Atlantic and Pacific storm belts, so as to give the architect who will join you in Rio ample opportunity to determine what exactly is wrong with the ship... At this moment, Harinxma, the future of Holland's glory rests in your hands.

Confident of the outcome, I remain:

> Your friend,
> Arnold Kwel

At first it looked like a sincere plea from one old man to another. But somewhere a bell rang. A word, a phrase, a thought. Then it came back to me: The Hague, head office, Jim Kwel saying, "I gather you're the one who's taking our *Isabel* to Talcahuano." They had planned it way back then. The old buzzard had pulled a fast one on me.

I was outraged. I put the letter back in its envelope, handed it to Fransen and said, "Well, you'd better come clean. Does Chung know that KITCO is planning to crash-test his ship in the Forties?"

"I don't think so."

"You don't think so. And the architect—when is he supposed to arrive?"

"He's here. Probably on board ship by now, with his equipment."

"And the tow is supposed to sail tonight with me as captain?"

"With you as adviser to the captain. Exactly the way you came."

"What makes you think I will?"

He gave me a pensive look. "Harinxma, the old man has been dealing with captains for fifty years. There are certain kneejerk reactions none of us can suppress. He knew that if he gave you a ship, any ship, even this pig, you'd be hooked enough by now to take her through the Forties. With pleasure."

"Fransen," I said, "I don't want any part of this. I'm going to phone Chung. I have already written a full report, which I shall send to him."

He gave me a tired look. "You bullheaded old bastard, can't you get it through your thick skull that on this voyage KITCO speaks for Chung, that I represent KITCO and that if I say, 'The ship will sail,' she sails, captain or no captain? By the time you locate Chung, which may take days, the ship will have left with your precious Chinese crew. If you want to protect them, you'd better be on board. That, my friend, is the bottom line."

So it was. The old man had known that if he had proposed in The Hague that I take the ship through the Forties, I would have turned it down. He had reeled me in slowly, counted on my identifying with the crew until I had turned into a mother hen. The hell with him.

"How about some food?" Fransen asked.

"No, thank you." I rose. "I need to think this over, Fransen. I have to talk to my wife."

"Don't be stupid, Harinxma. Don't tell your wife anything. Just say, 'Guess what, honey! I've been asked to go on to Talcahuano. Nice trip. Just a few more weeks, and the money is very good.' It is, by the way; you'll be paid the same salary as you've received up to now, plus a ten per cent bonus on arrival. You'll be able to build two guestrooms by the time you get back."

So they even knew about that.

THERE WAS ONLY ONE PLACE I knew of where I could get away for a few hours. I took a taxi to the terminal of the funicular railway that went up the mountainside to the giant statue of Christ. When I arrived at the station, a train was about to leave.

At the top, I got out, climbed the steps and sat down at the foot of the colossal statue to look at the view. It was stunning; far below lay the city, a shimmering expanse of white stucco walls and red rooftops, studded with the spires of baroque churches and the slender towers of skyscrapers, looking small and elegant from this height. To the right, the immensity of the blue ocean; across the green-and-cobalt bay, the mountains, shrouded by haze. Maybe it was the serenity of the bird's-eye view, but as I sat there, gazing at the familiar little toy tugboat moored at the fuel dock far below, the trinkets on her paradise tree glinting in the sun, the idea that Chung was a mass murderer became ludicrous. My first concept of him had been correct: old Kwel had run rings round him and used him for his own purposes; he had done the same to me. Naturally I wanted to protect Ma Chang, Hopla and the rest from death by drowning; very commendable. I would have to fool Sylvia along those lines. But there was no point in trying to fool myself. I was going to take the ship to Talcahuano because I wanted to, because I had fallen off the wagon.

I gazed at the sparkling little toy below. I had no illusions about her. I knew that to keep her from sneaking up on me in the Forties would need constant vigilance. She was a killer ship and I would have to be aware of her slightest move, even as I slept. Yet, I could know all that, *all* that, and at the same time realize that I had fallen in love with the pig. She might be a killer, she might be treacherous and ready to play me false, but I was utterly infatuated. It was almost as if the *Isabel* and I were engaged in a lovers' combat, daring each other, in order to establish supremacy.

It was hardly a rational decision. It would certainly be hard to explain to any man who had never owned a sailboat. But as I rode back down the mountain, watching the toy tugboat disappear from sight, I found myself reflecting that every man should, at some point in his life, have a ship of his own, however small, if only to discover that it is better to have loved and lost than never to have loved at all.

THE CALL HOME WAS A TOUGH ONE. The line was bad, but even so Sylvia's distress and dismay came over loud and clear. Finally, I wore her down to weary acceptance, but I had the uneasy feeling that I had strongarmed her. "Now don't worry, love, I'll be fine. Take care of yourself, and give my love to Helen and the others. We'll be in touch. OK? Bye, Syl. Love you."

Back on board, Porks jumped me as I stepped on deck. "While you were ashore, that hotshot architect came on board and had a truckload delivered. The bosun made them pile it all into my workshop!" he cried.

"What kind of a load?"

"Junk! Garbage! A huge pile of it. I haven't got enough room to—"

"All right. Leave it to me. Bosun, go and find the architect and tell him I want to see him."

A few moments later there was a knock on the door and BB came in. "Oh, hello there, Martinus," he said jovially. "Nice to see you again! Well, what's the fuss about?"

"BB, good to see you. Look, it seems you brought some equipment with you which the bosun put into the chief's workshop, and now the chief's hopping mad. What kind of equipment is it?"

"Oh, just a few odds and ends. It seemed prudent to bring along some stores, for emergency repairs."

"Chances are we may have to leave half your junk behind."

"Junk!" he said bitterly. "How's that for gratitude? Sailors!" He slammed out. Just then, the bosun returned.

"Has Captain Fransen told you that you're going on to Talcahuano?" I asked him.

He grunted. "Yes, Ome."

"Has he seen Mate Slobkous yet?"

His face fell. "Sorry, Ome. I couldn't stop him."

"What shape is the mate in right now?"

"So-so. Not unconscious, but he isn't all there either."

"See if you can spruce him up a bit. I'm afraid he'll have to leave with Captain Fransen before we sail." I couldn't possibly take him along through the storm belts.

"I'll see what I can do, but he's not operational, Ome."

The bosun moved heavily out of the room, and I went to see Cho.

When I opened the door, I found him sitting up in bed, smoking his pipe, reading his little red book. The air was heavy with the sweet scent of alien tobacco.

"Captain," I started, "has Captain Fransen been to see you yet?"

His eyes narrowed. "No."

"In that case, I'd better tell you. The Dutch company I work for has decided that the skeleton crew will stay on board to see you and your staff through both the Atlantic and the Pacific Forties, as far as Talcahuano. Mate Slobkous is about to leave, so you and I will have to run the show. I hope that's agreeable to you?"

Suddenly I felt sorry for him. There he was, a young captain, Chung's protégé, yet somehow it had all crumbled to nothing. He stared at me with his small, dark eyes, in stonewalling defiance, and said, "I have no instructions from Mr. Chung to that effect."

"Captain Fransen is Mr. Chung's representative on this voyage. I see no reason why we should go over his head. So, you and I should get together and decide what measures to take as we enter the Forties. Once we start hitting the gales, it's going to be a circus with that windjammer behind us. Now, why don't we talk it through and discuss what needs to be done before it starts to blow?"

He stared at me stone-faced and said, "No. You captured this ship. I will compose telegram to Mr. Chung that I am prisoner on board."

This was ridiculous. "For God's sake, Captain," I said, "don't be childish! Nobody is keeping you prisoner." However grudgingly, I had to admire him for his stand. "Tell you what, you send a telegram to Mr. Chung, and so will I. I'm the adviser, and my advice will be that you are not competent to take this ship and this tow through the Forties. Let's wait and see what he says."

I got up to do it. Then, alas, he caved in. As I went to open the door, he

192

said behind me, "Commodore..." There was a melancholy look on his small unlined face, the sadness of defeat in his dark eyes. "If those are Mr. Chung's instructions to Captain Fransen, I will accept. But Captain Fransen must tell me face to face."

"I'll tell him that."

I left him to confront his moment of truth in private, and made my way back to my quarters, to compose a cable, which would have to be sent via a shore station, as regulations prohibited us from sending telegrams while in port. I made two copies, one to be sent to Kao Hsiung and one to Brussels, hoping that one of them would reach Chung before we were due to sail.

IN VIEW OF INEXPERIENCE OF STAFF AND CAPTAIN AS DEMONSTRATED DURING ATLANTIC CROSSING, I JUDGE IT ESSENTIAL TO WELLBEING OF VESSEL AND CREW THAT SELF AND DUTCH STAFF REMAIN ON BOARD THROUGH BOTH STORM BELTS TO TALCAHUANO STOP FULL REPORT IN MAIL STOP WILL HOLD DEPARTURE UNTIL REPLY RECEIVED SIGNED MARTINUS HARINXMA COMMODORE END.

I sweated through five increasingly tense hours that afternoon until finally the answer was delivered. It was addressed to MASTER, TUGBOAT ISABEL KWEL and it was therefore taken to Captain Cho before I could intercept it.

I found him on his bunk, as always, telegram in hand. He looked stunned; I knew the answer before he handed it to me.

DEAR COMMODORE HARINXMA, APPRECIATE YOUR FRANKNESS AND AM IN TOTAL AGREEMENT PLEASE ACCEPT FULL FACTUAL COMMAND THROUGH TALCAHUANO BON VOYAGE GRATEFULLY, CHARLES CHUNG.

"Well," I said, "that clears the air. Now let's go to the bridge."

He set his jaw. "No. If I am not fit to command, I wish no part of it."

"Cho," I said in a friendly tone, "don't be an ass. We've all had to learn. Why cut off your nose to spite your face?"

I saw from the look he gave me that he didn't know the expression and that it spooked him. He clamped his pipe between his teeth and picked up his little red book, a clear signal. Well, so be it. I had other things to do.

Fransen, whose return I had not been looking forward to, seemed morose when he entered my dayroom an hour before departure. "Mind if I help myself?" He poured himself a stiff one.

"By the way," I said, "I think you should know that I had an exchange of telegrams with Mr. Chung."

He stopped pouring and stared at me. "You crazy, crazy bastard."

I handed him a copy of my telegram and Chung's reply. He read them carefully, folded them and put them inside his black notebook. To my surprise, he grinned. "Good work. The old man will be pleased."

"He will?"

"So should you be. If ever you wanted proof that the murderous little Chink was counting on Cho to scuttle the ship, here it is."

I gazed at him in disbelief. "Run that past me again, will you?"

"Did you expect him to say, 'No, damn it, get off my ship, you old busybody'? In that case, if anything happened to the ship, there would be one expert witness ashore ready to testify that Mr. Chung had been warned, and that the warning was ignored. It would amount to proof of criminal intent. Excellent! You're a chip off the old man's block, apart from providing work for unemployed assassins."

"Now, what's *that* about?"

"How grateful do you think Charlie will feel towards you now you've loused up his game, at least as far as Talca? I'd watch my back from now on, while you're ashore. You wouldn't be the first to be rubbed out by the Chinese Mafia."

I was about to voice a protest, but there was no arguing with him. To Fransen, Chung's evil intent had become an article of faith.

I said, "So now everybody's happy!"

In the thick of our predeparture flurry, with harbour tugs churning alongside, a pilot cutter banging against our flank in the wash of their propellers and the aft deck full of Chinese, a bumboat wormed its way alongside and Fransen got ready to leave with Slobkous.

I went to the port wing of the bridge to watch him being lowered into the bumboat and spirited away. Fransen waved to me and I waved back, and there went poor Slobbo, off in a bumboat, pitching and rolling among the harbour tugs and police launches. I saw that the bosun must have shaved him and filled him up with black coffee and aspirin, for Slobkous looked quite presentable, despite the phoney suntan which was in fact hepatitis yellow. It couldn't be long before his liver packed up, the alcoholic's suicide.

"Well, old fellow," I had said to him with forced good cheer, "I'm sorry to see you go. I could have used you in the Forties."

The *Isabel*, with *Agnes* in tow, sailed at midnight. When the long hawser had been paid out for the two-thousand-mile journey to the Strait of Magellan, I went off watch, and returned to the bridge a few hours later, just as dawn was breaking like a rose over the ocean. We had a brief Happy Hour to celebrate our smooth departure, then the rhythm of shipboard life took hold as Whittier, bless his jolly soul, struck four twins on the ship's bell, starting another chapter in the brief, troubled life of the *Isabel Kwel*.

194

Chapter Seven

During the first week or so after Rio the weather remained beautiful and warm, the sky clear, the wind light and pleasantly cooling. But the moment we crossed the fortieth parallel we began to battle against the Falkland current, which put us back about twenty-four miles a day, and the trouble started.

It began with a beam swell that came heaving in from the southeast, rapidly growing in size until, for the first time on this voyage, I was forced to break the cycle of the *Isabel*'s rolling with the thrusters.

Feeling the change in vibration, BB came up from below in a flash, cried, "Beautiful!" and hurried back to collect his measuring devices, which he took up to the bridge. After a few minutes I saw Porks join him there.

During the past week those two had become fast friends, despite their initial run-in about the stores in the workshop. They were like boys in their enthusiastic hunt for the *Isabel*'s deadly secret. Porks had become young BB's right hand, and after hours of whispered conferences, BB ended up installed on a stool lashed to the console of the starboard aft engine telegraph, surrounded by toys anchored to the bridge deck with adhesive tape, and holding what looked like a toggle switch connected by a cable to an improvised outlet in the wheelhouse wall. Their main area of interest was the foot of the paradise tree, where I spotted them several times during the first days.

This time they came down after twenty minutes and set up BB's clock shop in the corner of the wheelhouse. Porks hovered over the architect, watching dials and whispering readings into his ear. After a quarter of an hour BB muttered, disgruntled, "Too damn tame!" But even so he started to cipher.

A few days later the barometer began to fall. According to the weather charts, a disturbance was coming from the southeastern quarter. This was unusual; I had been hugging the coast, to seek shelter from the prevailing westerly gales. If we were hit by high winds and seas from the southeast there was no way I could keep the dock from being blown into the Bay de los Nodales, off the Argentian coast, an unhealthy place to be in and impossible to get out of.

So I went to put Captain Cho in the picture and to discuss with him the only way to safeguard both the ship and old *Agnes*: to take the runners off the dry dock and sink it.

When I told him that, he looked at me goggle-eyed, momentarily dropping his carefully studied mask of hostile superiority.

"*Sink* the dock?"

"It's a standard operation, Captain," I explained. "Submerging it is not going to endanger it. It's the only way to keep it stationary. If we leave it to float, it will end up on the rocks. After the gale we'll have to pump the water out of the dock again to raise her from the seabed. We have no choice. Also, I intend to cast off the *Isabel*. I want this ship to ride out the gale on her own."

"But what about the yacht?"

"We'll cut her loose and let her float free, attached to the dock by a hawser which will keep her headed into the seas."

"But what if the cable snaps and she breaks loose?"

"We'll give her a sheet anchor." I said that only to pacify him; realistically, if the yacht broke loose she would almost certainly end up as jetsam among the rocks on the beach of the Bay de los Nodales. But that was the name of the game, and no doubt she was well insured.

His jaw set; his face back in its imperial scowl, he stated, "I cannot permit that. I forbid you to put the yacht at risk. I command you to ride out the gale with the dry dock afloat."

So far I had been careful not to throw my weight around more than was strictly necessary. This time I said, as pleasantly as I knew how, "Captain, all I can say is: enter your protest in the ship's log. Now, if you don't mind, I'd like to get cracking."

I left and went to the bridge, where I raised Harakiri on the walkie-talkie. The crackly voice responded, "This is *Agnes*, this is *Agnes*, do you read?"

"*Agnes*, this is *Isabel*. I'm going to submerge you and cut you loose. We have a full gale threatening from the southeast."

There was a silence full of static, then the voice crackled, "I read you, *Isabel*. What about the yacht?"

"I suggest you start cutting the supports and stream her, to ride out the gale. You might also prepare a sheet anchor. Do you read?"

"Affirmative, *Isabel*. Glad you're ordering this in good time. I'd hate to be marooned on this pig's bladder close to the coast. Over."

"Go ahead, *Agnes*. Let me know when you and your runners are ready to be picked up. I'll have a boat standing by, over."

"Roger, *Isabel*. Give me a couple of hours. Over and out."

A few minutes later I spotted through my binoculars runners scurrying on the walls of the dry dock, opening valves and air vents. On the dock floor a few of them were dragging acetylene tanks about; welding cutters started to flicker in the gathering dusk.

I was watching the hawser being winched in on one of the television screens when the bosun turned up in a huff. "Damn it, Ome, I can't get those Chinks to prepare the boat! They refuse." The men on watch were standing about on the boat deck, looking surly and defiant.

"Number One," I asked, "what's going on?"

Before he could answer, Hopla piped up. I hadn't noticed him coming to the bridge with coffee. "They do not want dogs here," he cried dramatically. "No room for pregnant dogs! Wah!"

The telephone on the chart desk shrilled. It was Harlingen. "Skipper? We've got the dock on the blower. Would you take it?"

"Thanks, Harlingen." I picked up the walkie-talkie. "Yes, Harakiri?"

"We have a problem, Harinxma," the crackling voice said. "My Chinks refuse to leave the yacht. They don't want to join your crew. Over."

"That yacht is a derelict! If we get the kind of seas I expect, she's not going to stay in one piece. I won't allow them to risk their lives, so tell them to get ready. I'm sending a boat. Over."

"They're an ornery bunch, Harinxma. If they don't come, it won't be because I haven't tried. Over."

"What's the yacht doing?"

"Standing free now. The moment it has flotation it'll be off and running. Over."

"All right. Expect a boat. Tell your men to stand by on the lee side. Over and out."

Five minutes later he was back on the blower. "I've had an argument with the *mandur*, now he's turning ugly. They're staying aboard the yacht, period. Over."

"But her deck may stove in if she's broached!"

"I told them that, but they won't listen. They refuse to join the Chinks on the tug. What do I do now?" There was a silence while he waited for my answer, then the scratchy voice repeated, "*Isabel*, do you read?"

"Yes, I read. Hold everything. I'm coming over myself. Over and out."

I switched off the walkie-talkie, turned and found the bosun staring at me. "You can't do that, Ome!" he cried. "Look at those seas!"

"I have no choice, Bosun. I must convince those idiots that they're about to commit suicide."

"But, man, you . . . Send someone else! Send *him!*" He pointed at Cho.

I turned to Cho. "Think you could convince them, Captain?"

The Chinese quickly shook his head.

"Well, I'm going to give it a try. Come on, Bosun, you and I'll go. We can handle this boat between us."

At first he looked doubtful, then the spirit of the occasion got to him. "Sure," he said. "We'll show 'em." I heaved myself over the edge of the boat, grunting and huffing. He climbed in with the ease of a gorilla.

A voice beside the boat called, "May I come, Martinus?"

I looked over the edge and found BB standing there, holding fluttering oilskins.

"Have you handled boats before?"

197

"Ever since I was a boy!"

"All right, hop in. Let's go, Bosun."

The bosun reached down and hauled him on board, then switched on the electric motor that worked the davits.

When the boat was lowered and the pulleys had been cast off, the seas seemed much bigger and angrier than they had looked from above. The wind was picking up; if I spent too much time on the dock, we would have a problem getting back. Even now I needed all my strength to hold on to the gunnels. Maybe it was a bit crazy for me to attempt this. I was no longer the man I used to be.

Agnes, as we approached, looked way down; but the yacht was not yet afloat, even though the dock floor was awash. The boat swerved into the lee of the starboard wall like a roller coaster; the swell was running high and fast—there *must* be a big blow on its way to generate this surge. The bosun manoeuvred the boat in for a mooring; I told him and BB to stay where they were.

Harakiri stood waiting for me in whipping oilskins, occasionally up to his calves in the water that came slopping down the length of the dock floor. He threw a line, which BB caught; then he pulled the boat in. I grabbed his outstretched hand the moment a surge brought me level with the dock floor. Before I had found my balance, I was soaked to my knees.

"Good of you to come!" Harakiri shouted into the wind. "Let's hurry! Going to be dark soon! Careful on this ladder! It's very loose!"

When we reached the yacht, I saw that the companionway had been taken down. My heart in my mouth, I climbed the slippery Jacob's ladder against the flank of the yacht, was hauled over the rail and welcomed by staring Chinese faces.

Harakiri joined me. I asked, "Where is the *mandur?*"

"In the lounge with his cronies."

The inside of the old yacht seemed to reek even more pungently of toadstools than it had in Antwerp. Harakiri slid open a glass door. I stepped inside and found myself in a large solarium. A row of windows overlooked the foredeck of the yacht. Lolling in broken-down lounge chairs with stuffing hanging out, were some black-pyjamaed men; one of them got up and came over to us. I recognized the iron-faced *mandur* who had confronted me on the quayside in Rotterdam. He ignored my outstretched hand.

"You must leave this ship, *Mandur*. Your lives will be in danger unless you do. Do you understand what I'm saying?"

He gazed at me with pebble eyes. I was wasting my time.

"Listen," I said. "Wind! Wind is coming: hoo, hoo! Waves: whoosh! This ship: glug-glug! If you stay on board, you're going to be dead, all of you." I pointed at him, then made a throat-slitting gesture.

"So, come with me. Come."

I went to the door, beckoning.

The *mandur* made a gesture as if he were ripping off a mask.

"What does he mean?" I asked.

"He means that if he went on board the tugboat, he would lose face. Well, it's his face or ours. Let's beat it, Harinxma."

I was overcome with anger. I had, somehow, managed to make myself understood by his compatriots on board the *Isabel* at least some of the time, so he must understand the gist of what I was saying. "Friend," I said, "I understand that you and the people of the other island have a feud of long standing. I understand that you'd rather risk your life than lose face to them. But *I* am commander of this convoy. All souls under my command are my responsibility. If you don't come with me, you'll die. And if you die, *I* will lose face. Do you understand that?"

Behind me, Harakiri said, "Come on!"

The cast-iron face remained implacable.

"Very well," I said. "As you wish." I turned away, sick at heart. "Let's get out of here." Outside, I shouted against the wind, "Can you finish lowering the dock and make it to the boat?"

"No problem. I'll close the vents. After that she'll go on filling until the air pressure puts a stop to it! Have we got ten minutes?"

I nodded, but I didn't like it. Time was running out. Harakiri's presence in the boat would be a help; when the *Isabel*'s crew saw us return without the runners—without any pregnant dogs—they might assist us by hoisting the boat back on board.

In the boat I found the bosun and BB who looked as green as a frog. We waited while Harakiri clambered up and down the walls of the dock with impressive agility. It was going down fast and despite the whistling and hooting of the wind, I could hear the roar of air escaping through the vents overhead. Then the yacht started to move.

The bosun saw it first. "Watch out!" he yelled. "Here she comes!"

So she did. Iron beams came crashing into the water as the yacht, with groans of shifting iron, started to drift astern, her bowsprit scraping along the dock's starboard wall with a screeching sound, striking sparks. We cast off to get out of her way; from a distance we watched the old vessel float out of the dock, listing over to starboard, dragging the hawser attached to her anchor chains. For a few moments it looked as if she would turn violently to windward; she rolled heavily, loose objects slid off her decks, doors slammed, windows reflected the sunset in brief orange flashes. Then the hawser sprang taut, the bridle was whisked out of the water and the old ship straightened out with her bow in the seas. She began to rise and pitch like a giant bird. She looked like a good sea ship, as long as she held together. I saw men on her foredeck working lines; then I heard a whistle over the roar of the wind. Harakiri beckoned to us from the top of the starboard wall. "Let's pick him up, Bosun!" I shouted.

We did, with difficulty; when Harakiri was in the boat, we set out towards the *Isabel*, rearing and plunging in the distance. "Let's go! I need a drink!" Harakiri yelled.

Alongside the *Isabel*, Harakiri and the bosun managed to hook in the pulleys simultaneously and a few seconds later the boat was swinging above the water. The Chinese at the winches were on the ball; we were hauled home before the next roller came snorting by, as big as a bungalow.

"All right," I said when we were secure in the blocks, "let's get into some dry clothes and meet in my dayroom. This calls for a moment of relaxation before the gale hits."

Harakiri looked back at the yacht, now sheering behind the dock, streaked by bursts of spray. "Good luck to them!" he said.

We had a brief Happy Hour in the dayroom, before supper. Harakiri seemed to enjoy the communal meal, but for some reason the crew was unusually silent. I took it to be Harakiri's presence until, when dessert came round, Ma Chang placed a new dish in front of me. It was half a canned pear with a little bit of white fluff on top; in it was stuck a thin black stick. Only when she lit it did I recognize it as incense. Pear with incense? I sat looking at it in dismay when, suddenly, there was a sound of handclapping. I looked up to find everyone grinning at me.

Ma Chang stood in the doorway to her galley, clapping her hands and showing the gap in her teeth.

"What's going on, Harinxma?" Harakiri asked. "Is it your birthday?"

"No, it isn't," I replied. "I think they're just pleased to see me."

Pear with incense certainly had its drawbacks, but it was the thought that counted.

A FEW HOURS LATER the full gale hit with the impact of a freight train. I was lying on my bunk for a catnap when the windows were lashed by the first bursts of spray. I had hoped that the old yacht wouldn't be subjected to a force-nine blow, but we seemed to be in for one.

I dressed, hopping about on one leg, grabbing hold of the wardrobe and bunk to keep my footing. When I entered the wheelhouse, the windows were opaque with spray. Night had fallen but when I peered through the revolving clearview disc I saw, in the light of our for'ard floods, mottled black mountains combing towards us, crowned with phosphorescent foam. The low sky seemed to spew water; spray was whisked across the foredeck in horizontal sheets. The ship cleaved the combers with crunching blows, but her gyrations communicated joy rather than agony. She took the seas with ease; she was in her element.

"She takes it well, doesn't she?" I discovered BB was standing

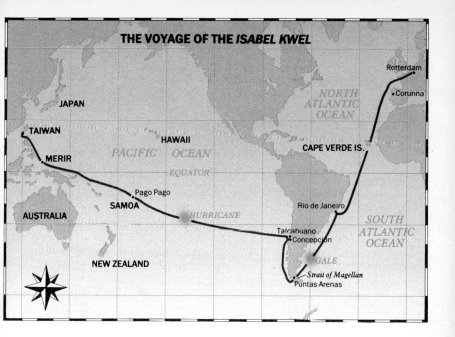

THE VOYAGE OF THE *ISABEL KWEL*

beside me. He still looked pale, but seemed to share the exuberance of the ship. "Let me get my instruments!" He hurried to the door.

I took Number One's place at the radar scanner. The dock appeared as parallel echoes; the yacht, discernible only intermittently among the ridges of the waves, seemed to have remained in place.

BB returned with his folding stool and attaché case, installed himself in the starboard aft corner, and took out his instruments. Then Porks turned up. He appeared to be measuring list, pitch and speed of recovery; BB, with some difficulty, made notes.

At one point we ran into a wave that seemed to stop the ship dead in her tracks; a moment later the for'ard windows were hit by a whiplash of spray that sounded like buckshot. BB came scooting towards us on his stool. Porks and I caught him. Once back on his feet, BB was ecstatic. "This is invaluable, Martinus," he said. "Let's see if we can pinpoint the danger zone by making a few sweeps."

"Wait until this gale's over. I don't want to push our luck."

"But this is perfect!"

"Too rough, BB."

He and Porks collected their toys, muttering.

Number One detached himself from the radar scanner. "Come and look, please, Commodore."

I looked at the screen. Behind the two rectangular islands of the submerged dock the intermittent echo of the yacht, frequently obscured by the ridges of the waves, appeared to be sheering wildly.

"Harakiri! Take a look at this."

The runner captain peered down at the scanner for a long time; then he said, "Looks to me as if one leg of the bridle's come loose."

"So she's hanging on by only one shackle?"

"It's belayed on an anchor chain. The shackle should stand up; the one that broke must have had a crack in it. One should be able to hold."

"Even when she's sheering like this?" The crew must be pretty uncomfortable."

"You told them what the score was, Harinxma. Is it OK if I go below for a while?"

"Take the couch in my dayroom. I'd like to have you around, just in case."

"Let's face it, the only thing that can happen is that the other shackle breaks. In that case, there's nothing I can do. They'll be on their way to the angels."

"What about the sheet anchor? Won't that keep them headed into the seas if they break loose?"

"It may prolong the agony, but it won't hold in this wind. What's to leeward?"

"A reef and a rocky beach. Wherever they end up, it's curtains."

Porks had gone down below; BB was making calculations in his corner; Number One was glued to the radar scanner; the bosun concentrated on the wheel. The wind and the seas seemed to be increasing in fury. There were now frequent crunches when the ship ran into the blank walls of huge waves; the whiplashes of spray were continuous and drowned all conversation. I charted the dock's position and ours every ten minutes; so far it seemed to remain stationary.

Suddenly, Number One called out, "Commodore! Come here, please!"

I hurried to the radar scanner. The ridges of the waves now kept obscuring even the twin echoes of the walls of the dock. But behind them no speck arose, however briefly. The yacht's echo was gone.

Number One asked, "What do you think?"

"Maybe the seas are too high now for the echo to register, or maybe she's out of range. Put the scanner on forty miles."

The screen changed. The waves ran closer together and became faint. The coast of the Bay de los Nodales registered now: the rock towers of Punta Lobos, the mass of Punta Medanosa. Nowhere within the crescent of the coastline was there any sign of a ship.

I looked up. "I'm afraid we've lost her."

Nobody appeared to be shocked, or even affected. The bosun said, gazing up at the compass, "They had it coming."

202

I STAYED ON THE BRIDGE all night, occasionally dozing in a deckchair Hopla had lashed to the console. From time to time I asked Number One—after the watch had changed, Number Two—if there was any sign of life on the radar. There was none.

I slept fitfully, plagued by guilt. By now there could no longer be any doubt: the ancient yacht with its Tiffany lamps and its murals had foundered and was being pounded to flotsam on the rocks of the Bay de los Nodales, and ten men were lost.

But why? The question haunted me. Why had they deliberately sacrificed their lives to save face? All night long I fretted and grieved, like any captain who has lost members of his crew. It was like a parent who has lost a child.

Meanwhile the *Isabel* soared and plunged with sickening surges as the tremendous swell of the angry ocean lifted her to the sky and dropped her into the troughs. When a bleak sun finally rose through clouds like roiling smoke over an ocean in blind fury, I rose arthritically from my deckchair and looked out through the clearview disc at the scene of cosmic violence. It seemed, in the grey daybreak, that I had never seen such a wild and confused sea before. I went to the radar scanner. The two parallel lines of the dry dock were still there, though washed under continuously by racing mountain ridges of oceanic swell; there was no other echo, no ship, nothing but the ridges of the waves for miles around.

Around eleven the wind suddenly dropped. The hills of the swell went on heaving massively, one huge range after the other, but spray no longer lashed the windows. The wind ceased to whistle and shriek in the rigging, and in that sudden stillness, there sounded thin and fragile, but of an inexpressible beauty, the screeching of a bird.

I went out onto the port wing and there it was, planing overhead, white and beautiful, a seagull looking down at us. It seemed a messenger of grace, Noah's dove.

"Commodore!" It was Number Two. "An echo at ten miles, due west."

I went inside to check. At ten miles to the south-sou'west an echo flashed with each sweep. "Looks like a fair-sized vessel," I said. "Probably a coast-guard cutter."

"I'll take a look," said Harakiri, who was now back on the bridge. He took the binoculars out onto the wing. Hopla came with coffee for the watch and a mug of Ma Chang's tea for me, followed by the bosun carrying a tray of sandwiches.

Suddenly Harakiri hollered, "Harinxma! Come and have a look!"

I joined him outside; he handed me the binoculars. "There, on the horizon! Tell me what you make of it."

I had to readjust the binoculars before the image emerged of the inhospitable coastline of Argentina's most desolate region. Profiled against it—vaguely, blurred by haze—was a triangular sail like that of an Egyptian dhow. "What the devil is that?"

"I'll tell you what it is," Harakiri said, taking back the binoculars. "It's that damned yacht."

"It's what?"

"The yacht, I tell you! They must have found a way to *hoist* the sheet anchor! She's under sail, heading our way."

If that was true, the ten dour men in their black pyjamas would have done something worthy of Sinbad the Sailor.

The minutes ticked by. The triangular sail became clearer. Then the superstructure of the antique yacht rose from the horizon. There she was, rising and falling with the swell, her ungainly sail adding a note of panache. I was struck with the most enormous admiration. I set the *Isabel*'s foghorn roaring. It was an irresistible impulse—they must still be too far away to hear us. But a minute later a flare soared skyward from the yacht and burst into a shower of red sparks against the black backdrop of the Punta Medanosa.

"Well, well," Harakiri said. "Now they're even setting off fireworks."

"Fancy that," I said.

My first impulse was to have myself ferried across to the yacht to congratulate the ten men who had pulled off this impressive feat, but the seas were too rough still and I was dead on my feet. When I finally reached my quarters, Louis leaped onto my shoulder, so I took him with me to the bedroom and fell asleep with him on the pillow beside me.

THE YACHT SLOWLY DREW NEARER to the *Isabel* during the afternoon. When I returned to the wheelhouse, it lay to at about three ships' lengths to starboard. Although there was still a fair swell running, I ordered the boat out and, despite the protestations of the bosun, had myself ferried across to the yacht together with Harakiri.

We were swung aboard in a sling. Dangling between sky and heaving sea, with my heart in my mouth, I tended to agree with the bosun.

Once I stood on the yacht's deck, I did something I had rarely done before: I embraced a man. And not just one; all ten. After a startled first reaction, they all responded in kind, even the cast-iron *mandur*, who took Harakiri and me on a guided tour of the deck and showed us the jury-rigged sail.

It was a marvel of creative invention; not only had they lashed it professionally to the mainmast, they had even managed to create a boom by using the central spar of the awning on the aft deck. To trawl in the sheet anchor—which they must have done, as I had seen it go overboard myself—meant risking capsizing her altogether. Yet, under those catastrophic circumstances they had done a job that would have taken the senior class of a naval academy half a day to accomplish on firm ground. There could only be one conclusion: they were superlative sailors.

Afterwards the *mandur* took us to the solarium, where we all sat on the deck in a circle and went through an elaborate ceremony of passing cans of beer from one to the other. Each man took a polite sip, toasting me in the process; I toasted them back. All of this without a word, and, as the swell was still running fast and long, so we all sat swaying in unison, like monks at prayer.

The whole thing brought tears to my eyes. That is a bewildering aspect of ageing: suddenly you cry.

One of them brought in some sinister snacks on sticks, which looked like worm kebabs; I declined with a mute expression of regret. The beer turned out to have a kick like a mule. When I finally rose to leave, I was unsteady on my feet, as well as inclined to resume the embracing. I was helped by many hands into the sling that lowered me back into the bobbing boat below. I landed in an untidy heap at the bosun's feet. Harakiri yelled from above like a concerned parent, "Is he hurt?"

The bosun yelled back, "No! There's a God for drunks!" He heaved me into a sitting position and said, "Now you sit still, Ome. You're lucky you didn't bash your skull in, you crazy old coot."

I forgave him and waved at the Chinese faces lined up at the rail. They waved back and shouted incomprehensible words between cupped hands.

I don't remember the crossing. At a given moment I found myself back in my bunk, being cradled with a sense of exquisite security, with Louis observing me from the shelf above me.

I sang, "Be embraced, ye millions" from the final chorus of Beethoven's Ninth; it set Pete in the dayroom warbling the descant. Then I heard the bosun's voice saying, "Now you calm down, Ome. You're getting everybody upset. Go to sleep."

I obeyed. When I woke, shaking like a leaf, it was dark. On my bedside table stood a tray with the familiar three little bowls of Ma Chang's prison fare. Louis was curled up on my pillow; Pete was silent. The ship was silent too, apart from some secretive creaking and clanking as she slowly rolled in the tail end of the swell.

I looked at my alarm; it was ten o'clock. I drifted back into sleep with the happy thought that I knew where my children were, every single one of them: back under the wings of the hen.

WE BEGAN RAISING THE DOCK again the next morning. Still weary from my visit, I moved the *Isabel* alongside the submerged port wall. Porks and his Number Two were ferried across to the pumping shed to start the motor. But after the dousing the old engine had received,

it was out of action, so we had to empty *Agnes* with our own equipment.

We towed across by boat our six-inch hose, with its bright orange floats, and Porks connected its coupling to the port bilge pipe. Then he and the Number Two were ferried back and hc started our large-capacity pump, which proceeded to empty the dock at the rate of five hundred tons an hour. It would take us forty hours to bring it back to its original flotation.

The problem was what to do with the yacht. I discussed it with Harakiri on the walkie-talkie and decided to have her towed by the dock.

The weather had turned; as I looked at the sea now, the whole episode seemed like a bad dream. The sky was clear, as always after a big blow, the sea a glassy infinity of slowly heaving swell, as if breathing in its sleep.

The next morning the ship's pumps finished bailing out the dock and I went to the bridge to move the *Isabel* into position to pick up the bridle.

That evening we sailed into the night, still on the short hawser to give the dock momentum before paying out the full length. The yacht was streamed behind *Agnes*. Now afloat at its normal height, the citadel looked forbidding with its rust-streaked ramparts, vermilion and orange in the glow of the setting sun, and beyond her the yacht's lamps and lanterns began to mingle with the stars as darkness fell.

Chapter Eight

I had worried about the Strait of Magellan; I remembered it as a tricky passage with fierce currents and sudden squalls of cyclonelike winds. As it turned out, Fransen showed his mettle as a professional this time. He turned up with a fleet of harbour tugs, five for the dock and one for the yacht, and took control of the operation. Four of the tugs sucked onto the flanks of the dry dock like leeches, two on each side, the fifth acted as tailholder, and so, with the *Isabel* roaring at full speed, the convoy churned through the first two narrows on the Atlantic side, with tugs providing steerage. It looked deceptively easy.

We made Punta Arenas, the stark little harbour town at the tip of the South American continent, within forty-eight hours. There the yacht was moored and delivered to her owner, a man so rich, Fransen told me, that he collected antique yachts the way simple millionaires collect antique cars. The *Isabel* was boarded by a bevy of government officials from a launch.

Fransen took me to meet the owner the moment we were cleared. We found Mr. Salan in the solarium of the yacht, surrounded by officials studying the murals with museumlike earnestness. He was blond, blue-eyed, in his thirties. "Hey," he said to Fransen when he saw us come in, "please dine with me! There is an excellent restaurant in my hotel." He moved towards the door. "Let's have a drink first, then dinner."

I would have preferred to relax, read my mail and go to bed; I had been on my feet for the better part of the past forty-eight hours. But after a nudge from Fransen I gave in gracefully and the owner took us to his hotel, a yellow building I had spotted from the bay. There he tried to force some local hooch on me while waiting for the menu.

"I'm afraid that's out," I said. "I'll take a pot of Chinese tea."

"*Madre de Dios!* What is this diet?" He turned to call the waiter; as he did so, Fransen looked at me meaningfully, then nodded in the direction of a set of glass doors behind our host. At a small table in the next room sat Captain Cho; he was listening earnestly to a black-haired gentleman sitting with his back to us.

"Let's order," our host said.

While explaining to him why I was restricting myself to a salad and an apple, my mind was on the scene next door. Had Cho been to Punta Arenas before? How else could he know anyone here well enough to have a meal with him? Then the waiter brought them a second round of drinks and the other man turned. It was Chung.

The meal seemed endless. While Mr. Salan explained his plans for the yacht I asked myself why Fransen hadn't told me that Chung was here. And how had Cho heard? Harlingen would have alerted me if the information had come through the radio room. Probably there was nothing to it. Chung was the owner ... It was time for me to retire. I excused myself, and left Salan and Fransen ordering coffee and Tia Marias.

The moment I was outside I nearly took off. There was a full gale blowing, howling down the street, which was empty even of cars.

As I struggled downhill towards the harbour, the only living thing I met was a cat trying to cross the street; it was whisked across diagonally as the gale hit it. I finally reached the ship, stumbled to my dayroom, and fell into bed.

THE NEXT MORNING, when I was about to go ashore, and already had my greatcoat on, there was a knock on the door. I shouted, "Come in!" and there was Mr. Chung, radiating bonhomie, eyes twinkling with good humour.

"Good morning, Commodore! How was the trip from Rio?" He caught me unawares; I hadn't expected him to turn up wreathed in smiles, for Cho must have told him that BB was crash-testing the *Isabel* at his expense during the voyage.

"Good morning, Mr. Chung. Good to see you." I continued recklessly, "I caught a glimpse of you last night at the hotel with Captain Cho. Fransen and I were having dinner there with the owner of the yacht."

"Ah," he said, "I wish you had made your presence known. We could have settled it last night." He moved to the couch. "May I sit down? There's something we should discuss."

"I see." I took off my coat and sat down to face him.

He smiled. "Commodore, how would you like to stay on as mentor to Captain Cho? Well, let's be precise: remain in your role of convoy commander *de facto* after Talcahuano?"

"Stay on to where?"

"Taiwan. After delivering the dry dock, this ship is to pick up a new tow for Kao Hsiung: a forty-thousand-ton liner that has been used as a prison ship by the Chilean navy and sold to my company for scrap. She's big, but no problem for this ship. I presented the situation to Captain Cho, who does not feel qualified to take on an object of that size. Especially since we're in the hurricane season in Polynesia."

He said it without a hint of guile, his eyes were like a baby's.

"I'll have to think it over, Mr. Chung."

"Of course. You have ten days before Talcahuano, plenty of time to think it over. There are a few details that may help you reach a decision. First, I'll pay you the same salary for the rest of the voyage, with a ten per cent bonus on arrival. And if it would amuse Mrs. Harinxma, she would be welcome to sail part of the way with you—say, from Samoa to Taiwan. We'd pay for her air fare, of course." He smiled and rose. "Think it over, Commodore. Let me know your decision in Talcahuano. By the way, let's keep this confidential until you have made up your mind. *Bon voyage*."

"But what about Captain Cho?" I asked as I followed him to the door. "Shouldn't he be replaced?"

He turned, and for once he did not smile. "Captain Cho will serve only to conform with the legal regulations. When it comes to sailing the ship, he will be a figurehead. He is happy with that arrangement, and so am I. Good day, Commodore."

"Good day, sir."

He slipped out, leaving me staring at the door.

WHEN WE LEFT, early the next morning, it was strange to see the dry dock behind us without the yacht. *Agnes*'s silhouette was different too. Two aluminium trailers had been welded to the top of the starboard wall, one to accommodate the runners and one for Harakiri; they looked flimsy on the ramparts of the old citadel.

As the convoy slowly made its way west, snow-capped mountains began to crowd in on us. It was a grim, desolate landscape with a strange beauty of its own. At nightfall we anchored in a chilly fjord that was already dark while the main channel was still lit by the setting sun.

Our last day was a voyage through the Ice Age. Glaciers descended to the blue-green water, a hazy sun occasionally appeared from behind the clouds, and whirling gusts spiralled down the canyons. When we entered the channel north of Isla Desolacion, the wind howled, night was falling and the incoming tide nearly brought us to a standstill. By the time we reached Cape Pilar it was pitch dark, and the weather stormy. I had my hands full keeping ship and dock headed into the wind and tide. I was too preoccupied for a gracious goodbye to the pilot, who was picked up by a launch which vanished amidst whorls of lashing rain, instantly swallowed up by primeval darkness.

As soon as we came out of the lee of the cape, we met the Pacific greybeards: foam-mottled black waves, awesome in size. The slowly rising hills of water lifted the three-thousand-ton ship effortlessly to where the wind whistled and the rain streaked green and red through the beams of the navigation lights; they held her there for a moment, then sent her tobogganing down into the windless valley before lifting her to the crest of the next hill. The dry dock's lights disappeared in the valleys so I lengthened the hawser to a full mile, to lessen the stress.

Once the *Isabel* was settled on her course, I handed the bridge to Number One. There had been no sign of Captain Cho since Punta Arenas; and after Chung's offer I had decided to forget the moody young man in his cabin altogether. When I entered my suite I lay down on the bed fully dressed, ready to return to the bridge if I was called.

The swell seemed to strain the entire body of the ship. The wainscoting creaked and the door to the dayroom rattled as the propellers accelerated each time a giant wave lifted the stern to the surface. Sleep was out of the question; I lay there listening, waiting for the call from the bridge, until I was woken by the bosun putting down a tray on the bedside table and saying cheerfully, "Breakfast, Ome."

When I came back to the wheelhouse, day was breaking behind the immense and sombre range of the Andes. We were passing the outer island of the Evangelistas. The lonely lighthouse high up on a cliff flashed its last signal of the night and went out when the sun rose over the mountains, just as we wallowed past, rising and falling with the massive swell. The first rays of the sun were reflected by the aluminium trailers on the wall of the dry dock when it rose momentarily to the top of a wave, a mile behind us. To the west, bright patches of early sunlight raced across the stormy sea, chased by slanting squalls of rain. The sight was breathtaking; Number One and I gazed at it with awe. We were not alone. The bosun, who came to take over the wheel, was stopped in his tracks. When BB entered the wheelhouse, he too was silenced by the spectacle.

After a while he took me aside. "Say, this wave action is perfect for our final testing! I'm ready when you are."

I thought the swell was too steep and dangerous to dare it with this sick ship, but as it was essential that the *Isabel*'s deadly secret be ferreted out or there would be no sister ship, I decided not to be overcautious, and he got his way.

Even so, while trying to induce *Isabel*'s suicidal rolling cycle among the greybeards of the South Pacific, I very nearly turned her over because of the relentless urging by BB, who egged me on, his wretched toggle switch always in hand. During a few endlessly protracted seconds I was certain she was capsizing; she seemed to lie flat on her side while tobogganing down a slope that looked like the Matterhorn.

As proof that it was not all in the mind, as soon as she righted herself a bug-eyed Carleton came streaking up to the bridge, yelling something which Hopla translated as "Ma Chang stove walking in the kitchen!" I went to have a look and, indeed, the three-ton range in the galley had broken loose from its foundations and was setting fire to the plastic wall covering. The blaze was put out, but everyone on board was sleepwalking with shock after that little episode. BB, proving that genius was closely related to lunacy, chortled with glee as he sat ciphering on his stool lashed to the console, oblivious of the yawning jaws of death outside. At the end of his calculations, he cried, like Archimedes in his bath, "*Eureka!* She *will* capsize!"

"He has to do *sums* to find that out?" the bosun asked, incredulous. An hour later, when I was about to take a nap before my watch, BB and Porks burst into the dayroom in a state of euphoria. "Martinus! Listen to this! It's—it's *elegant!*"

"Got any paper I can draw on, Skipper?" Porks asked.

I went to my desk and handed him a pad and a pencil.

"Let's start with the general subject of stability," BB began.

"Stability is determined by the distance between centre of gravity and metacentre. Show him, Porks."

Porks drew a cross-section of a ship with a mast in the centre. On the mast he made a cross and marked it 'M', in the body of the ship he drew a cross marked 'G'.

"The distance between these two is known as MG," BB continued. "The smaller the MG, the less stable the ship; when the centre of gravity coincides with the metacentre, the ship turns turtle. In the case of this ship, in seas coming in at a specific angle of attack, height, speed and wave train, a rapid diminution of MG takes place, which will be catastrophic if not instantly corrected. Draw it for him, Porks."

An engineering student would have grasped it; I soon lost my way, so Porks elaborated. "The danger zone is very confined: this narrow sector of incoming seas, over both starboard and port bow. If we hit this precise angle, together with the critical combination of other factors, she'll start the cycle."

"And if you allow her to continue on that cycle for more than a few minutes," BB added, "she'll capsize."

"Who would leave her on that cycle? The moment the officer of the watch realizes she's cycling, he'll correct it with the thrusters, as I've been doing all along."

"You realize that on a course to Taiwan she'll be crossing the hurricane belt at the height of the hurricane season?" Porks asked ominously.

"I do."

He and BB exchanged a look. "In that case, now that we know that she may eventually turn over," BB said, "we feel morally obliged to prevent that happening under any circumstances."

"I don't understand."

"Suppose the ship is on automatic and the angle of attack changes imperceptibly. If she starts the deadly rolling cycle while the officer of the watch happens to be incapacitated, she would go down with all hands within minutes."

"What are you driving at?" I asked, bemused. "There are never less than two people on the bridge, the helmsman and the officer of the watch. Not only the Chinese mates but the helmsmen know the procedure, so the one who isn't incapacitated would take her off automatic and throw her head off course with the bow thruster."

"Suppose both are incapacitated at the same time," Porks persisted.

"What exactly are you two proposing?"

They exchanged another look; then BB replied, "We would take down the paradise tree in Talcahuano before she sails."

"That would make her safe under any and all conditions," Porks added.

I had difficulty keeping my face straight. "Gentlemen," I said earnestly,

"I appreciate your concern. But I'm afraid we can't do that without specific instructions from Mr. Chung. Sorry, the answer is 'no'."

Porks stared at me, then said cryptically, "None so blind as those who will not see." He gathered up his drawings and they left in a huff.

After they had gone, I mulled over what they had said. It had now been established that the ship's flaw, which had become a sort of joke among the crew, was indeed a mortal danger to the inexperienced or the amateur. Captain Cho might be either or both; in any case, the West Pacific during the hurricane season was an unhealthy place for a man like him. If I still doubted whether or not I should accept Mr. Chung's offer, this should settle it for me: it was no longer merely a question of my wanting to take the ship to Taiwan, it was—well, my sacred duty. I had pledged myself to the wellbeing of ship and crew in Rio; this was merely the follow-up.

Take down the paradise tree? Over my dead body.

A WEEK LATER WE ARRIVED off Concepcion Bay in a thick, warm fog. I was all set to wait offshore for the weather to clear when, suddenly, the local naval authorities at Talcahuano, twittering on the VHF, insisted we move inside to the quarantine anchorage for fear that local traffic might pass between tug and dry dock and get fouled in our hawser.

As this operation was against my better judgment, I decided I needed to be legally covered, so I sent Whittier down with my compliments to Captain Cho requesting his presence on the bridge, as we were entering port. When he did not turn up, I went myself. As usual I found him in his dressing gown, lying on his bunk, smoking his pipe, reading quotations from, I assumed, Chairman Mao.

"Cho," I said breezily, "get yourself to the bridge at the double; we have to enter Concepcion Bay in a pea souper and your presence is legally required." As I left, I managed not to slam the door.

Five infuriating minutes later he turned up and headed straight for his corner. I stopped him in his tracks by saying, "Captain, the Chilean navy requests that we enter port despite weather conditions. Do you give your approval and wish me to execute the manoeuvre for your instruction?" He nodded imperceptibly. Then I added, with the best of intentions, "Would you also be so good as to man the radar, Captain? Both mates are with the lookouts on deck. We need an extra pair of eyes."

He said tonelessly, "I wish you to execute the manoeuvre, Commodore."

I really did need the extra pair of eyes, so I said in a reasonable tone of voice, "Captain Cho, I'm going to pull rank on you. Get yourself to that radar screen at the double!"

Too late, too late. Not only had I made him lose face, I had decapitated him in front of Whittier and Hopla, who had appeared on the bridge with tea. Deeply offended, Cho slowly paced towards his corner, where he turned round to face me and took root.

To make matters worse, I added, "I'll have to report this to the owner." I flicked the switch of the automatic repeat on the foghorn. Braying like a brontosauran ass, the *Isabel* barged into the fog, full speed. This being a fairly standard operation, I ventured into the cloud without any undue surge of gastric juices; then, suddenly, the bosun sang out, "Small echo approaching at twelve o'clock, one mile, Ome!"

I went to take a look. The little vessel, approaching fast on a collision course, turned out to be a launch carrying Fransen and a number of important-looking uniformed gentlemen wreathed in gold braid.

On board there was a flurry of saluting and handshaking. "The admiral would like to take command of the convoy," Fransen said, deadpan.

"It will be my pleasure," I said, equally deadpan. "But as I am only the adviser to the captain, may I present to you Captain Cho?" I strode to Cho's corner. "Captain Cho, the admiral requests permission to take over command of the tow. What are your wishes?"

He gave my jugular a look of mute contemplation, then he nodded.

I said, "Thank you," turned on my heel and announced, "Captain Cho gives his consent."

Fransen looked at me through narrowed eyes and asked, in Dutch, "What are you trying to do, Harinxma? Toss a cigar into the gunpowder?"

"Sorry, he got my goat this morning. Can these people handle it?"

He shrugged his shoulders. "It's their dock," he said.

"But it's my boat," I retorted.

"I see," he said. "You've decided to accept Chung's offer?"

"Yes," I said.

"In that case, take a look at this at your leisure." He pulled out an envelope with KITCO's logo. The address was handwritten.

"Commodore? Are we ready to proceed?"

It was the admiral, short on patience.

"Absolutely, sir," I replied, stuffing the envelope into my pocket. "What are your orders, sir?"

"I want Captain Gonzales to take over. He is the pilot."

"At your service," I said, smiling. Between the two of us, we managed to nudge the convoy into the quarantine anchorage in the southwest corner of the bay. All this purely by radar, with a visibility of less than a hundred feet.

Then, just as I was wondering how to convey to the gentlemen that we couldn't just stop and anchor with old *Agnes* behind us, an irresistible mass in motion, the fog suddenly thinned. A breath of a wind blew the haze away and revealed a deep blue bay, a green shore, the white tumble of a city, the massive mountain range of the Andes. We turned out to be

214

surrounded by a reception committee of harbour tugs, launches and, obscurely, landing craft, all waiting to put *Agnes* to bed. The harbour tugs got hold of her, we reeled in the hawser and the stretcher; then the admiral and his entourage were taken off by landing craft and I took over. I collected the bridle, waved at Harakiri and the runners and headed for a customs wharf, while Captain Cho stood in his corner.

After customs had come and gone, I collapsed on the couch in my dayroom and Fransen made for the fridge. "Before you zonk out, old buddy, you'd better read the letter from the old man."

I pulled the envelope out of my pocket, and started to read.

Dear Harinxma,

I was alarmed and distressed to learn of Mr. Chung's surprising and highly suspect request that you stay on in your present capacity after Talcahuano, which was conveyed to me in the same letter in which he lodged a formal complaint about our abusing his ship by stress-testing her for our own purposes. In my opinion—this, of course, is to be strictly confidential—you would be toying with what is potentially an extremely dangerous situation.

I do not wish to sound unduly alarmist, but I must urge you to leave the ship together with the others in Talcahuano. I have no idea what form Mr. Chung's action might take, but of this you can be sure: he would exact retribution, or his honour and self-esteem would suffer. You have done a sterling job on this assignment; now, at the height of your achievement, the time has come to withdraw ... I cannot tell you, dear Harinxma, how seriously I view the situation.

I look forward to seeing you on your return and assuring you in person of my sympathy and appreciation. Miss Bastiaans joins me in sending you our most friendly greetings. I ask you to burn this letter without delay.

"Well, did he write what I think he did?" asked Fransen.

"I suppose so," I said, folding the letter.

He sighed and shook his head. "Mind if I pour myself another shot?"

"Help yourself."

At the fridge, pouring, he said, "Don't do it, Harinxma. Don't stick your head in a noose. Chung sure as hell doesn't want someone on the bridge capable of keeping her upright in force-twelve weather."

"For God's sake, Fransen! If Chung is planning to scuttle the ship, why hire me to keep her afloat? His offer is perfectly straightforward. Cho couldn't handle a forty-thousand-ton tow in a hurricane."

He gave me one of his appraiser's looks. "Harinxma, old buddy, if you ask me, Captain Cho is perfectly capable of towing anything, on condition he hasn't got *you* breathing down his neck."

"Don't be ridiculous! The man's totally incompetent."

"Seriously: when have you seen him do his job? When has he had a chance to act as master?"

"What the hell are you talking about?" I sat there, stunned. Had I not given Cho a chance to take control of the ship? I had, but he hadn't taken it. On the other hand, as recently as an hour ago I had treated him as an apprentice and told him I would report him to the owner ... "But he *is* incompetent!" I cried. "You have a nerve to tell me that I'm riding roughshod over the poor devil! Not giving him a chance to sail the ship! I don't know what your game is, buddy, but—"

Suddenly he turned on me. Not in anger; it was as if a mask dropped and I was suddenly faced with the real man—weary, shrewd, but with an unexpected concern for me as a person. "Harinxma," he said, "I hate to do this to you, but let me tell you what the old man's *real* worry is. He's afraid he conditioned you too thoroughly, that now you're smitten with the pig and your Chinks to the point where he can no longer control you and order you off the ship."

"What in God's name are you talking about?"

"Listen to me, I'm serious. I'm not going to tell you this twice. If you stayed on and kept this ship upright in the hurricane zone the way you did in the Forties, you'd be lousing up Kwel's endgame."

"His what? For God's sake, Fransen, stop talking in riddles!"

"Now that the old man has the information he needs for building the sister ship, he is happy for Chung to execute his little scheme and let this pig scuttle herself under the command of the young Chinese captain. This ship is a killer of the inexperienced. Now, the way I see it is that as from this moment, Chung's and old Kwel's interests converge: they both want her dead and gone. Chung because he wants the insurance jackpot, Kwel because he doesn't want the Chinks to start competing with KITCO in the Far East, with one of our own capital ships. It's as simple as that. And now forget I ever told you."

He knocked back the rest of his drink, put down the glass and pulled another envelope from his pocket. "So"—he tossed the envelope onto the coffee table—"here are the airline tickets for your bosun, Porks, Harlingen, Harakiri, BB and yourself. Departure time twenty-two hundred hours tonight, by LAN Chile to Santiago." He took out his notebook and leafed through it. "You're all booked in at the Sheraton Cristobal. Tomorrow you leave for Amsterdam by KLM." He produced another envelope. "Here's one thousand bucks; you'll have to pay the hotel in cash." He put it on the coffee table with the tickets and gave me another of those looks. "Don't be a fool, Harinxma. I don't know what Chung's game is, inviting you to stay on. It doesn't make sense to me, but then I don't have a Chinese mind. Maybe Cho is in league with him, after the

216

buddy-buddy way we saw them talking together in the hotel in Punta Arenas. Maybe they were plotting to push you over the edge, who knows? But of one thing you can be damn sure: there's something in the wind. So, be wise and scram before Chung pulls the lever and you find yourself dangling from a rope." He lit another cigarette and rose. "You're an ornery old bastard, but we'd like to have you around for a little while longer." He went to the door. "Oh, wait a minute: your mail." He produced a handful of letters from a pocket of his raincoat. "This little parcel is pills, I had to sign for them at customs. Well, I'll go and see the others. I want everybody off the ship and on board that ten-o'clock flight for Santiago."

Before I could say anything, he had stepped into the corridor and closed the door behind him. I pocketed the envelope with the money, but left the tickets with my mail. I had to get off the ship; I had to think this through.

At the top of the companionway to the deck I was waylaid by Porks. "What's this I hear, Skipper? You're carrying on to Taiwan?"

"It's been suggested," I said, brushing past.

It was a relief to get off the ship. Right opposite was a square, very Spanish, with a terrace cafe in its centre. I sat at an ornate iron table and ordered a glass of Pisco Sour to help me think.

I would have fallen for old Kwel's concern about my becoming the butt of Mr. Chung's ire if Fransen hadn't revealed that, from here on in, Kwel's and Chung's interests converged—if Chung was indeed bent on scuttling the *Isabel* for the insurance money. It seemed painfully obvious to me that Fransen was right: old Kwel's real concern was that if I were to remain on board, the ship was likely to arrive at the destination and might start to compete with KITCO in the Far Eastern market. And as for Kwel's suggestion that Chung wanted my scalp because I had despoiled his honour? To my mind, he had used it as a ploy to stop me staying on. As usual, all this plotting and scheming had the opposite effect from what Kwel had intended. I was more determined than ever to see the ship to Taiwan.

"Commodore?"

I looked up and, talk of the devil, there stood Captain Cho, frail and challenging. "Captain! Sit down. Can I buy you a drink?"

He sat down without a word.

"Well," I said, "what'll you have? If you like peach brandy, I can recommend the local cocktail."

He shook his head, then said as if in response to a radioed command, "Commodore, I honour you."

"Well—er—look, Cho—"

The waiter came and flicked the table with his napkin. "*Si?*"

"One Pisco Sour and one mango juice, *por favor.*"

217

The waiter flicked the table again and walked off.

"I honour you," Cho repeated. "We do not always see eyes to eyes, but you are an honourable person, a great commodore distinguished in wars. I can submit to you without losing face."

"Cho, I'm glad you brought that up. I just sat here, thinking—"

"But if you go and a new captain comes, I will be disgraced. You say, 'Captain Cho cannot sail tow across the Pacific, someone else must be sent to take his place.' If that happens, I am dishonoured. I cannot continue in this profession." He fixed me with a baleful stare that, for some reason, gave me a chill of discomfort. "Please—" He was interrupted by the waiter putting two glasses in front of us.

"Don't take it so hard," I said, "there's no need. I'm sorry I told Mr. Chung that you were—er—expendable. I suggest that from now on you make it known whenever you feel in need of instruction or enlightenment. Any time you wish to consult me or—er—confide in me, that sort of thing, just shout." It wasn't much of a fatherly speech, but it was the best I could come up with. He really had touched a chord.

The boy said abruptly, "Mr. Chung sends greetings."

"Ah? Thank you."

We sat in uncomfortable silence. "Why don't you start by joining the Happy Hour?" I suggested jovially. "You know: join in, be one of the boys. We're a friendly bunch—I mean, you're welcome any time."

He looked at me without replying. His face seemed to take on a fleeting expression of melancholy, defeat. For a moment, it was as if a door were opened briefly, a sudden perception revealed; then it passed.

"I must go," he said, rising. "Thank you for the drink."

I said, "My pleasure."

He bowed slightly and walked away, an alien figure among the pigeons.

I sat sipping my drink. How could I refuse the appeal of a youth I had wronged, however unintentionally? I could see his point, it was as plain as a pikestaff: if I turned down Chung's offer, he would fly in another Chinese captain and Cho would lose face beyond hope of recovery. I owed it to the poor boy to stay on.

Before ingesting the last of my drink, I raised my glass to the pigeons, the sky, the sun, all the good things in life. "All right, Polynesian hurricanes," I said happily, "let's dance."

I PLACED A CALL to Sylvia from a small hotel behind the plaza. The telephone in the booth rang after a surprisingly short time. Sylvia was on the line.

"Martinus?" she asked. "When are you coming home?"

"Well, love, that's what this call is about. Mr. Chung has asked me to stay on board as acting convoy commander as far as Taiwan. I think I should accept. He suggests you join me in Pago Pago for the trip to Kao Hsiung."

There was a long silence.

"Sylvia? Are you there?"

"Yes." Even across all those miles of ocean I could hear her shock and distress. "But why you? Can't they replace the Chinese captain? If they need an adviser on board, can't Kwcl appoint someone else?"

"It's too late for all that, Syl. To find a replacement for the Chinese captain would take forever. And for Kwel to start shopping around for another retired captain—"

"But why Taiwan, love? I can understand you wanting to stay on as far as Pago Pago to see them across the Pacific, but from there on it's all plain sailing, isn't it? And with the loose boat, no tow to worry about? Surely the captain, however incompetent he may be, can take a loose boat through Polynesia at this time of year?"

"There's going to be another tow, love. A forty-thousand-ton derelict liner to Kao Hsiung for scrap. He won't be able to handle that, not in the hurricane season."

"For God's sake, Marty, you're seventy years old, you have hypertension, and you've had one gale already in the South Atlantic! And now the hurricane season! They *must* bring in someone else!" She sounded desperate.

"Syl, you must understand—"

"I understand all too well!" she cried.

There wasn't much else to say; she didn't know if she'd be able to join me in Pago Pago, she thought probably not. She made the dog bark into the telephone, which was always the last resort; then we said goodbye until Pago Pago and she wished me Godspeed and happy sailing. It was a sad conversation, really; it left me depressed.

I walked back to the ship across the square, pushing other thoughts aside. I had a ship to sail.

When I reached the dockside, I had the shock of my life: the ship was gone! She must be at the fuel dock; Captain Cho had taken her there without me, and without my permission!

I called a taxi and raced to the fuel dock on squealing tyres. When we arrived, I saw the *Isabel* approaching, half a mile offshore.

I paid the driver and waited, arms akimbo, for the ship's arrival. When she swung round to back into her mooring, I recognized young Cho peeking from the bridge. It was all very well, my decision to encourage him to gain self-confidence, but this was reckless to a degree.

I had to admit that he moored her deftly, but that was as far as it went. I leaped on board, gave him my honest opinion of his rash behaviour and told him in a fatherly fashion how extraordinarily lucky he had been. I also told most of Talcahuano; even the gulls on the bollards ashore seemed interested. I left his emotional and spiritual remains on the boat deck, where our discussion—walking slowly, he mostly backwards—had taken us, and went to my dayroom.

As I entered, I received the second shock of the day: lounging on the couch, glass in hand, lay Fransen. He gave me a broad grin and said, "Well, well. How to make friends and influence people. That was a vintage performance, old chap."

"What the hell are *you* doing here? Didn't you notice that Cho was taking the ship out?"

"Of course. I told him to. I thought it would be an educational experience for you to see it demonstrated that he can actually sail this ship. I thought it might help change your mind."

I could have strangled him with my bare hands. "Now, you stay off my goddamn bridge and stop giving orders to my staff! What's more, there's one hell of a difference between taking this ship from one side of town to the other on a windless bay and sailing her across the West Pacific hurricane zone with a tow of forty thousand tons!"

"Harinxma," he said amiably, "you're the stubbornest old mule in the fleet. You should give the poor little fool some room to breathe. You're going on to Taiwan, I gather?"

"I sure as hell am."

"Then may I have my thousand bucks back? And the air tickets?"

I fetched them from my desk and tossed them onto his chest.

"OK," he said. "Now, Chung has wired through the details of the hulk. As you're going to tow the damn thing, let me tell you about it." He produced his dog-eared notebook. "You may have known her in her heyday. She was built in '33 as the *Princess of Orange*.".

My anger suddenly subsided. "What? How did the *Princess* get here?"

"Let me see." He flicked the pages. "Present name, *Alfonso Mendozo*, navy brig stationed in Talca since '65. Ex *Sun Queen*. Ex *Helios*. Ex *Principessa Antonia*. . . ."

While he reeled off the stages of the great ship's decline, I saw her as I had seen her as a young man before the war, when I had served as skipper of a harbour-tour boat in Amsterdam. The departure of the *Princess of Orange* had been one of the most romantic sights in the busy port. The flagship of the Netherlands Steamship Company, she sailed between Amsterdam and Indonesia, then the Dutch East Indies. She was the most graceful and luxurious liner under the Dutch flag.

"What condition is she in?"

He shrugged his shoulders. "What do you expect, after twenty years as a navy brig? For one thing, she must be stuck on a shoal of kidney beans of her own making. You may have to help the harbour tugs by giving her a heave tomorrow. Twenty hundred hours is cast-off time. Oh, before I forget, her oil tanks and three of her four water tanks are being filled right now with fuel for you to use under way, whenever the need arises. All you do is wait for a calm day in mid-Pacific, put out a boat towing the female end of a two-hundred-foot fuel hose with floats, take off one of the watertight hatches bolted from the outside, six feet above the waterline, marry the hose to the nipple, and slurp. The hulk has no power of her own, so your hose has to be hitched to one of your own pumps, of course. The runners will have to work by candlelight."

"Harakiri isn't going to like that."

"Harakiri is going home, like everyone else."

"Who's taking over?"

"I don't know yet, I suppose his *mandur*. Now—the stores to be brought on board here: fruit and Chinese catfood from the chandlers, the new charts from the Institute ..." He hoisted himself to his feet. "Are you seeing them off at the airport tonight?"

"We'll probably have a farewell dinner. Do you know of a good place?"

"Yes. Come with me to the fuel office here, and book a table." He slapped my shoulder in a sudden excess of chumminess. "See you tomorrow, six hundred hours, for a visit to the hulk. I'll have a taxi." He went to open the door. "And take it easy on Cho, the poor devil, or when you're all by yourselves out in the Pacific, he may go berserk and nail you to the old rugged cross."

WHEN I CAME BACK from the fuel office, I found, to my surprise, BB and Porks at work in my dayroom. "What the devil are you doing?" I said.

They had moved the desk, which was covered with tools and electric wire, and were in the process of putting back a wall panel above it. In the centre of the panel I saw a red push-button and underneath it a notice screaming FIRE!

"Sit down, Martinus," BB said, keeping his voice low. "This has to remain a secret."

"It's not a fire button, Skipper." Porks took my arm and guided me away from the desk. "It's a panic button."

"Who's supposed to do the panicking? Me?"

"Hush!" BB whispered. "We don't want this all round the ship! Remember those stores I brought on board in Rio?" he began. "Well"— he tried to charm me with a smile—"the purpose of my joining you there was to test the ship's stability to the limit, right?"

"I know all that."

"So we—that's to say, me and the other architects—agreed that 'testing to the limit' meant just that: under the right creative circumstances I would have to push the ship to the point where she would start to capsize."

"I like the word 'creative'."

"The trouble was," BB continued, "that no one could say exactly when that point would be reached. Yet I had to push her that far to find the answer we needed. So we decided to make certain provisions, in case—"

"In case you turned the goddamn ship over?"

"Well—not quite. It was decided that I would take the ship's chief engineer into my confidence and together we'd install a dynamite charge at the foot of the paradise tree, to be detonated if I pushed the ship to the point of no return. The explosion should be strong enough to hurl the paradise tree well away from the hull and thereby restore stability. But as it was likely to cause some damage to the flying bridge and the wheel-house—"

"God almighty! You *are* insane! Destroy another man's ship for the sake of some lousy information? Was *that* the toggle switch you were clutching all the time? The trigger to blow up the ship?"

He looked sheepish. "Well, yes."

"We were planning to dismantle the charge here," Porks continued. "But then we heard that you'd decided to stay on by yourself—"

"What do you mean, by myself? Who do you think you are, the world's only engineer? Chief Liu makes you look like a goddamn amateur!"

They took it well. Their earnestness kept me in check.

"We've been through a few gales with you, Martinus," BB said with the voice of sweet reason, "and not once have we seen you leave the bridge to Number One or Number Two, let alone to Captain Cho. The moment there was a hint of a blow, you'd be on the bridge. You'll have to keep that up for days on end, maybe for weeks, in the hurricane zone."

"We want you to get sufficient rest, keep your wits about you," Porks continued, "and the only way of achieving that is by leaving the dynamite charge in place. The moment the ship starts to cycle, if you're down here in your quarters, all you'll have to do is press that button, trigger the charge and bang! Off flies the paradise tree and the ship rights herself. It's no joking matter, Skipper! We know it's farfetched, but there is a chance that the ship could start to cycle when there's no one on the bridge to take action. That's not likely, but it's a possibility. What we're leaving you is an emergency brake."

"I appreciate the thought—"

"At least look at the drawing," BB pleaded. He unrolled the blueprint on the coffee table. From the foot of the paradise tree radiated red lines representing the direction of the blast and the area of destruction. It was not minor at all; the flying bridge would be destroyed, the aft section of the wheelhouse and the stacks severely damaged.

"If having the button on the wall bothers you," Porks said, "we can put it on the desk."

I visualized the red button on the desk and Louis, with his insatiable curiosity, demolishing half the ship.

"And Mr. Chung?" I asked. "How do you think he'll react when I deliver his ship in Taiwan and he discovers there's a dynamite charge at the foot of his paradise tree?"

"He need never know," Porks replied. "I'm leaving a letter for Chief Liu with instructions on how to dismantle it. Give it to him as you approach Taiwan, then he can toss the whole lot overboard."

"We could put up a picture to cover that button," BB mused. "No one need ever know."

They gathered their tools and their coils of wire, rolled up the blueprint and headed for the door. Porks said, "Do me a favour, Skipper: don't mention it to Captain Fransen. I'm in enough trouble with the company as it is."

"OK. By the way, I appreciate the thought."

"Any day, Skip," Porks said, opening the door.

After they had left, I went to have a look at the ghoulish button on the wall. I could foresee Fransen's reaction. So, for Porks's sake, I took the picture of the old *Isabel* from the wall of the dayroom, drove in a nail— gently!—and put up the picture. It looked odd, higher than the others, but not enough to raise questions.

I went to feed Pete. Stuffing himself, he shook his head furiously and spilled most of his seed on the floor. This was usually the signal for Louis to stir on my shoulder so that I would put him beneath the cage to clean up, but this time he wasn't there. He wasn't on the copy of Bowditch either. I took a perfunctory look round, then shrugged my shoulders and sat down. He must have found a new place to hole up in, probably a slipper or something. He would show up when he was hungry.

I had barely started to open my mail when there was a knock on my door. Harakiri stuck his head in. "Listen, I just popped in to tell you I'm staying on to Taiwan. I thought you'd like to know."

"But didn't Captain Fransen tell you to go home? He has a ticket to Amsterdam for you."

"I told him to stuff it. My Chinks have kind of taken to me; when Fransen turned up and told me to get off, the *mandur* blew his top. You should have seen him! He took off like a bat out of hell. Those jokers don't mess around. So, I'm on. We won't see much of each other, but let's keep the daily chinwag going. Have to run now."

"Hold it! Have you seen the new tow?" He nodded.

"What's she like?"

"Oh, just another old rustbucket. Seen one, seen 'em all. Ta-ta."

"We're having a farewell meal tonight. Join us."

"Sure thing." And he was gone.

Sighing, I went back to my mail. It was going to be lonely without the bosun and the others but at least Fransen had met his match in Harakiri. For some reason, it made me feel a lot better.

THE SIX OF US—Porks, Harlingen, the bosun, BB, Harakiri and myself— had dinner that night in a Chilean version of an American diner. I ordered a bottle of champagne. The cork popped and the glasses foamed; I rose for a toast. "To the *Isabel Kwel*, God bless her soul. She has carried us halfway round the world, which was a bit of a miracle if one believes in rumours, and we owe it in large part to the four of you now about to leave. So: BB, Porks, Marco, Bosun—thank you, God bless you, hope to see you again soon." We did not clink glasses, as each glass that rings means a sailor drowns.

The bosun responded. Standing up, he spoke as if he had to make himself heard above a gale. The clientele in the diner fell silent; they had no choice. "Men! Brothers!" he bellowed. "We are gathered together to say farewell to Ome Tinus—"

"Hey!" Porks interrupted. "This isn't a funeral! Keep it light."

"Ome," the bosun continued, "the time has come to say farewell, but not goodbye. We've had a good trip together, with a few ups and downs. Let's drink to Ome and wish him Godspeed and happy sailing."

"Godspeed and happy sailing," the others chimed in, raising their glasses.

"Ome," the bosun bellowed, "here's looking at you!" He sat down to loud applause from the diners at the tables, which must have been from sheer relief, as they couldn't have understood a word he was saying. I ordered another bottle of champagne.

After the farewell at the airport and the long taxi ride back to the ship, I felt depressed as I made my way to my dayroom. With the others gone, the ship had become a floating Chinatown.

I went to put some decent music on the hi-fi, but discovered that Hopla, in a dramatic access of tidiness, had gathered all loose objects in the cabin and stacked them on my desk: crates of booze sealed by customs, a pair of open-toed sandals, a pile of official documents. I had to dig before I found the tapes under a box of oranges. I put on Handel's "Water Music" and settled down to read my letters at last. Louis was not on my shoulder. I looked at Bowditch again; he was not there either. Finally I called Hopla. "Hopla, Louis must have got out. Did you leave the door open while you were cleaning in here?"

"Who, me? No, no, Co'dore! No, no, never."

"Well, he'll turn up, I suppose. Take a look round the ship for him, will you? Tell the others. Well, goodnight. See you in the morning."

I went back and tried to read my letters, but I couldn't concentrate. If he *had* slipped outside, where would he have gone? The galley seemed most likely. I got up and went to look. I found Ma Chang setting out the dishes for tomorrow's breakfast. "Have you seen Louis?" I asked.

She gazed at me with a look of incomprehension. I went back to the door and called down the corridor, "Hopla! Hopla, come here!"

He turned up at once. "Hopla, ask Ma Chang about Louis. Has she any idea where he can be?"

Hopla translated. She said something in her bird language.

"She say: no idea. She say: him ashore looking for a bride."

Ashore . . . the idea didn't bear thinking about.

"Well, thank you, Ma Chang." As I turned to leave, Hopla called, "She say: wait!"

She rummaged in her pockets and produced her pendulum. She made it oscillate back and forth, her face took on a faraway expression, then she grinned as the pendulum started to swing in a circle; she uttered a few twittering sounds and pocketed it with a giggle.

"What was that, Hopla?"

"She say: him on—on—I do not know word. Pinge? Him visit wine shops. Him will turn up drunk. She think very funny."

"But where *is* he?"

He translated my question; she shrugged. I left, feeling certain that my little friend and I would never see each other again.

The next morning, after I had made everybody search the ship for Louis once more, I was picked up by Fransen and taken to inspect the huge liner. It was a grim and depressing experience, having known the *Princess of Orange* in her days of glory. It was like looking in a mirror at the age of twenty-five and seeing a man of seventy.

The moment I was back on board the *Isabel*, I checked to see if Louis had returned; he hadn't. Pete sat quietly in his cage; even he seemed to miss him. There could no longer be any doubt: Louis had slipped ashore under cover of darkness and got lost among the sheds and the containers and the stacks of cargo. It seemed final, for what chance had he among the tribes of vicious wharf rats?

I was surprised by my own reaction. I had had no idea how emotionally attached I had become to my little companion. It all added to the depression which darkened the rest of that day.

At sunset three harbour tugs tried to dislodge the *Princess of Orange* from the harbour bed; the fact that in the meantime her tanks had been filled from fuel barges did not help.

The *Isabel* was called upon; it took her full moon-rocket power to tear the old hulk from the mud with a gigantic sucking sound, an overwhelming stench of tropical marshes, and a cloud of mosquitoes that swarmed like bees and headed straight for the tugboat. On the aft deck the

Chinese sailors started to dance around, slapping themselves as the vicious insects zeroed in on them.

By the time we were set to leave, darkness had fallen. Our departure was an unexpectedly solemn occasion. The *Isabel*, with the aid of the three harbour tugs, slowly moved the *Princess* out into the Pacific. Her silhouette, outlined against the stars and the glow of the city across the bay, was majestic even in death. As I watched, the lights of Concepcion, diffused by night haze, seemed to surround the dead hulk with a halo. It briefly gave her a magical life; as I gazed at her from the bridge, I saw what Turner must have seen before he painted *The Fighting Temeraire*.

I gazed at the sight until darkness engulfed us, and mourned for Louis, a little speck of evanescent life lost among the stars.

BY THE TIME I had set the ship on her course and started the slow paying out of the hawser, it was too late for our traditional departure Happy Hour. I left the bridge feeling bereft and lonely.

Of course, it was all in the mind. Porks would have been in his engine room, Harlingen in his cubicle, the bosun below at the winches, BB asleep in the hospital. Practically speaking, they might all have been still on board. Yet still I missed them. Or maybe it was just the underlying awareness of the vastness of the Pacific Ocean we were now set to cross: five thousand four hundred miles of loneliness between here and Samoa, and no landfall before Pago Pago. Fifty-four days before Fransen would come sauntering onto the bridge again.

I was so dejected, so depressed, that I hoisted myself out of my chair and headed for the crate with the bottles.

Then I thought, No, damnit! I'm not going to sit here and drink myself to a standstill in maudlin self-pity! I spotted the untidy stack of junk Hopla had left on my desk. It should all be stowed away: the drink in the fridge, the box of oranges in the pantry ... Wait a minute: an orange! How healthy, how sane. I removed the ship's document from customs, the booze sealed by customs, opened the box and—"*Whaaaow!!*" Instead of the smooth, round globes of fruit, I felt a soft, furry—

Furry?

I tore open the box and there he lay: on his back, white belly exposed, paws spread, eyes closed, snoring—surrounded by the hollowed-out ghosts of oranges as empty as eggshells. Ma Chang, God bless her, had been right! He *was* drunk—on orange juice, fermenting in his stomach— and snoring it off surrounded by empties.

I lifted him out of his fruit rat's heaven; he was as floppy as a doll. He was blotto, a corpse with a heartbeat.

I carried him to the bedroom and put him on the bed, eyes closed, spreadeagled, out for the count.

I went to bed, put him on my chest and turned off the light. In the stillness, I listened to the ship's lazy, protracted creaking as she heeled, slowly, in the long, lazy swell of the Pacific.

Chapter Nine

After twenty-four hours at sea, the spell of the Pacific began to take hold of us.

Up to now, we had followed the coast; the eastern horizon had been dominated by the jagged ramparts of the Andes, their icy peaks, white with snow, turning the colour of coral when the sun went down. They had balanced the emptiness of the ocean to the west; now we were alone under the stars, a black beetle guiding a blind mole, for once we were out of sight of land, the old liner seemed not dead but blind. It was the first intimation of the spell of the Pacific.

The *Princess* lumbered behind us a mile away. The maximum speed we could make, with the *Isabel*'s engines churning at their most economical number of revolutions, was only four knots. Inevitably, this deepened the spell of the vastness through which we were crawling by day and in which we seemed to be lying still, under an overwhelming dome of blazing stars, by night.

The succession of identical days in the timeless void brought about a new intimacy with the staff, especially Chief Liu. I had always liked him, not just because he was an articulate, occasionally funny, man but because he was, at fifty-three, the nearest to me in age. We talked philosophy, Chinese art and, ultimately, war. He was reticent about it, so was I; I wasn't even sure which war he was talking about. But it somehow brought us closer: two old bores among the twittering young.

Happy Hour became a lot livelier now that the Chinese staff were no longer inhibited by the presence of Porks, Harlingen and BB. They swapped stories, told jokes, frequently slipping into Chinese. But Chief Liu quickly brought them back to our private brand of English, and Harakiri kept up his daily chat on the walkie-talkie.

The only one who didn't share in the general amusement was Captain Cho. A week after my bawling him out in Talcahuano, which had led to his total disappearance, he decided to take up his watch on the bridge again. But even though he was back in circulation, I rarely set eyes on him, and he still had all his meals served in his cabin.

After eighteen days at sea I decided to bunker from the old *Princess*. We still had plenty of oil in our tanks, but the wind had died down overnight and the sea was exceptionally peaceable that morning. Harakiri came on board the *Isabel* for a couple of hours while we refuelled.

The next morning, waking early, I dressed and went out on deck. The wind had not picked up; the weather was hot, still and muggy. There was a haze in the sky; the barometer was lower than the night before. I heard Hopla curse behind my back because he had spilled a mug of tea on the deck of the wheelhouse; only then did it penetrate to me that the *Isabel* was rolling heavily. The sea looked torpid and oily; the swell, long and fast, slid by, glinting in the misty light. I checked the night's log. Just after midnight the swell had started to increase sufficiently for Number One to make a note of it.

Although there was no mention of hurricanes in the official weather report, I decided to take no chances. I raised Harakiri on the walkie-talkie. "We're running into the fringe of some bad weather. I'm heading into the swell. Tell your men to stand by, over."

"I don't hear any wind. Are you sure about this?"

"Yes. At this latitude depressions build up very fast. I'll try to work my way round it, but I don't want to be caught with my trousers down when it starts to blow. Over."

"All right, Harinxma. You're the boss. Over and out."

An hour later the swell had become faster, but there still was no wind, which made it impossible to locate the centre of the disturbance. I called the radio room: Marco Two said no weather station had reported a hurricane threat. No wonder. We were in the largest no-man's-land on the globe; cyclones could be spawned here, range and die without anyone knowing.

I went through the ship to make sure that everything was stowed seafast. Ma Chang took her pots and pans off the range and secured the contents of her shelves. Carleton and Bryn Mawr put up hand lines on the aft deck. The boat covers were taken off and the decks cleared of loose objects by Wellesley, Haverford and Yale. After that, all I could do was wait for developments.

An hour or so later a distant mountain range of cumuli appeared on the horizon. There was still no wind, but the sky was overcast. I gave the order that everyone now on deck should get some rest while they still had the chance. I myself went below after arranging with Number One that he would call me when the going got rough. Then I went to see Captain Cho.

To my surprise, he was sitting at his little desk in his number-one uniform, counting money.

"Captain," I said, "we're in for bad weather, maybe a hurricane. I'll try to skirt it, but for the time being there's no wind and the centre is hard to locate. I've sent everyone to their bunks for rest, but as you're up and about—"

"Very well," he said with an eagerness he hadn't shown before, "I will take Number One's place. I will go at once."

"No need to break your neck, Captain. There's no emergency yet. Thanks all the same."

"My pleasure," he said, with the first smile he had given me since Rotterdam.

On my way to my quarters I reflected how odd it felt to thank the master of a ship for going to the bridge when bad weather threatened, but at least he had joined the human race. Who knows, after the hurricane if we were in for one—he might even join Happy Hour.

I entered the dayroom and headed for my bunk. I saw Louis's intelligent little eyes peeping at me over Bowditch. Obviously, he sensed something was coming and had found himself a secure place. Pete was practising his mating call, apparently unaware that the cage was swinging wildly. I took it down and lashed it to the radiator.

I called the bridge to tell Number One he was about to be relieved, but Captain Cho answered. He reported that he was alone in the wheelhouse with the helmsman, there was no one left on deck. I put back the receiver, closed my eyes and slid into sleep.

I HAD A DREAM. I was lying helpless as a baby in my bunk, being rocked more and more violently. I was about to be thrown out when suddenly my head hit the side and I was wide awake. The ship was rolling crazily; all around me things were sliding, crashing to the floor. The *Isabel* was in her deadly cycle!

I swung myself out of my bunk, was picked up bodily and hurled against the wall. The ship swept over onto her other side and hurled me back against the bunk. I couldn't keep my footing, yet I managed to pull myself into the dayroom and made a dash for the door. The ship picked me up and flung me against the room divider. My head exploded in pain and I lay there for a moment, paralysed by terror. I heard a voice shriek. I didn't know where it came from or who it was, but it brought me to my senses. The deck rose in a sickening surge as the ship rolled onto her other side; I tried to crawl to the door and was thrown down the length of the room again. Somehow I managed to direct my fall towards the desk, and grabbed it; it was bolted to the deck. The ship heeled over onto her other side; everything loose in the room tumbled past me. It was too late, I would never make it to the bridge in time.

Where the hell was Cho? Why didn't he use the thrusters? The ship was totally out of control. There was nothing for it: I must get to the panic button. The ship hovered for a second before sweeping onto her other side. I managed to throw myself across the desk and held on for dear life as it heaved. Every muscle in my body screamed to let go, my arms were being torn out of their sockets, but I was able to hang on, and waited for the moment she would start to swing back. The moment came, but she didn't do so. I realized with horror that she was lying on her side; she wasn't going to swing back, but would go on turning over and capsize. With a despairing lunge I hauled myself across the desk, pushed aside the picture and pressed the red button.

What followed was not an explosion but a convulsion of the whole ship, as if a shell had struck and slammed through two decks before it exploded with a sound of splintering wood and a shower of glass. I had a last, wordless thought of Sylvia, followed by a terrible sense of sorrow for my men about to go down with the ship while I was trapped in the dayroom. I waited for the water to engulf me; I was as ready to go as a man could be. Then the strain of my hands clutching the edge of the desk seemed to lessen. With a slow, tormented sigh, the *Isabel* began to right herself. There was a sound of sliding wood and slithering glass in the corridor, a tumult of slamming, tearing; then it ceased. A hill slid under her, lifted her martyred body, passed under her, and she started the deadly cycle of her rolling again. The thrusters! Why was there no one at the thrusters?

I staggered to the door and tore it open. The corridor was a chaos of glass and splintered wood. I heard a cry for help somewhere near, but what passed through my head with unnatural clarity was BB saying, "Unless it's been hurled well away from the ship, the destruction of the paradise tree will only give you a few minutes' respite. Get yourself to the thrusters immediately!" I clawed my way up the companionway.

When I reached the top I stood still, at a loss, facing a tangle of metal, gigantic shards of bulkheads, bits of rail angled crazily at the sky. Above me, hanging across a section of rail, wearing a life jacket, a man looked down at me, motionless. I saw something move in the tangle of steel that barred my way: a glint, a turning movement. The steering wheel! The ship was on automatic!

My confusion cleared. I clambered across the shards of metal. I reached the wheel, flicked the switch and turned off the automatic pilot. Now for the thrusters. I waited for the next heave of her wallowing hulk to pass, crawled across a pile of wreckage, grabbed the handle of the forward thrusters and gave full starboard power to the bow, praying that the lines that transmitted the signal hadn't been severed. They hadn't; with a mighty surge, her bow was swept off course. The fight was over. Only then did I become aware of blood trickling into my eyes.

It had been a supreme effort; as I felt myself collapsing, a voice cried, "Commodore! Commodore?" from the direction of the companionway. I saw Number One emerge and clamber towards me across the debris.

"Commodore! What happened?"

"No idea," I heard myself say. "Seems the bridge was unattended while the ship was on automatic."

"What happened to Captain Cho? Why is he dead?"

I stared at him. "Dead?"

"Yes! His body is hanging in the rail up there, look!"

I looked up; but then, as in a dream, I heard a small, metallic voice call, "*Isabel! Isabel!* Do you read?" It was the walkie-talkie, somewhere in the rubble. "*Isabel!* This is *Princess!* Do you read? Do you read?"

I groped for the walkie-talkie under the pile of wreckage. I found the talk switch, pressed it and shouted, "*Princess,* this is *Isabel! Princess,* this is *Isabel!* Harinxma here! Over!"

"Harinxma, what happened? Was that your engine? Was that your engine that exploded?"

"No, Harakiri, no! It was an explosive charge at the foot of the paradise tree! We nearly capsized!"

"Do you need assistance? Harinxma, do you need assistance?"

"I don't know, Harakiri! I'll contact you again in ten minutes, over and out."

"Omi! Omi!" Bryn Mawr loomed over me, distorted by the blood running into my eyes. "All right, Omi? All right?"

"Take the wheel, keep her headed into the seas."

I scrambled to my feet, made my way across the wreckage to the back of the wheelhouse and clambered across the jagged barrier of glass and metal to where I could see Cho. He was leaning over a slanting section of rail which must have been part of the flying bridge. Then I realized he was not leaning over the rail, but buried in it, stuck there like a smashed fly, his torso in a life jacket, his legs gone.

I gazed up at him, sickened by the sight. How could he have ended up there? He should have been inside the wheelhouse. Yet, judging from his position, the explosion must have flung him against the rail of the flying bridge with such force that his legs were sheared off.

I looked around me. Not only was the paradise tree gone and the stacks blown sideways, but the whole of the flying bridge and the walkway on which the paradise tree had rested were gone.

"What happened?" Chief Liu was standing beside me.

"There's been an explosion. The paradise tree was hurled overboard. Are the engines OK?"

"Hokay! Hokay! But what—"

A voice called from below, "Commodore! The radio is dead!"

I looked down at the anxious young marco standing among the wreckage. "There's been an explosion. The paradise tree is gone and all our equipment with it. Forget about the radio. Help me down and let's check out the rest of the ship."

The distance I had to lower myself in order to reach the remains of the companionway scared me. The marco waiting below me caught me in his arms as I made the jump.

The voice that had feebly called for help in the corridor was Hopla's—a crumpled white form, covered with debris. His leg was broken. I sent the marco to the hospital to get splints and bandages; when he came back, I put on the splints and got help to carry him to the hospital.

The first man I saw as I left the hospital was little Whittier, who should have been at the wheel. His eyes had a glazed expression; he was carrying a plate with a sandwich. "For Captain Cho."

"Did Captain Cho ask for that?"

He shook his head vigorously: that meant that Cho had.

Mate Number Two came running, visibly shaken. "Bad news, Number Two," I said. "Captain Cho has been killed. Take Whittier with you to the bridge and collect his body. Put him in his cabin."

"Yes, Commodore ..." They hurried off.

The main deck was a shambles: the crew's corridor looked as if the shell had exploded in it. Anything loose in the cabins had been thrown into the corridor by the wild gyrations of the ship. The men were dazed, some of them had blood on their faces. I went from one to another, checking that they were all right. The injuries were minor, mostly cuts and bruises, but the men were scared and bewildered.

Ma Chang, when I got to her in the chaos of the galley, was profuse in her welcome. I said, "Hopla—ouch! Leg! Broken!" and tried to act it out for her. She caught my meaning at once and hurried off.

In the engine room I checked on the Chinese engineers, who proved to be remarkably calm. They assured me that all was well and the engines were running normally; then the telephone rang. It was Number One on the bridge. "Commodore, please come up! Boat is coming from liner!"

I reached the bridge with difficulty, even though Chief Liu and his men had replaced the broken companionway with a ladder. The wind had freshened, the sea looked angry; a rain squall swept the ship. Out of the squall came, pitching and rolling, a white lifeboat. As it drew closer, I could see Harakiri at the rudder, with four runners rowing. When it was within hailing distance, Harakiri yelled, "The raft! Have you seen the raft?" He pointed.

I went to the broken starboard window and spotted an orange inflatable as it was lifted by the swell, swept along by the wind. I pulled the switch for the alarm bell and bells started to ring all over the ship: MAN OVERBOARD!

"Number One, I'll take the wheel. You go and have the men swing out the motor launch. Tell the runner captain to go after the raft in it. They'd never make it in a rowing boat."

He hurried off. In response to the alarm bells, the rest of the crew appeared on deck. I could see the raft clearly now, each time a wave lifted it. When the motor launch, with Harakiri at the wheel, reached the raft, the *mandur* grabbed hold of it and pulled it on board.

"Empty!" cried Number One, lowering his binoculars.

"OK," I said, as the launch headed back to the ship, "you take the wheel. Keep her headed into the seas. No course. Steady as she goes."

I made my way down to the boat deck. The launch was just being hauled up. Chief Liu was there. "How did the raft get into the sea?" he asked. "What happened? What was that explosion?"

"The moment Harakiri is on board, let's go to the dayroom and I'll tell you."

The launch was swung on board, lowered and settled into the blocks by Bryn Mawr and two sailors; when the *mandur* and his companions climbed down, they stood staring at each other. Oh, my God, I thought.

But it seemed that under the pressure of the emergency a truce had come about; the three runners started to help Bryn Mawr and the sailors cover the launch with its tarpaulin. The *mandur* followed us as Harakiri, Chief Liu and I set out for the dayroom; to prevent his losing face, I signalled Bryn Mawr to join us.

With Harakiri and Chief Liu each in a club chair among the debris, and the bosun and the *mandur* side by side on the couch, I told them about the ship's cycling and the dynamite charge, showed them the panic button and told them that there had been no one on the bridge. "Now, what do we do?" I asked. "The last I saw, the barometer was dropping. It's building up to quite a blow out there."

"I gather the Chinese captain is dead?" said Harakiri.

"Smashed into the rail of the flying bridge by the explosion."

"What was he doing up on walkway?" Chief Liu asked.

"I don't know."

"Harinxma," Harakiri said, "if we're in for a blow, you've got a problem. You've lost most of your wheelhouse, your stacks, your flying bridge. Is your steering gear still operational?"

"Yes. But we've lost the automatic."

"You'll need help."

"What kind?"

"I'm leaving my *mandur* with you. I would stay myself, but I can't leave the old girl—and I have to go now or I may not be able to get back on board."

"How are you going to haul up your lifeboat?"

"Oh, I'll let it ride, I've got thirty of 'em. Give the *mandur* any job you like, he's terrific. And you can do no wrong as far as those jokers are concerned. They may be part of the Chinese Mafia, but you're the one who risked an arm and a leg to try and get them to run for cover. So don't be shy: he may not look it, but he's your man."

I glanced doubtfully at the *mandur*. He stared at me as if he were about to wring my neck.

"Captain Cho was on watch, yes?" the chief asked, from his own world. "Who was at the wheel?"

"Whittier. But I met him in the corridor afterwards carrying a plate with a sandwich to the bridge."

"Captain was alone on bridge?"

"He must have been."

"And wearing life jacket?"

"Well, folks," Harakiri said, rising. "I hate to break this up, but I don't want to get my feet wet. Have the *mandur* clear the wreckage on your bridge." He nodded at the *mandur*. "He's good at that. Well— Godspeed, and happy sailing." He let himself out.

"Life rafts not inflate alone," the chief mused. "Must be triggered on purpose." Slowly he turned his head and gave me a smiling look. "How come life jacket? How come life raft inflate? How come ship on automatic on bad course? Questions will be asked, Commodore. Questions will have to be answered."

"Not now, Chief. A hurricane may be barrelling down on us, we have to get cracking. Would you take charge of clearing the wheelhouse? There's so much debris, the helmsman can barely stand at the wheel."

"If hurricane, who will stand at wheel, please?" he asked politely.

"I suppose I will."

"Well," he said, rising, "in that case we better look for seat for you. Maybe long hurricane. Come, *Mandur*."

The *mandur* hesitated, then he followed the chief into the corridor, while I set out on a search for an oilskin suit.

I DISCOVERED LONG AGO that the way to handle a crisis is to be as relaxed as possible and not to take oneself too seriously. But I could find little to laugh about in a seventy-year-old looking for oilskins in which to face a hurricane on the open bridge of a crippled ship. It was only after I had suited up and looked at myself in the mirror that I cracked a smile. I looked like an ad for a fish restaurant.

The wind had picked up during my absence. The sea was angry now, full of white horses. The ship was labouring; I had a problem hoisting myself up the temporary ladder to the wheelhouse in my stiff outfit. When I saw the interior of the wheelhouse, my heart sank. There was nothing left, only a vast empty space, like a stage, with the jagged remains of the for'ard bulkhead for a backdrop, its windows, miraculously, still intact. All the navigational wizardry connected with the paradise tree had been wiped out—we were back in the days of sextant and chronometer. Number One was at the wheel; beside him two space-age creatures in helmets were welding something to the steel dividers between the planking of the deck. As I approached, I saw what they were marrying to the ship. I could hardly believe my eyes: it was half a bicycle. It took a moment before I recognized the rear end of the exercise bike from the recreation room.

"My God!" I said. "Whose idea was this?"

One of the spacemen stopped welding and lifted his mask; it was Chief Liu. "Solid as rock!" he beamed. "Now you need seat belt!"

"Chief," I said, relieved from stress, tension and old man's terror by a sudden sense of comedy, "I don't think I'll need a seat belt."

"Oh, but you do!" he persisted. "You may be blown away, if big hurricane! Try it." He scrambled to his feet. "You see, I have blocked pedals."

The other spaceman stopped sparking away and flipped up the front of his helmet; I saw to my surprise that it was the *mandur*. The chief spoke to him in Chinese; he rose, gave me a mortifying look and pointed at the saddle. I climbed onto it, put my feet on the pedals and took the wheel, a child in a toy car.

"Yes?" Chief Liu asked expectantly.

"Excellent," I said with feeling. "Thank you. Now everybody should get back to their posts; we may have a good deal more wind than we bargained for."

It was an understatement. The sky to starboard looked as black as night. The rain would soon be upon us. This being the southern hemisphere, cyclones whirled clockwise; if we were lucky, we would find ourselves in the left quadrant. I had been making light of the possibility of our being hit by a hurricane, saying that I would skirt it, but at a speed of four knots, towing a forty-thousand-ton liner, I couldn't do any skirting, only head into the seas and hope for the best. This was simply going to be a trial of strength lasting between eight and sixteen hours, depending on the size and the forward speed of the cyclone.

"Number One," I called, "you'd better suit up and tell Number Two to do the same. I want you to take turns on the aft deck, keeping an eye on the hawser, but I need one of you on the bridge at all times to man the thrusters. Now, before you do anything else, do me a favour. Go to my dayroom. On my desk you'll see a cardboard box and inside, a number of earthenware crocks. Bring one of those up for me, will you?"

"Yes, Commodore," he said almost reverently, like an acolyte hurrying for the consecrated wine.

The *mandur* came back, accompanied by Bryn Mawr; together they strapped me into the wire harness they had made. I felt secure; if the baling wire that held me together lasted, and if the eye of the hurricane passed to the north of us instead of barrelling down upon the two pieces of jetsam in its path, I would have plenty of time to ponder on the questions Chief Liu had posed, to which answers had to be found.

It was not a happy prospect.

AS IT TURNED OUT, there was not going to be any pondering. The moment I took control of the *Isabel* and headed her into the seas, total identification with the ship took place, to the exclusion of all else. I was no longer an old man teetering in a saddle, feeble and faintly silly; I became the eyes, the ears, the will and the spirit of the ship. It was an instant transformation: one moment I was an ad for a fish restaurant, the next the nerve centre of the huge, lumbering body of the blinded ship. The two of us became one.

The *Isabel* took the seas with the same curious elation that had struck me the first time I handled her, in the sea off Flushing. Even with her paradise tree and her flying bridge gone, she seemed to face what was coming with anticipation, as if this were what she had been created for: to be turned by mountainous waves from a wallowing pontoon into a thing of grace and beauty.

That was what she became, as the first gale winds hit and the spray and spindrift started to fly. The swell came in fast, huge, precipitous; the parasite waves on its back grew in size and fury. The wind whisked the foam off their crests into horizontal sheets of water, lashing the windows of the wheelhouse in blinding torrents. The wind, in increasing gusts of tremendous, sustained force, occasionally stopped her dead in her tracks. But she never wavered. By some miracle, the clearview discs were still whirling; so, despite the fact that there was a lot of flying water inside the wheelhouse, I never lost contact with reality outside. Number One had hoisted a storm pennant on the foremast; in the confusion of whirling water I could keep the head of the tow into the wind by watching the whipping pennant, hoping it would survive the beating it took.

With the increase of the wind, the sheering of the *Princess* became a problem. Despite the *Isabel*'s massive power, occasionally the gale won out. The old liner's head veered away, her windage acted as a sail and gave her forward momentum as well as broaching her. Number One or Two stood by at the thrusters, watching me. Whenever I felt the ship's stern yanked aside, straining the hawser, I gave the signal to throw in one of the thrusters to compensate for the skid. It worked; the thrusters were indeed the greatest invention of the century for tugboat masters. Instantly the ship lined up, her powerful forward thrust no longer diminished by the angle; in short order the huge, wallowing mass behind us would heave to again, until another major gust came to blow her off course once more.

As night fell, I ordered that a floodlight be directed at the pennant. Sailing the ship now became entirely a matter of following the shifting direction of that tattered rag. It looked as though the eye of the hurricane was sweeping by at a fair distance to the north. At one moment we were at right angles to our original course.

My problem was not tiredness; on the contrary, I seemed to be as exhilarated by the challenge as the ship was. What got to me was the cold, despite frequent swigs from the earthenware crock. When dawn broke we had changed course a hundred and thirty-six degrees. The hurricane, though at its height the wind was over seventy-five knots, had been a minor one on the scale of the monsters that often sweep the region at this season. Harakiri's small, crackling voice over the walkie-talkie sounded relieved when it shouted, "Well, the worst seems to be over! Good show, Harinxma! You can start thinking about bed!"

But I didn't feel tired at all. I patted the little wheel and muttered, "Well done, old girl. Terrific." Somebody patted my shoulder as if to convey the same. I looked up and saw it was Bryn Mawr.

"Woo, Bryn," I said.

"Woo, Omi!" he replied, grinning.

The sun was beginning to break through the cloud cover of the hurricane's tail when Chief Liu appeared on the bridge. The moment had come for me to hand over the watch to Number One. The rain had stopped, the wind had died down, spray no longer lashed the windows. The clearview disc spun idly; the tattered remains of the pennant flapped limply.

"All right," I said. "Number One, time for you to take over. Would someone please help me out of this harness?"

This turned out to be less easy than strapping me in; twelve hours of sustained drenching had made the straps swell and in the end they had to be cut. When helped to my feet, I discovered that all that was left of me was my brain. My legs simply gave way. Bryn Mawr and Chief Liu supported me as I staggered towards the ladder. Number One called anxiously after me, "Commodore! What's the course?"

A good question. Where the hell were we? Satellites were coursing overhead, but we could no longer receive their signals telling us our position. Not that it mattered; there certainly was plenty of room. At that moment Whittier's head appeared above the deck as he climbed the ladder. "Whittier, take the wheel," I said. "Number One, come down with me to my quarters and I'll give you my sextant. You'll have to sight the sun the old-fashioned way, my friend."

The prospect appeared to alarm him.

I CANNOT REMEMBER GOING TO BED, but I found myself there, in my pyjamas with the lights on. Chief Liu was standing beside my bunk.

"Sorry," he said, "I think you should see this." He held out his hand and showed me a small black object. "A microphone. *Mandur* found it among wreckage on bridge."

I couldn't understand what it was all about. I glanced at the clock; I had been asleep for only two and a half hours. "So?" I asked wearily.

He pulled something out of the pocket of his boiler suit: another small black object. "I found this in Captain Cho's cabin."

"What is it?"

"Speaker. Sister to other one. You speak on bridge, he hear you."

So Captain Cho had had a listening device that enabled him to follow what was being said on the bridge. But my potential for excitement had been depleted and all I wanted was to sleep—I felt quite sick with exhaustion.

The chief pressed on. "You must get up. Number One Mate cannot use sextant. We must bury captain's body before he stink, but we do not know what service. Maybe he was Christian."

"I see," I said. "OK. I'll be right up."

"While you dress, we must talk. I found answers to questions. Captain Cho did it," the hectoring voice hammered on. "Captain Cho tried to scuttle ship. Captain alone on bridge, with helmsman. He send helmsman to galley for sandwich, then put on life jacket and inflate life raft. Then put ship on bad course, on automatic. Ran out of wheelhouse, tossed raft overboard, climbed onto walkway between the stacks."

"Why the walkway?"

"I think a long time for that: with ship lying on side, walkway furthest you can get from ship when she turn over. Less chance to be pulled down with her when she sink."

Suddenly I realized I had known all along that Cho was the culprit. "But why?" I asked. "What drove him to do such a thing?"

Chief Liu looked at the door, then whispered, "Mr. Chung! Insurance."

My heart sank. I knew in my gut it wasn't so, that there was another reason. "Look, Chief, we should talk more about this, but not now."

"You must write report!" he cried, bent on retribution. "You must report on Captain Cho death! Include ship's log, take testimony from all members of staff, then give big document to authorities. Mr. Chung must have no more chance to kill people for money."

I could understand his rage. Yet I knew in my bones it was all part of a bigger conspiracy, a nightmare web of plots and counterplots. Greedy Chung might be, but I couldn't see him callously engineering the death of forty people.

I would have to think about it all later. Now I had to get up, oversee the burial, sight the ship's position, put the tow back on course, decide what to do about the damage, make the rounds of the ship to see if everyone was all right, visit Hopla in the hospital. I swung my legs out of bed. "OK, Chief, you go ahead, and let me get dressed. I'll join you in a minute."

When I came out on the aft deck, I found everyone lined up for the burial. The scene seemed to have a haunting clarity: the clean, new sky, the silent ranks of the crew, the wind catching the Taiwanese flag which covered the bier, the foot of which rested on the rail. The other end was supported by the two junior engineers; Chief Liu joined them.

The sea swished past in foaming waves; the deck heaved slowly with the swell. In the far distance the last of the cumuli, white and harmless, were still massed above the horizon.

I had brought along a Bible and a Book of Common Prayer, but the standard hymn, "Father, in Thy gracious keeping, Leave we now Thy servant sleeping", seemed inappropriate. Instead, I read a few passages from Ecclesiastes which appeared universal.

"Remember now thy creator in the days of thy youth ..." The wind stirred the flag on the bier. It seemed as if all the young men I had buried at sea during my life as master were present among us. "...*And the grasshopper shall be a burden, and desire shall fail, because man goeth to his long home, and the mourners go about the streets.*"

As I read, it occurred to me that this must be totally meaningless to the crew lined up in their clean T-shirts; they didn't even understand the language. So I ended with, "*Then shall the dust return to the earth as it was, and the spirit shall return unto God who gave it.*"

I nodded at Chief Liu, who signalled his companions to start lifting the bier. According to tradition, I should now have read the Lord's Prayer; instead, I said, "Farewell, Captain Cho. Rest in peace."

The small bundle slid down the bier and dropped over the side. We all stood for a moment motionless, in silence, while the flag flapped in the wind. Then I put my cap back on and turned away.

There was only the foremast left on which to hoist a flag halfway.

THE MOMENT THE CEREMONY WAS OVER I went up to the wheelhouse. Number One followed me with an embarrassed apology about being out of practice at working the sextant.

"Don't worry," I said. "I'll run through it with you now. I have just the book for you, Bowditch's *American Practical Navigator*. My rat sleeps on it, but he'll have to rough it until you can give it back."

He thanked me profusely. I proceeded to shoot the sun. The horizon was beautifully clear, as always after a hurricane, and the sun was at an easy angle in the cloudless sky. Together we computed our exact location. I had to reintroduce him to the tables and the almanac; he obviously needed the Bowditch. I gave it to him to take to his cabin.

In the hospital I found Hopla sitting upright, his leg in plaster. The morphine must have worn off, for the moment he set eyes on me, he cried, "Co'dore! I have much, much pain! I cannot move. I cannot serve you! I am desolated! Are pregnant dogs still on board?"

"Hopla," I said, "the time of pregnant dogs is past. If I catch you starting that all over again, you'll be in trouble."

"But who is to replace me?" he wailed, nimbly changing the subject. "Who is to look after co'dore? I would like leg back!" he cried dramatically. "I would like hobble-hobble on crutches, serve co'dore!"

"I appreciate the thought, but that leg will need a couple of weeks at least before you can move around."

After a few more minutes of bedside chat, I decided to leave him to his woes and have a look at Cho's cabin, before his possessions were stowed away or divided among the crew.

I found myself in an arid little world. I went through his wardrobe, his desk, his chest of drawers; what struck me was that there was nothing there of his own culture. Everything was Western: clothes, shoes, a few pornographic paperbacks and the little red book he had been reading each time I went to see him. I discovered to my surprise that it was not, as I had thought, *The Thoughts of Chairman Mao*, but a second-hand copy of *The Rubaiyat of Omar Khayyam*, in English.

What had attracted the troubled youth from Taiwan to these elegiac Victorian poems, so utterly British? If Chief Liu was right, and Captain Cho had planned the whole operation in detail over a long period of time, he must have been clinically insane. I remembered the eagerness with which he had offered to take the watch while everyone else on board rested, before the hurricane. He must have been patiently waiting for an opportunity to execute his plot. After he got rid of Whittier by sending him down for a sandwich, the whole operation must have gone as planned, ending with his climbing the ladder to the walkway, intending to paddle in the raft to the liner, after the ship had gone down, as the sole survivor of the disaster. But for the dynamite charge, he would have succeeded.

But why? I looked round the cabin in search of a clue. There was none. Perhaps Chung was at the bottom of this sad boy's madness after all. Cho must have known that the ship was overinsured; had he been motivated by the desire to be successful in the eyes of Chung, his master, at last? Had he fantasized about turning up in front of Chung's desk to say, "I did it for you"? No one would ever know. I put the little red book back on the desk and left, closing the door softly behind me.

Chief Liu was waiting for me in the corridor. "Come with me to bridge," he said. "We must discuss what to do. There is dangerous damage."

He was right; the results of the bomb blast were dangerous to the watch on the bridge. The remnants of the walls and the aft bulkhead had sharp, jagged edges; what was left of the roof covered only the for'ard third of the wheelhouse; two thirds were exposed to the fierce sun.

Chief Liu and I decided that he and his staff would cut the jagged wheelhouse walls and aft bulkhead down to railing height and weld lengths of two-inch pipe on top for safety. The roof would be cut at the point where it could be done in a straight line; then BB's eight-foot lengths of galvanized pipe would be used to form a cage meant to support an awning made from BB's rolls of tarpaulin. The truncated stacks, at present spewing noxious fumes onto the bridge in the following wind, would be restored to their original height by using BB's stovepipe.

Before turning in, I arranged for the *mandur* to be taken back to the *Princess*, now a mouse lost in the blue infinity of the ocean under a vast, empty sky. I said farewell to him with a feeling of gratitude, but he stared at me exactly as he had when we first set eyes on each other on the quayside in Rotterdam.

Chapter Ten

The days that followed were glorious days of sunlight and blue skies; the ship was full of life and activity. Chief Liu and his crew were busy reconstructing the bridge and the wheelhouse, erecting a sort of veranda to shade the deck with a billowing awning of tarpaulin. A spirit of renewal pervaded the ship, even though, with the destruction of her electronic wizardry, the *Isabel* had been thrown back in time.

Without computers, calculators, satellites and hourly weather charts, the Chinese mates were virtually helpless, or pretended to be. As a result, I found myself, despite my bone-weariness, not only standing watches but making frequent visits to the bridge during my periods of rest to help them shoot a star, enter the tables and calculate our position.

My periods of rest were no great shakes. As a result of the destruction of the stacks, the air-conditioning units had been damaged beyond repair. My bedroom was an oven; I spent my off-watch hours stark naked on top of my bunk, tepidly bathed in warm air from a little fan the chief had dug up from his storeroom, trying to shoo away Louis who persistently curled up on my stomach, generating heat like a little furnace. I could not shut him out without shutting out whatever fresh air the fan could draw from the dayroom, so my periods of rest were troubled by his sneaky return to the mysterious attraction of my solar plexus.

Because of the open windows, the sounds of the ship came closer, invading my private world: singing and laughing on deck, hammering and drilling on the bridge overhead. It depressed me that I couldn't share in the general spirit of cheerfulness and camaraderie that had taken hold of the ship after our miraculous escape from destruction. Not only did I have a problem getting over the explosion, followed by the exertion of my hurricane watch at the wheel, but I could not shake off the memory of the sad, neurotic youth who had come to such a tragic end.

In retrospect, I felt I was partly to blame for the desperate isolation in which he lived, which had finally driven him to this act of sheer insanity. I think it was the little red book turning out to have been *Omar Khayyam* that did it. The error of judgment on my part had been typical of our entire relationship. I had taken his ship away from him, stomped on him until he locked himself in his cabin to nurse his powerless hatred and dream of revenge—Fransen had been right when he had warned me to go easy on the boy or, out in the Pacific, when we were by ourselves, he might go berserk and nail me to "the old rugged cross".

Weariness made me lie down on my couch and doze at odd hours of the day. The fact that Hopla wasn't there to act as my steward passed unnoticed, as different members of the crew started to visit me, bringing tea, and Ma Chang's concoctions. Every single member of the crew turned up at some time or another; even the oilers, whom I hardly knew. I began to look forward to their visits. They looked at my books, stroked the nude statue, wandered into my bedroom, the bathroom, flushed the toilet, made the bed; occasionally one would fiddle with my alarm clock and I would hear the bell go off. After a few days I barely noticed them coming in and out. I just sat at my desk writing my report, or went on reading on the couch.

From time to time Ma Chang turned up in person to check me over with her pendulum, pat my cheek and give me a gap-toothed grin.

My most frequent visitor was a big oiler called Tulane. He would turn up daily, immediately after his watch, sit down on the floor and browse through my books. He could not read them, but they seemed to have a fascination for him that for some reason was deeply moving. I tried to communicate with him verbally, but it was impossible. He was so backward, so prehistoric, that he didn't even speak Chinese. One day, on the spur of the moment, I produced a travel chess set I had found in a drawer of my desk. Tulane hooted with glee; I set up a game and invited him to play. As I might have expected, his game of chess was different from the one I knew—more like halma or mah-jong. The moment we started to play, others turned up and soon I found myself sitting in a crowd of excited sailors and oilers, being taught their form of gambling chess.

It was a mother hen's dream-come-true; not only were all the chicks accounted for, they turned up continuously, in ones, twos, droves, for a few moments under her wings before wandering off again, whistling, as if some solace had been received. I began to feel a lot better, but it took me days to realize that I was drawing vitality from them, the way the *Isabel* drew fuel from the old *Princess*.

Finally, I was charged up sufficiently to start writing my report in earnest. As I worked my way, in painstaking detail, through the chain of events which ended with Captain Cho's demise, a decision formed in my mind. When I had finally handed my report and the ship's log to the authorities in Pago Pago, I would have attained my objective of protecting my crew from harm. We had passed the hurricane zone of the southern hemisphere; after Samoa, any tug driver of reasonable experience could sail the ship to Taiwan. I would go home from Pago Pago.

When the cloud-shrouded mountain ridge of Tutuila Island was sighted, Hopla suddenly reappeared, crying, "Disgrace! Co'dore look disgrace! There is harbour coming up, and co'dore look like vagabond! You need haircut!"

I expected him to cut my hair himself, but instead he arranged for a professional to perform the operation: Ma Chang. So, ten minutes later, I found myself sitting on a stool on the aft deck under the fascinated eyes of a small crowd. Ma Chang draped a sheet round my neck and placed on my head a small copper wok. She had also brought a galley knife that glittered in the sun. When the wok was in place the knife started to scrape audibly, while tugging at my hair. I worried about my ears, but told myself not to be childish. Finally the wok was removed, she whisked the sheet away like a matador, the spectators applauded and Wellesley bellowed, "Woo, Omi!" I bowed to her, she bowed in return; but a twinkle in her eye made me hasten to my bathroom to take a look at myself in the mirror.

The creature that gazed back at me seemed to have nothing to do with the man I had known for seventy years. It was no longer Martinus Harinxma, or even Ome Tinus; it was one of the old Chinese drunks I remembered from years ago staggering out of Shanghai wine shops. I opened the wardrobe door and looked at myself in the long mirror through, say, Sylvia's eyes: a skinny old Chinese with a wino haircut, sweat-drenched shirt, flaring shorts like a tutu, thin hairy legs and open-toed sandals. There was a thud; the apparition was completed by a rat on his shoulder. When I thought of myself coming down the steps from the aeroplane, the possibility that Sylvia would flee, screaming, was a real one. And I would be carrying a cage containing a canary as well.

FRANSEN CAME ON BOARD the battered *Isabel* with the pilot, off Pago Pago. He looked shellshocked. "For God's sakes, Harinxma, what in God's name happened to the ship?"

Conscious of the pilot's presence, I thought it wiser not to go into dramatic details at that point. I said vaguely, "We passed through a hurricane and, as you see, sustained some damage. Otherwise, all is well." Addressing the pilot, I asked, "Where are you going to put us?"

He was a short, stocky Samoan. They are known for their composure, but he too looked nonplussed by the ship's appearance. "We can make room for you at the Station Wharf, but you'll have to be out in twenty-four hours. We're expecting one container and two Ro-Ro vessels tomorrow." He started to mutter into his walkie-talkie.

In the meantime two small harbour tugs had got hold of the *Princess*, all the port had to offer; the *Isabel* would have to do most of the mooring herself.

"And why is Captain Cho not on the bridge?" Fransen inquired.

"I'll tell you the whole story after we've put the *Princess* to bed," I replied "Let's have dinner somewhere."

THREE HOURS LATER, when darkness had fallen and it had started to rain, Fransen and I shared a meal in a dark little restaurant smelling of tropical decay, in the village of Fagatogo.

The heat was oppressive; the evening rain cascaded off the awning of the terrace on which we were having a drink. It was like dining behind a waterfall. The whole island seemed to be full of waterfalls; a distant drumbeat throbbed in the air.

Fransen polished off a tumbler of neat whisky, lit a cigarette, and said, "Well, let's have it. What happened to the ship? And to Cho?"

I told him the bare facts. Even so, it was a long story. He listened without comment, and apparently without emotion. However, he chain-smoked continuously and did not touch his food. When I had finished, he gazed at the cascade of water splashing off the awning, then ground out the cigarette he had just lit. "All right," he said. "Now what?"

"Now I hand you the ship's log and my report, for you to give to the authorities. Let them decide what should be done with the ship."

He looked at me with amazement. "You mean—you're planning to report everything? Explosive charge and all?"

"Of course," I replied, equally amazed. "What else? That's the crucial part, isn't it?"

"Do you realize what that would mean, man? If you report that the architect put an explosive charge on the walkway to prevent it capsizing, it means the ship was unseaworthy to start with! That KITCO sold Chung a ship they knew was unstable!"

"We have no choice, Fransen. As acting master, I have to report the events as they happened."

"You're not the acting master, damn it! The first mate is!"

I took a deep breath. "Officially, maybe. The fact remains that whoever is the master has to report the facts and hand over the log to the proper authority. That's the law."

He lit another cigarette and heaved a smoky sigh. "Harinxma, let me spell it out for you. If we hand in that report, the first thing they'll do is chain the ship to the quay for months while they investigate. After that, she'd have to be modified or she'd lose her certificate, which would mean that Chung couldn't sell her except for scrap. Apart from that, because the damage is self-inflicted, the insurance company would reject any claim. So what Chung would do is take KITCO and the architects to court, the kind of international litigation that can go on for years ..."

"Fransen, all I'm concerned about is the safety of my crew, and future crews of this ship. If she's rebuilt the way she was before ..."

"All right, I'll tell you what we're going to do. We'll submit another report, stating that the damage to the ship was caused by a rogue wave during a hurricane. The wheelhouse was smashed, the paradise tree toppled, the captain washed overboard; in short, the effect of an explosion."

"And the ship's log?"

"We'll state that was washed away with the chart desk when the wave smashed the wheelhouse."

It was vintage Fransen: unscrupulous, shameless, brazen. "The insurance will only pay for the damage done if it's an act of God. So, prepare an itemized list of the damage tonight, we'll shoot it off to Chung tomorrow and get the tow out of town."

"Sorry, Fransen," I said calmly. "It's no deal. You didn't get my point at all, did you? I want to protect my crew. If we do what you suggest, what is to stop Chung from rebuilding the ship into the death trap she was before? I want to force him to keep her as she is now, and only a court ruling will do that. I demand that you hand in my report and the ship's log to the authorities. And that's final."

He gave me a look I couldn't interpret. Then he raised his hands in mock surrender. "OK," he said. "On your head be it." He pushed away his plate.

A tired-looking waitress took the plates away and an insipid dessert was placed in front of us. We sat listening to the torrential rain for a while, then he said, "All right, let me try this on you for size. When I get to Kao Hsiung, twenty-four hours from now, I'll go straight to Chung. I'll show him the log and your report and tell him to have his architects design a safe profile for the ship along the lines of what you have now. If he refuses, the report and the log go to the authorities, in which case he'll be put through the mangle of an international court case with KITCO while his ship is chained to the quay. If you ask me, he'll play."

"Suppose he does, what kind of report will you file meantime?"

"None. I'll wait until I've talked to him. Let him decide."

"I don't know if I'll go along with that."

He stared at me for a moment through narrowed eyes, then said pleasantly, "Harinxma, old boy, sorry to be blunt, but you don't figure in this at all. Nobody will call you as a witness. You're not an officer but an adviser, and tomorrow you go home. When the captain was killed, the first mate took over command; he'll take the ship and the tow to Taiwan. Don't give me any problems; I'm the one who'll be taking the heat, not you.

Now—is this all we're going to get in the way of a lousy dessert? Yuck!"

He called for coffee. When, ten minutes later, we stepped out into the street, we found ourselves in a downpour and had to put our jackets over our heads while crossing the road to the taxi.

"I need the log and your report," Fransen said, once we were seated inside. "I'll take you to the ship and pick 'em up."

"Why? We'll be passing your hotel on the way to the ship. Tomorrow morning I'm going to call my wife from the hotel. I'll bring the documents along and leave them for you at the desk."

"OK, thanks. Boy, I'm beat. It's the heat." After a few moments he asked, "You want to pick up your plane ticket at the same time?"

"I don't think so."

"You changed your mind?"

"Yes."

"Mind telling me why?"

"I want to make sure the ship stays as she is. I want to be there when she arrives, talk to Chung myself."

"Also, your number one isn't up to the job. Right?"

"Right."

He sighed. "The mate you're waiting for, Harinxma, is Admiral Drake."

We drove the rest of the way in silence.

BEFORE LEAVING THE DOCUMENTS with the hotel porter for Captain Fransen the next morning, I had them photocopied by a helpful young lady at reception. She gave me two medium-sized envelopes and one large one; the originals went into one of the medium envelopes, addressed to Captain Fransen, the photocopies into the other, which I then inserted into the large envelope, addressed to Sylvia, together with a letter asking her to put the sealed envelope in the safety-deposit box in the bank.

In my letters I hadn't told her about Cho's attempt to capsize the ship, just that in the hurricane it had been necessary to activate the emergency dynamite charge, making it sound as casual as I could.

The rest of the day was hectic. We had to do in twelve hours what would normally take twenty four. Kao Hsiung was about five thousand miles away; we put plenty of fuel in the old *Princess* to get us there, but drinking water might become a problem if we weren't careful.

Just before we were due to sail, Fransen turned up with some documents for Number One to sign as acting master and he came into the dayroom for a quick final drink.

"Sorry, Harinxma," he said. "My plane leaves at twenty-one hundred and I don't want to cut it too fine. Well, cheers, Godspeed and happy sailing. See you in Kao Hsiung."

"Before you go," I said, "I think I should tell you that I had photocopies made of the log and my report."

He carefully put down his glass. "Let me see if I understand you rightly," he said. "Unless everybody does exactly what you want them to do with this ship, you're going to resort to blackmail. Is that it?"

"I want to be sure that this whole business is handled according to the law, that's all."

He sighed and went back to the fridge. "Harinxma, I'm worried about you. When I first knew you, you were a genial, chubby old boy the crew instantly called 'Uncle'. Now look at you. You eat catfood, you're as thin as a rake, with a crazy haircut and a nipped-in waist—"

"Damn it, Fransen," I exploded. "I was nearly killed by this ship! Together with forty others! What the hell do you want? A genial old boy who says, 'Oh, well . . .'?"

"Don't go for me," he said amiably, "I'm just the middleman." He knocked back his drink. "Don't worry, your precious Chinks will be safe. Now I've got to be going or I'll miss the plane." With that he left.

Two hours later I took the *Isabel* and the old *Princess* out of Pago Pago harbour into the deepest blood-red picture-postcard sunset any tourist could wish for. When our course was set and Number Two had taken over the watch, the rest of the staff and I gathered for Happy Hour.

"Well," Chief Liu said, raising his glass, "here's looking at us."

Louis got his cocktail nibbles and Pete a drop of Kirschwasser in his drinking water. Hopla hobbled around on his crutches dramatically, in death-defying devotion to duty.

AT DAYBREAK THREE DAYS LATER, towards the end of my watch, I saw in the growing light of the dawn a bizarre edifice emerging on the horizon. It looked like a stack of native houses on stilts.

It took me a while to make out what it was: a floating hotel structure, towed by a large tugboat. As I stood looking through my binoculars, trying to get a glimpse of the flag that hung limply in the windless morning, the telephone rang.

"Commodore," said the voice of Marco Two, "Netherland tugboat *Piano* make contact. The captain—Prong?—ask, will you visit?"

"Prong?"

"Sorry about name. Marco there not good Morse."

"*Bron!* You mean the *Fiona*?"

"Oh? Oh, yes, see now. What shall I signal, Commodore?"

"Say 'Yes'. Tell him I'll come over as soon as we're alongside." How about that? Beast Rufus! I remembered his telling me in Flushing that he would be pushing and pulling in Indonesia; but this was like two needles meeting in a haystack.

An hour later I was on my way to the *Fiona*, a beautiful tug of the doomed old class, as elegant and feminine as a yacht. As I approached her in the workboat, a flutter of wind stirred her flag. I realized it was flying at half-mast. One of the crew must have died.

It certainly wasn't Beast Rufus himself. He stood waiting for me at the rail. I had never seen him in his tropical working outfit: he looked like the butcher of a small town, complete with apron and straw boater, wild red beard and matted hair. "Hey!" he yelled as we drew within range. "What have you done to my pig, Ome Tinus?" So my nickname was common coinage now in the fleet.

I waved by way of answer. When we drew alongside, he reached down to haul me up like a sack of flour, plonked me on my feet on deck and yelled, "Hello there! Come to my dayroom. Let's have a snort. What the hell happened to your ship?"

"I'll tell you. Just fancy us meeting like this!"

"Nuts," he said, "my marco's been tracing you since you left Samoa. I changed course twice to hit you on the button. Why didn't your marco reply to our calls? Or do they only speak Chinese?"

"We lost our electronic gear," I explained. "We're back to Morse, ten minutes twice a day."

He led the way to his dayroom, which was smaller and scruffier than I had expected; I had forgotten how tugboat captains used to be housed, even in the recent past. "Sit down and have a drink," my host said, opening the door of the fridge and letting out a blast of polar air.

I sat down in a twanging armchair. He handed me a glass so cold that my hands almost froze to it. "I gather you ran into trouble with the pig?" he said.

I began to tell him the story. I told him how, nineteen days into the Pacific, we would have capsized but for the dynamite charge.

"Capsized?" He peered at me as if I had made a shameful confession. "You let the pig sneak up on you?"

I told him how it had come about. He was fascinated; he rose and picked up my glass. "No more for me," I said.

"You've got to be kidding. Here—" He handed me my glass. "So what did you report? That your Chink captain ran amok and tried to turn over the ship in a fit of madness?"

"Just about. But that isn't the critical part."

"Then what is?"

"Why the dynamite charge was installed in the first place."

His eyes widened. "You reported *that?*"

"Of course, I had to. Wouldn't you?"

"Like hell I would! Have myself blackballed as a tug driver for life?" Then he added, "Who did you file your report with?"

"I left that to Fransen."

His face was a study. "To *Fransen?*"

His astonishment was so genuine that I felt a twinge of doubt. "Why not?"

"Don't you know that when you talk to Fransen you talk to KITCO? Harinxma—you practically asked them to sweep it under the mat! He must have ditched the lot. You played right into their hands."

"I don't think so," I protested. "Before giving it to Fransen I had photocopies made."

"So you have photocopies! By now they aren't worth the paper they're printed on."

"I don't understand. . . ."

"You gave them all they needed, brother: time. It's going to take you fifty days to tow that hulk to Kao Hsiung. By the time you get there, the whole thing will be over and done with. They'll have filed a fraudulent claim without mentioning any explosion. The insurance company will have accepted it and paid up. All maritime reports will have been dutifully filed. The dead captain's next of kin will have received a nice letter and a little pension so they won't make trouble. The case will be closed, and your story about dynamite charges and captains running amok and trying to scuttle the ship will just seem crazy. You'll be a threat to everybody, even the civil servants involved, and if you're not careful you'll end up in a Taiwanese nut farm."

His dramatization was so exaggerated that I felt relieved. He was just another Fransen, seeing plots and assassins under every bed. Either that, or he was getting drunk.

"You don't believe me?"

"Frankly, no."

The look he gave me was one of commiseration. "No, I guess you don't." He took a swig from his glass. "OK, I'll spell it out for you. You told Fransen—when?"

"Oh, I don't know. During a meal, after I came in."

"You told him you were going to report the whole story exactly the way it happened? Dynamite charge and all?"

"Yes. He suggested reporting it as hurricane damage."

"And you said no?"

"I said—well, never mind. We ended by agreeing that he would go straight to see Chung, show him the log and my report, get him to agree not to rebuild the ship the way she was originally, but to have the architects design a lower profile along the lines she has now—"

"And if Mr. Chung didn't agree, he'd hand your report and the log to the authorities. Right?"

"Yes."

He rose to get himself a third drink. "OK, I'll tell you what happened. The same night he talked to you, Fransen called The Hague and warned them they had a loose cannon on deck: you. That he'd stalled you for the moment, but what should he do next?"

I shifted uneasily. "So?"

"So they told him: 'Here's what you do: play the old man along. Agree to whatever he says, as long as you get that convoy out of there on the double. But before you do, have the acting master sign a report stating that the damage was caused by a hurricane.' And that's exactly what he must have done."

I remembered Fransen coming on board with a sheaf of documents for Number One to sign. My heart sank. "But he couldn't! The boy knew I'd written a full report, that I had the log—"

"Harinxma, who are you kidding? You sincerely believe that Fransen, the wiliest hyena in the business, couldn't make a Chinese babe-in-the woods sign a bunch of papers saying it was a hurricane? That the captain was killed by a rogue wave? I can hear him saying it: 'Captain'—he's sure to have called the poor devil 'Captain'—'it's been decided by Mr. Chung that we should report that the damage was caused by a hurricane.' He'll have told him some so-called inside stuff, very hush-hush, about insurance, corporate responsibility—hell, you could write his sales pitch yourself. The kid would have signed his own death warrant within three minutes."

"But what difference would that make? I have photocopies of everything! My report, the log—if Chung doesn't agree to keep the ship's profile as it is now, I'll telephone my wife and she'll hand the documents to the authorities!"

"Your wife has them?" He shook his head. "Harinxma, you may be a great sailor, but 007 you ain't." He bent over and slurped the top off his drink before picking up the glass. "Fransen and KITCO know you better than you know yourself, man. You'll never do it, and they know you won't. All you've done is bellow 'Boo!' as far as blackmail is concerned. They have you over a barrel, friend. You'll never do it."

"You're dead wrong, I tell you! Boy, even if I end up in prison—"

"You in prison? No, Harinxma, not you. The little Chink. That gullible child, the 'acting master' who must have signed the fraudulent declaration. If you bring out your report and the log, every page of which he initialled at the end of his watch, they can have him for perjury. What do you think they'll do to him? Not only will his career be shot, *he'll* end up in prison, not you. Jim Kwel knows, Fransen knows, and I bet you Chung knows, you'll never do it; your hands are tied. So forget it, Harinxma. Chung is going to rebuild the pig the way she was, to have another shot at picking up the insurance money. And this time you can bet your life he's not going to put another old salt on board who could sail the world in a bathtub, and who fights for his crew like a tiger. He'll have a wide choice of dopes, like your Captain Cho, who don't even *know* that their souls are for sale."

My God, I had forgotten about Number One. He was right. I could never do that. But then, maybe it wasn't necessary. Old Kwel might be a tough, hard-nosed old devil, but when the chips were down, he had always proved to be decent in the end. I said, more to myself than to Beast Rufus, "I'll talk to old Kwel."

He fixed me with a strange stare. "You don't know? Of course—all you had left was Morse."

"Why? What happened?"

"Haven't you seen my flag? All ships of the fleet are under orders to observe one week of mourning." He raised his glass. "Here's to Arnold Kwel. May his soul roast in hell."

"My God . . ."

I suddenly wanted to get out of there. "I have to be going," I said putting down my glass.

"Why?" he asked, hurt. "You just got here!"

I rose and went to the door. "So long, Bron. Godspeed and happy sailing."

"And nuts to you," he said. "You didn't even finish your drink!"

Out on deck I looked up at the flag, now flying free in the freshening wind, at half-mast.

Old Kwel was dead.

I couldn't understand why the news affected me as deeply as it did. I was stunned. The sunlit world had suddenly darkened, transforming everything. Back on board and alone in my cabin, the full realization hit me. On impulse, I went to the desk, sat down and took a sheet of paper out of the drawer.

Dear Miss Bastiaans,

I have just received the news of Arnold Kwel's passing. My immediate response is to write to you. As you know, he and I knew each other for a long time, over fifty years in fact, and I find myself deeply affected by his death. But you probably knew him better than I did; the few times that I saw you together, I was struck by your dedication to him and your concern for his wellbeing.

He put his indelible stamp on the ocean towage business. That may not sound like much, compared to the movers of empires and the shakers of men, but he will be remembered as long as there are long-distance tugboats sailing the seas.

Miss Bastiaans, I'm far away, in Polynesia, after five months at sea.

I wish I could stand with you at his grave and bid farewell to the Old Man.

I feel as if I had lost part of my life, and thereby of myself.

Yours, in sympathy and mourning,
Martinus Harinxma.

ALTHOUGH THERE WAS NOTHING I could do about it, not for weeks, I had to know the truth. So that evening, after supper, I invited Number One to my dayroom. He accepted with alacrity. I asked, "Number One, before we left Pago Pago, did Captain Fransen ask you to sign any documents concerning the damage to the ship?"

I expected a shifty look, or one of bewildered innocence; instead, he beamed at me. "Don't worry, Commodore. It's been taken care of."

"Captain Fransen did give you a report to sign?"

"Of course, I acting master."

"So it's hurricane-wave damage now, officially?"

"Yes. Very good solution, OK."

"And the log?"

"Shh," he said. "Gone. He said he deep-six it." Suddenly, a doubt crossed his mind. "That mean what I think it mean, no?"

"It means 'to destroy'."

He looked relieved. "I told you," he said smugly, "everything taken care of. Don't worry."

I could no longer contain myself. "You stupid idiot!" I cried. "Can't you see what you've done? You've ruined my only chance of stopping this ship from being turned back into the death trap she was!"

He looked as if he had been hit by a bucket of water.

"Chung will get the money to rebuild her the way she was! I could have stopped him, because I have copies of the original log and my report, but now, damn it, if I do that, you'll end up in jail and you can forget about any future as a ship's officer! You idiot!"

I realized I was yelling at Fransen, Jim Kwel, myself, not the poor, hoodwinked youth. "Get out of my sight," I said. "I'll talk to you later," and I slammed the door after him.

Alone in my dayroom, pacing like a caged bear, I began to see that Beast Rufus was right: I might be a good sailor, but I was a lousy plotter. I had been an easy mark: a seventy-year-old man with hypertension who had been out of the running for nine years, and who had never involved himself in the subterfuges of the owners whose ships he sailed.

But no, it had nothing to do with age; it had to do with my lack of insight when it came to dealing with Fransen's demonic world. I had painted myself into a corner. There was no way out of the dilemma: either go along with them, cover up for Number One and save his career, or throw him to the wolves and protect the lives of the rest of the crew, and of all future crews that might sail on a reconstructed version of this killer ship. There simply was no alternative: I was utterly stymied. No matter what other plan I might come up with, by the time I reached Kao Hsiung, Bron's prophecy would have been fulfilled. They had me over a barrel.

The telephone on my desk rang shrilly. Sighing, I answered.

"Dayroom, Harinxma."

"Oh, Commodore, excuse me, a light show in far distance, not on chart, could you come identify, please?"

"Who is this? Number Two?"

"No, Co'dore, this is Number One. I am sorry for disturb you, but light flashes dot dot dot dash dot dot, not on chart, not in *Pilot*."

"Have you taken our position recently?"

"Yes, Commodore, we are exactly where we suppose to be, Commodore. . . ."

"In that case, stand on your own feet. What would you do if you were the captain of this ship, without me on tap? Call the marco on duty, ask if he's received any notices to mariners for this area. If not, let him contact Rabaul or Truk and find out."

"Yes, Commodore. . . ."

I went back to the couch.

Somebody banged on the door. I opened it, and there stood Hopla, bright-eyed, toothy-smiled, carrying a tray. "Co'dore like tea?"

I did not know what the time was. "All right, put it on the table."

"Yes, Co'dore. . . ." He limped to the coffee table, put down the mug, and tiptoed out, looking saintly and servile, but forgetting to limp. He found his way barred by Number One, standing in the doorway, his face sick with fear. "You must come!" he yelled in a highpitched, querulous voice. "I can't handle it alone! I can't!"

"I'm coming," I said. I hastened to the door, took my cap off the hook and set out at a run. When, out of breath, prepared for the worst, I arrived on the bridge, I found it strangely quiet. There were plenty of people about, but they were all standing gazing ahead into the night. The sky was full of stars.

I joined them and looked through the for'ard windows. On the horizon, right across our course, a row of lights was strung out, each of them flashing in groups of dots and dashes. I breathed easier; there was no emergency, they were at least five or six miles away. But what could they be? Fishermen? A convoy? No wonder Number One had got into a panic.

I called the radio room and a chipper voice answered. "Marco Two, Commodore. Yes, please?"

"Did you pick up any notices to mariners recently?"

The voice said cheerfully, "Moment, please!" I heard a rustling of papers. "I tell him already: about erections of Australian navy flashers."

It took a moment to get out of him what the message had actually said; it turned out to be an official warning to local traffic that the Australian navy would start night-bombing practice at 0:00 hours in an area delineated by pontoons, each showing a different sequence of flashing lights. I had come up just in time or we might have been dive-bombed by the latest version of World War II Stukas.

I changed course; the tow headed north into the open; we were safe. Even so, I felt I should stay on the bridge until we were far enough away from the danger zone for the faint-hearted to breathe easier.

Half an hour later, I went to my dayroom, and began to face, once again, the insoluble dilemma of how to save Number One's silly neck without endangering the lives of the present and future crews of the ship. Again I realized that I couldn't find the answer on my own; I decided I would discuss it with Chief Liu. He was intelligent, experienced, and as involved in the fate of the *Isabel* as I was. As a matter of fact, he was the one who had raised all the questions in the first place. I invited him for a drink.

He came up to the dayroom at once. But the moment he realized what I wanted to talk about, the jolly, mischievous man I knew changed back into an inscrutable member of an alien race. He refused a drink and sat silently listening, eyes averted, to the summary of my conversation with Beast Rufus. When finally he spoke, I knew that my idea of our finding an answer together had been an illusion.

"I am old man with large family," he said carefully. "I have children in school, in university. Two daughters needing dowry. I am no slave, but I— what you call?—behold to Mr. Chung. If Mr. Chung say, 'It was hurricane,' I say, 'Down in engine room there is much noise. Suddenly, "Bang!" upstairs. I rush up, find wheelhouse gone, stacks gone, captain killed. No idea what happen, none. No knowledge of anything.' "

"You mean to say that's the story you're going to tell if there is an inquiry?"

This time he looked me straight in the eye. "As I told Captain Fransen, I in no position to contradict Captain Hu's report."

"Who in hell is Captain Hu?"

"The one you call Number One," he replied, smiling.

I should have known. While I had been worrying about stores and drinking water that day in Pago Pago, Fransen had got not only to Number One but to Chief Liu as well, and probably all the other members of the staff. Beast Rufus was right: the report had been filed by now, the claim made, the testimonies of captain and staff registered, the insurance compensation paid. The case was closed.

"Thank you, Chief," I said. "How about a drink?"

"I would be ravished, thank you," he said.

We sat there chatting pleasantly. My Chinese friend was telling me, in effect, that Don Quixotes must tilt at their windmills alone.

Chapter Eleven

As the days went by, sunny, somnolent days which I spent on the bridge in my deckchair in the cool shade of the awning, while the tow slowly coursed across the blue seas, past islands large and small, some mountainous, others a mere fringe of palms on the horizon, all of them asleep in the tropical sun, I found myself arriving at a number of surprising conclusions. I became confident, despite the time lapse, that the existence of photocopies of my report and the ship's log would be sufficient to make Chung agree to repair the *Isabel* along the lines of her present safe profile and not reconstruct her to her original design. But to stop him from weaselling out of our agreement, someone would have to keep tabs on what happened to the ship. Who? The Dutch consul? I could hardly take him into my confidence ...

It was only at this point that it became clear to me, belatedly, that there was just one thing I could do—keep an eye on the ship myself. Rent a room on the waterfront in Kao Hsiung and make a daily round past the yard!

IN THE EARLY-MORNING HOURS of the one hundred and ninety-first day of our voyage we approached Kao Hsiung. The weather was stormy, with low, racing clouds and an angry, slate-coloured sea. The awning over the bridge flopped and thundered in the breeze. To the north I could see the barren peak of Tung Shan mountain, half obscured by rain, a mile and a half from the entrance to Kao Hsiung harbour.

I was quite calm, surprisingly so. Ever since Merir Island, our last fuelling stop, two weeks ago, I had resigned myself to the prospect of having to live on the Kao Hsiung waterfront until the *Isabel* had acquired her permanent low profile. So I was feeling resigned, even serene, when we approached the quarantine area outside the breakwater and the pilot launch came out, snorting and sneezing alongside.

Fransen didn't turn up until we were well inside the pierheads and swinging the *Princess* in the second harbour's turning basin. He climbed on board from a tender. A minute later he appeared on the bridge, holding on to his fedora, sparks flying off his cigarette, his raincoat billowing in the wind. I was surprisingly moved to see him; if the bridge hadn't been full of Chinese officers slapping one another's shoulders in the excitement of homecoming, I would have embraced him.

He was not in that mood. As he came towards me he shook his head.

"Well, boy, while you were frolicking on the waves, the china cupboard fell on its face at home. God! Your missus is something else."

My heart skipped a beat. "Sylvia? What's the matter?"

"I'm not going to tell you, Harinxma," he said, "I'm going to leave that to someone bigger than you and me. Don't worry, she's OK, but you'd better put on your helmet and your breastplate, as the Good Book says, before you meet Mr. Chung." He shook his head again.

"Captain?" the pilot called sharply. "Would you mind joining me for this manoeuvre?"

So I had to assist the pilot in taking the old *Princess* to her graveyard, a pier with a forest of cranes and a huge shed saying in man-size letters: CHARLIE S. CHUNG, KAO HSIUNG STEELWORKS. What could be the matter with Sylvia? What had happened?

I tried to get more out of Fransen, but he wasn't forthcoming. "Wait till Mr. Chung tells you," he said, "and hold onto your hat." Then glancing round, he muttered, "For openers, after the old man died, who do you think inherited his half of the business?"

"Look, Fransen, all I want to know is—"

"The Bastiaans woman! So, whatever you do, watch your step. Well, here's your mail." He pulled out a small stack of letters. "Most of them are from Mrs. Harinxma; let her tell you in her own words."

Now what was in store for me? I felt myself sliding into a panic of worry, speculation, confusion. I heard Fransen say, "O-oh! Here he comes ..." I looked up and saw a limousine approaching down the quayside and I suddenly became aware that the ship had fallen silent, as when old Kwel's limousine had stopped at the *Isabel*'s gangway in Rotterdam.

The ship was moored, the gangway lowered. I pulled the engine telegraph back and forth, signalling, "Finished with Engines." All vibration ceased. The ship was as silent as the grave. "Thank you, Pilot," I said, "it was a pleasure."

"Likewise, Captain," the unsmiling Taiwanese replied.

As I passed him on my way down, Fransen whispered, "If you need me, I'll be in the hospital, preparing bandages!" I didn't respond, but hurried to my dayroom, hoping to have a chance to read Sylvia's letters before Chung turned up. I tore open the first one.

My dear Martinus,

After all these months of subterfuge and dissimulation, how did you expect me to put a sealed envelope into the safe-deposit box—I was sick with worry. I could get no sense out of anyone at head office when I called. So I did what any wife would do who is worried sick. I opened the envelope and read what was inside. At last, at long last, I was told the truth! There it was, from the beginning ...

The door opened and there, smiling, eyes twinkling, stood Mr. Chung.
"Welcome to Taiwan, Commodore! Mind if I come in?"
"Of course—hello—good afternoon, sir."
We shook hands. "May I sit down?" he asked pleasantly.
I gestured to the couch. He sat down. His small, dark eyes, as enigmatic as a baby's, stared at me without expression.
"The ship is quite a sight. Captain Fransen gave me a report describing the damage sustained, but I could not quite visualize it."
"Indeed, it must have been difficult."
"I'm distressed about Captain Cho," he continued. "What a sad occurrence. Well, we were lucky to have you on the team, Commodore. You did a sterling job. Thank you very much."
Trying to sound casual, I asked, "Did Captain Fransen inform you of the cause of the damage? I may have a different report for you from the one you received."
"Ah?" He said it lightly. His smile didn't waver.
"I must tell you, sir, that I am determined this ship shall never sail again unless her present profile is maintained. She was a death trap. She would be again, if you restored—"
"Commodore, you are worrying unduly." He gave me a look that suddenly was unnervingly kind. "Tomorrow at six o'clock we start breaking up the ship for scrap."
I stared at him, thunderstruck.
"The operation should take little time; a month from now, at the latest, all her components will have been stacked ashore and sorted out. I will then mail you a certified surveyor's statement of demolition, with photographs, for your records."
"But, sir, *why?*" I couldn't believe this.
"In exchange, I expect you to mail me by return all photocopies of the ship's log and of your report. I wish to include those when we close her file. Now—" He put his hand in an inside pocket and brought out an envelope. "Here is a cheque for what we owe you."
I accepted the envelope mechanically.
"You'll also find in there your flight ticket to France. You leave tomorrow for T'ai-pei, where you change planes. I want everybody off this ship by six o'clock tomorrow morning." He rose; I just sat there, staring at him in disbelief.
"Well," he said cheerfully, "I think that takes care of everything. Thank you very much, Commodore, and have a good flight. No, no! Don't get up, I know the way out."
After he had left, I didn't know if I should rush to the hospital to see Fransen. It could not be true!
I ran to the hospital.

THE AIR WAS BLUE with cigarette smoke. On the bedside table stood a bottle and a tumbler. Fransen was lying on the high bed in his shirtsleeves, fanning his face with his fedora.

"Fransen, what the hell is going on? I mean, who—"

"Sit down, Harinxma. Calm down. Want a drink?"

"Fransen, listen to me! Chung has just told me the ship's going to be broken up! Did you know that?"

He peered at me through the smoke of his cigarette. "I told you that your missus had dropped the atom bomb. Didn't she tell you why, in her letters?"

"I haven't read them yet! Tell me what happened! For God's sake, Fransen, it can't be true, they can't break up this ship! She's the best tugboat I ever sailed, she's—"

"Harinxma," he said with an authority he had never used on me before,"take it easy, man! You're as tight as a drum. Here, have a swig. Either that, or grab a fistful of tranquillizers from your medicine cupboard."

"Why, for God's sake?" I cried. "The ship is perfectly all right the way she is now! Why break her up? Why?"

"Because," he said, handing me a glass, "no one has any use for a barge with thirty thousand horsepower. All Chung could use her for, the way she is now, would be pushing and pulling outside the harbour here, maybe some tootling to Japan and back with a piece of junk. That's not an economical proposition. He'd be crazy to do it. Go on, drink up."

Shaking, I took a swig, suddenly overcome by grief. This hadn't been my intention at all, I had never thought in terms of killing her! My God, what had I done? "Fransen, please," I said, "explain to me. Why—"

"Harinxma, I know," he interrupted kindly. "I don't blame you. I would have reacted the same way if she'd been mine. You can't sail a ship this far and go through what you went through with her without thinking she's the greatest bucket ever built. But you know as well as I do, if you look at it soberly: she's a killer. Everybody, including yourself, will be better off when she's put down. So don't stand there as if you'd murdered your own mother. You did a good job, but the job is over, and you and everybody else were lucky to get here in one piece. Now, you had better start packing. You'll have to be off this ship by six tomorrow morning, boy. These men mean business."

"But when was it decided? What brought it about?"

"It's simple, really. Your missus got that envelope with the log and your report and she opened it. Once she had read it, she took the first plane to Holland, turned up at head office and marched straight into Jim Kwel's office. She slammed your little contribution on his desk, accused him of trying to murder her husband and his crew, and threatened to publish your report in the newspapers. It seems Jim Kwel wanted to take the stuff away from her, but—so goes the tale—she hit him with her handbag, stuffed it all back inside and marched out. And there, in the corridor, who did she run into? One guess: our new director, Miss Bastiaans. They took off to have lunch together, leaving Jim Kwel going berserk in his office. At least, that's how the secretaries tell it."

I asked incredulously, "Don't tell me it was *she* who decided? Not Miss Bastiaans?"

He lifted one hand in a gesture of blessing, raising his glass with the other. "I told you, I warned the old man you'd never leave this ship unless somebody shot you. Well, leave it to a woman. As no one seemed prepared to shoot you, she shot the ship."

"But how could she decide all by herself?"

"Not she alone. She and Jim and the architects, with a couple of whiz kids from our legal department. They decided that, things having gone this far, and what with Mrs. Harinxma ready to pull the pin on the hand grenade, it would be best if somebody went to see Mr. Chung to remind him that he too was up to his neck in this, that his little stooge had tried to scuttle the ship with forty people on board for the insurance money, and that nobody would look too good if this ever came out in the open. So, as far as I can see—mind you, I'm just a flunkey—it's a good bet that KITCO paid him some compensation, and that he decided to take the honest man's way out and destroy the evidence."

"But this is crazy! This must cost them—"

"Harinxma," he said soothingly, "when you're in their league, you know when to cut your losses. What they lose on the swings, they gain on the roundabouts. Chung has his fingers in many pies. Now, would you like to hear what little Bastiaans is planning to do?"

"Fransen, I think I—I would—I'll see you later."

"Don't take it too hard," he said, as I headed for the door. "Remember, tomorrow, six hundred hours."

I was about to go down the corridor when he added, "Harinxma, once more: watch your step. Mr. Chung is a pussycat in comparison to little Bastiaans. I thought I'd warn you, because the lady is in town."

I desperately needed some time alone. I was still in a state of shock. It hadn't penetrated fully yet, but I knew that all my plotting and scheming had merely contrived to kill my ship. I opened the door and found Number One waiting for me in the dayroom.

I was about to tell him to come back later; then I saw the expression on his face. He was in agony—had he been fired?

It took me a moment before I realized why he looked so worried. "Don't worry, Number One, things look better for you than you could have dared hope, my friend. Tomorrow morning they're starting to break up this ship. All photocopies of the log and my report will be destroyed. It's all over and done with. Your fraudulent report will never be challenged, it's already forgotten."

The poor devil burst into tears. I put an arm round his shoulders and said, "OK, OK now. Pull yourself together. But let it be a lesson. Never sign anything that distorts the facts, stick to the truth." I was a fine one to talk. I shooed him out.

"Will we—will we have Happy Hour...?" He asked as if it were a sacrament. Maybe it was.

"Of course we will." I closed the door on his anxious face.

Finally alone, I felt so tired that all I could do was drag myself to the bedroom, climb into my bunk and pass out.

At least, that's what I thought. Once I lay on my bed, I became aware of a small, familiar vibration. I remembered lying like this the very first night on board; my mind a blank, my hand pressed against the wall, feeling that faint vibration of the main generator, the living body of the ship. Now I experienced again the physical union between captain and ship, that most ancient, mystical relationship between man and matter. Without knowing it, the *Isabel* and I had shared the last voyage of our lives, the long voyage home.

And the grasshopper shall be a burden, and desire shall fail: because man goeth to his long home, and the mourners go about the streets.

Mourning for us both, our brief, star-crossed lives, I fell asleep.

"COMMODORE?"

I was dreaming. I was lying on my bunk. I stared at the figure in the doorway. I saw a beautiful young woman.

"Sorry to wake you," the beautiful young woman said, "but my plane leaves in a few hours and you and I have things to discuss. Don't hurry, I'll be waiting for you in the lounge." She gave me a smile that lit up the room; only then did I realize who it was.

I got up, washed my face, wetted my hair, combed it, straightened my crumpled shirt and my tutu shorts and went to face the beautiful young woman who Fransen had said was more cunning than Chung. Another phantasm from his demonic universe.

When I came in, she was sitting on the couch in the dayroom, scratching Louis's belly. Pete strutted in his cage, noisy with jealousy.

"He's charming," she said. "Where did you get him?"

"In Antwerp. He was brought on board in a basket of fruit—a farewell gift from Mr. Chung. Can I offer you something?" I asked, heading for the fridge.

"Whatever you are having, Commodore."

"I'm afraid all I have is Dutch gin. But it's from the freezer."

"Thank you, that'll be fine." Well, she certainly knew her way around tugboats. I would only have to tell her that "the lounge" was called "the dayroom" and she could be one of the boys.

I poured us each a dainty one and carried them carefully to the coffee table, trying not to spill anything. My hands were shaking badly.

"You may have a problem importing him into Europe," she said, driving Louis to ecstasies with her delicate, persistent scratching. Soon I would have to cover Pete's cage with a towel; in his jealousy he was beginning to sound like a burglar alarm. "You'd have no problem in Curaçao."

Again she gave me the smile that had beguiled me when first we met. I lifted my glass and said, "Cheers, Miss Bastiaans." We each took a nip and put our glasses down. I said, "All right, tell me."

She looked at me with an expression that I could only define as soulful, then said, "I must thank you for your very kind letter on the occasion of Mr. Arnold's passing. You were the only one who spoke from the heart."

"Well," I said uncomfortably, "I had known him for a long time. I just felt—well, I thought you would understand."

"It was quite mutual, Commodore. I appreciated what you said."

It all sounded sincere and spontaneous, yet there was something I couldn't put my finger on. "Tell me about Curaçao," I said.

She smiled. "I don't know how much Captain Fransen has told you, but after Mr. Arnold's death I was put in charge of a new branch of the company based in Willemstad. Mr. Jim will stay in The Hague, he'll have the more powerful and modern ships; I have been asked to take charge of a small fleet of older ones, very modest, which would be put on station in the Caribbean and the Gulf during the hurricane season. There will also be some oil work to do. The company will be called KITCO N.A., for Netherland Antilles. I would like you to take charge as head of operations." Again she gave me one of those smiles that would melt a heart of ice.

"If you'll forgive me for being frank, Miss Bastiaans, I think that's a crazy idea. I can tell you here and now that there's no question of my accepting. But why choose me?"

"Because," she said, "KITCO N.A. will be different from the parent company in so far as all ships will be manned by Chinese or Indonesian crews. It seems you have a particular affinity with the Chinese."

"Well, I appreciate your confidence in me, but I'm through with the sea. For good, this time. I'm going home to spend the years that are left to me with my wife. To be quite frank, Miss Bastiaans," I added, "head of operations is the most exhausting job in the business. You don't want a man in his seventies for that."

Her blue eyes remained unmoved. "Mr. Arnold was ninety when he

262

died." She finished her drink and rose. I could tell that she had given me up as a lost cause. "I would have liked to have lunch with you, but there won't be time. Instead, what I'm going to do is take you to a tailor and put you in some decent clothes. You cannot travel in what you are wearing now, your wife would never forgive me. You've lost a lot of weight, haven't you? Your dress uniform must be much too large."

"But I have a tailor on board, an oiler who—"

"Commodore, you're about to meet your wife. I want her to recognize you when you step off the plane. Mr. Chung phoned the man for me. I was promised it could be done before you leave for T'ai-pei. Let's go." She opened the door.

"Miss Bastiaans," I said, with a feeling of tenderness at all this dazzling efficiency, "I'm grateful for your kind offer, but I cannot go to see a tailor. I have too much to do on board before we leave."

"But the ship is about to be broken up! What is there for you to do?"

It was comforting to know that owners remained owners, whatever their gender. "There are *people* on board, Miss Bastiaans. I cannot walk out on them just like that. We've just spent six and a half months together."

Suddenly she gave me a fleeting view of something deep down, behind those hard blue eyes. "You see, it isn't just for your know-how that I need you, Commodore. I've always been guided and protected by the wisdom of someone much older than myself."

It was manipulation worthy of old Kwel. She was certainly a chip off the old block. "There's not much wisdom I have to give you, Miss Bastiaans," I said, "except, maybe, don't try to become one of the boys. When the jokes start, go and play Chopin. In memory of Arnold Kwel and me."

"That was a pompous remark, Commodore," she said. "But you are forgiven."

"Thank you," I said.

Happy Hour that afternoon would have been a strained affair but for Harakiri. Marco One's and Mate Number Two's wives had appeared and were invited to join us; Chief Liu's three daughters and four sons also turned up, shutting out the clamour of children as they closed the door. I gathered there were grandchildren, and that Mrs. Liu had been detailed to look after them.

Harakiri had had the foresight to bribe someone ashore and harvest six packs of Taiwanese beer. We all drank beer; even the ladies sipped delicately. Harakiri handed round more cans, saying, "Let's polish 'em off, folks, plenty more where these came from. Well, here's mud in your eye." He must have been drinking before he arrived, because there was no stopping him. He told his audience about the yacht, about life in two aluminium trailers on top of a dock, the murals on board the liner, which I had not seen, but which I could imagine when he said that his crew had spruced them up in their spare time.

When the time came to break it up—not an easy thing to do with Harakiri going full blast—fate came to my aid in the person of a roly-poly Chinese gentleman who entered with beaming apologies, produced a note pad and rolled-up tape measure and asked, "Excuse. Who of you be Condor Eczema?" Harakiri pointed at me and said, "Who do you think, bozo? There's only one of us dripping with gold."

The gentleman bowed and handed me a little note which read, *Allow me this for old times' sake, Eleanor B.* "Please be upstanding," he said, bowing; he must have seen *Rumpole of the Bailey* on Taiwanese TV.

I complied; he began to measure my neck, my chest, the length of my arms, my hips—the audience became restless. When he proceeded to the inside leg seam, the ladies rose and bowed and I bowed in return, and in no time at all everyone was gone. Then the gentleman left too, after saying, "Will be at plane tomorrow, Condor."

I went to the bedroom to pack my suitcase and holdall. When I came back to the dayroom, Harakiri was still there. He joined me for the evening meal; together we went down the corridor of the officers' quarters, from which everyone seemed to have vanished.

The desolation of an empty ship was getting to me, until I saw the messroom. Not only was it as full as always, but more so. The runners, with their *mandur*, had come on board, not mingling with the rest but seated at a separate table, scowling. Harakiri put a stop to that with the insouciance of inebriation, saying, "Come on, boys, join the crowd. Bring the beer."

The *mandur* rose, his crew followed suit, and they joined the main table, when Ma Chang's tribe had shuffled down the benches to make room for them. The *mandur* produced more six-packs from somewhere, and when everyone had an open can in hand, Harakiri tried to lead us in song by bursting into raucous bawling, pounding time with his fist on the table. The *mandur* and two of the runners, who obviously had seen him like this before, picked him up and carried him off, singing.

There were no speeches at the end of the meal, but lots of grins, and no toasts, except "Woo, Omi!" from Wellesley, followed by his own manic laughter. It was a comfort of sorts to realize that even among prehistoric Chinese tribes there was sure to be one crashing bore.

When finally I got back to my dayroom, Louis jumped on my shoulder and Pete drew his beak back and forth across the bars of his cage with a harplike sound. I fed him, covered the cage with a towel, went to my bedroom and found that I had packed my pyjamas. But it was stiflingly hot, so I lay down on top of my bunk in my shorts, realized I should have called Sylvia, and fell asleep.

Chapter Twelve

At dead of night I suddenly found myself wide awake, staring at the ceiling, feeling tearful. The ship was silent. It felt as if there were not a soul left on board: a feeling of finality and desolation. Well, someone had to say goodbye to her, it might as well be me. So I put on my shortsleeved shirt with shoulder tabs, shorts, sandals and cap, and started my farewell tour.

I walked down the empty corridor, down the companionway to the boat deck, exactly as I had done that first night in Rotterdam when everything was new, saying goodbye without undue emotion, other than occasionally patting a handrail or touching a bulkhead. Goodbye, old girl. Goodbye.

As I came up the companionway to the next deck, I saw right opposite me the entrance to the galley; at the table inside sat a motionless figure—Ma Chang. She and I must be the only ones awake on board. She beckoned to me without a word; I stepped inside.

She pointed to a stool; I sat down. Then she took a couple of teacups from the shelf, reached down and produced a curiously shaped bottle without a label from under the table. With little glugs, loud in the silence, she filled both cups, pushed one across to me, raised hers and stared at me without a smile.

I followed her example, raised my teacup; when she drank, I drank. It nearly blasted me off my stool. Never before in my life had I drunk anything remotely like it. I gazed at her, wide-eyed with disbelief, as she put the empty cup in front of her, smacking her lips.

I could hardly spit it out, so I swallowed it. I cannot describe the sensation; it was as if my soul and body were separated. She and I were sitting opposite one another in some other dimension, beyond space, and she was solemnly trying to blow us up. She went on pouring the stuff, lifting her cup without a smile, and sipping it, forcing me to do the same. There came a moment when it all flowed together: gratitude, sorrow, friendship, wordless understanding. Suddenly I wanted to give her something; a token, however small, that would somehow embody it all. On an impulse, I took a shoulder tab, with commodore's gold, off my shirt and held it out to her.

Without looking at it, she picked it up, put it in a pocket of her smock and stared at me. I took off the other shoulder tab and put it on the table too. Again, she didn't even look at it but picked it up, put it in her pocket and stared at me again. Then her hand went into the other pocket and brought out a small object which she put in front of me. It was her pendulum.

I looked up at her, not believing. She stared at me without a smile, then shook her head: yes, that was her present to me. It was just a bead on a bit

of string, but it was her symbol of power. Well, so were my shoulder tabs. I picked it up and put it in my shirt pocket.

She filled the cups once more; I knew this was the zero in the countdown, but it seemed unthinkable for me to refuse it. She drank hers in small, sensuous slurpings, I downed mine in one. When I opened my eyes, we were still staring at each other with total understanding. Or misunderstanding; it no longer seemed to matter.

She bowed. I bowed. I rose slowly to my feet and floated back to bed.

I WAS WOKEN BY A VOICE calling, "Harinxma! Harinxma, wake up, man!"

Groaning, I opened my eyes and saw that it was Fransen. "Get up!" he urged, shaking me. "You have to be off this ship in ten minutes! The wrecking crew is here, the funeral service is in progress on the dockside."

"Funeral service?" My tongue felt as if it had grown hair overnight. "Where's Harakiri?" I asked, closing my eyes because of the transparent worms wriggling in front of them.

"He's out there already. Everybody's lined up for the funeral service. Come on, man. What's the matter with you?"

I dressed, unstable on my feet as if the ship were rolling, and went to the dayroom.

Fransen stared at me. "No!" he cried, as if I were a cat bringing in a dead bird. "You can't go out like that! For God's sake, man, you're the commodore! You look like—" Words failed him. "Don't you give a damn that you're leaving your ship for good? That she's going to be broken up? There's a Chinese religious service going on outside, damn it! Put on your number-one uniform ... You're drunk."

"Don't talk nonsense. I took a sleeping pill last night, that's all."

But I went back to the bedroom wondering if he was right. When I caught sight of myself in the mirror, I looked ten years older, but perfectly sober. I dressed in my number-one uniform. It looked ludicrous, but I didn't want to run into Fransen's buzz-saw again. The jacket hung round me in folds, the sleeves seemed longer than when I had last seen them, the ribbons commemorating forgotten sea battles added a final touch of drollery.

I found Louis hiding behind the books on the shelf; it took some persuasion before he would let himself be zipped into the flight bag, despite the apples and the piece of bread soaked in Kirschwasser I put in there. I covered Pete's cage with a towel and took it off the hook.

"Is that it?" Fransen asked. "What can I carry? You must hurry, man!"

"You take my holdall and my suitcase. I'll take the animals. Lead on, Macduff."

When we came out on deck, I saw that the yard was bright with floodlights and the blinding pinpoints of welding. The giant skeletons across the basin were silhouetted against a skyline yellow with the dawn. At the foot of the gangway the staff, the crew and Harakiri and his runners were lined up, watching a Chinese priest dressed in unfamiliar robes make sweeping gestures with an incense burner over the gangway, intoning a chant. He stood aside to let us pass; after we had stepped off the gangway, he put lighted candles on it and began to swing his incense burner again. Fransen and I joined the staff and watched the ceremony. To one side, a group of workmen in blue overalls and welding helmets were waiting, ready for action. The whole thing had an unearthly quality.

Fransen nudged me and whispered, "OK, that's that. Now, say goodbye to them. Go on! Go down the line, Harinxma!"

I put the cage down, but held on to the flight bag, as I could feel Louis wriggling inside it. I started with the staff, and shook hands with the officers who were left: Number One, Chief Liu, Engineer Number Two, Marco One; then Bryn Mawr, little Whittier, Yale, Loyola, Nebraska, Swarthmore, Notre Dame. The last in the row was Wellesley, who pumped my hand long and hard and whispered, "Woo ..."

I went down the line of oilers: Carleton, Purdue, Harvard, Dartmouth; when I shook Tulane by the hand, I felt something hard being pressed into my palm. I looked at it; it was a brass nameplate, like the ones on the doors of the officers' cabins; this one said, on two lines: KOMM ODOR.

"Him make," a voice whispered beside me. "Him make himself, for *you*." It was Hopla, bright eyes beaming. "He not read, me tell him how to spell: Co'dore. For your door at home, him make. Him and me."

I looked at the little plate and its bizarre legend. It was beautifully made; he must have spent hours on it, filing, scraping, tapping ... For some reason, that did it. Suddenly I could take no more.

I shook him by the hand, said, "Thank you, Tulane, thank you very much, I'll use this always," and hurried on down the line of oilers to the runners, where I found myself facing the *mandur*. He took my hand, bared his stainless-steel teeth and said, "Co'dore."

"Godspeed, *Mandur*," I said, "happy sailing." Finally I got to Ma Chang, the last in line. She stared up at me poker-faced; on her shoulders were my commodore's tabs. I wondered if I should bring out her pendulum and wear it in my buttonhole, but I didn't have it on me; it was still in the breast pocket of my short-sleeved shirt. I bowed to her, she pulled my head down and kissed me on both cheeks. The only response I could think of was to kiss hers; they were bristly. "Godspeed, Ma Chang."

"Woo poos," she said.

I went back to where Fransen and Harakiri were waiting and picked up Pete's cage. Harakiri took my luggage. As I walked away, a whistle sounded behind me; I heard the gangway rumble.

It was a long walk to the gate. Before leaving the quayside, I turned to look back. A crane was swinging something off the ship onto the dock: the lifebelt locker.

"Come on, Harinxma," Fransen said, putting his arm round my shoulders, "let it be." He took me through the gate to where a taxi was waiting.

WE WERE ABOUT TO PASS through security at Kao Hsiung airport when the Chinese tailor barred my way, bowing, and handed me a large cardboard box; Fransen took it from him. "Many happy return, Condor," he said bowing.

I bowed back; then I heard Fransen say, "Come on, Harinxma, give me that rat, you carry the box."

"No, I want to hang on to him."

"Harinxma," Fransen said patiently, "if you send that animal through the X-ray machine, he'll be cooked. And if you hand that bag to the maid on the other side for inspection, she'll scream the place down. I have a diplomatic passport, I'll take him through without inspection."

So he did; I passed through the metal-detector gate with Pete in his cage; Fransen flashed a piece of paper full of stamps and sauntered past with Louis in the bag.

In T'ai-pei, Harakiri took the KLM plane to Amsterdam that same night. Fransen and I stayed in a motel at the airport; the next morning he was to leave for Curaçao and I for France.

That evening, in my room, Fransen lay down on my bed, cracked open a bottle of Taiwanese Scotch and watched me feed Pete, with Louis on my shoulder. "Don't worry about getting your act through French customs," he said. "I've got a health certificate for him—and for the bird."

"You have? That's nice of you! Where did you get it? When?"

"From a little Chink who sells stamped documents. Any document, any stamp. Must have been the most innocent document he ever forged." He raised the bottle. "Well, here's to the pig. God rest her oinking soul." He took another swig, rubbed the neck of the bottle dry with his hand and asked casually, "Are you going to Curaçao with little Bastiaans or are you going to be a good boy and stay at home?"

"What ships has she got so far, do you know?"

"As far as Jim Kwel's concerned, only those who were about to be junked, like the *Fiona*, leaving him all the good ones, especially the pig's little sister on the stocks. What he doesn't realize is that she's taken all the top-notch captains along with them—Beast Rufus for one."

"Who's getting my crew and runners, do you know?"

"Beast Rufus, I gather. Why? Are you worried about them? Don't be, Harinxma. Beast Rufus may not look or sound like you, but he's just the same as you are when it comes to his crew. You must stop thinking that after God made you, He broke the mould. If He did, then where's your immortality?"

I stared at him as he lay there, bottle raised, Adam's apple bobbing: a skinny, tired, disreputable man; it was the last thing I would have expected him to say.

"What do you mean by that?"

He waved it away. "Oh, just some cheap wisdom out of a bottle."

I thought it was time to work him out of the room; I should ring Sylvia, in France it was eight o'clock in the morning. "I'd like to place a call to my wife, if you don't mind."

"Righto. See you tomorrow, bright and early." He got off the bed. "Here—want this?" He held out the bottle to me.

"No, thank you."

"Then be a friend and pour it down the drain for me, will you? A man should know when to stop." Before closing the door behind him, he added, "That goes for you too, old buddy."

"I know," I said.

WHILE WAITING FOR MY CALL to France, I eased myself down onto the bed. As I lay there, I was overcome by an inexpressible feeling of happiness, which made no sense. This was the end of my career, my life; by all standards, I should be steeped in sorrow and hopelessness. But, gazing out at the thin blue line of the horizon now ahead, I was filled with that strange happiness, a sense of fulfilment and anticipation, as if I were heading for the most exciting adventure of my life.

I heard the telephone ring. I took it off the hook and was about to say, "Bridge, Harinxma," when a girl said, "*Ne quittez pas! Je vous donne Cannes.*"

Suddenly there was her voice, very close. "Martinus, is that you?"

"Yes, love," I said. "I'm in."

JAN DE HARTOG

Jan de Hartog was born in 1914 in Haarlem, Holland, the second son of a Calvinist minister and a Quaker mother. At the age of ten he ran off to sea aboard one of the fishing smacks that worked the Zuyder Zee, and later became a cabin boy on a two-masted schooner. At sixteen he entered Amsterdam Naval College, but was later dismissed with the report, "This school is not for pirates". Packed off to sea again, this time as a messboy, he eventually joined the oceangoing tugboat service. Thus began his love of the sea and of tugboats in particular.

When war broke out in 1940 Holland was occupied by the Nazis and de Hartog was trapped in his native country. During this time he wrote his first major novel, *Holland's Glory*, which became a symbol of Dutch resistance and was banned by the Germans. The young writer fled to England in 1943, a journey which took him six months, during which time he was imprisoned five times, involved in a plane crash, wounded as he crossed the Spanish border and sentenced to death *in absentia* by the Germans. In London de Hartog was appointed war correspondent for the Dutch merchant marine and during this time gathered material for his postwar novels, *The Distant Shore* and *The Captain* (which featured the young Martinus Harinxma as a captain during the second world war).

In the late sixties Jan de Hartog, himself a Quaker, undertook the ambitious project of a multivolume novel on the history of the Religious Society of Friends, which started with *The Peaceable Kingdom*. He has also written plays and several volumes of essays.

Today, Jan de Hartog and his wife live in Somerset.

IN A PLACE AND DARK SECRET

A CONDENSATION OF THE BOOK BY
Phillip Finch

ILLUSTRATED BY WALTER RANE

Joseph Sherk was a tormented man.
Any man would be who had lost his
only child. His precious daughter.
His Margaret.

He wasn't sure how it had happened.
He couldn't remember. It had been
something awful. Something to
do with blood and fire. And now
Margaret was gone . . .

But he was determined to find
her. And when he found her,
he'd know what to do. He'd
make sure he'd never lose her
again. Not ever.

CHAPTER ONE

Wednesday, August 22

From the sharp spine of a hill, beneath an old bent ash, Sherk waited for Margaret. He watched the cabin below him, a four-room bungalow with yellow asbestos shingles and a rusty tin roof. Outside the back door was a five-year-old Ford pickup truck, a vegetable patch, a shed, and a creek that ran black with coal dust from the mines upstream. The front porch nudged a gravel road that led from the mines to a paved highway. Cabin, creek and road filled a six-acre hollow between two steep ridges that rose up like prison walls. Beyond were more hills of the Appalachian range, aligned north to south, a frothy green sea that lapped against the horizon.

While he waited, Sherk stripped the bark from a length of fallen branch and began to whittle. He sat with his long legs bent, slowly pushing a buck knife the length of the stick. A paper-thin strip rose up from the knife's edge, then curled and fell away. His eyes moved between the stick and the cabin and back. Once he heard the rumble of a coal truck, and stopped to watch it pass. Then the hollow was quiet once more. Sherk went back to the stick. He was a patient man who knew how to wait.

When he heard gravel crunch again, he came alert and peered down at the road. In a few seconds a blue convertible came into view beneath him. The top was down, and Sherk could see three figures in the front seat, four more in the back, teenage boys and girls wearing shirts over swimsuits. There was laughter as the car stopped in front of the cabin. Sherk's eyes sought out a girl who clambered out of the back seat and ran up onto the porch: Margaret. Sherk's throat was dry. The car turned round and went back down the road, and Margaret went inside.

At first Sherk didn't move. He felt the fire rising within him, the cleansing flame that roared and burned everything until he was empty inside. Empty and pure and clean.

He had sensed the fire coming on when he climbed the hill to wait. The other vices that were supposed to capture men—lust, drink, sloth—had never seriously tempted him. But this was different, this rage. It had begun to blossom in him about a year earlier, but he suspected it had always been there, ready to claim him. He craved these moments when he could stop being Sherk and let what was inside take hold.

The fire. He let it smoulder. His pulse was quicker now, his breathing short. While he stared down at the cabin, the buck knife slashed at the stick. Finally Sherk stood, dropped the stick, and replaced the knife in the scabbard he wore at his hip. There was a rawness about Sherk: knobbly elbows and knuckles, hair like the nest of a careless bird, whiskers that darkened his cheeks even after he had shaved. His face was gaunt. He could soften it with a smile, but now the mouth was tight, eyes narrow.

He began to scuttle down the hillside, a tall, gangling figure in blue bib overalls and red flannel shirt. When he walked, Sherk had about him the awkwardness of a heron, all legs, moving in arrhythmic starts. But he could cover the ground. Now he was moving fast, and every stride brought him closer to the cabin.

WHEN SHE CAME HOME from swimming, Margaret called for her father. She got no answer. His truck was parked out back, but there was no sign of him anywhere. She changed into jeans and a shirt, and went into the kitchen to start dinner. She knew that he would be home soon. He was on the night shift this month, and he would want to eat before he left for work. She lit a burner on the stove and started water for coffee. She had always done most of the cooking. Somewhere there was supposed to be a mother, but she had left before Margaret was a year old. For as long as she could remember, there had only been the two of them, father and daughter, alone in the cabin.

She was standing at the kitchen counter, with her back to the entrance, when Sherk came through the front door. She knew the footsteps. She called over her shoulder, "Hi, Daddy."

He stood in the kitchen doorway and stared at her in silence.

She turned and looked at him closely. Something in his stance, his silence, disturbed her. Then she knew. Her shoulders sagged, and she whimpered, "Oh no, Daddy, not again."

He glared at her, then began to pace. He strode into the front room and back, then into the front room again. Margaret followed. As he walked, his fists clenched and opened, clenched and opened. Margaret had seen him this way twice in the last year: suddenly changed, angry, hard, not the father she knew. Both times it had been bad while it lasted. She had dreaded its happening again, had prayed that it would not.

She sat in an armchair in the front room, head bowed. She bit her bottom lip and waited for the tempest. He stopped in front of her. When he spoke, his voice was low and harsh. "You was swimming," he said.

"At the pool."

There was a community pool in town, built with government money. She went there often in the summer.

"There was boys," Sherk said. "I seen 'em."

"Three or four," she said. "No one special."

"They's dead meat if I get my hands on 'em."

She cringed at the violent words. Tears came to her eyes.

"I told you, no running off to go swimming," Sherk said. His voice was louder. "You been a bad girl, sneaking off."

"Daddy, you knew. You said I could go." He had waved goodbye to her in the car that morning.

"Sneaking off."

"You said—"

He slapped her hard, knocking her head against the back of the chair. When she looked up again, he was still looming over her, his eyes narrowed down to two small flints.

There was a noise from the kitchen—the kettle whistling. He looked towards it, and at that instant she bolted for the front door. She had nearly reached it when one big hand clamped down on her shoulder and yanked her back. Her feet flew out from under her and she fell to the floor.

He hauled her up and slung her into the chair. When she opened her eyes, he was leaning down, his face close.

"Why do you make me do these things?" he said.

Margaret tasted blood-salt and tears. His hands grasped her arms so tightly she wanted to cry out.

"You been a bad girl," he said in a tone that was colourless, detached. His right hand loosened its grip. Suddenly it swung and cracked against her cheek, snapping her head sideways. "A bad, bad girl." The hand smacked against the side of her mouth again and again.

Margaret closed her eyes and tried to shut out the words and the blood and the awful pain in her heart, which hurt even more than the pain from his blows. It would end, she told herself, and he would be right again. Most times he was gentle and loving. He was the best daddy a girl could want.

SHERK KNEW HE MUST HAVE DONE something wrong. He didn't know what it was, for when the fire passed, it always took away the memory. But now he was here, at the kitchen table. The hollow was in evening shadow, and Margaret was sobbing, and he knew he had done wrong.

He went to her. She was sitting cross-legged on the floor of her room. It was a small room, furnished with a bed and a dressing table and a hooked rug on the floor. She had slept here since she was an infant, and all around him Sherk could see the evidence of the childhood that she was just now outgrowing; a stuffed bear in one corner, pasteboard angels dangling from a mobile, Little Bopeep stitched into the quilt folded at the foot of the bed.

He felt ashamed of what he had done, whatever it was. He could see that it must have been bad. Her face was swollen and streaked with dried blood, and her fear showed when she saw him.

"Margaret, sweetness, I'm sorry," he said in the gentle voice she had always known. He held out a hand. In a moment she touched it, and she let him pull her up.

"Kneel down with me," he said. "Let's pray."

They knelt together at the foot of the bed.

"Dear God," he whispered. "We want to be good. Life makes it hard for us, but we want to do right. Give us your grace, Lord. Let us be good."

"Amen," they said together. Her voice was small.

They stood. She was crying again, but without urgency.

"I have to go," he said. "Shift'll be starting soon."

He waited for her to kiss him, as she always did when he left for work. But she looked away. He touched his lips briefly to her forehead and mumbled a goodbye at the door.

Sherk was a mechanic at a truck stop on the interstate highway. It was thirty miles away, forty-five minutes each direction on the mountain roads that twisted down into the flatland. But the trip didn't bother Sherk. He would have driven even further for a job that kept him above ground; mine work paid too little for what it took out of a man. Besides, Sherk had always been good with machines and tools. He knew how to make things run.

He started his shift that evening replacing the piston rings on a farm truck, a long job that required concentration. He had been at it for about an hour when the night manager interrupted him.

"Joseph," the manager said. "I want you to knock off." It was the first time the man had called Sherk by his given name.

"You got to go home," the manager was saying. "Now. The police just called from Harben."

That was the closest town to the cabin in the hollow. Sherk put down the wrench he had been holding. "About what?" he said.

"I don't know, Joseph. He didn't say."

Sherk turned without a word, went to his truck, and roared it up into the hills.

The cabin was three miles back off the highway. Sherk had just turned onto gravel when a pair of headlights and a pulsing red light poked out of the darkness in front of him. A police car, he thought, but when it passed him, Sherk saw it was an ambulance.

He spun his wheels as he hurried on to the hollow. A county cop was parked there in his patrol car. The night was dark, but in his pick-up's high beams Sherk could see a charred jumble where the cabin was supposed to be. Sherk's heart thumped. He jumped out of the truck and ran towards the cabin. He smelled the dankness of wet ashes. He yelled, "Margaret! Margaret!"

The county cop was walking towards him. Sherk was sure that she must be in the patrol car. He brushed past the cop to see her.

The car was empty. Sherk heard himself calling his daughter's name again. It came out as a wail. The cop was reaching to him.

"Propane . . . the stove," Sherk heard the cop saying. "Must have been a valve open. It blew. Bad fire. She never got out, mister. I'm sorry."

Thursday, August 23

When the movers loaded the truck, they carted all the life out of the house on Berry Road. It was a house outside a town called Johnson, in Vermont. The rooms were empty now and the walls were bare. With the curtains gone, summer sunlight lay in big patches on the living-room floor.

Sarah Stannard stood in one of the bright splashes, her eyes moving round the room. She had never before seen it this way, stripped and desolate. She was aware of her mother standing at the front door, one hand fidgeting on the knob.

"Sarah, love, we have to be on the road," Elise Stannard said. "We have a long way to go."

"A little while longer, OK?"

"Dragging this out can only make it worse," her mother said.

"Please. Just a minute or two. Is that so much to ask?"

"I only want what's best for you," Elise said.

"I wonder when you'll let me decide what's best for myself."

Elise stiffened. "I don't want to see you hurt, that's all."

Sarah shrugged. "This little bit more won't make a difference. Just a couple of minutes. Please."

"Very well, then. I'll wait for you in the car." Elise left, and the door closed hard behind her.

Same old argument, Sarah thought. For as long as she could remember, there had been this tug-of-war, this rivalry of pride and will. The crazy part was that they really loved each other. Strangers wouldn't have fought so passionately. It was worse now that they were alone, without her father. He had been dead for over nine months, dead at forty-three of a heart attack, and he had left a great empty spot in their lives.

As she stood alone in the warm light, Sarah told herself that this was the last time she would see these walls. She was fifteen years old. This was the only home she had ever known.

From the driver's seat Elise Stannard watched her daughter in the house. Sarah was standing at a window, sunshine blanching her long, yellow hair. She was tall and thin, gawky, her body stalled awkwardly in adolescence. But in her face there were undertones of the woman she would be in a few years. Her eyes were dark and expressive, cheekbones high-set, chin straight.

Standing framed now in the window, Sarah stared out over the front lawn. Her eyes avoided the car, and Elise was reminded of a zoo animal, remote and melancholy behind plate glass. The girl sometimes seemed so distant, baffling, beyond reach.

Sarah's eyes lifted, and she turned away from the window.

HEY, HEY, BUCK UP, her father would say. Sarah could hear him now, could feel his strong hands gripping her shoulders as he looked into her liquid eyes. It might have been a skinned knee, a slight from a classmate— anything that would bring a little girl to the brink of bawling. *Chin up, champ. Don't let 'em see you cry.*

It was the kind of thing that a father would say to a son. But Jack Stannard had no son, only Sarah, and she would do anything for him. She could be tough if he wanted.

Sarah wandered through the empty house, memories crowding in on her. So far she had kept it together all right. There was one room left, a little nook beyond the laundry. She had saved it for last. It was going to be the hardest of all to say goodbye to.

Get it together, champ. Don't lose it now.

She stepped into the room and looked around. It had been her father's study. He had taught history at the state college in Johnson, and there had always been books stacked on the floor and jammed into shelves. Now the shelves were empty, the books in crates on a moving van headed south.

Jack Stannard could spend hours here, his feet resting on the desk top, tilting back in a chair, a book in his lap. It was a place to be alone with his books and with his little girl. Sarah would match him hour for hour, happy to be near him. She had a spot. The desk was an old oak rolltop, and she would curl up in the foot well. Plenty of room for her in there.

While he read she would draw, bracing a sketch pad against her knees. She had been taking art lessons since she was ten, and her father thought she had promise. She would work on a drawing, then tear out the page and pass it up for his inspection. He would study it, and when he found a really good one, he would tack it up on the one wall that wasn't covered with shelves. Sarah would be proud. She would know that she had done well.

Now Sarah walked across the empty room. She put out a hand and touched the tiny holes in the wall that his tacks had left. It brought her close to tears, and she gulped air to level out her ragged breathing.

Keep it together, champ.

He had taught her to be strong, had given her the face she showed the rest of the world. But here, alone with him, she could be just Sarah, scared and vulnerable. He understood what lay within her, knew things that not even her mother fully grasped. It wasn't fair, she thought. The father she mourned was the one person with whom she could have shared this terrible grief. But he was gone, and she knew what he would expect of her.

Tighten up. Be tough. That's a champ.

She squared her shoulders, held her head up, and left the room. She had finished what she wanted to do. She walked quickly to the front door, paused to look around one last time, then went outside. Down the front walk, round the car, into the front seat beside her mother.

"I'm sorry," Elise said. "I tried to keep us here."

Sarah leaned across the seat and kissed her mother. "It doesn't matter," she said. "I was afraid to leave, because I thought I might forget him. But I won't let that happen. I'm ready to go, really I am."

Elise started the engine and they pulled into the road. Soon the house was out of sight. They were going to start a new life. They were going to live near Annapolis, where Jack's parents had made a place for them.

The country road stretched out ahead.

He was the best father, Sarah thought. The best ever. She still needed him, and she didn't know what she was going to do without him.

CHAPTER TWO

Saturday, August 25

John Burwell paused when he reached the top of the stairs. Before him was the door to the spare bedroom of his home, a two-storey house in Harben, where he lived with his wife. Sherk was on the other side of the door, and Burwell had stopped to gather himself before he went in. There was something wrong with Sherk. Burwell couldn't say what it was, but he felt it all the same, and he dreaded seeing Sherk again, talking to him.

Burwell was a storekeeper in Harben, a stoop-shouldered man with wispy hair. In his left hand now he carried a blue worsted suit Sherk was supposed to wear today to his daughter's funeral.

Outside, the air was hot and stagnant. A clammy rivulet ran down Burwell's spine as he stood on the landing. The door was open a crack. He rapped on it lightly.

"Joseph? Can I come in? Joseph?"

There was no answer. Slowly Burwell pushed open the door.

Sherk was in a chair, hands folded in his lap, staring out across the room. He was expressionless, so still he reminded Burwell of a wax figure. Burwell could believe he had been sitting that way for hours. After a few seconds Sherk turned an empty face to him.

Burwell held out the suit and spoke quickly. "The missus, she found this in a closet last night," he said. "Anywhere it's too loose, she can take it in with pins. It'll do."

Sherk's face didn't move. He didn't seem to have heard.

"You're going to need this today," Burwell said gently.

Sherk did not respond.

It had seemed the Christian thing to do, to take Sherk in. He and the Burwells had belonged to the same church for more than ten years, and almost every Sunday they had attended services in the meetinghouse outside town. The night that Margaret had died Sherk had called the pastor, and the pastor had called the Burwells, who had an empty room. Just for a few days, the pastor had said, and so they had brought him into their home.

The first hours had been bad, Sherk moaning and shouting desperate prayers upstairs. But awful as that grief had been, it was no more than you would expect from a man who had lost his only child so suddenly. Since that first night, though, Sherk had been subdued and distant. Burwell thought such calm was unnatural.

He held out the suit and waited for Sherk to move. Sherk looked at him without seeing him; disconnected.

"Joseph," he said. "We'll need to leave by noon. Better get ready."

A quiet smile came over Sherk. "I'm going to be all right," he said, speaking slowly, as if the thought had travelled a great distance from an obscure part of his mind.

"That's right," Burwell said. "You've got people who care about you, people who'll see you through this."

Sherk looked serene. That was wrong, Burwell thought. This wasn't bereavement; this was emptiness.

Sherk nodded several times with increasing conviction.

"Going to be all right," he said firmly.

Burwell wanted to be away from him. Quickly he hung up the suit, shut the door on Sherk's placid face, and hurried out.

"DAD-DY," SAID A GIRL'S VOICE, singsong. "Dad-dy."

Sherk's head snapped up and he looked round the room. He was alone. The voice lilted in his head again.

"Dad-dy. Down here."

Sherk looked through the open window beside his chair. Margaret was in the Burwell's backyard, her face lifted up to him. Sherk saw that she

282

wore a pink taffeta dress, the fanciest she owned, her favourite. She waved a welcome.

"Margaret," Sherk shouted, feeling his heart leap. He leaned out of the window. "It's you. It's really you."

"I wanted to see you," she said. Her face seemed full of light. She was so beautiful. "I wanted to tell you I love you, Daddy."

"And I love you," he yelled. He put out a hand. "Come to Daddy."

She shook her head. "I can't."

"Then I'll be down. Just wait. I'll be right there."

She shook her head again. "I have to go," she said.

"No!" he howled. "I love you!"

She ignored him and walked slowly through the backyard gate. There she looked over her shoulder at him. She whispered, and even at that distance Sherk could hear her clearly.

"Come find me," she said. "I'm awful lonely. Come get your little girl." Then she turned away and ran down the alley behind the house, the pink dress dancing brightly. Sherk's eyes didn't leave her until she was gone.

BURWELL'S WIFE WAS WAITING for him when he got out of the shower. She looked troubled.

"He's talking to somebody up there," she said.

Burwell listened. He heard nothing.

"He just stopped," she said. "But he was yelling out the window." After a pause she added, "There was nobody out there."

"He wasn't talking much, last time I saw him," Burwell said.

"Poor man, I'm worried about him. He's been through so much. You'd better go see if he needs anything."

Burwell dried himself and slipped into trousers and a fresh shirt. He was immediately damp with sweat again.

In bare feet he padded up the stairs. He hesitated, then addressed the closed door. "Joseph? Everything all right?"

"Just fine, John." Sherk's voice was muffled, but Burwell thought that it did not sound as leaden as before.

"How's that suit? Passable?"

"I don't need the suit," Sherk said.

Burwell knew that the man had no clothes but what he wore. Everything else had been burned.

"Sure you do," Burwell said. "Wouldn't be fitting otherwise, Joseph. Got to have a dark suit for a funeral."

"No funeral," Sherk said loudly.

Patience, Burwell thought. He said, "What do you mean?"

"I'm not going to no funeral today."

Burwell felt suddenly weary. He pushed the door open. Sherk stood facing him, hands at his sides. His face was alive again. That was an improvement anyway, Burwell thought.

"You're going to do what's proper, Joseph," he said. "A father doesn't skip out of his daughter's funeral. No way."

Sherk shook his head emphatically. "My little girl is alive."

Burwell went to him and put a hand on his shoulder. "Now Joseph, that just ain't so. Your daughter is dead. Remember?"

"No." Sherk's eyes flamed.

"She's laying in a casket this minute, waiting to be buried."

"No!" Sherk grunted like an animal, and one arm flew upwards, striking Burwell's face, knocking him off balance.

"Hey!" Burwell said.

Sherk stepped forward and grabbed the front of Burwell's shirt and threw him against the wall. Burwell hit it hard, jarring loose a picture frame, and slid down to the floor. Sherk strode towards him, his features contorted. Burwell had never seen anything so frightening. Frantically he tried to move, but now Sherk was kneeling over him, across his chest.

"She's alive," Sherk said fiercely.

Burwell wanted to say, Sure, sure, she's alive, my mistake. But his mouth wouldn't work and it came out a babble.

"She's alive," Sherk said again, glaring. His eyes never left Burwell's as he reached back with one hand. He came up with the buck knife. In a second he had it open.

"Don't hurt me," Burwell said. The knife was at his throat. "Oh no, Joseph. Oh, my God, no."

Unhurried, deliberate, Sherk began to increase the pressure of the blade. Burwell felt it at his throat. He told himself that Sherk was the last of this world that he would ever see.

A scream shrilled in Burwell's ears. Sherk's head jerked round. It was Burwell's wife, standing in the open doorway. She put her hands to her face and screamed again.

Sherk looked away from her, down at the knife, then back at Burwell's wife. Without haste he rose and straightened. Burwell felt the lifting of an enormous weight. The blade made a snicking sound as Sherk folded it into the handle. He put it away and looked down at Burwell.

"I'll find her," Sherk said. "She's waiting, and I'll git 'er."

Sherk moved for the door, past Burwell's wife. His feet banged on the stairs and in the hall, and then he was gone.

SHERK DROVE TO THE BANK in Harben, keeping to the back streets so that he wouldn't be spotted. Better that way, he thought. No more trouble today; he had a job to do, and he wanted to get on with it.

Inside, a couple of electric fans pushed around stale air. Sherk went to the end of a line at the bank clerk's cage, and he let his mind retreat to a memory he had recalled two nights earlier, at a time when he was sure that sorrow would crush him. The remembrance had given him strength then, and it buoyed him now, a warm and comforting image that, though ten years old, was more real to him than the summer heat and the hum of the fans.

Margaret was lost. It was a cool May morning, and she had wandered away from the cabin while Sherk turned earth in the garden patch. She was almost five, old enough to cover plenty of ground before Sherk realized she was missing. He shouted himself hoarse calling her, feeling panic seize him as he scrambled wildly up and down the hills around the cabin.

After about an hour Sherk realized that Margaret had somehow found a way past the curtain of high hills that surrounded the hollow. She could be anywhere. A phone call brought a sheriff's deputy and some searchers, who fanned out over the slopes as the sun began to fall. Sherk and a man named James Vansil started down the far side of one hill. They pushed through the forest, Sherk thinking, She's gone, my baby's gone.

Nearly four miles from the cabin they reached a creek called Weam's Run, which ran beneath a dense overhang of trees. In the mud beside the creek they found a set of tiny footprints, headed upstream. Sherk and Vansil ran along the creek, shouting the girl's name. Sherk was splashing through calf-high water when he saw Margaret, her golden hair shining even in the forest's deep shadows. She was perched on a rock, looking pleased with herself, watching him approach. Sherk grabbed her and held her so hard that she squeaked a protest. He wanted to cry for joy.

Sherk could feel Margaret pressed to his chest as he stood in the creek. Then someone tapped his back. He looked round. A fat woman in a blue shift had appeared behind him.

"Mister, you're next," said a highpitched voice.

When Sherk turned back, he was facing the bank clerk. The forest and the creek and Margaret were gone. The memory drained away, leaving mild euphoria. He walked to the window.

"I want to cash out my savings," he said. "Same with my current account. Comes to something like nine hundred dollars."

Minutes later he was in the truck, heading east out of the hills. About a mile along the highway was the meetinghouse where he had worshipped for so many Sundays. Sherk stopped across the road. Parked outside were a hearse and mourners' cars. Inside, sorrowful voices battled with a hymn in a minor key.

Somehow Sherk knew that the funeral was for a teenage girl. He couldn't have said how he knew this, but the thought made him sad. A father was burying his daughter. It was pitiful.

Welling tears distorted Sherk's vision. He wiped his eyes roughly with the back of a sleeve. This was a tragedy, but it had nothing to do with him. He blinked his eyes and turned away, and accelerated the truck down the road. The sound of the dirge faded. There was work to do. He had a daughter to find.

He drove fast and didn't stop again until he had reached the cloverleaf junction of the interstate highway, where he pulled over to the side. The slip road was a two-lane entrance, demanding a choice. The right lane joined southbound traffic; the left lane crossed an overpass to merge with the northbound traffic.

Sherk reached round to a back pocket and took out his wallet. From it he extracted a photograph of Margaret standing outside the cabin. The photo showed a slim, almost frail girl with golden hair bound in a pigtail that fell over one shoulder. She was squinting slightly, and she was smiling. Smiling at her daddy.

Something was happening in his head, a mingling of the real and the imagined. Part of the jumble was a pain that would sear his soul if he looked at it directly, so he turned aside from it. He knew that Margaret was gone. Lost. Like the day ten years past when she had wandered away. Exactly. Margaret was ... out there, somewhere, waiting for him. He had seen her.

The question was, Where to begin? He might have gone to Weam's Run, but the creek did not exist any longer. It had been diverted several years earlier by a new mine upstream. Anyway, he sensed that Margaret had gone further, beyond immediate reach. It was going to take some work this time, and patience.

He turned to a road atlas that he kept in the cab. From the spot on the map where he now sat, beside the heavy green line of the interstate, he traced the line southwards, to Knoxville, Chattanooga, Birmingham. Then to the north, up through Virginia, past Washington DC and Baltimore, and into Pennsylvania.

His eyes moved from the map to the ramp ahead, then back to the map. It showed a welter of roads, hundreds more decisions to be made. Sherk tossed the atlas aside. This was a journey of faith. As long as he believed, there would be no wrong turns for him. He tucked the photograph into a corner of the sun visor so that Margaret would be smiling down on him whenever he looked up. Then he put the truck in gear.

He felt full of confidence as he approached the slip road. Where the lanes diverged he glanced to the right; southbound traffic was heavy, and three cars were stopped, waiting to merge. Sherk didn't want to wait. He moved to the left lane and sped over the bridge that spanned the interstate. His tyres screeched round the sweeping curve that launched him out onto the highway, part of the endless mass of people and machines moving north.

286

WHEN BURWELL WIPED THE BLOOD from his neck, he saw that Sherk's blade had left a small mark, little more than a shaving cut; the police weren't likely to be impressed. A couple of Band-Aids covered the wound. Burwell told only the pastor about what had happened. Anyway, he was sure that he had nothing more to fear. He would never see Sherk again. None of them would.

So while others at the funeral mourned the departed Margaret Sherk, Burwell prayed for her father, who had departed on a journey of his own, Burwell thought, with a destination that was much less certain.

CHAPTER THREE

Sunday, August 26

"She oughta be up and around by now," said Harry Stannard. "It's— what? Quarter after ten, f'crying out loud."

"Harry," said his wife. "You told Sarah that today would be a good day to do something together, maybe take her for a drive. You said maybe. And you didn't say when. You'll drive all of us nuts, the way you go on."

Harry held up his hands, miming surrender. He was a small, stocky man, with a head sunburned from his brow to the back of his skull. Knotty calves showed between his yellow socks and his Bermuda shorts. He wore loafers and a pink golf shirt that stretched over a belly as round and solid as a medicine ball.

"What am I doing that's so bad?" he said. "Waiting for my grand-daughter is all. Sure, I'm anxious to see her. It's a crime now, a man wants to see his granddaughter?"

His vehemence might have startled someone else. But Joy Stannard had lived with him for forty-five years, and she knew that he did nothing mildly. Without a word she sipped from her teacup and returned to the glossy pages of a mail-order catalogue.

Harry and Joy were seated at a butcher-block table in their breakfast room, a bright place with walls the colour of egg yolk. Designed and built by Harry, their home near Annapolis sat on a twenty-acre estate that fronted on the Severn River.

Harry had supervised its construction with a knowing eye. His business was property and development—Harry's thumbprint was prominent on the great smudge of suburban housing that lies beyond Washington's Capital Beltway. Nothing he had built, however, approached the magnificence of his own home, a classic Georgian colonial house with a gabled roof and salmon-tinted brickwork. A swimming pool and a tennis court reposed side by side behind the house. He had also spent a lot of money on a new wing. It was the only way he could coax Elise out of Vermont, Sarah with her. Sarah, of course, being the real prize. Eighty-eight thousand for the construction of the new addition. It had also cost him a promise of privacy: separate entrances, separate lives. No interference. Now Harry regretted these concessions. Hell, this was his house, his granddaughter.

"I figured I'd see Sarah after breakfast," Harry said. "I mean, how long can it take to eat breakfast?"

He picked up a spoon and tapped it on the tabletop. Harry was never totally at rest. Even at his most composed, some part of him was moving: a toe dancing, head bobbing, eyes darting in the manner of a predatory bird.

Joy looked up. "The girl will *be* here," she said.

Harry sighed elaborately and got up from the table. He paced round the room a few times and finally stopped at a window. Outside, the rolling green lawn dropped away to a bluff that hid the Severn below.

"Maybe she forgot," Harry said, speaking to the window. "Sure. Kids that age, nothing stays with 'em for long."

He walked out of the room. Joy called after him, "Harry, you promised those two you'd give them peace."

"Nobody disturbing the peace out here," he said.

He went to the end of the hall and tried the door. Locked.

Joy followed him. "This is the wrong way to start," she said. "Barging in on them."

"It'll give you some time alone with Elise," he said. "You'll have a chance to talk with her about you know what."

"That's your idea. You do it," Joy said, but Harry ignored her. He rapped sharply on the door.

HARRY HAD COME AND LEFT, dragging Sarah away, bludgeoning the morning quiet. Now he was gone, and stillness surrounded Elise again. She looked round her new living room and told herself that she had traded her home for an ice palace.

The new wing was cold and austere. Its walls were snowbank white, pristine. Kitchen appliances glistened, and a transparent glaze covered the oak floors. She didn't know if she would ever feel comfortable in such relentless perfection.

At least Harry hadn't skimped, she thought. The addition was two storeys. It included two big bedrooms, a kitchen and dining room, a sitting room, and a top-floor solarium that might serve as Sarah's studio. The new wing was, in effect, a separate residence.

For a while Elise had resisted Harry's pleas to leave Vermont. She wanted to be independent, she had told him. She would support Sarah and keep the house. Harry was unfazed. He continued the construction, sending Elise more plans, more photos.

288

Meanwhile, she was trying to earn a living for the first time ever. There was no work in Johnson, and Burlington was an hour's drive each way. The bills arrived as regularly as the letters and calls from Harry, nudging her, reassuring her. In the end, Harry's determination had won out. He had wanted them here. Sarah most of all. And here they were.

Elise caught a glimpse of herself reflected in the mirror over the sofa. She shared her best features with her daughter: prominent cheekbones, large and expressive eyes; a long, slim nose, slightly turned up at the tip. The years had treated her gently, but too frequently these days she felt like an old woman. Jack's death, the struggle to keep the house, all had ground away at her. She realized that at forty-one she might be past the midpoint of her life. And lately she had begun to fear that the best of that life might be behind her.

There was movement beyond the living room. Elise looked up; Joy Stannard, her mother-in-law, was standing hesitantly in the hall.

"The door was open," she said. "Maybe Harry forgot to close it. We could talk, if you're not too busy."

"Please." Elise gestured to a chair beside her. She liked Joy, admired her resilience for surviving four and a half decades of marriage to a human steamroller.

"You're settling in?" Joy said. "I know it's hard, uprooting yourself. Anything I can do, let me know."

"It'll take some time to feel at home."

"I'm sorry about Harry," said Joy. "You know he means well. I tried to tell him this morning that he was going to make a pest of himself. But when he decides he wants something, there's no stopping him. If you understand that what he does is out of love, that he really wants the best for all of us, then it's not so hard to live with."

"I'm trying," Elise said.

"He had this idea ..." Joy said, looking away, and Elise realized that there was a point to this conversation.

"Maybe you'd better tell me."

"Harry doesn't think public schools are right for Sarah."

"I suppose he has a better idea."

"A girls' academy in Annapolis," Joy said. "It's called Nordbrook. It has the highest standards. Art courses, too. You won't find a better place, Elise. And Harry thinks that Sarah ought to have the best."

Elise happened to agree. And she could even forgive Harry for pushing it on her. But there was a problem. Sarah didn't like to be forced into anything. She would resist any coercion. And the harder she was forced, the stiffer her resistance would be.

"A school like that can't be easy to get into," Elise said. "Especially when we're so late."

"All taken care of. Just fill out an application. Harry says he's greased the skids. His words. I didn't ask how."

"Tuition must be high," Elise said. "I have some money."

"Keep it, dear. Harry's taken care of that, too. He's a terrible bully, I know, the way he pushes people around. But he's no skinflint."

HARRY HAD A BMW SEDAN—big and fast and sleek—and he knew some roads through the countryside where he could open it up. Cold air blasted out of the air-conditioner. Past the Chesapeake Bay Bridge, east of Kent Narrows, he turned south onto a two-lane road that skirted the Eastern Shore. The countryside streamed past, low and flat.

To Sarah it was a bleak vista. She missed the hills of Vermont. They imparted a feeling of security, as if they protected the farms and homes that nestled down among them. And no Vermont day was ever as hot as it was here. They drove in silence. It was unusual for her grandfather, she thought. He seemed restive.

He had promised her lunch—the best crab cakes in Maryland, he had said—and after they had driven for a few minutes he turned down a dirt road that cut between tobacco fields. It ended beside the bay, at a low clapboard building, one end resting on a concrete mooring, the other extending out over the water, supported by pilings. DOT'S GOOD FOOD, read a faded sign on the roof.

They ate on a screened porch overlooking the bay. Sarah watched a speedboat pulling a skier, about a hundred yards offshore. The air was hot and clammy and she felt bereft, far from what she knew and loved.

Harry reached across the table and took her hands. "Poor kid," he said. "You're feeling low, I can tell."

So that was it, Sarah thought. Harry was trying to play father. No, thank you. As a grandfather, Harry was OK, but she wanted nothing beyond that.

"I'm fine," she said, "just sleepy. I stayed up late."

"I thought maybe it was something else. Maybe moving to a new place, you don't like it so much." He was wrestling with the words. "You could tell me if something's bothering you. You're entitled to a few rough days, the troubles you've had."

"I'd tell you, Grandpa, if I had something to talk about."

He nodded and looked relieved, as if he had discharged some difficult duty and could now put it behind him. When he spoke to her next, his tone was lighter.

"So," he said. "What do you want to be when you grow up?"

"I don't know, Grandpa. I think maybe I'm a little young yet to make up my mind." She looked straight at him. "What do you want to be when you grow up?"

290

He chuckled. "Young lady, my ambition has always been to end up a rich, old pain in the neck. And I think I may be getting close to it."

She patted his hands, which were resting on the table.

"You're not *that* old, Grandpa," she said. She smiled brightly. "But two out of three isn't bad."

SARAH WAS SUBDUED when she returned. She gave Elise a quick hello and then disappeared upstairs into the solarium. Elise waited a few minutes, going over in her mind what she wanted to do. Maybe she could force Sarah into Nordbrook School. Maybe, if she pushed hard enough. But there would be weeks of friction between them if she did. There had to be another way.

She went upstairs. Sarah was seated in a corner, partly hidden by a sketchbook on an easel. A tray of watercolours sat on a table beside her. She dabbed a brush into one of the colour wells and lightly touched it to the paper.

"Sarah, honey, did you have fun today?"

She spoke without looking up. "It wasn't so bad."

"Harry didn't talk to you about school?"

Now Sarah turned to her, interested and wary. "What about school?"

"Apparently he's got this idea that you should go to a private girls' school in Annapolis. Joy told me he insists on it. But I told her no. No way would I let Harry dictate to you."

She turned to leave. Before she reached the door, Sarah's voice stopped her. "Mom, you could have talked to me first," she said. "I should have a say in it."

Bull's-eye, Elise thought, She turned to face her daughter again. "Maybe you should. I'm sorry if I spoke too soon. Look, Harry can tell you more about the school. Go and speak to him. If this school is what you really want, that's fine with me."

Sarah walked out of the room, carrying herself like a fighter, with shoulders thrust back, head high. Elise watched her go. With Sarah, she thought, it was always a battle.

She crossed the room to look at Sarah's work on the easel. Usually Sarah worked with pencil, or pen and ink. Watercolors were new, and Elise was curious to see the result.

What she saw was so startling it took her breath away. Jack Stannard looked out at her from the paper. He was about thirty years old, grinning the go-to-hell smile that had always made her melt inside. Sarah had been working from an old photo. But she had caught things the camera had missed: the kindness, the intelligence, the love—most of all the love—that had set him apart from any other man Elise had known.

For a moment Elise had to look away. Then she studied the painting again. It wasn't finished, and it lacked a professional's polish. But it *was* Jack Stannard. That was talent—a gift. Elise had to hold the sketchbook at arm's length, because she didn't want her tears to smear the work.

THE NEXT DAY Sarah filled out an application form for Nordbrook School. She was quickly accepted as an incoming sophomore, or second-year student. Another occurrence that took place in the afternoon, several miles away, proved to be even more significant. Though at the time it escaped the notice of everyone in the showpiece house above the Severn, it would shortly affect the lives of all the Stannards.

A seventeen-year-old boy, having consumed six cans of beer in less than an hour, climbed into his father's speedboat, started the engine, and shoved the throttle forward. With prow raised, the craft bolted across the crowded harbour. Within seconds it struck an unoccupied dinghy tied up at a jetty. The wheel was wrenched out of the boy's hands, and the boat became an aimless missile. Miraculously, the teenager managed to leap from the craft an instant before it destroyed itself against a bridge piling.

The incident took place in one of the narrow tidal fingers that extend inland near Annapolis. It is called Weems Creek.

Monday, August 27

Fifty-six hours after he left Harben, Sherk's daughter ran across the highway, at the edge of the glow cast by his headlights. He had been driving most of that time, frenzied, fuelled by hope. He drove up through Virginia, over to Pittsburgh, on to Chicago and Louisville in an erratic circle that brought him within two hundred miles of Harben again as he tracked south.

She ran across the highway about five miles north of Bowling Green, Kentucky. Sherk could see her face clearly. Oblivious to traffic, laughing, she leaped lightly over the steel barrier beyond the gravel shoulder and disappeared down an embankment.

Sherk braked suddenly and jerked the wheel to the right. He cut across two lanes of traffic and nearly collided with a station wagon. When his pick-up had skidded to a stop, he scrambled out and ran round to the grassy slope. It was empty. She was gone. Beyond was a farmer's pasture, also empty. Sherk felt his heart collapse. Something was happening, and he groped for an answer. He was astonished. Not because he had seen her—he expected that—but because she had disappeared so suddenly.

Then he knew. He was being tested. He had been foolish to hope that she would be delivered up to him so easily. His faith was on trial, and before it was finally rewarded he might have to prove it against unimaginable setbacks and disappointments.

He returned to the truck. Suddenly he was weary and incredibly hungry.

TO ALMA NETTLES HE WAS WILDEYES. Alma faced dozens of people every day. She didn't name them all. She was a truck-stop waitress, and most of the customers who sat at the counter were as plain as rice pudding. Wildeyes was different. She spotted him while he was still outside, filling up his pick-up. Afterwards he came in, sat at her counter, and asked for coffee and an omelette. It was a slow night, so when Alma had put in the order she had a chance to study him. His cheeks were sunken, and he looked as if he had started a beard without intending it. He seemed oblivious to his surroundings—not unaware, but hostage to something churning inside him.

At first he sipped his coffee and stared at the wall behind the counter. Then he saw a newspaper on the seat beside him, left there by a trucker. He picked it up and scanned the headlines. Alma was standing off to the side, watching him. Suddenly she saw his haggard face come to life. He leaned closer to the page with an intense expression. Then he put the paper down, hurried out through the door, and headed for his pick-up.

The cook was flipping over his omelette, and Alma considered running out to tell Wildeyes that his meal was ready. But she knew that there was no point. He had forgotten food. He had forgotten everything but what he had seen in the paper.

She went over to where he had sat, and picked up the paper he had been reading. It was a morning edition of the Baltimore *Sun*, turned to an inside page of statewide news. She read the first paragraph of each article, wondering which one had gotten Wildeyes out the door so fast. Two boys in Aberdeen are burned by fireworks. A four-year-old girl drowns in the Patuxent River. In La Plata, four teenagers are killed in a single-car accident. And in Annapolis, a runaway speedboat is demolished at a place called Weems Creek.

SHERK found Maryland in his atlas. Annapolis. He would find her there. Not immediately, maybe, but he would persist. Any place that had a Weems Creek would have his daughter, too. That was not logic but faith.

All along he had only needed a sign.

SHERK REACHED ANNAPOLIS around midday on Tuesday. At the city limits he crossed over a bridge with a sign that identified Weems Creek below. He stopped beside the highway and got out to look. The creek was a curled finger of water, motionless, glaring under a high sun; much wider than the little stream in the hills had been. He stared at the creek with mild curiosity. Already he had decided that Margaret wasn't going to be perched there, waiting. He realized that much work lay before him. Up the road he could see the low skyline of Annapolis, a steeple and some squat office buildings.

293

She was there, somewhere, and Sherk felt ready to start his search immediately. But first he needed a place to stay.

At a filling station up the road, the pump attendant recommended a motel on the other side of town, clean and not too expensive. It had kitchens and weekly rates. He drew a map, which Sherk followed round to the north side of the city. Checking in at the motel, Sherk paid a week's rent. He stopped in the room long enough to look around and splash some water on his face. Then he was ready. He felt like a soldier marching into battle, nervous and elated and desperate.

He drove into downtown Annapolis, passing the State House and the US Naval Academy. While the city was large by hill standards, it wasn't the Behemoth that Sherk had feared. He might not have to search too long before he found his daughter.

He made his way towards the harbour, a narrow notch of water intruding two blocks inland, into the heart of the city. Traffic was slow, clogging the street. Ahead he saw the masts of sailboats. The harbour seemed a busy place. The area was full of people, some of them shopping in the galleries and boutiques near the dockside. Most appeared to be sightseers. That was good, he thought. He wouldn't be conspicuous as he wandered the streets looking at the faces in the crowd.

Sherk spotted a parking space at the kerb and slid into it. He jumped from the truck, locked the door, and walked down to the city dock.

Several hundred people were gathered there, and tourists were perched on the seawall, like magpies on a telephone wire. Sherk found an open spot on the wall and leaned against it to watch the people flow past him. His eyes moved among them, sorting through them, discarding one after another.

Suddenly Sherk straightened. Through the crowd he saw a long blonde pigtail. It belonged to a girl who was turned away from him, headed up Main Street. He watched, alert. She was tall and slight, wearing jeans and red running shoes—Margaret often wore both. He hadn't seen her face, but everything else fitted.

Sherk pushed off from the wall and began to move towards her, avoiding those who got in his path, or brushing them aside. His stride lengthened and quickened, until he was almost running. He felt his heart surge, breath coming shorter and faster. She stopped to look at a shop window. In turning she showed her profile, and Sherk pulled up short about thirty feet away. She was not Margaret, but a woman, at least twenty-five years old.

Sherk looked at her with disgust. He hated her for not being Margaret. He felt the urge to go to her, grab her, thrash the life out of her. It would have happened if they had been alone.

Though the sidewalk was crowded, she became aware of his presence.

She turned her head towards him and saw the naked antipathy in his face. It startled her, and she walked away hastily. Sherk felt the fire subside. He turned and headed back towards the harbour.

ST. BARTHOLOMEW'S CHURCH was almost always a cool, sombre place. It had high, narrow, stained-glass windows, so even on the brightest days the sunlight was dim inside. Monsignor Frank Herrity, who saw it at all hours, liked it best when it was quiet and empty, when a whisper would carry to the furthest corners. He was pastor of the parish; with three other priests, he ministered to a congregation that numbered more than three thousand.

Catholics had been worshipping on this spot for more than three centuries. What served now as the lobby had once been a small chapel of pre-Revolution vintage. The main church was built in the mid-nineteenth century. The grey granite walls were more than forty feet high. The pews and the altar rail were of brown mahogany. It was an imposing place.

Tonight he sat on a padded bench in a confessional box that was built into one wall in the church. It had been at least a quarter of an hour since the last penitent left. There would be no more tonight. After a few more minutes he let himself out of the box and walked slowly by a side aisle up to the sacristy. At the head of the aisle a bank of votive candles winked and wavered in their red glass cups.

He loved the church. While he knew that prayer ought to be in the heart, that worship required no roof, the truth was that people often needed a special place to feel close to God. Most had no trouble believing that this was His house. Its walls were a fortress against the rancorous and profane. It was a sanctuary where life eddied undisturbed. It was a place apart.

CHAPTER FOUR

Wednesday, September 5

Nordbrook School was a large, three-storey brick structure that, at first appearance, might have been an exceptionally grand manor house. It was situated on a thirty-acre plot surrounded by grass and trees. From the street it could be reached only by a long asphalt driveway that ended in a circle at the school's front steps.

Sarah found the place imposing. As she sat beside Elise in the car, she nervously smoothed the pleats in her charcoal-grey skirt, part of a uniform that included a white blouse and burgundy blazer with the Nordbrook crest on the breast pocket. She had never attended a school that required a uniform. She was dismayed to think that she would have to make a niche for herself in these surroundings.

296

"Don't be nervous," Elise said as she drove up the driveway. "Just be yourself. Everything will go fine."

"I know. Can we hurry, please? I don't want to be late."

To the left the car passed a line of tennis courts. On the other side was a grassy playing field bordered by a row of maple trees. The maples made Sarah think of Vermont, and she wished she were there now, ready to walk into a school that she knew, about to see friends and familiar faces.

They reached the circular turning space in front of the building. The car slowed and stopped.

"I'll pick you up at half past three," Elise said. "And for goodness' sake, don't worry. You'll fit in just fine."

"I'm not worried," Sarah said.

She got out of the car and watched it pull away. A couple of girls nearby broke off their conversation to gaze at Sarah. Looking me over already, she thought. But then she imagined that her father was watching, and that gave her strength. Shoulders back, eyes straight ahead, she turned and marched up the broad stone steps that led to the school's front door.

Inside, Sarah found her name on a seating chart taped to the door of homeroom 2-C, and took her place among twenty-three other sophomore girls.

She felt a tap on her shoulder and turned.

"You're new, right?" said the girl behind Sarah: plump-faced, freckled, with curly red hair. "Ever go to private school before?"

Sarah shook her head.

"Then you never had to wear glad rags like these." The girl gestured towards the uniform. "You get used to it after a while. Coming to a new school, I guess you feel strange, huh?"

Sarah nodded. At that moment a teacher walked into the room, took the seating chart off the door, and introduced herself. She began reading from the seating chart. Looking out at the class, she spoke the names of the girls. When she reached Sarah, she asked her to stand.

"You're Sarah Stannard?" She sounded doubtful.

"Yes, I am," Sarah said. She felt uncomfortable, and thought, Let me sit down. Please.

"You're a new girl?"

"Well, I've been a girl all my life. But this is my first day at Nordbrook." There was a tittering around her. The teacher gave Sarah a narrow, level look, then allowed herself a smile.

"I don't suppose you've had a chance to meet Emily Caldwell yet," the teacher said. "She's a sophomore, too."

"I don't think I've seen her."

The teacher laughed. "You would know if you had," she said. "You've got a real surprise ahead of you."

SHERK DROVE SLOWLY through the city. He idled down streets and through intersections, dividing his attention between the traffic and the sidewalks. He was tireless. She was here: he *knew*, and that kept him going. And as he drove, Margaret smiled down at him from the sun visor.

AT LUNCH THAT DAY in the cafeteria, Sarah started on an overnight reading assignment. She was just getting into it when a voice said, "You must be Sarah."

A girl was standing in front of her, holding a tray of food. Sarah looked up into a face that was a fair likeness of her own.

The girl put down her tray and stuck out her hand.

"Emily Caldwell," she said. "I heard about you this morning, and when I saw you sitting here, I knew you had to be the celebrated impostor."

The girl had a commanding, throaty voice, and a manner to match. Sarah envied her her effortless composure.

"Come on, stand beside me. Let's see how we measure up."

Sarah obeyed. Emily was perhaps half an inch taller, four or five pounds heavier. But both girls had the same small-boned build. Each had a fair complexion and long blonde hair pulled back over the ears and fastened with slides.

"What do you think, Stannard? Close enough to fool anybody in a low light, I'd say. We could be sisters." Emily clapped Sarah on the arm. "Tell you what. I'll make you a deal. You try not to do anything that'll make me look bad, and I'll do the same for you. Fair enough?"

Sarah nodded and the girl thumped her on the arm again.

"That's fine," she said. "It'll be fun to have you here, Stannard. Between us we'll keep 'em on their toes."

WHILE MOST OF HER CLASSMATES streamed out of school with the final bell that afternoon, Emily Caldwell went to a lavatory in the basement of the school auditorium and replaced the Nordbrook uniform with jeans and a rumpled cotton shirt. She took a series of deep, deliberate breaths to slow her pulse and loosen the tightness in her stomach. In a few minutes she was going to read for the part of Millie in William Inge's *Picnic*.

Nordbrook's drama department was producing the play with a boys' school nearby. Emily had studied the part for three weeks before school began; now she thought she was ready. The denims and shirt were clothes that Millie might wear. But something looked wrong. When she examined herself in the mirror, she realized her hairstyle was out of place for the role.

She took out the slides, quickly combed out her hair, and put it in a single long plait. Now it looked right.

The fist in her stomach tightened, and she went up the stairs.

ELISE WAS PARKED and waiting when school came out. She spotted Sarah at the top of the stairs. Then Sarah saw her and made her way to the car. Getting in, she slammed the door behind her. Elise leaned across to kiss her. Sarah responded with a quick peck and slouched in the seat, as if to make herself less conspicuous.

"Mama, do you think we could pull out of here?"

"Good afternoon," Elise said. "I missed you, too." She drove round the circle and started up the driveway.

"I'm sorry, Mama. But do you know how many other girls were getting picked up by their mothers today? About three. And they were freshmen. I feel out of it enough already. Now everybody thinks I can't get back and forth to school without my mother."

Elise listened carefully. It was the first time in months that her daughter had even come close to confessing insecurity.

"What would you rather do?" she said.

"I found out there's a bus that goes up the Ritchie Highway. It'll pick me up and drop me off right at Whittier Lane, and it's not a long walk from there."

Elise knew that the lane must run at least half a mile, some of it through dense woods, before it reached the back of Harry's land. The thought of her daughter walking alone every day through the forest made her nervous. But she also knew that Sarah ought to be rewarded for opening up—however narrowly and obliquely.

"I'll make a deal with you," Elise said. "The bus can't get you to school as fast as I can. So in the mornings let me bring you in. After school you can try the bus. We'll see how it works. Deal?"

"Deal," Sarah said.

"Just be careful. Don't let anybody give you a problem, OK?"

"Come *on*. Really!"

"I can't help it," Elise said. "I'm a mother. You know I worry."

EMILY CALDWELL'S THROAT WENT DRY the moment she stepped on stage, but somehow she got the lines out anyway. When the scene ended, the director asked her to come down. He was a thin, serious young man with a wispy moustache; she wanted desperately to please him.

"A good job," he said. "The part is yours, if you think you can handle it. By the way, I like the pigtail. Nice touch."

He called one of the two senior girls who were going to read for the part of Millie's older sister. Without looking at Emily, he said, "Rehearsals start tomorrow. Count on two hours an afternoon."

Emily kept herself gathered up long enough to walk quietly out of the auditorium. But when the door closed behind her, she whooped and took the stairs three at a time, down to where she had left her uniform.

Quickly she put on her skirt and blouse. The blazer she slung over a shoulder. She was about to comb out the plait when she stopped. It had been good to her, she thought. She would wear it for a few more hours. She crammed the clothes with her books into a canvas bag and went outside.

This late in the afternoon the school buses were long gone, and today she had no patience for the city bus. Home was just a mile and a half away, and she felt as if she could do handstands for a mile and a half. She began to walk.

IT WAS BY THE DOCK that Sherk saw her first. In the last week he had spent most of his time here, looking at the faces in the crowd. Now the sight of her made him draw in his breath. She was so beautiful he wanted to cry.

As Sherk watched from the truck, she walked out of a shop along the market square. Sherk inched the truck closer, studying her. Yes. This time it really was Margaret.

Now she was crossing an intersection, turning up a one-way street, leaving the harbour. Sherk called to her. She didn't turn her head. Too far, he thought; she couldn't hear.

A car pulled out of a meter space at the end of the block. Sherk hurried the truck into it, jumped out, and followed her.

THE CALDWELLS LIVED in Hanover Street in a stately old town house, across the street from the Naval Academy. If she had walked directly home, Emily's route would have taken her above Main Street, past the State House which crowns the hill. But she liked to go by way of the harbour. Its stores and boutiques were worth a detour.

She browsed for about half an hour, then started for home. Within a couple of minutes she was in a residential area, where a low wind rustled the black oaks and sycamores overhanging the street.

There, about four blocks from home, she heard the shouts. At first she didn't pay attention. A man's voice was shouting, "Margaret," and she was sure that he wanted someone else. But his voice got louder as he came up behind her, and she could see nobody else on the sidewalk.

"Margaret, stop!"

She looked round and saw a tall, gaunt-faced man walking purposefully, arms and legs jerking him forward, propelling him towards her. His eyes connected with hers, and a chill came over her. She realized that he wanted *her*.

"Margaret!" he shouted, and he waved a hand to stop her. She turned away and began to walk faster.

His footsteps came thumping up the sidewalk behind her. She heard his voice again, pleading. "Margaret, turn around, sweetie. It's me. It's your old daddy."

She was nearly running now. She thought, I can't believe this is happening to me. She hurried to the end of the block, an intersection, her head low so that he wouldn't catch her eyes again.

Halfway home, almost there.

Emily stepped off the kerb. A car slewed round the corner, directly across her path. She pulled back quickly, felt a rush of air as the car rocked past her, inches away.

His hand came down on her shoulder, turning her to face him.

"It's me," he said fiercely. "Look!"

"I don't know you." She tried to keep her voice calm.

He looked stunned. She tried to slip away, but the hand held her. Finally he spoke the name again. "Margaret." It came out tenderly, but she was still frightened.

"I'm sorry. You're mistaken," she said. Her eyes shifted from side to side. "I'm not Margaret. Please, let go of my arm. I'm sorry, but I'm not the person you want."

This seemed to astonish him. His grip relaxed. She turned on her heel and crossed the street, putting distance between them, listening for his footsteps, hearing only her own.

IT WAS HER, SHERK THOUGHT. It *was*. He had touched her, looked into her eyes. He had imagined this moment a hundred different ways, but never had it come out like this, Margaret looking at him as if he were a stranger, being frightened and bolting away.

He found the truck still running where he had left it.

SHE DIDN'T DARE LOOK ROUND. But there were no more shouts and no more footsteps behind her, and soon she slowed down. She was breathless. He had left. A crazy man. Scary, but no harm done.

She was on King George Street now, one block from home. Bisecting the block was a cobblestone alley that ran between brick walls enclosing backyard gardens. She turned down the alley. At the end of it she could see Hanover Street. She had got about halfway through when a blue pick-up truck stopped momentarily on Hanover, then turned into the alley, moving slowly in her direction. It was a wide truck in a passage built for carriages, and she moved to one side so that it could pass.

Sunlight was glaring off the windscreen. She couldn't see the driver. As the truck approached, it rolled into a spot of tree shade. Then she saw.

Oh, God, it's him. He's got me.

She turned and ran. The truck accelerated. She heard it accelerating, closer, closer, and she flattened against a wall so that she wouldn't be run over. The truck roared past and she could see her pursuer's face, thin and grizzled and haunted.

She fled back towards Hanover. Blue smoke rose from the tyres as he braked. She could smell burned rubber. Behind her the truck's door opened, and the man's feet thumped after her.

He was too fast. Before she could get ten steps down the alley he threw out a hand. It swiped her in the back, knocked her forward, and she sprawled. Before she could recover he caught her by an arm and held tight.

"Margaret!" he said. "Look at me, baby. Don't run away."

"Please . . ." She tried to twist free. "You're wrong. I'm not her."

He shouted, "Don't do this to your daddy. Don't hurt me this way."

He was pulling her by one arm, pulling her to the truck. She fought against him, but his grip was solid.

"Somebody, help!" she cried, but it came out weakly.

"We're going," he said, muttering now, impatient, determined.

"You're crazy," she gasped.

The words seemed to jolt him. He flung her against the wall.

"Bad girl," he shouted. Before this he had seemed by turns confused and irritated and hurt. Now he was seething.

"You're a *bad* girl," he said, and the back of his hand flashed out and cracked against her mouth.

His strength seemed multiplied by fury. With an arm round her waist, he swept her up and carried her to the truck. He threw her into the cab and shoved her over to make room for himself.

Then she saw two teenage boys enter the alley off Hanover. They were muscular kids, young guys. Noticing the struggle in the truck, they stopped, uncertain of what was happening and what they ought to do.

Her captor saw, too. When his head turned to them she moved fast, pulling up the lock button, yanking the door handle. As he reached across the seat for her, Emily pushed against the door and tumbled out onto the cobblestones.

The back of the truck blocked the alley between her and the boys, who were now approaching at a hesitant trot. The King George end was open, but she knew that if she ran that way the man would scoop her up again. Already he was stretching across the seat, his fingers inches away, clutching for her. Emily got up. Behind her was the wall, about five feet high. She couldn't climb it. Instead she scrambled up onto the bonnet of the truck. The man looked startled to see her there. The boys were running towards her now, and she knew that they would help her if she gave them a few more seconds.

From the bonnet she looked down into the garden on the other side of the wall. One step up, and she was standing on it. The gaunt man got out of the truck and moved to grab her. She jumped away from him, into the garden, landing in a patch of daisies. She could see the rear entrance of the house and a half-open door. She ran for it, without looking back.

SHERK WATCHED HER RUN. The two boys were still coming on, but Sherk couldn't look away from her. An overwhelming sadness replaced his rage. His own daughter had looked at him with fear and hatred. His instinct was to chase her again. But he couldn't bear any more humiliation.

The two boys came near, moving at a careful walk. Puppies, Sherk thought. Snarling, he shot them a stare of such loathing that they stopped short and let him return to his truck. He got in and retreated up the alley to King George Street.

TERENCE DEAN, A PATROLMAN with the Annapolis Police Department, answered the call on Hanover Street. As he listened to the story he got the feeling that what had happened to the girl was an incomprehensible part of something bigger.

"You're sure he called you his daughter?" he said.

"Yes. No. Not exactly."

Emily Caldwell, seated on a couch between her parents in their living room, held an ice pack against her swollen right cheek. Her eyes were red from weeping, and she stammered slightly when she spoke. "What he said was, 'Don't do this to your daddy.' He believed I was his daughter."

If that was so, Dean thought, he was some father. His blow to her face had raised a livid welt. Dean wondered what the man might have done if he hadn't been interrupted.

"Could be he just made a mistake," Dean said. He felt the need to explain it, to understand. "Maybe he saw you from a distance, really did think you were his daughter, and got surprised when he had a good look at you."

She shook her head. "When I first turned round, he was closer to me than you are now."

That bothered Dean. The school uniform set the girl apart; even from a distance she couldn't be just anyone.

He tried once more. "It's possible he has a daughter who looks like you and goes to your school, and he just assumed . . ."

Emily smiled for the first time. "Officer, this was not somebody who'd have a daughter at Nordbrook."

Dean repeated the physical description she had given him: blue pick-up truck of unknown make, model, and licence; suspect about forty-five, six foot two inches or slightly taller, slender and bony—"with crazy eyes and sunken cheeks," Emily added—wearing a red flannel shirt and bib overalls. Nothing more; the teenage boys had vanished. He got up to leave.

"Can you catch this maniac?" her father said.

"We'll get the description out right away."

The truth was that though the man's description would be mentioned at roll-call briefings the next day, he would soon be forgotten unless he repeated his act. Whatever that had been, Dean thought. Mistake a girl for his daughter? How often was that likely to happen?

Terry Dean and the girl's father went outside together. They stood on the sidewalk. "I don't think you've got a lot to worry about," Dean said. "You might want to see that she doesn't go out alone for the next couple of weeks. And tell her to keep away from the harbour for the time being."

Still, Terry Dean drove away dissatisfied. He could not explain what had happened in the alley, but he believed that there were no truly inexplicable occurrences, only obscure ones, which fascinated him. He knew that he would toss this one around for a while.

SHERK SAT UP PAST MIDNIGHT trying to reason things out. Part of his mind was a stew of fantasy and illusion, while another part lived by rules of logic. But it was all one mind, and the two parts met so seamlessly that Sherk couldn't tell them apart, and he had stopped trying. So that night he reasoned the unreasonable.

He had found Margaret. That much he knew. But something had happened to her. She didn't know him, and she was scared of him, and there would be trouble if he wasn't careful. It was a cruel turn, but he couldn't change it.

He could leave or he could stay. Leaving was unthinkable, but if he stayed, he would have to be cautious. Watch and wait. Sherk didn't know what came after waiting, but he would see.

EVERY TIME SHE SHUT HER EYES to sleep, Emily Caldwell saw the gaunt-faced man, and felt his grip on her wrist, his knuckles cracking against her mouth.

Like the policeman Terry Dean, she wanted to understand. She recalled what Dean had suggested: "A daughter who looks like you and goes to your school . . ."

For the first time she remembered the new girl who resembled her so closely. But that girl's name was Sarah. And Emily could still hear the gaunt man crying for Margaret, Margaret. So she put away the thought that there could be any connection between her assailant and the new girl. It was weeks before anyone mentioned it again.

CHAPTER FIVE

Thursday, September 6
Five Nordbrook girls stood at a street corner and waited for the bus. An unshaven man in flannel shirt and bib overalls crossed the street and stopped in front of them.

"'Scuse me," he said. "I noticed you was all wearin' the same jackets and I was wonderin', is that a school uniform?"

Any one of them, alone, would have been frightened of him. But in a group they felt safe.

"Uh-huh," said the boldest. "Nordbrook School."

"And where's that?"

She told him the address and gave him general directions.

"Well, thank you," he said. "I was just wonderin'."

He headed back across the street.

SHERK STUDIED THE AD in the newspaper. "Wanted," it said. "Maintenance engineer. Local institution seeks experienced individual with full range of mechanical, plumbing and carpentry skills. Some janitorial required. $900/mo. Apply in person to J. Davis, 220 Ivy, Annapls."

Two twenty Ivy turned out to be the rectory of St. Bartholomew's Catholic Church, and J. Davis was a crew-cut young priest in a short-sleeved black shirt. Sherk told him why he had come.

"Call me Father Jim," the priest said, pumping Sherk's hand. They went into the rectory's front room. Sherk felt somewhat apprehensive; he had known few Catholics, and the religion had always seemed mysterious to him. He wasn't sure he wanted to work for a Catholic church.

"We're looking for a handyman really," the priest said. "There are four priests here, including Monsignor Herrity, and we need somebody who can keep this place together."

"With the right tools I can do almost anything," Sherk said.

The priest looked doubtful. "Some of the plumbing is at least thirty years old," he said. "The heating system for the church and the hall is oil-fired steam heat, a real antique. There's some minor wiring to do, and odd carpentry jobs as well. Also the landscaping and gardening. How much of that can you handle?"

"I've done it all at one time or another," Sherk said. "Where I come from, you learn to do for yourself."

"Where is that?" the priest said. "I don't place your accent."

"Southwest Virginia. In the Appalachians."

"And what brings you to Annapolis?"

Sherk's gaze narrowed briefly. "I come to be near my daughter."

"I see. Well, maybe I should give you the grand tour," the priest said. "Show you what you'd be getting yourself into."

The church grounds occupied an entire block about a mile west of downtown Annapolis. Rectory, elementary school and convent faced Ivy Street. Behind them was a huge, paved parking lot, which also served as a school playground. Across the car park were the church and the parish hall, which fronted on Bellflower Street.

The priest led Sherk out of the rectory, through the school building, then across the parking lot. It was lunch hour and the playground was full of children, running and laughing; the priest told Sherk that the school had nearly five hundred students.

They went into the back of the parish hall, a low brick structure. Downstairs, the hall's basement was close and dark, the ceiling low. The pipes and ducts of the heating system cast long shadows from a couple of bare light bulbs. It was a secluded place, with the look of neglect and the smell of machinery, and Sherk immediately felt at ease. Beside one wall was a tool cabinet. Sherk found a torch, studied the boiler, and told the priest it was not hard to understand; he could keep it working.

The priest wanted to know whether Sherk had found a permanent place to live yet. No, Sherk said. He was going to look today.

Then the priest led him to a one-room apartment across the basement. It was clean and plain, furnished with a bed, a dressing table, a table, and a couple of chairs. There was a two-coil hotplate and a grill, and a bathroom with a shower.

"The apartment goes with the job," the priest said. "You wouldn't have to use it. But it would save you paying rent."

Sherk didn't say anything.

"We'll take a quick look at the church," the priest said.

Sherk followed him upstairs and through a covered passageway that connected the hall and the church. They came out into the church sacristy, a small room with two doors. One opened into the chancel, and Sherk got a glimpse of a huge raised slab of marble with a gold tabernacle in the middle. Then the priest led him through the other door.

Sherk looked around him, enthralled. The church was cool and vast, with narrow stained-glass windows and mahogany woodwork. Its grey walls were high, and the roof rose up steeply to the peak, dim and distant from where Sherk stood. The place reminded him of a cavern, with far corners that never felt a human touch.

The priest crossed to the wide centre aisle, dipped his knee in the direction of the altar, then turned and walked towards the rear of the church. Sherk followed a few feet behind him. When they walked past the last pew, they were in the lobby.

"This was once a chapel," said the priest. "It's at least three hundred years old. I suppose it meant too much to tear down, so when the main church went up, about a hundred and twenty years ago, they put the two churches together." What had been done was obvious to Sherk. The big church had been built exactly against the back of the chapel. The back wall of the chapel had been torn out, and the front door enlarged. They had turned the old chapel into a good-sized entrance hall.

Sherk went back into the church. Its silent vastness fascinated him. He could imagine himself passing many hours in this moody quiet. Besides, it was the perfect job. The priests had other concerns; he would be left alone, and as long as the work got done he would not have to account for his hours.

"I want the job," Sherk told the priest. "I'm what you need."

Back in the rectory, Sherk filled out an application form.

AT THREE O'CLOCK that afternoon, while Emily Caldwell was at home nursing the purple bruises that had blossomed overnight on her cheek, Sarah Stannard was joining the nearly one hundred other girls who waited to board the school's shuttle buses.

There were three shuttles. The first wound through Annapolis proper. The second headed over the South River Bridge into the western suburbs. The third followed a route east, round the peninsula that is bounded by the Severn and the Magothy rivers. This was the bus that Sarah would ride on.

Three queues formed as the buses pulled up in the drive. Sarah got in line and filed on with the others. She was pleased that her mother hadn't changed her mind and driven down to meet her after all. It was a start, she thought. She had to grow up sometime.

BY A QUARTER TO THREE Sherk had found a parking place across the street from Nordbrook. He saw that the school was set back from the street. About two hundred yards, he guessed.

When the first burgundy blazers appeared on the front steps, he got out of the truck and crossed the road. He stood on the sidewalk. The view was distant, but he was sure that he would be able to find Margaret when she appeared.

Three school buses turned into the driveway. At that moment he saw her on the steps, in the group of girls who were waiting for the buses. There was something different, he thought. Her hair. The pigtail was gone. For a moment he was unsettled, and he questioned whether this was Margaret. But the doubt passed quickly. Even at this distance there was no mistaking her slender form and fine features.

The buses pulled up in front of the school. Margaret boarded the last one. Sherk crossed the street, got into his truck, and watched as the buses headed back up the drive. At the street the third one turned left. Sherk pulled into the traffic behind it.

He followed the bus across the Old Severn River Bridge. It made several stops. Each time Sherk saw who got off.

They were two or three minutes beyond the bridge when the bus stopped again and Margaret got out. Traffic was stopped in both directions; she ran across the highway.

The bus pulled away. Sherk drove slowly past. In his rearview mirror he saw her enter a shady lane that disappeared into a heavy stand of trees. It took all his strength to keep from calling out her name. But he stayed silent. Still fresh in his mind was the shock and shame he had felt when she ran from him in Annapolis. He couldn't bear such humiliation again. Today he would just watch. Today, and until he decided what he must do to reclaim his daughter.

JIM DAVIS FOUND Monsignor Frank Herrity in his rectory office, wolfing a slice of chocolate cake. Herrity was a small, round man who was perpetually either beginning or breaking a diet.

"Come in, Father," the monsignor said. He put down the empty plate. "And please close the door behind you. Yvonne will be merciless if she finds that I've been cheating." Yvonne Duranleau was the housekeeper, a French-Canadian grandmother who supervised his diets.

"Sit down," Herrity said. "What can I do for you, Father?"

"Monsignor, I think I've found a handyman," Davis said. He held out Sherk's application. Herrity took the form and looked at it.

"Notice how cold the air-conditioning is," Davis said. "You mentioned a few days ago that it didn't seem to be keeping the house cool. He noticed the same thing, and he told me he'd fix it right away. He says he can fix anything. He's down from the hills—Virginia—and he looks it."

"Family?"

"A daughter living here. He says that he came here because of her. He'd use the apartment in the hall basement."

Herrity's brows lifted. "That would be convenient."

"He's a Baptist," Davis said. Sherk had given the pastor of his church in Harben as a reference. "I told him it didn't matter; that if you approved, the job was his."

"He can start tomorrow, if you think he's a good man." He looked closer at the priest. "You do think he's a good man, Father?"

Davis didn't answer at first. The truth was, people didn't open up to him quickly, and he was slow—too slow—to get a feel for others. He was not the best judge of character. He answered after a few seconds. "I believe so."

"Then you should hire him."

Down the hall a woman shouted, "Someone's been into the cake! Oh no, Monsignor, not again."

"That woman is astounding," Herrity said. "Clairvoyant."

Davis let himself out of the office. That evening he realized that he had left Sherk's application with the monsignor. He reminded himself to retrieve it in the morning. He wanted to call the Baptist minister to ask about Sherk. But he was busy the next day. He never saw the application again, and he never did call.

MARGARET WAS SCREAMING. Her mouth was open, her face contorted in fear. Her eyes were looking straight at him, beseeching. An awful shriek welled up out of her throat. Sherk saw that she was terrified of something—no, of some *person* he could not see. A horror was about to occur, and Margaret knew it, and there was nothing he could do to help her.

A hand gripped her throat, and she screamed again.

Sherk sat up in bed, snapped awake by the nightmare. His hands were trembling. For a second he didn't know where he was. Then he remembered. Annapolis. The motel. He lay back. It was just a bad dream, he told himself. But it felt real, not so much a dream as a dreamed memory.

Sherk lay awake in the dark. The silence in the room felt fragile. Even the room, the bed, seemed insubstantial, more dreamlike than the dream itself had been. He was still awake, tense, when morning light bled through the curtains.

CHAPTER SIX

Thursday, November 1

Howard Warner was driving to his best friend's retirement party. Half an hour before the end of his shift he had answered a call on an armed robbery of a liquor store. By the time he had finished there, he was an hour late, but he knew that Frank Gephardt would understand.

The hall where Frank was having his send-off was a flat-roofed breeze-block building behind a cemetery. Perfect, Warner thought as he pulled into the parking lot.

He got out of the car and walked towards the hall. Once he had been an athlete, and he still had an athlete's step—weight forward, arms swinging in measured arcs at the sides, head up. But his body was now far from lithe. His chest, always broad, no longer tapered to the hips the way it once had. At forty-six, he figured, he was fighting to hold the line, nothing more. Two things he would never be again: young and slim.

He stopped outside the front door of the hall and listened to the garbled noise inside. Warner had dreaded this evening since Gephardt announced he had decided to take early retirement at the age of fifty-five. Warner had always seen in Gephardt a vision of what he himself would be in a few years. So the idea of Gephardt's getting tired and kissing it all away—which he had been doing by degrees for the past few years—was unsettling for Warner.

He went inside. The door opened on a reception room. At least half of the Annapolis Police Department was there, plus friends and mates.

Warner found Gephardt at the bar. He grinned when he saw Warner, and raised his glass in a toast.

"Hey, boy, I didn't think you'd make it."

"Duty calls."

Gephardt made a derisive snort. He curled an arm round Warner's neck, and they walked into the dining room. On the walls were enlarged photographs of Gephardt. They showed a marine in Korea, a proud rookie patrolman, a father balancing his four-year-old girl on the bonnet of a Studebaker. Warner had a hard time looking at the thin-waisted, dark-haired man in the pictures.

They reached the table where the chief of police was sitting with the captain of detectives. The chief motioned Warner towards an empty chair beside him.

"No way," Gephardt roared. "This is my party. You're sitting with the good folks tonight."

Warner let himself be led to the head table. There sat Gephardt's wife, Alice, and their two daughters with their husbands. Warner felt that he belonged with Gephardt's family. The two men had worked the last fourteen years as plain-clothes partners, and they had shared more than most brothers. After he got divorced, in 1978, Warner had found himself eating two or three dinners a week with the Gephardts. Now he kissed Alice and the girls and shook hands with their husbands. He sat down and made small talk and pretended that tonight was not the end of something that mattered.

Dinner consisted mostly of crabs and beer. After that came the speeches. It was awful: beery detectives telling stories everyone had heard a dozen times, the chief telling Gephardt what a credit he had been to the force. Even Warner had to take his turn; the chief had insisted that he present Gephardt with his retirement gift. He started by saying that Annapolis wasn't good enough for Frank Gephardt now; he and Alice had bought a bungalow on the shore, and instead of chasing bad guys he was going to go after the real big ones. Warner asked Gephardt if he was going to read the riot act to every rockfish that he hooked. Then a couple of men carried in the new Evinrude outboard motor they had all bought. That gave Warner a chance to escape. He went out through a side door of the hall to a narrow deck that looked over the cemetery.

He was watching a half moon rising when the door opened behind him. "Hey," Gephardt said. "You like the company better out here?"

Warner made a waving movement with one hand. "You know, Frank, all the smoke ..."

"And the hot air," Gephardt said.

"That, too." Warner looked out at the moon. "You lousy creep," he said abruptly. "Why'd you have to go quit on me?"

Gephardt looked amused. "Couldn't you tell? You never once noticed that Frank Gephardt wasn't quite the cop he used to be?"

"We all change," Warner said.

"I changed all right. I started thinking. A very dangerous practice. I started thinking that if I stayed here for the rest of my life, where would it get me? What difference would it make?"

"You're a cop. Cops are supposed to make a difference."

"And you," Gephardt said, "are old enough to recognize a lie like that one when it comes around. I worked hard for thirty years." He smiled and shrugged. "OK, twenty-five. Maybe I have been skating by a little, these last few. The old bones get tired. But I'll tell you, I earned this time and I'm gonna enjoy it."

"I know you. You're going to miss it. It's part of you, and you'll be sorry you ever left."

"Nope. I know the signs. When you stop caring, that's the time to give back the badge and let another cowboy have a go at it."

His smile—a smirk, almost—made Warner uncomfortable.

"B'sides," he said, "it's done. All washed and put out to dry. Who you trying to convince? Me? Or yourself?"

Warner changed the subject so he wouldn't have to answer.

Friday, November 2

There he was again. Seven minutes before three in the afternoon, and there was Sherk, leaving.

From his office Monsignor Herrity could see the parking lot between the church and the rectory. For the fourth time in as many days he had watched Sherk walk out of the church hall and drive off in his pick-up truck. Each day it had happened at about the same time, just before three in the afternoon.

The monsignor remembered having seen Sherk leave like this several times in the past few weeks. But it had never struck him until this week. The monsignor liked to think that not much around him went unnoticed and unexamined, and Sherk was by far the most intriguing new figure to have entered his world in some while. They had spoken several times. Sherk reminded him of an iceberg, hard and stolid.

Now here Sherk was, once again driving off. The monsignor wondered what duty might move him so regularly, so punctually. Nothing to do with the church, as far as he knew.

He turned away from the window. There was work on his desk, and he reminded himself that as a priest of the church, he of all people should be willing to abide some of life's mysteries, great and small.

SHERK PARKED HIS TRUCK beside the Ritchie Highway, about three hundred yards south of the spot where the school bus stopped every afternoon. On the other side of the road was a stand of forest. Sherk crossed

311

over to a narrow trail that ran in among the trees, virtually invisible.

He took the trail into the woods. He found his spot, behind a berry bush. There he crouched and waited.

AT THREE TWENTY Sarah Stannard got off the school shuttle, crossed Ritchie Highway and entered Whittier Lane, the private road that ran between her grandparents' home and the highway. Here were maples and pin oaks, and some evergreens as well. Among the trees it was easy for Sarah to pretend she was back in Vermont, and the few minutes she spent alone on the lane every afternoon were often the most pleasant of her day.

This afternoon, as always, the road was empty. Sarah took off her blazer; the day was warm and still. As she walked, a grey squirrel skittered in front of her, hurrying for cover.

Her grandparents' home was on the southernmost of six twenty-acre estates that were situated side by side along the east bank of the Severn River. A wooded grove sprawled across the rear of the properties, and Whittier Lane cut through the grove. The woods were thinnest near the beginning of the lane, but soon the right of way swung left and into the heart of the grove, tunnelling through the foliage. It was a still, secluded spot.

Now, as Sarah approached that stretch, a tune came into her head. She sang quietly, and her pace picked up.

SHERK CROUCHED IN THE BRUSH and waited. Berry bushes and tall grass grew thick along the edge of the lane, and Sherk knew that he was perfectly concealed. He had tried several spots in the past weeks as he hid to watch his daughter, but this one was best.

It reminded Sherk of deer hunting. You didn't go out and get a deer. First you had to watch them, learn where they fed and watered. You had to know their habits. Then you found a place along their path where you could hide. Sherk was good at that. He was on one knee in the brush, hunched over. Cautiously he lifted a leaf so that he could see the lane more clearly. She ought to be along any time now.

Presently he heard footsteps; his daughter appeared round a bend. Sherk did not question that this was Margaret. The girl who came towards him, kicking a pebble in front of her and singing to herself, had become the Margaret of his memory and his imagination.

She was closer now. Sometimes she passed him on the far side of the lane, but today her path brought her within an arm's length of where he hid. Now she was so close he could see only the grey of her skirt as she went by. It took all his effort to remain still.

As he watched her stride away, Sherk's vision blurred moistly. The lane curved, the foliage swallowed her up, and she was gone.

Sherk didn't move at first. He let his eyes clear. Once, these moments in the woods had been joyful. Just seeing Margaret again was enough. But now it was agony. The past few days he had barely restrained himself from rushing out and taking her. It wasn't fair, he thought. He had found his daughter, but he couldn't have her.

Sherk got up. He picked his way through the underbrush, back to the trail and the highway. He returned to the church forlorn and angry. He thought about having a daughter who didn't know him, who feared him and would scream at the sight of him. He felt the fire inside. It made his hands sweat. He knew a place that would ease his mind, a soothing place, and he needed to be there now.

"HE'S A STRANGE ONE," Yvonne Duranleau said. "You can see right through an honest man. But not him."

They were in Monsignor Herrity's office, watching Sherk getting out of his truck. The monsignor was at his desk, the housekeeper dusting bookshelves behind him.

"He's reserved," the monsignor said. "No harm in that."

"He looks like he's dried up inside. And to talk to him—half the time it's like he's not there. I don't like him."

"He's a good worker, Yvonne."

"I wish he had never showed up." Sherk was walking out of sight, round the church. "I'm telling you, he's trouble."

THERE WERE TWO STEPS up to the door of the lobby. Sherk went round to the side of the steps and wriggled into the tight space beneath them. He pushed aside several loose boards that lay across the stone foundation, revealing a rectangular opening barely wide enough for his hips and shoulders. He slid his legs in first, and then pulled his upper body through. His feet dropped and touched solid ground.

He was standing in a cellar beneath the lobby, the old chapel. The floor was packed dirt. Above him were the lobby's exposed floor joists. There, cobwebs hung thick. The cellar was crypt-like, the air cool and undisturbed.

Sherk sat cross-legged on the floor, comfortable in the darkness. He could be alone here. Really alone. It was unlikely that anyone else knew of this spot. When he had first opened it up, expecting to find a crawl space where he might store some tools, the boards across the entrance had been fastened with square-cut nails at least fifty years old.

He let his mind drift, let the quiet overtake him. He must have dozed, he told himself later, because his dream returned.

It started differently this time, but he recognized the peculiar feel of it, the strange texture that was unlike any other dream he had ever known.

313

Somebody was up on a hill, looking down at the cabin. Waiting. Waiting for Margaret.

Sherk couldn't see the face, but somehow he felt the malevolence inside this evil man up on the hill.

There was Margaret, getting out of a car, laughing, skipping up into the cabin. Up on the hill, the evil one was thinking, Bad girl, bad bad girl, then starting down towards the cabin.

Sherk tried to shout to her, Run! But he knew that the dream-Margaret couldn't hear, that he was powerless to interfere in what was taking place.

Now the evil one was walking through the front door. Now standing over Margaret as she sat paralysed in a chair. Now shouting at her as she tried to talk. Now slapping her hard across the face, coldly, snapping her head to the side.

He bent over her, saying, "Why do you make me do this?"

His hands were on Margaret's arms. He raised them, rested them lightly on her throat. The fingers tightened. She screamed. The fingers got tighter and she screamed again.

Sherk writhed in the dirt and somehow escaped from the dream. He had seen much more this time, but he knew that there was still more to see. It was inside his head somehow, behind a door, pounding to get out. Awful stuff.

THE CAPTAIN OF DETECTIVES—a man named Blatchford—leaned forward in his swivel chair, hands clasped on his desk. He was a small and trim man, a couple of years younger than Warner, unbelievably dapper. He wore suits that fitted him close to the body and never showed a wrinkle.

"I thought we ought to have a talk, Howard," the captain said. "With Frank gone, there'll have to be some adjustments. Obviously you'll be the most immediately affected."

Warner thought this sounded ominous.

"It may be a while before we fill the position full-time. That means we'll all have to pull harder to take up the slack. I'd go so far as to say you might have further to pull than others."

"Wait a minute. I work hard." Warner sounded more defensive than he wanted.

The captain sat back in his chair. "I don't want to be harsh. But I think we'd both agree that Frank Gephardt has not exactly been a whirlwind of enthusiasm. After a while that has to reflect on his partner. Bad habits are contagious."

"You're talking about my friend," Warner said.

The captain shook his head. "Frank Gephardt's gone. The point is, the people who are left will have to do that much more if we're going to keep up to standard. I'm sure you'll do your part."

314

He picked a piece of lint off a sleeve and flicked it away. "I give Frank full marks in one respect. He knew that when you lose the fire in your belly, it's time to get out." He looked directly at Warner. "Otherwise you're cheating everybody. The force, the city, yourself."

WARNER'S SHIFT ENDED AT SIX He was typing reports at six fifteen, when the captain went home, giving him a curt nod. As Warner's big fingers jumped at the keyboard he recalled the captain's words about fire in the belly. The man wanted to hang him because he was no longer a crusader. And it was true. Nobody could keep that up.

He finished the report, filed it, and left for the day. Driving away, he was still thinking about the captain's lecture, the part about cheating the force and the city. That hurt. He wanted to tell the captain that only three things were really important in his life. Two of them were the force and the city. The third was *Amaranth*.

He pulled into the parking lot of a marina on the South River. *Amaranth* was at the end of the dock: a thirty-eight-foot sloop, trimmed in brown teak. Warner stepped aboard, careful not to leave a mark on the white fibreglass, and looked round anxiously; nothing was amiss. He went below, changed into corduroys and a cotton pullover, then came up on deck.

On a cop's salary a thirty-eight-foot yacht is a remarkable extravagance. Warner had swung the deal six years ago, when he sold his house to settle accounts with his ex-wife. His share of the profits had made a good down payment on the boat, and he eked out the monthly instalments. He lived frugally, had a studio apartment, and off duty he got by with a nine-year-old Toyota. For *Amaranth* he would have sacrificed a great deal more.

In four years his loan on the boat would be paid. At the same time he would have chalked up twenty-five years in the force. He would be fifty. Warner had never taken *Amaranth* out of the bay, but she was built for blue-water sailing. She could be sailed round the world single-handed, if the one hand was up to the job.

For now he had the weekend. The forecast was for fair weather, warmer than was seasonable. Warner knew an anchorage on the other side of Kent Island that he could make in a short time. He cast off and set sail.

Saturday, November 3

Sherk was painting the lobby when he heard a scratching behind the wall. It was the sound of an animal's claws brushing the other side of the plaster, moving up the space between the inside and outside walls. He put down the roller and listened. The scratching moved slowly upwards, stopping at the ceiling.

Too big for a rat, he thought. Maybe a coon. Beneath the floor was his hidden cellar, which was surely where the animal had got in. But he wondered where it could have gone when it came to the ceiling. He went back to work, thinking about how the lobby had changed over the centuries, thinking about old buildings and the secrets their walls conceal.

Later he baited and set a couple of live traps in the cellar. Then he went up into the church with a torch and climbed an enclosed staircase in the back corner that led to the choir loft, a balcony that extended over the last ten rows of pews.

He tapped the wall at the top of the stairs. It was solid. He crossed the landing, where the stairs doubled back, and climbed up to the doors that opened into the loft. The walls were solid all the way. Then he was in the loft itself, moving along the back wall, where the smooth grey granite was exposed. A pipe organ sat against the wall. He came to a walk-in closet where the choir members hung their robes. It was built into wall, near the far corner of the loft.

Sherk walked in. He pushed the robes aside. The closet was wainscoted from belt level down to the floor, and in the corners were stacks of hymnals and boxes of candles.

He closed the door behind him. The church was empty, and nobody noticed that Sherk was in the closet for more than an hour, marvelling again at the secrets that old buildings hold.

Sunday, November 4

Sarah was laughing. Elise didn't know the last time she had heard the sound. The girl was playing tennis with her grandfather, bantering with him, really enjoying herself.

"Grandpa, it was out by a foot!" Sarah yelled.

"Nicked the line," said Harry Stannard. "Play on."

"The ball hit right here," she said, tapping her racket at a spot beyond the baseline. "Mama, Grandma, you tell him."

"Out," said Elise, sitting in a deckchair near the court.

"Out," said Joy, sitting beside Elise.

"That makes it three to one," Sarah said.

"So what? Only my vote counts. Thirty all. Serve the ball."

"You're terrible," she said, laughing.

Was it possible, Elise wondered, that Sarah had forgotten what day it was? Exactly one year ago they had all lost Jack Stannard: son, husband and father. Elise had had a good cry before she came outside with the others. She glanced at Joy's eyes, red-rimmed and puffed, and guessed that she, too, had remembered.

Sarah slammed a shot down the middle of the court.

"Try and steal that one." She was grinning as she said it.

"It was close. I'll give it to you this once."

Now Sarah tossed the ball and hit a hard serve that Harry grounded into the net. She whooped. "All right, my game!"

"The sun," Harry said. "The sun was in my eyes."

Maybe she had put it behind her, Elise thought. The young are resilient. Let it be so, she told herself.

USUALLY SHERK DIDN'T GO NEAR the church on Sunday. There were five Masses through the day, and the church would be nearly full for each one. But this morning Sherk had his traps to check. He clambered down into the cellar and turned the torch on the cages. A pair of green eyes shone back at him from one cage; the other was empty. Sherk went over to the animal and squatted beside it: a raccoon, fat and healthy.

The floorboards rumbled overhead. People arriving for Mass. Sherk didn't want to give away his secret, so he decided to wait until the service was under way. Then he could climb out unseen.

He turned off the torch and sat listening to the noises overhead. Heard murmuring and shuffled feet, a wailing infant—the sounds of life going past him, oblivious to him. He thought about home, about all the days and nights he had known with Margaret in the little cabin there, the two of them hidden away and untouchable, life passing them by. The coon's sharp claws clicked on the bare wire of the cage. And at that moment Sherk knew what he was going to do. He could see it all. He knew.

"SHE'S TOUGH," HARRY SAID. "You'd think she might give an old man a break, but I couldn't get a single close call."

"Spare me," Sarah said. They were sitting with Joy and Elise, drinking lemonade.

"How 'bout another set?" Harry said.

"No way, Grandpa. You're too much for me. I think I'll go in."

Sarah got up and headed for the house, relieved that she wouldn't have to show her face to anyone for a while. A year ago today, she told herself.

Up in her room, she stretched out on the bed, face buried in a pillow. There was nothing harder than keeping in grief, feeling it weigh her down. But she told herself that she had done pretty well today. Nobody would have guessed.

Then she felt it come spilling out, and she sobbed into her pillow, sobbed, "Daddy, Daddy, I need you," feeling very small and very helpless.

Monday, November 5

Sherk was at the hardware store in Parole Plaza when it opened. He needed plenty: insulating tape, a canvas tarpaulin, screw eyes, webbed rope. A strong hammock, buckles, a glass kerosene lamp. At an army-

317

navy surplus store, he picked out a sleeping bag and some camping gear. Then he found a leather-goods store and bought a supple, soft piece of deerskin.

That night he went to work. If something could be made with hands and tools, Sherk would find a way. He had never worked with leather before, but he turned the deerskin into what he needed. And with heavy thread and needle, he made what he wanted out of the buckles and the canvas.

After four nights' work, he was ready.

CHAPTER SEVEN

Friday, November 9
For nearly a week Joy Stannard had been trying to talk Elise into a day trip to Washington, DC. It was a shame to live within fifty miles of the capital and not visit the city as often as possible. They would go on a White House tour, have lunch downtown, spend the afternoon at the National Gallery of Art. Maybe even squeeze in some shopping.

Elise, without knowing why, put her off at first. But finally she agreed.

"There won't be anyone here when you get home," she told Sarah. "We'll be out until at least five. And with rush hour, who knows?"

"Take all the time you want," Sarah said. "I'll be fine."

There was still a trace of doubt in Elise's face.

"I'll be fine. Really."

A short time later they pulled into the school's driveway and stopped in the turning space. Sarah leaned over and kissed Joy and her mother.

"You've got your key?" Elise said.

"Got it."

"And don't worry if we're a little late," Elise said.

"If you don't get going, you'll never get back," Sarah said. She climbed out of the car, closed the door, and gave them a wave before she went up the steps.

HOWARD WARNER OPENED HIS EYES and looked at the clock on the bedside table. Just past noon. He got up, showered and shaved, and boiled water for instant coffee in the kitchen of his apartment. All week he had been on the late shift, subbing for a detective who had court duty, never asleep before three in the morning. Brushing his teeth and reading the sports pages at an hour when everyone else was on lunch break made him feel vaguely estranged from society.

He looked outside. A low, tweedy layer of rolling clouds covered the sky as far as he could see. Snow, he thought, the clouds have that look about them. Annapolis rarely saw snow until December, but today the air

318

seemed cold enough and the clouds looked right. The thought brightened Warner, and he decided he would go to work early. Snow was a drag on the traffic detail, maybe, but to almost every other cop it meant relief. Muggers and rapists found few potential victims on the streets, and burglars knew that it kept people at home. Crime, for at least a few hours, would be out of the hands of all but the maddest and the most desperate.

SHERK ENTERED THE GROVE OF TREES, a shadowy figure moving silently under the bare limbs and low grey sky of winter. He wore a dark blue watch cap and a black wool jacket, and he carried a brown gym bag.

Snow was falling thickly, large wet flakes. All day it had been threatening. Now here it was. Sherk plunged into it, and in a moment the snow and the muted woods swallowed him up.

"COME ON, SARAH, it'll be fun."

"I shouldn't," she said. She and Stephanie, a friend from school, were in the Nordbrook cafeteria, eating lunch.

"Sarah, he's a senior. He's six feet tall, and gorgeous. I'd go for him myself, except that I'm kinda hooked on his friend. Don't tell me you've got so many boys on hold that you can pass this up."

Actually Sarah had no boys at all. Since coming to Annapolis she had met none. Now Stephanie wanted to introduce her to one. Stephanie's older brother had a Trans-Am, and after school he and his car and two of his friends were going to be waiting.

"I'd like to," Sarah said.

"Then do it. Call your mother, tell her you want to run around with some friends, and we'll get you home by four thirty."

Sarah couldn't call her mother, but if she were back by four thirty, Elise would never know.

"I'll have to think about it," she said.

"Sarah, I have to know. If you can't come, I have to find somebody else. I promised I'd get two other girls."

The bell rang for fourth period. Sarah gathered up her books.

"I'll do it," she said.

"Stannard, you're OK. Meet you at the front door."

"I'M SORRY," Joy Stannard said.

"It's all right," said Elise.

She had known they were in trouble when they left the restaurant on Connecticut Avenue and walked out into the sleet. In Vermont she had often driven through ice and snow. But aware of the reputation of DC drivers for panicking under such conditions, she had suggested starting back, cutting the day short.

319

"Nonsense," Joy had said. "Harry would rib us without mercy if we let a little bad weather chase us home."

She had insisted on going across the city to Georgetown. Later they had spent two hours covering ten miles to the Beltway. Now at last they were nearing Annapolis. The clouds had dropped about three inches of soggy snow, and the road was clogged with cars grinding through brown slush at fifteen miles an hour.

In the back seat was a large pile of packages. Almost all of them were Joy's. Under her direction the trip had turned into a shopping expedition. For Elise the day had been a waste. No White House, no museum, and much tedium behind the wheel. Now she wanted nothing more than to be home in a hot bath.

When they finally turned down Whittier Lane, the clock on the dash said six twenty-two. Sarah would be worried, Elise thought. She rounded a bend. Home at last. But it looked dark; not a light was showing.

Elise parked beside the main house and hurried over to the new wing. She opened the door, switched on the lights and went into the living room. "Sarah!" she called.

She heard only silence. She checked the kitchen, then ran upstairs, suddenly frantic. "Sarah!" she called again. No answer.

She tried the studio. Sarah's room. The bed was rumpled, but exactly as it had been left that morning. Not a trace of the Nordbrook skirt and blazer that festooned chairs after she had changed.

Elise ran back into the main wing. She found Joy bringing in an armload of packages.

"Have you seen Sarah?" Elise said breathlessly.

"No. She wouldn't be here."

Elise covered the entire house. Afterwards she found Joy in the dining room, heaping packages on the table. "Sarah's not here," Elise said. "She should have been home three hours ago."

After a moment Joy said, "The snow. Maybe the school bus had trouble. Call the school and find out."

Elise did. She was back to Joy quickly, her voice quavering.

"They said the buses were late, but that the last one finished its run before five. Joy, something has happened to my girl."

"Nothing serious, I'm sure. It can't be long before Harry's home. He'll know what to do. Until then, let's not panic."

Harry Stannard had spent the day in southern Maryland, where he was in a partnership to build two hundred town houses. As they waited for his return, Elise kept going to the window, looking out at the lane, where the grove swallowed it up.

It was now after seven. She put on her coat and walked up the lane. She had to do something. The snow was already melting, sloppy underfoot.

320

She shouted Sarah's name, walked further into the woods, and shouted again. She was walking back when headlights overtook her from behind. Harry's car stopped, and she got in. Elise felt a surge of gratitude. The old dinosaur. His stubborn strength was exactly what she needed at this moment.

"Sarah's missing," she said. "Harry, I'm so worried."

"Not a word from her?"

"Nothing."

"Did she make it back home?"

"Harry, I don't know anything except she's gone."

HOWARD WARNER HAD NEVER been down Whittier Lane before, but even in the dark he knew that this was an enclave of real money. The name Stannard was unknown to him, but he told himself that it must mean a great deal to someone who mattered. It was hardly routine for the department to react so quickly to the disappearance of a fifteen-year-old, especially one who lived outside the city, in Anne Arundel County.

Warner had been assigned to the case because the girl was last known to have been in Annapolis, at school. But let him find a witness to place her outside the city limits, and he would be able to leave it to the county. With any luck, he thought, he would be off the case before morning.

Warner reached the end of the drive. Outside the house were a county patrol cruiser and an unmarked county detective's car.

A man in his late sixties met Warner at the door.

"I'm Harry Stannard," he said. "Sarah's my granddaughter."

They shook hands. Then they walked into the living room. Two women were there, talking to a detective and a couple of uniformed officers. Warner glanced around him. The room was at least three times the size of his apartment.

Stannard introduced his wife, a blue-haired woman with a bewildered expression, and Sarah's mother, Elise, who extended a slim hand. Warner stepped forward to take it, noting that the woman's face was strained and pale. She was good-looking, with dark and searching eyes. He knew he must have stared too long, because after a moment she averted her eyes.

"You know your colleagues," Harry Stannard went on, motioning to the three cops. Warner knew one of them, a puffy-faced county detective named Tarver. He nodded a greeting.

Elise turned back to the two officers. She was telling them how punctual Sarah was, how she caught the same school bus every afternoon. Tarver motioned Warner out to the hall.

"First thing we need to do is find the bus driver," Warner said when they were alone. "See if she caught that bus."

"Want to get her out of the city, huh? Wriggle off the hook. I don't blame you. We've got a patrolman with the driver now. But you want my opinion, the kid up and split."

"A good guess," Warner said.

"You haven't heard the half of it. Three months ago, mom and the girl move here from out of state. The father died a year ago. Kid took it hard. They move in with the grandparents. She starts at a new school; her grades are just so-so."

They were standing with their backs to the living room. Warner realized that the mother had stopped talking. He put up a hand to quiet Tarver, but the detective ground on, loudly.

"Is this starting to sound familiar? A big emotional upset. A new home, new school, new friends. A runaway, pure and simple."

Elise had come up behind him. "She's not!" she shouted. "She didn't run away."

Warner touched her arm lightly and turned her aside. "Hey," he said soothingly. "Maybe you'd show me her room. Would you mind? It might help."

She looked angrily over her shoulder at the county detective. Then she took Warner to the new wing, up the stairs to Sarah's bedroom. To Warner it was standard issue: stuffed animals, posters of rock stars, ruffles and a flowery spread on the bed.

He looked at the top of the dressing table. A bottle of eau de cologne. A wooden jewellery box. A sketch pad, which he opened.

"This hers?"

"Yes. She has taken lessons for several years."

"A quiet girl, I bet. Probably doesn't mind being alone."

She looked closely at him. "How did you know that?"

"A lot of time went into this." He held up the sketch pad. "Drawing's a solitary pastime, and you don't get it done if you're the type that has to be out running around."

"My daughter *is* quiet. She's a very sensitive child."

He thumbed past a couple more pages. "I could see that, too."

"Now you're going to tell me that's just the type who'd get upset over something and run away. She fits the profile, right?"

"Most kids do, at one time or another. That doesn't stop you from going crazy when it happens to one of yours. I know. I had one run out on me."

She looked at him with interest. Warner pulled up a chair and sat down. She faced him from the edge of the bed.

"It's bad, I know that, Mrs. Stannard," he began.

"Elise," she said.

"OK, Elise. And I'm Howard." He felt her softening up, the inner tension losing its grip.

"Like I say, I've been through it. My daughter was just a few months older than yours. My wife and I were having a hard time. The marriage was coming apart. And one day Sharon—that's my girl—is gone. Just like that. Probably decided that what she found out there couldn't be worse than home." Warner shook his head. "They think they're so tough at that age," he continued. "They're growing up. They have to prove it. But they know nothing about the world and how it can be. Inside, they're just kids."

Elise nodded eagerly. "And did you find her?"

"She came back on her own, three weeks later. She'd found some crash pad down at Virginia Beach. When she got tired of peanut-butter sandwiches for dinner, she came home."

"Was she all right?"

"Oh yes. They make out, you know." He shrugged. "Now she's twenty-six, lives in Seattle. Got her nursing degree last year, found a good job. She's doing OK." Warner leaned forward. "Most of these cases turn out fine. It's the very few exceptions you hear about."

"You're telling me that most runaways make their way home. But my daughter didn't run away."

"Maybe we should hope that she did," Warner said.

"Because if she didn't run away, then somebody is preventing her from coming home. Isn't that it? And that's a lot more serious."

"There are a lot of possibilities," was all he would say.

They went back to the main part of the house. There Tarver took Warner aside to relay some news. "We've got a history teacher says the girl was definitely in her two o'clock class this afternoon. And the bus driver says no way did she get on the bus. This one is all yours."

MONSIGNOR HERRITY HAPPENED to be reading in his bedroom on the second floor of the rectory at St. Bartholomew's when he heard the scream. He only heard it once, so he couldn't say for sure what it was. But his first impression was that it had been a woman screaming from somewhere near the church. He put the book down, went to his window and pushed aside the curtains.

His bedroom looked out across the parking lot to the church and the hall. But from here he could see nothing amiss.

He went back to bed. It was late, and he was saying a seven o'clock Mass in the morning, so he turned out the light. For a few minutes he lay awake listening. But he heard nothing more, and soon sleep overcame him.

"IT'S ONE THIRTY IN THE MORNING," Warner said. "If I were you, I'd crawl into bed and get some sleep."

"I couldn't sleep," Elise told him.

She had wanted to be near her own phone, so she had gone back to the new wing, and Warner had followed her. They had sat in the living room for about an hour, talking. Warner was staying at the house through the end of his shift. Captain's orders. There was little else to do now. Sarah's description had been broadcast to patrol cars. In a few hours her photo would be distributed to policemen in Annapolis and surrounding jurisdictions. The county was sending a patrolman soon, just to stand by, and a technician was coming to wire the telephones with recorders in case the Stannards received a ransom demand.

"The waiting is awful," she said. "Not knowing. Imagining ... I keep asking myself what could have happened."

"I've got a piece of cop wisdom," he said. "Don't torture yourself with speculation. It does no good."

A shy smile passed over her face. It was the first Warner had seen from her, and he was sorry when it left. He got up from the chair. "Coffee's still on, right? No, sit. I can take care of myself."

He went into the kitchen and filled his cup from the percolator. Standing at the kitchen window, he looked out into the night and thought about the girl, wondering where she was at this moment. All the statistics insisted that she was a runaway. Elise had said it: "She fits the profile. . . ." But there were angles that didn't mesh. Like the school uniform. It wasn't an outfit a kid would wear to run away in. And her savings account. Elise had found the passbook. No recent withdrawals. Yet a kid planning to run away would want to put together all the money she could.

A county patrol was coming up the drive. Warner's shift was nearly finished. He decided he could leave now.

Elise had stretched out on the couch. When he got closer, he saw that she was asleep. Draped over an arm of the couch was a shawl. Warner unfolded it and let it fall lightly over her. She didn't move. He turned out all the lights but one table lamp, and he took a business card out of his wallet. He wrote his home number on the front of the card and left it on the coffee table. He checked in with the patrolman, then went out to his car.

Late night was warmer than the afternoon had been. On the front lawn the snow cover had melted down to a scattered white archipelago. Warner drove back up the lane through a thin fog that hung down to about waist height. It was crazy weather, he thought, gone from summer into winter and back again.

He was about a hundred yards into the grove when a speck beside the road gleamed in his headlights. He stopped and got out to look. It was a small gold charm. He picked it up by its edges and read the enamelled emblem. "Mont Tremblant", it said. Then he dropped the charm in an envelope. A long shot, he thought. But you never know.

He walked back to the car and drove home.

"HOWARD," SAID THE CAPTAIN'S VOICE from the telephone receiver. "We need to talk about the Stannard girl."

The clock said quarter to ten. Warner had been asleep when the call snapped him awake.

"I want to know how we handle it," the captain went on. "Is this something serious, or just a runaway? I've got three men who're going to spend all weekend running down the kid's classmates, and I don't want them wasting their time on a flier."

"I had the feeling that there was some pull involved," Warner said, digesting this.

"Somebody asks for a favour, I don't mind. But we've done all right by these people. Starting now, the case gets what it deserves. Nothing more. So tell me where we go with it."

Warner forced his mind back a few hours. He remembered the passbook, the school uniform that a girl would never wear to run away. "I want to go out to the house again. Give me an hour."

"An hour won't break my back," the captain said.

"Hey, I've got one for you," Warner said. "You ever hear of a place called Mont Tremblant?"

"Sure. It's a resort area in the Laurentian Mountains, not far from Montreal."

"That would make it close to Vermont."

"Maybe a hundred miles from the border."

"Uh-huh," Warner said. "One hour, right?"

He dressed quickly and hurried out.

SHERK DIDN'T ANSWER his door. He wasn't in the church and wasn't in the school, or anywhere else the monsignor looked.

Yvonne was right, he thought. Sherk was a queer one, materializing suddenly where you least expected him, or disappearing just when you wanted him. Well, the blocked toilet in the church hall would have to wait.

ELISE WAS IN JEANS and a Mexican-style blouse when Warner walked into her living room.

"Good morning," she said. Warner thought he saw a stirring of that smile. "I don't suppose you've brought good news."

"Brought something for you to look at."

Warner took a chair opposite the couch, and Elise sat across from him. Harry and Joy had followed him in and they looked curiously over his shoulder as he removed the envelope from his jacket. He slid the charm out on the coffee table.

Elise reached for it, and he caught her hand.

"Don't," he said. "There might be prints. Do you know it?"

"Sarah wears it on a bracelet."

"Was it lost?"

"I don't know. No ... she'd have said something if it was gone."

"She wear it yesterday?"

"Every day. Her father gave it to her. Where did you find it?"

"Not far up the road that goes through the woods."

She looked at Warner, up at Harry and Joy, back to Warner.

"So she *was* here," she said, hopeful. Then it hit her. "She was here. But she never got home." Her eyes filled with tears.

Warner found a phone and called the captain, told him about the charm and the uniform and the savings account. Warner conceded that it might mean nothing. "But I can't get away from it all," he went on. "I get the feeling something funny is going on here." Good cops all knew the flutter of instinct that told them some element was misplaced in the correct order of life.

"Then we won't let it go," the captain said after a moment. That was half of what Warner wanted to hear. "You're on top of it; you stay with it." And that was the other half.

Warner was hanging up when Elise appeared. Her mouth was tight, and there was concern on her face.

"Please come," she said.

Warner followed her to the hall. In the front doorway stood a tall boy of about seventeen. He was holding a couple of textbooks and a loose-leaf binder, and he had a startled look. Harry and Joy were standing in front of him, Harry glaring.

"Look," the boy said. "I don't want any trouble, I just wanted to bring back her books."

Warner saw a name penned on the cover of the binder. A precise script: "Sarah Stannard". Warner took out his badge and showed it to the boy.

"Oh, God. I didn't do anything. Really."

"First tell me your name."

"Timothy Witherspoon," the kid said.

"And tell me how you got the books."

"This girl, Sarah, left them in the car yesterday. My friend Larry's car, I mean. There were three of us guys, and we met three girls at Nordbrook, and we went bumming around for a while. That's Larry outside."

Over the kid's shoulder Warner could see a black Trans-Am with another boy at the wheel.

"We drove out to Sandy Point Park," Timothy volunteered.

"In the snow?" Warner asked.

"It wasn't snowing bad at first. We just wanted to goof around a little. We stayed about an hour, and then we took the girls home."

"You brought Sarah here?"

"Sure. Well, almost. By then the snow was pretty bad. Sarah told us her house was at the end of the road, but the lane wasn't ploughed, and Larry was worried he'd slide off. She said not to worry, she walks home all the time. So we let her out."

"Where, exactly?"

"About halfway down the road," the kid said.

Elise leaned against Harry for support, and gave a low moan.

TERRY DEAN WAS AMONG the first patrolmen on the force to see Sarah's photo. He stopped by the station house before his lunch break and found the five-by-seven glossies in the squad room. He pulled one off the top of the stack and glanced at it. The glance became a stare.

He told himself that he had met this girl. Where, or how, he couldn't say. But the long blonde hair, the pale skin, the deep eyes; he had seen them all somewhere before.

He read the label on the back of the photo: Sarah Stannard. It meant nothing. As a cop he encountered at least a thousand people every year, names and faces that came and went. He was sometimes shaky with names, but the faces never got away from him. He was sure that he had seen this girl.

ON SATURDAY AFTERNOON the county police search team gathered on Harry Stannard's lawn. There were nearly forty of them, mostly volunteers, and they were subdued as they waited, for the odds were high that they might find the body of Sarah Stannard as they tramped through the woods.

Timothy Witherspoon's story had been corroborated by his friends and by the other two girls who had been in the car. It meant that Sarah had entered the grove at about four forty-five the previous afternoon, and apparently had not left it—at least, not of her own free will.

Warner, standing nearby, looked back at the house and thought about the grief that might descend upon it tonight. He walked over to the county detective, Tarver. The case was now the county's, since the girl had disappeared outside city limits.

"Go on home," Tarver said "It's outa your pocket now."

"I'm in," Warner said. "I can use the walk."

"Up to you. But it'll be cold and wet." Tarver looked at the searchers, and yelled, "OK, people, let's spread out."

The team, strung out at ten-foot intervals, like a skirmish line, advanced on the woods. It was slow work. They were supposed to examine every inch of ground, turn over every fallen branch. They had been at it for half an hour, and had reached the area where Warner had found the gold charm, when one of them came upon a patch of electric blue among the greens and browns. He ran to it and held it up: a flimsy nylon bag.

"What's this?" he said.

Some of the others had joined him. "It's a sack," said a young reserve officer, "for a sleeping bag."

They moved on. The light was dimming when they reached the north end of the grove. They had found no body, only the blue stuff sack. Nothing else seemed to have even the faintest possible connection to Sarah's disappearance.

ELISE SAT IN A ROCKING CHAIR in her room. The blinds were drawn, the lights off. Outside, she heard car doors slamming, engines turning over. The searchers had come to look for Sarah, and now they were leaving. Sarah was gone. Really gone.

A shadow moved across the low light in the doorway.

"Elise? It's me. Howard Warner."

"Hello, Howard," she said dully.

"I wanted to tell you goodbye." Warner's thick fingers nibbled at the hem of his jacket. "Wanted you to know I'll be thinking of you, hoping all this comes out right."

"You won't be back?"

"It's not my case any more. a matter of jurisdiction. But don't get discouraged. Be thankful that she wasn't out there. It's the best you could hope for at the moment."

She gave no sign that she had heard, and after a few seconds he left, and she was alone. Her chair rocked forward and back in slow, tiny arcs. Elise folded her arms across her chest, in the manner of someone painfully cold.

BY SUNDAY THE NEWSPAPERS had the story. It appeared on the front page of the Metro section of the Washington *Post*. The story quoted a county police spokesman to the effect that all possible leads were being developed.

At three pm the number of those leads increased from none to one, when the state crime lab completed its analysis of the blue stuff sack. The material was common 1.5-ounce ripstop nylon of unidentifiable manufacture. Microscopic examination disclosed fragments of goose down. The police compiled a list of sporting goods outlets in Anne Arundel and the surrounding counties. Soon they would visit each of those stores, hoping to discover where the sack had been bought, and by whom.

The gold charm yielded no fingerprints.

Warner, reading the newspaper accounts, imagined a girl he had never met, but whom he knew from her reflection in Elise's eyes. He saw her in the woods, saw her alone in the lane, making tracks in the snow as she walked to meet a horror. Little girl lost. And gone, he thought. Some people are going to miss you, kid.

CHAPTER EIGHT

Sarah couldn't move. Bound at hands and feet, trussed and gagged, she could do no more than breathe. There were voices and footsteps, but they seemed to belong to a distant reality, nothing to do with her. She was hidden and alone and beyond the reach of the world. But she was alive ...

It had been late Friday afternoon when she got out of Larry's Trans-Am. She had watched it leave, and then she was alone, with the snow still falling in big flakes all around her.

The walk wouldn't be bad, she thought. At least she was dressed for it, in her green vinyl jacket and low-cut rubber shoes. But somehow she felt incomplete. Then she remembered. Her books. She must have forgotten them in the back seat.

She looked back to where the car had disappeared. Long gone. She turned towards home and put aside her worries about the books. Stephanie would bring them on Monday.

She began to walk. Soon she was in dense woods. The stranger appeared from nowhere. She was looking down at her feet scuffing the snow, and when she looked up again he was standing directly in her path, about twenty paces away.

He startled her. She always had the lane to herself. And this interloper was looking at her so strangely, his mouth bent in a chilling perversion of a smile.

She glanced away, veered slightly to avoid him, and continued walking. As she passed him she noticed a strip of wide grey insulating tape dangling from his right hand. Tape, she thought. Now why—

Suddenly one arm whipped round her neck and his right hand went up to her face. Tape over her mouth. A squeal died in her throat, and she tasted adhesive. With one arm locked round her neck and the other grasping a wrist, he pulled her out of the lane. She kicked and tried to jab him, but he was unstoppable.

"You was late," he muttered.

He dragged her into deep brush that hid them from the lane. Sarah tried to scream, but the tape smothered it. With a deft movement he forced her to her knees and brought her arms back, pinning her wrists together. Then he wrapped a length of rope round her wrists and drew it tight. Next he threw her to the ground and tied her ankles. He stood over her. She was trussed and supine, limp from struggle.

"You was late," he said. "You been swimming."

She shook her head no. The man was crazy.

"Yes," he said. "Swimming. With boys. You been a bad girl."

His voice was a rumbling threat. She shook her head violently.

"Yes!" he shouted, and he picked her up by the jacket, no effort at all, and tossed her backwards into the brush.

"You been a *bad* girl," he said.

A guttural noise came from her throat. She saw the man blink, look at her in wonderment, and then his anger seeped away.

"Margaret," he said. "Margaret, sweetness, you all right?"

She writhed against the rope and the tape, trying to speak, trying to tell him what a mistake he was making.

"Come on, don't fight it. There's nothing you can do."

He walked away a few steps and returned with a gym bag. He sat beside her. Exhausted from squirming, she lay quiet.

"That's it," he said. "Nice and easy. Your daddy doesn't want you hurting yourself."

She shook her head. You're not my daddy!

He showed a knowing smile. He understood. "I am. Yes, I am." His confidence was unnerving.

He dug in the gym bag and produced two belts of webbed nylon. The belts had loops at each end, adjustable with toothed clamps. He replaced the rope round her legs with one of the belts, and with the second one replaced the rope around her wrists. After that he swiftly replaced the tape at her mouth with a handkerchief gag.

All at once she felt cold. She began to shiver. It sent him to the bag again. This time he came up with an electric-blue sack that he peeled away to reveal a sleeping bag. He shook it out.

"This'll do you," he said. "I don't want you getting cold."

He laid her out in it and zipped it round her.

"Not so bad, huh? Better?"

She nodded sullenly, and the stranger grinned.

A few feet away was a large elm. He cleared snow from a spot at the base of the trunk and sat. She saw that he meant to wait. As they waited, his eyes didn't leave her. Patient and vigilant, he hunched beside her as night closed in and the falling snow dwindled to nothing.

How much time passed, she didn't know. Eventually she heard a car in the lane, rolling away from the highway and towards the Stannard house. It rounded the bend, and then it was gone.

A little later she heard her mother shouting her name from somewhere along the lane. "Sarah! Sarah!" Sarah fought the gag. Just one scream, she thought, but the gag was too tight.

Again, "Sarah! *Sa-a-r*-ah!"

Sarah felt her eyes water. The gag choked all sound in her throat, but there was nothing to stop the tears. They poured out. The stranger dried her cheeks with his coat sleeve. "Now don't you pay no 'tention to that. Don't get all upset over nothing."

330

A second car ground up the lane; then it too was gone. They heard no more cars, and no more of Elise, but the stranger was restive now, shifting his weight as he sat, his eyes scanning the trees. "Dark enough," he finally said. "Time we was gone."

SHERK GOT UP OUT OF HIS PICK-UP and looked around. He had parked beside the church hall at St. Bartholomew's, in a space that was hemmed in on three sides by the hall, a high hedge, and a stockade fence along the sidewalk. So far, all had gone as planned. The forest had been a haven for a couple of hours, and under darkness he had been able to bring the truck into the lane, carry Margaret out of the woods, and drive away. Then he had driven around for more than three hours, letting the streets empty before he came into the city.

He walked round the side of the hall and saw nobody. A single light shone behind an upstairs curtain in the rectory, but the hall was dark, and the only movement he could discern was the sluggish stirring of ground fog under a streetlamp. Sherk went down the concrete steps that led to the basement of the hall. He undid the padlock on the metal door at the bottom and left the door open a crack. Then he returned to the truck, lifted her out, and carried her down the stairs to his apartment.

HE SAT HER IN A CHAIR beside a small round kitchen table.

She knew that they were in a building near a large church. But this room didn't have the feel of a church. It was more like an animal's den. As he loomed over her, she wondered what he was going to do next. Never had she been more frightened. He reached down. She flinched. But his fingers only loosed the cord that drew the sleeping bag tight against her face.

"Don't try shouting," he said. "Won't nobody hear you."

He pulled the gag loose. Then he stood her up, unzipped the bag, peeled it off. "Go on. Sit down," he said. "You must be hungry. I know I am. I fixed us something. A surprise."

She spoke for the first time. "Please don't hurt me," she said.

"Aw, sweetness, you know I wouldn't do that. You be a good girl, you've got nothing to worry about."

"I have to use the bathroom," she said.

He removed the nylon belts from her hands and feet.

"Bathroom's there," he said, pointing to a door across the room. "But don't get any ideas. You'll just make Daddy unhappy."

She went to it on unsteady legs. Inside, she closed the door and looked around. There was a window, up at ground level. She tried it: locked and painted shut. The door had no lock. He would be there in seconds if she broke the window and tried to climb out. She was powerless. The thought was disheartening.

When she came out, he was boiling water and heating a casserole on a hotplate. He poured the water into a cup with some instant cocoa, gave it to her as she sat down. Then he spooned out the casserole onto two dishes. It was macaroni and cheese, ground beef, some slivers of onion.

"Your favourite," he said. "Go on. Eat."

"I'm not her," she said. "You think I'm your daughter, but you're wrong. My name is Sarah Stannard. I grew up in Vermont."

His hands made hard fists on the table. "I said *eat*."

He took a few bites, staring down at the table. When he looked up again, the harshness was gone. "I knew it'd be hard," he said. "Now listen. I know it'll come to you. My name is Joseph Sherk. Your name is Margaret. You're my little girl. We live together, you and me, in a cabin in a hollow near Harben, Virginia."

He corrected himself. "We *used* to live in a cabin near Harben. But something happened ..." His voice trailed off and he seemed to be searching his memory. "Anyway, we'll go back there one of these days. It won't be like this for long. Soon we'll be back the way we was."

Sarah was discouraged, but it was no use arguing. She turned to her food and ate what was on her plate.

After she had finished, Sherk brought her jeans, a shirt, and a sweater.

"Get rid of that"—he gestured towards her uniform—"and into something more like you."

She put on the clothes in the bathroom. They fitted perfectly, and Sherk grinned when he saw her. He wasn't nearly so frightening when she was doing what he wanted, what he expected.

"That's it; that's my girl," he said. "Now sit."

She did. Sherk replaced the belts at her ankles and wrists, binding her hands in front of her. "Now stay. I won't be long."

He went into the bathroom and closed the door behind him. Sarah thought of the cellar door, and beyond that the parking lot, the city streets.

If you've got the nerve, kiddo.

She tested the belt at her ankles. The loops were tight round each ankle. But he had left a few inches of slack between the loops, maybe enough for some short, shuffling steps.

She stood up and managed to wobble to the front door. Over her shoulder she could see the bathroom door, still shut. There was water running. She put both hands on the knob, turned it, pulled. The door swung open, and she went through, into the basement.

To the right was a lighted stairwell that seemed to go up to the main floor. To the left was the metal door where he had carried her in. She shuffled over to it, yanked on the handle. The door didn't budge. She felt in the darkness, around the frame. Down at the bottom was a sliding bolt. She pulled it up.

Still the door wouldn't move. Had to be another catch somewhere. She pawed frantically. There. At the top of the door, a second bolt. She released it. The door came back suddenly and knocked her down. The blessed cold air of freedom poured in.

She struggled up. The bindings tripped her when she tried to climb the stairs. She crawled, pulling herself over the cold, wet concrete, hauling herself up, fighting gravity and the sharp angles of the steps that dug into her arms and her shins.

Finally the top step. Up on her feet again. Between her and the street was a high fence. It met a hedge, nearly as tall, that ran beside a driveway. To get away she had to get round the hedge.

In her imagination she could feel Sherk behind her, closing in. The hedge grew thinner near the ground. She fell flat and began to crawl through mud and melting snow. The branches' sharp ends were like thorns, tearing at her face, her hands, and then she was free, dragging herself into the driveway. She stumbled out into the empty street.

She shouted, "Help me, somebody. He's going to get me."

IN THEIR UPSTAIRS BEDROOM at 270 Bellflower, the Corwins were watching *Nightline* when the shout reached their window.

"You hear that?" said Marie Corwin. "Somebody's screaming."

"Punks," said her husband. The neighbourhood had a problem with teenagers, especially at weekends. There would be car horns, blaring music, yelling. Of course it did no good to call the cops; they always seemed to arrive after the kids had peeled off.

Marie got up, went to the window, and pushed up a slat on the blinds. She could see nothing amiss, so she returned to bed.

SHERK WAS BRUSHING HIS TEETH when he heard the scream. At first it didn't register. Margaret was in his room, a few feet away. This came from outside.

Then he understood. The fire was suddenly huge in him. He burst out of the bathroom into the empty apartment. His stork's lope carried him into the basement and up the steps outside. He looked around. No Margaret. Then she helped him. She yelled again. Beyond the hedge, other side of the fence.

Sherk ran round into the driveway. Margaret was in the middle of the street, looking over her shoulder at him and stumbling as she did. She fell.

He hurried out to her, looking up and down the street as he approached. Nobody round. Another yell starting in her chest. He reached her and slapped a hand over her mouth.

Then all the fight seemed to leave her. She gave a helpless groan and went limp as he carried her back round the hedge. As he leaped down the basement steps with her, Sherk could see a figure backlit behind a curtain in the rectory. The curtain parted and the monsignor peered out. Sherk kept a hand clamped over her mouth. He knew that they couldn't be seen.

The curtain closed. With that, Sherk went into the cellar and dropped her to the floor. As he reached back to shut the door, she scrambled away. He lunged and caught her and dragged her back. Then he knelt over her. One hand found her mouth. The other was reaching for her neck when she raised her arms feebly to push him off. Sherk swatted them away.

He felt the fire. In his mind a picture played out for him, an image of what was going to happen next. Or maybe something that had happened already—he couldn't quite bring it into focus. One hand pressed harder on her mouth as the other encircled her throat. She kicked the air and exhaled in rapid gasps.

His fingers squeezed, and now the left hand joined the right at her throat. Margaret stopped struggling. He was choking the fight out of her. Choking the badness and the evil out of her.

He looked at her face. Her eyes bulged and rolled. He had seen that somewhere before. The dream. Terror on Margaret's face, and the faceless man's hands on her throat.

Memory and fantasy and the present all became one, and Sherk could see it clearly, a single illuminating flash.

He pulled his hands away as if scalded. He stood and swayed over where she lay with her mouth agape. A thermostat clicked across the basement, and the oil jets flamed, roared, under the boiler.

SARAH BREATHED IN. Her vision cleared, and she breathed again. I could be dead right now. She knew it had been that close.

"Get up," he said. He was standing over her. She staggered to her feet and stumbled ahead of him into his room.

"Sit down." She sat in the chair where he had left her before.

He slammed the door and turned back to her. "You think you can spit in my face, nothing happens?" His shouting made her cringe.

"You don't know what you're doing," he went on. "What you're playing with here. Things . . . things . . ." His voice was softer, tortured. "I don't know . . . things. Not quite right. Not the way they were." He stood in front of her, hands going up to his head. Then his eyes found hers again. "Get up. We're going," he said.

She got up. He checked the belts. Then he went to a cupboard and came out with a pillowcase. He shook it out and placed it over her head, and she saw only white cotton, faintly suffusing the room light.

"Where am I going?" she pleaded. Her throat was sore; the words came out raspy.

"Home," he said. "We're going home."

She heard a silken noise that sounded like the sleeping bag. He must be putting it over his shoulder. Then he picked her up and carried her out. They turned right and went up some steps, then down a long corridor on a hard floor that sounded like linoleum.

One step up and they were on carpet. A small space that he crossed in a few strides. Two steps down. A hard surface again. This space was much larger—he took longer to cross it. And there was a faint smell that eluded her, fragrant and smoky.

Another set of stairs—wooden ones that doubled back at the landing. At the top he stopped and stood her up. She heard a door swing open, followed by a sound like coat hangers scraping on a pipe. He pushed her forward and turned her to the right.

"Down on your knees," he commanded. He loosened the belts on her wrists and ankles, enabling her to move. "Now crawl."

She did as he said. She was in a passage hardly wider than her shoulders. She imagined a tunnel about two feet wide. She continued forward. As she advanced, the passage seemed to constrict. The walls were closing in on her, smothering her.

"Now stop," he said. "Off to your left is a space. Go through it."

She put out her left hand, felt a gap in the wall. She crawled through and stretched out her arms. The walls had retreated.

He came in behind her. A flaring match gave a saffron glow to the inside of the pillowcase. The glow brightened. A lamp, she thought. He lifted the cloth off her face. She could see.

They were in an attic about the size of her bedroom at her grandparents' house. The floor was unfinished wood planking. Rough-hewn beams angled upwards from two sides of the floor and peaked about five feet overhead. At no place was there room to stand straight under the sloping roof.

Now her eyes took in a folding camp bed, blankets, a collapsible canvas chair. A string hammock hung across the far end of the room, suspended from a set of beams.

"Going home," he had said. Her heart sank. He meant to keep her here.

Sherk made her stretch out on the floor, and he fastened the restraints round her arms and legs. He pulled the sleeping bag over her again. Then he dragged out a shapeless pile of canvas. There were straps and buckles sewn on. It looked like a shroud. Sherk was laying it out on the floor, open, unbuckled.

"No," she said, suddenly comprehending. "You can't."

Sherk picked her up and placed her in the middle of the canvas. "Have to," he said. "Can't take chances."

The shroud enclosed her. He pulled it tight, closed the buckles. She was encased in a cocoon. She wiggled her fingers and toes, and canted her head to one side. Nothing else would move.

"Good. One last thing, we'll be set."

He was holding what looked like a surgeon's mask, made of leather, and it had a row of small holes at the mouth.

"Deerskin," he said. "Nice and soft."

He put it on her. It pulled upwards on her jaw as he tightened the straps.

"Can you breathe?" he asked. She nodded.

"Now say goodnight."

There was just enough room to slightly part her lips. All that came out was a throaty mumble.

"Just right," he said.

He picked her up, set her in the hammock. There were two more belts yet, both passing through loops in the shroud, one tying her into the hammock at the feet, the other holding her in at the shoulders. When he had finished, she was completely immobile.

He stood over her, sombre. "You know who you are?" he said.

She nodded. Yes.

"Are you Margaret?"

Maybe it was foolish, but she couldn't lie. She shook her head. No. And waited for him to explode.

Sherk didn't change expression. His eyes looked tired.

"It'll come," he said. "In its time."

He left her side and extinguished the lamp. Night surrounded them. She heard him stretch out on the bed, pull up the blankets.

She thought of home and school, and of her mother, all so far from this dark prison. She could not imagine anyone finding her here. Wherever she was. If she was to survive, to see the light again, it might be up to her.

CHAPTER NINE

Saturday, November 10
Sarah woke in total blackness. She had the sensation of being buried in a deep, narrow cave. Her heart raced in panic. She tried to call Sherk, gulping in air, then shoving it up into her throat. It came out as a grunt.

She waited. Except for her own pulse, loud in her ears, there was no sound. She was alone. He had left her while she slept. To return—who knew when?

AFTER BOLTING THE APARTMENT DOOR, Sherk reached under his bed and retrieved the handbag that he had brought in from the truck. He took it to the table and sorted through the contents: half a roll of Life Savers, several pens and pencils, a hairbrush; these he returned to the bag. That left a red leather wallet. In it he found photographs. Margaret posing with strangers, a man and a woman about his age. Then a small portrait of this same man. There was also a library card in the name of Sarah Stannard, an ID card from Nordbrook School in the same name, and a newspaper obituary of a man named John Stannard.

He took all these to the kitchen sink, where he touched a match to them and watched them burn. Then he rinsed the ashes down the drain.

By now, Sherk thought, Margaret would be awake and hungry. He replaced the wallet, tucked her handbag into his gym bag, put in a quart of orange juice and a box of crackers, and went to rejoin his daughter.

She was whimpering softly when he returned, the beam from a torch preceding him. He lit the glass lamp, came over to her in the yellow light, and removed the mask.

"You been crying," he said.

"Hardly at all."

He unbuckled the straps next, and she filled her lungs with air and tried twisting her neck. A band of pain embraced her throat where his hands had gripped her.

"What was it, exactly, that bothered you?" He was distant, but not unfriendly.

"I woke up," she said. "And it was dark."

"I never knowed you to be afraid of the dark."

"I'm not. But this was different." The words were out before she remembered that they were talking about two different girls.

"I'm sorry you got scared." He sounded as if he meant it. "Next time I'll leave the lamp burning."

He removed the straps from her wrists and her ankles.

"Hungry?" he asked.

"Yes. But first I'd like you to take me down to the bathroom."

His eyes showed amusement. "Suppose I bring the bathroom to you instead."

She watched him go to a corner and wrestle a large cardboard crate into the middle of the floor. He tore it open and lifted out what looked like a green toilet bowl without the tank.

"Camper's loo," he said.

He took a blanket and began draping it across the attic, hanging it from nails that protruded from a couple of the beams. This would give her some privacy.

"You're not letting me out?" she said.

"Sweetheart, I wish I could." Sherk's tone was wistful. "But it ain't such a good idea. Not now."

"When?" she said.

"When I can trust you." It was the voice of an unrelenting father. "When you're back the way you should be."

"But how long?"

"Long as it takes, Margaret."

He finished hanging the blanket, then crawled into the passage to wait.

SHERK'S FIRST VICTORY came when she ate all her crackers. For breakfast? Margaret had asked him. But she had eaten eagerly, proof that the daughter he knew was not far out of reach. Many times he had seen her make a meal of water biscuits and orange juice.

Now she was brushing her hair—long, slow strokes that pulled the yellow strands halfway down her back.

"You used to go out on the front porch to do that," he said.

She looked at him without understanding.

"Don't you remember? You'd wash it in the sink. Then if it was a sunny day, you'd go out on the porch and brush it dry."

She shook her head slowly. "There's nothing to remember. Don't get angry. But I'm not her."

He put out a hand to caress her cheek, thinking, Poor girl, she needs kindness. She flinched at his touch. That riled him.

"OK, let's get up," he said brusquely. "I been gone long enough, and it's time you got back in the bag."

Her expression was morose as he buckled the cocoon. To Sherk it looked as if she was trying mightily to hold back tears.

"What's your name?" he said.

She looked away. "My name is Sarah."

"You ain't even *tryin'*," he said.

HE WAS GONE. Sarah was grateful that she would not have to see him for a while. Claustrophobia didn't kill, but Sherk might. She had nearly set him off again by drawing away from his touch.

He could almost be nice, she thought, as long as he wasn't challenged. As long as she didn't contradict him. She couldn't afford petulance or even pride. Had to keep him happy.

Kid, we're talking survival here.

Sunday, November 11

The tower bell at St. Bartholomew's pealed with a deep, sonorous clanging that shook the attic. It struck nine times, and then there was silence.

To Sarah, the sound was like divine thunder. Obviously the attic was somewhere very close to the bell. She had glimpsed a church when Sherk brought her here in the truck; this place couldn't possibly belong to the stone edifice that she had seen. But it was close, she thought. She hoped she would hear it again. Anything to break the boredom. Anything to remind her that there was a reality beyond the roof's slanting rafters.

Sherk had left. Again he had slept in the camp bed, before rousing himself in what Sarah assumed was early morning. Through half-open lids she watched as he crawled out, while she wondered where he was going and—more important—where he was leaving from. The attic existed somewhere.

Now she heard a muddy humming. Voices and footsteps wafted up to the attic. Suddenly she recalled the smoky fragrance she had smelled while Sherk was bringing her here. It was incense.

She was telling herself this when an organ bellowed through the back wall of the attic. It was playing a hymn. Voices lifted and chased the melody line, and she was surrounded by song.

Amid the din Sarah realized that Sherk had carried her through the church, but he had never taken her out. He had found a place in God's house as far from light and life as she could imagine.

Every now and then the organ played another hymn. Then she heard the low babble and the footsteps, and then again the bell, but no more choir, no more organ.

The bell rang twice more, four times in all, at intervals, she guessed, of about an hour. All the while, Sherk was absent. Then the light in the glass lamp trembled and died. Out of fuel.

This time the darkness wasn't so bad. There were fewer unknowns to weigh on her. She was hidden away, maybe, but not buried. And she knew that Sherk would not desert her. Crazy as he was, he loved his daughter.

At that moment she realized that Sherk's delusion could keep her alive. But she had to nurture it. He had nearly killed her on Friday night, when she had reacted liked a frightened stranger. Daughters don't flee from their fathers. And fathers don't kill their daughters. It was something to think about.

SHERK'S GYM BAG had become her lifeline. This time it held salami sandwiches and canned lemonade. They ate sitting cross-legged on the floor, with paper towels spread in front of them. "I want to know where we are," she told him.

His grin was at once coy and sinister. "All the racket on a Sunday morning, ain't you figured it out?"

"In a church."

"More or less," he said. Still grinning.

"You get here through the back of the church, is that right?"

"Questions, questions," he said, in the light way that fathers will use with insistent children. "You'll find out soon enough."

She knew better than to press him. She finished her meal without another word. Sherk watched her constantly, and for the first time she tried not to shrink from his gaze. Instead she smiled what she hoped he would interpret as a shy, daughterlike smile. He caught it, and she thought she saw his face soften.

When they had both eaten, she thanked him for the meal and gathered up the empty cans and paper towels. She could see that this pleased him. A good daughter would do housekeeping.

"How you doing?" he said. "You do all right, alone up here?"

"I get bored," she said.

"Well, bored is better than scared, huh? Anything else?"

"I get lonely."

"Do you? Is that right?" He was prodding, testing. "You get lonely for your daddy?"

She nodded once. Sherk suddenly reached out and grabbed one of her wrists. His face was taut, intense.

"What's your name?" he said.

What could it hurt? she thought. But not all at once. "I don't know ... I have trouble remembering."

He let go of her wrist. The tightness dissolved around his jaw, and his face split into a wide smile.

"That's a start," he said.

He put her back in the cocoon anyway; but he left happy, and Sarah felt more secure than at any time since the moment she had encountered him in the snowy lane.

Monday, November 12

Monsignor Herrity, hidden in shadow, watched Sherk walk through the dimness of the church: a silent, fleeting figure.

The monsignor had been praying in a tiny chapel to the left of the altar, opposite the sacristy. This evening was the anniversary of his parents' marriage, and he had come there to remember them.

The chapel was dark; prayer required no lights. Through a half-open door to his right, the main altar sat under a couple of weak spotlights.

As the monsignor knelt in the darkness of the chapel, Sherk had come out of the sacristy and passed beneath one of these lights. The movement had made the monsignor turn his head, and that's when he had seen Sherk.

At another time the monsignor would have called out; he had been meaning to tell Sherk about the blocked drain in the church hall. But he watched Sherk pass through the gate in the altar rail and glide soundlessly down the main aisle in and out of the shadows, to the rear of the church.

Inexplicably disturbed, the monsignor rose and went to the back door of the small side chapel; there he could see Sherk making his way up the stairs to the choir loft.

The monsignor knelt again to resume praying. Instead, he found himself wondering what Sherk could want in the loft at this hour.

He crossed himself and got up. Leaving the chapel by the rear door, he walked up the aisle towards the stairs to the choir loft. He reached them, hesitated uncertainly, then began to climb. Halfway up was a landing, where the steps reversed direction. His footfalls sounded loud, and he was sure that Sherk would hear him coming. He reached the top step, came through the short passage and out into the loft.

It was empty. Softly he spoke Sherk's name. No reply.

Two minutes ago, he thought, he had seen Sherk come up here. Then he had turned his back to pray. There was only one way up into the loft and one way down. Sherk would have had to come back down the stairs almost immediately. Or he would be here.

The monsignor walked across the loft and looked around. He came to the cupboard door in the far corner and pulled it open. It was dark. He felt along the wall until he found the light switch.

Choir robes, a few boxes. That was all.

He closed the door and crossed to the passageway at the top of the stairs. There he paused and looked around again. It was as quiet as he had ever known it. As quiet and as empty.

EVEN THROUGH THE MASK Sarah caught the aroma: hamburgers and french fries. "I needed to get away from home cookin'," Sherk said, removing the mask. "I thought maybe you did, too."

With his help she shed the cocoon, and they sat as before, with the gym bag between them. It was his third trip to the attic today, and each time he had seemed satisfied. Seemed calm.

"You can serve," Sherk said. He pushed the bag towards her.

She opened it. On top was a checked tablecloth. She spread it on the floor. Then she pulled out the treasure trove of junk food.

"I don't believe this," she said in wonderment.

As Sherk watched, she arranged the feast on the tablecloth. He seemed pleased with himself, pleased with her, and Sarah told herself that if she could only keep him that happy, she would survive until the time came for escape or rescue. In the gym bag was one last package, oblong and wrapped in brown paper, a little smaller than a shoe box.

"Go on and open it," he said.

Hesitantly she pulled off the wrapping. Inside was a tiny radio, smaller than a pack of cigarettes, with earphones.

"For me?" she said.

"I don't see anybody else in this room that needs a radio." He was hugely pleased with himself. "Something to make the time pass. You said you was getting bored. I put the battery in already."

She was speechless.

"It's really nice." She felt a rush of gratitude that was all out of proportion to the gift itself. "Thank you, Mr. Sherk," she said. "Thank you so much."

The smile left his face. "You don't have to call me Mister."

She thought for a moment.

"Thank you, Joseph," she said. But that didn't seem to help. He was impassive, but she saw a touch of sadness in his look.

"Better eat," he said. "Food's getting cold."

BEFORE HE LEFT, Sherk adjusted the earphones to her head— the mask didn't interfere. He had put the tiny radio receiver in her hands before fastening her in the cocoon. She could adjust the volume and change the tuning by moving thumbs and fingers.

She worked across the dial before settling on an FM station in Baltimore. There was a sequence of songs, followed by the news.

She listened to a story about the Ayatollah Khomeini, one about a prison riot in Virginia. Then she heard her own name. The announcer was talking about Sarah Stannard, a teenage girl apparently abducted on Friday afternoon near her home in Anne Arundel County.

"As of this hour," the announcer was saying, "the young woman remains missing."

But I'm not, Sarah thought. I'm here. It was a moment as unreal as anything she had experienced in the past three days.

Wednesday, November 14

Sarah Stannard's photo—the same one that had perplexed him for days now—greeted Patrolman Terry Dean when he opened his evening paper. He thought he had finally succeeded in putting it out of his mind, having convinced himself that he was either mistaken or that the answer to the puzzle was beyond him, but now she was looking out at him again. Those deep-set, searching eyes. The photo accompanied a story. Dean tried to read the piece, but the photo kept distracting him. He knew that it would be that way all day, nagging at him, prodding his mind.

ELISE WAS ALONE in her bedroom, buried in sheets and blankets, when she heard her name spoken on the other side of the door. It was Joy. Elise didn't bother to answer, and after a few moments Joy opened the door and tentatively entered the darkened room.

"Elise, honey." Joy moved closer to the bed. "Are you OK?"

Elise gave her a hard look. Sarah had been gone for five days. County Detective Tarver had assured them that all possible was being done to find her. But this far no progress had been made.

"That was a dumb question, I guess," Joy said. "Look, this has hit us all hard. But Harry and I, we're as worried about you as we are about Sarah. We can't stand to lose either of you."

"Save your concern for Sarah."

"We can't do anything about Sarah. But you, that's different. We won't let you shrivel up on us."

Elise turned away. She put an arm across her face.

"I'll be all right," she said. "Please. Just go."

"WHAT'S YOUR NAME?"

Up in the attic. A languid yellow splash from the kerosene lamp playing across the beams and the wooden sheathing of the roof. The canvas cocoon was tight round her.

A little coyly she answered, "I'm not sure."

All day Sherk had been in a light mood. He leaned over her with a grin in his eyes.

"What kind of girl don't know her own name?"

"A forgetful one, I guess."

"Maybe I can help," he said, the voice still playful. "Is your name ... Amy?"

"I don't think so."

"Is your name ... Ernestine?" He mugged outlandishly as he said it.

"No!" She giggled. This exchange had a familiar feel, and in a second she realized what it was. This was a father-and-daughter game. Daddy and little girl. She knew how to play that.

"You got to have a name. Every little girl does. Let's see. Maybe your name is Sarah." He looked sidelong at her, watching her reaction.

"No," she said after a moment. "That doesn't sound familiar."

"Well, now." He looked thoughtful. "How about Margaret?"

"I've heard that name before," she said.

"So have I. Could that be you?"

"It might be," she said. "Yes, that could be it."

His embrace was real and fervent. She didn't try to avoid him; there was safety in his arms around her. If playing by his rules would keep him happy, keep her alive, then she would do it. From now on she would be Margaret, only Margaret.

He extinguished the lamp, and night surrounded them. She heard him stretch out on the cot, pull the blankets over him.

His voice began, low and satisfied.

"Your room was painted pink till you was six years old," he was saying. "Then I painted it white, 'cause you told me you didn't care for pink. Your best friend was a girl named Susie that lived about a mile down the road, and her mother took her away. You was about eight then. Your favourite

344

shoes was some red tennis sneakers that said P.F. Flyers on the heel, and I always told you the P.F. stood for Purty Fancy."

The sentences were strung out aimlessly, but Sarah understood. He was talking about home and about the girl named Margaret, about things that she was supposed to have known. He realized that Margaret had forgotten, so he was trying to help. She closed her eyes and listened.

"You had a tabby cat named Banana that run away when you was nine. Broke your heart. In fourth grade you fell off a climbing frame and busted your right arm in three places. You wore a cast for two months."

He went on for a while, about coal trucks that shook the house when they rumbled by, about skinned knees and dolls and a maiden aunt named Beatrice. Sarah thought about the girl named Margaret, wondered where she could be, what could have happened to her.

Whoever she is, he must really love her.

It was the last thought in her mind before she fell asleep.

CHAPTER TEN

Thursday, November 15
Howard Warner was in the car, stopped on Ritchie Highway. He waited for a break in the oncoming traffic; then he turned left into Whittier Lane and followed it through the grove.

Part of him didn't want to be here. He'd done his duty in this case. Yet the people who lived here—and the girl who once had—would not leave his mind. He couldn't say exactly what had brought him back. A sense of unfinished business was part of it. And Elise. Even in her grief he wanted to see her again.

He pulled into the driveway. The car had hardly stopped before Harry was standing at the front door, waiting to meet him.

"I was in the neighbourhood," Warner said as he got out. "Thought I'd look in, see how you're all doing."

"We've been better," Harry said. "It's a rough time."

Joy appeared as they walked into the hall. She looked weary. "I hope you can stay a few minutes," she told Warner. "I know Elise will want to talk to you. Why don't I take you in?"

Harry took his coat and Joy led Warner into the living room of the new wing. There she stopped him with a hand on his elbow.

"This has been hard on Elise," she said. "You'll see."

They found Elise in Sarah's room. A mess. The bed was heaped with clothes. Drawers had been opened, contents strewn about the floor. Elise was on hands and knees, picking through a pile of socks. She looked desperate. But when she glanced up, Warner saw her expression soften.

"Elise, you remember the detective from Annapolis," Joy said.

"Howard," she murmured. "I didn't know you were coming."

She was wearing jeans and a red V-neck sweater over a blouse. As she stood up, her right hand went up to her face and swept away some invisible wisps of hair. An endearing gesture, Warner thought.

"Should've called, I guess. But I was nearby," he said, "and I thought maybe you'd want some company."

"I'd like that. I really would."

Joy left, and Warner felt suddenly stranded. He looked round at the disarray. "Everything all right here?" he asked.

"I remember what one of the officers said the other night. Any little thing might help. I thought maybe I'd find something."

"Yeah, well. Could be. You come across anything?"

She shook her head.

"Look," he said. "Why don't we just put this stuff away? I'll help you. We'll get it done in no time."

They worked without a word for a while. Elise replaced clothes on hangers, and Warner carried them over to the closet. Then he sat with her on the floor, filling the drawers that she had dumped.

They had nearly finished when Elise left the room. She returned carrying a shoe box. Warner sat beside her on the edge of the bed and watched as she opened the box and began to pick through what appeared to be an incomprehensible pile of rubbish. She plucked out a printed card marked with ink strokes.

"Her first report card," Elise said. "See? 'Satisfactory' in every subject. She was always a good student. She's a hard worker, and very intelligent."

She replaced the card and took out a piece of lavender paper.

"A note she wrote us on her thirteenth birthday." Elise smiled and showed it to Warner. "Dear Mom and Dad," Sarah had written. "I can't think of a better day to tell you how much I love you, and how lucky I am to have you as my parents."

More exhibits. The tiara Sarah had worn at a school pageant. A blue ribbon for drawing, from the Lamoille County Fair. A hospital ID bracelet from the time she had her tonsils removed.

"She was so scared," Elise said. "She was just seven, and she knew that her grandfather, my dad, had gone into the hospital and never come out. She kept saying, 'I don't want to die, Mommy. If I die, I'll never see you and Daddy again.'"

Her mouth was tight and strained. She turned to Warner.

"Every morning," she said, "I wake up, and for a second I don't remember what's happened. It's like everything is the way it was—she's here, in this room next to mine, and if I walk a few steps I can look in on her. Then it comes back to me."

346

She slumped over, head bowed. Warner saw that she was crying, her shoulders shaking.

"Don't," he said. "Please don't."

He got up and crouched in front of her. From here the natural thing was to put his arms round her. He patted her on the back; it had no effect. He pulled her closer, and then they were holding each other, her arms tight around him, her face pressed against his collar and dampening the bare skin of his neck.

THE GOLD CHARM WAS GONE. Sarah hadn't noticed until now.

She was out of the cocoon. Sherk had come to visit, as he often did around midafternoon. He was a few feet away, whittling a piece of wood that was about a foot long and several inches round. As always, the hammock had knotted her muscles, so she was trying to stretch out the stiffness.

She was doing sit-ups when she realized that the bracelet wasn't ringing. Usually the single charm that she wore on it chimed when she moved.

She sat up and examined the bracelet. Gone. Her father's gift. Gone like everything else in that faraway existence.

Sherk had stopped whittling. "What's the matter?" he said.

"Nothing. I'm OK."

He saw that she was looking at the bracelet. He put down the piece of wood and came over to her. He held her wrist.

"I don't think that's yours anyway," he said. "Is it?"

She sensed a challenge in his words.

"No," she said. "I don't know how it got there."

He took off the bracelet and put it in his pocket.

"Now don't be upset," he said. "No reason for it." He reached across the floor for the wood that he had been working. "Here, look. Almost finished."

She took it from him. It was a figure of a girl, primitive but not crude. She wore a dress and an apron; there was a plait etched down her back.

"Remember?" he said. "Your first doll. I made you one like this when you was just a little thing. I know you don't play with dolls any more. But I thought it might be a reminder. You recall it?"

She fingered the smooth wood. "Sure, I remember."

"You named it Daisy, for the flower I put on her apron."

"Daisy. I remember," she said.

"I knew you would. Now let me see a big smile. That's it."

"IT WOULD BE GOOD to see you again," Elise said. "If you could drop by for a few minutes tomorrow ..."

They were in the hall, Warner with his coat over one arm.

"Oh sure," Warner said. "I was a big help. Fifteen minutes and I've got you blubbering."

"Next time I won't."

"Friday is a bad day. Even if I don't leave the desk, I've got a ton of paperwork."

"Do you work Saturdays?"

"As a rule I get weekends off," he said. "I guess I could drop by on Saturday, not too early."

She squeezed his hand.

Friday, November 16

Once Sherk and Margaret had seen a mama bear and her cub playing in the summer-high grass of a meadow near the cabin.

"We were downwind of her," Sherk said, "so she didn't smell us. It must have been a couple minutes we got to watch her."

"Is that the meadow where we went for picnics?" Sarah said.

"No, no. That's down the road. The one where we saw the bear was on the other side of Drolsom's Ridge."

Sherk liked to go on this way. As he spoke, Sarah could see the cabin, the rooms, the furniture. She could see the hills, too, high and steep, keeping the hollow in shadow for most of the day. At first vague, the pictures were now sharp in her mind. She saw the happy life of a father and daughter alone in the hills.

It was past midnight when Sherk finished talking. He wrapped her up, put her in the hammock, and blew out the lamp. Sarah's mind was still in the hills, and she tried to put herself to sleep with a soothing image.

The first that came to her was Sherk and Margaret in their cabin, a small cabin out of the world's way, shelter for a loving father and a loving daughter. Only she put herself in Margaret's bed, and the father was both Sherk and her own father. It was nonsense the mind might accept in those minutes when consciousness and logic give way to sleep. Sarah nestled herself in the image, let it envelop her and put her to sleep.

Saturday, November 17

Fifteen minutes after he arrived Warner knew he had to get out of the house; the taint of tragedy was everywhere.

Elise put on a coat and they walked together down to the river. The day was overcast, with scudding clouds and a clawing wind. They made their way to the edge of the river's high bank, then down to the end of a pier that stood about six feet above the water. Warner looked around. Below him the Severn was green and choppy. Elise stood to his left, and he could feel a slight pressure at his elbow, where the wind bent her towards him.

"This morning they took out the tape recorders," she said. "The ones on the telephones. They said if we were going to get a ransom call, it would have come by now."

In the corners of her eyes Warner saw a wetness that might have been from the bite of the wind. "That's not good, is it?" she asked.

"Don't feel let down. The chances were against it anyway."

"I thought it might mean they were losing hope." She struggled to get the words out. "That they had decided, you know, something must have happened to her."

He looked towards the far shore. "I'd say it's way too early to talk like that. It's only been a week."

A gust of wind rocked them. Her hands went to his arm for support. It was a few seconds before she spoke again, her voice choked. "I need her, Howard. She's all I've got. This waiting is killing me."

He turned to face her. "Don't take this wrong," he said. "But there are psychiatrists. I'm told they know how to listen."

"I'm not ruling them out. But it seems premature for that."

He nodded and was silent. Then he asked, "You go to church?"

"Not for a long while. We had Sarah baptized Catholic, but Jack didn't really go in for it. And I got out of the habit."

"Some people find it helps."

"You?"

He shrugged. "I go sometimes. I was brought up Catholic. Eight years with the sisters in grade school. Then the Jesuits for four years after that. Some of it is bound to stick."

She smiled. "Church," she mused. "I've heard worse ideas. Where could I go? I don't know this town."

"I know of one," he said. "I could show you if you want."

HE CAME TO TAKE HER to Mass the next morning, dressed in an ink-blue suit. It was eleven minutes before nine when they turned onto the highway, and Elise was sure they would be late. But Warner knew the streets. He got them over the river, across town, and into the church car park without meeting a traffic light.

He gave her his arm as they walked towards the church. The bell in the tower was clanging when they walked up the front steps, and she barely had time to notice the brass plaque beside the door: St Bartholomew's Roman Catholic Church.

WHEN SARAH HEARD THE BELL, she thought of Sherk. He had said when he left this morning that he would be back with breakfast. But she guessed he wouldn't be coming for a while. The bells meant Mass, meant people.

She thought of how far she had come. She was no longer fearful, only lonesome. The attic had first seemed cramped and stifling; now it was still monotonous, but she also found it cosy and almost homelike. And though she still feared Sherk's quicksilver moods, she believed she understood him. Pitied him, too, because of the sadness that seemed to permeate him. She was unable to hate him, in spite of what he had done to her, and clearly he cared about her. He was happy when she fulfilled his expectations. His pleasure, in turn, made her giddy with relief.

The bell's tolling ended. She clicked on the little hand-held radio and awaited his return.

"I WILL GO TO THE ALTAR of God," the priest was saying.

Elise listened attentively. For nine days she had been desolate. But here, as Howard had predicted, she seemed to find relief.

It wasn't as if she expected a miracle: Sarah walking into the kitchen as though she had never been missing. Elise prayed simply for her daughter's wellbeing; to ask anything more seemed presumptuous. Mostly she just felt that in this magnificent church she was in the presence of a force much greater than herself. Somehow it diminished her pain. She would come again tomorrow and the day after. It was just what she needed.

Monday, November 19

It was a few minutes before eleven at night. Patrolman Terry Dean was parked at an intersection when the silver Peugeot blew past the stop sign. The cruiser was already running. Dean put it in gear, whipped round a left, and had the sedan pulling over within a block and a half. He parked behind it, got out, and walked towards the driver's side. The window came down about halfway as he approached.

"This is awful," the driver said. It was a young woman's voice. Dean flicked on his torch and shone it down into the car, where he could see hands. Always want to know what the hands are doing.

"Your licence, please," Dean said. "And the registration." The driver got her handbag and fumbled through it.

"I went through the stop sign, didn't I?" she said, talking into the bag. "I never saw it, but they told me I did." In the dim interior Dean could make out one passenger in the front and two others in the back. All young women.

"Here," the driver said. She handed over the papers without looking at him. "This is awful. I just got my licence last week. My dad's going to kill me." Dean took the licence and registration back to the patrol car, where he kept his summons pad. He turned on the overhead light and took out a pen and the pad. Then he looked for the first time at the licence and at the colour ID photo that was laminated into it.

Seconds later he was hurrying back to the Peugeot. He was holding a clipboard and the licence as he jogged up to the door.

"Please get out of the car," he said to the driver. She obeyed. "Now, walk with me into the light."

She followed him to a streetlamp near the corner. "Hey. I know you," she said.

He was studying her features in the light, then looking down at the clipboard. "Tell me your name," he said.

"It's right there. Emily Caldwell. You came to my house, remember?"

"You go to a private school," he said.

"Nordbrook."

"That's it. Nordbrook." He looked at the photograph one more time. The hand that held the clipboard dropped to his side.

"Good God almighty," he said.

ONE OF THE YOUNGER PRIESTS was sick with a virus, so Monsignor Herrity took Tuesday-night confessions. It was a quiet hour, and while he waited in the box he read his office by the soft light of an overhead bulb. After reading uninterrupted for nearly half an hour, he checked his watch: eight twenty. The church must have been empty for some time.

He had just turned off the light when he heard footsteps. They grew louder, passed the box without pausing, headed towards the back of the church. The monsignor drew the curtain of the box and saw Sherk turn up the stairs that led to the loft. Then he heard steps on the wooden floor above. From the sound of it, Sherk was crossing the loft from one side to the other. There was a noise like a door closing. Then silence.

Determined this time to find out what Sherk was up to, the monsignor left the confessional, crossed to the stairwell and climbed the stairs. But when he came out into the loft, it was empty. There was a low dim light from the ceiling fixtures. He looked around, then went to the cupboard door and opened it.

No one. Inside were the same boxes and choir robes. The monsignor looked in the corners, moved the robes around. The idea that Sherk would hide among the choir robes was ridiculous. But not nearly as ridiculous, the monsignor thought, as the idea that he would come up here and disappear.

Sherk had come up, he told himself. Had come up, hadn't come down. But he wasn't here any more. For some time the monsignor considered this, before he left the cupboard and made for the stairs.

Tuesday, November 20

Claire Johansen was fifty years old, weighed nearly two hundred pounds, and maintained at all times an air of command. The Annapolis Police Department didn't keep a psychologist on staff—there wasn't enough demand; but it sent plenty of business her way.

Now she faced three nervous men across her desk. There was Carl Caldwell, father of Emily. Flanking him were Howard Warner and the county detective named Tarver, who were anxious because they believed that Emily Caldwell might have seen Sarah Stannard's abductor. The two girls were almost identical in appearance, Tarver had explained. In September Emily had been accosted by a man claiming to be her father. Nine weeks later Sarah had disappeared.

"You're sure this won't harm her?" Carl Caldwell said.

"I promise," Claire said. "Look. Hypnosis isn't dangerous. There are entertainers in Las Vegas who do this without ill effect. I've never played the halls, but my training is better."

She stood up, her bearing almost regal. "Now, if you'll let me get on with it, I have business in the other room."

Transcript: INTERROGATION UNDER HYPNOSIS
Conducted by Claire F. Johansen, Ph.D.

Subject: Emily Caldwell
Time: 7.38 pm, November 20, 1984

CFJ: How are you feeling? Comfortable?
EC: I'm fine.
CFJ: I want you to think about a day last September. You won a part in a play.
EC: I remember. Millie. In *Picnic*.
CFJ: Right. Now you're walking home. Tell me what happens.
EC: I'm walking down Main. Looking in the shop windows. I go into a store down by the dock to check out some blouses. Then I leave, cross the street, and set out for home.
CFJ: You're on what street now?
EC: I'm heading up King George.
CFJ: And then what happens?
EC: (With some distress.) He's coming after me!
CFJ: Who is?
EC: Him. The guy who thinks I'm somebody else.
CFJ: Tell me about him.
EC: He's a block away. He's yelling for some girl named Margaret. I get scared, and I keep walking. I can hear him. He's coming after. I don't like this. Can I stop?
CFJ: You're all right. He can't hurt you. Tell me what you see.
EC: I'm hurrying. Not far from home. He says, "Margaret, turn around, Margaret, it's your daddy." But I know it's me he wants. I can hear him breathing, he's so close. I try to get across the street. There's a car ... oh! Almost hit me.

352

CFJ: The car?

EC: Yes. Then he puts his hand on me. He's real strong.

CFJ: You see his clothes?

EC: Farmer's overalls. Work shoes. And a red flannel shirt rolled up to his elbows. He looks like a hillbilly. Talks like one, too.

CFJ: You see his face? Tell me what you see.

EC: Those eyes. Like he's real mad at me or something. Except he's not mad. He just doesn't understand. He's got a long face. Bushy eyebrows. Tall, skinny guy. Maybe six three. He needs a shave.

CFJ: How old, would you say?

EC: About forty.

CFJ: What happens next?

EC: I get away. He sort of lets go, he's so surprised. I start walking fast. Got to get home.

CFJ: But something happens before you get there.

EC: Uh-huh. I'm walking down the alley. There's a pick-up truck coming towards me. I can see him driving it.

CFJ: Tell me about the truck.

EC: It's a Ford. It says so on the bonnet. Blue. (Pause.) And it's been in a wreck. The right wing is slightly bent.

CFJ: This is important. Can you see the licence plate?

EC: Yeah. It's from Virginia. Z ... F ... B. Eight. Oh. One.

CFJ: You're doing great. What happens next?

EC: The truck rushes past. I start to run. He stops the truck and grabs me.

CFJ: So you see him up close again. Anything else you notice about him?

EC: He's got a knife. Like a big jackknife. It's in a black holder, but I can tell a knife's in there.

CFJ: Anything more?

EC: Just that I feel sorry for him. He really loves her.

CFJ: The other girl?

EC: Uh-huh. Margaret. I'm not her, but he doesn't believe me. I can tell he doesn't understand. (Pause.) And there's something else. I can see it in his eyes. In the way he acts. No doubt about it. The guy is totally crazy.

WARNER PHONED IN the licence-plate number from the psychologist's office, and ten minutes later got a call back. Virginia Motor Vehicles Division reported that ZFB801 belonged to a blue 1978 Ford pick-up, registered to Joseph Toller Sherk (6'3", 185, black hair, brown eyes, date of birth 7/27/41), last known address Colgan Road, Harben, Lee County, Virginia. No outstanding warrants.

Within thirty minutes a description of Sherk and the truck was broadcast to patrols throughout the county, with instructions to hold the suspect for questioning.

CHAPTER ELEVEN

Wednesday, November 21

Sherk thought of everything. At dinner Sarah had mentioned that she needed a bath. He had left, returning a few minutes later with a dishpan and a two-gallon insulated jug of hot water, a towel and a face flannel, and a bar of soap.

The attic was cold, and she scrubbed hastily. Sherk waited outside the entrance, as he always did when she had to be alone. She dried herself, then pulled on her jeans and a sweater.

"All done," she said, and in a couple of seconds Sherk emerged through the low opening.

"Better?"

"Much better," she said, and Sherk smiled.

Story time now. In the last few days the routine had been unvarying. They arranged two cushions on the floor, sat facing one another, and Sherk put the lantern between them. When they huddled close to it, the flame provided some warmth.

"I was thinking about the time you went to the hospital in Abingdon to have your tonsils out," Sherk said. "You was ten years old. You remember?"

"I was scared," she said.

"That's right. Scared they wouldn't let you come home. It must have been the first night you ever slept away from your own bed. I remember how quiet you was when we put your things in a bag and drove off."

"Did we have the hot-rod Chevy then?"

"Right. The souped-up Impala. You was in the front seat, like always, looking out the window, and your eyes was big as the rising moon."

THE MONSIGNOR WALKED OUT of the rectory and across the parking lot. He headed for the back entrance of the church. He used a key to let himself in. The door opened into the sacristy; he went through, came out beside the altar and continued up the aisle of the empty church. By the doorway to the lobby he stopped. He stood there, listening.

He heard a voice. An indistinct monotone, so faint it could have been a muttering of the subconscious. He stepped into the lobby. There it was louder, but only a little. He could make out none of the words. From the sound alone he would have said that it came from outside. But he believed otherwise.

Back in the church, he went to the stairway that led to the choir loft and pressed the light switch. Nothing happened. Bulb must be out, he thought. He had no trouble until the stairs doubled back. Beyond that he had to feel his way up, across the landing, then through the doors that opened onto the loft. There he could see by the light from the ceiling fixtures. He walked slowly along the back of the loft, following the wall until it ended.

He opened the cupboard door and flipped on the light. All was as before. Hymnals and boxes, and robes hanging from a pole across the width of the space. He looked at the ceiling. It was unbroken, seamless. Same for the plaster wall above the wainscot. He shoved the robes aside and went to the back of the closet. He went down on one knee, and began to tap his knuckles against the wainscot. He worked his way to the front, his knuckles thudding on the vertical strips of dark wood.

SHERK WAS TELLING about the trip back from Abingdon when he heard the tapping. He shut up and listened. The sound seemed to emanate from the far end of the passage that lay on the other side of the narrow entryway. Sarah watched Sherk's face become stony.

Without a word he got the mask and buckled it over Sarah's face. He put the straps on her wrists and ankles, and he hissed, "Stay!" At the entryway his hand went to his side and came up with the folding knife. There was a snick as the blade locked into place. Then he crawled into the passage and out of sight.

WHEN HE HAD SOUNDED his way all along the wainscot, the monsignor stood up and turned off the light. He closed the door behind him and left the loft. No longer than a heartbeat afterwards, the door opened and Sherk stepped out with the knife held low. He looked around, saw nobody. He walked silently to the front of the loft, in time to see a figure he recognized going up the main aisle towards the altar. Sherk watched with scorching eyes until the monsignor disappeared into the sacristy. Only then did he fold the blade into its handle and sheathe the knife.

He went into the closet and closed the door. About halfway along the inside wall he went onto one knee and pushed with visible effort against the wood stripping. There was a mechanical click, and a section of the wainscot swung inwards.

The raccoon's scratching had brought him here, and he had found a hollow spot in the closet wall. When he tore out some of the wainscot, he had discovered the crawl space that led behind the organ into the attic over the lobby. That same day he had fitted a door over the opening, with hinges and a snap lock. The wood strips, applied to the door, camouflaged it completely. The wainscot appeared to be unbroken.

Now he crawled through the opening and pulled the door shut behind him. He could see the lamp's glow through the entryway. Not once in the last two weeks had that rectangle of light failed to lift his heart. Because there, hidden from the world, waited Margaret.

Thanksgiving afternoon. The monsignor was rummaging through a crate in the basement of the rectory. It must be here somewhere, he thought. Finally he found what he was looking for: a large album, bound in cracked red leather.

He opened it carefully. Inside was a full set of building plans for the church—architects' and engineers' drawings more than a century old. He looked for the detailed chart of the lobby, found it, studied it; then the choir loft and what lay behind it. The diagrams showed everything. He looked at them for nearly twenty minutes before he replaced the album in the crate.

IN THE BIG HOUSE above the Severn, they didn't have Thanksgiving dinner. The main meal was soup and sandwiches, which Harry would not touch until Joy badgered him.

Elise didn't like to see the way his face had lost its ruddy tone, its animation. She ate quickly and then went outside for a walk, following the lane to the road and back. For the first time she felt that she was ready for the worst, if it came. The strength would be there. She was ready, but she still believed. She believed.

THANKSGIVING WAS A QUIET DAY in the detectives' squad room. Warner had volunteered for the shift so that one of the younger detectives could have the day with his family. He looked down at his desk. On it was a copy of the photo on Joseph Sherk's driver's licence, which had been wired from the Virginia MVD.

Warner studied the picture. Emily Caldwell had described the man's bushy brows, his rough-edged look; both were there. She had talked about crazy eyes, too. Those were there as well.

"HAS ANYONE SEEN JOSEPH?" the monsignor said. There were five at the rectory dinner table, including the housekeeper and the other three priests of the parish. The wreckage of Thanksgiving dinner lay before them. One plate was clean: Sherk's.

"I invited him to dinner a couple of days ago," said the youngest priest, Jim Davis. "But I couldn't get him to answer. And I haven't talked to him since."

The monsignor patted his stomach and stood. "The man doesn't know what he has missed. Yvonne, you've outdone yourself."

She was blushing with pleasure as the priest left the room. He went upstairs and looked out across the parking lot. Sherk's truck was in its usual place beside the hall. The monsignor had hoped it would be gone. He had a task in mind, and if Sherk was around he could only complicate it.

But not stop it, the monsignor thought. Something was happening behind the loft. It might be trivial or it might not, but whatever it was, tonight he was going to discover it.

"I'd be glad to take confessions tonight," Father Keegan said. "Business will be slow." Martin Keegan, a good priest with eleven years at St. Bart's, was second only to the monsignor in service to the parish.

"Thanks, but I'll have my Thursday-night regulars," the monsignor told him. "I look forward to it. Anyway, I have a small chore to take care of when I'm finished."

They were standing in the hall of the rectory as the monsignor put on his windcheater. He was about to leave, but a thought that he had been mulling over for several days returned to his mind, and he wanted to share it.

"Did it ever occur to you," he said to Keegan, "what an unusual building a church is? It's a house. But unlike most houses, it has no tenants except the Lord. Nobody knows it totally, brick by brick. Priests come and leave, and none of us really knows it. Even simple things like the wiring, for example. If we had to draw a wiring diagram to save the building, it would be lost."

"That's why we have a custodian. That's Joseph's job."

"Our Mr. Sherk." The monsignor laughed dryly. "Yes, we're very fortunate to have found someone who learned his way around so quickly."

He bade Keegan goodnight and went out by the kitchen. Yvonne kept a utility drawer in one of the cabinets, and he opened it and dug out a hammer, a screwdriver and a putty knife that seemed sturdy enough for light prising. With the tools in his pocket he walked across the pavement to the church.

USUALLY AT THIS HOUR SHERK would be up in the attic to stay until morning. But this evening he surprised Sarah as she was gathering up rubbish after the meal. He had to leave for a while, he said. Something important to do.

"Don't worry," he said as he bound her up. "It might be a few hours, but I'll be back before you know it."

He kissed her on the cheek before he fastened the mask, then disappeared into the passage.

WHEN HE WAS SURE that the last penitent had left, the monsignor stood in the confessional and removed his sacramental stole. He folded it, kissed it reverentially, and placed it on the seat beside his windcheater. He wouldn't need either for a while. In one hand he held the tools from the kitchen. He opened the door and stepped out into the church.

It was quiet and dark. Peaceful. For a few seconds he was immobile, peering into the shadows, checking for Sherk's lurking form. Certain that he was alone, he slipped down the side aisle to the staircase at the back.

He tried the light. Out. And he hadn't brought a torch.

He started up the stairs. He was all right as far as the first landing. After that he was in deep darkness. He continued upwards, feeling his way. At the top step, he knew, was a set of swinging doors. He groped across the second landing and pushed them open.

Out into the loft. There was more light now, from the hanging fixtures. He went across to the cupboard.

The cupboard, he thought. It didn't appear in the original plans. Instead they showed a small, open room with a square hatch in the wall, hardly more than knee high. "Service Access" was the notation on the diagrams. The hatch led into a crawl space. Follow it to the end and you would find yourself above the lobby, under the rafters of the old chapel.

He had seen no hatch in the cupboard wall, only unbroken wainscot. But he knew that Sherk had found a way into the passage. Tonight, even if it meant tearing out the wainscot, he too would find it. And find what it was that kept bringing Sherk up here.

He opened the door, turned on the light, and closed the door behind him so that he wouldn't be noticed. He tried to remember the old plans of the church—where the hatch had been, where he should begin. Towards the back, he thought. Behind the robes. He pushed them aside, glanced down, and looked into Sherk's leering, hateful eyes.

The monsignor recoiled. "Joseph," he bleated.

From his crouched position Sherk sprang forward, snarling. He slammed into the monsignor's chest, knocking him backwards. The monsignor reeled; the tools dropped from his hands. He was sprawled, with his right hand reaching back, feeling for the doorknob. At that moment there was no question in his mind but that Sherk meant to kill him. But if he could open the door and get out, he might have a chance.

Sherk gathered himself up again and leaped. The monsignor's hand fell on the knob and he wrenched at it. Sherk fell upon him, the door flew open, and they tumbled together into the loft.

Sarah, dozing lightly in the cocoon, heard a single loud thump that came from down the crawl space. Then a brief scuffling noise. Then silence. Ten days earlier the noise might have excited or alarmed her, but now what happened outside the attic seemed increasingly unreal. She heard nothing more, and after a couple of minutes she was sound asleep.

Sherk had known the priest would come skulking around again. Trying to take Margaret away. The thought made him livid with rage, and he had plenty of time to let it boil, let it roar, as he waited for the priest who came to the church every Thursday evening.

358

Now they were grappling on the floor of the loft, Sherk's hands clutching at the monsignor's throat, yanking the stiff white collar, straining for a grip.

The loft was banked downwards, like a theatre balcony. It had a solid facing topped by a rail. Somehow the monsignor pulled free, but Sherk caught him by an ankle and tripped him, and the monsignor crashed onto the rail. Then Sherk was on him for sure, a good grip right on the throat. He held the monsignor in close, denying him leverage to push away.

The monsignor's mouth was moving, forming words, without breath to give them sound. He was struggling, but Sherk felt invincible. Fury kept building in him until he could stand it no more.

He lifted the monsignor by the throat, lifted him ten, twelve, eighteen inches off the floor. They were against the edge of the railing. With all his strength Sherk lifted and heaved. He pushed the monsignor over the edge and let go.

YVONNE DURANLEAU PUSHED ASIDE the curtain at the kitchen window to look again across the parking lot. "Past ten. He should have been back two hours ago."

Behind her, Father Martin and Father Jim were making sandwiches from the evening meal's leftovers.

"I told you," Keegan said. "He had something to do when he was finished with confessions."

"And I'm asking you, what does he have to do on Thanksgiving night that takes almost two hours?"

"His car's there," Davis said. "Can't be far."

"You worry too much," said Keegan.

She left the room and came back in her coat.

"Such friends he has," she said. "It's quite touching, the concern they show for his welfare." She wrapped a scarf round her head. "At least save him some pie. He'll want it when he gets back."

She went out, crossed the car park, and tried the church doors. Locked. Fine. The church was supposed to be locked after nine o'clock. But the monsignor would have kept it open if he was still inside.

Which meant that he was gone. He was gone but had not taken his car. And he was not one to walk even two blocks if he could avoid it. Something was wrong.

SHERK WATCHED THE OLD WOMAN tug at the front door of the church and hesitate. He stood outside, peering round the corner of the parish hall. Behind him, in the bed of his pick-up, lay what appeared to be a long, bulky roll of painter's tarpaulins. Sherk wasn't worried. He knew that in the church, the smooth flagstone where the monsignor had fallen was perfectly clean. He had scrubbed away every taint of blood.

With evident reluctance the housekeeper left the church and shuffled across the parking lot, returning to the rectory. Sherk watched her go inside. Then he got into his truck and drove off, heading for the open country outside town.

Sherk had no trouble finding a clay farm road that ran beside a cornfield, a spot where he couldn't see a single light. The ground was soft, and he dug the earth with ease. When the hole was ready, he lugged the body out of the pick-up. He laid it in the hole, threw in the screwdriver, the hammer and the putty knife, and the stiff white clerical collar. Also a pair of his own overalls, which had soaked up blood when he knelt to scrub the floor.

The dirt made a slight mound when he was finished. Sherk packed it down with the spade and threw on some corn stubble so that it wouldn't look so fresh.

CHAPTER TWELVE

Friday, November 23

A couple of minutes before eight in the morning, Warner was walking down the hall to the squad room, ready to start his shift, when he passed two policemen hurrying for the door.

One of them called back to him, "Hey, Warner. They been trying to raise you. Tried to get you at home."

"So here I am," Warner said. He'd had breakfast at a diner.

"The guy you were looking for? Farmer John type with a Ford pick-up, Virginia plates? We got 'im. At St. Bartholomew's."

Warner got into his car and drove to the church.

THE HOUSEKEEPER WARNER LEARNED, had reported the monsignor missing just before six in the morning.

The young patrolman first ordered to the rectory had checked the confessional where the monsignor was supposed to have been. There he found the stole and the windcheater, which now lay folded on a table in the rectory living room.

Warner looked them over.

"Were they folded like that?" he asked the patrolman.

"Like he was coming right back to pick them up."

"What about the janitor? Have you talked to him?"

"No, sir. But I questioned the priests. When one of them mentioned a custodian living in the basement of the hall, the name sounded familiar. As I was walking over to question him I noticed a truck parked beside the hall that fit the description on the duty board. I figured you'd want first crack at him. He's in the school cafeteria—one of the ovens is on the blink."

"Call headquarters," Warner said. "Tell them to send three more officers. Start questioning people in the neighbourhood, four blocks in every direction." He jammed his hands into the pockets of his overcoat. "I'll talk to Mr. Sherk."

Warner walked down the street to the school building, thinking, This is too strange for words. The man who tried to snatch Emily Caldwell—and maybe has done much worse to Sarah—is the janitor of a church where a monsignor disappears.

As he went in at the front door he thought about what he would say to Sherk. Instinct told him to go easy. Ask a few questions, nothing tough. But watch his eyes. See how he reacts.

"THING'S ON THE FRITZ, huh? Is it serious?"

Sherk took his head out of the oven to see who belonged to the voice. It was a man about his age, but heavier. A city man, with vacant eyes and a false, city smile.

"Heating element slipped off the bracket, shorted out," Sherk said. He was sitting cross-legged on the floor.

"Dinosaur like this, I bet you have trouble finding parts."

"Do I know you?" Sherk said.

"Howard Warner, Annapolis police." He flipped out his wallet and exposed his badge. The smile didn't waver. "And you're Joseph Sherk, right? Can I talk to you for a couple of minutes?"

Police. Sherk had known they would come, though not so soon and not in this form. But it didn't matter, he thought.

"Sure," he said. "What is it you want?"

"We can't find the monsignor. Remember the last time you saw him?" Suddenly the cop seemed to be looming over him. Sherk felt uneasy. He stood up, and found that he was two or three inches taller than the other man. It restored his sense of security.

"Day before yesterday. Saw him in the church." Sherk had rehearsed the answer.

"You live down in the church basement, don't you?"

"In the basement of the parish hall."

"He came in around seven to hear confessions."

"Well, I didn't see him. I was in my room the whole evening."

"Who was with you?"

"Wasn't nobody with me. I was by myself."

The cop nodded. He took out a notebook and riffled through it. "You're from Virginia," he said. "Outside Harben." He levelled his eyes at Sherk over the top of the book.

361

"That's right," Sherk said after a pause. He wondered how the police knew that already.

"Let's see," the cop said. "Last time you saw the monsignor was day before yesterday. You were alone in your room all yesterday evening. You never saw or heard anything; you don't know where he is or where he might have gone. Is that about right?"

"That's right," Sherk said.

"Then I guess we can wrap this up." The cop put away his notebook. "You think of anything, let me know."

The cop turned to leave. Sherk returned to work, getting down on his knees and leaning into the oven. Then the cop spoke again.

"Hey," he said. "I forgot to ask. You got any family?"

Sherk withdrew his head from the oven slowly. This was the last question he had expected. He wondered what the cop knew and what was the right answer among all the wrong ones.

"A daughter," he said after he had straightened up. "But I don't see her much."

"That's too bad," the cop said. Then he turned and walked away. This time Sherk watched him until he was gone.

"THAT'S HIM, ALL RIGHT," Emily Caldwell said, looking through binoculars. "What a creep!" She was sitting with Warner in his car, parked on Bellflower Street. Half a block away Sherk was assembling a Christmas crib on the front lawn of the church hall.

As evidence, Warner knew, this was weaker than a lineup ID. This was for himself. An idea was coming together in his mind, and he had to make sure the pieces fitted.

"When I was a kid," he said, "there used to be these booths in drugstores. For a quarter you could take three or four pictures of yourself. Any of those contraptions around here?"

"There's a booth at Annapolis Mall," she said. "But you only get one picture."

"One is fine," he said. "What do you say we run up there?"

THIS DAY THE SKY over Harben was a flawless blue. From his desk in the sheriff's station Hap Ammen could see at least half the town's dwellings draped over the hillside. He heard a car pull up outside. That would be his deputy, Eddie Fitt, back from the wreck on the highway.

"Bad one, Eddie?" he said when Fitt entered.

"I seen worse," Fitt said as he homed in on the coffee urn. "One fella got tore up pretty bad. But he'll make it."

He poured two cups of coffee and handed one across the desk. Ammen took it and said, "Joseph Sherk has showed up in Maryland. Annapolis."

362

"No kidding," the deputy said.

"Nope. I just got off the phone with a detective there. Wanted to know all about him. Asked if he had a daughter. Get this. Two months ago Sherk stops a girl on the street, says he's her father, tried to get her into the truck with him. Tell me *that* don't give you something to ponder."

Fitt wrinkled his lips in thought.

"Two months ago," he said. "His girl was just buried."

"The ashes hadn't even cooled over in the hollow."

The deputy looked at Ammen. "What'd you tell him?"

"All I know. I said the whole thing smelled bad to me. I thought so then and I always will."

He recalled again how the cabin had been ripped apart by the fire. It just didn't *look* right. Then Sherk's leaving so soon afterwards. The whole subject still rubbed him raw. He had wondered a thousand times what an autopsy of the girl's body would have showed if there had been enough left for an autopsy.

"I want you to get over to the high school," he said. "Pick up a copy of last year's yearbook. Then find out if they've got Express Mail in Abingdon. I want to get something out this afternoon."

THE COPS HAD BEEN ALL OVER the neighbourhood, rooting through trash-cans, looking behind hedges, knocking on doors. They had gone through the parish buildings, including Sherk's apartment, with even more care. Sherk had cheerfully let them in when they asked permission.

"I'M COLD," SARAH SAID. Sitting on the floor, she drew her legs up and wrapped her arms round them. "It's so cold in here."

Sherk fetched the sleeping bag and hung it, unzipped, over her shoulders. She thanked him morosely.

"What's the matter?" he said. "Feeling blue?"

That was one way to put it, she thought. She was empty and drained, stultified by the bleak, endless hours. Even the radio had become just another condition of her imprisonment.

"Kind of like that," she said.

"Want to hear a story?"

"Yeah," she said. "That would be nice." It was the only recreation her mind ever got.

"It's a special story," he said. "I was saving it for a time when you was ready to hear it. You never knew this one before."

She pulled the quilted nylon tight around herself. Sherk turned down the lamp until only a sprite of flame fluttered above its wick. Darkness collapsed around them, and they both edged in as close as possible to the sooty glass chimney.

"It's about somebody that tried to take you away from me," he said. "You don't remember your mother, I guess. When you was first born, we lived in Kentucky."

"What was her name?" Sarah said.

"Evelyn. And a beauty she was. You got her looks. Anyway, I fell hard for her. We got married; then along you came. She weren't much of a wife and sure not much of a mother."

His voice was heavy. She had never seen him so solemn.

"We had it out plenty of times. She'd say she was leaving, and I'd say, go on. One day she did leave. And she took you with her. I 'bout went crazy when I saw you was gone.

"She had family, so I knew how to find you. Keeping you was another thing. Her family woulda come after you, see? So I bided my time. Let everybody think I didn't care. I looked for a place I could take you, where we could live and nobody'd find us. Once I found the cabin in the hollow, I was ready."

As she watched him she could see the determined young father, unswerving in his love. It all made sense now, all that he had done. He wanted his daughter and he would do anything to get her back. Of course he had made one huge mistake. Except for that, there was a touching logic to all that he said and did.

"She had a sister without any kids of her own. I would drive by the place and see your aunt out on the porch, rocking a cradle, and I knew it had to be you. I made my move one afternoon. I drove past the house and there was your aunt, rocking the cradle. I waited a few minutes and drove past again. The cradle was still there, but wasn't nobody with it. I parked and run up on the porch. I looked into the crib. There you was. You knew me. You put your hand out to me. I picked you up and drove off with you, straight to the hollow. And that's where you grew up.

"They never found us. But I don't think they looked too hard. See, they didn't want you as much as I did. Nobody ever could. I loved you with all that was in me, and I still do. I always will."

To Sarah he no longer looked menacing, just sad. She couldn't believe she had ever feared him. "I'm sorry, Joseph," she said.

"You used to call me Daddy," he murmured.

There was a wet light in his eyes, and Sarah felt her own eyes moisten. It had been so long since she had spoken that word.

"I'm sorry, Daddy," she said, and she reached out.

His arms enfolded her, a father's arms, strong and loving. She couldn't remember the last time she had been held like this. It was a distant memory, a father's arms around her, security in his words and his manner and in the arms themselves. His strength surrounded her, and she was a little girl again, scared and alone and tired of living inside herself.

364

Saturday, November 24

As Elise Stannard walked up the front steps of the church for early Mass she thought about the monsignor. A story about his disappearance had been in the morning paper.

She remembered him. He had said Mass on Sunday, and once again early in the week. His eyes were kind, and she had told herself that she should talk alone with him, ask his guidance.

Now he was gone. Awful, she thought. It was depressing, as if she were under a cloud that rained tragedy wherever she went.

WARNER HAD SPENT THE NIGHT parked along Bellflower Street in a plain brown Chevy, watching the parish hall, the blue pick-up that was vaguely visible through the hedge, and the lighted window of Sherk's apartment. Sometime in the night, he had imagined, Sherk would be leaving and he had intended to follow, but Sherk had not appeared.

Now the detective was with the psychologist, Claire Johansen, treating her to breakfast in a diner.

"I'm glad you could come," he told her. "In a couple of hours I'm going up against more brass than I ever wanted to see in one place, and I've got an idea I want to sell them. But first I'd like to know it isn't totally off the wall."

"Go ahead," she said. "We'll see if it holds up."

Warner told her his theory. When he had finished, she nodded and said, "It's possible."

"That's what I wanted to hear," he said, exultant.

"I said it's possible. But it would be one for the journals, if you're right."

"That's still good enough."

She didn't say anything for a moment, and Warner knew there must be something else, something she hadn't told him.

"You have some interest in this?" she said finally. "Something more than putting away a bad guy?"

"You get caught up in it," Warner said. "Especially when there's a kid involved. You know how it goes."

"Then I'll tell you what I'd tell her family," she said. "So they won't be disappointed. If she is alive, and you do find her, she may not be grateful. She may not even want to leave him."

"You're kidding, right?" Warner said.

"No. No joke. He's had two weeks with her. That's enough time for him to have turned her into anything he wants."

"In only two weeks?" Warner said.

"It can happen faster than that. In a hostage situation, everything is compressed. The kidnapper and his captive immediately establish an intense relationship. At first it's based on fear, the threat of death. When

365

that doesn't happen, the hostage is often relieved and full of gratitude.

"The kidnapper typically realizes how easily he can shape the behaviour of his captive. Threat, followed by submission. Before long the captive is volunteering the submissive response, anticipating the intimidation. That may be just a ploy at first, but it's not unusual for genuine sympathy and affection to develop. So you should know," she said, "if you do get to her, she may not be the girl you expect to find."

"I'll just stick to finding her," Warner said. "Sort out the rest later."

"Something else you should know," she said. "The sympathy can work both ways; the more time a kidnapper spends with his hostage, the less likely he is to do physical harm."

"That's good," Warner said.

"It's true," she said, "in most cases. Political kidnappings, kidnappings for ransom. But if you're right, this is something else entirely. The man would be seriously ill. In which case all bets are off. She may think that she's figured out the rules. And it may seem to work. But I'm telling you, Warner. You want to find her before she discovers that he isn't playing by any rules at all."

THE CAPTAIN'S OFFICE was panelled in glass, so when Warner rushed into the squad room, already fifteen minutes late, he could see them all: the captain and the chief of police and their counterparts on the county force, all here to decide how to handle Sherk.

The captain waved him in. Warner stuck up an index finger and hurried over to his desk. He spotted the Express Mail envelope—the package had arrived. He ripped it open.

Inside was a page from a high-school yearbook. It showed a dozen head-and-shoulders photos, arranged in rows of three each. The sheriff in Harben had circled one in the second row, but Warner didn't need the help. He could have selected the picture from among thousands. He tore the photo out of the page and walked into the captain's office.

"Howard," said the captain. "The thinking is, we would get Sherk off the street. With the Caldwell girl, we've got enough for assault. Bring him in, let him stew for a day and a half in lockup. Who knows what he might decide to talk about."

"No," Warner said with conviction. "That'd be a big mistake right now. Sarah Stannard may be alive, and our best chance of finding her is to keep Sherk out where he can get to her."

The captain and the others looked sceptical.

"What's more," Warner went on, "I've talked to this guy, and he's tough. You couldn't crack him with ten years of hard time, let alone a weekend in county detention."

"So let's hear your ideas," said the captain.

"Right," Warner said. He got up and went to the bulletin board along the side wall. Four pairs of eyes followed him. He took out the five-by-seven glossy of Sarah.

"We all know this young lady," Warner said, and he tacked the photo to the board. "Sarah Stannard, at age fifteen years, four months." Beside it he tacked a second photo, a head shot in colour. "This one you've heard about. Emily Caldwell, at the age of sixteen and three months. Normally she wears her hair swept back. But for comparison I got her to put it in a pigtail, and she remembered that's how it was the day she was attacked."

"We know the connection," one of the chiefs said.

"Not this one, you don't." Warner had his back turned. When he moved aside, a third photo was tacked to the board.

"Margaret Anne Sherk, at about age fifteen. It's a yearbook photo, taken almost nine months ago."

They all peered at the photos. The girls were nearly identical, their features and colouring and hair interchangeable. The effect was startling and powerful.

"This is his daughter?" said one of the chiefs.

"His late daughter. Died last August in a house fire. Sherk disappeared before her funeral. Two weeks later he accosts Emily Caldwell near the harbour. He calls her by his daughter's name and is angry when she doesn't respond. He's ready to haul her away, but she escapes. Two months later Sarah—her schoolmate and nearly her double—goes missing. I don't know how Sherk ended up here, but I think he came looking for his daughter. And he found her. Only her name is Sarah Stannard."

The captain and the others listened as Warner laid it out for them, telling them what he knew, what he had learned from Claire Johansen, and what he guessed.

"We've searched the church property," Warner said. "Sherk even let us into his rooms. So I'd say he's rented an apartment, maybe a garage, to hold her. He'd want to see her as often as possible, so it'd be nearby. But he has to visit her periodically."

The two chiefs and the captains looked at one another, and one of them asked, "What do you need?"

"A couple of days," Warner said. "Keep two people at the church, rotating shifts. One county, one from us. I can double-shift. County has a surveillance van with one-way glass. It would help. We ought to tell the priests that Sherk is a suspect, but leave him where he is."

The captain looked at his chief and got a nod. The two county officers signalled their agreement.

The captain said to Warner, "You can have until early Monday morning. I don't want him anywhere near when the kids come to school.

367

He'll have to go to her at least once between now and then. If that doesn't cut it, we bring him in."

"Good," Warner said. "I'll get on it right now."

The captain couldn't remember the last time Warner had moved so fast.

IT WAS A WARM MORNING for November. Sarah was sweating inside the sleeping bag when she woke. She reached for the zipper tab. Only when she had unzipped it did she realize what she had done: she had moved her hands. There was no cocoon. No straps round her arms and legs. And no mask.

"Mornin'," Sherk said from across the attic. He filled a glass with orange juice and brought it to her. So he had gone for breakfast already. He had gone and left her unbound as she slept.

"Sleepyhead," he said as he craned over the hammock. "I thought you'd never wake up." He bent closer and kissed her on the cheek. It didn't feel unnatural to her. Then she remembered: the sadness in his eyes, holding him, being held.

She swung her feet to the floor and took the juice. The roof pinched in directly above her, its underside just inches from her face. She could feel warmth radiating from the wood.

"It ain't too cold," he said. "A good day for a bath."

"I'd enjoy that," she said.

She followed him to the cushions, where they always sat to eat. He reached into the gym bag. Without thinking, she knew that he was going to pull out crackers. She had always liked crackers and orange juice for breakfast.

They ate. Sherk wouldn't take his eyes away from her. She didn't mind. They weren't sad this morning, his eyes, but proud and happy. She basked in his pleasure.

When he was finished, he told her that he was leaving to bring hot water. "Anything else you want?" he said.

"I'd like some shampoo." She looked at her hands. "And maybe some clippers. My nails are getting long."

He got up. The straps and the mask were on the floor, beneath the hammock, and she expected him to cross over and get them. Instead he went to the passage opening.

"I'll have to go to the drugstore for clippers, so I'll be a while. Maybe an hour," he said. His eyes narrowed slightly. "You'll be a good girl? Won't do anything you shouldn't do?"

"No." Her voice was tentative. "I'll be good."

"I know you will," he said. Then he turned and crawled through the opening. A few seconds later she heard the door snap shut at the end of the passage.

368

At first she didn't budge. She stared at the exit, telling herself that Sherk had left and she could do what she wanted—she was free. The idea was slow to root. Finally something nudged her off the cushion. She crawled to the threshold, stopped, summoned all her courage, and looked out.

At the end of the passage, invisible in the darkness, Sherk watched her. He had opened the door and shut it without going through. Now he watched and waited.

The lantern in the attic illuminated the first few feet of the crawl space. The rest was completely dark, and she knew that somewhere in that blackness, at the indeterminable end of the passage, was a door to the world.

The thought made her shrink inside. Beyond that black buffer was noise, confusion, the disordered unknown.

Outside, a dog barked. She had never been afraid of dogs, but the barking frightened her. She knew that she should leave, that it was almost a duty. But she didn't understand why. At first the attic had nearly suffocated her, and she tried to remember how that had felt. Then the desire to escape—she tried to remember why she had sought the jumble and the brightness and the noise. The reason was incomprehensible now.

She pulled her head back. Sherk spoke, and the surprise nearly lifted her off the floor.

"Where was you going?" he intoned.

"No place," she said. Her voice cracked.

"Who are you?"

"I'm Margaret. I'm your good little girl."

"A good girl don't run off."

"I wasn't. I just wanted to look."

"Don't even look. Nothing for you out here."

"I won't. I won't even look."

She scrambled over to the hammock, crawled into the sleeping bag, and zipped it up in spite of the warmth. She drew her arms into the bag, clutched the fabric around her shoulders, and gently rocked, rocked in the hammock.

WARNER THOUGHT THE STANNARDS ought to be informed. He sat with them in the big living room and gave a shortened version of what he had told the brass. Elise interrupted only once, to say, "He works at the church? At St. Bartholomew's?"

She didn't speak again until he had finished. "I only want to know one thing," she said then. "Can we really hope?"

Warner looked at her. There seemed to be a new dignity about her, an inward solidness. "Why not?" he said. "I do."

FROM AN UPSTAIRS WINDOW in the rectory, Warner could see the black surveillance van take up its position on Bellflower Street. Warner and a young officer in plain clothes had been in the monsignor's room for almost an hour. They needed this second post to cover the rear of the church and the parish hall.

In a few seconds there was a squawk from the radio transmitter that lay on the monsignor's bedside table.

"Orchid One," said the voice. "This is Two in place."

Warner picked up the transmitter and keyed it. "Two, check. Our man went down the basement steps of the hall about fifteen minutes ago. Possibly gone to his room."

The schedule that Warner had devised called for one county officer and one from the city to be on post at all times. His own shift didn't begin until midnight, but he had to be here.

The young plain clothesman, sitting at the window in the monsignor's straight-backed desk chair, fidged on the hard wooden seat and said, "Let's hope he's decided he has to see her soon. Otherwise it'll be a lo-o-ong eight hours."

Warner stood behind him and watched the back of the church, the hall, Sherk's truck. One more time he ran over his theory, the reasoning of it. From Margaret to Emily to Sarah. It made sense if you understood fathers and daughters, and Warner believed that he did.

He remembered a girl who had once got off a bus from Virginia Beach. A small, scared girl who had let her long hair get too dirty. Who stood on the top step of the bus in Baltimore and wouldn't move until she had spotted him in the crowd. Who came down the steps shyly at first, then ran to his arms.

Father and daughter, he thought—that was something special.

THE CLIPPERS SNAPPED as Sarah trimmed the last of her nails. It was a small device of chromed steel, with sharp curved jaws; she slipped it absently into a side pocket of her jeans.

"How's your hair?" Sherk said.

It lay straight, fanned out across her back. "It's about dry."

"Do something for me," he said. "Plait it down the back."

She thought of the wooden doll with plaited hair, and remembered that Margaret wore her hair that way.

"Sure," she said.

He came over and put an arm round her. "You've been a good girl," he said. "Made me real happy. I couldn't ask for more."

He was beaming when he let her go. Sarah returned his smile and had begun to brush her hair when she saw him frown.

"Blood," he said. "Blood on your face."

"I don't think so."

"I can see it," he said. "All over your face."

She reached up and felt around. There was nothing.

"I'm sorry," Sherk said. His voice was distressed, his breathing fast and shallow. "I didn't mean to. It just came over me, I couldn't stop it. So much blood."

"It's OK," she said. She put her hands on his shoulders and shook him gently. "I'm all right."

His breathing evened out. There was still the trace of a question on his face, but in a few seconds even that vanished. He squeezed her hand and was calm again.

A FEW MINUTES BEFORE MIDNIGHT Warner stood at the rectory window, thinking of Sarah. He told himself that she was alone tonight, a prisoner in what must be some dingy hole.

Sherk would be in his room. The lights were low in the church and the hall was dark, so he had to be down in the basement.

Some father, he thought. Go to her. Go.

THE CABIN WAS A MESS. A chair was on its side in the front room, a lamp lay smashed in the corner, and an end table beside the sofa had been overturned. Margaret kept a spun-glass figure of a horse there, a gift he had found for her at a shop in Abingdon. He went over to the table and found a thousand gleaming splinters on the floor. There was also a trail of blood. It led to the back of the cabin, to Margaret's room. Margaret was there now.

If he tried hard, concentrated, he could see her sleeping in a rope hammock under the attic's roof beams. But he knew where she really was. He could feel himself drawn to her room, the pull inexorable, and he knew that he would have to go in and look. It had to be. Maybe not now, not right away. But soon he would have to go into the room and see what he had done.

CHAPTER THIRTEEN

Sunday, November 25

For more than six hours Warner had been peering through a night-vision scope that stripped away darkness and rendered life in a grainy green monochrome. Now he pulled back from the eyepiece and looked eastwards. A flock of gulls scattered across a mother-of-pearl sky, and a boy wearing a black jacket was delivering Sunday papers to the homes across Bellflower Street.

Warner spoke into the radio. "Orchid Two, you still with me?"

"Oh sure, wide awake." It was Tarver in the county van.

Warner put the radio aside. The lights went out along all Bellflower Street.

SHERK WAS GETTING BREAKFAST when morning arrived. He had left the attic early so he could return and spend the day with Margaret. He put two pieces of bread into the toaster, peeled some bacon into a frying pan, and began to heat milk for cocoa.

"Oh no, Daddy. Not again," Margaret said behind him.

He spun round. Nobody there.

"No, Daddy, no. Please don't."

A tortured plea, full of pain. This time it came from under the kitchen counter. He rushed to look, but she wasn't there.

She screamed. The sound seared inside his head. He clapped his hands over his ears, but he couldn't block it out. The shriek was excruciating. He reached out and she was there. His hands were on her throat, and he was choking off the scream. Only way to stop it—he couldn't take it any more. He put all his strength into the grip. The scream died to a moan and then to nothing. He was soaked with sweat, hands still held out in front of him, clenching air.

Off to his left there was a hiss. He ignored it and tried to control his breathing. Tried to understand what had happened. There was another hiss, louder than the first. He turned around to see milk boiling over the pan, onto the coils of the hotplate.

THE WATCH CHANGED AT EIGHT. Warner gave up his seat to the new man but stayed near the window. About half an hour later the housekeeper brought him a bowl of cornflakes for breakfast. Warner ate standing up, watching the first worshippers arrive for the nine o'clock Mass. He was more alert now than ever. With all the activity they could easily miss one man leaving.

At about ten minutes before nine he reached for his binoculars, brought them to focus on a woman who was walking alone towards the church. It was Elise.

She approached the walkway that led to the front of the church. There she stopped and looked around. He knew she was trying to find Sherk. Just to look at him, that would be enough now.

"Get something?" said the cop in the chair.

Elise turned her back and started up the walk.

"An old friend," Warner said. He resumed his scan. Rear of church, side door of church. Rear of hall, side door of hall. Basement steps, Sherk's truck. And then back again, again, again.

WHEN SHERK RETURNED with breakfast, Sarah knew that something was wrong. He had put a distance between them, an almost palpable barrier that she sensed the moment he came in.

He pulled a foil-wrapped bundle out of the gym bag and tossed it on the floor between them. She opened it—cold toast, some black shards of bacon. He hadn't yet looked into her eyes. For the first time in days she was scared.

He poured orange juice out of a carton into a plastic cup, and handed it to her. "No cocoa," he said. "I burned the milk."

"I don't mind," she said. She tried to catch his gaze, but he avoided her, and she thought maybe she would be better off away from him. She went to the hammock and sat beside it.

He appeared not to notice. He bit the corner off a piece of toast and stared out morosely. For a while they sat in silence, Sherk with a wall around him, Sarah trying to be unobtrusive.

Some sounds below marred the silence. There were voices and foot-steps, people coming to church. Then the first shattering clap of the steeple bell. Sherk jumped and looked up. But before the bell had finished pealing he had withdrawn into himself again.

The organ piped alive a couple of minutes later. The choir joined in, and music surged through the room. Sarah ignored it. She was watching Sherk. He got to his feet and came over to her. He was stooped under the peak of the roof. To Sarah on the floor, he looked gigantic.

"I think I done something bad," he said. He had to raise his voice to be heard. "Tell me what I done to you. Something bad."

Sarah didn't know how to answer. By an unspoken pact they both had put aside what happened that first night.

"I can almos' *see* it," he said. "I have to know."

The last bars of the hymn dropped away, and the attic was silent. He crouched beside her. "Tell me," he whispered.

"You've always been good to me," she said.

Sherk rubbed his temples. He looked doubtful, distraught.

"My head hurts. Got to get rid of this headache." He got up and retreated to the furthest corner of the attic. His face was dismal in the lamplight.

Beyond the wall there was a low murmur, like distant thunder. Sarah couldn't make out the words, but she knew it was people praying out loud, praying together.

Sherk looked at her, almost accusingly, then buried his face in his hands. He remained that way a long while. The Mass ended and the church emptied. Sarah sat on the floor, looking at Sherk and at the way out, a few feet away, trying to find a grip on the slippery truth of who she was and how she had got here.

WHEN THE TEN FIFTEEN MASS was under way and the view was uncluttered again, Warner told the relief officer that he was going to try for a nap while he had the chance.

He took off his shoes and stretched out on the monsignor's bed. Within minutes he was dozing.

FOR HOURS SARAH HAD SAT at one end of the attic, away from Sherk, watching him where he crouched. Sometimes he would mumble down at the floor, ignoring her; at other times he would look up and glare at her—not a hostile look, really, but a piercing one.

She had listened all morning to the bell and the prayers and the sound of people periodically passing below. When the familiar pattern had stopped, she knew the church must be empty. As more hours passed and Sherk disintegrated, the attic seemed to shrink. Now it was oppressively close, and she didn't understand how she had managed to grow comfortable here.

Across the attic Sherk could feel the wall coming down, the wall he had built in his mind without even knowing. Images and feelings and memories that he had hidden away were coming together. There in the room. Her bedroom in the cabin.

He looked up and saw Margaret. Who was not Margaret. Because Margaret was in the room, waiting for him.

"You're not here," he said. "You can't be here."

Sarah went over to him, knelt beside him.

"Look, I'm real," she said. "You can touch me." She squeezed his right hand, brought it up to her face. "See?"

Sherk caressed her cheek, fingered the pigtail down her back. Verifying her existence. But one thing he knew. One truth he could hold on to. Margaret was in the room. He looked closer.

"Who *are* you?" he said.

Sarah was stunned. She tried not to let it show, because that would ruin her. That would end it all.

Get it together, champ. Don't lose it now.

"I'm me. I'm Margaret." This was her life.

He shook his head wistfully, as if he wished it were so.

"I am," she said. "And you're my daddy. We lived in a little cabin in a hollow near Harben, in Virginia. Just the two of us. I never knew my mama—she ran off when I was a baby and took me with her, and you had to steal me back. Remember?"

"I'll never forget." He closed his eyes, bringing it back.

"I had a tabby cat named Banana that got lost one day, and we never found it." She rummaged through her mind, dredging for details. "We saw a mother bear and her cubs once in a meadow on the other side of

Drolsom's Ridge. A beautiful meadow. Remember the grass—so tall and thick and green?"

His eyes were still closed and his head was thrown back, and on his face was an emotion she had never seen before: bliss somehow coexisting with misery. "Yes," he said. "Yes."

"When I got up on cold mornings, and the windows were iced over, do you remember what I used to do?"

"You used to scratch our names on the frost," Sherk said fervently. "You'd write 'Daddy and M'." His eyes were closed, but a tiny wet gleam had appeared at each corner.

"And why I did always write the two together?" she asked.

"Because you said that's how we'd always be. Together." A sob caught in his throat. "You made me promise that whatever happened, we'd always be together."

"And we are, aren't we?" she said.

"Yes."

"And aren't I your little girl?"

"My little girl," he whispered. Still with his head thrown back, eyes closed, suddenly limp and wrung out.

"Then tell me everything's OK."

"It's OK," he mumbled. Leaning towards her, he opened his eyes. A leering corpse's head looked back at him. It lolled on a broken neck. One eye swollen, one cheek sliced deep.

"Daddy?" she said, putting her hands on his shoulders. "What's the matter?"

Sherk roared with fright and outrage. He roared with grief, and threw up his arms to break the grip of her ghastly dead fingers. He struck out at her, shoving her as hard as he could.

When she picked herself up, she was just a girl again, wide-eyed and ready to flinch. "What did I do wrong?" she asked.

His head hurt something awful. He had to think, but he couldn't get things straight, not near her. She was part of his problem. Sherk ducked through the opening, into the passage.

SHE HAD FORGOTTEN how strong he was. Her shoulders were sore where the explosive blow had fallen.

She listened to his boots scraping along the passage. The sound diminished. He was really leaving, she thought. When the noise ceased, she knew he was out of the passage, out and gone.

Standing up, she hit her head on a beam. Too low, she thought. The place was suffocating, the lamp's light woefully dim.

She made her way to the opening. She wanted to get away. Now. Only the thought of Sherk out there somewhere held her back; for about a minute she hesitated at the threshold. Then she imagined being there when he returned, and that was enough to send her through the opening and into the blackness.

The passage was even darker than it looked. She advanced slowly, sliding her hands across the floor in front of her, blindly feeling her way along. Then her right hand touched something solid. She moved closer. The barrier was flat and wooden, standing directly in her path. Boxing her in. Her heart accelerated.

Keep it together. Keep it together. Think!

OK. Sherk went through here all the time. There had to be an entry. The last thing she heard when he left was a hard click that sounded like a door being firmly closed. She moved her palms along the surface in front of her, and her fingers fell across a metal handle. She pulled. The snap clicked and the door swung open. She crawled through, emerging behind the rack of choir robes. She shoved past them, stumbled over a box, and came out through the cupboard door.

The light burned her eyes. It was only indirect evening light through the stained-glass windows, but it was more than she had seen in weeks. She blinked and turned aside until her vision had adjusted. Then she looked around.

The church seemed huge. Its walls and arched ceiling overhead seemed to go on for ever, the scale overwhelming after the confines of the attic. She looked upwards to take it all in. Instantly she was dizzy, and her legs began to wobble under her. She reached back and steadied herself against the doorpost.

Deep breath. Deep breath. Her equilibrium returned. She released her hold, and for the first time she straightened out of the constant stoop that the attic demanded. She could move. Breathe. Stand. Walk.

She went out into the loft, looked around, and saw the double doors at the far end. She crossed over and opened one. In the meagre light she could make out a wide landing and some stairs. She held the rail and made her way down to the bottom, through another set of doors, and out into the side aisle of the church.

WHEN HE LEFT THE CUPBOARD, Sherk went to the first dark and quiet place he could find. His head buzzed. Something inside was trying to get through. He didn't want to see, but he knew there was no more running from it. He sat and looked out dumbly, and he saw.

The fire burns inside him as he scuttles down the hillside. He knows what's going to happen and he knows it's wrong, but he can't stop it. Doesn't know how. Doesn't want to.

Margaret's in the kitchen. He stands in the doorway until she notices.

Oh no, Daddy. Not again.

He ignores her. You was swimming. There was boys. Blows crack against her face. For a while she just sits there, taking it, until she wriggles out of his grasp. But she's off balance and the chair tips back and she falls with it, slamming against the side table, turning it over.

She gets up, dazed. He could grab her but he doesn't. No hurry. She stumbles off to her room, locks the door. He follows. Open the door. No, I can't. I'm your father. Let me in. No, Daddy. I'm scared. He steps back and raises his foot and kicks the door right beside the knob. The lock rips out of the mortise. She screams.

And now it really starts.

Next he knows he's sitting at the kitchen table. The hollow is in shadow. He knows he's done wrong. Isn't sure what it is.

Margaret's in her room. He knows that. Already he's got it in his mind how it'll go. She'll be cowering in the corner, naturally. She'll be afraid. But he'll show her it's over, hold out a hand, pull her up. Then they'll kneel, say a prayer, pray about how life makes it hard for us to be good.

He gets up and goes to her room. She's propped up in the corner. He gets sick when he sees her. Blood on her face, one eye bruised and swollen, her left cheek split open.

"Margaret," he says in a small voice. "Wake up, honey. Come on, wake up. Don't pretend."

He prods her. She doesn't move.

Somebody's screaming, howling. He wishes it would stop, and realizes it's him, he's the one screaming. Then he does stop.

Inside his head is a tiny hard-shelled kernel, unperturbed and unmoved. He surrenders to it, lets it take over.

It sends him out to the shed for a bit and a brace. He picks a spot in the front room and drills a hole through the floor, near the wall. Next he goes through the house, shutting windows, stuffing towels into the cracks under doors. He leaves Margaret's room for last, and when he's finished there, he picks her up, carries her into the kitchen, sits her in a chair in front of the stove.

It's an old-fashioned stove, with pilot lights that are always going out. He blows them out. Then he turns up the oven's control; the propane gas makes a throaty sound coming out of the jets. He goes out and shuts the front door behind him.

Now he goes to the shed again. He comes out with a smudge pot. It's about the size and shape of a cannonball, made of tin, slightly flattened at the bottom, with a wick at the top. Highway crews use them as long-burning flares to mark road repairs at night. Sherk shakes it. Plenty of fuel inside.

The cabin has no basement, and no foundation except for concrete blocks at the corners and at six-foot intervals along the base of the walls.

There's a foot of space between the ground and the floorboards. He gets on his back, finds the hole he has drilled, positions the smudge pot directly beneath it.

He lights it with a match.

It's already hazy in his mind why he is doing this, what has happened.

His drive down to the truck stop will be three quarters of an hour, and by then he'll have forgotten completely. By the time he starts work the house will be filling up with gas, and when it gets thick enough, some of it will get pushed out through the hole, down into the burning smudge pot.

"Propane ... the stove. She never got out," the deputy will say, and Sherk's mournful moan will be full, real, unrehearsed.

Sherk was sweat-drenched as he sat in the darkness, remembering. What these hands have done, he thought.

He knew now that the fire was inside him every moment. It was there now, and he could feel it rising.

He couldn't stop it. Didn't want to.

There were footsteps, coming his way.

WHEN SARAH came out into the side aisle, she could see nobody else around. Further down this aisle was a side exit. She started towards it. To her right was a section of pews. To her left was the side wall of the church, and as she hurried to get out she passed two purple-curtained confessional boxes.

The side door was close now. She passed a pillar on her right and came upon a third confessional. She was almost running, and didn't notice the tremor in the purple curtain of the last box.

Sherk stepped out from behind the curtain, blocking her way. She tried to slow down, slipped on the smooth marble floor, and fell into him.

He grabbed her by the arm.

"Well now, girlie," he said. His voice could have chiselled stone. "Well now. What are we doing down here?"

CHAPTER FOURTEEN

After supper Father Keegan went upstairs to visit Warner. The detective had been a presence in the rectory for more than a day, mostly unseen, an object of curiosity. Now, finding the door to the monsignor's room open a crack, the priest saw that all the lights were turned off. Warner was standing at the window, looking out.

Keegan knocked. Warner turned round, said, "Come on in, Father," and went back to the window.

"I thought you could use company," Keegan said.

"Glad you came." He remained fixed at the window.

"I have to admit that I wondered what a stakeout was like," Keegan said. "I've never seen one before."

"As you can tell, the drama is relentless." Warner's tone was wearily dry. "I don't suppose anybody down there has seen him since yesterday afternoon?"

"I did," Keegan said. "Early this morning. I was changing the altar linen when he came in through the sacristy. I think I surprised him. When he saw me, he mumbled something and then went back the way he came."

"Back to the hall," Warner said.

"Yes. He must have been coming to make a repair, because he had a gym bag with him. I think he carries tools in it."

"Then he really is there. I was beginning to wonder."

"We all know the feeling. You'll think that he can't be far. Yet if you go looking for him, you can't find him. Sometimes I think that we find him only when he wants to be found."

Warner said nothing more for a while. He gave the window complete attention.

"I need a favour," he said abruptly. "Will you cover for me for a few minutes?"

"You think I can handle it?" the priest said.

"Nothing to it. Just keep watching. I don't suppose you'll see him, but if you do, get on the radio here. Press this button to talk. Just say you've spotted him and which way he's headed."

Warner stepped aside and Keegan took his spot at the window.

"Hey," Warner said as he was putting on his overcoat, "keep holy the Sabbath is the way I was taught."

"It still is. We try."

"But Sherk was working this morning."

"Emergencies come up," Keegan said.

"What was the emergency this morning?" Warner said.

Keegan thought for a moment. "I have no idea."

"OK. Won't be long. Any questions, push the button and talk."

About half a minute later Warner was out in the moonlit night and walking across the parking lot towards the parish hall.

KILL ME IF THAT'S WHAT YOU WANT, Sarah thought. Stop waiting and just do it.

The mask was over her face, tighter than ever before, and she was bound and trussed in the cocoon. The canvas restricted her chest. A set of three belts held shoulders and waist and ankles, holding her fast in the hammock.

Sherk had broken her jaw, she thought. It was swelling against the mask. He had hit her just once, but that was enough to subdue her. Then he had led her back. Since then, for more than two hours, he had sat on a box in the middle of the room. Not like this morning, when he had seemed to be coming apart. Now he was hard and cold, as if he had sloughed off an uncomfortable human skin to reveal a centre of pure vileness. Just seeing him that way made her fear for her life.

He was waiting, she thought. Waiting and watching in a world that existed for him alone. She wondered what he saw as he sat on the box, sitting there and slowly whittling down the wooden doll he had made for her, drawing his open knife the length of the wood, raising paper-thin strips that curved up and fell at his feet.

AFTER NEARLY THIRTY HOURS of looking out from the rectory window, Warner had to get closer. He couldn't say why. But he believed that he had earned the right to indulge an urge when all else had failed. And all else had, he thought.

He walked round to the front of the church, then towards the parish hall on the other side. Sherk's apartment was a corner room on the far end. It was completely blocked from view of the rectory: its window faced out onto Bellflower Street.

The window sat just a couple of inches above ground level. There was a light in it. Warner didn't want Sherk to see him, so he passed it quickly on the sidewalk, turning his head to look.

It was painted over. One window in the place and it had been whitewashed. Somebody likes privacy, he thought.

There was nothing else to see, so he crossed Bellflower and went over to the black van—another impulse. When he got there, the rear door popped back at him. Tarver was holding it open. Warner climbed in and shut the door behind him.

The van had a carpeted floor, a small refrigerator, and two contoured swivel chairs in the back. Warner took the empty chair as Tarver got two cans of cola from the refrigerator.

"I thought I had him figured," Warner said. "I really did."

"He's a head case," Tarver said. "You can go goofy trying to figure head cases. Sometimes they seem OK. They walk, they talk fine. But there's nothing there. Night of the living dead. Lights are on, nobody's home. You know what I mean?"

"I guess." Warner kept looking at the lighted window, imagining Sherk behind it, behind painted glass. "I'd like to know how he spends his time. What does he do with himself?"

Holed up all weekend, Warner thought, alone in a tiny basement room for thirty hours. Except when he's walking around in the church on Sunday morning, carrying a gym bag.

"I think he must sleep in the daytime," Tarver said. "Either that or he's afraid of the dark. He can't sleep with the light off."

"What do you mean?" Warner said.

"The light in his room. I was here midnight to eight, and it was on the whole time. I get back about an hour ago, thing's still on. Maybe he sleeps with his head under the covers." Tarver swigged from the can of cola, swallowed. "So what do we do? You want to take him now, fold the tent?"

"No," Warner said. "Let's give it a couple more hours."

He got out and began to walk back to the rectory. Head case, he thought. Find him only when he wants to be found. Came in through the sacristy, Keegan had said; saw me and turned around. Sleeps with his head under the covers.

And Tarver had said something else. What was it? A head case. Night of the living dead. Lights are on, nobody's home.

Light's on. Nobody's home.

Warner stopped in the middle of the parking lot, turned on a heel, and went back to the painted-over window of Sherk's apartment. He dropped to one knee on the grass in front of it, placed an ear against the pane. He couldn't hear anything. He tapped on the glass.

Knock on the door, he thought, somebody might ignore that. But not this. He tapped again, harder.

Or this. Half buried in the turf was a stone about the size of a walnut. He pried it out, stepped back a few feet, and cocked his arm. He told himself that in five seconds he was going to be either one brilliant or else one very silly cop. He flung the rock.

A fist-size hole appeared in the window, and chunks of glass fell out of the frame, shattering on the floor inside.

Nothing happened. No shouts, no angry face at the window. He went close, kicked out some of the hanging glass, and bent down to look. He could see almost the entire apartment, and there was nobody. Not now, probably not all weekend.

Tarver was coming out of the van. Warner waved him back.

"There's a priest on the radio," Warner said. "Tell him we need keys for every lock in these two buildings—to bring 'em down. The radio too. She's here. The bastard, he's got her here."

SARAH FOUND THAT SHE COULD move her hands in the cocoon. A strap outside the canvas pinned her arms tight against her sides, but her hands were free and she could move them at the wrists. Sherk was oblivious. He was still rapt, enmeshed in his fantasy.

Under her right hand, in her jeans, she could feel a flat metal object. It might work, she thought. If she could somehow get it out of the pocket. Maybe. If Sherk would leave. Maybe.

WARNER AND TARVER stood beside the van, watching Father Keegan coming with a big hoop of keys and a torch.

"I could call for backups," Warner said.

"Bad idea," Tarver said. "If you call for the cavalry and find nothing, you only make yourself look bad."

"I don't mind," Warner said.

"I do. It's my reputation too."

Keegan crossed the street and came over to them. "I'd like to help," he said. "I know my way around in there."

Warner pursed his lips for a few seconds and said to Tarver, "OK. The Father and I'll start in the hall, work our way towards you. You stay back in the church. If we flush out Sherk, he'll be coming your way."

"Right," Tarver said.

They all went across to the front door of the church. It was locked. The priest picked out a key, unlocked the door and pushed it open. They walked into the darkened lobby. There was a switch by the door, and when Keegan touched it, a series of fluorescent lights popped on overhead. The church remained dark.

"We'll start next door," Warner said.

Tarver said, "I'll stay right here. Behind the doors. I can see out; he won't see me. And if he comes my way, I'll get him."

He watched Warner and the priest go up the main aisle, cross in front of the altar, and walk into the sacristy.

SARAH SAW SHERK CHANGE AGAIN. He seemed to have seen something, something he had been waiting for. He was alert. If anything, his demeanour turned even colder.

Under his knife the carved doll had become a smooth wooden shaft. Now he suddenly lost interest in it. His knife hacked at the wood and sliced off two thick chunks, and he let the piece of wood slide out of his hand, hitting the floor. Sherk got up and came to her, looking directly at her for the first time since he had tightened the mask. He stood stooped over her, the arm with his knife hanging loosely at his side.

TARVER HEARD THE THUMP, something hard hitting the ceiling immediately overhead. Then silence.

He looked up. Fluorescent fixtures and acoustic tiles in a low ceiling. But he had heard something.

"Sarah?" he said out loud. And again, louder, "Sar-ah!"

THE NOISE ARRESTED SHERK. First low voices—he had ignored that—then somebody down below calling out.

He lifted his eyes from her. When he heard the name a second time, he looked down at the floor where the voice had come from, glanced at her, then back to the floor. He was torn, she thought. The knife twitched at his side, flicking small slices out of the air. Then silently he folded himself into the entryway and slithered out of sight down the passage.

The door closed; the catch clicked. Sarah realized what she had heard, what it meant. Somebody calling her name. Somebody looking for her. But how hard it would be for anyone to find her, anyone except Sherk. She would have to help herself, couldn't count on anyone else.

The nail clippers. In her right pocket. The outside straps were binding, but she managed to slide her hand up on her hip. She slid her fingers into the pocket. They touched smooth metal.

She withdrew her hand and brought the clippers out. They had a small lever that had to be swung round before they would work. She tried to manipulate it between her thigh and the close-fitting sleeping bag. She wriggled in the bag, momentarily created about an inch of space, and managed to twist the lever into place.

Now she held the clippers against the sleeping bag. She closed the crescent jaws. There was an audible snap as the clippers nipped a tiny hole in the nylon. She was elated and shoved the jaws against the fabric again. Again they grabbed nylon and bit. She repeated the action a dozen times, then felt with her fingers where she had been working. The cloth was ragged, chewed, but not yet completely ripped. She set to work once more.

TARVER WAITED ABOUT half a minute, wondering what he had heard, what he ought to do. Then he heard a second noise—like the quiet shutting of a door. He decided to investigate.

He went into the church, let the lobby door swing closed behind him, and looked around. He saw only one way up, a set of doors to his left that had to go to a staircase. He walked behind the last row of pews and went through the doors.

He found stairs, tried the light switch. Nothing. But there was a weak, hooded light set into the wall. He started to climb the steps. When he got to the first landing, he faced thick darkness. He drew his pistol, a nickel-plated, snub-nosed thirty-eight, and continued to climb.

At the top of the stairs he stumbled in the soupy blackness. He caught at the handrail, found his balance, and stepped across the landing, thinking that he had to run into a door.

He felt around and found a handle.

Behind him a voice said, "Dead meat if I get him."

SARAH COULD FEEL A TATTERED PATCH where she had been working. There was at least one hole big enough for the tip of her finger. She put it in and pulled at the fabric. It tore raggedly.

Now she could feel feathers, the down stuffing. She pawed through it until she could feel nylon again. The outside covering of the bag, she thought. After that the canvas of the shroud.

The tips of her fingers ached. But she could feel the rough canvas through the nylon, and that gave her strength. She took up the clippers and went back to work.

The canvas, though, was tougher than the second layer of nylon. She could nip it, but it wouldn't tear when she pulled it. She was losing strength in her arm. Will could do only so much.

Then she thought of Sherk coming back. She fitted the clipper's jaws over the ragged edge of canvas and set to work again.

WARNER FINISHED GOING through the hall in ten minutes. Now he and Father Keegan were down in the basement. The jets were roaring in the furnace, a hellish racket, and it made him think this would be the place. Dark and full of nooks.

They started at the corner furthest from the outside entrance and began to search. It was just a room full of fifty one-gallon cans of paint, a storage cupboard.

No good, Warner thought. People had checked these places two days ago. Had to be some place else, the kind of place nobody would think to look. *Think!*

THERE WAS MORE THAN ONE, Sherk thought. His mind was mostly a void now, but he could reason, the thoughts pinging and echoing through his head. He had heard at least two voices below the floor. So there was more than one, and one would come looking for the other. He could wait. What was in the attic for him would be there when he got back.

WARNER HAD COBWEBS IN HIS HAIR, and a smear of grease across his face, when he trudged up the stairs with Father Keegan. They came into the hall and turned down the corridor towards the church. They hadn't found Sherk. Yet Warner knew he was here somewhere. But not in the hall, not in the basement. Had to be in the church, hidden somewhere.

Unless Tarver had seen him. Warner wanted to start in the sacristy and work back, but he thought he ought to check in with Tarver first.

The priest followed as Warner left the sacristy and walked down the main aisle. Warner couldn't see the detective at the door where he was supposed to be. He looked in the lobby. There was nobody. Gone to the van, maybe. Only other place he could be was the second set of doors, in the corner to the right.

He motioned to them and asked, "Where do they go?"

"Up to the choir loft," Keegan said.

Could be he was there, Warner thought. It was worth checking. He slipped behind the back row of pews. The priest followed.

There was blood on the floor. A dark crimson puddle of it was leaking out from under the stairwell doors.

Warner automatically stopped, put out his left hand to halt the priest, reached with his right to the holster he wore at the small of his back and brought the pistol out.

He went forward, stepped over the puddle, grasped the door handle. Paused. Then whipped the door open suddenly and swung round it. He looked. There was only blood. A pool of it lay in the stairwell.

Warner put out his hand and said, "Torch." The priest put it in his palm, crowding in behind him, trying to see. Warner heard a gasp and then a guttural, hurried Hail Mary. He found his own lips moving to the words.

"Stay," he said. He picked his way round the puddle, then upstairs, gun in his right hand and torch in his left.

He got to the first landing and started up the next flight. Slowly. Flashing the torch around. At the top of the last step the light fell on a hand, fingers curled upwards. He went closer and saw a body. It was Tarver's, a bloody cut straight across his throat.

Warner tried to contain himself, tried to keep his voice steady as he leaned over the handrail and spoke to the priest below.

"Father," he said. "Listen. I want you to go to the rectory. Run. Dial nine one one. Tell the dispatcher an officer needs assistance at this address. Understand?"

"I understand." The priest sounded shaky.

"Hurry," Warner said.

He listened until he could no longer hear the priest's footsteps. He was out, Warner thought. Help was coming, and there would be no disgrace in going downstairs, waiting for it.

But he knew he couldn't do that. Tarver had come here for a reason; something had brought him up these stairs.

Warner steadied his gun hand, stepped over the body, and put his hand on one of the swinging doors, ready to push through it.

THERE WAS A HOLE in the canvas now. Sarah could get two fingers through it. Three fingers. Her entire right hand.

A few inches above the hole was the belt at her waist. Sarah turned her wrist and felt for the fastener. There. Piece of metal with teeth.

She pressed and prodded it as she had seen Sherk do. Suddenly it let go. The pressure disappeared round her middle. She could move her arms. The left was still tucked inside the cocoon, but she poked the right one through the hole. Unbuckled the cocoon halfway up her chest.

Now she had some movement. There were still straps at her shoulders and her feet, holding her to the hammock. She released the top one, freeing herself from the hips up. She was bending forward to release her ankles when she heard the shot.

WARNER PUT HIS LEFT HAND on the door and pushed it outwards. He took one step into the loft and was turning to look around when a thunderclap filled his head. He felt himself lifted, picked up by an unseen force, thrown against the door.

He fell, dazed. He knew that he had lost his gun. His first thought was to search for it, but when he tried, his right arm wouldn't work. It burned terribly at the shoulder. He looked, and saw a small neat hole in the upper front of his jacket. There was blood coming from it. The sight was so fascinating that at first he didn't notice Sherk coming towards him. When he looked up, Sherk was a couple of paces away, standing over him with a nickel-plated, snub-nosed revolver pointed at his head.

SARAH HURRIED TO FREE HERSELF. But when she bent at her waist to release her ankles, the buckle was beyond reach. She rocked forward to get closer, and the hammock spilled her out.

She fell with her legs still strapped to the foot of the hammock. Her left arm flew out as she tried to break her fall. It struck the lantern on the floor. She knocked it backwards, and heard the breaking of glass as it smashed into the corner, out of sight.

The light should go out, she thought. A lamp breaks, the light should go out. But it didn't. It grew brighter behind her. She was hamstrung, legs suspended above her head, tied into the hammock. By twisting, she was able to get on her side and look back.

The attic was on fire. In one corner the wooden floor shimmered red and orange, and flames were starting up the back wall, spilling across the floor in front of the entryway.

Her ankles were out of reach, but she could get to the mask on her face. She ripped it off and screamed.

"YOU!" SHERK EXCLAIMED.

"Talk to me," Warner said. In a couple of minutes there would be cops all over. If he could hold out that long. "Tell me what's bugging you. We can work things out."

"I don't think so," Sherk said. "I think it's time to die."

He thumbed the hammer back. Warner heard the click.

Sarah screamed.

Sherk swung his head towards the sound.

"What did you do to her?" Warner said.

"Didn't do nothing."

Another scream, long and sustained. Sherk looked alarmed.

"Help her," Warner said. "She's in trouble."

"No," Sherk said. He stared at Warner. The gun was waving, circling, and he used both hands to steady it.

"It's fire," Warner said. Almost softly. "Look."

Smoke was streaming out around the edges of the organ, patterned waves that grew thicker as Sherk watched.

Sarah screamed again.

"Get her," Warner said. "Go get your daughter."

"I'll kill you," Sherk said.

"Kill me, but don't wait," Warner shouted. "'She's your girl. She's Margaret. You love her, go get her."

Margaret? Sherk thought. Maybe. His head hurt and he was very tired, and there were things he was supposed to remember but couldn't. Margaret, he thought. Margaret was somewhere.

She screamed. A single long continuous scream. Sherk couldn't stand it. Had to make it stop. He dropped the gun.

SARAH WAS ON HER SIDE, legs tangled in the hammock, watching the fire advance. She could feel its heat, and she could see it creeping across the floor towards her. Overhead, the steep angle let it burn faster, and one side of the roof was aflame.

She wasn't going to scream any more. The air she sucked in was too hot. It singed her throat and her nostrils, so she was going to try not to breathe again.

A figure appeared in the flames at the entry, a gaunt, stooped figure. He walked through the fire without even picking up his feet. When he got to her, the bottoms of his overalls were burning.

For a second he stood above her, reeling. Then he bent over the foot of the hammock. Her feet fell out onto the floor, and she kicked free of the canvas. But there was fire all around, flames knee high on the floor that she would have to cross.

He reached down and picked her up. So strong, she thought. He carried her in his arms, his feet dragging through the flames, and he put her down in the passageway.

"Go," he shouted. The fire was deafening, and the smoke choked her. She looked across the flames at him, and he shouted again, "Go!"

WARNER WATCHED SHERK throw the gun down and run for the cupboard. He dragged himself to the revolver, picked it up, and stood. By leaning against the wall, he was able to make his way over to the door.

The wainscot door was open, and there was smoke coming out. He could hear sirens. Not much longer, he thought.

He looked in the opening and saw a girl coming towards him. She clambered out, and when she was clear, he planted himself in front of the opening. He held the pistol in his left hand, braced it with his right as best he could, and waited.

Then she touched him on the sleeve.

"He's not coming," she said. "You don't have to worry. He's not coming out."

EPILOGUE

Saturday, April 27

Two county detectives were on elbows and knees in a freshly ploughed farm field west of Annapolis. Before them was a shallow pit that had been dug between two of the dark furrows ploughed in preparation for spring planting. The detectives' hands were caked with dirt from sifting through the moist loam.

The coroner had left, and they were putting the rest of their finds in a bag, which they closed with a tie-wrap and marked with a numbered tag. So far they had come up with a hammer, a screwdriver, and a curved white clerical collar.

"I'VE BEEN DOING OK," Sarah Stannard said. "Better. I guess this is sort of a ten-thousand-mile checkup, huh?"

"Something like that," said Claire Johansen. "It's been a month since we talked, and I didn't want to lose touch."

Sarah had seen the psychologist almost daily at first, then less often. Almost from the start she had felt at ease with Claire. You could talk to this lady, she thought. Tell her anything.

"What's been happening in your life?" the psychologist said.

"I guess the big thing is that my grandparents are moving to Arizona. Scottsdale. They said we can stay in the house, but I think we're going to get another place."

"Staying in Annapolis?"

"For a while. It's OK with me. School is great. My marks are getting better, and they hung my drawings in the hall for Parents' Day."

"What else have you been up to?"

"Not much. We went out on the boat last Sunday. Howard—Mr. Warner—is trying to teach us to sail. He keeps saying that we have to learn before we sail to the Caribbean."

"Do you want to do that?"

"I think I'll let Mom do it. Anyway, it sounds like one of those things adults talk about and never get around to doing."

"How goes it with you and your mother?"

"Better. At first it was pretty hard. I couldn't go anywhere; she always had to be there. I told you that. But lately I can tell she's trying. I can feel her letting go. A little bit."

"What about all the rest? Do you think about it often?"

"You mean with Sherk and me? I think about it sometimes. But it doesn't get to me so much any more. Mostly I look back on it and think, Wow, that actually happened to me. It's hard to believe."

"And your nightmare? Does that bother you any more?"

"Once in a while. But like I said, it's not really a nightmare. It actually happened. I remember. I try not to think about it, but when I'm asleep, I can't control what I think about, so it comes to me. It's not something I'll ever forget."

SHE COULD STILL SEE IT. The attic was full of fire. Sherk had carried her through the sea of flames to the entryway of the passage. Then he had backed away into the middle of the floor.

"Go," he shouted at her. "Go."

She ducked into the passage. But before she crawled away, she turned back to see him.

Sherk was kneeling on the floor. His legs were aflame, and he was crying. When he saw her, he reached out, extending his hand to her over the inferno. As if he wanted to touch her one last time. Their eyes met and in his face was sorrow and pain, and a last look of perfect understanding that lingered until she turned and fled.

PHILLIP FINCH

In a Place Dark and Secret is Phillip Finch's eighth published book—an extraordinary record for a man still in his mid-thirties. What's even more extraordinary is that writing books is the *second* successful career of this energetic native of Washington DC.

As one might expect, Finch started early. "I knew I wanted to be a writer by the time I was ten," he says. While still in high school he worked part-time as a reporter for a major Washington daily paper, and during his college years he held down a full-time job as a sportswriter. So when he left college to work for a San Francisco newspaper, he was already a veteran journalist.

Finch's goals began to change, however, when he was about twenty-five. "I went through a premature career crisis. I had covered a lot of important sports events and done a lot of feature stories, but I realized I didn't want to continue doing that for the rest of my life. I wanted to branch out." He wrote *Haulin'*, a novel based on a magazine article he had written about long-haul truckers, and when he had finished it he left the newspaper world for good. Two nonfiction books and five more novels have followed, including *Texas Dawn*, which was also a Condensed Books selection.

Clearly, Finch loves what he does. "Being a writer has given me the time and opportunity to do things that might otherwise have been beyond me." In the course of researching his various books and articles, he has driven racing cars, climbed mountains, visited the Arctic, and flown across the Atlantic in a 1939-vintage DC-3. And with more books planned, more adventures are likely.

Phillip Finch now lives in Maryland, with his wife, a television newscaster. He is currently hard at work on book number nine, a novel set in the mountains of Montana.

Windmills
of the Gods

A CONDENSATION OF THE BOOK BY
SIDNEY SHELDON

ILLUSTRATED BY WALTER RANE

It all begins with an astounding call from the White House. One minute Mary Ashley, a smalltown political science professor, is chatting over dinner with her family; the next minute the President of the United States is asking her to become the new ambassador to Romania!

That call changes everything for Mary Ashley. She becomes an instant celebrity, hounded by the press, courted by politicians. Finally, Mary arrives in exotic Bucharest to take up her duties, confident, refreshingly candid—and dangerously innocent.

For watching her closely is an invisible network of powerful men, whose aim is to sabotage the President's bold new peace plan. They are about to set a diabolical trap. And the inexperienced young diplomat is the perfect bait.

We are all victims, Anselmo.
Our destinies are decided
by a cosmic roll of the dice,
the whims of the stars,
the vagrant breezes
of fortune that blow from
the windmills of the gods.

A FINAL DESTINY
H. L. Dietrich

Prologue

Perho, Finland

The meeting took place in a comfortable weatherproofed cabin in a remote wooded area two hundred miles from Helsinki, near the Russian border. The members of the Western branch of the Committee had arrived discreetly at irregular intervals. They came from eight different countries, but their visit had been quietly arranged by a senior minister in the Valtioneuvosto, the Finnish council of state, and there was no record of entry in their passports. Upon their arrival, armed guards escorted them into the cabin, and when the last visitor appeared, the cabin door was locked and the guards took up positions in the full-throated January winds, alert for any sign of intruders.

The members seated around the large rectangular table were men in powerful positions, high in the councils of their respective governments. They had met before in their official capacities, under less clandestine circumstances, and they trusted one another because they had no choice. For added security, each had been assigned a code name.

The meeting lasted almost five hours, and the discussion was heated. Finally the chairman decided the time had come to call for a vote. He rose, standing tall, and turned to the man seated at his right. "Sigurd?"

"Yes."

"Odin?"

"Yes."

"Balder?"

"We're moving too hastily. The danger—"

"Yes or no, please?"

"No."

"Freyr?"

"Yes."

"Sigmund?"

"*Nein*. If this should be exposed, our lives would be—"

"Thor?"

"Yes."

"Tyr?"

"Yes."

"I vote yes. The resolution is passed. I will so inform the Controller. We will observe the usual precautions and leave at twenty-minute intervals. Thank you, gentlemen."

Two hours and forty-five minutes later, the cabin was deserted. A crew of experts carrying paraffin moved in and set the cabin on fire, the red flames licked by the hungry winds.

When the fire brigade from Perho finally reached the scene, there was nothing left to see but the smouldering embers that outlined the cabin against the hissing snow.

The assistant to the fire chief approached the ashes, bent down, and sniffed. "Paraffin," he said. "Arson."

The fire chief was staring at the ruins, a puzzled expression on his face. "That's strange," he muttered.

"What?"

"I was hunting in these woods last week. There was no cabin."

Chapter One

Washington DC

Stanton Rogers was destined to be President of the United States. He was a charismatic politician, highly visible to an approving public and backed by powerful friends. Unfortunately for Rogers, his libido got in the way of his career.

It was not that Stanton Rogers fancied himself a Casanova. On the contrary, until that one fatal escapade, he had been a model husband. He was handsome and wealthy, and although he had had ample opportunity to cheat on his wife, he had never given another woman a thought.

There was a second, perhaps greater, irony: Stanton Rogers's wife, Elizabeth, was social, beautiful and intelligent, and the two of them shared a common interest in almost everything, whereas Barbara, the woman Rogers fell in love with, and eventually married after a much-headlined divorce, was five years older than Stanton, pleasant-faced rather than pretty, and seemed to have nothing in common with him. Stanton was athletic; Barbara hated all forms of exercise. Stanton was gregarious; Barbara preferred to be alone with her husband. The biggest surprise was the political differences. Stanton was a liberal, while Barbara was an archconservative.

Paul Ellison, Stanton's closest friend, had said, "You must be out of your mind, chum! You and Liz are the perfect married couple. Do you have any idea what a divorce is going to do to your career?"

Stanton Rogers had replied tightly, "Back off, Paul. Half the marriages in this country end in divorce. It won't do anything."

Rogers had proved to be a poor prophet. The newspapers kept the story of the bitterly fought divorce alive as long as they could, and when the furore died down, Stanton Rogers's powerful political friends had found a new white knight to champion: Paul Ellison.

Ellison was a sound choice. While he had neither Stanton Rogers's good looks nor his charisma, he was intelligent, likable, and had the right background. He was short in stature, with regular, even features and candid blue eyes. He had been happily married for ten years to the daughter of a steel magnate.

Stanton Rogers and Paul Ellison had grown up together in New York. Their families had had adjoining summer homes in Southampton. They were in the same class, first at Yale and later at Harvard Law School. Paul Ellison did well, but it was Stanton Rogers who was the star pupil. Once out of law school, Stanton Rogers's political star began rising meteorically, and if he was the comet, Paul Ellison was the tail.

The divorce changed everything. It was now Stanton Rogers who became the appendage to Paul Ellison. The trail leading to the presidency took almost fifteen years. First Ellison became a highly popular, articulate senator. He fought against waste in government and Washington bureaucracy. He believed in international détente. When he was finally elected President of the United States, his first appointment was Stanton Rogers as presidential foreign affairs adviser.

MARSHALL MCLUHAN'S THEORY that television would turn the world into a global village had become a reality. The inauguration of the forty-second President of the United States was carried by satellite to more than one hundred and ninety countries.

In The Black Rooster, a Washington DC hangout for newsmen, Ben Cohn, a veteran political reporter of the Washington *Post*, was seated at a table with four colleagues, watching the inauguration on the television set over the bar.

The camera panned to show the massive crowds gathered on Pennsylvania Avenue, huddled inside their overcoats against the bitter January wind. Jason Merlin, Chief Justice of the United States Supreme Court, finished the swearing-in oath, and the new President shook his hand and stepped up to the microphone.

"Look at those idiots standing out there freezing their tails off," Ben Cohn commented. "Do you know why they aren't home like normal human beings, watching it on television?"

"Why?" asked one of the other reporters.

"Because a man is making history, my friends. One day all those people are going to tell their grandchildren that they were there the day Paul Ellison was sworn in."

"You're a cynic, Cohn."

"And proud of it. Every politician in the world comes out of the same cookie cutter. They're all in it for what they can get out of it."

The truth was that Ben Cohn was not as cynical as he sounded. He had covered Paul Ellison's career from the beginning, and while it was true that he had not been impressed at first, as Ellison moved up the political ladder Ben Cohn had begun to change his opinion. This politician was nobody's yes-man. He was an oak in a forest of willows.

Outside, the sky exploded into icy sheets of rain. Ben Cohn hoped the weather was not an omen for the four years that lay ahead. He turned his attention back to the television set and President Ellison's speech.

"I speak today not only to our allies, but to those countries in the Soviet camp. I say to them now, as we prepare to move into the twenty-first century, that there is no longer any room for confrontation and that we must learn to make the phrase 'one world' become a reality. Vast chasms lie between us, but the first priority of this administration will be to build unshakeable bridges across those chasms."

His words rang out with a deep, heartfelt sincerity. He means it, Ben Cohn thought. I hope no one assassinates the guy.

IN JUNCTION CITY, KANSAS, it was a potbellied stove kind of day, bleak and raw and snowing hard. Mary Ashley cautiously steered her old station wagon towards the centre of the highway, where the snowploughs had been at work. The storm was going to make her late for the class she was teaching.

From the car radio came the President's voice: ". . . because I believe that there is no problem that cannot be solved by genuine goodwill on both sides, the concrete wall around East Berlin and the iron curtain that surrounds the other Soviet satellite countries must come down."

Mary Ashley thought, I'm glad I voted for him. Paul Ellison is going to make a great President.

IN BUCHAREST, THE CAPITAL OF ROMANIA, it was evening. President Alexandros Ionescu sat in his office, surrounded by half a dozen aides, listening to the American President on a shortwave radio.

"As you are aware, three years ago, upon the death of Romania's President, Nicolae Ceausescu, Romania broke off diplomatic relations with the United States I want to inform you now that we have approached the government of Romania, and its President, Alexandros Ionescu, has agreed to reestablish diplomatic relations with our country.

"One of our first official acts will be to send an ambassador to Romania. And that is merely the beginning. I have no intention of stopping there. Albania broke off all diplomatic relations with the United States in 1946. I intend to reestablish those ties. In addition, I intend to strengthen our diplomatic relations with Bulgaria, with Czechoslovakia and with East Germany.

"Sending our ambassador to Romania is the beginning of a worldwide people-to-people movement. Let us never forget that all mankind shares a common origin, common problems, and a common ultimate fate. Let us remember that the problems we share are greater than the problems that divide us, and that what divides us is of our own making."

Over the shortwave radio came the sound of cheers and applause.

IN A HEAVILY GUARDED VILLA in Neuilly, a suburb of Paris, the Romanian revolutionary leader, Marin Groza, was watching the President on Chaîne 2 television.

"I think our time has come, Lev. He really means it," said Marin Groza thoughtfully.

Lev Pasternak, his security chief, replied, "Won't this help Ionescu?"

Marin Groza shook his head. "Ionescu is a tyrant, so in the end nothing will help him. But I must be careful with my timing. I failed when I tried to overthrow Ceausescu. I must not fail again."

PETE CONNORS HAD DOWNED almost a fifth of Scotch while watching the inaugural speech. He poured himself another glassful and turned back to the image on the television set. "You filthy Communist," he yelled at the screen. "This is my country, and the CIA's not gonna let you give it away. We're gonna stop you, Ellison. You bet your bottom dollar on it."

Chapter Two

Paul Ellison said, "I'm going to need your help, old friend."

"You'll get it," Stanton Rogers replied quietly.

It was their first meeting together in the Oval Office, and President

Ellison was uncomfortable. If Stanton hadn't made that one mistake, he thought, he would be sitting at this desk instead of me.

As though reading his mind, Stanton Rogers said, "I have a confession to make. The day you were nominated for the presidency, I was bitterly jealous, Paul. It was *my* dream, and you were living it. But I came to realize that if I couldn't sit in that chair, there was no one else I would want there but you."

Paul Ellison smiled at his friend, and pressed the button on his desk. Seconds later a white-jacketed steward came into the room.

"Yes, Mr. President?"

Paul Ellison turned to Rogers. "Coffee?"

"Sounds good."

"Want anything with it?"

"No, thanks. Barbara wants me to watch my waistline."

The President nodded to Henry, the steward, and he quietly left the room.

Barbara. She had surprised everyone. The gossip around Washington has been that the marriage would not last out the first year. But that was almost fifteen years ago now, and it was a success. Stanton Rogers had built up a prestigious law practice in Washington, and Barbara had earned the reputation of being a gracious hostess.

Paul Ellison rose and began to pace. "My people-to-people speech seems to have caused quite an uproar. I suppose you've seen all the newspapers."

"Yes," said Stanton Rogers. "And quite candidly, Paul, you're scaring the pants off a lot of people. The armed forces are against your plan, and some powerful movers and shakers would like to see it fail."

Ellison sat down and faced his friend. "It's not going to fail."

The steward appeared with the coffee. "Can I get you something else, Mr. President?"

"No. That's it, Henry. Thank you."

The President waited until the steward had gone. "I want to talk to you about finding the right ambassador to Romania."

"Right."

"I don't have to tell you how important this is. I want you to move on it as quickly as possible."

Stanton Rogers took a sip of his coffee and rose to his feet. "I'll get State on it right away."

IN THE LITTLE SUBURB of Neuilly, it was two am. Marin Groza's villa lay in darkness, the moon nested in a thick layer of storm clouds. The streets were hushed at this hour, as a black-clad figure moved noiselessly through the trees towards the brick wall that surrounded the villa. Over one shoulder he carried a rope and a blanket, and in his arms he cradled a dart gun and an Uzi submachine gun with a silencer. When he reached the wall, he stopped and listened. He waited, motionless, for five minutes. Finally, satisfied, he uncoiled the nylon rope and tossed the scaling hook attached to the end of it upwards until it caught on the far edge of the wall. Swiftly the man began to climb. When he reached the top of the wall, he flung the blanket across it to protect himself against the poison-tipped metal spikes embedded on top. He stopped again to listen. He reversed the hook, shifting the rope to the inside of the wall, and slid down into the grounds. He checked the *balisong* at his waist, the deadly Filipino folding knife that could be flicked open or closed with one hand.

The attack dogs would be next. The intruder crouched there, waiting for them to pick up his scent. There were two Dobermans, trained to kill. But they were only the first obstacle. The grounds and the villa were filled with electronic devices and continuously monitored by television cameras. All mail and packages were received at the gatehouse and opened there by the guards. The doors of the villa were bombproof. The villa had its own water supply, and Marin Groza had a food taster. The villa was impregnable. Supposedly. The figure in black was here this night to prove that it was not.

He heard the sounds of the dogs rushing at him before he saw them. They came flying out of the darkness, charging at his throat. He aimed the dart gun and shot the one on his left first, then the one on his right, dodging out of the way of their hurtling bodies. And then there was only stillness.

The intruder knew where the sonic traps were buried in the ground, and he skirted them. He silently glided through the areas of the grounds that the television cameras did not cover, and in less than two minutes after he had gone over the wall, he was at the back door of the villa.

As he reached for the handle of the door he was caught in the sudden glare of floodlights. A voice called out, "Freeze! Drop your gun and raise your hands."

The figure in black carefully dropped his gun and looked up. There were half a dozen men spread out on the roof, with a variety of weapons pointed at him.

The man in black growled, "What the devil took you so long? I never should have gotten this far."

"You didn't," the head guard informed him. "We started tracking you before you got over the wall."

Lev Pasternak was not mollified. "Then you should have stopped me sooner. I could have been on a suicide mission with a load of grenades. I want a meeting of the entire staff tomorrow morning, eight o'clock sharp. The dogs have been stunned. Have someone keep an eye on them until they wake up."

Lev Pasternak prided himself on being the best security guard in the world. He had been a pilot in the Israeli Six-Day War, and after the war had become a top agent in Mossad, one of Israel's secret services.

He would never forget the morning, two years earlier, when his colonel called him into his office and said, "Lev, Marin Groza wants to borrow you for a few weeks."

Mossad had a complete file on the Romanian dissident. Groza had been the leader of the popular Romanian movement to depose Alexandros Ionescu, and was about to stage a coup when he was betrayed by one of his men. More than two dozen underground fighters had been executed, and Groza had barely escaped with his life. France had given him sanctuary. Then Ionescu had put a price on his head. So far half a dozen attempts to assassinate Groza had failed, but he had been wounded in the most recent attack.

"What does he want with me?" Pasternak had asked. "He has government protection."

"Not good enough. He needs someone to set up a foolproof security system. He came to us. I recommended you."

"I'd have to go to France?"

"Only for a few weeks, Lev. Our information is that he has enough popular support in Romania to knock over Ionescu. When the timing is right, he'll make his move. Meanwhile, we have to keep the man alive."

Lev Pasternak thought about it. "A few weeks, you said?"

"That's all."

The colonel had been wrong about the time, but he had been right about Marin Groza. He was a white-haired, fragile-looking man whose face was etched with sorrow. He had deep black eyes, and when he spoke, they blazed with passion.

"I don't give a damn whether I live or die," he told Lev at their first meeting. "We're all going to die. It's the *when* that I'm concerned about. I have to stay alive for another year or two."

Lev Pasternak went to work on the security system at the villa in Neuilly. He used some of his own men, and all outsiders were checked out thoroughly. Every single piece of equipment was state-of-the-art.

Pasternak saw the Romanian rebel leader every day, and the more time he spent with him, the more he came to admire him. When Marin Groza asked him to stay on, Pasternak agreed, saying, "Until you're ready to make your move."

At irregular intervals, Pasternak staged surprise attacks on the villa, testing its security. Now he thought, Some of the guards are getting careless. I'll have to replace them.

402

He walked through the hallways, checking the heat sensors, the electronic warning systems, and the infrared beams at the sill of each door. As he reached Groza's bedroom he heard a loud crack, and a moment later Groza began screaming in agony.

Lev Pasternak passed Marin Groza's room and kept walking.

THE MONDAY MORNING executive staff meeting was under way in the seventh-floor conference room at CIA headquarters in Langley, Virginia. Seated round the large oak table were Ned Tillingast, Director of the CIA; General Oliver Brooks, Army Chief of Staff; Secretary of State Floyd Baker; Pete Connors, Chief of Counterintelligence; and Stanton Rogers.

Ned Tillingast, the CIA director, was in his sixties, a cold, taciturn man, burdened with maleficent secrets. There is a light branch and a dark branch of the CIA. The dark branch handles clandestine operations, and for the past seven years Tillingast had been in charge of that section.

General Oliver Brooks was a West Point soldier who conducted his personal and professional life by the book. He was a company man, and the company he worked for was the United States army.

Floyd Baker, the Secretary of State, was of southern vintage, silver-haired, distinguished-looking, with an old-fashioned gallantry. He owned a chain of influential newspapers around the country, and was reputed to be enormously wealthy.

Pete Connors was black Irish, a stubborn bulldog of a man, hard-drinking and fearless. He faced compulsory retirement in August. Connors was chief of the counterintelligence staff, the most secret, highly compartmentalized branch of the CIA. He had worked his way up through the various intelligence divisions, and had been around in the good old days when CIA agents were the golden boys. In fact, Pete Connors had been a golden boy himself. As far as he was concerned, no sacrifice was too great to make for his country.

Now, in the middle of the meeting, his face was red with anger. "This idiotic people-to-people programme has to be stopped. We can't allow the President to give the country away. We—"

Floyd Baker interrupted. "The President has been in office less than a week. We're all here to carry out his policies and—"

"He sprang his plan on us. We didn't have a chance to get together a rebuttal."

Ned Tillingast turned to Stanton Rogers. "Connors has a point. The President is actually planning to *invite* the Communist countries to send their spies here posing as attachés, chauffeurs, secretaries, maids. We're spending billions to guard the back door, and the President wants to throw open the front door."

403

General Brooks nodded agreement. "I wasn't consulted, either. In my opinion, the President's plan could destroy this country."

Stanton Rogers said, "Gentlemen, some of us may disagree with the President, but let's not forget that the people voted for Paul Ellison. We have to support him in every way we can." His words were followed by a reluctant silence. "All right, then. The President wants an update on Romania. What's the situation with President Ionescu?"

"Ionescu's riding high in the saddle," Ned Tillingast replied. "Once he'd got rid of Ceausescu, all of Ceausescu's allies were assassinated, jailed or exiled. Since he seized power, Ionescu's been bleeding the country dry. The people hate his guts."

"What about the prospects for a revolution?"

Tillingast said, "Ah. That's rather interesting. Do you remember a couple of years back when Marin Groza almost toppled the Ionescu government?"

"Yes. Groza got out of the country by the skin of his teeth."

"With our help. Our information is that there's a popular ground swell to bring him back. Groza would be good for Romania—and good for us. We're watching the situation."

Stanton Rogers turned to the Secretary of State. "Do you have that list of candidates for the Romanian post?"

Floyd Baker took an envelope from a leather attaché case and handed it to Rogers. "These are our top prospects. They're all career diplomats. Naturally," he added, "the State Department favours a career diplomat, rather than a political appointee. Someone who's been trained for this kind of job. Romania is an extremely sensitive post."

"I agree." Stanton Rogers rose to his feet. "I'll discuss these names with the President and get back to you."

As the others got up to leave, Ned Tillingast said, "Stay here, Pete. I want to talk to you." When they were alone, Tillingast said, "You came on pretty strong, Pete."

"But I'm right," Pete Connors said stubbornly. "The President is trying to sell out the country. What are we supposed to do?"

"Keep your mouth shut, Pete. And be careful. Very careful."

Ned Tillingast had been around longer than Pete Connors. He had been a member of Wild Bill Donovan's OSS before it became the CIA. He too hated what the bleeding hearts in Congress were doing to the organization he loved. It had been Tillingast who had recruited Pete Connors out of college, and Connors had turned out to be one of the best. But in the last few years, Connors had become a cowboy—a little too independent, a little too quick on the trigger. Dangerous.

"Pete—have you heard anything about an underground organization calling itself Patriots for Freedom?" Tillingast asked.

Connors frowned. "No. Can't say that I have. Who are they?"

"All I have is smoke. See if you can get a lead on them."

"Will do."

AN HOUR LATER Pete Connors was making a phone call from a public booth. "I have a message for Odin," he said.

"This is Odin," General Oliver Brooks replied.

PAUL ELLISON THREW the list of candidates down on his desk. "They're dinosaurs," he snapped. "Every one of them."

"Mr. President," Rogers protested, "these people are all experienced career diplomats."

"And hidebound by State Department tradition. You remember how we lost Romania three years ago? Our *experienced* career diplomat in Bucharest screwed up, and we were out in the cold. The pinstripe boys worry me."

"But if you put an amateur in there, someone with no experience, you're taking a big risk."

"Maybe we need someone with a different kind of experience. Romania is going to be a test case, Stan." He hesitated. "I'm not kidding myself. I know that there are a lot of powerful people who don't want to see this work. If it fails, I'm going to get cut off at the knees. I don't intend for that to happen."

"I can check out some of our political appointees who—"

President Ellison shook his head. "Same problem. I want someone with a completely fresh point of view. Someone who can thaw the ice. The opposite of the ugly American."

Stan Rogers was studying the President, puzzled. "Mr. President—I get the impression that you already have someone in mind. Do you?"

"As a matter of fact," Paul Ellison said slowly, "I have."

"Who is he?"

"She. Did you happen to see the article in *Foreign Affairs* magazine called 'Détente Now'?"

"Yes."

"What did you think of it?"

"I thought it was interesting. The author believes that we're in a position to try to seduce the Communist countries into coming into our camp by offering them economic and—" He broke off. "It was a lot like your inaugural speech."

"Only it was written six months earlier. She's published brilliant articles in *Commentary* and *Public Affairs*. Last year I read a book of hers on Eastern European politics, and I must admit, it helped clarify some of my ideas."

"OK. So she agrees with your theories. That's no reason—"

"Stan—she went further than my theory. She outlined a detailed plan that's brilliant. She wants to take the four major world economic pacts and combine them."

"How can we—"

"It would take time, but it could be done. Look. You know that in 1949 the Eastern-bloc countries formed a pact for mutual economic assistance, called COMECON, and in 1958 the other European countries formed the EEC—the Common Market."

"Right."

"We have the Organization for Economic Cooperation and Development, which includes the United States, some Western-bloc countries and Yugoslavia. And don't forget that the Third World countries have formed a nonaligned movement of their own."

The President's voice was charged with excitement. "Think of the possibilities. If we could combine these plans and form one big marketplace—it could be awesome! It would mean *real* world trade. And it could bring peace."

Stanton Rogers said cautiously, "It's an interesting idea, but you don't know anything about this woman."

"Except that she's extremely bright and that we're on the same wavelength. Her name is Mary Ashley. I want you to find out everything you can about her."

TWO DAYS LATER President Ellison and Stanton Rogers breakfasted together.

"I got the information you asked for." Rogers pulled a paper from his pocket. "Mary Elizabeth Ashley, twenty-seven Old Milford Road, Junction City, Kansas. Age, almost thirty-five. Married to Dr. Edward Ashley. Two children: Beth, twelve, and Tim, ten. Assistant professor, East European Political Science, Kansas State University. Grandfather born in Romania." He looked up thoughtfully. "I must admit she sounds interesting."

"I think so, too. I'd like to have a full security check run on her."

"I'll see that it's done."

"I DISAGREE, PROFESSOR ASHLEY," said Barry Dylan, one of the twelve graduate students in Mary Ashley's political science seminar. "Alexandros Ionescu is worse than Ceausescu ever was."

· "Can you back up that statement?" Mary Ashley asked.

The waiting lists to get into Mary Ashley's classes were longer than any other professor's at Kansas State University. She was a superb teacher, with an easy sense of humour and a warmth that made being around her a pleasure. She had an oval face that changed from interesting to beautiful, depending on her mood. She had the high cheekbones of a model and almond-shaped hazel eyes. Her hair was dark and thick. She had a figure that made her female students envious, and the males fantasize, yet she was unaware of how beautiful she was.

"Well," said Barry, "when Ionescu took over Romania, he cracked down on all the pro-Groza elements and reestablished a hard-line, pro-Soviet position. Even Ceausescu wasn't that bad."

Another student spoke up. "Then why is President Ellison so anxious to establish diplomatic relations with him?"

"Because we want to woo him into the Western orbit. Also—"

The bell sounded. The time was up.

Mary said, "On Monday we'll discuss the possible consequences of President Ellison's plan to penetrate the Eastern bloc. Have a good weekend."

Mary Ashley loved the give-and-take of the graduate seminars. Foreign names and places became real, and historical events took on flesh and blood. This was her fifth year on the faculty at Kansas State, and teaching still excited her. She especially enjoyed teaching about Romania, because her grandfather had instilled in her a deep curiosity about his native land. She taught five political science classes in addition to the graduate seminars, and each of them dealt with the Soviet Union and its satellite countries. At times she felt like a fraud. I've never even been to any of these countries I teach about, she thought. I've never even been outside the United States.

Mary had planned a trip abroad after she received her master's degree, but that summer she met Edward Ashley, and the European trip had turned into a three-day honeymoon at Waterville, fifty-five miles from Junction City, where Edward was taking care of a critical heart patient.

"We really must travel next year," Mary said to Edward shortly after they were married. "I'm dying to see places like Rome and Paris—and Romania."

"So am I. It's a date. Next summer."

But that following summer Beth was born, and Edward was caught up in his work at the Geary Community Hospital. Two years later Tim was born. Mary had got her PhD and gone back to teaching at Kansas State University, and somehow the years had melted away. Except for brief trips to Chicago, Atlanta and Denver, Mary had never been out of the state of Kansas.

One day, she promised herself. One day . . .

Mary gathered her notes together, put on her coat and a scarf, and headed out to where she had parked her car. As she passed Denison Hall a stranger with a Nikon camera aimed it at the building and pressed the shutter. Mary was in the foreground of the picture. One hour later the photograph was on its way to Washington DC.

EVERY TOWN HAS ITS OWN distinctive rhythm, a life pulse that springs from the people and the land. Junction City, in Geary County, is a farm community, one hundred and thirty miles west of Kansas City. It has a population of 20,381, and prides itself on being the geographical centre of the continental United States. The downtown shopping area consists of a series of scattered stores, fast-food chains and filling stations—the types of establishment that are duplicated in hundreds of small towns across the United States. But the residents of Junction City love it for its bucolic peace and tranquillity. On weekdays, at least. At weekends, Junction City becomes the rest-and-recreation centre for the soldiers at nearby Fort Riley.

MARY ASHLEY STOPPED to shop for dinner at Dillon's Market and then headed home. When she walked through the door, Tim and Beth ran to greet her.

"Guess what?" Tim said. "We're going to have our pictures in the paper!"

"Help me put away the groceries," Mary said. "What paper?"

"The man didn't say, but he said we'd hear from him."

Mary stopped and turned to look at her son. "Did he say why?"

"No," Tim said, "but he sure had a nifty Nikon."

ON SUNDAY, MARY CELEBRATED—although that was not the word that sprang to her mind—her thirty-fifth birthday. Edward had arranged a surprise party for her at the country club. Their neighbours, Florence and Douglas Schiffer, and four other couples, were waiting for her. Edward was as delighted as a small child at the look of amazement on Mary's face when she walked into the club and saw the festive table and the happy birthday sign. After dinner, as Mary blew out the candles on her birthday cake, she looked across at Edward and thought, How lucky can a lady be?

On Monday morning she woke with a hangover. There had been a lot of champagne toasts the night before, and she was not used to drinking alcohol. She eased her way out of bed and went down to the kitchen, where she set about preparing breakfast for the children.

Beth, Mary's twelve-year-old daughter, walked into the room carrying an armful of books.

Mary put a box of cereal on the table. "I bought a new cereal for you. You're going to like it."

408

Beth sat down at the kitchen table and studied the label on the cereal box. "I can't eat this. You're trying to kill me."

"Don't put any ideas in my head," her mother cautioned.

Tim, Mary's ten-year-old, ran into the kitchen. He slid into a chair at the table and said, "I'll have bacon and eggs."

"Whatever happened to 'good morning'?" Mary asked.

"Good morning. I'll have bacon and eggs. Can I go to the skating rink after school, Mom?"

"You're to come right home and study. Mrs. Reynolds called me. You're failing maths. How do you think it looks for a college professor to have a son who's failing maths?"

"It looks OK. You don't teach maths."

They talk about the terrible twos, Mary thought grimly. What about the terrible tens? She had packed lunch for each of them, but she was concerned about Beth, who was on some kind of crazy new diet.

"Please, Beth, eat all of your lunch today."

"If it has no artificial preservatives. I'm not going to let the greed of the food industry ruin my health."

Whatever happened to the good old days of junk food? Mary wondered.

Tim plucked a loose paper from one of Beth's notebooks. "Look at this!" he yelled. "'Dear Beth, let's sit together during study period. I thought of you all day yesterday and—'"

"Give that back to me!" Beth screamed. "That's mine!"

"Hey! It's signed 'Virgil'. I thought you were in love with Arnold."

Beth snatched the note away from him. "What would you know about love? You're a child."

At that moment they heard the horn of the school bus outside. Tim and Beth started towards the door.

"Wait! You haven't eaten your breakfast," Mary said. She followed them out into the hall.

"No time, Mother. Got to go."

"Bye, Mom."

And they were gone. Mary felt drained.

She looked up as Edward came down the stairs.

"Morning, darling," he said.

"Sweetheart—would you do me a favour?"

"Sure, beautiful." He gave her a kiss. "Anything."

"I want to sell the children."

"Who'd buy them?"

"Strangers. They've reached the age where I can't do anything right. Beth has become a health-food freak, and your son is turning into a world-class dunce."

Edward said thoughtfully, "Maybe they're not our kids."

"I hope not. I'm making oatmeal for you."

"Sorry, darling. No time. I'm due in surgery in half an hour."

Mary looked at Edward and felt a glow. Even after all these years, she thought, he's still the most attractive man I've ever known.

"OK, let's keep the kids. I like their father a lot."

"To tell you the truth, I'm rather fond of their mother." He took her in his arms and held her close.

MARY AND EDWARD left the house together, bowing their heads against the relentless wind. Edward strapped himself into his Ford Granada and watched Mary as she got behind the wheel of the station wagon.

"Drive carefully, sweetheart," he called.

"You too, darling." She blew him a kiss, and the two cars drove away from the house, Edward heading towards the hospital and Mary towards the university.

Two men parked half a block from the Ashley house waited until the vehicles were out of sight. "Let's go." They drove up to the house next door to the Ashleys'. Rex Olds, the driver, sat in the car while his companion walked up to the front door and rang the bell. The door was opened by an attractive brunette in her middle thirties.

"Mrs. Douglas Schiffer?"

"Yes?"

The man reached into his jacket pocket and pulled out an identification card. "My name is Donald Zamlock. I'm with the Security Agency of the State Department." He smiled. "I wanted to ask you a few questions about your neighbour, Mrs. Ashley."

She looked at him with concern. "Mary? Why would you be asking about her?"

"May I come in?"

"Yes." Florence Schiffer led him into the living room.

"I'll only take a few minutes." He smiled reassuringly. "This is just a routine check. She's not suspected of any wrongdoing."

"I should hope not," Florence Schiffer said indignantly. "Mary Ashley is one of the nicest persons you'll ever meet." She added, "*Have* you met her?"

"No, ma'am. This visit is confidential, and I would appreciate it if you kept it that way. How long have you known Mrs. Ashley?"

"About thirteen years. Since the day she moved in next door."

"Would you say that you know Mrs. Ashley well?"

"Of course I would. Mary's my closest friend. What—?"

"Mrs. Schiffer, would you say, in your opinion, Mrs. Ashley is an emotionally stable person?"

410

"Of course she is."

"Mary Ashley's grandfather was born in Romania. Have you ever heard her discuss Romania?"

"Oh, once in a while she'll tell stories her grandfather told her about the old country."

"One last question. Have you ever heard Mrs Ashley, or Dr. Ashley, say anything against the United States government?"

"Absolutely not!"

"Then in your estimation, they're both loyal Americans?"

"You bet they are. Would you mind telling me—?"

The man rose. "I want to thank you for your time, Mrs. Schiffer. And I'd like to impress upon you again that this matter is highly confidential. I would appreciate it if you didn't discuss it with anyone."

A moment later he was out of the door. Florence Schiffer stood there staring after him. "I don't believe this whole conversation took place," she said aloud.

BRIDGE WITH THEIR NEIGHBOURS, the Schiffers, was a Monday-night ritual for Mary and Edward Ashley. The fact that Douglas Schiffer was a doctor and worked with Edward at the hospital made them even closer. Douglas Schiffer was normally a pleasant, easygoing man, but at the moment there was a grim expression on his face. They were in the middle of the game, and the Schiffers were a thousand points behind. For the fourth time that evening, Florence Schiffer had revoked.

"Florence!" Douglas exploded. "Which side are you on?"

"I'm sorry," she said nervously.

"Is anything bothering you?" Edward Ashley asked Florence.

"I can't tell you." They all looked at her in surprise.

"What does *that* mean?" her husband asked.

Florence Schiffer took a deep breath. "Mary—it's about you."

"What about me?"

"I'm not supposed to tell. I promised."

"You promised who?" Edward asked.

"A federal agent from Washington. He was at the house this morning asking me all kinds of questions about Mary."

"What kinds of questions?" Edward demanded.

"Oh, you know. Was she a loyal American? Was she stable?"

"Wait," Mary said excitedly. "I think I know. I'm up for tenure. The university does some sensitive government research on campus, so I suppose they check everyone thoroughly."

"Well, thank God that's all it is." Florence Schiffer breathed a sigh of relief. "I thought they were going to lock you up."

"I hope they do," Mary smiled. "At Kansas State."

Abbeywood, England

"WE ARE MEETING under the usual rules," the chairman announced. "No records will be kept, this meeting will never be discussed, and we will refer to one another by the code names we have been assigned."

There were eight men inside the library of the fifteenth-century Claymore Castle. Two armed men kept vigil outside, while a third man guarded the door to the library.

The chairman continued. "The Controller has received some disturbing information. Marin Groza is preparing a coup against Alexandros Ionescu. A group of senior army officers in Romania has decided to back Groza. This time he could very well be successful."

Odin spoke up. "How would that affect our plan?"

"It could destroy it. It would open too many bridges to the West."

Freyr said, "Then we must prevent it from happening."

Balder asked, "How?"

"We assassinate Groza," the chairman replied.

"Impossible. All Ionescu's attempts have failed. His villa is impregnable. Anyway, no one in this room can afford to be involved in an assassination attempt."

"We wouldn't be directly involved," the chairman said. "The Controller has discovered a confidential dossier that concerns an international terrorist who's for hire. He's called Angel."

"Never heard of him," Sigmund said.

"Exactly. His credentials are most impressive. According to the Controller's file, Angel was involved in the Sikh Khalistan assassination in India. He helped the Khmer Rouge in Cambodia. He's masterminded the assassinations of half a dozen army officers in Israel and the Israelis have offered a million-dollar reward for him, dead or alive. He's expensive. If he agrees to take the contract, it will cost us two million dollars."

"How do we get to this Angel person?" Sigmund asked.

"All his contacts are handled through his mistress, Neusa Muñez. Angel has set her up in an apartment in Buenos Aires."

Thor said, "Who would get in touch with her for us?"

The chairman replied, "The Controller has suggested a man named Harry Lantz. He was thrown out of the CIA for setting up his own drug business in Vietnam. While he was with the CIA, he did a tour in South America, so he knows the territory. He'd be a perfect go-between." He paused. "I suggest we take a vote. All those in favour of hiring Angel, please raise your hands."

Eight well-manicured hands went into the air.

"Then it's settled." The chairman rose. "The meeting is adjourned. Please observe the usual precautions as you leave."

412

Chapter Three

In his hotel room in New York, Harry Lantz was woken in the middle of the night by the ringing of the telephone.

Who the devil knows I'm here? he wondered. He looked blearily at the bedside clock, then snatched up the phone. "It's four o'clock in the morning! Who the—"

A soft voice at the other end of the line began speaking, and Lantz sat upright in bed, his heart beginning to pound. "Yes, sir." He listened for a long time. Finally he said, "Yes, sir. I understand. I'll be on the first plane to Buenos Aires. Thank you, sir."

He replaced the receiver and lit a cigarette. His hands were trembling. The man he had just spoken to was one of the most powerful men in the world, and was going to pay him fifty thousand dollars to deliver a message. It would be fun going back to Argentina. Harry Lantz loved South American women.

THE 747 ARRIVED at Ezeiza Airport in Buenos Aires at five pm the following afternoon. Harry Lantz felt a surge of excitement as he stepped out of the plane, but the blast of hot air startled him for a moment. Of course, he realized, it's summer here.

Yes, it was good to be back. Siesta was over, and the streets were crowded with people. When the taxi arrived at the Hotel El Conquistador, in the heart of the fashionable Barrio Norte sector, Lantz paid the driver with a million-peso note.

"Keep the change," he said. Their money was a joke. I'll take care of my business with this Neusa broad tomorrow, Harry decided, and stay around a few days and enjoy myself.

IT WAS MORE THAN TWO WEEKS before Harry was able to track down Neusa Muñez. His search began with the city telephone directories, but none of them had a listing for a Neusa Muñez.

Where the hell is she? Lantz wondered.

He took to the streets, looking up old contacts.

He walked into La Biela, and the bartender cried out, "Señor Lantz! *Por dios*—I heard you were dead."

"I was, Antonio. But I missed you so much, I came back."

"What are you doing in Buenos Aires?"

Lantz let his voice grow pensive. "I came here to find an old girlfriend. Her name is Neusa Muñez."

The bartender scratched his head. "Never heard of her."

The answer was the same everywhere. No one had ever heard of

413

Neusa Muñez. Harry Lantz began to feel he might be on a wild-goose chase.

It was at The Pilar, a small bar in the *barrios* of Floresta, that his luck suddenly changed. It was a Friday night, and the bar was filled with working men. It took Lantz ten minutes to get the bartender's attention. Before he was halfway through his prepared speech, the bartender said, "Neusa Muñez? *Sí.* I know her. If she wishes to talk to you, she will come here *mañana*, about midnight."

The following evening Harry Lantz returned to The Pilar at eleven o'clock, and watched the bar gradually fill up. As midnight approached, he found himself getting more and more nervous. If she doesn't show up, he thought, I can kiss the fifty grand goodbye.

He wondered what she looked like. She had to be a stunner. He was authorized to offer her boyfriend, Angel, a cool two million dollars to assassinate someone, so Angel was probably up to his ears in millions. He would be well able to afford a beautiful young mistress.

The door opened, and Lantz looked up expectantly. A woman was walking in, alone. She was middle-aged and unattractive, with a fat, bloated body and huge, pendulous breasts that swayed as she walked. Her face was pockmarked and she had dyed blonde hair. A hooker down on her luck, Lantz decided.

The woman looked round the bar with vacant, listless eyes, then pushed her way over to Harry, standing at the bar. "Wanna buy me a drink?" She had a heavy Spanish accent.

She looks like a fat cow, Lantz thought. And she's drunk. "Get lost, sister."

"Esteban, the bartender. He say you are lookin' for me, no?"

"He must have made a mistake. I'm looking for Neusa Muñez."

"*Sí. Yo soy Neusa Muñez.*"

But the wrong one, Harry thought.

"Are you Angel's friend?"

She smiled drunkenly. "*Sí.*"

Harry Lantz recovered swiftly. "Well, well." He forced a smile. "Can we go to a corner table and talk?"

They fought their way across the smoky bar, and when they were seated, Harry Lantz said, "I'd like to talk about—"

"You buy me a rum, *sí*? A double."

Lantz nodded. "Sure." When the waiter left, he said, "I want to meet with Angel. I have a little present for him."

She studied him. "*Sí*? What kin'a presen'?"

"Two million dollars."

Their drinks arrived. She downed hers in one gulp. "Wha' for you wanna give Angel two million dollars?"

414

"That's something I'll have to discuss with him in person."

"Tha's not possible. Angel, he don' talk to nobody."

"Lady, for two million dollars—"

Neusa Muñez struggled to her feet. "I tol' you, he don' talk to nobody. *Adios*."

"Hey! Wait a minute! Don't go."

She looked down at him with bleary eyes. "What you wan'?"

"Sit down," Lantz said slowly, "and I'll tell you what I want."

She sat down heavily. "I need a rum, huh?"

Harry Lantz was baffled. What kind of man is this Angel? he wondered. His mistress is not only the ugliest broad in all of South America, but she's a lush.

Lantz did not like dealing with drunks. On the other hand, he hated the thought of losing his fifty-thousand-dollar commission. He summoned the waiter and ordered the drink, then smiled and said reasonably, "Neusa, if I can't talk to Angel, how can I do business with him?"

"Ess simple. You tell me what you wan'. I tell Angel. If he say *sí*, I tell you *sí*. If he say *no*, I tell you *no*."

Lantz distrusted using her as a go-between, but he had no choice. "You've heard of Marin Groza."

"No."

He patted her fat hand. "Angel will know who Groza is. You just say Marin Groza. He'll know. The people who sent me want him blown away. Killed."

"Oh. I'll ass' Angel. Wha' you say the man's name is?"

He wanted to shake her. "Groza. Marin Groza."

"Yeah. My baby's outa town. I'll call him tonight an' meet you here tomorrow. Kin I have 'nother rum?"

Neusa Muñez was turning out to be a nightmare. How could a man who was supposed to be as smart as Angel was get hooked up with such a rum dummy? Harry Lantz prided himself on being a pro. He was too smart to walk into a deal like this without first checking it out. He had cautiously asked around, and the information that impressed him most was that the Israelis had put a price of a million dollars on Angel's head.

THE FOLLOWING NIGHT Harry Lantz was seated at the same table in The Pilar, intermittently chewing peanuts and his fingernails. At two am he saw Neusa Muñez stumble through the door.

"Hi," she mumbled, and slumped into a chair.

"Neusa—did you remember to talk to Angel?"

She looked at him vacantly. "Angel? *Sí*."

He ordered a double rum for her and a double Scotch for himself. He needed it desperately. "What did Angel say, Neusa?"

"Angel? Oh, he say yeah. Ess OK."

Harry Lantz felt a surge of relief. "That's wonderful!" He no longer cared about his messenger-boy mission. He had thought of a better idea. This drunken floozy was going to lead him to Angel. He was going to collect the one million dollars reward money from the Israelis.

He watched her slop down her drink, spilling some of it on her already soiled blouse. "What else did Angel say?"

"Angel say he wanna know who your people are."

Lantz gave her a winning smile. "You tell him that's confidential, Neusa. I can't give him that information."

She shrugged. "Then Angel say to tell you to get lost."

Harry Lantz's mind started working at top speed. "Neusa, I'll telephone the people I'm working for, and if they give me permission, I'll give you a name. OK?" She nodded, indifferent. "You tell Angel I'll have an answer for him by tomorrow. Is there some place I can reach you?"

"I guess so."

He was making progress. "Where?"

"Here."

LANTZ MADE THE CALL reverse-charge from a telephone box so it could not be traced. It took him one hour to get through.

"No," the Controller said. "I told you, no names."

"Yes, sir. But there's a problem. Neusa Muñez, Angel's mistress, says he's willing to make a deal, but he won't move without knowing who he's dealing with."

"What is this woman like?"

"She's a fat, ugly moron, sir."

"It's much too dangerous for my name to be used."

Harry Lantz could feel the deal slipping away from him. "Yes, sir," he said earnestly. "The only thing is, sir, Angel's reputation is based on his being able to keep his mouth shut. If he ever started talking, he wouldn't last five minutes in his business."

There was a long silence. "Very well. You may give Angel my name. But he is never to divulge it, and never to contact me directly. He'll work only through you."

Harry Lantz could have danced. "Yes, sir. I'll tell him. Thank you, sir." He hung up, a big grin on his face. He was going to collect the fifty thousand. And then the million-dollar reward.

WHEN HARRY LANTZ met Neusa Muñez late that evening, he immediately ordered a double rum for her and said happily, "Everything's set. I got permission."

416

She looked at him indifferently. "Yeah?"

He told her the name of his employer. It was a household word.

She shrugged. "Never hearda him."

"Neusa, the people I work for want this done as quickly as possible. Marin Groza is hiding out in a villa in Neuilly, and—"

"Where?"

"It's a suburb of Paris," he said patiently. "Angel will know."

"I need 'nother drink."

An hour later Neusa was still drinking, and Harry Lantz was encouraging her. When she's drunk enough, he thought, she's going to lead me to her boyfriend. The rest will be easy. "When is Angel coming back to town?" he asked.

She focused her watery eyes on him. "Nex' week."

Harry Lantz took her hand and stroked it.

"Why don't you and I go back to your place?" he asked softly.

"OK."

He was in.

NEUSA MUÑEZ LIVED in a shabby two-room apartment that was as messy and unkempt as its tenant. When they walked through the door, Neusa made straight for the little bar in the corner.

Lantz watched as she poured a drink and downed it. She's the most ugly, repulsive pig I've ever met, he thought, but the million dollars is going to be beautiful.

Lantz walked over to her and put his arms round her huge, flabby waist. "You're really cute, do you know that? You've got a really great body."

"Wha'?" Her eyes were glazed.

He was getting nowhere. He had to think of an approach that would get this amazon into bed. But he knew he had to make his move carefully. If he offended her, she might report him to Angel, and that would be the end of the deal.

As Lantz was desperately trying to think of a clever gambit, Neusa mumbled, "Come on 'n the bedroom."

He grinned in relief. "That's a great idea, baby."

She stumbled as Lantz followed her into the small bedroom. It contained one cupboard with the door ajar, a large unmade bed, two chairs, and a chest of drawers with a cracked mirror above it. It was the cupboard that caught Harry Lantz's attention. In it he glimpsed a row of men's suits hanging on a rack.

He went into the bathroom to undress, and when he returned, Neusa was propped up in bed like a leviathan. He sat down beside her. She was drunker than he had thought. That's good, he said to himself. It will make things easier. "You're a pretty woman, honey. You know that?"

"Yeah?"

He began to caress her. "I'll bet you live an exciting life."

"Huh?"

"I mean—being Angel's girlfriend. That must be really interesting. Tell me, baby, what's Angel like?"

There was a silence, and he wondered if Neusa had fallen asleep. "Don't go to sleep, sweetheart. Not yet. What kind of man is Angel? Is he handsome?"

"Rich. Angel, he's rich."

Lantz continued to caress her. "Tell me about Angel. Who are his friends?"

Her voice was drowsy. "Angel got no frens. I'm his fren." Neusa closed her eyes. "Hey, I'm sleepy. Let's go to sleep."

Lantz stayed there quietly until he was certain Neusa was asleep. Then he carefully rose from the bed and padded over to the cupboard.

There were a dozen suits hanging on the rack and six pairs of men's shoes on the floor. Lantz opened the jackets and examined the labels. The suits were all custom-made by Herrera, Avenida la Plata. I've hit the jackpot! Lantz gloated. They'll have a record of Angel's address. I'll go and ask a few questions. Then all I have to do is tip off my friends in the Mossad and collect the reward.

Lantz thought he heard a sound from across the room. He quickly walked over to the bed. Neusa's eyes were closed. He tiptoed to the chest and began looking through the drawers, hoping to find a photograph of Angel. No luck. He crept back to bed.

PRESIDENT PAUL ELLISON put down the last security report on Mary Ashley and said, "Not a blemish, Stan."

"I know. I think she's the perfect candidate. Of course, State isn't going to be happy."

"We'll send them a big handkerchief. Now let's hope the Senate will back us up."

WHEN HARRY LANTZ woke in the morning, he heard Neusa singing off-key in the bathroom.

She was standing in front of the bathroom mirror. Her hair was in fat curlers, and she looked, if possible, even more unattractive than before. She pointed to the bath full of water. "I fix a bath for you. When you're finish', I fix breakfast."

"Sounds great," he lied.

"You like omelettes? I make good omelettes. Angel teach me." She began to dry her hair.

418

Lantz stepped into the bath and lay back in the warm water, thinking, Maybe I should get a gun and take Angel myself. If I let the Israelis do it, there'll probably be an inquiry into who gets the reward. This way there won't be any questions. I'll just tell them where to pick up his body.

Neusa said something, but Harry Lantz could barely hear her over the roar of the hairdryer.

"What did you say?" he called out.

Neusa moved to the side of the tub. "I got a presen' for you."

She dropped the electric hairdryer into the water and stood there watching as Lantz's body twitched in a dance of death.

Chapter Four

Mary Ashley's nerves were on edge during dinner. The children were being impossible again. Beth refused to touch her food.

"No one eats meat any more. It's a barbaric custom carried over from the caveman. Civilized people don't eat live animals."

"It's not alive," Tim argued. "It's dead, so you might as well eat it."

"Children! Quiet. Beth, go make yourself a salad."

"She could go graze in a field," Tim offered.

"Tim! Finish your dinner." Mary's head was pounding.

The telephone rang.

"That's for me," Beth said. She leaped out of her chair and raced towards the telephone. She picked it up and said seductively, "Virgil?" She listened a moment, and her expression changed. "Oh, sure," she said disgustedly. She slammed down the receiver and returned to the table.

"What was that all about?" Edward asked.

"Some joker. Said it was the White House, calling Mom."

"*The White House?*" Edward asked.

The telephone rang again.

"I'll get it." Mary rose and walked over to the telephone. "Hello." As she listened, her face grew grim. "We're in the middle of dinner, and I don't think this is funny—What? Who? The President?" There was a hush in the room. "Wait, I—Oh, good evening, Mr. President." There was a dazed expression on her face. Her family was watching her, wide-eyed. "Yes, sir. I do. I recognize your voice. I'm sorry about hanging up a moment ago. Beth thought it was Virgil, and—Yes, sir. Thank you." She stood there listening. "Would I be willing to serve as *what?*" Her face suddenly flushed.

Edward was on his feet, moving towards the phone, the children close behind him.

"There must be some mistake, Mr. President. My name is Mary

Ashley. I'm a professor at Kansas State University, and—You read it?
Thank you, sir . . ." She listened for a long time. "Yes, sir, I agree. But
that doesn't mean that I . . . Yes, sir. I'm sure it's a wonderful
opportunity, but I . . . Of course. I will. I'll talk it over with my husband
and get back to you." She picked up a pen and wrote down a number.
"Yes, sir. I have it. Thank you, Mr. President. Goodbye." She slowly
replaced the receiver and stood there, in shock.

"What was that all about?" Edward demanded.

"Was that *really* the President?" Tim asked.

Mary sank into a chair. "Yes. It really was."

Edward took Mary's hand in his. "Mary—what did he want?"

Mary sat there, numb, thinking, So that's why that man was
questioning Florence. She looked up at Edward and the children and said
slowly, "The President read my book, and the article in *Foreign Affairs*,
and he thought it was brilliant. He said that's the kind of thinking he
wants for his people-to-people programme. He wants to nominate me for
ambassador to Romania."

There was a look of total disbelief on Edward's face. "*You?* Why
you?"

It was exactly what Mary had asked herself, but she felt Edward could
have been more tactful. He could have said, "How wonderful! You'd
make a great ambassador."

"You haven't had any political experience."

"I'm well aware of that," Mary responded tartly. "I agree that the
whole thing is ridiculous."

"Are you going to be the ambassador?" Tim asked.

Edward turned to the children. "You two finish your dinner. Your
mother and I would like to have a little talk." Edward took Mary's arm
and led her into the library. "I'm sorry if I sounded like a pompous jerk
in there. It—"

"No. You were perfectly right. Why on earth should they choose
me?"

"Honey, you'd probably make a great ambassador. But you must
admit it came as a bit of a shock."

"Try thunderbolt. I still can't believe it." Mary laughed. "Wait until I
tell Florence. She'll die."

"You're really excited about this, aren't you?" asked Edward.

She looked at him in surprise. "Of course. Wouldn't you be?"

Edward chose his words carefully. "It *is* a great honour, honey, and I'm
sure they must have had good reasons for choosing you." He hesitated.
"We have to think about this very carefully."

She knew what he was going to say, and she thought, Edward's right.
Of course he's right.

"I can't just leave my practice and walk out on my patients. I have to stay here. I don't know how long you'd have to be away, but if it really means a lot to you, well, maybe you could go over there with the children and I could join you whenever—"

Mary said softly, "You crazy man. Nothing means as much to me as you and the children. I could never live away from you."

He took her in his arms. "Are you sure?"

"I'm positive. It was exciting being asked. That's enough."

Next morning Mary dialled the number the President had given her. "This is Mrs. Edward Ashley. The President's assistant is expecting my call."

"One moment, please."

A male voice on the other end said, "Hello. Mrs. Ashley?"

"Yes," Mary said. "Would you please give the President a message for me? That I'm very, very flattered by his offer, but my husband's profession ties him down here, so I'm afraid it would be impossible for me to accept. I hope he understands."

"I'll pass on your message," the voice said noncommittally. "Thank you, Mrs. Ashley." The line went dead.

Mary slowly replaced the receiver. It was done. For one brief moment a tantalizing dream had been offered her. But that was all it was. A dream. I'd better get ready for my first class, she thought.

Manama, Bahrain

THE WHITEWASHED STONE HOUSE was anonymous, hidden among dozens of identical houses a short walk from the *souks*, the large, colourful outdoor markets. It was owned by a merchant sympathetic to the cause of the Patriots for Freedom.

The chairman was speaking to the men gathered in the living room. "A problem has arisen. The motion that was recently passed has run into difficulty. The go-between we selected—Harry Lantz—was murdered. His body was found floating in the harbour in Buenos Aires."

"Do the police have any idea who did it?" Balder asked. "I mean—can they connect this to us in any way?"

"No. We're perfectly safe."

Thor asked, "What about our plan? Can we go ahead with it?"

"Not at the moment. We have no idea how to reach Angel. However, the Controller gave Harry Lantz permission to reveal his name to him. If Angel is interested in our proposition, he will find a way to get in touch with him. All we can do now is wait."

THE MAN DIRECTLY RESPONSIBLE for Marin Groza's safety was Roland Passy, the French Minister of Defence. Gendarmes were stationed in front of the villa in Neuilly on twenty-four-hour shifts. But it was the knowledge that Lev Pasternak was in charge of the villa's inner security that gave Passy confidence. He had seen the security arrangements himself and was firmly convinced that the house was impregnable.

In recent weeks rumours had been sweeping the diplomatic world that a coup was imminent, that Marin Groza was planning to return to Romania, and that Alexandros Ionescu was going to be deposed by his senior military officers.

Lev Pasternak knocked on the door and entered the book-crammed library that served as Marin Groza's office. Groza was seated behind his desk, working.

"Everybody wants to know when the revolution is going to happen," Pasternak said. "It's the world's worst-kept secret."

"Tell them to be patient. Will you come to Bucharest with me, Lev?"

More than anything, Lev Pasternak yearned to return home to Israel. "I'll only take this job temporarily," he had told Marin Groza. "Until you're ready to make your move." Temporarily had turned into weeks and months, and finally into three years. And now it was time to make another decision. In a world peopled with pygmies, Lev Pasternak thought, I have been given the privilege of serving a giant. Marin Groza was the most selfless and idealistic man Lev Pasternak had ever known.

When Pasternak had come to work for Groza, he had wondered about the man's family. Groza would never speak of them, but the officer who had arranged for Pasternak to meet Groza had told him the story.

"Groza was betrayed. The *Securitate* picked him up and tortured him for five days. They promised to free him if he would give them the names of his associates in the underground. He wouldn't talk. They arrested his wife and his fourteen-year-old daughter and brought them to the interrogation room. Groza was given a choice: talk, or watch them die. It was the hardest decision any man ever had to make. It was the lives of his beloved wife and child against the lives of hundreds of people who believed in him." The man paused, then went on more slowly. "I think in the end what made Groza decide the way he did was that he was convinced that he and his family were going to be killed anyway. He refused to give them the names. The guards strapped him in a chair and forced him to watch his wife and daughter being tortured until they died."

The officer had looked into Lev Pasternak's eyes and said, "The most important thing for you to understand is that Marin Groza does not want to return to Romania to seek vengeance. He wants to go back to free his people. He wants to make certain that such things can never again happen."

Lev Pasternak had been with Groza from that day on, and the more

time he spent with the revolutionary, the more he came to love him. Now he would have to decide whether to give up his return to Israel and go to Romania with Groza.

PASTERNAK WAS WALKING down the hallway that evening, and as he passed Marin Groza's bedroom door he heard the familiar screams of pain ring out. So, it's Friday, Pasternak thought; Marin Groza's day of penance. Every Friday night the halls of the villa resounded with Groza's screams. That was the day of the week when Groza would shut himself in his room and whip himself mercilessly, until his blood flowed, even though no amount of self-inflicted pain would ever eradicate the terrible guilt that consumed him. Each time he felt the lash of the whip he would see his wife and daughter screaming for help, and would cry out, "I'm sorry! I'll talk. Oh, God, please let me talk . . ."

THE TELEPHONE CALL came ten days after Harry Lantz's body was found. The Controller was in the middle of a staff meeting in the conference room when the intercom buzzer sounded. "I know you asked not to be disturbed, sir, but there's a Miss Neusa Muñez calling from Buenos Aires. It sounds urgent. I told her—"

"It's all right." He kept his emotions under tight control. "I'll take the call in my private office." He went into his office and locked the door. "Hello. Is this Miss Muñez?"

"Yeah. I got a message for you from Angel. He din' like the nosy messenger you sent."

The Controller chose his words carefully. "I'm sorry. But we would still like Angel to go ahead. Would that be possible?"

"Yeah. He say he wanna do it."

"Excellent. How shall I arrange his advance?"

The woman laughed. "Angel, he don' need no advance. Nobody cheats Angel." Somehow the words were chilling. "When the job is finished, he say you put the money in—wait a minute—I got it wrote down—here it is—the State Bank in Zurich. Thas some place in Switzerland." She sounded like a moron.

"I'll need the account number."

"Oh, yeah. Hol' on. I got it here somewhere." He heard the rustle of papers, and finally she was back on the telephone. "J three four nine zero seven seven."

"How soon can he handle the matter?"

"When he's ready, señor. Angel say you'll know when 'ees done. You'll read 'bout it in the newspapers."

"Very well. I'm going to give you my private telephone number in case Angel needs to reach me."

Tbilisi, Russia

THE MEETING WAS BEING HELD in an isolated dacha bordering on the Kura River.

The chairman said, "Two urgent matters have arisen. The first is good news. The Controller has had word from Angel. The contract is moving forward:"

"That's very good news!" Freyr exclaimed. "What's the bad news?"

"I'm afraid it concerns the President's candidate for the ambassadorship to Romania, but the situation can be handled . . ."

IT WAS DIFFICULT FOR MARY ASHLEY to keep her mind on her lecture. Too much had changed. The Junction City newspaper had carried a feature story on Mary's rejection of the ambassadorship to Romania. The fact that she had declined the President's offer made the story even bigger than if she had accepted it. In the eyes of the community and her students she had become a celebrity. It was a heady feeling.

Romania, she mused. Welcome to Romania, Madam Ambassador. Your limousine is here to drive you to your embassy. Her embassy. She had been invited to live in Bucharest, one of the most exciting capitals of the world, reporting to the President, being at the centre of his people-to-people concept. She could have been a part of history.

Mary was roused from her reverie by the sound of the bell. Class was over. Time to go home and change. Edward was taking her out to the country club for dinner. As befitted an almost-ambassador.

It was late by the time Edward and Mary arrived at the country club, and there was only a sprinkling of guests left in the dining room. They stared, watching as Mary sat down, and whispered to one another.

Edward looked at his wife and felt guilty. He was responsible for her turning down the President's offer, and his reasons were valid. But there's more to it than that, Edward admitted to himself. I was jealous. I reacted like a spoiled brat. What would have happened if the President had made me an offer like that? I'd probably have jumped at it. All I could think of was that I wanted Mary to stay home and take care of me and the kids.

He sat there admiring Mary. I'll make it up to her, he thought. I'll surprise her this summer with a trip to Paris and London. Maybe Romania. "Any regrets?" he asked.

Of course there were regrets. But they were castles-in-Spain regrets about the kind of glamorous, impossible dreams that everyone has. Mary smiled. "None, darling. It was a fluke that they even asked me." She took Edward's hand in hers. "I'm glad I refused the offer."

Edward leaned across the table and kissed his wife. "I love you."

"I love you twice as much, darling."

AT THREE O'CLOCK IN THE MORNING, when Edward and Mary were fast asleep, the phone exploded into sound. Edward sleepily reached for the instrument and brought it to his ear. "Hello?"

A woman's urgent voice said, "Dr. Ashley?"

"Yes . . ."

"Pete Grimes is havin' a heart attack. He's in pain somethin' awful. I think he's dyin'. I don't know what to do."

Edward sat up. "Don't do anything. Keep him still. I'll be there in half an hour." He slid out of bed and started to dress.

"Edward . . . what's wrong?" Mary mumbled.

"Everything's fine. Go back to sleep."

Five minutes later, Edward was on his way to the Grimeses' farm. It was a cold, raw morning, with a northwesterly wind. Edward turned the car onto Route 18, the two-lane highway that went through Junction City. The town was asleep, its houses huddled against the bitter, frigid wind.

When Edward came to the end of Sixth Street, he made the turn that took him onto Route 57. How many times had he driven over these roads on hot summer days with the sweet smell of corn and prairie hay in the air, past haystacks piled up alongside the road? And how many winters had he driven on this road through a frosted landscape, with power lines delicately laced with ice, and lonely smoke from far-off chimneys?

Edward thought of Mary lying in their warm bed, waiting for him. He was so lucky. I'll make everything up to her, he promised himself.

Ahead, at the junction of Highways 57 and 77, was a stop sign. Edward came to a halt and looked up and down the deserted road. Then, as he started over the crossroads, a truck appeared out of nowhere. He heard a sudden roar, and his car was pinned by two bright headlights racing towards him. He caught a glimpse of the giant army truck bearing down on him, and the last sound he heard was his own voice screaming.

IN NEUILLY CHURCH BELLS PEALED out across the quiet noon air. The gendarmes guarding Marin Groza's villa had no reason to pay attention to the dusty Renault cruising by. Angel drove slowly, but not slowly enough to arouse suspicion, taking everything in. Two guards in front, a high wall, probably electrified, and inside, of course, the usual electronic nonsense of beams, sensors and alarms. It would take an army to storm the villa. But I don't need an army, Angel thought. Only my genius. Marin Groza is a dead man. If only my mother were alive to see how rich I have become. How happy it would have made her.

In Argentina, poor families were very poor indeed, and Angel's mother had been one of the poorest. Through the years Angel had watched friends and relatives die of hunger and sickness. Death was a way of life, and Angel thought philosophically, Since it is going to happen anyway, why not make a profit from it? In the beginning there were those who doubted Angel's lethal talents, but any who tried to put roadblocks in the way had a habit of disappearing. Angel's reputation as an assassin grew. I have never failed, Angel thought. I am Angel. The Angel of Death.

Chapter Five

The snow-covered Kansas highway was ablaze with vehicles with flashing red lights that turned the frosty air blood red. In the centre, ringed by headlights, sat the five-ton M871 army tractor-trailer and, partially beneath it, Edward Ashley's crumpled car. A dozen police officers and firemen were milling around, trying to keep warm in the predawn freeze. In the middle of the highway, covered by a tarpaulin, was a body.

A sheriff's car skidded to a stop and Mary Ashley ran out of it. She was trembling so hard that she could barely stand. Sheriff Munster grabbed her arm. "I wouldn't look at him if I were you, Mrs. Ashley."

"Let go of me!" She was screaming. She shook loose from his grasp and started towards the tarpaulin.

"Please, Mrs. Ashley. You don't want to see what he looks like." He caught her as she fainted.

She woke up in the back seat of the sheriff's car. Sheriff Munster was sitting in the front seat watching her. The heater was on, and the car was stifling. Mary stared out of the window at all the flashing red lights and thought, It's a scene from hell. In spite of the heat in the car, her teeth were chattering. "How did—how did it h-happen?"

"He shot the stop sign. An army truck was comin' along Seventy-seven and tried to avoid him, but your husband drove right out in front of him."

She closed her eyes and saw the truck bearing down on Edward and felt his panic. All she could say was, "Edward was a c-careful driver. He would n-never shoot a stop sign."

The sheriff said sympathetically, "Mrs. Ashley, we have eyewitnesses. A priest and two nuns, and a Colonel Jenkins from Fort Riley. They all said your husband shot the stop sign."

Everything after that seemed to happen in slow motion. Finally, she watched as Edward's body was lifted into the ambulance.

Sheriff Munster said, "They're takin' the body to the morgue. I'd best get you back home."

LATER, MARY REMEMBERED walking up to the house and Sheriff Munster leading her inside. Florence and Douglas Schiffer were waiting for her in the living room. The children were still asleep.

Florence threw her arms round Mary. "Oh, darling, I'm so terribly, terribly sorry."

"It's all right. Edward had an accident." Mary giggled.

Douglas Schiffer looked into her eyes. They were wide and vacant. He felt a chill go through him. "Come on, I'm putting you to bed."

He gave her a sedative, helped her into bed, and sat at her side. An hour later she was still awake. He gave her another sedative. Then a third. Finally, she slept.

IN JUNCTION CITY there are strict investigative procedures involved in the report of a 1048—an injury accident. An ambulance is dispatched from the County Ambulance Service, and a sheriff's officer is sent to the scene. If army personnel are involved in the accident, the CID—the Criminal Investigating Division of the army—conducts an investigation, along with the sheriff's office.

Shel Planchard, a plain-clothes officer from CID headquarters at Fort Riley, and the sheriff were examining the accident report in the sheriff's office.

"It beats me," Sheriff Munster said.

"What's the problem, Sheriff?" Planchard asked.

"Well, looky here. There were five witnesses to the accident, right? A priest and two nuns, Colonel Jenkins and the truck driver, Sergeant Wallis. Every single one of them says *exactly* the same thing: Doc Ashley's car turned onto the highway, shot the stop sign, and was hit by the army truck." Sheriff Munster scratched his head. "Have you *ever* seen an accident report where even *two* eyewitnesses said the same thing?"

"It just shows that what happened was pretty obvious."

"There's somethin' else nigglin' at me. What were a priest and two nuns and a colonel doing out on Highway Seventy-seven at three thirty in the mornin'?"

"Nothing mysterious about that. The priest and the sisters were on their way to Leonardville. Colonel Jenkins was returning to Fort Riley."

The sheriff said, "I checked with the Department of Motor Vehicles. The last ticket Doc Ashley got was six years ago, for illegal parking. He had no accident record."

"Sheriff," said the CID man, "just what are you suggesting?"

Munster shrugged. "I'm not suggestin' anythin'. I jest have a funny feelin' about this."

"If you think there's some kind of conspiracy involved, there's a big hole in your theory. If—"

The sheriff sighed. "I know. If it wasn't an accident, all the army truck had to do was knock him off and keep goin'. There wouldn't be any reason for all these witnesses and rigamarole."

428

"Exactly." The CID man rose and stretched. "Well, I've got to get back to the base. As far as I'm concerned, the driver of the truck, Sergeant Wallis, is cleared. Are we in agreement?"

Sheriff Munster said reluctantly, "Yeah."

MARY ASHLEY DECIDED LATER that the only thing that saved her sanity was being in a state of shock. Everything that happened seemed to be happening to someone else. She was under water, moving slowly, hearing voices from a distance.

The church was filled to overflowing. There were dozens of wreaths and bouquets. One of the largest wreaths had a card that read, simply, "My deepest sympathy. Paul Ellison."

The casket with Edward's body in it was closed. Mary could not bear to think about the reason.

The minister was speaking: "Lord, thou has been our dwelling place in all generations. Before the mountains were brought forth, or ever thou hadst formed the earth and the world, even from everlasting to everlasting, thou art God. Therefore, we will not fear, though the earth doth change, and though the mountains be shaken into the heart of the seas . . ."

She and Edward were in the small sailing boat on Milford Lake.

"Do you like sailing?" he had asked on their first date.

"I've never been sailing."

"Saturday," he'd said. "We have a date."

They were married one week later.

"Do you know why I married you, lady?" Edward used to tease. "You passed the test. You laughed a lot and you didn't fall overboard."

When the service ended, Mary, Beth and Tim got into the long black limousine that led the funeral procession to the cemetery. Because of the numbing cold, the graveside ceremony was kept brief.

"I am the resurrection and the life; he that believeth in me, though he were dead, yet shall he live; and whosoever liveth and believeth in me shall never die. I am he that liveth and was dead; and, behold, I am alive for ever more."

Finally, mercifully, it was over. Mary and the children watched the coffin being lowered into the frozen and uncaring earth. *Goodbye, my darling.*

IN AN OFFICE at CID headquarters Shel Planchard, the CID officer, was talking to Colonel Jenkins. "I'm afraid I have some bad news, sir. Sergeant Wallis, the driver of the truck that killed the civilian doctor. He had a fatal heart attack this morning."

"That's a shame," said Colonel Jenkins. "Well, I won't be here much

429

longer. I'm being transferred overseas." He allowed himself a small smile. "A rather important promotion."

"Congratulations, sir. You've earned it."

EDWARD'S DEATH WAS THE BEGINNING of an unbearable hell for Mary Ashley. Everything within her screamed in denial of what had happened to Edward, but the reality kept hitting her in fresh waves of shock.

Florence and Douglas and other friends stayed with her, trying to make things easier, but Mary wished they would go away and leave her alone. When it was time to dispose of Edward's personal things, Florence offered to help her, but Mary said, "No. Edward would have wanted me to do it."

There were so many small, intimate things. She ran her fingers over suits he would never wear again. The blue tie he had worn on their last night together. His gloves and scarf that kept him warm. He would not need them in his cold grave.

She found love notes they had written to each other, bringing back memories of the lean days when Edward started his own practice, a Thanksgiving dinner without a turkey, summer picnics and winter sleigh rides, her first pregnancy and both of them reading and playing classical music to Beth while she was in the womb, the love letter Edward wrote when Tim was born, and a hundred other wonderful things that brought tears to her eyes. His death was like some cruel magician's trick.

Edward was everywhere. He was in the songs Mary heard on the radio, in the hills they had driven through together. He was in bed at her side when she awoke at sunrise.

She began to talk to him: *I'm worried about the children, Edward. They don't want to go to school. Beth says they're afraid that when they get home I won't be here. The dean wanted to know whether I planned to go back to teaching at the university. I told him, not now. The children need me too much. Do you think I should go back one day?*

Edward would never leave her and the children. He was there with her, somewhere.

THERE WAS A POPULAR BAR on the Boulevard Bineau that Marin Groza's guards frequented when they were not on duty at the villa in Neuilly. Angel selected a table where conversations could be overheard. The guards, away from the rigid routine of the villa, liked to drink, and when they drank, they talked. Angel listened, seeking the villa's vulnerable point. There was always a vulnerable point. One simply had to be clever enough to find it.

It was three days before Angel overheard a conversation that gave the clue to the solution of the problem. A guard was saying, "Groza sure whips the hell out of himself. You should hear the screaming that goes on every Friday night. Last week I got a look at the whips he keeps in his cupboard . . ."

It was all Angel needed.

Early the following morning, Angel changed his hire car and drove a Fiat into Paris. The shop was on the Place Pigalle, in a quarter populated by prostitutes. Angel went inside, walking slowly along the aisles, carefully studying the merchandise for sale. At length Angel selected a whip, paid cash for it, and left.

The next afternoon, Angel brought the whip back to the shop. The manager looked up and growled, "No refunds."

"I don't want a refund," Angel explained. "I feel awkward carrying this around. I would appreciate it if you would post it for me. I'll pay extra, of course."

That evening, Angel was on a plane to Buenos Aires.

THE WHIP, CAREFULLY WRAPPED, arrived at the villa in Neuilly the following day. It was intercepted by the guard at the gatehouse. He opened the package and examined the whip with great care: You would have thought the old man had enough of these already. He passed it through, and another guard took it to Marin Groza's bedroom cupboard, where he placed it with the other whips.

MARY WAS PREPARING DINNER when the telephone rang, and when she picked it up, an operator said, "This is the White House. The President is calling Mrs. Edward Ashley. Please hold."

Moments later the familiar voice was on the line. "Mrs. Ashley, this is Paul Ellison. I just want you to know how terribly sorry we are about your husband. I understand he was a fine man."

"Thank you, Mr. President. It was kind of you to send flowers."

"I don't want to intrude on your privacy, Mrs. Ashley, and I know it's been a very short time, but now that your domestic situation has changed, I'm asking you to reconsider my offer."

"Thank you, but I couldn't possibly—"

"Hear me out, please. I'm having someone fly out there to talk to you. His name is Stanton Rogers. I would appreciate it if you would at least meet with him."

She did not know what to say. How could she explain that her life had been shattered, that all that mattered now were Beth and Tim? "I'll meet with him, Mr. President," she said. "But I won't change my mind."

Stanton Rogers telephoned Mary directly after the President's call. "I promise to make my visit as brief as possible, Mrs. Ashley. I plan to fly in on Monday afternoon to see you, if that's all right?"

He's such an important man and he's being so polite, Mary thought. "That will be fine." In a reflex action, she asked, "Would you care to have dinner with us?"

He hesitated, thinking what a boring evening it would be. "Thank you," he said.

STANTON ROGERS WAS A FORMIDABLE MAN, Mary decided. She had seen him on "Meet the Press" and in news photographs but, she thought, he looks bigger in person. He was polite, but there was something distant about him.

"Permit me to convey again the President's sincere regrets about your terrible tragedy, Mrs. Ashley."

"Thank you." Mary introduced him to Beth and Tim. They made small talk while she went into the kitchen.

When Mary told Florence Schiffer that Stanton Rogers was coming for dinner and that she was making a pot roast, Florence had said, "People like Mr. Rogers don't eat pot roast."

"Oh? What do they eat?" Mary had asked.

"Chateaubriand and crêpes suzette."

"Well, we're having pot roast."

Along with the pot roast Mary had prepared creamed mashed potatoes, fresh vegetables and a salad. She had baked a pumpkin pie for dessert. Stanton Rogers finished everything on his plate.

During dinner Mary and he talked about the colourful history of Junction City. Finally he brought the conversation round to Romania. "Do you think there will be a revolution there?" he asked.

"Not in the present circumstances. The only man powerful enough to depose Ionescu is Marin Groza, who's in exile."

The questioning went on. Mary Ashley was an expert on the iron-curtain countries, and Stanton Rogers was impressed.

The President was right, he thought, she really is an authority on Romania. And what's more, she's beautiful. She and the children make an all-American package that will sell. Stanton found himself getting more and more excited by the prospect. Mary Ashley could be more useful than she realized.

At the end of the evening Stanton Rogers said, "Mrs. Ashley, I'm going to be frank with you. Initially I was against the President appointing you to a post as sensitive as Romania, but I've changed my mind. I think you would make an excellent ambassador."

Mary shook her head. "I'm sorry, Mr. Rogers. I'm no politician. I'm an amateur."

"Mrs. Ashley, some of our finest ambassadors have been amateurs. That is to say, their experience was not in the Foreign Service. Walter

Annenberg, our former ambassador to the United Kingdom, was a publisher. John Kenneth Galbraith, our ambassador to India, was a professor. I could give you a dozen more examples. These people were all what you would call amateurs. What they had, Mrs. Ashley, was intelligence, a love for their country, and goodwill towards the people of the country where they were sent to serve."

"You make it sound so simple."

"As you're probably aware, you've already been investigated. You've been approved for a security clearance. You're an expert on Romania, and last but not least, you have the kind of image the President wants to project in the iron-curtain countries."

Mary listened, a thoughtful expression on her face. "Mr. Rogers, I appreciate everything you've said. But I can't accept. I have Beth and Tim to think about. I can't just uproot them like—"

"There's a fine school for diplomats' children in Bucharest," Rogers told her. "It would be a wonderful education for them. They'd learn things they could never learn in school here."

The conversation was not going the way Mary had planned. "I don't— I'll think about it."

"I'm staying in town overnight," Stanton Rogers said. "I'll be at the All Seasons Motel. Believe me, Mrs. Ashley, I know what a big decision this is for you. But this programme is important not only to the President but to our country. Please think about that."

When Rogers left, Mary went upstairs. The children were waiting for her, wide awake and excited.

"Are you going to take the job?" Beth asked.

"We have to have a talk. If I did decide to accept it, it would mean that you would have to leave school and all your friends. You would be living in a foreign country where we don't speak the language, and you would be going to a strange school."

"Tim and I talked about all that," Beth said, "and you know what we think? Any country would be really lucky to have you as an ambassador, Mom."

Mary talked to Edward that night: *He made it sound as though the President really needed me, darling. I have the chance again, and I don't know what to do. To tell you the truth, I'm terrified. This is our home. How can I leave it? This is all I have left of you.* She found that she was crying. *Please help me decide . . .*

She sat by the window for hours, looking out at the trees shivering in the howling, restless wind.

At nine o'clock in the morning, Mary telephoned Stanton Rogers. "Mr. Rogers, would you please tell the President that I will be honoured to accept his nomination for the ambassadorship."

As he always did on Friday nights, Marin Groza shut his bedroom door, went to the cupboard and selected a whip. Once he had made his choice, he took off his robe, exposing his back, which was covered with cruel welts. His expression was full of anguish as he raised the leather whip and cracked it down hard against his back.

Marin Groza flinched with pain each time the tough leather beat against his skin. Once . . . twice . . . again . . . and again until the vision he had been waiting for came to him. With each lash, scenes of his wife and daughter being tortured seared through his brain. With each lash, he could hear them scream for mercy. Suddenly he stopped, holding the whip in midair. He was having difficulty breathing. "Help— Help—" His voice was a croak. His lungs felt paralysed.

Lev Pasternak heard Groza's cry for help and came running in, gun in hand. He was too late. He watched as Groza toppled to the floor, his eyes open, staring at nothing. Lev summoned the doctor who lived in the villa and came into Groza's room within minutes. He bent down to examine the body. The skin had turned blue, and the muscles were rigid. He picked up the whip and smelled it.

"What is it?" asked Pasternak. "Poison?"

The doctor nodded. "It's curare. It's an extract from a South American plant. The Incas used it on darts to kill their enemies. Within three minutes the entire nervous system is paralysed."

The two men stood staring helplessly at their dead leader.

The news of Marin Groza's assassination was carried all over the world by satellite although Lev Pasternak was able to keep the details away from the press. In Washington DC, the President talked to Stanton Rogers.

"Who do you think's behind it, Stan?"

"Either the Russians or Ionescu. In the end it comes to the same thing, doesn't it? They didn't want the status quo disturbed."

"So we'll be dealing with Ionescu. Very well. Let's push the Mary Ashley appointment through as quickly as possible."

"She's on her way here, Paul. No problem."

"Good."

On hearing the news, Angel smiled. It had happened sooner than he had expected.

At ten pm the Controller's private phone rang. He picked it up. "Hello."

He heard the sound of Neusa Muñez's guttural voice. "Angel say to deposit the money in his bank account."

434

"Inform him that it will be taken care of immediately. And Miss Muñez, tell Angel how pleased I am. Also tell him that I may need him again very soon. Do you have a telephone number where I can reach you?"

There was a long pause, then: "I guess so." She gave it to him.

"Fine. If Angel—" The line went dead.

IT WAS MORE THAN PACKING up a household, Mary thought. It was packing up a life. It was bidding farewell to thirteen years of dreams, memories, love. It was saying a final goodbye to Edward.

Besides packing, there were so many other practical details. An indefinite leave of absence from the university had been arranged with the dean. The children had been withdrawn from their school. There had been travel arrangements to make, the house to rent out. In the past Mary had taken all the financial transactions for granted because Edward had been there to handle them. Now there was no Edward, except in her mind and in her heart, where he would always be.

Finally, miraculously, everything was ready. It was time to leave. Mary walked upstairs to the bedroom she and Edward had shared for so many wonderful years. She stood there taking a long last look.

Chapter Six

When their plane landed at Washington's Dulles Airport, Mary and the children were met by a young man from the State Department.

"Welcome to Washington, Mrs. Ashley. My name is John Burns. Mr. Rogers asked me to meet you and see that you get to your hotel safely. I've checked you in at the Riverdale Towers. I think you'll all be comfortable there."

"Thank you."

Mary introduced Beth and Tim.

"If you'll give me your baggage-claim checks, Mrs. Ashley, I'll see that everything is taken care of."

Twenty minutes later they were all seated in a chauffeur-driven limousine, heading towards the centre of Washington.

PETE CONNORS, head of the counterintelligence section of the CIA, was working late, and his day was far from over. Every morning at three am a team reported, to prepare the President's daily intelligence checklist, collected from overnight cables. The report, code-named Pickles, had to be ready by six am so that it could be on the President's desk at the start of his day. An armed courier carried the list to the White House, entering at the west gate. Pete Connors had a renewed interest in the intercepted-cable traffic coming from behind the iron curtain, because much of it concerned the appointment of Mary Ashley as the American ambassador to Romania.

The Soviet Union was worried that President Ellison's plan was a ploy to penetrate their satellite countries, to spy on them or seduce them.

The Commies aren't as worried as I am, Pete Connors thought grimly. If the President's idea works, this whole country is going to be open house for their slimy spies.

Pete Connors had been informed the moment Mary Ashley landed in Washington. He had seen photographs of her and the children. She's going to be perfect, Connors thought happily.

THE RIVERDALE TOWERS, one block away from the Watergate, is a small family hotel with comfortable, nicely decorated suites.

No sooner had Mary checked in than Stanton Rogers telephoned. "Good morning, Mrs. Ashley." It was like hearing the voice of an old friend. "I thought it would be a good idea if we met to discuss some of the procedures you'll be going through. Why don't we make it lunch today at the Grand?"

It was starting.

Mary arranged for the children to have room service, and at one o'clock a taxi dropped her off at the Grand Hotel. She looked at it in awe. It was an elegant building, with an imposing lobby and a landscaped courtyard with a fountain. Heads of state and diplomats from all over the world stay there. A marble staircase leads down to the promenade restaurant, where Stanton Rogers was waiting.

"Good afternoon, Mrs. Ashley."

"Good afternoon, Mr. Rogers."

He laughed. "That sounds so formal. What about Stan and Mary?"

She was pleased. "That would be nice."

They ordered lunch. "Stan, will I be in Washington long?" Mary asked.

"About a month. We'll do everything we can to expedite your move. Just between us, there have already been private discussions between the two governments. There will be no problem with the Romanians, but you still have to pass the Senate."

So the Romanian government is going to accept me, Mary thought. Perhaps I'm better qualified than I realized.

"There will be an open hearing of the Senate Foreign Relations Committee. That's scheduled for nine o'clock on Wednesday morning. They vote, and when they turn in their report, the full Senate votes."

Mary said slowly, "Nominations have been voted down in the past, haven't they?"

436

"Yes. But you'll have the full backing of the White House. The President is eager to push your appointment through as quickly as possible. Incidentally, he would like to meet with you this afternoon. Would three o'clock be convenient?"

Mary swallowed. "Yes, I—of course."

"Excellent. A car will be downstairs for you at two thirty."

PAUL ELLISON ROSE as Mary was ushered into the Oval Office. He walked over to shake her hand, grinned, and said, "Gotcha!"

Mary laughed. "I'm glad you did, Mr. President. This is a great honour for me."

"Sit down, Mrs. Ashley. May I call you Mary?"

"Please." They sat down on the couch.

President Ellison said, "You're going to be my doppelganger. Do you know what that is?"

"It's a kind of identical spirit of a living person."

"Right. And that's us. I can't tell you how excited I was when I read your latest article, Mary. It was as though I were reading something I had written myself. There are a lot of people who don't believe our people-to-people plan can work, but you and I are going to fool them."

Our people-to-people plan. He's a charmer, Mary thought. Aloud, she said, "I want to do everything I can to help, Mr. President."

"I'm counting on you. Very heavily. Romania is the testing ground. Since Groza was assassinated, your job is going to be more difficult. If we can pull it off there, we can make it work in the other Communist countries."

They spent the next thirty minutes discussing some of the problems that lay ahead, and then Paul Ellison said, "Stan Rogers will keep in close touch with you. He's become a big fan of yours." He held out his hand. "Good luck, doppelganger."

THE NIGHT BEFORE the Foreign Relations Committee hearing, Mary was in panic. *Oh, Edward, how I wish you were here with me. What am I going to tell them, darling? That in Junction City I was homecoming queen?*

Then the irony struck her. If Edward were alive, she would not be here. *I'd be safe and warm at home with my husband and children, where I belong.*

She lay awake all night.

THE HEARING WAS HELD in the Senate Foreign Relations Committee room, with the full fifteen committee members seated on a dais. Along the left side of the room was the press table, filled with reporters, and in

437

the centre, seats for two hundred spectators. The room was filled to overflowing. Pete Connors sat in a back row. There was a sudden hush as Mary entered with Beth and Tim.

Mary was wearing a dark tailored suit and a white blouse. The children were in their Sunday best.

Ben Cohn, political reporter for the Washington *Post*, watched as they came in. Goodness, he thought, they look like a Norman Rockwell magazine cover.

An attendant seated the children in a front row, and Mary was escorted to the witness chair facing the committee.

The questions started innocently enough.

Senator Campbell, the chairman of the committee and a supporter of President Ellison, spoke first. "According to the biography we've been furnished with, Mrs. Ashley, you're a native of Kansas, and for the last several years you've taught political science at Kansas State University. Is that correct?"

"Yes, sir." Mary was so nervous she could barely speak.

"Your grandparents were Romanian?"

"My grandfather. Yes, sir."

"An article you wrote was published in *Foreign Affairs* magazine and came to the attention of the President?"

"That's my understanding."

"Mrs. Ashley, would you kindly tell this committee what the basic premise of your article is?"

"Several regional economic pacts currently exist in the world, and because they are mutually exclusive, they serve to divide the world into antagonistic and competitive blocs." She felt as though she were conducting a seminar, and her nervousness began to disappear.

"My premise is simple," she continued. "I would like to see our country spearhead a movement to form a common market that includes allies and adversaries alike. Today, as an example, we're paying billions of dollars to store surplus grain while people in dozens of countries are starving. The one-world common market could cure inequities of distribution, at fair market prices. I would like to try to make that happen."

Senator Harold Turkel, a senior member of the committee and a leader of the opposition party, spoke up. "I'd like to ask the nominee a few questions. Is this your first time in Washington, Mrs. Ashley?"

"Yes, sir."

"Have you ever been to New York?"

"No, sir."

"California?"

"No, sir."

"Have you, in fact, ever been outside the state of Kansas?"

"Yes. I gave a lecture at the University of Chicago and a series of talks in Denver and Atlanta."

"That must have been very exciting for you, Mrs. Ashley," Turkel said drily. "You expect to represent the United States in an iron curtain country, and you're telling us that your entire knowledge of the world comes from living in Junction City, Kansas?"

Mary held back her temper. "No, sir. My knowledge of the world comes from studying it. I have a PhD in political science and I've been teaching at Kansas State University for five years, with an emphasis on the iron curtain countries. I'm familiar with the current problems of the Romanian people and what their government thinks of the United States, and why. I—" She broke off, afraid she had gone too far. And then, to her surprise, the committee started to applaud. All except Turkel.

The questioning went on. One hour later Senator Campbell, the chairman, asked, "Are there any more questions?"

"I think the nominee has expressed herself very clearly," one of the senators commented.

"I agree. Thank you, Mrs. Ashley. This session is adjourned."

Pete Connors studied Mary thoughtfully for a moment, then quietly left as the members of the press swarmed round her.

"Turn this way, Mrs. Ashley. Smile, please. One more."

"Mrs. Ashley—"

Ben Cohn stood apart from the others, watching and listening. She's good, he thought; she has all the right answers. But there was something about her nomination that puzzled him. The problem was that he was not sure what it was.

WHEN MARY ARRIVED BACK at the hotel, emotionally drained, Stanton Rogers telephoned.

"Hello, Madam Ambassador."

She felt giddy with relief. "You mean I *made* it? Oh, Stan. I can't tell you how excited I am."

"So am I, Mary." His voice was filled with pride. "So am I."

THE FINAL CONFIRMATION was almost a formality. The full Senate voted Mary in by a comfortable majority. President Ellison said to Stanton Rogers, "Our plan is under way, Stan. Nothing can stop us now."

Rogers nodded. "Nothing," he agreed.

PETE CONNORS WAS IN HIS OFFICE when he heard the news. He immediately wrote out a message and encoded it. One of his men was on duty in the CIA cable room.

"I want to use the Roger Channel," Connors said. "Wait outside." The Roger Channel is the CIA's ultraprivate cable system, only for top executives. The cable was addressed to Sigmund.

MARY ASHLEY WAS SWORN IN as the ambassador to the Socialist Republic of Romania, and the treadmill began. She was ordered to report to the European Affairs Section at the State Department. There she was assigned a small, boxlike office next to the Romanian desk.

James Stickley, the Romanian desk officer, was a career diplomat, with twenty-five years in the service. He was considered the foremost expert on the Romanian desk, and had fully expected to be appointed ambassador to Romania. The news about Mary Ashley had been a bitter blow. It was bad enough to have been passed over, but to have lost out to a political appointee—a nobody from Kansas—was galling.

He studied Mary Ashley now, as she sat across from his desk.

Mary was also studying Stickley. There is something mean-looking about him, she thought.

"I'll be reading the cables you send in," Stickley informed her. "They will be yellow copies for action, or white copies for information. Duplicates of your cables will go to Defence, the CIA, the USIA, the Treasury Department, and a dozen other departments. One of the first issues you'll be expected to resolve is the matter of the Americans being held in Romanian prisons. We want their release."

"What are they charged with?"

"Espionage, drugs, theft—anything the Romanians want to charge them with."

Mary wondered how on earth one went about getting a charge of espionage dismissed.

"Right," she said briskly.

"We're going to have to make an instant expert out of you." He handed her an armful of files. "You can start by reading these."

"I'll dedicate my morning to it."

"No. First I want to introduce you to your military attaché, Colonel William McKinney. Then, in thirty minutes, you're scheduled to begin a language course in Romanian. The course usually takes months, but I have orders to push you through the mill."

BILL MCKINNEY WORE MUFTI, but his military bearing was like a uniform. He was a tall, middle-aged man, with a seamed, weathered face. "Madam Ambassador." His voice was rough and gravelly, as though his throat had suffered an injury.

"I'm pleased to meet you," Mary said. Colonel McKinney was her first staff member, and meeting him gave her a sense of excitement. It seemed to bring her new position much closer. "Have you been to Romania before?"

The colonel and James Stickley exchanged a look.

"He's been there before," Stickley replied.

EVERY DAY MARY and Stickley went through the files of the Romanian desk together.

"I'm going to give you a package," Stickley announced one afternoon. "It's for your eyes only. Read it and digest it, and return it to me personally tomorrow morning." He handed Mary a thick manila envelope sealed with red tape. "Sign for it, please."

She signed.

During the ride back to the hotel Mary clutched it to her lap, feeling like a character in a James Bond movie.

The children were dressed up and waiting for her.

Oh, dear, Mary remembered, I promised to take them to a movie. "Fellas," she said, "we'll have to make our excursion another evening. I have some urgent work to do."

"Sure, Mom."

"OK."

And Mary thought, before Edward died, they would have screamed like banshees; but they've had to grow up. She took them both in her arms.

"I'll make it up to you," she promised.

The material James Stickley had given her was incredible. No wonder he wants this right back, Mary thought. There were detailed reports on every important Romanian official, from the President to the Minister of Commerce. There was a dossier on their private habits, financial dealings, friendships, personal traits and prejudices. Some of the reading was lurid. Mary was up half the night memorizing the names and peccadilloes of the people with whom she would be dealing.

In the morning she returned the secret documents.

Stickley said, "Now you know everything you should know about the Romanian leaders."

"And then some," Mary murmured.

"There's something you should bear in mind: by now the Romanians also know everything there is to know about *you*."

"That won't get them far," Mary said.

"No?" Stickley leaned back in his chair. "You're a woman, and you're alone. You can be sure they've already marked you as an easy target. They'll play on your loneliness. Every move you make will be watched and recorded."

He's trying to frighten me, Mary thought. Well, it won't work.

TIME BECAME A BLUR, a whirlwind of activity that left Mary exhausted. Besides language lessons, her schedule included a course at the Foreign Service Institute, briefings at the Defence Intelligence Agency, meetings with the secretary of the ISA—International Security Affairs—and with Senate committees. They all had demands, advice, questions.

On top of all this, a media blitz began. Mary found herself in front of the cameras on "Good Morning America", "Meet the Press", and "Firing Line". She was interviewed by the Washington *Post*, the *New York Times*, and half a dozen other important daily papers. She did interviews for the London *Times*, *Der Spiegel*, *Oggi* and *Le Monde*. *Time* magazine and *People* did feature articles on her and the children. Mary Ashley's photograph seemed to be everywhere, and whenever there was a newsbreak about an event in some far-off corner of the world, she was asked for her comments. Overnight Mary Ashley and her children became celebrities.

Tim said, "Mom, it's really spooky seeing our pictures on the covers of all the magazines."

"Spooky is the word," Mary agreed. Somehow she felt uneasy about the publicity, and spoke to Stanton Rogers about it.

"Look on it as part of the job. The President wants to create an image. By the time you get to Romania, everyone will know who you are."

"THERE'S SOMETHING WEIRD happening in this town," Ben Cohn said. He and his girlfriend, Akiko Hadaka, were watching Mary Ashley on "Meet the Press". The new ambassador to Romania was saying, "I believe that China is heading for a more humane, individualistic Communist society with its incorporation of Hong Kong and Macao."

"Now what does that lady know about China?" Ben Cohn muttered. He turned to Akiko. "You're looking at a housewife from Kansas who's become an expert on everything overnight."

"She seems very bright," Akiko said.

"Bright is beside the point. Every time she gives an interview, the reporters go crazy. It's like a feeding frenzy. How did she get on 'Meet the Press'? I'll tell you how. Someone decided that Mary Ashley was going to be a celebrity. The question is who, and why?"

"I'm supposed to be the one with the devious Oriental mind," Akiko said. "I think you're making more out of this than necessary."

Ben Cohn lit a cigarette and took an angry puff at it. "You could be right," he grumbled.

LATER THAT EVENING Ben Cohn telephoned Ian Villiers, chief of press relations for the State Department.

"Benjie, my boy—what can I do for you?" asked Ian.

"I need a favour. I understand you're in charge of press relations for our new ambassador to Romania."

A cautious, "Yes . . . ?"

"Who's behind her buildup, Ian? I'm interested in—"

"I'm sorry, Ben. That's State Department business. I'm just a hired hand. You might drop a note to the Secretary."

Hanging up, Ben made a decision. "I think I'm going to have to go out of town for a few days," he told Akiko.

"Where are you going, baby?"

"Junction City, Kansas."

AS IT TURNED OUT, Ben Cohn was in Junction City for only one day. He spent an hour talking to Sheriff Munster, then drove a rental car to Fort Riley, where he visited the CID office. He caught a late-afternoon flight home.

As Ben Cohn's plane took off, a person-to-person telephone call was placed from the fort to a number in Washington DC.

MARY ASHLEY WAS WALKING down the long corridor of the European Affairs section of the State Department, on her way to report to James Stickley, when she heard a deep male voice behind her say, "Now, that's what I call a perfect ten."

Mary spun round. A tall stranger was leaning against the wall staring at her, an insolent grin on his face. He was rugged-looking, dressed in jeans, T-shirt and tennis shoes, and he looked scruffy and unshaven. There were laugh lines round his mouth, and his eyes were a bright, mocking blue. There was an air of arrogance about him that was infuriating. Mary turned on her heel and angrily walked away, conscious of his eyes following her.

The conference with James Stickley lasted for more than an hour.

When Mary returned to her office, the stranger was seated in her chair, his feet on her desk, looking through her papers.

"What the devil do you think you're doing?"

The man gave her a long, lazy look and slowly got to his feet. "I'm Mike Slade. My friends call me Michael."

She said icily, "What can I do for you, Mr. Slade?"

"Nothing, really," he said easily. "We're neighbours. I work here in the department, so I thought I'd come by and say hello."

"You've said it. And if you really are in the department, I assume you have your own desk. So in the future you won't have to sit at my desk and snoop."

"Well, well, it has a temper! I heard the Kansians, or whatever you people call yourselves, were supposed to be friendly folks."

443

"Mr. Slade, I'll give you two seconds to get out of my office."

"I must have heard wrong," he mumbled to himself.

"And if you really work here, I'd suggest you go home and shave and put on some proper clothing."

He waved his hand at her. "Bye, honey. I'll be seeing you."

Oh, no, Mary thought. No, you won't.

The next morning, when Mary arrived for her daily session with Stickley, Mike Slade was there as well.

He grinned at Mary. "Hi. I took your advice and shaved."

Stickley looked from one to the other. "You two have met?"

Mary gritted her teeth. "Not really. I found him snooping at my desk."

James Stickley said, "Mrs. Ashley, Mike Slade. Mr. Slade is going to be your deputy chief of mission."

Mary stared at him. "*He's what?*"

"Mr. Slade is on the East European desk. He usually works out of Washington, but it's been decided to assign him to Romania."

"No!" she protested. "That's impossible."

"Mrs. Ashley, Mike Slade happens to be our top field expert on East European affairs. Your job is to make friends with the natives. My job is to see to it that you get all the help I can give you. And that means Mike Slade. I really don't want to hear any more about it."

Mike said mildly, "I promise to shave every day."

Mary turned to Stickley. "I thought an ambassador was permitted to choose her own deputy chief of mission."

"That is correct, but—"

"Then I am unchoosing Mr. Slade. I don't want him."

"Ordinarily you would be within your rights, but in this case I'm afraid you have no choice. The order came from the White House."

MARY COULD NOT SEEM to avoid Mike Slade. The man was everywhere. She ran into him in the Pentagon, in the Senate dining room, in the corridors of the State Department. He was always dressed in either denims and a T-shirt or in sports clothes. Mary wondered how he got away with it in an environment that was so formal.

One day Mary saw him having lunch with Colonel McKinney. They were engaged in an earnest conversation, and Mary wondered how close the two men were. Could they be old friends? And could they be planning to gang up on me? I'm getting paranoid, Mary told herself, and I'm not even in Romania yet.

BEN COHN WAS SEATED at a corner table at Mama Regina's restaurant when his guest, Alfred Shuttleworth, arrived. The proprietor, Tony Sergio, seated him.

444

"Would you care for a drink, gentlemen?"

Shuttleworth ordered a martini.

"Nothing for me," Ben Cohn said.

Alfred Shuttleworth was a sallow-looking middle-aged man who worked in the European section of the State Department. A few years earlier he had been involved in a drunk-driving accident that Ben Cohn had covered for his newspaper. Shuttleworth's career had been at stake and Cohn had killed the story. Shuttleworth showed his appreciation by giving him news tips from time to time.

"I need your help, Al."

"Name it and you've got it."

"I'd like the inside information on our new ambassador to Romania."

Alfred Shuttleworth frowned. "What do you mean?"

"Al, there's this Cinderella who comes out of nowhere, is touched by the magic wand of our President, and suddenly becomes Grace Kelly, Princess Di and Jacqueline Kennedy rolled into one. Now, I'll admit the lady is pretty—but she isn't *that* pretty. The lady is bright—but she isn't *that* bright. I'll tell you something else that's strange. I flew to Junction City and talked to the sheriff there." Ben Cohn paused.

"Go on," Shuttleworth said.

"Mrs. Ashley originally turned down the President because her husband couldn't leave his medical practice. Then he was killed in a convenient auto accident. *Voilà!* The lady's in Washington, on her way to Bucharest. Exactly as someone had planned from the beginning."

"Someone? Who?"

"That's the jackpot question."

"Ben—what are you suggesting?"

"I'm not suggesting anything. Let me tell you what Sheriff Munster suggested. He thought it was peculiar that half a dozen witnesses showed up in the middle of a freezing winter night just in time to witness the accident. And do you want to hear something even more peculiar? They've all disappeared."

"Go on."

"The driver of the army truck that killed Dr. Ashley is dead. Heart attack. Twenty-seven years old. Colonel Jenkins—the officer in charge of the army investigation, as well as one of the witnesses to the accident—he's been promoted and transferred. No one seems to know where."

Shuttleworth shook his head. "Ben, I know you're a darn good reporter, but I think you've gone off the track. You're building a few coincidences into a Hitchcock scenario. People *do* get killed in auto accidents. You're looking for a conspiracy where there is none."

"Al, have you heard of an organization called Patriots for Freedom?"

"No."

"I keep hearing rumours, but there's nothing I can pin down."

"What kind of rumours?"

"It's supposed to be a cabal of high-level right-wing and left-wing fanatics from a dozen Eastern and Western countries. Their ideologies are diametrically opposed, but what brings them together is fear. The Communist members think President Ellison's plan is a capitalist trick to destroy the Eastern bloc. The right-wingers believe his plan is an open door that will let the Communists destroy us. So they've formed this unholy alliance."

"I don't believe it."

"Fair enough. But do you think you could check it out for me?"

"I don't know, Ben. I'll try."

"Thanks. Let's order lunch."

The spaghetti carbonara was superb.

ALFRED SHUTTLEWORTH WAS SCEPTICAL about Ben Cohn's theory. He liked Ben, and he wanted to help, but he had no idea how to go about tracking down a probably mythical organization. If it really did exist, it would be in some government computer. He himself had no access to the computers.

But I know someone who has, Alfred Shuttleworth said to himself, I'll give him a call.

ALFRED SHUTTLEWORTH WAS ON his second martini when Pete Connors walked into the bar.

"Sorry I'm late," Connors said. "A minor problem at the pickle factory."

Pete Connors ordered a Scotch, and Shuttleworth ordered another martini. "Pete," Shuttleworth said, "I need a favour. Could you look up something for me in the CIA computer? It may not be in there, but I promised a friend I'd try."

"Sure," said Connors. "I owe you a few. Who do you want to know about?"

"It's not a *who*, it's a *what*. And it probably doesn't even exist. It's an organization called Patriots for Freedom. Have you heard of it?"

Pete Connors carefully set down his drink. "I can't say that I have, Al. What's the name of your friend?"

"Ben Cohn. He's a reporter for the *Post*."

THERE WAS NO WAY to get directly in touch with the Controller. He had organized and financed the Patriots for Freedom, but he never attended Committee meetings, and he was completely anonymous. He was a telephone number—untraceable (Connors had tried)—and a recording

that said, "You have sixty seconds in which to leave your message." The number was to be used only in case of emergency. Connors stopped at a public telephone booth to make the call. He talked to the recording.

The message was received at six pm. The Controller listened to it twice, then dialled a number in Buenos Aires. He waited for three full minutes before Neusa Muñez's voice came on.

"*Sí?*"

The Controller said, "I am the man who made arrangements with you before about Angel. I have another contract for him. Can you get in touch with him right away?"

"I don't know." She sounded drunk.

Damn the woman. "Listen to me. Tell Angel I need this done immediately. I want him to—"

"Wait a minute. I gotta go to toilet."

The Controller heard her drop the phone. He sat there, filled with frustration, until she came back on the line. "A lotta beer makes you go," she announced.

He gritted his teeth. "This is very important. I want you to get a pencil and write this down. I'll speak slowly."

"I WANTED TO BRING YOU the good news in person, Mary," said Stanton Rogers. "We just received official word that the Romanian government has approved you as the new ambassador from the United States. Now President Ellison can give you a letter of credence, and you'll be on your way."

It was one of the most thrilling moments of Mary Ashley's life. "I—I don't know how to thank you for everything you've done, Stan."

"I haven't done anything," Rogers protested. "It was the President who selected you." He grinned. "And I must say, he made the perfect choice. You can do more for our country over there than anyone else I can think of."

"Thank you," she said soberly. "I'll try to live up to that."

ON THURSDAY MORNING ANGEL was in a bad mood. The flight from Buenos Aires to Washington DC, had been delayed because of a telephoned bomb threat. The world isn't safe any more, Angel thought angrily.

The hotel room that had been reserved in Washington was too modern, too—what was the word?—plastic. That was it. In Buenos Aires, everything was *authentico*. I'll finish this contract and get back home, Angel thought. The job is simple, almost an insult to my talent, but the money is excellent.

Angel's first stop was an electrical supply store, then a paint store, and finally a supermarket, where Angel's only purchase was six light bulbs. The rest of the equipment was waiting in the hotel room in two sealed boxes marked "Fragile. Handle with care". Inside the first box were four carefully packed army-green hand grenades. In the second box was soldering equipment.

Working very slowly, with exquisite care, Angel cut the top off the first grenade, then painted the bottom of it the same colour as the light bulbs. The next step was to scoop out the explosive from the grenade and replace it with a seismic explosive. When this was tightly packed, Angel added lead and metallic shrapnel to it. Then he shattered a light bulb against a table, preserving the filament and threaded base. It took less than a minute to solder the filament of the bulb to an electrically activated detonator. The final step was to insert it gently inside the painted grenade. When Angel had finished, it looked exactly like a normal light bulb.

Then he began to work on the remaining light bulbs. After that, there was nothing to do but wait for the phone call.

The telephone rang at eight o'clock that evening. Angel picked up the phone and listened. After a moment a voice said, "He's gone."

The taxi ride to the apartment building took seventeen minutes.

There was no doorman in the lobby. The target apartment was on the fifth floor, at the far end of the corridor. The lock was an early-model Schlage, childishly simple to manipulate. Angel was inside the dark apartment within seconds.

It was the work of a few minutes to replace six light bulbs in the living room of the apartment. Afterwards, Angel headed for Dulles Airport to catch a midnight flight back to Buenos Aires.

THE FOLLOWING DAY Ben Cohn was killed by a mysterious explosion in his apartment. There was a brief item in the press attributing the accident to a leaky gas stove. That same day Alfred Shuttleworth was reported missing by his wife. His body was never found.

STANTON ROGERS ACCOMPANIED Mary and the children to Dulles Airport in a State Department limousine.

"Remember, Mary," he said, just before she boarded the plane, "if you have any problems with anyone once you're in Romania, I want you to let me know. I intend to make sure that you get every bit of help I can give you."

"I appreciate that."

"One last thing. If you have any messages that you want to send to me without anyone else reading them, the code at the top of the message is three *x*'s. I'll be the only one to receive that message."

IT WAS ONLY AFTER she and the children were airborne that the enormity of what was about to happen really struck Mary Ashley. It was so incredible that she had to say it aloud. "We're on our way to Romania, where I'm going to take up my post as ambassador from the United States."

Beth looked at her strangely. "Yes, Mother. We know that."

I'm going to be the best ambassador they've ever seen, Mary thought. Before I'm finished, the United States and Romania are going to be close allies.

The next instant Mary's euphoric dreams of great statesmanship evaporated, giving way to panic. I'm not a real ambassador, she thought, I'm a fake. I'm going to get us into a war. God help us. I should never have left Kansas.

Chapter Seven

Otopeni Airport, twenty-five miles from the heart of Bucharest, is a modern airport, built to facilitate the flow of travellers from nearby iron-curtain countries as well as to take care of the lesser number of Western tourists who visit Romania each year.

Inside the terminal were soldiers in brown uniforms, armed with rifles and pistols, and there was a stark air of coldness about the building which had nothing to do with the frigid temperature. Unconsciously Tim and Beth moved closer to Mary. So they feel it too, she thought.

Two men were approaching. One of them, a slim, athletic man, introduced himself. "Welcome to Romania, Madam Ambassador. I'm Jerry Davis, your public affairs consul. This is Tudor Costache, the Romanian chief of protocol."

"It is a pleasure to have you and your children with us," Costache said. "Welcome to our country."

In a way, Mary thought, it's going to be my country too. "*Mulţumesc, domnule*," she said.

"You speak Romanian!" Costache cried. "*Cu plăcere!*"

"A few words," Mary replied hastily.

Tim said, "*Bŭnadimineaţa*," and Mary was so proud she could have burst. She introduced Tim and Beth.

There was a long queue waiting to go through customs, but Mary and the children were outside the building in a matter of minutes. There were reporters and photographers waiting again, but instead of the free-for-alls that Mary had encountered at home, they were orderly and controlled. When they had finished, they thanked Mary and departed.

Colonel McKinney, in army uniform, was waiting at the kerb. He held out his hand. "Good morning, Madam Ambassador. Did you have a pleasant trip?"

"Yes, thank you."

"Mike Slade wanted to be here, but there was some important business he had to take care of."

Mary was relieved.

A long black limousine with an American flag on the right front wing pulled up. A cheerful-looking man in a chauffeur's uniform held the door open.

"This is Florian."

The chauffeur grinned. "Welcome, Madam Ambassador. Master Tim. Miss Beth. It will be my pleasure to serve you."

"Thank you," Mary said.

"Florian will be at your disposal twenty-four hours a day. I thought we would go directly to the residence, so you can unpack and relax. In the morning Florian will take you to the embassy."

"That sounds fine," Mary said.

The drive from the airport to the city was fascinating. They drove on a busy two-lane highway, but every few miles the traffic would be held up by plodding gipsy carts. On both sides of the highway were modern factories next to ancient huts. The car passed farm after farm, with women working in the fields, colourful bandannas knotted round their heads. Then they drove by an ominous blue and grey building off the highway.

"What is that?" Mary asked.

Florian grimaced. "The Ivan Stelian Prison. That is where they put anyone who disagrees with the Romanian government."

At last they reached the centre of Bucharest and Mary was in the homeland of her forefathers. It was very beautiful. There were parks and monuments and fountains everywhere one looked. The streets were crowded with people and trams, and the limousine had to honk its way through the traffic.

"The residence is just ahead," Colonel McKinney said, as the car turned into a small, tree-lined street.

The ambassador's residence was a large and beautiful old-fashioned three-storey house surrounded by lovely grounds. The staff was lined up outside, waiting to welcome Mary.

Jerry Davis made the introductions. "Mihai, your butler; Rosica, your housekeeper; Cosma, your chef; and Delia and Carmen, your maids."

Mary moved down the line, receiving their bows and curtsies. They all seemed to be waiting for her to say something. She took a deep breath. "*Bună ziua. Mulţumesc. Nu vorbesc—*" Every bit of Romanian she had learned flew out of her head. She stared at them helplessly.

Mihai, the butler, bowed. "We all speak English, ma'am. We welcome you and shall be happy to serve your every need."

Mary sighed with relief. "Thank you."

"Let me show you around," Jerry Davis said.

On the ground floor there was a library, a music room, a living room and a large dining room, a kitchen, and a pantry. A terrace ran the length of the building outside the dining room, facing a park. At the rear of the house was an indoor swimming pool.

"Our own swimming pool!" Tim exclaimed. "Can I go swimming straight away?"

"Later, darling. Let's get settled in first."

The *pièce de résistance* downstairs was the ballroom, built near the garden. It was enormous. Glistening wall lights lined the walls, which were decorated with flocked paper.

Jerry Davis said, "This is where the embassy parties are given. Watch this." He pressed a switch on the wall. There was a grinding noise and the ceiling began to split in the centre, opening up until the sky became visible. "It can also be operated manually."

"Hey, that's neat!" Beth exclaimed.

"It's called the Ambassador's Folly," Jerry explained. "It's too hot to keep open in the summer and too cold in the winter. We use it in April and September." As the cold started to descend, Jerry pressed the switch and the ceiling closed.

They followed him upstairs to a large central landing with two bedrooms separated by a bathroom. Further down the landing was the master bedroom, with a sitting room and a bathroom.

"The second floor has servants' quarters," Jerry continued. "In the basement is a wine cellar."

"It's—it's enormous," Mary said.

"Which is my bedroom?" Beth asked.

"You and Tim can decide that between yourselves."

"You can have this one," Tim offered. "It's frilly. Girls like frilly things."

The master bedroom was lovely, with a queen-sized bed with a goose-down quilt, a dressing table, a fireplace, a luxurious bathroom and a wonderful view of the gardens. Mary was so exhausted she could hardly wait to get into bed.

She lay awake most of that first night, filled with a deep, cold loneliness, mingled with a growing feeling of excitement about starting her new job.

It's up to me now, Edward. I don't have anyone to lean on. I wish you were here with me, telling me not to be afraid, telling me I won't fail. I mustn't fail, darling.

452

THE AMERICAN EMBASSY in Bucharest is a white, semi-Gothic, two-storey building with an iron gate in front. The building is patrolled by a marine officer, and a second guard sits inside a security booth at the side of the gate. The lobby is ornate. It has a marble floor, two closed-circuit television sets at a desk guarded by a marine, and a fireplace. The corridors are lined with portraits of US Presidents. A winding staircase leads to the first floor, where a conference room and offices are located.

A marine guard was waiting for Mary. "Good morning, Madam Ambassador. I'm Sergeant Hughes. They call me Gunny. They're waiting for you in your office. I'll escort you there."

"Thank you, Gunny." Mary followed him upstairs to a reception room where a middle-aged woman sat behind a desk.

She rose. "Good morning, Madam Ambassador. I'm Dorothy Stone, your secretary."

"How do you do?"

Dorothy said, "I'm afraid you have quite a crowd in there."

She opened the office door, and Mary walked into the room. There were nine people seated round a large conference table. They rose as Mary entered, and she felt a wave of animosity that was almost palpable. The first person she saw was Mike Slade.

"I see you got here safely," Mike said. "Let me introduce you to your department heads. This is Lucas Janklow, administrative consul; Eddie Maltz, political consul; Patricia Hatfield, your economic consul; David Wallace, head of administration; Ted Thompson, agriculture. You've already met Jerry Davis, your public affairs consul. This is David Victor, commerce consul, and you already know Colonel Bill McKinney."

"Please be seated," Mary said. She sat at the head of the table and surveyed the group. *Hostility comes in all sizes and shapes*, Mary thought. *It's going to take time to sort them all out.*

Mike Slade was saying, "All of us are serving at your discretion. You can replace any of us at any time."

That's a lie, Mary thought angrily, *I tried to replace you.*

There was general inconsequential conversation, until Mike Slade said, "Madam Ambassador, the individual consuls will now brief you on any serious problems."

Mary resented his taking charge, but she said nothing.

Ted Thompson, the agriculture consul, was the first to speak. "The Romanian agriculture minister is in worse trouble than he's admitting. They're going to have a disastrous crop this year, and we can't afford to let them go under."

The economic consul, Patricia Hatfield, protested, "We've given them enough aid, Ted. Romania's already operating under a favoured-nations treaty. It's a GSP country." She looked at Mary and said patronizingly, "A GSP country is—"

"Is a generalized system of preferences," Mary cut in. "We treat Romania as a less developed country so that they get import and export advantages."

Hatfield's expression changed. "That's right . . ."

"I'll see what I can do," Mary promised.

Eddie Maltz, the political consul, spoke up. "I have an urgent problem. A nineteen-year-old American college student was arrested last night for possession of marijuana. That's an extremely serious offence here. The usual penalty is a five-year prison sentence."

How awful, Mary thought. "What can we do about it?"

Mike Slade said lazily, "You can try your charm on the head of *Securitate*. His name is Istrase. He has a lot of power."

Eddie Maltz went on, "The girl says she was framed, and she may have a point. She was stupid enough to have an affair with a Romanian policeman. He turned her in."

Mary was horrified. "I'll see what I can do." She turned to the public affairs consul, Jerry Davis. "Do you have any urgent problems?"

"My department is having trouble getting approvals for repairs on the apartments our embassy staff live in. Some of our people are without heat, and in several of the apartments the toilets don't work and there's no running water."

"Can't they just go ahead and have their own repairs made?"

"No. The Romanian government has to approve all repairs."

"Have you complained about this?"

"Yes, ma'am. Every day for the last three months."

"It's called harassment," Mike Slade explained. "It's a war of nerves they like to play with us."

Ambassador Ashley was beginning to get a headache.

After the meeting broke up and she and Slade were alone, Mary asked, "Which one of them is the CIA agent attached to the embassy?"

Mike looked at her for a moment. "Why don't you come with me?" He walked out of the conference room.

Mary followed him down a long corridor. He came to a large door with a marine guard standing in front of it. The guard stepped aside as Mike pushed the door open. He turned and gestured for Mary to enter.

She stepped inside and looked round. The room was an incredible combination of metal and glass, covering the floor, the walls and the ceiling.

Mike closed the heavy door behind them. "This is the Bubble Room. Every embassy in an iron-curtain country has one. It's the only room in the embassy that can't be bugged."

He saw her look of disbelief.

"Madam Ambassador, not only is the embassy bugged, but you can bet your residence is bugged, and that if you go out to a restaurant, your table will be bugged. You're in enemy territory."

Mary sank into a chair. "How do you handle that?" she asked. "I mean, not ever being able to talk freely?"

"We do an electronic sweep every morning. We find their bugs and pull them out. They replace them, and we pull *those* out."

"Why do we permit Romanians to work in the embassy?"

"It's their playground. They're the home team. We play by their rules or blow the ball game. They can't get their microphones into this room because there are marine guards on duty in front of that door twenty-four hours a day. Now—what are your questions?"

"I just wondered who the CIA man was."

"Eddie Maltz, your political consul."

Eddie Maltz . . . Ah, he was the middle-aged one, very thin, a sinister face. Or did she think that now because he was CIA? "Is he the only CIA man on the staff?"

"Yes." Mike Slade looked at his watch. "You're due to present your credentials in thirty minutes. Florian is waiting for you outside. Take your letter of credence. You'll give the original to President Ionescu and put a copy in our safe."

Mary found that she was gritting her teeth. "I *know* that, Mr. Slade."

HEADQUARTERS FOR THE ROMANIAN GOVERNMENT is a forbidding sandstone building in the centre of Bucharest. It is protected by a steel wall and surrounded by armed guards.

An aide escorted Mary up to the first floor, where she was greeted by President Ionescu. He was dark, with curly black hair, hawklike features, and one of the most imperious noses Mary had ever seen. His eyes were blazing, mesmerizing. He took Mary's hand and gave it a lingering kiss. "You are even more beautiful than your photographs."

"Thank you, Your Excellency." Mary opened her bag and took out the letter of credence from President Ellison.

Ionescu gave it a careless glance. "Thank you. You are now officially the American ambassador to my country." He beamed at her. "I have arranged a reception this evening for you. You will meet some of our people who will be working with you."

"That's very kind of you," Mary said.

He took her hand in his again and said, "I hope you will grow to love our country, Madam Ambassador." He massaged her hand.

"I'm sure I will." He thinks I'm just another pretty face, Mary thought grimly. I'll have to do something about that.

MARY RETURNED TO THE EMBASSY and spent the rest of the day catching up with her reading. There were the English translations of Romanian newspaper and magazine articles, the wireless file and the summary of news developments reported in the United States, a thick report on arms-control negotiations, and an update on the United States economy. There's enough reading material in one day, Mary thought, to keep me busy for a week, and I'm going to get this every day.

But the problem that disturbed Mary most was the feeling of antagonism from her staff. She sent for Harriet Kruger, her protocol officer. "How long have you worked here at the embassy?"

"Four years before our break with Romania, and now three glorious months." There was a note of irony in her voice.

"May we have an off-the-record conversation?"

"No, ma'am."

Mary had forgotten. "Why don't we adjourn to the Bubble Room?" she suggested.

When Mary and Harriet Kruger were seated in the Bubble Room, Mary said, "Something just occurred to me. Our meeting this morning was held in the conference room. Isn't that bugged?"

"Probably," Harriet said cheerfully. "But it doesn't matter. Mike Slade wouldn't let anything be discussed that the Romanians aren't already aware of."

Mike Slade. "What do you think of Slade?" Mary asked.

"He's the best."

Mary decided not to express her opinion. "I got the feeling today that morale around here isn't good. Is it because of me, or has it always been that way?"

Harriet studied her a moment. "It's a combination of both. The Americans working here are in a pressure cooker. We're afraid to make friends with Romanians because they probably belong to the *Securitate*, so we stick together. We're a small group, so pretty soon that gets claustrophobic." She shrugged. "The pay is small, the food is lousy, and the weather is bad." She studied Mary. "None of that is your fault, Ambassador Ashley. You have two problems: the first is that you're a political appointee and you're in charge of an embassy manned by career diplomats." She stopped. "Am I coming on too strong?"

"No. Please go on."

"Most of them were against you before you even got here. To them, you're an amateur telling professionals how to run their business. The second problem is that you're a woman. The men in the embassy don't like taking orders from a woman."

"I see."

Harriet Kruger smiled. "But you sure have a great publicity agent. I've never seen so many magazine cover stories in my life. How did you do it?"

Mary had no answer to that. She was, in fact, disturbed by the comments about the amount of publicity she and the children had been getting. There had even been an article in *Pravda*, with a picture of the three of them.

Harriet Kruger glanced at her watch. "Oops! You're going to be late. Florian's waiting to take you home so that you can change. Aside from President Ionescu's reception you have three parties tonight."

Mary was staring at her. "That's impossible. I have too—"

"It goes with the territory. There are seventy-five embassies in Bucharest, and on any given night some of them are celebrating something."

"Can't I say no?"

"That would be the United States saying no to them. They would be offended."

Mary sighed. "I guess I'd better go and change."

AS SOON AS MARY ARRIVED, President Ionescu walked over to her. He kissed her hand and said, "I have been looking forward to seeing you again."

"Thank you, Your Excellency. I too."

She had a feeling he had been drinking heavily. She recalled the dossier on him: Married. One son, fourteen, the heir apparent, and three daughters. Is a womanizer. Drinks a lot. A shrewd peasant mentality. Charming when it suits him. Generous to his friends. Dangerous and ruthless to his enemies.

Ionescu took Mary's arm and led her off to a deserted corner. "You will find us Romanians interesting." He squeezed her arm. "We are a very passionate people." He looked at her for a reaction, and when he got none he went on, "We are descendants of the ancient Dacians and their conquerors, the Romans. For centuries we have been Europe's doormat. The Huns, Goths, Avars, Slavs and Mongols wiped their feet on us, but Romania has survived. And do you know how?" He leaned closer to her. "By giving our people a strong, firm leadership. They trust me, and I rule them well."

Mary thought of some of the stories she had heard. The arrests in the middle of the night, the atrocities, the disappearances.

Ionescu was about to continue talking when a man came up to him and whispered in his ear. Ionescu's expression turned cold. He hissed something in Romanian, and the man hurried off. The dictator turned back to Mary, oozing charm again. "I must leave you now. I look forward to seeing you again soon." And he was gone.

457

To GET A HEAD START on the crowded day that faced her, Mary had asked Florian to pick her up at six thirty am. During the ride to the embassy she read the reports and communiqués that had been delivered to the residence during the night.

As Mary walked past Mike Slade's office she stopped in surprise. He was at his desk working. "You're in early," she said.

He looked up. "Morning. I'd like to have a word with you. Not here. Your office."

He followed Mary through the connecting door to her office, and watched as he walked over to an instrument in the corner of the room. "This is a shredder," Mike informed her.

"I know that."

"Really? Last night you left some papers on top of your desk. By now they've been photographed and sent to Moscow."

"Oh, no! I must have forgotten. Which ones?"

"A list of personal things you wanted to order. But that's beside the point. The cleaning women work for the *Securitate*. Lesson number one: at night everything must be locked up or shredded."

"What's lesson number two?" Mary asked coldly.

Mike grinned. "The ambassador always starts the day by having coffee with her deputy chief. How do you take yours?"

"I—black."

"Good. You have to watch your figure around here. The food is fattening." He started towards the door that led to his office. "I make my own special brew. You'll like it."

Mary sat there, infuriated by his arrogance. I have to be careful how I handle him, she decided. I want him out of here as quickly as possible.

He returned with two steaming mugs of coffee.

"How do I arrange for Beth and Tim to start school?" she asked.

"I've already arranged it. Florian will deliver them mornings and pick them up afternoons."

She was taken aback. "I—thank you."

"The school is small, but excellent. Each class has eight or nine students. They come from all over—Canadians, Israelis, Nigerians—you name it." Mike took a sip of his coffee. "I understand that you had a nice chat with our fearless leader last night."

"President Ionescu? Yes. He seemed very pleasant."

"Oh, he is. Until he gets annoyed with somebody. Don't let Ionescu's charm fool you. He's a dyed-in-the-wool s.o.b. His people despise him, but there's nothing they can do about it. The secret police are everywhere. The general rule of thumb here is that one out of every three people works for *Securitate* or the KGB. A Romanian can be arrested for merely signing a petition."

458

Mary felt a shiver go through her. "They do have trials here?"

"Oh, occasionally they'll have show trials, but most of the people arrested manage to have fatal accidents while they're in police custody. In general, conditions here are horrifying, but the people are afraid to strike back because they know they'll be shot. The standard of living is one of the lowest in Europe. There's a shortage of everything. If people see a queue in front of a store, they'll join in and buy whatever's for sale while they have the chance."

"It seems to me," Mary said slowly, "that all these things add up to a wonderful opportunity for us to help them."

Mike Slade looked at her. "Sure," he said drily. "Wonderful."

AS MARY WAS GOING THROUGH some newly arrived cables from Washington that afternoon, she thought about Mike Slade. He was arrogant and rude. Yet he'd arranged for the children's school. He may be more complex than I thought, she decided. But I still don't trust him.

THE INSIDE OF THE IVAN STELIAN PRISON was even more forbidding than its exterior. The corridors were narrow, painted a dull grey. There was a jungle of crowded, black-barred cells patrolled by uniformed guards armed with machineguns. The stench was overpowering.

A guard led Mary to a small visitor's room, saying, "She's in there. You have ten minutes."

Mary entered and the door closed behind her.

Hannah Murphy was seated at a small, battle-scarred table. She was handcuffed and wearing prison garb. Her face was pale and gaunt and her eyes were red and swollen. Her hair was uncombed.

"Hi," Mary said. "I'm the American ambassador."

Hannah Murphy looked at her and began to sob uncontrollably.

Mary put her arms round her and said soothingly, "It's going to be all right. Tell me what happened."

Hannah Murphy took a deep breath. "I met this man—he was a Romanian—and I was lonely. He was nice to me and we—we spent the night together. A girlfriend had given me some marijuana. I shared it with him. When I woke up in the morning, he was gone, but the police were there. And they brought me to this hellhole." She shook her head helplessly. "Five years."

Mary thought of what Lucas Janklow had said as she was leaving for the prison: "There's nothing you can do for her. If she were a Romanian, they'd probably give her life." Now Mary looked at Hannah Murphy and said, "I'll do everything in my power to help you."

Mary had examined the official police report. It was signed by Captain Aurel Istrase, head of *Securitate*. It was brief and unhelpful, but there was no doubt of the girl's guilt. I'll have to find another way, Mary thought. Aurel Istrase. The name had a familiar ring. She thought back to the confidential dossier James Stickley had showed her in Washington. She remembered something in there about Captain Istrase . . .

Mary arranged to meet the captain the following morning.

AUREL ISTRASE WAS A SHORT, swarthy man with a scarred face. He had come to the embassy for the meeting. He was curious about the new American ambassador.

"You wished to talk to me, Madam Ambassador?"

"Thank you for coming. I want to discuss Hannah Murphy."

"Ah, yes. The drug peddler. In Romania we have strict laws about people who sell drugs. They go to jail."

"Excellent," Mary said. "I'm pleased to hear that. I wish we had stricter drug laws in the United States."

Istrase was watching her, puzzled. "Then you agree with me?"

"Absolutely. Anyone who sells drugs deserves jail. Hannah Murphy, however, did not sell drugs. She offered to *give* some marijuana to a Romanian citizen."

"It is the same thing. If—"

"Not quite, Captain. The Romanian was a lieutenant on your police force. He smoked marijuana too. Has he been punished?"

"He was merely gathering evidence of a criminal act."

"Your lieutenant has a wife and three children?"

Captain Istrase frowned. "Yes."

"Does the lieutenant's wife know about her husband's affair?"

Captain Istrase stared at her. "Why should she?"

"Because it sounds to me like a clear case of entrapment. I think we had better make this whole thing public. The international press will be fascinated."

"There would be no point in that," Istrase said.

She sprang her ace. "Because the lieutenant happens to be your son-in-law?"

"Certainly not! I just want to see justice done."

"So do I," Mary assured him.

According to the dossier she had seen, the son-in-law specialized in making the acquaintance of young tourists, seducing them, suggesting places where they could trade in the black market or buy drugs, and then turning them in.

Mary said in a conciliatory tone, "I see no need for your daughter to know how her husband conducts himself. I think it would be much better if you released Hannah Murphy from jail and I sent her back to the States. What do you say, Captain?"

460

He sat there fuming. Finally he shrugged. "I will use what little influence I have."

"I'm sure you will, Captain Istrase. Thank you."

The next day a grateful Hannah Murphy was on her way home.

"How did you do it?" Mike Slade asked unbelievingly.

"I followed your advice. I charmed him."

Chapter Eight

The day Beth and Tim were to start school, Mary got a call at five am from the embassy that a NIACT—a night action cable—had come in and required an immediate answer. It was the start of a long and busy day, and by the time Mary returned to the residence, it was after seven pm. The children were waiting for her.

"Well," Mary asked, "how was school?"

"I like it," Beth replied. "Did you know there are kids there from twenty-two different countries? This neat Italian boy kept staring at me all through class. It's a great school."

"They've got a keen science laboratory," Tim added. "Tomorrow we're going to take some Romanian frogs apart."

"Well, I'm glad you had no problems."

Beth said, "No, Mom. Mike Slade took care of us."

"What does Mike Slade have to do with your going to school?"

"He took us and introduced us to our teachers. He knows them all."

"He knows a lot of kids there too," Tim said. "And he introduced us to them. Everybody likes him. He's a neat guy."

A little too neat, Mary thought.

THE FOLLOWING MORNING when Mike walked into Mary's office, she said, "I understand that you took Beth and Tim to school."

He nodded. "It's tough for youngsters trying to adjust in a foreign country. They're good kids. And speaking of kids, we have a sick kid here you'd better take a look at."

He led her to one of the small offices down the corridor. On the couch was a white-faced young marine, groaning in pain.

"What happened?" Mary asked.

"My guess is appendicitis."

"Then we'd better get him to a hospital right away."

"Not here. He has to be flown either to Rome or Zurich. No one from an American embassy ever goes to a hospital in an iron-curtain country."

"But why?"

"Because we're vulnerable. We could be put under ether or given

461

scopolamine. They could extract all kinds of information from us. It's a State Department rule. We fly him out."

"Why don't we have our own doctor?" Mary snapped.

"Because we're a C-category embassy. We haven't the budget for our own doctor. An American doctor pays us a visit here once every three months. In the meantime, we have a pharmacist for minor aches and pains. Just sign this and he's on his way."

"Very well." Mary signed the paper. She walked over to the young marine and took his hand in hers. "You're going to be fine," she said softly, "just fine."

Two hours later the marine was on a plane to Zurich.

THE TIME-ZONE PROBLEM was exhausting. When it was daylight in Washington, it was the middle of the night in Bucharest, and Mary was constantly being woken by telegrams and telephone calls at three and four in the morning. Afterwards, she would be too keyed up to go back to sleep.

It's exciting, Edward. I really think I can make a difference here. Anyway, I'm trying. I couldn't bear to fail. Everyone is counting on me. I wish you were here to say "You can do it, old girl." I miss you so much, Edward. Can you hear me my darling? Are you there, somewhere where I can't see you? Sometimes not knowing the answer to that drives me crazy . . .

MARY SPENT EVERY POSSIBLE MOMENT she could with the children. They did a lot of sightseeing. There were dozens of museums and old churches to visit, but for the children the highlight of all their trips was to Dracula's castle in Brasov, located in the heart of Transylvania, a hundred miles from Bucharest.

"The count was really a prince," Florian explained on the drive up. "Prince Vlad Tepes. He was a great hero who stopped the Turkish invasion."

"I thought he just sucked blood and killed people," Tim said.

Florian nodded. "Yes. Unfortunately, after the war Vlad's power went to his head. He became a dictator, and he impaled his enemies on stakes. The legend grew that he was a vampire. An Irishman named Bram Stoker wrote a book based on the legend. A silly book, but it has done wonders for tourism."

Bran Castle was a huge stone monument high in the mountains. They climbed the steep stone steps leading to the castle and went into a low-ceilinged room containing guns and ancient artifacts.

"This is where Count Dracula murdered his victims and drank their blood," the guide said in a sepulchral voice.

462

The room was damp and eerie. A spider's web brushed across Tim's face. "I'm not scared or anything," he said to his mother, "but can we get out of here?"

EVERY MORNING WHEN MARY rode to work she noticed long queues of people outside the gates, waiting to get into the consular section of the embassy. She had taken it for granted that they were people with minor problems they hoped the consul could solve. But on this particular morning she went to the window to take a closer look, and the expressions she saw on their faces impelled her to go into Mike's office.

"Who are all those people waiting in line outside?"

Mike walked with her to the window. "They're mostly Romanian Jews. They're waiting to file applications for visas."

"But there's an Israeli embassy in Bucharest."

"They think there's less chance of the Romanian security people finding out their intention if they come to us. They're wrong, of course." He pointed out of the window. "That apartment house has several flats filled with agents using telescopic lenses, photographing everybody who goes in and out of the embassy."

"That's terrible!"

"That's the way they play the game. When a Jewish family applies for a visa to emigrate, they lose their green job cards and they're thrown out of their apartments. Then it takes three to four years before the government will tell them whether they'll even get their exit papers, and the answer is usually no."

"Can't we do something about it?"

"We try all the time. But Ionescu enjoys playing a cat-and-mouse game with the Jews. Very few of them are ever allowed to leave the country."

Mary looked out at the expressions of hopelessness on their faces. "There has to be a way," she said.

"Don't break your heart," Mike told her, handing her her morning coffee.

What a cold man, Mary thought, I wonder if anything ever touches him. I'm going to do something to help the Jews, she promised herself.

Mike rose. "There's a Romanian folk dance company opening tonight. They're supposed to be pretty good. Would you like to go?"

Mary was taken by surprise. The last thing she had expected was that Mike would invite her out.

And now, even more incredibly, she found herself saying yes.

"Good." Mike handed her a small envelope. "Here are three tickets. You can take Beth and Tim, courtesy of the Romanian government. We get tickets to most of their openings."

Mary sat there, her face flushed, feeling like a fool. "Thank you," she said stiffly.

"I'll have Florian pick you up at eight o'clock."

Beth and Tim were not interested in going to the theatre. Beth had invited a schoolfriend for dinner. "It's my Italian friend."

"To tell you the truth, I've never really cared much for folk dancing," Tim added.

Mary laughed. "I'll let you two off the hook this time."

She wondered if the children were as lonely as she was. She thought about whom she could invite to go with her. She mentally ran down the list: Colonel McKinney, Jerry Davis, Harriet Kruger? There was no one she really wanted to be with. I'll go alone, she decided.

The folk theatre, an ornate relic of more tranquil times, was on Rasodia Romana, a bustling street filled with small stands selling flowers, and blouses and pens. The entertainment was boring, the costumes tawdry and the dancers awkward. The show seemed interminable, and when it was finally over Mary was glad to escape into the fresh night air. Florian was standing by the limousine in front of the theatre.

"I'm afraid there will be a delay, Madam Ambassador. A flat tyre. And a thief has stolen the spare. I have sent for one. It should be here in the next hour. Would you like to wait in the car?"

Mary looked up at the full moon shining above. The evening was crisp and clear. She realized she had not taken a walk since she had arrived in Bucharest. "I think I'll walk back."

She turned and started walking down the street towards the central square. Bucharest was a fascinating, exotic city. Even at this late hour most of the shops were open, and there were queues at all of them. Coffee shops were serving *gogoaşe*, the delicious Romanian doughnuts. The pavements were crowded with late-night shoppers carrying *pungi*, string shopping bags. It seemed to Mary that the people were ominously quiet. They were staring at her, the women avidly eyeing her clothes. She began to walk faster.

When she reached a street called Calea Victoriei, she stopped, unsure of which direction to take. She said to a passerby, "Excuse me—" He gave her a quick, frightened look and hurried off.

How was she going to get back? It seemed to her that the residence was somewhere to the east. She began walking in that direction. Soon she was in a small, dimly lit side street. In the far distance she could see a broad, well-lit boulevard. I can get a taxi there, Mary thought with relief.

There was the sound of heavy footsteps behind her and she turned. A large man in an overcoat was coming towards her.

"Excuse me," the man called out in a heavy Romanian accent. "Are you lost?"

She was filled with relief. He was probably a policeman.

"Yes," Mary said gratefully. "I want to go back to—"

There was the sudden roar of a car racing up behind her, and then the squeal of brakes. The pedestrian in the overcoat grabbed Mary. She could smell his hot, fetid breath and feel his fat fingers bruising her wrist. He started pushing her towards the open door of the car. "Get in the car!" he growled.

"No!" Mary was fighting to break free. "Help! Help me!"

There was a shout from across the street, and a figure came racing towards them. The man stopped, unsure of what to do.

The stranger yelled, "Let go of her!"

He grabbed the man in the overcoat and pulled him away from Mary. The man behind the wheel got out of the car to help his accomplice.

From the far distance came the sound of an approaching siren, and the two men leaped into the car, which sped away.

A blue and white car with the word MILITIA on the side and a flashing light on top pulled up in front of Mary. Two men in uniform hurried out. In Romanian one of them asked, "Are you all right?" And then in halting English, "What happened?"

Mary was fighting to get herself under control. "Two men—they—they tr-tried to force me into their car. If—if it hadn't been for this gentleman—" She turned. But the stranger was gone.

MARY FOUGHT ALL NIGHT LONG, waking in a panic, falling back to sleep and waking again. She kept reliving the scene. Had they known who she was? Or were they merely trying to rob a tourist?

When Mary arrived at her office, Mike Slade was waiting for her as usual. He brought in two cups of coffee and sat down opposite her. The coffee was delicious, and she realized that having coffee with Mike had become a morning ritual.

"How was the theatre?" Mike asked.

"Fine." The rest was none of his business.

"Did you get hurt when they tried to kidnap you?"

"I—how do you know about that?"

His voice was filled with irony. "Madam Ambassador, Romania is one big, open secret. It wasn't very clever of you to go for a stroll by yourself."

"I'm aware of that now. It won't happen again."

"Good." His tone was brisk. "Did they take anything?"

"No."

He frowned. "It makes no sense. If they had wanted your coat or purse, they could have taken them from you in the street. Trying to force you into a car means it was a kidnapping."

465

"Who would want to kidnap me?"

"It wouldn't have been Ionescu's men. He's trying to keep our relations on an even keel. It would have to be some dissident group." He took a sip of his coffee. "May I give you some advice?"

"I'm listening."

"Go home."

"What?"

Mike Slade put down the cup. "Send in a letter of resignation, pack up your kids, and go back to Kansas, where you'll be safe."

Mary could feel her face getting red. "Mr. Slade, I made a mistake. It's not the first one I've made, and it probably won't be the last one. But I was appointed to this post by the President of the United States, and until he fires me, I don't want you or anyone else telling me to go home." She fought to keep control of her voice. "I expect the people in this embassy to work with me, not against me. If that's too much for you to handle, why don't *you* go home?"

Mike Slade stood up. "I'll see that the morning reports are put on your desk, Madam Ambassador."

The attempted kidnapping was the sole topic of conversation at the embassy that morning. How had everyone found out? Mary wondered. And how had Mike Slade found out?

Mary wished she could have learned the name of her rescuer, so that she could thank him. In the quick glimpse she had had of him, she had got the impression of an attractive man, probably in his early forties. He had had a foreign accent.

An idea kept gnawing at Mary, and it was hard to dismiss. The only person she knew of who wanted to get rid of her was Mike Slade. What if he had set up the attack to frighten her into leaving? He had given her the theatre tickets. He had known where she would be.

THERE WAS A COCKTAIL PARTY at the French embassy that evening in honour of a visiting French concert pianist. Mary was tired and nervous, but she knew she had to go.

When Mary arrived, the embassy was already crowded with guests. As she was exchanging pleasantries with the ambassador she caught sight of the stranger who had rescued her from the kidnappers. He was talking to the Italian ambassador.

"Please excuse me," Mary said. She moved across the room towards her rescuer.

He was saying, "Of course I miss Paris, but I hope—" He broke off as he saw Mary approaching. "Ah, the lady in distress."

"You know each other?" the Italian ambassador asked.

"We haven't been officially introduced," Mary replied.

467

"Madam Ambassador, may I present Dr. Louis Desforges."

The expression on the Frenchman's face changed. *"Madam Ambassador?* I beg your pardon! I had no idea." His voice was filled with embarrassment. "I should have recognized you."

"You did better than that." Mary smiled. "You saved me."

The Italian ambassador turned to Mary. "I heard about your unfortunate experience."

"It would have been unfortunate if Dr. Desforges hadn't come along. Thank you."

Louis Desforges smiled. "I'm happy that I was in the right place at the right time."

The ambassador excused himself. Mary was alone with the doctor.

"Why did you run away when the police came?" she asked.

The doctor studied her for a moment. "It is not good policy to get involved with the Romanian police. They have a way of arresting witnesses, then pumping them for information. I'm a doctor attached to the French embassy here, and I don't have diplomatic immunity. I do, however, know a great deal about what goes on at our embassy." He smiled. "So forgive me if I seemed to desert you."

There was a directness about him that was very appealing. He had the same openness that Edward had had, and almost the same smile.

"If you'll excuse me," Dr. Desforges said, "I must go and become a social animal."

"You don't like parties?"

He winced. "I despise them."

"Does your wife enjoy them?"

"Yes—she did. Very much." He hesitated, then said, "She and our two children are dead."

Mary paled. "Oh—I'm so sorry. How—?"

His face was rigid. "I blame myself. We were living in Algeria. I was in the underground, fighting the terrorists. They found out my identity and blew up the house. I was away at the time."

"I'm so sorry," Mary said again. Hopeless, inadequate words.

"There is a cliché that time heals everything. I no longer believe it. If you will excuse me, Madam Ambassador." He turned to greet a group of arriving guests.

He reminds me a little of Edward, Mary thought. He's a brave man. He's in a lot of pain, and I think that's what draws me to him. I'm in pain too. *Will I ever get over missing you, Edward? It's so lonely here.*

THE FOLLOWING DAY Mary could not get Dr. Louis Desforges out of her mind. He had saved her life and then disappeared. She was glad she had found him again. On an impulse she bought a beautiful silver bowl for him and had it sent to the French embassy. It was a small enough gesture after what he had done.

That afternoon Dr. Desforges telephoned. "Good afternoon, Madam Ambassador." The phrase sounded delightful in his French accent. "I called to thank you for your thoughtful gift. I assure you that it was unnecessary. I was delighted that I was able to be of some service."

"It was more than just some service," Mary told him.

There was a pause. "Would you—" He sounded suddenly shy. "I was wondering if you might care to have dinner with me one evening—but I know how busy you must be and—"

"I would love to," Mary said quickly.

"Really? Are you free tomorrow night?"

"Yes."

"Ah, splendid."

They agreed to meet at the Tarv restaurant at eight o'clock.

IN THE LIMOUSINE, on the way to the restaurant, Mary asked Florian to stop at the embassy. She had left a silk scarf in her office and wanted to pick it up.

Gunny was on duty at the desk. He stood at attention and saluted her. Mary walked down the corridor to her office and turned on the light. She stood there, frozen. On the wall someone had sprayed in red paint GO HOME BEFORE YOU DIE. She backed out of the room, white-faced, and ran down the hall to the reception desk. "Gunny—wh-who's been in my office?" she demanded.

"Why, no one that I know of, ma'am."

"Let me see your roster sheet." She tried to keep her voice from quavering.

"Yes, ma'am." Gunny pulled out the visitors' access sheet and handed it to her. Each name had the time of entry listed after it. She scanned the list. There were a dozen names.

Mary looked up at the marine guard. "Were all the people on this list escorted to the offices they visited?"

"Always, Madam Ambassador. Is something wrong?"

Something was very wrong. Mary said, "Please send someone to my office to paint out that obscenity on the wall."

She turned and hurried outside, afraid she was going to be sick.

DR. LOUIS DESFORGES was waiting for Mary when she arrived at the restaurant. He stood up as she approached the table.

"I'm sorry I'm late." Mary tried to sound normal. She wished she had not come. She pressed her hands together to keep them from trembling.

"Are you all right?"

469

"Yes," she said. "I'm fine." *Go home before you die.* "I think I'd like a straight Scotch, please."

The doctor ordered drinks, then said, "It can't be easy being an ambassador— especcially a woman—in this country. Romanians are male chauvinists, you know."

Mary forced a smile. "Tell me about yourself." Anything to take her mind off the threat.

"I am afraid there is not much to tell that is exciting."

"You mentioned that you fought in the underground in Algeria. That sounds exciting."

He shrugged. "We live in terrible times. I believe that every man must risk something so that in the end he does not have to risk everything. The terrorist situation is literally that—terrifying. We must put an end to it." His voice was filled with passion.

He's like Edward, Mary thought. Edward was always passionate about his beliefs.

Dr. Desforges was saying, "If I had known that the price would be the lives of my family—" He stopped. His knuckles were white against the table. "Forgive me. I did not bring you here to talk about my troubles. Let me recommend the lamb. They do it very well here."

He ordered dinner and a bottle of wine, and they talked. Mary began to relax, to forget the frightening warning painted in red. She was finding it surprisingly easy to talk to this attractive Frenchman. In an odd way, it was like talking to Edward. It was amazing how she and Louis shared so many of the same beliefs and felt the same way about so many things. Louis Desforges was born in a small town in France, and Mary was born in a small town in Kansas, five thousand miles apart, and yet their backgrounds were similar. His father had been a farmer and had scrimped and saved to send Louis to medical school in Paris.

"My father was a wonderful man, Madam Ambassador."

"Mary."

"Thank you. Mary."

She smiled. "You're welcome, Louis."

Mary wondered what his personal life was like. He was handsome and intelligent. "Have you thought of getting married again?" She could not believe she had asked him that.

He shook his head. "No. My wife was a remarkable woman. No one could ever replace her."

That's how I feel about Edward, Mary thought. And yet it was not really a question of replacing a beloved one. It was finding someone new to share things with.

Louis was saying, "So when I was offered the opportunity, I thought it would be interesting to visit Romania." He lowered his voice. "I confess I feel something evil about this country. Not the people. They are lovely. But the government is everything I despise. There is no freedom here for anyone." He glanced around to make sure no one could overhear. "I shall be glad when my tour of duty is over and I can return to France."

Without thinking, Mary heard herself saying, "There are some people who think *I* should go home."

"I beg your pardon?"

And suddenly Mary found herself telling him about the paint scrawl on her office wall.

"But that is horrible! You have no idea who did this?"

"No."

Louis said, "May I make an impertinent confession? Since I found out who you were, I have been asking questions. Everyone who knows you is very impressed with you."

She was listening to him with intense interest.

"You have brought here an image of America that is beautiful and intelligent and warm. If you believe in what you are doing, then you must fight for it. You must stay. Do not let anyone frighten you away." It was what Edward would have said.

THE FOLLOWING MORNING Mike Slade brought in two cups of coffee. He nodded at the wall where the message had been painted. "I hear someone has been spraying graffiti on your walls."

"Yes. Have they found out who did it?"

Mike took a sip of coffee. "No. I went through the visitors' list myself. Everyone is accounted for."

"That means it must have been someone here in the embassy."

"Either that, or someone managed to sneak in past the guards."

"Do you believe that?"

Mike put down his coffee cup. "Nope."

"Neither do I."

"What exactly did it say?"

"'Go home before you die'."

He made no comment.

"Who would want to kill me?"

"I don't know. But we're doing everything we can to track down whoever it is. In the meantime, I've arranged for a marine guard to be posted outside your door at night."

"Mr. Slade, I would appreciate a straight answer. Do you think I'm in any real danger?"

He studied her thoughtfully. "Madam Ambassador, they assassinated John Kennedy, Martin Luther King and Marin Groza. We're all vulnerable. The answer to your question is yes."

THREE DAYS LATER Mary had dinner again with Dr. Louis Desforges. He seemed more relaxed with her this time, and although the core of sadness she sensed within him was still there, he took pains to be attentive and amusing. Mary wondered if he felt the same attraction towards her that she felt towards him.

After dinner, when Louis took Mary back to the residence, she asked, "Would you like to come in?"

"Thank you," he said. "I would."

The children were downstairs doing their homework.

"Would you all like some hot chocolate?" Mary asked.

The four of them sat in the huge kitchen drinking hot chocolate and talking. The children were utterly enchanted with Louis. He focused entirely on them, telling them stories and anecdotes and jokes until he had them roaring with laughter.

It was almost midnight when Mary looked at her watch. "Oh, no! You children should have been in bed hours ago. Scoot."

Tim went over to Louis. "Will you come to see us again?"

"I hope so, Tim."

Mary saw Louis to the door. He took her hand in his. "They're beautiful children." His voice was husky. "I won't try to tell you what this evening has meant to me, Mary."

"I'm glad." She was looking into his eyes, and she felt him moving towards her. She raised her lips.

"Goodnight, Mary." And he was gone.

DAVID VICTOR, THE COMMERCE CONSUL, hurried into Mary's office. "I have some very bad news. I just got a tip that President Ionescu is going to approve a contract with Argentina for a million and a half tons of corn, and with Brazil for half a million tons of soybeans. We were counting heavily that they'd buy from us."

"How far have the negotiations gone?"

"They're almost concluded. We've been shut out. I was about to send a cable to Washington—with your approval, of course."

"Hold off a bit," Mary said. "I want to think about it."

"You won't get President Ionescu to change his mind. Believe me, I've tried every argument I could think of."

"Then we have nothing to lose if I give it a try." She buzzed her secretary. "Dorothy, set up an appointment with President Ionescu as quickly as possible."

ALEXANDROS IONESCU INVITED MARY to the palace for lunch. As she entered she was greeted by Nicu, his fourteen-year-old son. He was a handsome boy, tall for his age, with beautiful black eyes.

"Good afternoon, Madam Ambassador," he said. "I am Nicu. Welcome to the palace. I have heard very nice things about you."

"Thank you. I'm pleased to hear that, Nicu."

"I will tell my father you have arrived."

Mary and Ionescu sat opposite each other in the formal dining room, just the two of them.

The President had been drinking and was in a mellow mood. He lighted a Snogov, the vile-smelling Romanian cigarette.

"Mr. President," said Mary. "I was eager to meet with you, because I have something important to discuss with you."

Ionescu almost laughed aloud. He knew exactly why she had come. The Americans wanted to sell him corn and soybeans, but they were too late. The American ambassador would go away empty-handed this time. Too bad. Such an attractive woman.

"Yes?" he said innocently.

"I want to talk to you about sister cities."

Ionescu blinked. "I beg your pardon?"

"Sister cities. You know—like San Francisco and Osaka, Los Angeles and Bombay, Washington and Bangkok . . ."

"I—I don't understand. What does that have to do with—?"

"Mr. President, it occurred to me that you could get headlines all over the world if you made Bucharest a sister city of some American city. It would get almost as much attention as President Ellison's people-to-people plan."

He said cautiously, "A sister city with the United States? It is an interesting idea. What would it involve?"

"Mostly, wonderful publicity for you. You would be a hero. It would be your idea. You would pay the city a visit. A delegation from Kansas City would pay *you* a visit."

"Kansas City?"

"That's just a suggestion, of course. Kansas City is Middle America. There are farmers there, like your farmers. Mr. President, your name would be on everyone's lips. No one in Europe has thought of doing this."

He sat there, silent. "I—I would naturally have to give this a great deal of thought."

"Naturally."

"Kansas City, Kansas, and Bucharest, Romania." He nodded. "We are a much larger city, of course."

"Of course. Bucharest would be the big sister."

"I must admit it is a very intriguing idea. Is there any chance of a rejection from the American side?" Ionescu asked.

"Absolutely none. I can guarantee it."

He sat there reflecting. "When would this go into effect?"

"Just as soon as you're ready to announce it."

Ionescu thought of something else. "We could set up a trade exchange with our sister city. Romania has many things to sell. Tell me—what crops does Kansas grow?"

"Among other things," Mary said innocently, "corn and soybeans."

"YOU REALLY MADE THE DEAL? You actually fooled him?" David Victor asked incredulously.

"Not for a minute," Mary assured him. "Ionescu knew what I was after. He just liked the package I wrapped it in. He's already rehearsing his television speech."

WHEN STANTON ROGERS heard the news, he telephoned Mary. "You're a genius." He laughed. "We thought we'd lost that deal. How in the world did you do it?"

"Ego," Mary said. "His."

"The President asked me to tell you what a really great job you're doing over there, Mary."

"Thank him for me, Stan."

"I will. By the way, the President and I are leaving for China in a few weeks. If you need me, you can get in touch with me through my office."

"Have a wonderful trip."

Chapter Nine

Over the swiftly moving weeks the dancing March winds had given way to spring and then summer. Trees and flowers blossomed everywhere, and the parks were green.

In Buenos Aires, it was winter. When Neusa Muñez returned to her apartment, it was the middle of the night. The telephone was ringing. "*Si?*" It was the *gringo* from the United States.

"May I speak with Angel?"

"Angel no here, *señor*. Wha' you wan'?"

"Tell Angel I need him for a contract in Bucharest."

"Budapes'?"

The Controller found his irritation mounting. "*Bucharest*. Romania. Tell him it's a five-million-dollar contract. He has to be in Bucharest by the end of June. That's three weeks from now. Do you have that?"

"Wait a minute. I'm writin'. OK. How many people Angel gotta kill for five million dollars?"

"A lot . . ."

THE DAILY QUEUES in front of the embassy continued to disturb Mary. She discussed the subject again with Mike Slade.

"There must be something we can do to help those people get out of the country."

"Everything's been tried," Mike assured her. "We've applied pressure, we've offered to sweeten the money pot—Ionescu refuses to cut a deal."

"I'm going to have another talk with Ionescu."

"Good luck."

Mary asked Dorothy Stone to set up an appointment with the dictator. A few minutes later the secretary walked into Mary's office. "I'm sorry, Madam Ambassador. Something weird is going on at the presidential palace. Ionescu isn't seeing anybody. In fact, no one can even get in."

"Dorothy," Mary said, "see if you can find out what's going on there."

An hour later Dorothy reported back. "They're keeping it very hush-hush. Ionescu's son is dying."

Mary was aghast. "Nicu? What happened?"

"He has botulism poisoning. There was an epidemic in East Germany a few months ago. Apparently Nicu visited there and someone gave him some canned food as a gift. He ate some of it yesterday."

"But there's an antiserum for botulism!" Mary exclaimed.

"The European countries are out of it. The epidemic used it all up."

"Oh no!"

When Dorothy left the office, Mary sat there thinking. It might be too late, but still . . . She remembered how cheerful and happy young Nicu had been. He was fourteen years old—only two years older than Beth. "Dorothy, get me Walter Reed Hospital in Maryland."

Five minutes later she was speaking to the director.

"Yes, Madam Ambassador, we have an antiserum for botulism poisoning, and I'll be happy to supply some, but botulism poisoning works very rapidly. I'm afraid that by the time it gets there . . ."

"I'll arrange for it to get here. Just have it ready. Thank you."

Ten minutes later Mary was speaking to airforce general, Ralph Zukor in Washington.

"Good morning, Madam Ambassador. Well, this is an unexpected pleasure. My wife and I are big fans of yours. How are—?"

"General, I need a favour. I need your fastest jet."

"I beg your pardon?"

"I need a jet to fly some serum to Bucharest right away. Can you do it?"

"Well, yes. But first you'll have to get approval from the Secretary of Defence. There are requisition forms to fill out—"

Mary listened, seething. "General, a boy's life is at stake. He happens to be the son of the President of Romania. If that boy dies because some form hasn't been filled out, I'm going to call the biggest press conference you've ever seen. And I'll let you explain why you let Ionescu's son die."

"I'm sorry, but I can't possibly authorize an operation like this without an approval from the White House. If—"

Mary snapped. "Then get it. The serum will be delivered to Andrews Air Force Base. And, General, every single minute counts."

When Mary hung up, she sat there, silently praying.

GENERAL ZUKOR'S AIDE said, "What was that all about, sir?"

"The ambassador expects me to send up an SR-71 to fly some serum to Romania. It's ridiculous. But we might as well cover ourselves. Get me Stanton Rogers."

Five minutes later the general was speaking to the President's foreign adviser. "I just wanted to go on record with you that the request was made, and I naturally refused. If—"

Stanton Rogers said, "General, how soon can you have an SR-71 airborne?"

"In ten minutes, but—"

"Do it."

NICU IONESCU'S NERVOUS SYSTEM had been affected. He lay in bed, disorientated, sweating and pale, attached to a respirator. There were three doctors at his bedside.

President Ionescu strode into the bedroom. "What's happening?"

"Your Excellency, we have communicated with our colleagues all over Eastern and Western Europe. There is no antiserum left."

"What about the United States?"

The doctor shrugged. "By the time we could arrange for someone to fly the serum here—" He paused. "I'm afraid it would be too late."

Ionescu picked up his son's hand. "You're not going to die." He wept. "You're *not* going to die."

AN ARMY HELICOPTER DELIVERED the antibotulism serum, packed in ice, to Andrews Air Force Base. Three minutes later an SR-71 was in the air, on a northeast heading. The SR-71—the US airforce's fastest supersonic jet—flies at three times the speed of sound. It slowed down once to refuel over the mid-Atlantic. The plane made the five-thousand-mile flight to Bucharest in a little over two and a half hours.

MARY HAD REMAINED IN HER OFFICE all night, getting up-to-the-minute reports. At six am, McKinney telephoned. "They gave the boy the serum. The doctors say he's going to live."

"Oh, thank God!"

Two days later a diamond-and-emerald necklace was delivered to Mary's office with a note: "I can never thank you enough. Alexandros Ionescu."

"I don't believe this!" Dorothy exclaimed when she saw the necklace. "It must have cost half a million dollars!"

"At least," Mary said. "Return it."

The following morning President Ionescu sent for Mary.

An aide said, "The President is waiting for you in his office."

"May I see Nicu first?"

"Yes, of course." He led her upstairs.

Nicu was in bed, reading. He looked up as Mary entered. "Good morning, Madam Ambassador."

"Good morning, Nicu."

"My father told me what you did. I wish to thank you."

"I couldn't let you die. I'm saving you for Beth one day."

Nicu laughed. "Bring her over, and we'll talk about it."

President Ionescu was waiting downstairs for Mary. He said without preamble, "You returned my gift."

"Yes, Your Excellency."

He indicated a chair. "Sit down." He studied her for a moment. "You saved my son's life. I must give you something."

Mary said, "I don't bargain for children's lives."

"You must want something! Name your price."

Mary said, "Your Excellency, there is no price. I have two children of my own. I know how you must feel."

"Do you? Nicu is my only son. If anything had happened to him—" He stopped, unable to go on.

"I went up to see him. He looks fine. If there's nothing else, Your Excellency, I have an appointment." She rose and started to leave.

"Wait! You will not accept a gift, but—" He thought for a moment. "If you were to make a wish, what would you wish for? Anything at all that you want."

Mary stood there studying his face, thinking. Finally she said, "I wish that the restriction on the Jews waiting to leave Romania could be lifted."

"I see." Ionescu was still for a long time. Finally he looked up at Mary. "It shall be done. They will not all be allowed out, of course, but— I will make it easier."

When the announcement was made public two days later, Mary received a telephone call from President Ellison himself. "I thought I was sending a diplomat, and I got a miracle worker. Congratulations, Mary, on everything you've done over there."

"Thank you, Mr. President." She hung up, feeling a warm glow.

IN CELEBRATION OF HER DIPLOMATIC COUP, Louis invited Mary to a candlelit dinner in the rooftop restaurant at the Intercontinental Hotel. They saw each other whenever possible now, and more and more Mary had come to rely on him as an island of strength and sanity. Before they parted that night, Mary found herself accepting an invitation to go away to the mountains with him the following weekend.

Once she got into bed, she lay in the dark talking to Edward: *Darling, I'll always, always love you, but it's time I started a new life. You'll always be a part of that life, but there has to be someone else too. Louis isn't you, but he's strong, and he's good, and he's brave. That's as close as I can come to having you. Please understand, Edward. Please . . .*

"JULY IS JUST AROUND the corner," Harriet Kruger told Mary. "In the past the ambassador always gave a Fourth of July party for the Americans living in Bucharest. If you'd prefer not to—"

"No. I think it's a lovely idea."

"Fine. I'll take care of all the arrangements. A lot of flags, balloons, an orchestra—the works."

"Sounds wonderful. Thank you, Harriet."

A big party would eat into the residence's expense account, but it would be worth it. The truth is, Mary thought, I miss home. She had only been here for four months, but it seemed an eternity.

Junction City had meant peace and security, an easy, friendly way of life. Here, there was fear and terror and a death threat scrawled on her office wall in red paint. Suddenly Mary felt a sharp pang of loneliness, a sense of being totally isolated from her roots, adrift in an alien and dangerous land. Then she thought about Louis, and the loneliness began to disappear.

MARY WAS HAVING her usual morning coffee with Mike Slade, discussing the day's agenda.

When they had finished, he said, "I've been hearing rumours about you. It seems that you're seeing a lot of Dr. Desforges."

Mary felt a flare of anger. "Whom I see is no one's business but my own."

"I beg to differ with you, Madam Ambassador. The State Department has a strict rule against getting involved with foreigners, and the doctor is a foreigner. He also happens to be an enemy agent."

Mary was almost too stunned to speak. "That's absurd!"

"Think about how you met him," Mike suggested. "The damsel in distress and the knight in shining armour. That's the oldest trick in the world. I've used it myself."

"I don't care what you've done," Mary retorted. "He's worth a dozen of you. He fought against terrorists in Algeria, and they murdered his wife and children."

Mike said mildly, "That's interesting. I've been examining his dossier. Your doctor never had a wife or children."

THEY STOPPED FOR LUNCH at Timisoara on their way up to the Carpathian Mountains. The inn was decorated in the period style of a medieval wine cellar.

"The speciality of the house is game," Louis told Mary. "I would suggest the venison."

"Fine." She had never eaten venison. It was delicious. There was an air of confidence about Louis, a quiet strength that gave her a feeling of security.

After lunch they started out again. They passed farmers driving primitive, homemade wagons made from branches that were twisted together, and caravans of gipsies.

Louis was a skilful driver. Mary studied him as he drove. *"He's an enemy agent."* She did not believe Mike Slade. Every instinct told her he was lying. She trusted Louis. No one could have faked the emotion I saw on his face when he was playing with the children, she thought.

The air was getting noticeably thinner and cooler. The mountains ahead looked like pictures she had seen of the Swiss Alps, their peaks covered by mist and icy clouds the colour of steel.

It was late afternoon when they reached their destination, a lovely mountain retreat built like a chalet. Their suite had a comfortable living room, simply furnished, a bedroom, a bathroom and a terrace with a breathtaking view of the mountains.

"For the first time in my life," Louis sighed, "I wish I were a painter."

"It *is* a beautiful view."

He moved closer to her. "No. I wish I could paint you."

He took her in his arms and held her tightly. She buried her head against his chest, and then his lips were on hers, and she forgot everything except what was happening to her. He led her to the bed. There was a frantic need in her for someone to reassure her, to protect her, to let her know that she was no longer alone. She needed to be one with him.

Louis was an incredible lover, passionate and demanding, tender and caring. After a long, long time they lay contented. She nestled in his strong arms and they talked.

"It's so strange," Louis said. "I feel whole again. Since Renée and the children were killed, I've been a ghost, wandering around lost."

"I've felt helpless too. Edward was my umbrella, and when it rained and he wasn't there to protect me, I almost drowned."

They made love again. It was almost perfect. *Almost.* Because there was a question Mary dared not ask: Did you have a wife and children? She knew that the moment she asked the question, everything between them would be over for ever. Louis would never forgive her for doubting him. Curse Mike Slade, she thought.

Louis was watching her. "What are you thinking about?"

"Nothing, darling."

On Saturday they went by tram to a mountain peak. In the evening they drove to Eintrul, a rustic restaurant in the mountains, where they had dinner in a large room that had an open fireplace with a roaring fire. There were hunting trophies on the walls, and through the windows they could look at the snow-covered hills outside. A perfect setting.

And finally, too soon, it was Sunday, and time to leave.

As they neared the outskirts of Bucharest they drove past fields of sunflowers, their faces turning towards the sun. That's me, Mary thought happily. I'm finally moving into the sunlight.

THE NEXT MORNING, when Mary arrived at her office, there were a dozen red roses with a note: "Thank you for you."

Mary read the card. And wondered if he had sent flowers to Renée. And wondered if there had been a Renée, and two daughters. And hated herself for it. Why would Mike Slade make up a terrible lie like that? There was no way she could ever check it. And at that moment Eddie Maltz, the political consul and CIA agent, walked into her office.

They spent some time discussing a colonel who had approached Maltz about defecting.

"He'd be a valuable asset for us," Maltz told her. "He'll be bringing some useful information with him, but be prepared to receive some heat from Ionescu."

"Thank you, Mr. Maltz."

He rose to leave.

On a sudden impulse Mary said, "Wait. I—I wonder if I could ask you for a favour? It's—personal and confidential."

"Sounds like our motto," Maltz smiled.

"I need some information on a Dr. Louis Desforges. He's attached to the French embassy."

This was more difficult than she had imagined. It was a betrayal. "I— I'd like to know whether Dr. Desforges was once married and had two children. Do you think you could find out?"

"Will twenty-four hours be soon enough?" Maltz asked.

"Yes, thank you." Please forgive me, Louis, she thought.

A short time later, Mike Slade walked into Mary's office and put a cup of coffee on her desk. Something in his attitude seemed subtly changed.

480

Mary was not sure wha. it was, but she had a feeling that Mike Slade knew all about her weekend.

She took a sip of the coffee. Excellent, as usual. That's one thing Mike Slade does well, Mary thought.

"We have some problems," he said. And for the rest of the morning they became involved in a discussion that included the Romanian financial crisis and a dozen other topics.

At the end of the meeting Mary was more tired than usual.

Mike Slade said, "The ballet is opening tonight. Corina Socoli is dancing." She was one of the leading ballerinas in the world. "I have some tickets if you're interested."

"No thanks." She thought of the last time Mike had given her tickets. Besides, she was dining at the Chinese embassy.

As Mary was dressing for dinner she felt suddenly exhausted. She sank down on the bed. I wish I didn't have to go out tonight, she thought wearily. But I have to. My country is depending on me.

The evening was a blur of the same familiar diplomatic corps faces. Mary had only a hazy collection of the others at her table. She could not wait to get home.

When Mary woke up the following morning, she was feeling worse. Her head ached, and she was nauseated. It took all of her willpower to get dressed and go to the embassy.

Mike Slade was waiting in her office, coffee in hand. He took one look at her and said, "You don't look too well. You OK?"

"I'm just tired."

"What you need is a cup of coffee. It will perk you up. No pun intended." He handed her a cup of coffee. "Maybe you should fly to Frankfurt and see our doctor there."

Mary shook her head. "I'm fine." Her voice was slurred.

The only thing that made her feel slightly better was a visit from Eddie Maltz. "I have the information you requested," he said. "Desforges was married for fourteen years. Wife's name Renée. Two daughters, Phillipa and Geneviève. They were murdered in Algeria by terrorists as an act of vengeance against the doctor, who was fighting in the underground. Do you need any further information?"

"No," Mary said. "That's fine. Thank you."

By late afternoon Mary was feeling hot and feverish. She called Louis to cancel dinner. She felt too ill to see anybody. She wished that the American doctor was in Bucharest. Perhaps Louis would know what was wrong with her. If I don't get over this, she told herself, I'll call him back. Dorothy got the nurse to send up some aspirin. It did not help.

Somehow Mary managed to struggle through the rest of the day. When she finally arrived home, she fell straight into bed. Her whole body ached, and she could feel that her temperature had climbed. I'm really ill, she thought. I feel as though I'm dying. With an enormous effort she reached out and pulled the bell cord. Carmen appeared. She looked at Mary in alarm. "Madam Ambassador! What—?"

Mary's voice was a croak. "Please call the French embassy. I need Dr. Desforges."

MARY OPENED HER EYES and blinked. There were two blurred Louis figures bending over her.

"What's happening to you?" He felt her forehead. It was hot to the touch. "Have you taken your temperature?"

"I don't want to know." It hurt to talk.

Louis sat down on the edge of the bed. "Darling, when did you start feeling like this?"

"The day after we got back from the mountains."

Louis felt her pulse. It was very weak. As he leaned forward he smelled her breath. "Have you eaten something today with garlic?"

She shook her head. "I've hardly eaten anything in two days."

He gently lifted her eyelids. "Have you been thirsty?"

She nodded.

"Pain, muscle cramps, vomiting, nausea?"

"Yes. What's the matter with me Louis?"

"Do you feel like answering some questions?"

She swallowed. "I'll try."

He held her hand. "Do you remember having anything to eat or drink that made you feel ill afterwards?"

She shook her head.

"Do you eat breakfast here at the residence with the children?"

"Usually, yes," she whispered.

"And the children are feeling well?"

She nodded.

"What about lunch? Do you eat at the same place every day?"

"No. Sometimes the embassy, sometimes restaurants."

"Is there any one place you regularly have dinner, or anything you regularly eat?"

She closed her eyes.

He shook her gently. "Mary, listen to me." There was an urgency in his voice. "Is there any person you eat with constantly?"

She blinked up at him sleepily. "No." Why was he asking all these questions? "It's a virus," she mumbled. "Isn't it?"

He took a deep breath. "No. Someone is poisoning you."

482

It sent a bolt of electricity through her body. She opened her eyes wide. "What? I don't believe it."

He was frowning. "I would say it was arsenic poisoning, except that arsenic is not for sale in Romania."

Mary felt a sudden tremor of fear. "Who—who would be trying to poison me?"

He squeezed her hand. "Darling, you've got to think. Are you sure there's no set routine you have where someone gives you something to eat or drink every day?"

"Of course not," Mary protested weakly. "I told you, I—" *Coffee. Mike Slade. My own special brew.* "Oh, no!"

"What is it?"

She cleared her throat and managed to whisper, "Mike Slade brings me coffee every morning."

Louis stared at her. "Your deputy? No. What reason would he have for trying to kill you?"

"He— he wants to get rid of me."

"We'll talk about this later," Louis said urgently. "The first thing we have to do is treat you. I'm going to get something for you. I'll be back in a few minutes."

Mary lay there, trying to grasp the meaning of what Louis had told her. *"What you need is another cup of coffee. It will make you feel better. I brew it myself."*

She drifted off into unconsciousness and was awakened by Louis's voice. "Mary!"

She forced her eyes open. Louis was at her bedside, taking a syringe out of a small bag.

He felt for a vein in her arm. "I'm going to leave you an injection of BAL. It's an antidote for arsenic. I'm going to alternate it with penicillamine. Mary?" She was asleep.

The following morning Louis gave Mary another injection, and another one in the evening. The effects of the drugs were miraculous. The symptoms began to disappear. The following day Mary felt drained and weak, as though she had gone through a long illness, but all the pain and discomfort were gone.

"This is twice you've saved my life."

Louise looked at her soberly. "I think we'd better find out who's trying to take it."

"How do we do that?"

"I've been checking around at the various embassies. None of them carries arsenic. I have not been able to find out about the American embassy. So I would like you to do something for me. What I want you to do is go to the embassy pharmacy. Tell them you need a pesticide. Say that you're having trouble with insects in your garden. Ask for Antrol. That's loaded with arsenic."

Mary looked at him, puzzled. "What's the point?"

"My hunch is that the arsenic had to be flown into Bucharest. If it is anywhere, it will be in the embassy pharmacy. Anyone who checks out a poison must sign for it. When you sign for the Antrol see what names are on the sheet."

MARY WALKED DOWN the long corridor to the embassy pharmacy, where the nurse was working behind the cage. "Good morning, Madam Ambassador. Are you feeling better?"

"Yes, thank you."

"Can I get you something?"

Mary took a nervous breath. "My—my gardener tells me he's having trouble with insects in the garden. I wondered whether you might have something to help—like Antrol?"

"Why, yes. As a matter of fact, we do." The nurse reached towards a back shelf and picked up a can with a poison label on it. "You'll have to sign for it, if you don't mind. It has arsenic in it."

Mary was staring at the form placed in front of her. There was only one name on it.

Mike Slade.

Chapter Ten

When Mary tried to telephone Louis Desforges, to tell him what she had learned, his line was busy. He was talking to Mike Slade. Dr. Desforges's first instinct had been to report the murder attempt, except that he could not believe Slade was responsible. And so Louis had decided to telephone Slade himself.

"I have just left your ambassador," Louis Desforges said. "She is going to live."

"Well, that's good news, Doctor. Why shouldn't she?"

Louis's tone was cautious. "Someone has been poisoning her."

"What are you talking about?" Mike demanded.

"I think perhaps you know what I'm talking about."

"Hold it! Are you saying that you think *I'm* responsible? You and I had better have a private talk. Can you meet me tonight?"

"At what time?" asked Louis.

"I'm tied up until nine o'clock. Why don't you meet me a few minutes after, in Băneasa Forest? I'll meet you at the fountain and explain everything then."

484

Louis hesitated. "Very well. I will see you there." He hung up and thought, Mike Slade cannot possibly be behind this.

When Mary tried to telephone Louis again, he had left. No one knew where to reach him.

MARY AND THE CHILDREN were having dinner at the residence.

"You look a lot better," Beth said. "We were worried."

"I feel fine," Mary assured her. Thank God for Louis!

She could hear Mike Slade saying, *"Here's your coffee. I brew it myself."* Slowly killing her. She shuddered.

"Are you cold?" Tim asked.

"No, darling." Mary was thinking, There is only one person I can think of who could help me. Stanton Rogers. But what proof do I have? That Mike Slade made coffee for me every morning?

Beth was talking to her. "So can we watch a movie tonight?"

Mary had not planned on a movie, but she had spent so little time with the children lately that she decided to give them a treat. "Yes."

"Thank you, Madame Ambassador," Tim shouted. "Can we see *American Graffiti* again?"

American Graffiti. Suddenly Mary knew what proof she might show Stanton Rogers.

AT MIDNIGHT MARY asked Carmen to call a taxi.

"Don't you want Florian to drive you?" Carmen asked.

"No." This had to be done secretly.

"Good evening, Madam Ambassador," said the marine guard when Mary emerged from the taxi. "Can I help you?"

"No, thank you. I'm going to my office for a few minutes."

The marine walked her to the entrance and opened the door for her. He watched her walk down the hall.

Mary turned the lights on in her office and looked at the wall where the red scrawl had been washed away. She walked over to the connecting door that led to Mike Slade's office and entered. The room was in darkness. She turned on the lights.

There were no papers on his desk. The drawers were empty, except for brochures and timetables, innocent things that would be of no use to a snooping cleaning woman. Mary's eyes scrutinized the office. It had to be here somewhere.

She opened the drawers again and started examining their contents slowly and carefully. When she came to a bottom drawer, she felt something hard at the back, behind a mass of papers. She pulled it out and held it in her hand, staring at it.

It was a can of red spray paint.

AT A FEW MINUTES after nine pm Dr. Louis Desforges was waiting in Băneasa Forest, near the fountain. He wondered if he had done the wrong thing by not reporting Mike Slade. No, he thought, first I must hear what he has to say.

Mike Slade appeared suddenly out of the darkness. "Thanks for coming. We can clear this up very quickly. You said you thought someone was poisoning Mary Ashley."

"I *know* it. Someone was feeding her arsenic."

"And you think I'm responsible?"

"You could have put it in her coffee, a little bit at a time."

"Have you reported this to anyone?"

"Not yet. I wanted to talk to you first."

"I'm glad you did," Mike said. He took his hand out of his pocket. In it was a .357 calibre magnum pistol.

Louis stared. "What—what are you doing? Listen to me—"

Mike Slade pulled the trigger and watched the Frenchman's chest explode into a red cloud.

MARY WAS IN THE BUBBLE ROOM telephoning Stanton Rogers's office on the secure line. It was six pm in Washington and one o'clock in the morning in Bucharest. "This is Ambassador Ashley. I know that Mr. Rogers is in China with the President, but it's urgent that I speak to him. Is there any way I can reach him there?"

"I'm sorry, Madam Ambassador. His itinerary is very flexible. I have no telephone number for him."

Mary felt her heart plummet. "When will you hear from him?"

"It's difficult to say. They have a very busy schedule. Perhaps someone in the State Department could help you."

"No," Mary said dully. "No one else can help me. Thank you."

There she sat, surrounded by the most sophisticated electronic equipment in the world, and none of it was of any use to her. Mike Slade was trying to murder her. She *had* to let someone know. But whom could she trust? The only one who knew what Mike Slade was trying to do was Louis Desforges.

Mary tried his residence again, but there still was no answer. She remembered what Stanton Rogers had told her: "If you want to send messages you don't want anyone else to read, the code at the top of the cable is three x's."

Mary hurried back to her office and wrote an urgent message. She placed three x's at the top of the pad, took out the black code book from a locked drawer in her desk, and carefully encoded what she had written. At least if anything happened to her now, Stanton Rogers would know who was responsible.

486

Mary walked down the corridor to the communications room. Eddie Maltz, the CIA agent, happened to be behind the cage.

"Good evening, Madam Ambassador. You're working late."

"Yes. There's a message I want sent off right away."

"I'll take care of it personally."

"Thank you." She handed him the message and headed immediately for the front door.

WHEN EDDIE MALTZ finished decoding the message, he read it through twice, frowning. He walked over to the shredder and watched the message turn into confetti.

Then he placed a call to Floyd Baker, the Secretary of State, in Washington. Code name: *Thor*.

IT HAD TAKEN LEV PASTERNAK two months to follow the circuitous trail that led to Buenos Aires. SIS and half a dozen other security agencies around the world had helped identify Angel as the killer. Mossad had given him the name of Neusa Muñez, Angel's mistress. They all wanted to eliminate Angel. To Lev Pasternak, Angel had become an obsession. Because of Pasternak's failure, Marin Groza had died, and Pasternak could never forgive himself for that. He could, however, make atonement. And he intended to.

He located the apartment building where Neusa Muñez lived, and kept watch on it, waiting for Angel to appear. After five days, when there was no sign of him, Pasternak made his move.

He waited patiently until the woman had left, and after fifteen minutes he walked upstairs, picked the lock on her door, and entered the apartment. He searched it, swiftly and thoroughly. There were no photographs, memos, or addresses that could lead him to Angel. Pasternak discovered the suits in the cupboard. He examined the Herrera labels, took one of the jackets off the hanger and tucked it under his arm. A minute later he was gone.

The following morning Lev Pasternak walked unsteadily into Herrera's men's shop. His hair was dishevelled and his clothes were wrinkled, and he smelled of whisky.

The manager came up to him and said disapprovingly, "May I help you, *señor*?"

Lev Pasternak grinned sheepishly. "Yeah. Tell you the truth, I got in a card game last night. We all got drunk. Anyway, we ended up in my hotel room. One of the guys—I don't remember his name—left his jacket." Lev held up the jacket. "It had your label in it, so I figured you could tell me where to return it to him."

The manager examined the jacket. "Yes, we made this. Please wait."

A few minutes later, the man returned. "The name of the gentleman we made the jacket for is H. R. de Mendoza. He has a suite at the Aurora Hotel, suite four seventeen."

AT FOUR AM LEV PASTERNAK was silently moving down the deserted fourth-floor corridor of the Aurora Hotel. When he reached room 417, he looked around to make sure no one was in sight. He reached down to the lock and inserted a wire. When he heard the door click open, he pulled out a .45-calibre SIG-Sauer pistol with a silencer.

He sensed a draught as the door across the hall opened, and before he could swing round, he felt something hard and cold pressing against the back of his neck.

"I don't like being followed," Angel said.

Lev Pasternak heard the click of the trigger a second before his brain was torn apart.

THE TELEPHONE CALL HAD COME, and it was time to move. First, Angel had some shopping to do. There was a good lingerie shop on Pueyrredón, expensive, but Neusa deserved the best. The inside of the shop was cool and quiet.

"I would like to see a negligee, something very frilly," Angel said. "The best you have."

Fifteen minutes later Angel left the shop and hailed a taxi. He gave the driver an address on Humberto, alighted a block away, and hailed another taxi.

There would be a ticket for London waiting at the airport. Tourist. First class was too conspicuous.

Two hours later, Angel watched the city of Buenos Aires disappear beneath the clouds, like some celestial magician's trick, and concentrated on the assignment ahead, thinking about the instructions he had been given: "Make sure the children die with her. Their deaths must be spectacular."

Angel smiled and fell into a deep, dreamless sleep.

THE PASSPORT READ H. R. de Mendoza. The ticket waiting at Heathrow Airport was on Tarom Airlines to Bucharest. Angel sent a telegram from the airport: H. R. DE MENDOZA ARRIVING WEDNESDAY.

It was addressed to Eddie Maltz.

ALL MORNING MARY kept trying to telephone Louis at home. No answer. She tried the French embassy. They had no idea where he was. "Please have him call me as soon as you hear from him." She replaced the receiver. There was nothing to do but wait.

A few minutes later Dorothy Stone came into Mary's office. "There's a call for you, but she refuses to give her name."

"I'll take it." Mary picked up the phone. "Hello, this is Ambassador Ashley."

A soft female voice with a Romanian accent said, "This is Corina Socoli." The name registered instantly. She was Romania's prima ballerina.

"I need your help," the girl said. "I have decided to defect."

I can't handle this today, Mary thought. Not now.

"I— I don't know if I can help you." Her mind was racing. She tried to remember what she had been told about defectors: "Many of them are Soviet plants. We don't grant political asylum unless there's a darn good reason."

Corina Socoli was sobbing. "Please, I am not safe staying where I am. You must send someone to get me."

"Where are you?" Mary asked.

There was a pause. Then, "I am at the Roscow Inn in Moldavia. Will you come for me?"

"I can't," Mary said. "But I'll send someone to get you. Don't call on this phone again. Just wait where you are. I—"

The door opened, and Mike Slade walked in. Mary looked up in shock. He moved towards her.

The voice on the phone was saying, "Hello? Hello?"

"Who are you talking to?" Mike asked.

"To—to Dr. Desforges." She replaced the receiver, terrified. "He's— he's on his way over to see me." You're in the embassy, she told herself. He wouldn't dare do anything to you here.

There was a strange look in Mike's eyes. "Are you sure you're well enough to be back at work?"

The nerve. "Yes. I'm fine." She was finding it hard to breathe. Her intercom phone rang. "If you'll excuse me . . ."

"Sure." Mike Slade stood there staring at her, then turned and left.

Almost sobbing with relief, Mary picked up the phone. "Hello?"

It was Jerry Davis, the public affairs consul. "Madam Ambassador, I'm sorry to disturb you, but I'm afraid I have some terrible news. Dr. Louis Desforges has been murdered."

The room began to swim. "Are you— are you sure?"

"Yes, ma'am."

Memories flooded through her, and a voice over the telephone was saying: "*This is Sheriff Munster. Your husband has been killed in a car accident.*" All the old sorrows came rushing back, stabbing at her, tearing her apart.

"How—how did it happen?" Her voice was strangled.

"He was shot to death."

"Do they—do they know who did it?"

"No, ma'am. The *Securitate* and the French embassy are investigating."

Mary dropped the receiver, her mind and body numb, and leaned back in her chair, studying the ceiling. There was a crack in it. I must have that repaired, Mary thought. We mustn't have cracks in our embassy. There's another crack. Cracks everywhere, and when there is a crack, evil things get in. Edward is dead. Louis is dead. I can't go through this pain again. Who would want to kill Louis?

The answer immediately followed the question. *Mike Slade.* Louis had discovered that Slade was feeding Mary arsenic. Slade probably thought that with Louis dead, no one could prove anything against him. A sudden realization filled her with a new terror. *"Who were you talking to?"* Mike must have known that Desforges was dead.

She stayed in her office all day, planning her next move. I'm not going to let Mike Slade drive me away. I'm not going to let him kill me. I have to stop him. She was filled with a rage such as she had never known before. She was going to protect herself and her children. And she was going to destroy Mike Slade.

"Madam Ambassador . . ." Dorothy Stone was holding an envelope out to her. "The guard at the gate asked me to give you this." The envelope was marked: "Personal, for the ambassador's eyes only." Mary tore open the envelope. The note was written in a neat copperplate handwriting. It read:

Dear Madam Ambassador
    Enjoy your last day on earth.

                                           Angel.

Another one of Mike's scare tactics, Mary thought. It won't work. I'll keep well away from him.

COLONEL MCKINNEY WAS STUDYING the note. He looked up at Mary. "You were scheduled to appear this afternoon at the opening of the new library extension. I'll cancel it and—"

"No."

"Madam Ambassador, it's too dangerous for you to—"

"I'll be safe." She knew now where the danger lay, and she had a plan ready. "Please tell Mike Slade that I wish to see him right away."

"YOU WANTED TO TALK TO ME?" Mike Slade's tone was casual.

"I received a call from someone who wants to defect."

"Who is it?"

She had no intention of telling him. He would betray the girl. "That's not important. I want you to bring this person in."

Mike frowned. "This could lead to a lot of—"

Mary cut him short. "I want you to go to the Roscow Inn at Moldavia and pick her up."

He started to argue. "If that's what you want, I'll send—"

"No." Mary's voice was steel. "I want *you* to go. I'm sending two men with you." With Gunny and another marine along, Mike would not be able to play any tricks. She had told Gunny not to let Mike Slade out of his sight.

He was studying Mary, puzzled. "I have a heavy schedule—"

"I want you to leave immediately. You're to bring the defector back here to me."

Mike nodded slowly. "All right."

Mary watched him go, with a feeling of relief so intense that she felt giddy. With Mike Slade out of the way she would be safe.

THE OPENING CEREMONY for the new American library extension was scheduled to be held at four o'clock at Alexandru Sahia Square. By three pm a large crowd had already gathered. Colonel McKinney had a meeting with Captain Aurel Istrase, head of *Securitate*, and told him of the death threat. Istrase ordered all automobiles to be removed from the square, so that there was no danger of a car bomb. In addition, police were stationed around the entire area and a sharpshooter was on the roof of the library. At a few minutes before four, bomb experts swept the entire area and found no explosives; everything was in readiness for Mary's arrival.

AS MARY WALKED from her limousine towards the site where the ceremony was to take place, two armed members of *Securitate* walked in front of her and two behind her, shielding her with their bodies.

The onlookers applauded as she stepped into the small circle that had been cleared for her. The crowd was a mixture of Romanians, Americans and attachés from other embassies in Bucharest. As Mary looked at the people she thought: I should never have come here. I'm terrified.

Colonel McKinney was saying, "Ladies and gentlemen, it is my honour to present the ambassador from the United States of America."

The crowd applauded.

Mary took a deep breath and began. "Thank you . . ."

She had been so caught up in the maelstrom of events of the past week that she had not prepared a speech, but some deep wellspring within her gave her the words. She found herself saying, "What we are doing here today may seem a small thing, but it is important, because it is one more

491

bridge between our country and all the countries of Eastern Europe. The new buildings we are dedicating will be filled with information about the United States of America."

Colonel McKinney and his men were moving through the crowd. The note had said, "Enjoy your last day on earth." When did the killer's day end? Six pm? Nine pm? Midnight?

On the far side of the square a car suddenly raced past the police barrier and screamed to a stop at the kerb. As a startled policeman moved towards it the driver jumped out and began running away. As he ran, he pulled a device from his pocket and pressed it.

The car exploded instantly, sending out a shower of metal into the crowd. None of it reached the centre, where Mary was standing, but the spectators began to panic, trying to get away. The sharpshooter on the roof raised his rifle and put a bullet through the fleeing man's heart before he could escape.

It took the Romanian police an hour to clear the crowd away and remove the body. The fire department had put out the flames of the burning car. Mary was driven back to the embassy, shaken.

"Are you sure you wouldn't prefer to go to the residence and rest?" Colonel McKinney asked her. "You've just been through a horrifying experience that—"

"No," Mary said stubbornly. "The embassy." That was the only place where she could safely talk to Stanton Rogers. I must talk to him soon, Mary thought, or I'll go to pieces.

The strain of everything that was happening to her was unbearable. She had made sure that Mike Slade was safely out of the way, yet an attempt had still been made on her life.

So he was not working alone.

AT SIX O'CLOCK Mike Slade walked into Mary's office. He was furious. "I put Corina Socoli in a room upstairs," he said curtly. "Nice shot, not to tell me who I was picking up. You've made a big mistake. We have to return her. She's a national treasure—"

Colonel McKinney hurried into the office. He stopped short as he saw Mike. "We have an identification on the dead man. He's the Angel, all right. His real name is H. R. de Mendoza."

Mike was staring at him. "What are you talking about?"

"Didn't the ambassador tell you? She received a death warning from 'Angel'. He tried to assassinate her at the opening ceremony this afternoon. One of Istrase's men got him."

Mike stood there, his eyes fixed on Mary.

"Where's the body?" he asked.

"In the morgue at police headquarters."

THE BODY WAS LYING on a stone slab. He had been an ordinary-looking man, of medium height, with a small, thin nose that went with his tight mouth, very small feet and thinning hair. His belongings were piled on a table.

Mike examined the jacket label. It was from a shop in Buenos Aires. The leather shoes also had an Argentinian label. He turned to the sergeant. "What do you have on him?"

"He flew in from London on Tarom Airlines two days ago, checked into the Intercontinental under the name of de Mendoza. His passport shows his home address as Buenos Aires. It is forged. He does not look like an international killer, does he?"

"No," Mike agreed. "He doesn't."

TWO DOZEN BLOCKS AWAY Angel was walking past the residence. The photographs that had been sent were excellent, but Angel believed in personally checking every detail.

Angel grinned at the thought of the charade in the town square. It had been child's play to hire a junkie for the price of a noseful of cocaine. *Throw everyone off guard. Let them sweat.* But the big event was yet to come. *For five million dollars I will give them a show they will never forget. What do the television networks call them? Spectaculars. They will get a spectacular in living colour.*

"There will be a Fourth of July celebration at the residence," the voice on the phone had said. "There will be balloons, a marine band, entertainers." Angel smiled and thought, *A five-million-dollar spectacular in living colour.*

WHEN STANTON ROGERS CALLED from Washington, Mary grabbed the phone in the Bubble Room as if it were a lifeline.

"Mary—I can't understand a word you're saying. Slow down."

"I'm sorry, Stan—didn't you get my cable?"

"No. I've just returned. There was no cable from you. What's wrong?"

Mary fought to control her hysteria and took a deep breath. "Mike Slade is trying to murder me."

There was a shocked silence. "Mary—you can't believe—"

"It's true. I know it is. I met a doctor from the French embassy—Louis Desforges. I became ill, and he found out I was being poisoned with arsenic. Mike was doing it."

Rogers's voice was sharp. "What makes you think that?"

"Louis—Dr. Desforges—figured it out. Mike Slade made coffee for me every morning, with arsenic in it. I have proof that he got hold of the arsenic. Last night Louis was murdered, and this afternoon someone working with Slade tried to assassinate me."

This time the silence was even longer.

When Stanton Rogers spoke again, his tone was urgent. "Mary, think carefully. Could it have been anyone besides Mike Slade?"

"No. He's been trying to get me out of Romania from the beginning."

"All right," Rogers said crisply. "I'll inform the President. We'll handle Slade. I'll also arrange extra protection for you."

"Stan—on Sunday night I'm giving a Fourth of July party at the residence. Do you think I should cancel it?"

There was a thoughtful silence. "As a matter of fact, the party might be a good idea. Keep a lot of people around you. Mary—I don't want to frighten you any more than you already are, but I would suggest that you don't let the children out of your sight. Not for a minute. Slade might try to get at you through them."

She felt a shudder go through her. "Why is Slade doing this?"

"I wish I knew. It makes no sense. But I'm going to find out. In the meantime, keep as far away from him as you possibly can."

When Mary hung up, it was as though an enormous burden had been lifted from her shoulders.

EDDIE MALTZ ANSWERED on the first ring. The conversation lasted for ten minutes.

"I'll make sure everything is there," Eddie promised.

Angel hung up. Eddie Maltz thought, I wonder what Angel needs all that stuff for. He looked at his watch. Forty-eight hours to go.

THE MOMENT STANTON ROGERS finished talking to Mary, he placed an emergency call to Colonel McKinney. "I want you to pick up Mike Slade," he said. "Hold him in close custody until you hear from me."

"Mike Slade?" asked the colonel incredulously.

"I want him held and isolated. He's probably armed and dangerous. Don't let him talk to anyone. Call me back at the White House as soon as you have him."

"Yes, sir."

Two hours later Stanton Rogers's phone rang. He snatched up the receiver. "Hello, Bill? Do you have Slade?"

"No, sir. There's a problem. Mike Slade has disappeared."

Sofia, Bulgaria: Saturday, July 3

In a small, nondescript building, a group of Eastern Committee members was meeting. Seated round the table were powerful representatives from Russia, China, Czechoslovakia, Pakistan, India and Malaysia.

The chairman was speaking. "We welcome our brothers and sisters on the Eastern Committee who have joined us today. I am happy to tell you

494

that we have excellent news from the Western Committee. The final phase of our plan is about to be successfully concluded. It will happen tomorrow night at the American ambassador's residence in Bucharest. Arrangements have been made for international press and television coverage."

Code name Kali spoke. "The American ambassador and her two children—?"

"Will be assassinated, along with a hundred or so other Americans. We are all aware of the grave risks, and the holocaust that may follow. It is time to put the motion to a vote." He started at the far end of the table. "Brahma?"

"Yes."

"Vishnu?"

"Yes."

"Krishna?"

"Yes . . ."

When everyone had voted, the chairman declared, "It is unanimous. We owe a particular vote of thanks to the person who has helped so much to bring this about." He turned to the American.

"My pleasure," Mike Slade said.

THE DECORATIONS FOR the Fourth of July party were flown into Bucharest late on Saturday afternoon and transported directly to a United States government warehouse. The cargo consisted of a thousand red, white and blue balloons packed in boxes, three steel cylinders of helium to inflate the balloons, two hundred and fifty rolls of confetti, party favours, noisemakers, a dozen banners and six dozen miniature American flags. The cargo was unloaded in the warehouse at eight pm.

Two hours later a jeep arrived with three oxygen cylinders stamped with US army markings. The driver placed them inside.

At one am, when the warehouse was deserted, Angel appeared. The warehouse door had been left unlocked. Angel went inside, examined the cylinders carefully, and went to work. The first task was to empty the three helium tanks until each was only one third full. After that, the rest was simple.

AT FOUR O'CLOCK on the afternoon of July 4 a US army truck pulled up to the service entrance of the residence and was stopped. The guard said, "What have you got in there?"

"Goodies for the party tonight."

"Let's take a look." The guard inspected the inside of the truck. "What's in the boxes?"

495

"Balloons and flags and stuff."

"Open them."

Fifteen minutes later the truck was passed through. Once it was inside the compound a marine corporal and two marine guards began to unload the equipment. They carried it into a large storage room off the ballroom.

As they began to unpack, Eddie Maltz walked in, accompanied by a stranger wearing army fatigues.

One of the guards said, "Who's going to blow up all these balloons?"

"Don't worry," Eddie Maltz said. "This is the age of technology." He nodded towards the stranger. "Here's the one that's in charge of the balloons. Colonel McKinney's orders."

The other guard grinned at the stranger. "Rather you than me." The two guards finished unpacking and left.

"You have an hour," Eddie Maltz told the stranger. "Better get to work." Maltz nodded to the corporal and walked out.

The corporal walked over to one of the cylinders. "What's in these babies?"

"Helium," the stranger said curtly.

As the corporal stood watching, the stranger picked up a balloon, put the tip to the nozzle of a cylinder for an instant, and, as the balloon filled, tied off the tip. The balloon floated to the ceiling. The whole operation took no more than a second.

"Hey, that's great," the corporal smiled.

IN HER OFFICE at the embassy Mary Ashley was finishing off some action cables. She desperately wished the party could have been called off. There were going to be more than two hundred guests. She hoped Mike Slade was caught before the party began.

Tim and Beth were under constant supervision at the residence. How could Mike bear to harm them? Mary remembered how much he had seemed to enjoy playing with them. He's not sane, she thought.

Mary rose to put some papers in the shredder, and froze. Mike Slade was walking into her office through the connecting door. She opened her mouth to scream.

"Don't!" he ordered.

She was terrified. He could kill her before she could call for help, and he could escape the same way he had come.

"Colonel McKinney's men are looking for you. You can kill me," Mary said defiantly, "but you'll never escape."

"Angel's the one who's trying to kill you," Mike said.

"You're a liar. Angel is dead. I saw him shot."

"Angel is a professional from Argentina. The last thing he would do is

496

walk around with Argentine labels in his clothes. The slob the police killed was an amateur who was set up."

"I don't believe a word you're saying," Mary said. "You killed Louis Desforges. You tried to poison me. Do you deny that?"

Mike studied her for a long moment. "No. I don't deny it, but you'd better hear the story from a friend of mine." He turned towards the door to his office. "Come in, Bill."

Colonel McKinney walked into the room. "I think it's time we all had a chat, Madam Ambassador . . ."

IN THE RESIDENCE storage room the stranger in army fatigues was filling the balloons under the watchful eye of the corporal.

Boy, that's one ugly customer, the corporal thought to himself. Whew!

The corporal could not understand why the white balloons were being filled from one cylinder, the red balloons from a second cylinder, and the blue ones from a third. Why not use each cylinder until it's empty? he wondered. He was tempted to ask, but he did not want to start a conversation. Not with this one.

"LET'S START AT THE BEGINNING," Colonel McKinney said. "On Inauguration Day, when the President announced that he wanted to open relations with every iron curtain country, he exploded a bombshell. There's a faction in our government that's convinced that if we get too involved with the Eastern bloc, the Communists will destroy us. On the other side of the iron curtain there are Communists who believe that our President's plan is a trick to bring our capitalist spies into their countries. A group of powerful men on both sides had formed a supersecret alliance called Patriots for Freedom. They decided that the only way to destroy the President's plan was to let him start it, and then sabotage it in such a dramatic way that it would never be tried again. That's where you came into the picture."

"But—why me? Why was I chosen?"

"Because the packaging was important," Mike said. "You were exactly the image they needed—Mrs. America, with two squeaky-clean kids. They were determined to have you. When your husband got in the way, they murdered him and made it look like an accident so you wouldn't be suspicious and refuse the post."

Mary could not speak. The horror of what Mike was saying was too appalling.

"Their next step was your buildup. They used their press connections around the world and saw to it that you became everyone's darling—the beautiful lady who was going to lead the world down the road to peace."

"And—and now?"

Mike's voice grew gentle. "Their plan is to assassinate you and the children as shockingly as possible—to sicken the world so much that it would put an end to any further idea of détente."

Mary sat there in stunned silence.

"That states it bluntly but accurately," Colonel McKinney said quietly. "Mike is with the CIA. After your husband and Marin Groza were murdered, Mike started to get on the trail of the Patriots for Freedom. They thought he was on their side and invited him to join.

"We talked the idea over with President Ellison, and he gave his approval. The President has been kept abreast of every development. His overriding concern has been that you and the children be protected, but he dared not discuss what he knew with you or anyone else, because Ned Tillingast, head of the CIA, had warned him that there were high-level leaks."

Mary's head was spinning. She said to Mike, "But—you tried to kill me."

He sighed. "Lady, I've been trying to save your life. You haven't made it easy. I tried every way I knew how to get you to take the kids and go home where you'd be safe."

"But—you poisoned me."

"Not fatally. I wanted to get you just sick enough so you'd have to leave Romania. Our doctors were waiting for you in Frankfurt. I couldn't tell you the truth, because it would have blown the whole operation. Even now, we don't know who put the organization together. He never attends meetings. He's known only as the Controller."

"And Louis?"

"The doctor was one of them. He was Angel's backup. He was an explosives expert. A phony kidnapping was set up, and you were rescued by Mr. Charm." Mike saw the expression on Mary's face. "You were lonely and vulnerable, and they worked on that. You weren't the first one to fall for the good doctor."

Something was bothering Mary. "But Mike—why did you kill Louis?"

"I had no choice. The whole point of their plan was to murder you and the children as publicly and spectacularly as possible. Louis knew I was a member of the Committee. Poisoning wasn't the way you were supposed to die. When he figured out that I was poisoning you, he became suspicious of me. I had to kill him before he exposed me."

Mary sat there listening as the pieces of the puzzle fell into place. The man she had distrusted had poisoned her to keep her alive, and the man she thought she loved had saved her for a more dramatic death. She and her children had been used. *I was the Judas goat,* Mary thought. All the

498

warmth that everyone showed me was phoney. The only one who was real was Stanton Rogers. Or was he?

"Stanton," Mary began, "is he—?"

"He's been protective of you all the way," Colonel McKinney assured her. "When he thought Mike was the one trying to kill you, he ordered me to arrest him."

Mary looked at Mike. He had been sent here to protect her, and all the time she had looked on him as the enemy. Her thoughts were in a turmoil. "Then Louis never did have a wife or children?"

"No."

Mary remembered something.

"But—I asked Eddie Maltz to check, and he told me that Louis was married and had two daughters."

Mike and Colonel McKinney exchanged a look.

"He'll be taken care of," McKinney said. "I sent him to Frankfurt. I'll have him picked up."

"Who is Angel?" Mary asked.

Mike answered. "He's an assassin from South America. He's probably the best in the world. The Committee agreed to pay him five million dollars to kill you." Mary listened to the words in disbelief.

Mike went on, "We know he's in Bucharest, but we don't have a single description of him. He uses a dozen different passports. No one has ever talked directly to him. They deal through his mistress, Neusa Muñez. The various groups in the Committee are so compartmentalized that I haven't been able to learn what Angel's plan is."

"What's to stop him from killing me?"

"Us," said Colonel McKinney. "With the help of the Romanian government, we've taken extraordinary precautions for the party. We've covered every possible contingency."

"What happens now?" Mary asked.

Mike said carefully, "That's up to you. Angel was ordered to carry out the contract at your party tonight. We're sure we can catch him, but if you and the children aren't at the party . . ."

"You're asking me to set myself up as a target?"

Colonel McKinney said, "You don't have to agree."

I could end this now, Mary told herself. I could go back to Kansas with the children and leave this nightmare behind. Angel would forget about me. She looked up at Mike and Bill McKinney and said, "I won't expose my children to danger."

McKinney said, "I can arrange for Beth and Tim to be spirited out of the residence and brought here under escort."

Mary looked at Mike for a long time. Finally she spoke. "How does a Judas goat dress?"

Chapter Eleven

There was a tremendous feeling of excitement in the air. Hundreds of curious Romanians had gathered outside the residence, which was ringed with huge spotlights that lit up the sky. The crowd was kept moving by a detachment of American MPs and Romanian police. Plain-clothes men mingled with the multitude, looking for anything suspicious. Some of them moved around with trained dogs that were sniffing for explosives.

There were photographers and reporters from a dozen countries. They had all been carefully checked and their equipment searched before they were allowed to enter the residence.

"A cockroach couldn't sneak into this place tonight," the marine officer in charge of security boasted.

IN THE STORAGE ROOM the marine corporal was getting bored watching the person in army fatigues filling up balloons. He pulled out a cigarette and started to light it.

Angel yelled, "Put that out!"

The corporal looked up, startled. "What's the problem? You're filling those with helium, aren't you? Helium doesn't burn."

"Put it out! Colonel McKinney said no smoking here."

Grumbling, the corporal put out the cigarette.

Angel watched to make sure there were no sparks left. It was true that helium did not burn, but the cylinders were not filled with helium. The first tank was filled with propane, the second with white phosphorus and the third with an oxygen-acetylene mix. Angel had left just enough helium in each tank to make the balloons rise.

Angel was filling the white balloons with propane, the red balloons with oxygen-acetylene and the blue balloons with white phosphorus. When the balloons were exploded, the white phosphorus would act as an incendiary for the initial gas discharge, drawing in oxygen so that all breath would be sucked out of the body of everyone within fifty yards. The phosphorus would instantly turn to a hot, searing molten liquid, falling on every person in the room. The thermal effect would destroy the lungs and throat, and the blast would flatten an area of a square block. *It's going to be beautiful.*

Angel straightened up and looked at the colourful balloons floating against the ceiling of the storage room. "I am finished."

"OK." The corporal called over four guards. "Help me get these balloons out into the ballroom."

One of the guards opened the doors to the ballroom, which was already crowded with guests. The room had been decorated with

American flags and red, white and blue bunting. At the far end was the raised stand for the band.

"It's a lovely room," Angel said. *In one hour it will be filled with burned corpses.* "Could I take a picture of it?"

The corporal shrugged. "Why not? Let's go, fellas."

The marines pushed past Angel and started shoving the inflated balloons into the ballroom. "Easy," Angel warned. "Easy."

"Don't worry," a marine called. "We won't burst your precious balloons."

Angel stood in the doorway, staring at the riot of colours ascending in a rising rainbow, and smiled. One thousand of the lethal little beauties nestled against the ceiling. Angel took a camera from a pocket and stepped into the ballroom.

"Hey! You're not allowed in here," the corporal said.

"I just want to take a picture to show my daughter."

I'll bet that's some ugly-looking daughter, the corporal thought sardonically. "All right. But make it quick."

Angel glanced across the room. Ambassador Mary Ashley was entering with her two children. Angel grinned. Perfect timing.

When the corporal turned his back, Angel quickly set the camera down under a cloth-covered table. The automatic timing device was set for a one-hour delay. Everything was ready.

Five minutes later Angel was strolling down Alexandru Sahia Street.

BEFORE THE PARTY BEGAN, Mary had taken the children upstairs. She felt she owed them the truth.

They sat listening, wide-eyed, as Mary explained what had been happening and what might be about to happen.

"You'll be taken out of here, where you'll be safe," she said.

"But what about you?" Beth asked. "Can't you come with us?"

"No, darling. Not if we want to catch this man."

Tim was trying not to cry. "How do you know they will?"

Mary thought about that a moment and said, "Because Mike Slade said so. OK, fellas?"

Beth and Tim looked at each other. They were both white-faced, terrified. Mary's heart went out to them. They're too young to have to go through this, she thought.

Fifteen minutes later Mary, Beth and Tim entered the ballroom. They walked across the floor, greeting guests, trying to conceal their nervousness. When they reached the other side of the room, Mary turned to the children. "You have homework to do," she said loudly. "Back to your rooms."

The moment the children left the ballroom, they were escorted to a service entrance by Colonel McKinney. He said to the two armed marines waiting at the door, "Take them to the embassy. Don't let them out of your sight."

Mike Slade watched them leave, then went to find Mary.

"The children are on their way. I must check. I'll be back."

Mary tried to stop the pounding of her heart. How was Angel planning to assassinate her? She looked around the festive ballroom, but there was no clue.

"Don't leave me." The words came out before Mary could stop herself. "I want to go with you. I feel safer with you."

Mike grinned. "Now that's a change. Come on."

Mary followed him, staying close behind. The orchestra had begun playing, and people were dancing. Those who were not dancing were helping themselves from the silver trays of champagne being offered, or from the buffet tables.

The room looked spectacular. Mary raised her head, and there were the balloons, a thousand of them—red, white and blue—floating against the pink ceiling. It was a festive occasion, but her nerves were so taut that she was finding it difficult to breathe. Angel could be watching her this very minute.

"Do you think Angel is here now?" she asked.

"I don't know," Mike said. He saw the expression on her face. "Look, if you want to leave—"

"No. I'm the bait. Without me, he won't spring the trap."

He nodded and squeezed her arm. "Right."

Colonel McKinney approached. "We've done a thorough search, Mike. We haven't found a thing. I don't like it."

"Let's take another look round." Mike signalled to four armed marines standing by, and they moved up next to Mary. "Be right back," Mike said.

Mary swallowed nervously. "Please."

Mike and Colonel McKinney, accompanied by two guards with sniffer dogs, searched every room in the residence. They found nothing suspicious.

"What about poison?" asked McKinney.

"Not photogenic enough. Angel's going for the big bang."

"Mike, there's no way anyone could get explosives into this place. The place is clean."

"There's one way."

McKinney looked at Mike. "How?"

"I don't know. But Angel does."

They searched the library and the offices again. Nothing.

They passed the storage room where the corporal was shoving out a

502

few balloons that had been left behind. He watched them float to the ceiling.

"Pretty, huh?" the corporal said.

"Yeah," Mike said. He started to walk on, then stopped. "Corporal, where did these balloons come from?"

"From the US airbase in Frankfurt, sir."

Mike indicated the helium cylinders. "And these?"

"Same place. They were escorted to our warehouse as per Colonel McKinney's instructions, sir."

Mike said to McKinney, "Let's start upstairs again."

They turned to leave. The corporal said, "Oh, Colonel, the person you sent forgot to leave a time slip. Is that going to be handled by military payroll or civilian?"

Colonel McKinney frowned. "What person?"

"The one you authorized to fill the balloons."

"I never—who said I authorized it?"

"Eddie Maltz. He said you—"

Colonel McKinney said, "Eddie Maltz?"

Mike turned to the corporal, his voice urgent. "What did this man look like?"

"Oh, it wasn't a man, sir. It was a woman. To tell you the truth, I thought she looked weird. Fat and ugly. She had a funny accent. She was pockmarked and had kind of a puffy face."

Mike said to McKinney, "That sounds like the description of Neusa Muñez that Harry Lantz gave the Committee."

The revelation hit them both at the same time.

Mike said slowly, "Oh, my God! Neusa Muñez is Angel!" He pointed to the cylinders. "She filled the balloons from these?"

"Yes, sir. It was funny. I lit a cigarette and she screamed at me to put it out. I said, 'Helium doesn't burn,' and she said—"

Mike looked up. "The balloons! The explosives are in the balloons!" The two men stared at the high ceiling covered with the spectacular red, white and blue balloons.

"She's using some kind of a remote-control device to explode them." He turned to the corporal. "How long ago did she leave?"

"I guess about an hour ago."

Under the table, the timing device had six minutes left on the dial.

Mike was frantically scanning the huge room. "She could have put the timer anywhere. It could go off at any second. We'll never find it in time."

Mary was approaching. Mike turned to her. "You've got to clear the room. Fast! Make an announcement. It will sound better coming from you. Get everybody outside."

She was looking at him, bewildered. "But—why?"

"We found our playmate's toy," Mike said grimly. He pointed. "Those balloons. They're lethal."

Mary was looking up at them, horror on her face. "Can't we take them down?"

Mike snapped, "There must be a thousand of them. By the time—"

Mary's throat was so dry she could hardly get the words out. "Mike . . . I know a way." The two men stared at her. "The Ambassador's Folly. The roof. It slides open."

Mike tried to control his excitement. "How does it work?"

"There's a switch that—"

"No," Mike said. "Nothing electrical. A spark could set them all off. Can it be done manually?"

"Yes. The roof is divided in half. There's a crank on each side that—" She was talking to herself.

The two men were frantically racing upstairs. When they reached the top floor, they found a door opening into a loft and hurried inside. A wooden ladder led to a catwalk above, which was used by workmen when they cleaned the ballroom ceiling. A crank was fastened to the wall.

"There must be another one on the other side," Mike said.

He started across the narrow catwalk, pushing his way through the sea of deadly balloons, struggling to keep his balance, trying not to look down at the mob of people far below. A current of air pushed a mass of balloons against him, and he slipped. One foot went off the catwalk. He began to fall. He grabbed the boards as he fell, hanging on. Slowly he managed to pull himself up. He was soaked in perspiration. He inched his way along the rest of the walk. Fastened to the wall was the crank.

"I'm ready," Mike called. "Careful. No sudden moves."

"Right."

Mike began turning the crank very slowly.

UNDER THE TABLE the timer was down to two minutes.

MIKE COULD NOT SEE Colonel McKinney because of the balloons, but he could hear the other crank being turned. Slowly, very slowly, the roof started to slide open. A few balloons drifted into the night air, and as the roof opened further, more balloons began to escape. Hundreds of them poured through the opening, dancing into the star-filled night, drawing oohs and aahs from the unsuspecting guests below and the people out in the street.

Under the table there were forty-five seconds left on the remote-control timer. A cluster of balloons caught on the edge of the ceiling

504

just out of Mike's reach. He strained forward, trying to free them. They swayed just beyond his fingertips. Carefully he moved out on the catwalk with nothing to hold on to and strained to push the balloons free. *Now!*

Mike stood there watching the last of the balloons escape. They soared higher and higher, painting the velvet night with their vivid colours, and suddenly the sky exploded.

There was a tremendous roar, and tongues of red and white flames shot high into the air. It was a Fourth of July celebration such as had never been seen before.

Below, everyone applauded.

Mike watched, drained, too tired to move. It was over.

THE ROUNDUP WAS TIMED to take place simultaneously, in far-flung corners of the world.

Floyd Baker, the Secretary of State, was with his mistress when the door burst open. Four men came into the room. "FBI, Mr. Secretary. You're under arrest."

"You must be mad. What's the charge?"

"Treason, Thor."

General Oliver Brooks, Odin, was having breakfast at his club when two FBI agents walked up to his table and arrested him.

In London, Sir Alex Hyde-White, KBE, MP, one of the senior heads of the British Secret Intelligence Service, code name Freyr, was being toasted at a parliamentary dinner when the club steward approached him.

"Excuse me, Sir Alex. There are some gentlemen outside who would like a word with you . . ."

In Paris, in the Chambre des Députés de la République Française, a deputy, Balder, was called off the floor.

In the parliament building in New Delhi, the speaker of the Lok Sabha, Vishnu, was taken to jail.

In Rome, the deputy of the Camera dei Deputati, Tyr, was in a Turkish bath when he was arrested.

The sweep went on. In Mexico and Albania and Japan, high officials were arrested. A member of the Bundestag in West Germany, a deputy in the Nationalrat in Austria, the vice-chairman of the Presidium of the Soviet Union. The arrests included the president of a large shipping company and a powerful union leader, a television evangelist and the head of an oil cartel.

Eddie Maltz was shot while trying to escape.

Pete Connors committed suicide while FBI agents were breaking down the door to his office.

506

MARY AND MIKE SLADE were in the Bubble Room receiving telephone reports from around the world. Finally, Mike replaced the receiver and turned to Mary.

"They've got most of them. Except for the Controller and Neusa Muñez—Angel."

"No one knew that Angel was a woman?" Mary marvelled.

"No. She had all of us fooled. Lantz described her to the Patriots for Freedom Committee as a fat, ugly moron."

"What about the Controller?" Mary asked.

"No one ever saw him. He gave orders by telephone. He was a brilliant organizer. The group was broken up into small cells, so that one group never knew what the other was doing."

ANGEL WAS LIKE AN ENRAGED ANIMAL. The contract had gone wrong somehow, but she had been prepared to make up for it.

She had called the private number in Washington, and using her dull, listless voice, had said, "Angel say to tell you not to worry. There was som' mistake, but he weel take care of it, meester. They will all die nex' time, and—"

"There won't be a next time," the voice had exploded. "Angel bungled it. He's worse than an amateur."

"Angel tol' me—"

"I don't give a damn what he told you. He's finished. He won't get a cent. Just tell that incompetent moron to keep away. I'll find someone else who knows how to do the job." And he had slammed the phone down.

The gringo dog. No one had ever treated Angel like that and lived. The man was going to pay. Oh, how he would pay!

THE PRIVATE PHONE in the Bubble Room rang. Mary picked it up. It was Stanton Rogers. "Mary! You're safe! Thank God it's over. Tell me what happened."

"It was Angel. She tried to blow up the residence and—"

"You mean *he.*"

"No. Angel is a woman. Her name is Neusa Muñez."

There was a long, stunned silence. "*Neusa Muñez?* That fat, ugly moron was *Angel?*"

Mary felt a sudden chill go through her. "That's right, Stan."

"Is there anything I can do for you, Mary?"

"No. I'm on my way to see the children. I'll talk to you later."

She replaced the receiver and sat there, dazed.

Mike looked at her. "What's the matter?"

She turned to him. "You told me that Harry Lantz had informed only some Committee members what Neusa Muñez looked like."

"Yes."

Mary said, "Stanton Rogers just described her."

WHEN ANGEL'S PLANE LANDED at Dulles Airport, she went to a telephone booth and dialled the Controller's private number.

The familiar voice said, "Stanton Rogers."

TWO DAYS LATER, Mike, Colonel McKinney and Mary were seated in the embassy conference room. An electronics expert had just finished debugging it.

"It all fits now," Mike said. "The Controller had to be Stanton Rogers, but none of us could see it."

"But why would he want to kill me?" Mary asked. "In the beginning he was *against* my being appointed ambassador. He told me so himself."

Mike explained. "He hadn't completely formulated his plan then. But once he realized what you and the children symbolized, he fought for you to get the nomination. That's what threw us off the track. He was behind you all the way, seeing to it that you got a buildup in the press."

Mary shuddered. "Why did he get involved with—?"

"He never forgave Paul Ellison for being President. He felt cheated. He started out as a liberal, and he married a right-wing reactionary. My guess is that his wife turned him around."

"Have they found him yet?"

"No. He's disappeared. But he can't hide for very long."

STANTON ROGERS'S HEAD was found in a garbage dump in Washington DC two days later. His eyes had been torn out.

PAUL ELLISON WAS CALLING from the White House. "I'm refusing to accept your resignation. Mary, I know how much you've been through, but I'm asking you to remain at your post in Romania."

I know how much you've been through. Did anyone have any idea? She had been so unbelievably naive when she arrived. She had been going to show the world how wonderful Americans really were. And all the time she had been a cat's paw. She and her children had been placed in mortal danger. She thought of Edward, and how he had been murdered, and of Louis and his lies and his death. She thought of the destruction Angel had sown all over the world.

I'm not the same person I was when I came here, Mary thought. I've grown up the hard way, but I've grown up. I've managed to accomplish something here. I got Hannah Murphy out of prison, and I made our grain deal. I saved the life of Ionescu's son, and I rescued some Jews.

"Hello. Are you there?" the President asked.

"Yes, sir." She looked across her desk at Mike Slade, who was slouched back in his chair, studying her.

"You've done a truly remarkable job," the President said. "You're just the person we need over there. You'll be doing our country a great service."

The President was waiting for an answer. Mary was weighing her decision. Finally, she said, "Mr. President, if I did agree to stay, I would insist that our country give sanctuary to Corina Socoli."

"I'm sorry, Mary. I've already explained why we can't do that. It would offend Ionescu and—"

"He'll get over it. I know Ionescu, Mr. President. He's using her as a bargaining chip."

There was a long silence. "How would you get her out?"

"An army cargo plane is due to arrive in the morning. I'll send her out in that."

There was a pause. "I'll square it with State. If that's all—?"

Mary looked over at Mike Slade again. "No, sir. There's one thing more. I want Mike Slade to stay here with me. I need him. We make a good team."

Mike was watching her, a private smile on his lips.

"I'm afraid that's impossible," the President said firmly. "I need Slade back here. He already has another assignment."

Mary sat there, holding the phone, saying nothing.

The President went on. "We'll send you someone else. Anyone you want. Mary? Hello? What is this—some kind of blackmail?"

Mary sat, silently waiting.

Finally the President said grudgingly, "Well, I suppose if you really need him, we might spare him for a little while."

Mary felt her heart lighten. "Thank you, Mr. President. I'll be happy to stay on as ambassador."

The President had a final parting shot. "You're one ace of a negotiator, Madam Ambassador. I have some interesting plans in mind for you when you're finished there. Good luck! And stay out of trouble." The line went dead.

Mary replaced the receiver and looked at Mike. "You're going to be staying here. He told me to stay out of trouble."

Mike Slade grinned. "He has a nice sense of humour." He rose and moved towards her. "Do you remember the day I met you and called you a perfect ten?"

How well she remembered. "Yes."

"I was wrong. *Now* you're a perfect ten."

She felt a warm glow. "Oh, Mike . . ."

"Since I'm staying on, Madam Ambassador, we'd better talk about the problems we're having with the Romanian commerce minister." He looked into her eyes and said softly, "Coffee?"

Epilogue

Alice Springs, Australia

The chairwoman was addressing the Committee. "We have suffered a setback, but because of the lessons we have learned, our organization will become even stronger. Now it is time to take a vote. Aphrodite?"

"Yes."

"Athene?"

"Yes."

"Cybele?"

"Yes."

"Selene?"

"Considering the horrible death of our former Controller—"

"Yes or no, please."

"No."

"Nike?"

"Yes."

"Nemesis?"

"Yes."

"The motion is carried. Please observe the usual precautions, ladies."

SIDNEY SHELDON

The name Sidney Sheldon has become synonymous with the term bestselling novelist. But few of his fans know that before he composed a single line of any novel, Sheldon was a successful writer for stage, screen and television. Over the years he collected an Oscar (for the film *The Bachelor and the Bobby-Soxer*) and a Tony Award (for the Broadway play *Redhead*). Still broader popular success came to Sheldon later, with the television series *I Dream of Jeannie* and *Hart to Hart*, which he created and produced. It wasn't until he was fifty-three that he changed direction and turned to writing novels.

Why the change? Sheldon explains: "I came up with an idea for a television drama about a psychiatrist. In order for the plot to make sense, the viewer had to know what the psychiatrist was thinking, and I didn't know how to achieve introspection like that on television. The only way to do it was as a novel." That novel was *The Naked Face*. From then on, Sheldon wrote one bestseller after another. *Windmills of the Gods* is his seventh.

Thorough research and old-fashioned hard work are Sheldon's trademarks. He spent three and a half years on *Windmills*, rewriting it a dozen times. But hard work alone is not enough. Sheldon attributes his books' enormous appeal to the simple fact that *he* likes what readers like. "My characters are very real to me," he says, "and I think therefore very real to others." The same rule applies to his penchant for intriguing plot twists that keep the reader hooked. "I love that kind of book, and I think my readers do, too."

Sidney Sheldon lives in Holmsby Hills, California, and has a daughter, Mary. He was married for thirty-four years to Jorja, who died recently, lending the passages on Edward Ashley's death a bittersweet poignancy.

Does the man whose books sell millions of copies regularly have any secrets of success? "Just that I love to write. I can't help it."

THE CHOICE. Original full-length version © 1987 by Henry Denker. US condensed version © The Reader's Digest Association Inc. 1987. British condensed version © The Reader's Digest Association Limited 1987.

THE COMMODORE. Original full-length version © 1986 by Jan de Hartog. British condensed version © The Reader's Digest Association Limited 1987.

IN A PLACE DARK AND SECRET. Original full-length version © 1985 by Phillip Finch. US condensed version © The Reader's Digest Association Inc. 1986. British condensed version © The Reader's Digest Association Limited 1987.

WINDMILLS OF THE GODS. Original full-length version © 1987 by Sidney Sheldon. US condensed version © The Reader's Digest Association Inc. 1987. British condensed version © The Reader's Digest Association 1987.

PICTURE CREDITS: Page 119: Benn Mitchell; page 391: George H. Cook/ *Baltimore Sun*; page 511: Jerry Bauer.

© The Reader's Digest Association Limited 1987.
© The Reader's Digest Association South Africa (Pty) Limited 1987.

All rights reserved. No part of this publication may be reproduced, stored in a retrieval system, or transmitted in any form or by any means, electronic, mechanical, photocopying, recording or otherwise, without the prior permission of the copyright holders.

Reader's Digest, The Digest and the Pegasus logo
are registered trademarks of The Reader's Digest Association, Inc.